THE AHIMSA GAMBIT

"The humans can teach us much about ourselves," the Ahimsa Overone said. "I intend to force our stagnating people to deal with real things again, to regain the control which has atrophied and wasted. I will light a new fire in this galaxy, and perhaps we'll yearn to see the stars again. Not just think about them."

"What have you finally decided?" his mentor asked.

"I will take the humans to TaHaAk at the height of the cycles. The humans I have chosen have talents for destruction and anger. They are insane, violent, hideous in their own wonderful way. I shall unleash that on the Pashti race. And when the Pashti cycles are over, the cry of terror will shudder the very dimensions of space. . . ."

THE FINEST IN SCIENCE FICTION FROM W. MICHAEL GEAR available from DAW Books:

STARSTRIKE

THE ARTIFACT

The Forbidden Borders Trilogy:
REQUIEM FOR THE CONQUEROR (#1)
RELIC OF EMPIRE (#2) *(Spring 1992)*

The Spider Trilogy:
THE WARRIORS OF SPIDER (#1)
THE WAY OF SPIDER (#2)
THE WEB OF SPIDER (#3)

STARSTRIKE

W. Michael Gear

DAW BOOKS, INC.
DONALD A. WOLLHEIM, FOUNDER
375 Hudson Street, New York, NY 10014

ELIZABETH R. WOLLHEIM
SHEILA E. GILBERT
PUBLISHERS

Cover art by Sanjulian.

DAW Book Collectors No. 822

First Printing, July 1990

18 17 16 15 14 13 12 11 10 9

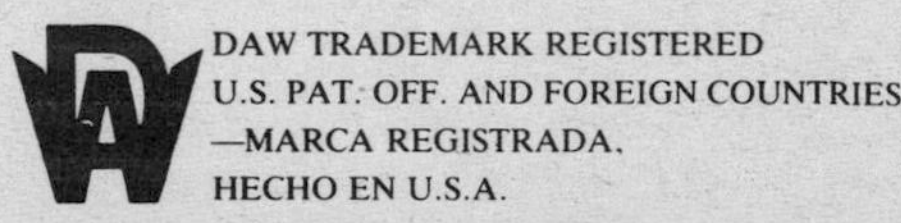

PRINTED IN THE U.S.A.

DEDICATION

TO DAN AND NANCY BELK
FOR SO MUCH HELP WITH HORSES,
SHELTIES, SADDLES AND—OF COURSE—
THE EXPLORATION OF SPACE.

ACKNOWLEDGMENTS

My goal in writing any book is to bring you, the reader, the finest story possible. In meeting that commitment, several people have played key roles in the writing of this novel. Kathleen M. O'Neal (author of the POWERS OF LIGHT trilogy by DAW Books) contributed numerous hours critiquing various drafts of the manuscript. Katherine and Joe Cook, of Mission, Texas, added their thoughts and observations. When I had need of a back pocket physicist, I called Dan Belk, of Billings, Montana, for his keen analysis. Nancy Belk made sure the medical assumptions were grounded in reality and kept me honest around the characters. Finally—as always—I owe a special debt of gratitude to Sheila Gilbert, my outstanding editor at DAW Books, who fit time into her crystal-lattice tight schedule to read the roughed out manuscript. She infused new energy into a fatigued mind and her comments challenged and enlightened.

CHAPTER I

James Atwood listened to his heels click smartly on the tiled floor of the hallway. Curious how the physical world ignored the reality of his changed status. A lesson in humility lay in that—in the fact that his heels sounded exactly the same on tile as they had before his election to the Presidency of the United States.

He rounded the corner to the final hall leading to the White House Strategic Operations Command and took a deep breath. The glassy eyes of the security cameras panned over him. The faint hum of air conditioning filled the otherwise silent hall. He hated the basement of the White House. It had been good enough for Johnson, Nixon, and Reagan to come skulking down here to keep tabs on their sand table models, but Atwood always experienced a distaste for the place. Decisions made so academically in those sterile rooms left people bleeding and dying somewhere—as he knew so painfully from his past. He scowled, as if the covert power that hummed in the very air might corrupt his soul.

"Damn it, Fermen, this had better be good." He shook his head. Any time an emergency interrupted a press conference, the administration was automatically on the defensive. The bloodhounds *knew* something hot had hit the tubes. *Damn it, Fermen!*

He stopped before the steel door and glanced up at the security cameras before nodding to the armed Marine guards. He tapped his code into the lock, and stooped to stare at the retinal camera for final ID. The heavy armored door clicked and swung open.

He could hear Fermen's strained voice. "Jesus! No way! This can't be happening! It's . . ."

Colonel Bill Fermen stared ashen-faced at the dead screen before him. His back hunched as if he expected a blow between the shoulder blades. Sweat beaded on his balding scalp to glisten in the glow of the fluorescent lights.

Blinking anxiously, the President stared around the room, cataloging the familiar computer equipment. Uniformed personnel sat stunned, their disbelieving eyes on the terminals before them. One woman shook her head in shock. The familiar outlines of the world land masses filled two walls—except the continents and oceans on the electronic map should have been lit by little flickers of light to represent the positions of submarines, aircraft, and land-based missiles.

Atwood shot a quick glance at the monitors. The entire wall of screens and status lights remained blank. Desperate fingers raced ineffectively over the command keyboards. Shouted queries into headsets brought nothing in return. Despite redundancy and shielding, the nerve center for North American strategic defense looked completely dead.

"What is it? I was in the middle of a press—"

"The whole system's failed!" Fermen spun his chair, expression panicked.

"That's impossible!" the President mumbled unsteadily. He could feel his heart thumping hollowly. *Failed? The entire defense net?*

"What does NORAD—"

"*Nothing!*" Fermen cried. "The phones, long wave communication, fax machines . . . everything's dead! Hell, I even sent Captain Marston to try the pay phones!"

Atwood hesitated in the center of the room, mind reeling, arms out as if to implore. "But that's impossible! We've dumped billions into making the system foolproof! We've . . . we've . . ."

Fermen wiped his bulldog face with a trembling palm. "I've got people running diagnostics on the power. Nothing. Their meters are just as dead as the rest of it . . . as if the power's just drained somehow."

"Drained? You can't just *drain* that much power." Atwood ran nervous fingers through perfectly combed hair. His long frame went curiously weak as he realized the implications. "My God, my God."

The security door clicked open to admit a disheveled captain. The man's face burned red as he struggled to catch his breath and blurted, "Just got through to Colorado Springs on a pay phone outside. Cheyenne Mountain's dead. Warren Air Force Base is the same. We can't reach the B2s, or the subs either."

Atwood gaped, refusing to believe.

Colonel Fermen looked up, dazed. "Mr. President, the entire defense net is down. The shielding. . . . No, it just can't happen in the blink of an eye!"

Around the room, worried faces looked to him for guidance. "Russians? Could they have . . ." *Don't even think it!*

Fermen's thick hands moved like spiders as they danced over the keyboard. "Impossible! They don't have anything that could drop the whole net! Russians? I can't believe that. They buy or steal all their electronics from *us!*"

"The *whole* defense net?" Atwood's mouth went dry as his gaze shot to the big world map. Had it been activated, incoming blips would have begun to race over the polar regions. How long did they have? Ten minutes? Were SS-26 missiles even now nosing over to their targets? And the Soviet sub fleet? Were depressed trajectory warheads homing in even as he stood staring? Was the United States dead? What could he do?

Atwood scrambled for the red phone, jamming the receiver to his ear. Not even a buzz. Panicked, he met their horrified gazes. "We can't even launch a counterstrike?"

"No, sir. We're sitting ducks."

He turned to the security door, pressing the button.

Nothing!

"Door's dead," he added woodenly.

"Huh?" Fermen turned to stare, his eyes glittering with fear.

Atwood fought the urge to cry out in rage and frustration as he tore the emergency cover loose and threw his weight against the winch handle. He barely noticed the odd, mirrorlike surface of the shiny ball that surrounded the lock mechanism. Shaking, he heaved again and again, frantically. He closed his eyes, taking a deep breath, seeking to calm himself.

"No use," Atwood's voice broke. "We're stuck. Intercom still out?"

Captain Marston licked his lips and inspected the mirror-bright sphere on the lock, pointing. "What's that?"

Marston's fingers slipped off the reflecting sphere as he probed at it.

Fermen hollered into the intercom, finger mashing the call button down. Nothing. He panted softly as he wiped his face.

"Then we'll die here," Atwood whispered, running clammy fingers down his suit, gaze darting to the ops computer.

"What's that?" he asked, a faint stirring in his breast.

Fermen ran for the chair, mouth open as he stared.

One by one, the words formed on the screen:

"TO THE PRESIDENT OF THE UNITED STATES OF AMERICA: GREETINGS! THE DEMONSTRATION OF POWER IS ALWAYS DISTASTEFUL; HOWEVER, WHAT WE ARE ABOUT TO DISCLOSE WILL BRING ABOUT THE END OF THE WORLD AS YOU KNOW IT. A SUITABLE METHOD HAD TO BE EMPLOYED TO ENSURE YOUR COOPERATION."

A technician cried out as he looked up from a sophisticated test meter, "Mr. President! The system's dead! This can't happen! My meters tell me there's no power in the mainframe!"

President Atwood sank slowly into a chair, staring woodenly as more words continued to fill the screen. He mumbled a hoarse, "Oh, my God!"

* * *

Uri Golovanov, General Secretary of the Soviet Union, had never been able to overcome the nausea that accompanied the drop down the escape shaft. His stomach jumped up into the hollow left by his heart as his lift shot down and almost flattened him when it slowed to a stop.

Stepping out, he found General Andre Kutsov, the KGB head, waiting. The general paced nervously, hands clasped behind his back. Not even during the "Days of December" when their lives had hung by a thread had Kutsov looked this jittery.

"Andre! Why did we have no warning?" Golovanov hated his too shrill voice.

Kutsov's hands spread wide. His voice conveyed a controlled throb of anger. "Who could have guessed? They did *nothing* to tip their hand! My people over there are the best! We have two top agents in the American NSC! Not even they heard! It is . . . *inconceivable!*"

Golovanov waved it away as the escape van pulled up.

"Inconceivable or not, they've done something. We missed some important clue, some bit of information somewhere." The plastic seats crackled under his weight as he pulled himself inside. The driver picked up speed.

"Do we have time?" he wondered, staring at the white tiled walls flashing by the window. The vehicle whooshed away from the guts of the Kremlin, down the Leningrad Prospekt beneath Red Square.

Kutsov's eyes narrowed. "I don't know. I sent a runner to Marshal Kulikov. If the Commander in Chief of the Strategic Rocket Forces doesn't know, who does? Radar's dead. Communications with the silos are dead. *We* are dead."

Golovanov leaned back in the seat, troubled fingers picking at his Italian suit. The chill in his heart matched that of the air. "Dead? So was the red phone. They've won. I only hope the Strategic Rocket Forces can be notified somehow. I can't understand, Andre. How did they manage to shut down only the defense system? They leave the rest of Moscow lighted!"

"They were always better at technology." Kutsov sniffed and wiped at his nose, looking ahead.

The icy wind-chill burned exposed skin as they climbed out of the Prospekt and hurried onto the grassy Central Airfield. The waiting jet whined as the turbines built thrust. Uri Golovanov started up the ladder and hesitated, letting his glance stray over the lights of Moscow. Squat buildings stood illuminated by the street lights.

People walked quickly along the sidewalks, hands thrust into coats, heads down so as not to see the official jet. Squares of light cast from the windows of official buildings mottled the streets. The trees were stark, waiting for a spring that might never come now.

He thought of all those lives—snuffed out like a Cuban cigar. How many dreams, hopes, and longings would die tonight? They wouldn't even know—all those people—they'd just die. Loves and hates, fears and triumphs vanishing in fire and death and radiation. How long until the MX missiles dropped from the sky? How long until Moscow, his home, exploded in a cloud of radiation and plasma?

"My people . . . my poor people." *Had Gorbachev been so wrong after all?* Jaws clamped against the answer, he shook his head. Feet rang out on the steps as he started up. They still had time to get off the ground. Within an hour they would all be safe at Zhiguli. From there, they would see how much of the Soviet Union could be salvaged from the American holocaust. He hadn't made it halfway to the hatch when he felt his stomach surge again. Uri Golovanov suffered a debilitating bout of vertigo seconds before he and Andre Kutsov disappeared into thin air.

The guards blinked and panicked, splashing flashlight beams about the grassy field, seeing nothing but occasional bits of paper tumbled by the late October wind.

* * *

Major Viktor Staka moved carefully as he drew the night scope from over his shoulder. He could feel rather than see Lieutenant Mika Gubanya to his right, eyes intent on the dark canyon. Viktor settled the night scope before him on the angular granite and adjusted the optics. In the rocky valley bottom, trucks and men sprang to life.

He nestled in the rocks, the night hiding his medium-framed, muscular body. Shutting one cold blue eye Viktor squinted through the eyepiece, studying the target below. The thrill of incipient combat tingled through his limbs, playing along muscles toned by constant exertion. Watching the trucks unloading below, he ran callused fingers along the firm line of his jaw. Time.

"Now!" he ordered, picking up his assault rifle.

Rockets trailed white smoke as they leapt for the concentration of trucks below. The white-hot flashes echoed with the *poomph-bam* of explosions as crates of mortars and rockets blew the parked convoy apart. Mules kicked and died as shouting men stumbled away from the inferno.

"Move!" Viktor snapped into his wrist radio. With the night scope, he could see his special Long Range SPETSNAZ unit leaping down the rocky cliff. A muffled chatter of assault fire crackled and popped.

Viktor quickly scanned the sky. He hated working so close to Kabul. He didn't like Afghanistan. Too much could happen here. In the past, too much had. He spit into the darkness, irritated. Afghanistan had been a sucking cesspool from the beginning. Curse Brezhnev for sending troops here in the first place. Gorbachev had been right to pull out—but he should have realized the effect the withdrawal would have on the Uzbeks.

The Mujahadin began to recover, firing back ineffectively, blinded, stunned by the rocket attack and the erupting fountains of fire and destruction that had been supply trucks. Pack animals screamed in death as SPETSNAZ snipers picked Afgnans off one by one with their NDM 86 rifles.

He checked the sky again. Still no enemy helicopters or aircraft. Could they have hit the radio first thing?

Group 3 closed in on the perimeter. Group 2 seemed to be held up by concentrated fire. Viktor studied the position. The Afghans had set up a light machine gun. "Mika, blast that overturned truck in Group 2's path. They have covering fire there."

Lieutenant Gubanya promptly settled his rockets on the area and Viktor nodded as the Afghan position rocked in a pall of dust, smoke, and flaring light. Relieved, Malenkov's Group 2 poured down the slopes, overrunning any remaining resistance.

Like fleas off a dead rat, the Afghans fled for the opposite side of the valley.

Ten minutes later, Viktor had his men racing for the

hills. He trotted along behind, fingers tapping out the recall signal on the radio. Behind them, a black column of smoke rolled out of the valley. Soft thuds echoed on the night breeze as fuel tanks and occasional mortar shells overheated in the burning trucks.

"Lost Suka and Tast is wounded," Malenkov called as he trotted up from the rear. "Pietre and Nikolai are bringing Suka's body."

Suka? Not Suka with all his pranks and fun and laughter. Viktor's heart hardened. *I ought to be used to it by now. Why can't I be like the damned Afghans, who live to fight? Why does each time hurt more? Suka . . . Suka . . .*

Their helicopters rose out of the next defile like black demons, rotors rattling like chattering teeth. Each of the ships hovered as his groups climbed aboard, then swung off to race for the canyons to the north and safety.

Viktor ducked under the down-wash, unslung his pack and threw it in, before he jumped for the strut and hauled his sweaty body into the aircraft.

He leaned out and scanned the ridge top through the night glasses, searching for stragglers—finding none.

"Go!" he called over the racket. The eerily illuminated ground dropped away, rocky, foreboding, the home of his ghosts and personal demons. Dust swirled in the wash, the blades chattering overhead. Chattering . . . chattering . . . drifting into the memory of the machine-gun fire that night outside of Baraki. Afghanistan remained the same—a trap for men's souls. For Suka's . . . for his.

Viktor felt the ship turn and throw him back and down as it accelerated into the canyon to race for the safety of Soviet air cover.

He pulled his way past grinning troops and into the cockpit where the din abated from a howling fury to a dull roar.

"Another shipment the Uzbeks won't get to shoot at us!" The pilot waved his welcome. "It went well?"

"One dead, one wounded." Viktor answered. *One by one, we're worn away. So what if we kill ten of them to each one we lose? They keep coming.* His jaw muscles cramped with the sense of loss. *Why does it hurt so?*

Images of Baraki, of the underground canals . . . of the smell of gasoline and burning flesh. In his mind, shadows of racing flames came roaring to cover the terrified screams of the hidden Afghans in a sanctuary turned to hell. *My hell—just as eternal and damning as God's.* An image flashed of the young woman rising from the flames, twisting, reaching. . . .

"No."

"You all right?" the pilot called, glancing worriedly at him.

He strangled the horror festering in his belly. To feel emotion, to wonder about justice and purpose could undo him. Like his men, Viktor forced himself to survive, to keep his mental armor in place. The world had become too dangerous for human frailties.

"Tired." He grinned weakly and leaned to stare out the window at the jagged walls of rock they flew between. The moon rose higher in the sky. Periodically, Viktor could make out the blades of the craft in front of them shimmering dragonflylike in the light before dodging back into canyon shadows. A man had to have skill to fly through these valleys of death. Did a Stinger home in on them even now, the trigger about to be pressed by a dirty goat herder's finger?

A cold gnawing began in Viktor's belly. Everything had looked so good—once. Perestroika had been a hope for the future. If only Gorbachev. . . . Hope had vanished, like blood into the frozen rocky Afghan soil.

"There's the border!" the pilot called, pointing down into the darkness. The Armundar'ya River lay somewhere in the shadows. A ghost-gray ridge rose before them. "On the other side we don't need to worry about hiding. We can get higher—out of small arms range."

Viktor nodded. Beaten by goat herders! The Uzbeks had taken too much courage from the Afghan success. He glanced at the pilot's face. The young man's features, lined with concentration, were etched in red by the instrument glow. So many like him had died and for what? What did they control? KGB and GRU tried to infiltrate, to buy collaboration and betrayal among the Uzbek tribes. Their attempts met with failure after failure. Soviet soldiers died by ones and threes, by platoons and companies. A constant attrition. Latvians tried to hold places like Murgab, Khorog, and Karshi. Georgians wandered about in ragged mountain valleys in the Alay Range gasping for breath in the thin air at the top of the world—only to die, ambushed by home-cast lead bullets fired from handmade rifles.

A wall of rock rose before Viktor's eyes as his pilot made a perfect flight up a narrow defile. They shot over into the shadow of the other side. Viktor drew a deep breath. Behind him, hidden in the shadows, lay the Kush: a twisted world of rock carved and dissected by ages of snow, wind, and rain, a maze of unscalable death. There, the Red Army had ground to a halt—defied by nature and a stubborn, indomitable people. That legacy of hate fueled the Afghans now as they infiltrated and spread unrest among their relatives, the Uzbeks.

The entire Islamic world—helped by the Americans—funneled guns, rockets, and mortars to the Uzbek uprising. Under Gorbachev, the whole Soviet Union had come unhinged from the Baltic to Uzbekistan. The iron fist of the Red Army had crushed the Baltics, the Georgians, and Armenians—but not the crazy Uzbeks.

Now he and his crack unit raided Afghanistan, snapping the primitive supply lines, seeking to stem the flow of Russian blood and deny the Uzbeks smuggled ordnance. Night after night, they raided Afghan positions. *And one day, the clock will run out. One day, we'll fly into a trap. We're dead men, each and every one of us.* He blinked, soul drained. *Afghanistan will finally reclaim my soul. For the moment, it only waits . . . so the end will be more terrible.*

The thought tried to suffocate him—pressing down like an anvil on hope and spirit.

He pulled up his personal iron curtain, the one that kept the world at bay, nodded to the radio man, and took the mike to report. "This is Winter Sable. Come in Central. Repeat, this is Winter Sable. We've had good hunting. Caught the mice in the wheat field. We need medical for one."

He waited, listening to the crackle of static.

"Viktor?" Lieutenant-Colonel Ashmov's voice sounded relieved. "Are you all right? How did it go?"

"Target destroyed, two casualties on our side, over." Staka stared sightlessly at the blackness below. He imagined the sharp granite teeth of the Alays waiting to tear them to bloody shreds.

"Viktor, you have a change of orders. You and your unit will not return to your quarters. You will land at the air base at Dushanbe. Aircraft will be waiting. They want you in Moscow by 1200 tomorrow, understood?"

Viktor took a deep breath, heart constricting in his chest. What had he done? Take the whole unit? But what—

"Understood." He fought to swallow, nervous fear building. Just such an order had sent him from a cushy job in Zossen-Wunsdorf, overseeing SPETSNAZ deployment for the Western Strategic Direction, to Tadzhik in the first place.

"I'll see you there, Viktor." Ashmov's voice sounded neutral. "Central out."

Viktor was still staring at the radio when he felt the helicopter settle at Dushanbe.

* * *

President Atwood pulled at his earlobe and looked up as Bill Fermen walked into the Oval Office, glancing wearily at the flag that stood behind the big polished desk. The white doors clicked shut after him. From the muss and wrinkles, the colonel looked like he'd slept in his uniform. The bulldog lines of his face had fallen, haggard and pinched.

"Sit down, Bill. All the recorders are off. I take it you've kept the lid on?"

Fermen's heavy jowls shook as he nodded. "I guess, but I don't know how. I've pulled all of our people out of the White Base. The Joint Chiefs of Staff are sniffing around like hound dogs after a fox. For the moment, they're panicked over the missiles. The reports are coming in. If the JCS goes berserk, you're going to have Congress and every reporter in the country howling."

Atwood leaned back in the big chair, rubbing a thumb

and forefinger to clear his gritty eyes. "Yes, they've been clogging the phone lines. Right now the Secretary of Defense has them under control, but how long that will last is anybody's guess. The DCI was here ten minutes ago, wanting to know what I was doing recalling his top agents. The Hill—as you can no doubt guess—has caught wind of it and they've initiated their own feelers."

Fermen sighed. "Look, everyone knows the defense net went down. We can't keep this thing under wraps forever."

Atwood winced. "No, but I've got to stall for another forty-eight hours. You've sent everyone who knows to White Base?"

"Last night, first thing. Jim, only you and I know about the Ahimsa. That scares hell out of me."

Atwood jumped to his feet, leaving the big over-padded chair rocking. "Damn it! I can't help it! They were very clear in the instructions."

Fermen looked up restlessly, licking his lips. "What if it's just a kid somewhere? You know, one of those computer hackers?"

Atwood paced anxiously, head back. "Then he's damn good. He's got the entire Soviet Union scrambling madly. They've called up the reserves and are breaking weapons out of mothballs. Everyone over there is going as nuts as we are. And what about that silver ball on the lock? No, it's *them*.

"Listen, Bill, I've talked to Golovanov. He was whisked off Central Airfield with General Kutsov—and right back into his office where he got the same message, word for word, that we did. Worse, I talked to him here, in this room. Face to face."

Fermen blinked, squinting.

"I don't know how, only that these Ahimsa—as they call themselves—projected his image into this room. Golovanov saw my image in his office in the Kremlin. Damn it, we talked on the red phone afterward, both of us baffled, looking for a trick. No, we've got to play by the rules these Ahimsa have given. Anything else could be suicide."

"Trust them?"

"Well, what else? If you've got any suggestions. . . ."

Fermen took a deep breath. "Every warhead in our arsenal is encapsulated in one of those mirror spheres. Laser reflects. The TAC team at Livermore shot one with a rail gun using some sort of trick ceramic lattice bullet. Didn't even mar the surface. The thing's opaque to X ray, ultrasound, CAT scan, you name it. Nothing we've got can even look inside to see if they used some device."

"The one on the lock downstairs just disappeared. Pop, and it was gone."

"But we've got to *do* something! This is all going to come apart . . . and *I'm* in the hot seat! I mean, how long before I'm on the Hill testifying before a committee? What do I tell them? That Bug-Eyed Monsters that we haven't even seen have put all our weapons in stasis?" Fermen lifted his arms, a wild look in his eyes. "Jesus, Jim, this isn't some movie! Damn it!"

"Bill, I had to tell the JCS something. I had them put our military on full alert. It bought a little time."

"Jesus, Jesus, Jesus!" Fermen shook his head slowly. "Didn't these Ahimsa know what they'd unleash with that stupid little trick? Remember that War of the Worlds broadcast? If they pirate every radio station and TV channel, we'll have a. . . . Oh, God, I can't even think about it!"

"Do you hear that?" Atwood called to the room, staring around at all the monitors and pickups and the security devices that hung down from the corners. "Do you understand what can happen?"

Silence.

* * *

The first law in Lebanon had been written in blood: Stay alive. The second law—radio silence—no longer had any applicability as the first mortar rounds pounded the dirt, seeking range. No Israeli commander would compromise his command by breaking radio silence during a covert raid. With Assaf tanks spotted, their location known, and their destination guessed, nothing remained now but the first law.

"Take them over the wall!" Colonel Moshe Gabi shouted into the mike as the road ahead of them erupted with exploding mortar shells. Chaim, his driver, complied immediately. The M1 spun on its tracks, shrapnel and dirt rattling off the armor. The treads fought for purchase as the tank climbed the low wall. Sun-baked rock and clay collapsed as they rocked over and through a dusty narrow enclosed yard, crushing chairs and a table.

"Between the buildings!" he ordered, hearing Arya's tank crashing through a structure somewhere behind them. The mortars continued to pound the road they'd been traveling. The M1 churned and clawed its way through a mud hut and swung onto a narrow goat trail, balancing precariously on the slope of the rocky windswept hill.

"See if you can keep the damage to a minimum," Moshe called down to his driver as he looked back at the devastation. Chickens ran, squawking and flapping wings, where the cleated tracks had marked the buff earth.

Moshe braced himself as Chaim raced for a low mud wall and smashed it down. Behind them, Arya broke through, drying laundry strung colorfully across the desert tan of his tank. Swirls of brown dust trailed after them, blocking the scabby dry hills of Lebanon.

"Assaf Company, anyone hit?" Moshe called into his radio net.

"Ben Yar here, sir. We took a hit. Turret's jammed. We're coming along behind."

The mortar barrage on the road had ceased.

"Wondering where we are," Moshe whispered to himself and rubbed his bearded chin, feeling the hot dry breeze on his face. He hated Lebanon.

Chaim geared down as they came to a narrow passage between two low rock houses. The M1 grumbled and groaned as the barrel slid between the structures and the tracks dug in. They bulled through collapsing walls in a clatter of dust. A woman ran screaming out the other side, two children clinging to her arms.

"God," Moshe whispered.

Mortars popped as shrapnel whistled through the air. Chaim throttled up, racing across a small plowed field.

Fonts of dirt blasted darkly as the mortars sought their range.

"Should be a road just beyond the next ditch." Moshe studied the map clipped just below the hatch. "Take a right and roll! They won't have mines on the road. According to DMI it's the only way in."

"Right!" Chaim called.

The dusty tanks of Assaf Company strung out in a staggered line as they crossed the field, commanders looking around warily, nervous at the continued mortar fire. So far, the PLO hadn't found their range.

Chaim bounced over the ditch and clawed the tank around to the right. Yeled, the gunner, swung the barrel to keep from clipping a low row of cedars. Gray dust boiled up from the parched road beneath them as they paralleled a whitewashed mud wall, palm fronds hanging over the side.

Roaring and singing in a high-pitched mechanical whine, the M1 raced past a blasted mosque and swung wide around a parked lorry. Moshe dropped until his eyes just cleared the hatch. A barbed-wire perimeter spread out from each side of a fortified gate. Dust jumped from muzzle flash as an anti-tank gun sought them. The shell whistled loud overhead.

Bullets spattered and splatted across the armor as Yeled targeted and blew the gate apart, the tank rocking with recoil. Moshe calmly laced the boiling dust with machine-gun fire. He could see men running and the mortars banged as fire lagged behind the racing tanks.

"Head for the SAM batteries!"

A Saggar missile ripped past as Yeled swiveled the turret and blew a bunker apart like a ripe melon. The piercing HE shell ripped through the concrete, dirt jetting from the fire and flame of the explosive. In the veil of dust, the heavy concrete roof collapsed, dust roiling.

Chaim overran a trench and Moshe caught a momentary glimpse of frantic men fleeing from walls that crumbled under the tank's weight. A grenade exploded behind the turret as barracks and bunkers died amid fire and explosions. Dust, noise, confusion, and the crackle of weapons and exploding shells boiled around them.

"Moshe! This is Shmulik! We're hit! Took a Saggar! We're powered down with machine-gun backup."

"Roger." *How bad, Shmulik? Stay alive, for God's sake. Hang on!*

Chaim thundered up a forty-five degree earth embankment and Moshe felt that tingle of nerves that comes when a tank crests an unknown obstacle. How much drop? What if an anti-tank gun fired into their defenseless belly? They pitched over almost straight down as Yeled pulled his gun up and around to keep from driving it into the ground.

He forgot the patter and rattle of small arms fire on the armor as he eyed the SAM batteries nestled in their sandbagged warrens. There, at last.

"Hit 'em!" Moshe cried. "That's what we came for!" The tank rocked with recoil as Yeled targeted a battery. Concussion blasted dirt and pebbles against the Ml.

Moshe ducked down and slammed the hatch shut. Over the din, he hollered into the radio, "Metzada One, this is Sword. We've got the launchers. Expecting you for tea soon. Look forward to your arrival."

"We're on the way, Sword. Metzada One out," the radio cackled.

"Let's clean up as much as we can before they get here," Yeled shouted as he triggered the big gun—the blast from another missile battery buffeted the tank. His ears rang from the explosion as the M1 shivered like a white-linen sheet in a high wind.

"Do it! The more we drive out, the less chance Metzada will get hit when they come in. Go! Go! Go!"

Another blast left the tank careening on its suspension. Ytzak must have cleared the wall to target the last launcher. Moshe raised his eyes above the hatch to look, seeing the remains of a man tumble before the tank, body splayed open, entrails scoured from the rib cage. One leg and both arms were missing along with the head. How much power did it take to do that to a human being?

Chaim sloughed them around and raced for the imposing wall. Moshe winced as the treads pressed those pitiful Palestinian remains into the hard clay, his toes curling at the thought of the shattered bones crushing and grating under the steel claws of the M1.

Going out scared him as much as coming in. From the vantage point of the earthworks, Moshe spotted one target after another in the burning pummeled perimeter while Yeled warmed up the big gun and hammered the PLO positions. Assaf tanks threaded the maze, blowing away resistance as it formed up in the tortured dust.

The wappity-wap of the helicopters came as welcome relief. They flew in from the south, gunning trenches, strafing the PLO attempting to set up Saggars and RPG-7 anti-tank fire. Ominous insects, they set down, commandos popping out to tackle the missile bunkers.

Shmulik's tank burned in a black smudge. Moshe's gut hollowed with that familiar feeling of dread. A second Saggar must have homed in on them while they sat motionless.

"Metzada? Can you pick up the wounded from my tank crew?"

"Roger, Sword."

Moshe chewed his lip nervously as one of the assault helicopters wheeled and hovered by Shmulik's tank. Through his glasses, Moshe watched as the bodies were transferred and the chopper rose. Yeled's gun continued to boom as he targeted the trenches. In twos and fours, commandos evacuated from the breached bunkers, Galils and Uzis chattering. Within seconds the helicopters rose like big ungainly bugs and climbed for altitude.

"Let's get out of here!" Moshe called into his net.

Chaim throttled up and they raced for the gate, pulling up where Shmulik hobbled out, waving. Moshe took one last glance at Shmulik's tank, the tread blown off one side, the diesel exposed under twisted metal. How many had survived? How many would live?

"Go!" Shmulik called as he and Iakob clambered up behind the turret. Shmulik's right arm hung limp, bloodsoaked.

"Why didn't you ride out on the helicopter?"

Shmulik grinned as the M1 growled forward. "Too noisy!" he bellowed over the roar of the diesel.

Moshe shook his head and looked back, seeing Assaf

emerging from the whirling dust, guns pointed this way and that. "Metzada One! Can you cover for us?"

"Roger. We'll clean up that mortar position for you, too. Thanks a lot, Sword. You just pulled a thorn from our side."

Moshe swallowed down a dry throat. The PLO hadn't planned on a tank force taking out the SAMs. The Air Force had already lost two F16s to the new missiles.

Behind them the missile site mushroomed in a pall of smoke, dust, and fire. The commandos had taken care of the underground bunkers with a passion.

He leaned out of the hatch, looking to where Shmulik and Iakob rode on the hot armor above the diesel. "How bad were the wounded?"

"They'll live."

The haunting emptiness filled and Moshe grinned happily at his remaining tanks. Not a bad mission. They pulled up beyond the village—beyond sniping range—and watched the helicopters wheeling in the dull sky. At the same time, yet another chopper homed in on them, settling in a whirlwind of dust and debris at the edge of the field.

Odd . . . and who's this? Moshe jumped down, slapping a hand on the tough armor of his idling tank. The dust of Lebanon clogged his nose, streaking his gnomish face. Perhaps forty, Moshe Gabi had dedicated his life to the IDF. Five feet, five inches tall, he stood in a creased uniform, fatigues tucked into his boots. Four days of beard clung to his round cheeks, somehow accenting his bent nose. The laugh lines around his eyes didn't hide the hard reality those brown orbs had seen.

The shock came when IDF Minister of Defense, Eliashev Natke, himself hopped sprightly from the chopper. Dressed in fatigues, the Minister ducked the whirling blades and trotted forward through the dust-choked down wash. Moshe had barely pulled himself to attention when Natke stopped before him. The Defense Minister studied the sere landscape for a second before smiling wickedly. "Good work, Moshe. Perfectly executed."

"I, uh . . . Sir, what are you doing here? You could be

killed! Why are you—" Moshe's arms had come up in protest.

"Later," Natke interrupted. "My friend, I don't have any idea what this is all about. I was called to the Prime Minister's office this morning. The American President wants you and your Assaf Company for immediate service. No! I see it in your eyes, Moshe. Don't ask. Even if I knew, do you think I could tell you?"

Moshe shrugged and looked to the south. Another fleet of helicopters slipped over the horizon. "Who are they?"

"Replacements . . . yours." Eliashev's thin, lined face looked grim behind his black sunglasses. "You and your men will go immediately. That's Maluk's company. They'll take good care of your tanks."

"But, Eli, where are we—"

"Relax, Moshe, I don't know. The Prime Minister simply ordered me to get you to Tel Aviv. El Al has a 747 waiting for you and your men. I hear you will be taken straight to Washington."

"But I . . ."

The helicopters drowned the rest, as they changed attitude, hovering for a moment before dropping in tornadoes of dust.

"Let's go, Moshe," Natke shouted and pointed to the waiting choppers.

Even after he'd strapped into the seat onboard the 747, a bottle of Gold Star beer in his hand, Moshe still couldn't convince himself this was real.

CHAPTER II

"What does this mean, Alexi?" Major Svetlana Detova looked up from the diplomatic pouch. She hated coming to the embassy—hated walking in the front door where any CIA camera could record her. The urgent summons hadn't given her time for any other course of action, couched as it was in top priority alert code.

For once, she didn't even mind Alexi's eyes devouring her. Her physical appearance had become her one vanity, as well as an asset in dealing with powerful men. Dark brown hair hung to the middle of her back and offered a striking contrast to her blue eyes. With facial features that rivaled the beauties displayed in the American magazines, she'd used her charms to augment her other talents. Men in positions of power and responsibility talked to beautiful women. To them an attractive woman became a decoration, a symbol of status and a reflection of their perception of self-worth. And if the potential consort appeared intelligent, so much the better. Svetlana had learned to use that quality against them. Now Alexi stared openly, worry mixed with his lust.

The basement room smelled stuffy. The walls needed paint and the floor felt gritty under her shoes. Somewhere in the background, the air conditioning hummed. Two fluorescent lights hung down from the concrete ceiling.

Alexi's face remained blank as he clasped his hands together. He sat half-hitched on the conference table. "I assure you, I don't know. I don't know why they didn't fax the information over your machine. All I know is that Kutsov's seal is on the documents."

Svetlana stared down at the passport and the airline

ticket. "I fly from here to Tokyo? Then an *American* military jet will pick me up? That's insane!"

Alexi's baffled look reassured her. "What do *I* know? I'm only an ambassador! You're the KGB department head here. You tell me. Maybe Kutsov has doubled an American air crew for something?"

She settled back in the chair, mind racing. Her Residency controlled all KGB operations on the Pacific rim. Her information nets rivaled anything in Europe. One by one, she'd weeded out the Oriental pipelines supplying the Uzbek revolt. She had successfully and ruthlessly stymied the CIA in the Orient during the Perestroika years. Her operatives and illegals had kept the Philippines in turmoil and even destabilized Thailand.

But then, could it be. . . . Her expression, like a steel mask, betrayed no hint of the sudden fear that ate deep within. Had someone stumbled onto her ability with computers? Could Kutsov have learned her secret? If they'd compromised her front company, found out about the big Cray computer . . .

She frowned at the passport and ticket. Assuming Kutsov knew about her bank accounts, knew about the computer, why not simply arrest her, smuggle her out to a submarine, and then to Vladivostok? From there, a quick flight would take her to Moscow under heavy guard.

For that matter, why not simply kill her? KGB had a variety of means to accomplish that.

She tapped her long fingernails on the counter, staring at the airline ticket. Events had taken them all by surprise. Gorbachev's failure; George Bush's catastrophic campaign after the crash of the American economy; Golovanov rolling the Red Army through the Baltic states; the civil war that broke out all over the Soviet Union; the violence in the Balkans; all contributed to the destabilization of the political situation. The old dogs had regained the Kremlin in the wake of Gorbachev's ousting. Could that be it? Had she become too powerful? Did Kutsov perceive a rival to threaten his position?

She had survived through her cunning and ability. No one—with the possible exception of a handful of advanced MIT students in the United States—knew as much about computers and how to manipulate them as Svetlana Detova. The big machines had become her passion, filling that loneliness she couldn't share with another human being. Now they might have become her downfall. If Moscow even suspected she'd broken every security system they'd laboriously placed on . . . *Better suicide than that!*

After breaking into Subic Bay, Sony, Hitachi, and the Bank of Hong Kong, the KGB computers had been child's play. If only she could have taken a crack at the Pentagon! She glared at the pouch lying so innocently before her. Asking to try the Pentagon would have exposed everything to her superiors. *And sent me straight to Siberia at best.*

Svetlana chafed at the increasing concern in Alexi's expression. Damn it! Did he *have* to be here?

She looked up and smiled. "Curious, don't you think? We haven't considered yet whether Kutsov's seal is authentic."

"It came through on the secure line. It would be impossible for anyone else to have—"

"Precisely." Svetlana stood in a fluid movement, walking to the fax. She could feel his eyes tracing her muscular legs, the swell of her bottom and her thin waist. She keyed her own KGB access. If the line had been compromised, CIA already knew her ID. She promptly sent a query to Kutsov's office, using a special clearance CIA could wind itself in knots trying to unravel. She smiled at the thought of their analysts adding it to the files. Such a code could be used once—and only once.

The machine remained silent. Svetlana's eyes narrowed. No answer?

Then the phone rang.

Alexi picked it up, answering, *"Da?"* His face went white, nervous eyes going to Svetlana. He swallowed and handed her the receiver. "It's Kutsov. He wants to speak with you."

Svetlana cocked her head, trying to make sense of it all.

"Da?"

"Tana?" The voice sounded like Kutsov's—and addressed her in a code CIA couldn't have compromised. "I should have expected you would double-check. To reassure you as to my identity, I, too, remember orange blossoms in the Sudan."

Kutsov! The joke had been shared privately after she'd broken an arms pipeline to the civil war there. "Andre, I have a ticket and a passport to—"

"And the plane leaves in thirty minutes, Hong Kong time. You had better be on it. Anticipating your suspicions, I assure you this is not a double cross. You aren't being set up. Everything will be explained when you arrive at the American base. I . . . Things have changed, Tana. Just do your sacred duty. Things have . . . changed, that's all."

"I'll be on the plane, Andre." Her whole body went numb. She stood mutely as the phone clicked dead.

She glared at Alexi's questioning expression. "Call me a cab. I must get to the airport. Now! I'm already late as it is."

* * *

"What could I have done differently, Andre?" Golovanov bent over his desk, elbows propped to support his head. "Gorbachev let loose the whirlwind. Hungary and Poland slipped away—and then the flight from East Germany and the opening of the borders. The elections, the riots in Czechoslovakia, the bloodbath in Rumania bled us dry. The Baltics, Georgia, Armenia, and finally Uzbekistan rose in revolt. What could we do? Sit by and idly watch the Soviet Union unravel like an old coat?"

"Marshal Rastinyevski has mobilized the army." Kutsov rubbed the back of his neck where he sat in an overstuffed chair. "He knows the Strategic Rocket Forces are worthless."

Golovanov stared hopelessly at him. "I know. I backed his decision. What else could I do? We're defenseless against attack."

"But the same thing happened to the Americans."

"Ah! And *you'll* tell Rastinyevski that we're at the mercy of Ahimsa aliens? You know the man; he's a dinosaur! *If* he believes you, and doesn't have you hauled off for psychiatric treatment, he'll go crazy! What then? He's lived all his life with the 'Sacred Duty' of protecting Mother Russia. What sort of response do you suppose the Ahimsa are capable of? Do you think they'll put little shiny mirrors around the firing pin of every Kalishnikov rifle? Or will they simply crush us like some sort of irritating bug?"

"Rastinyevski won't go without a fight." Kutsov picked up the glass of brandy from the table beside him, staring at the amber contents of the bourbon. "Funny, at this, of all times, I should be drinking vodka."

"Your people are on the way?"

"Yes. Now what, Uri?"

The General Secretary dropped his head to stare at the desktop. "Now, we wait. The next move is up to the Ahimsa. Whatever it is, we must hold onto the tiger's tail—and hope we survive."

* * *

Captain Sam Daniels hit the IP perfectly. He rolled, punched the release button, and shot to his feet while the parachute billowed in the darkness behind him. Unclipping his rifle, he charged for the main cell block. Only his reactions saved him as Phil Cruz dropped from the sky on top of him. So far so good, the Cubans still hadn't sounded an alarm. Behind him, booted feet thumped into the hard-packed dirt of the exercise ground, black chutes spilling around in silken waves as his people landed.

Muffled patters sounded as Murphy's sniper team took out the guards with their night-sighted weapons.

Sam reached the perimeter fence and checked the body of a dead guard. He leapt to the gate and slapped thermite onto the lock. He ducked back as it flared, neatly cutting the steel. The metal rang out hollowly as he kicked the gate in. Behind him, dark figures followed, the outline of mat-black weapons barely visible in the dim light.

Somewhere in the darkness a voice called out in Spanish. Damn! Well, had to happen sometime. Before long the place would be crawling with Cubans.

"Murphy!" Sam hissed. A figure trotted up next to him. *"Go!"*

Boots pounded as half his force split off. Murphy's team, with the perfect efficiency of slickly-oiled machinery, raced for the communications tower to cut Fidel's wires and mine the west side fence.

The main cell block rose out of the night as Sam brought his men up along either side of the big door. Black hands patted thermite on the hinges. Flares of light danced blindingly to illuminate the grim faces of his SOD team. They looked like weird aliens in their night-vision goggles. The huge door tottered and fell with a clanging thump.

"That's it!" Sam hollered. *"Go!"* He led the way through the acrid smell of molten metal and burning paint. Two wide-eyed guards leapt out of their seats fumbling for weapons. Sam kicked one hard in the throat and slashed wickedly at the other with his Wind River fighting knife. The Cuban backed onto Ted Mason's bayonet.

Pulling up his night goggles, Sam bit his lip as he studied the monitors and hit the buttons to open the cell block doors. Gene Anderson dove headfirst into the cabinet below, snipping the remote TV monitor wires, blanking off the security system. Somewhere, far away, an alarm peeled into the night. Sam palmed the right button and the barred door behind him slid back with a metallic crash. Mason had finished with the guards and taken a position to cover the outside—their only escape route. Anderson unslung his rifle and nodded while Kearney and "Slap" Watson covered the cell block hallway.

"Let's go," Sam muttered. "Pray we got here in time."

"Yeah," Simpson breathed from behind.

Watson's rifle burped a muffled staccato as a guard charged down the cell block. The guard's shirt jumped—the spatting sounds of bullets impacting flesh and bone loud in the confined hall. The man faltered and hit the floor headfirst, his Uzi clattering on the linoleum.

"Hit it!" Sam yelled, and they were off, advancing methodically through the cell block. Bullets slapped angrily off the white plaster by Sam's ear. Kearney's fire drove the Cuban back. Sam tossed a grenade, banking it off the walls and around the corner where the guard was

holed up. Concussion shot plaster dust and a severed hand into view.

From the map on his wrist, they needed only to make one more corner. Frightened voices rose as questions were called in Spanish up and down the cell blocks.

"Howard Cleftman?" Daniels bellowed at the top of his lungs. "Cleftman? Where are you? The USA's come to get you!'

"*Here!* I'm here!"

Sam sprinted down the dingy cell block. The floor—gray with dirt—grated under his boots. The air had a foul smell. "Where?"

"Here!" The voice sounded louder.

Something shook the detention center to be followed seconds later by a muffled bang.

"Here! Here! *Here!*"

Sam slid to a stop and shot a quick look inside to see the familiar face. He slid the bolt back and pulled the door open. The man staggered up, thin and pale, misery reflected in his drawn face. He limped forward and Daniels had to physically drag him from the cell.

"God . . . so glad . . . you came," the man whispered. "Knew you would. Knew you wouldn't leave me here. Knew you. . . ."

"C'mon, man. Let's get outta here!" Sam swung the frail CIA officer over his broad shoulder and smiled a toothy grin. "Clear out!" He hollered. "I got him!"

Slap Watson appeared from another cell block, yanking back bolts as he went. The prisoners boiled out of their cells, sliding back yet more bolts as others ran, panting, frantic, wide-eyed, to escape. The air filled with babbled Spanish.

Another bang sounded from outside.

Sam trotted easily down the halls, rifle swinging in one hand. Cleftman's limp body, thrown over his shoulder, bounced like a sack of rice.

Automatic fire—unsilenced—echoed through the hallways. Sam ran harder, not as careful of the whimpering burden he carried.

Anderson slid around a corner. "Move it, Captain! Intelligence blew it! Must be a couple hundred Cubans out there and they got ordnance!" As if to emphasize, a heavy *kumph-thud* sounded distantly.

"Damn!" Sam growled. "Sound recall. We gotta get to that landing field. Mason? How's Murphy doing?"

Mason looked up from his radio. "Got their communications. He's laying down a flanking fire and hammering Fidel's boys pretty good. Our ride's on the way in."

The *Cubano* prisoners continued to stream past them in a headlong flight for life and freedom.

"Cover me!" Sam yelled as he bolted out the door, almost slipping on the brass Mason's HK spewed out as he sniped at the Cuban military seeking to advance from the barracks into the compound.

With his burden quivering and limp, Daniels ran with all he had, bullets whupping loudly around his ears. Behind him, the night became a confusion of automatic weapons fire and screams as the fleeing prisoners ran into a maelstrom of wicked crossfire and death.

The hot humid air made sweat trickle down his cheeks as he pounded along. Cleftman had to weigh in at around one-eighty.

"Murphy?" Sam bellowed into the dark.

"Here, Captain! We're ready any time you are!"

"Blow it, man!"

Cuban tracers crisscrossed the night as a brilliant white flash illuminated guard towers and a woven-wire fence a split second before a concussion ripped them apart.

Murphy's stocky form pounded past followed by his squad. From behind, Cruz and Watson laid out a devastating fire, covering their retreat.

A loud pop coincided with the prison lights flickering off.

Sam passed the fence line. Softer dirt lay underfoot where it had been torn by the explosion. Here, away from the prison, the night smelled of damp earth, green plants, and grass. The hot muggy air lay heavy, torn by the sounds of machine guns and louder bangs of heavy stuff. Men called and screamed in Spanish.

"Murphy, get ahead of us! Secure that landing strip or we're all dead!"

Dark figures sprinted past, lungs gasping for air. Behind them, a burst of gunfire ended in a tortured shriek. Light flashed to their right followed by a blast.

A door burst open in a dark barracks across the road to expose a roomful of half-dressed soldiers illuminated by a dozen matches held in brown fingers. *"Que pasa?"*

Sam pulled up long enough to empty a magazine into the doorway, the HK bucking in his fist. He barely made out a dark form beside him chucking a grenade as he stumbled on. The barracks windows blew out in a spray of glass.

"Sam? This way!" Murphy called.

Sweating, Daniels sprinted along, wishing his Detroit-bred lungs could get just one full breath of cool air in the hot muggy hell of the Cuban night. Cleftman sobbed quietly.

Automatic fire chattered in the dark. How far had he run? A half mile? More? The weight on his shoulder ate into his stamina. What if the plane wasn't on time? What if the Cubans shot it up on the way down? A nasty tension built in Sam's breast.

A flare lit the sky and Sam could see Murphy's men fanning out, covering the approaches to the strip. A drone grew in intensity. Gunfire sounded from the thick vegetation to be answered by the soft stutter of muffled weapons.

"Come on, baby." Sam searched the sky, picking up the shape of the plane as it skimmed treetops.

The louder sound of a fifty caliber cut the night to be followed by the *CRAP-POW!* of a Soviet 73mm field gun.

"Come on." Sam wet his lips, blinking at the sweat that trickled down his face.

The plane dropped, settling onto the field. Sam swallowed hard as the craft taxied to his end of the strip, swinging around in the gaudy light of the flare.

Sam hunched his back to resettle Cleftman's weight as he scuttled under the wing, prop wash almost knocking him flat. The door opened, one of the CIA crewmen dropping the ladder.

Sam slipped Cleftman off his back and climbed up,

pulling the Station Chief after him. Mason appeared like magic, talking quietly on the radio.

"Get Cleftman strapped in," Daniels called over his shoulder as he pulled the members of his team in, counting heads. The dark forms of familiar figures scrambled forward to seats, clipping their rifles in silent efficiency.

"Mason? Any casualties?"

"Simon took one in the leg. Everyone else checks in."

"We ready?" the pilot called back.

"Pulling Kearney and Watson through the hatch now!" Murphy called back. Gunfire sputtered from the trees. "Go! Get us out of here!"

The engines moaned, then the plane shook as it started forward. Bullets made a snapping patter on the fuselage. "Fly, baby, fly," Sam whispered to himself as the g pulled him back and the props thundered.

The nose came up sluggishly and big plane lifted.

"We made it," Murphy whooped.

One of the CIA men slipped into the seat beside him. "Got Washington on the radio. We'll have air cover as soon as we cross the twelve mile limit."

Sam took a deep breath, pulling his goggles off. "Key West, here we come."

The CIA agent looked at him. "They want you in Washington ASAP. We're taking you straight there."

"You guys that anxious to get Cleftman back?" Sam grinned, teeth white against his black face.

"Cleftman's no longer the concern. They want *you*, Captain. Top priority. From the tone, I got the impression we could have dropped Cleftman in the drink for all they cared."

Murphy moaned, "Aw, man! Now what?"

Mason chuckled. "Must be that Senator's daughter you—"

"Shut up, man! That ain't funny in any way, shape, or form!"

"Drop Cleftman?" Sam frowned. "We in some sort of trouble again?"

* * *

Colonel Fermen jumped when the KGB Head, Andre Kutsov, appeared in the air across from him.

"Jesus!"

Fermen stared, realizing the man's lips had formed Russian, the words coming through in English.

"How did they get you here?" Fermen asked the first thing that came to his reeling mind.

"You came to me!"

"I'm in my office."

"So am I. I see my books here." Kutsov reached and plucked a volume out of thin air.

"Holographic projection with instant translation," Fermen muttered to himself. "Nothing else explains it. But we've just begun to work out the technology, and it takes lots of equipment. Damn it! How do they do it?"

Kutsov's lips pursed, gaze drifting uneasily around him. Fermen realized he'd done the same. What projector? Where?

Then Kutsov sighed and straightened. "I am supposed to inform you of the steps we have taken. We have located every person on the list supplied by the Ahimsa. They are on the way to your country."

Fermen nodded. "We're still trying to reach some of our people. A couple of . . . well, operatives, are still out of touch."

Kutsov smiled wearily. "I took the liberty of having Barbara Dix informed that Washington would like to speak to her."

"How . . . No, never mind." He leaned back, rubbing stubby fingers over his forehead. *Damned KGB!*

"You look tired, Colonel."

Fermen simply stared, elbows propped on his desk.

Kutsov chuckled hollowly. "Evidently you haven't slept any better than I have."

"What do they want from us?"

Kutsov turned, shaking his head. The man looked terrible, heavy bags under his bloodshot eyes. "I haven't the slightest idea, Colonel. Perhaps . . ." He waved his arms expressively.

"Let's hope not. I don't know how we'd resist."

Kutsov raised his eyes, a reminder they were under observation.

"Andre," Fermen said quietly. "It doesn't matter. If

they can project your image into *my* office in the basement of the White House, they can monitor us anywhere, anytime. I mean, think of the people they asked for. How did they get the information? They asked for our best people by name—using information from covert files. They tapped your best illegals, our best case officers. If they can do that, and place those damn mirror balls over our warheads . . . well . . ."

"And what else can they do, Colonel?"

"Let's hope we never have to find out."

General Kutsov fingered his books. "If only we knew *what* they wanted from us!"

If only . . . if only . . . Fermen met the KGB general's frightened expression with one of his own.

* * *

The Ahimsa Overone known as Wide wheeled on his tread foot, one eyestalk on the monitor which depicted Bill Fermen's office on the planet below. "You see, they have no choice."

His body had thinned, giving him a wheellike appearance. Two eyestalks protruded from either side along the axis of his yellow-brown body. Happily, he rolled back and forth, powered by the redistribution of mass within his leathery hide. A manipulator formed, flesh extending to touch a control panel; the scene he watched shifted to the American base on the polar cap below. Men and women worked to remove file cabinets, maps, and computer records, which parka-suited men trundled out to the waiting C-130s.

The second Ahimsa on the narrow bridge seemed to deflate, his sides sagging as the mottled reddish patches on his tread foot grew darker from changing pigment. From that trait, Spotted had derived his name. "I would ask you one last time, Overone. Why? This is madness. Interference with an interdicted species violates every moral code established by the Overones. Think of the ramifications, the potential for disaster. It's as if you're dealing with plague! What if they get loose somehow? What if—"

"Peace be with you, Nav-Pilot. I've given this a great

deal of thought. For the last three hundred years, I've planned each move, watching, studying their evolution. The only disaster will be suffered by the Pashti."

"The Pashti are a *civilized* species! Overone, what has happened to you? Where have your senses of responsibility—"

Wide wheeled, eyestalks swiveling, hard stare pinning his subordinate. "Are you questioning my intelligence? My authority?"

Spotted flattened even more, as if the air had run out of his boneless body, the filaments that webbed his interior going flaccid. "I do not question your intelligence, Overone. I simply can't understand your willingness to disgrace the Pashti. Despite the cycles they—"

"The cycles!" Wide shrilled, piping his disgust through the air spicules at the base of his eyestalks. "Am I to watch the power of the Ahimsa eroded? With each of their cycles, they are more . . . *and we are less.*"

The colors in Spotted's leathery surface deepened, a sign of emotional anxiety. "But, Overone, what you plan to do . . . it's as barbaric as these animals you study. What has happened to you?"

Wide rolled forward, his thinned height imposing to the flattened Spotted. "You know why we came here. For two million of their years, this species gradually increased in intelligence. Remember what they were the first time we came here? Naked, defenseless, shivering little beasts, that's what. They lived as scavengers, picking fruits and leaves, scaring other carrion eaters away from the carcasses of dead animals. Every galactic thousandth or so, we updated the information on their development. They progressed slowly, predictably."

"And were interdicted," Spotted reminded with a shrill piping.

"Yes. Yes. What would you expect? They killed each other—and anything else that got in their way."

Spotted whistled dismay. "Why can't we leave them alone now? Why can't we simply let them destroy themselves and allow evolution on the planet to change its course? What is this fascination with humans?"

"The last one hundred thousand years, Nav-Pilot."

"But we've proved it was only an anomly. They haven't been interfered with. No one tampered with their evolution to make them—"

"But that's exactly it! Why? After three million years of gradually paced evolution with long plateaus of homeostasis, why did their cultures suddenly explode? What brought them from scattered bands of nomadic hunters to an incipient space-faring culture in less than ten thousand of their years? They're an aberration, something we've never seen in millions of galactic years."

Spotted shivered, sides trembling.

"Yes, Nav-Pilot?"

"You've been suppressing information. None of the data we've collected have been sent to the Overones."

Wide's hide stretched tight with anger as he thinned further. "I have my reasons."

Spotted chirped and whistled. "You still haven't told me how you intend to use humans to disgrace the Pashti."

"No, Nav-Pilot. I haven't."

"Does it have anything to do with the records you keep studying? The humans who preoccupy you were all—"

"Do you question *me,* Nav-Pilot?"

"But these animals are dangerous! This planet has been interdicted. They—"

"They can't even travel to their moon anymore, Nav-Pilot. They are in cultural regression—decline. At the threshold of space, they gave up the stars. They abandoned the heavy lift technology which would allow them to explore their own solar system." Wide's round body thinned even more. "Humans are no more than primitives headed down a path of mutual self-destruction through their awkward fission weapons. Now, my friend, I will put an end to that. Like useful animals everywhere, I shall domesticate them."

"For what?"

Wide whistled through his spicules. "Mostly . . . for myself."

"And if they won't domesticate?"

"I'll destroy them."

* * *

Riva Thompson paced the small waiting room. Beyond the window, two F16s taxied past. The rising whine of their powerful engines left her wincing.

She crossed her arms, still uneasy, wondering at the sudden change in her life. The two agents had appeared at her desk, flashing Secret Service badges. Her supervisor had simply nodded as they escorted her out of the big white NSA building and into one of those nondescript, look-alike sedans Detroit cranked out like clones.

First she asked questions politely. Then she asked them with more vigor. She could have questioned a rock for all the response she got. As her fear and frustration grew, she took some measure of vengeance by cursing them in Arabic and Russian. After all, what better use could a language specialist have than that?

She stood five-foot five. Flame-red hair hung to her shoulders. Hard green eyes stared out of a lightly freckled face. Last April she'd survived her thirty-second birthday—and wondered where the time had gone since she graduated from Columbia so long ago. Ten years, years of excitement, anger, fear and heartbreak. Now a deep-seated worry chewed at her guts with razor teeth. What had she done to draw the Secret Service to her? Some old colleague?

She'd paced the room's dimensions: five paces wide, seven paces long, and nine paces on the diagonal. She'd emptied half of the coffeepot, and used the rest room that could be entered through a corner door. When she tried to leave, an armed air policeman politely told her to stay put. She presumed he still waited beyond the door.

What did I do? She ordered her mind, going back through the years. Undoubtedly she'd made some mistake during her CIA days. What? One by one, she cataloged the cases she'd worked on. Vienna? Had one of her team been doubled at the time? Who? Charlie? Ann? Dietrich? No matter how she tried, she couldn't make herself believe any of them had been recruited by the KGB.

Bill Casey himself had debriefed her over the Lebanese debacle. She couldn't take responsibility for what the analysts and policy makers did with her field reports once she'd filed them. Her evaluation of the situation had been succinct and emphatic—the predictions so painfully accurate. Damn it, she'd *told* them what would happen.

Lebanon had soured her. Why pay a case officer to risk her ass in the snake pit Lebanon had become if the desk-bound analysts in Washington weren't going to listen when the reports came in? She narrowed her eyes. Yes, that's where it had all gone wrong. Theoreticians—looking for the grand picture, seeking to prove their pet hypothesis—had missed all the signals. Of course, the reports by the field officers never made it to the policy makers—and people died. *Asshole Washington bureaucrats.* CIA was full of them.

"And then I jumped for the Israeli liaison," she whispered under her breath, shaking her head. A vague image of Ari's face tried to form. She forced it away, stopping the hurt before it could wound her again.

She jammed hands to her ears as the F16s thundered by, shaking the building and rattling the windows. Like lances, the deadly forms shot into the sky, rising at an impossible rate of speed.

Maybe she'd gone crazy after Ari's death. She'd worked desperately for a while, ruthlessly tracing out KGB networks that supplied the Intefada. Unlike the CIA, Mossad had been ruthlessly efficient.

She walked over to the window, staring out at the winter-bare trees just visible beyond the endless concrete. Her passion had broken the day she watched a young Palestinian girl shot down in front of her by Israeli soldiers.

At the height of her professional career, she'd asked for a transfer to NSA.

And now? Had the past come back to haunt her? In her dreams, Ari's eyes became those of a frightened young girl as the blood ran foaming from her mouth to stain her cheeks and mat thick black hair amid the dusty rubble of a Nablus street.

"What a world," Riva whispered. She watched an F111

settle on the runway, braking frantically as the building shook again.

What do they want of me? Why am I here? She shook her head, staring into the distance, hardly aware as the big jet taxied up, stopping just beyond her window. Trucks moved in like puppies around a bitch, connecting fuel lines, ground crew hurrying about as they inspected the aircraft.

"Riva Thompson?"

She started, irritated with herself for missing the sound of the door opening. The AP stood to one side as she walked out. He escorted her into the chill outside. The nippy Virginia air carried the scent of burned kerosene and solvent. Behind her, the buildings stood squat and military-ugly. Chain link fencing topped by Y brackets of razor wire rattled softly with the breeze blowing in off the coast. Overhead, leaden clouds cast a somber mantle over the day: gray as the chilled, stained concrete under her feet.

"Your plane is here, ma'am." He indicated the big jet.

"My . . ." Riva gaped.

"And I'm the chauffeur." A woman walked toward her, helmet under one flight-suited arm. "Barbara Dix," she introduced herself. "We'll need to get you suited up and we'll be on our way."

"Do you know what this is all about?"

Barbara Dix pushed mahogany hair back. She appeared to be a trim, athletic woman in her late twenties. Cool brown eyes stared levelly into Riva's. Dix had a slight squint, as if her eyes had been molded by bright sun—or danger. She had that look of cool, capable efficiency. "No, I don't. Uh . . . I'd kind of hoped you did."

CHAPTER III

Sheila Dunbar decided she could come to enjoy First Class on the Concorde. She looked back, seeing the stewardess standing in the hatch, still smiling. Sheila took a deep breath, listening to her heels thumping hollowly on the thin carpeting of the jetway as she walked up the slight incline. *Where is everybody? Not even a British Air attendant in here?* The air carried the odor of airports, nippy from the cold outside. *Bloody God, what's this all about?*

She stepped out onto the concourse, finding her gate abandoned. Kennedy International might have been evacuated just for her. Lines of chairs sat hauntingly empty. The passage of multitudes had left stains on the red carpeting of the international terminal. Spacious white walls bracketed the windows where passengers could look out at the planes. No one manned the British Air booth at the gate. No placard marked the arrival of the flight.

Eerie.

The thought that she had been the Concorde's only passenger unnerved her even more. She had still been trying to stifle her yawns when they hustled her on board half a world away at Heathrow. And now this? A shiver worked up her spine.

A severely dressed man walked out from a side door. As she smiled, two plainly dressed Secret Service men seemed to materialize at her elbow.

"Welcome to the United States. This way, Major Dunbar," he spoke in that toneless voice that had become cliche for security personnel.

"Indeed, no customs?" She cocked her head, long

blonde tresses bouncing over the cobalt blue of her coat. Her smile sagged as his face remained wooden.

"No, ma'am."

"Do at least let me freshen up a bit."

"Yes, ma'am."

The Secret Service waited, flanking either side of the women's room door. Inside, she washed, tried to blink some of the champagne out of her foggy system, and checked to see that none of the chicken parisienne was stuck in her teeth.

She studied the effect in the mirror. She stood five-nine and weighed only one-twenty. Not bad for twenty-nine years. She wore a knee-length skirt that did the best for her shapely calves. Her stomach was still flat and her narrow waist accentuated the swell of breasts that might have otherwise looked too small. She finished checking her appearance, meeting eyes that reflected a ravishing blue from either side of a decidedly straight English nose. Maybe, just maybe, a man might have said her lips were a little too wide, but then, when had she had time for men—or they for her?

Satisfied, she shot some breath spray into her mouth and pushed the door open, granting the stalwart Secret Service agents a smile before she followed the wooden man to an elevator. A black limo with those wretched tinted windows carried her across the airport. The car pulled up and she stepped out before a ladder—this one to climb into yet another aircraft, sleek and ominous, marked United States Air Force.

Morning had almost caught up with her. Her breath frosted in the chill air. A jet roared somewhere in the pre-morning darkness. The lights seemed too bright and hurt her eyes. The ladder chilled her fingers as she climbed.

At the hatch, a flight-suited officer saluted and led her to a spartan seat under the cockpit.

"And now where to?" she asked soberly.

"I'm sorry, ma'am. I don't have that information." The young lieutenant gave her a serious nod and bowed out after seeing her duly strapped into her seat.

"You'd think someone had died dreadfully from their faces," she mused, hearing the whine of the engines. The plane rolled and bucked slightly as it crossed the concrete. The taxi seemed unusually fast and after what could have been no more than thirty seconds, g force squashed her back into her seat then down as they lifted off.

Time passed and Sheila found herself preoccupied with her situation. At MI6, she specialized in systems theory, gaming, strategy, and tactics. She'd risen rapidly as a result of her uncanny talents during the Falklands scuffle. For the most part, she ruthlessly dissected the work of NATO strategists, attempting to see weaknesses in strategic planning and logistics.

Her mind clicked back to the morning—from her watch, only four hours ago. The painful jangle of the telephone had brought her to puffy-eyed wakefulness.

"Sheila? General Hardwick here. Sorry to wake you so early. Seems we're in a bit of a bind. I'll have a car in front of your flat within ten minutes. Pack light. Time is of the essence."

She'd said yes before it really sank in. First thing, she'd stepped on Tips, her black and white cat and sole companion in the world. Fortunately, she had remembered to open a tin of food for him and splash a glass of water into his bowl. Stumbling about in the dark, she'd dressed, grabbed her purse, and almost pitched head over heels as she tripped on the stairs. True to Hardwick's words, the car had been waiting. Only, she hadn't gone to her office.

Looking at the instrumentation that surrounded her, she couldn't help but ponder what she would wear in the coming day, days, or. . . . "Oh, poor Tips." She stared nervously at the tiny cubicle.

Hours later, she still couldn't fathom what Hardwick had done to her. Irritated, she realized she didn't have any puzzle pieces except that she was being transported somewhere by the American military. What did she have that they needed? Her stomach lurched as the aircraft dipped. She unbuckled, stood to get the circulation going, and opened the little door, realizing the champagne she'd had on the Concorde wanted out—now!

The young lieutenant sat before a radio. Through the

plexiglas bubble, a violet-blue sky beckoned. The sun seemed to be behind them.

"Excuse me," she asked, touching his shoulder. "Do you have facilities?"

He nodded and pointed. "Better hurry ma'am, we're on the descent."

She nodded, sighed wearily, and found the tiny head—not built for women. The experience proved militarily spartan.

"Where are we?" she asked, on the way back to her cubicle.

"I regret that I don't have that information, ma'am." He looked at her innocently. She detected a vulnerability in that gaze. No wonder the Yanks had caused so much consternation in England during the war. With a little coaxing, he could have been a real charmer with those big blue eyes and long lashes.

"I should have realized." She returned to her seat and buckled in. Minutes later she felt the gear go down. The tires chirped as the aircraft bumped down and g tried to throw her through the front of the aircraft.

The lieutenant appeared, leaning over her compartment. "Better put these on, ma'am," he said softly, eyes still blissfully innocent. He handed her a down-filled jumpsuit and an . . . Arctic parka?

"But I. . . . My word, Leftenant, where are we?"

He shrugged and grinned.

"Look, I was jolly well nipped out of bed at an ungodly hour this morning, bundled off to Heathrow, slapped into the Concorde and flown halfway around the world. My superior simply said it would all be arranged. Now, what is bloody well going on?"

The lieutenant shrugged expressively. "I don't know, ma'am. I'm simply following orders." He looked sheepish. "My CO said you should dress for the weather outside and I guess I'll have to make you."

She gave him a wicked smile and took the cold weather clothing. The jumpsuit went right over her dress—so much for looking professional! The coat hung heavily and immediately she started to perspire. She took the gloves the lieutenant offered and followed him to the rear. The wind practically ripped the door off the hinges as she made her way down the ladder.

Winter? Hell! The wind gusted by at twenty or thirty knots. Streamers of snow tinkled along the metal webbing of the landing mat. Above her the hatch banged closed, cutting off that direction of retreat. She turned, looking at a wilderness of wind-whipped sky and sculptured drifts. Horizon and heavens blended in a white haze of blowing snow that churned in wreaths of sub-zero cold.

Several domes, which might have been equipment storage or quonsets of some sort, lined the runway. Two snow-packed tractors with chained tires seemed to back up such an assumption as they rolled out from one of the buildings.

"Blessed be . . ." The gale of ice crystals ripped her words away as quickly as she spoke to tumble them about the frozen wastes. What appeared to be an Eskimo walked toward her.

"Major Dunbar?" he shouted in the blasphemous accent Americans called Texan.

"Here!" She waved, realizing the mucus in her nose froze with each breath.

"This way, you'll turn into a block o' ice out here." The figure waved and she trotted, stumbling along behind. When it came to functional practicality, high-heeled pumps would make it as far in the Arctic as a proctor in a gang of skinheads.

"What of my luggage?" she insisted. "I didn't quite expect to find myself playing Peary or Amundsen. I'm not prepared for the North Pole! And who will feed my cat?" She stepped awkwardly through the frozen snow in a staggering walk, buffeted by the relentless gale. She mistook the rising howl for wind at first. Rather, the building moan came from the Air Force jet turning and taxiing away.

"Don't worry. It will all be taken care of!" he called across the lashing wind. Her breath frosted white on the fur that lined her parka.

"But my cat!"

"Don't worry."

Images of Tips starving, dying of thirst, and over filling his cat box haunted her.

The entrance consisted of a hole that led into the side of a snowdrift. An insulated door opened and Sheila stepped through into another world. Had it not been for the ice around her hood, she might have just walked into an office building on Bond Street or in Brussels or Miami.

"Good heavens!" She mumbled numbly, pulling her hood back, upended by the changes wrought so quickly in her life.

The Texan smiled. "Here, I'll take your coat. Colonel Fermen will be here any second to take you to briefing."

"Yes. . . . Uh, thank you." She waved to his retreating back and added, "I think."

A printer chattered in the background. Blinking, she shook her head. She'd never believed a career in MI6 could have led to a real James Bond life. An Arctic base? What did that mean? Coolly she tried to catalog the options.

Insufficient data. I don't know the game yet.

The colonel who approached down the hall fit the stereotype of an American administrative officer. He wore the sweater Americans had effected for a uniform. His chunky body tended toward fat. A bald scalp reflected the light, hair graying along the temples. Serious eyes took her measure. He looked like he hadn't slept recently.

"Major Sheila Dunbar?"

"Yes, Colonel. I must say, your methods are rather dramatic." As she took his hand she noticed the strain on his face.

"Yes, well, sorry about that. We didn't know we needed you until yesterday evening. Uh, that would have been early morning your time. Had to wake the Prime Minister up to get you on such short—"

"Prime Minister! My word." For a second she wanted to pinch herself to make sure she wasn't caught in a bizarre dream. Her mind wrapped itself around that new bit of information and resorted the data in her head, searching for a pattern in global events. Did this involve the Soviets? Had they reacted to the nationalistic struggles by turning their efforts against external threats?

Fermen's voice interrupted her thoughts. "If you'll follow me. Briefing has been delayed pending your arrival."

Thick carpeting cushioned her feet and the office walls had been paneled in fake wood. Acoustical tiles hung overhead, interspersed with fluorescent lighting. Fermen turned abruptly and led her into an ordinary looking confcrcncc room. A long tablc fillcd thc middlc of thc floor. Women and men stood around the peripheries, talking quietly, watching her with sudden interest. The tall blond with Adonis features wore a Soviet major's uniform. The muscular black man appeared to be an American captain. The short stocky fellow looked like an Israeli fresh from the Sinai. A striking brunette woman stood in the rear, inspecting her thoughtfully. A redheaded woman gave her a hard scrutiny. The proverbial pin could have been dropped thunderously.

"Gentlemen, ladies, may I present Major Sheila Dunbar," Colonel Fermen turned to watch Sheila's expression as he added, "your commanding officer."

Sheila turned to stare. Her keen mind couldn't fit the announcement into any matrix of data. The whole situation couldn't be described as anything less than ludicrous. What possible reason could they have to put her in command of . . . what? Her stunned mind flopped, unable to grasp anything which would allow her to manipulate the crazy data. Instead, Sheila did the unthinkable.

She laughed.

* * *

"They are all assembled," Wide piped through his spicules as he watched the imaging monitor. He formed and extended a manipulator to adjust the audio input to a minimum. Humans wasted a lot of time over inanities. Wide knew a lot about humans. He'd been studying them for almost three hundred years.

"Overone, we still have time to withdraw. No one will know. Our presence will be forgotten by all parties," Spotted reminded, one eyestalk on Wide, the other on the humans gathered in the room so far below. He rocked back and forth on his tread foot.

Spotted formed a manipulator and punched the buttons to initiate the sequence which purged the moisture that had collected in one of the hydrogen tanks. A series of monitors displayed various status reports for the ship, all easily accessible from the central strip he rolled down. A reading rose as solar wind increased to effect the Earth's magnetosphere. Spotted detached one of his minds to deal with increasing hull ionization.

Wide flattened himself slightly, a sign of nervousness. "We won't . . . we can't." He rounded out with resolution and moved an eyestalk to watch Spotted. "Is this not the lesser of the evils? On one side we are eroded cycle after cycle by the Pashti. Here we deal with trainable animals—but animals nonetheless. Which would you rather? Humans we can control? Or Pashti who would control us after the next several cycles?"

Spotted bounced himself off the deck in irritation. "Neither. You claim to be concerned with the Pashti and their cycles. Theirs is a temporary and harmless insanity. What would you do with humans? Fight temporary insanity with permanent?"

Wide whistled his laughter. "Perhaps you have begun to learn from me after all, Nav-Pilot."

"There must be another way."

"There is," Wide whistled soberly. "We could employ a biological agent. There would be little difficulty in forming a parasite which would eventually wipe out the Pashti as a species."

Spotted flattened himself to a mottled white pancake. "If they ever found out, the Pashti would—"

"—sweep the Ahimsa aside like so much foamed cinder?" Wide answered, pulling in his sides, thinning into a wheel. "Pashti are condemned by their own benign natures."

"I suppose the consequences are no more severe than fooling with an interdicted planet like this Earth. If the Overones learn of this, we will—"

"I *am* an Overone!" Wide piped fiercely, an eyestalk whipping in Spotted's direction. "Ahimsa have lived far too long without risk! The Pashti are proof that intelligence is not everything. Why are we failing while they absorb more and more of the galaxy? Eh? What have we to lose?"

"Excommunication," Spotted almost wailed, falling flatter and flatter as his confidence ebbed. "If anyone learns of these humans, we'll be . . . oh, too terrible! If the Pashti learn what you're attempting, they'll—"

"Hush!" Wide shrilled through his spicules. "You make no sense. Keep your minds together. Perhaps you would flatten and lyse?"

Spotted recovered and sent an eyestalk to look at the humans. The woman had ceased laughing. "And if they are not so easily tamed? What then, Wide? Can you control them?"

Wide pulled himself even thinner. "Of course. They're animals. Clever perhaps—but animals for all that. I shall treat them as such." He paused, staring at the monitor. "What do you think I've been studying with so much intent these past three hundred years? If they become unruly, their recent history has provided more than one example of how to discipline them."

* * *

Fermen took her around the room. "Captain Sam Daniels, United States Army."

She shook the black man's hand, wondering at the faint scars along his cheeks and the hard look in his eyes. "My pleasure, Captain."

The short Israeli gripped her hand vigorously. "Colonel Moshe Gabi, Israeli Defense Forces."

"Colonel."

Fermen cleared his throat. "Major Viktor Staka, Red Army."

She stared into those cold eyes, fighting an involuntary shudder.

"My pleasure." Even the Russian's voice sounded deadly as he gave her a short bow.

"Major Svetlana Detova, KGB." Fermen's tone remained professional.

"Major." Sheila shook hands with the attractive woman, meeting piercing blue eyes.

"Major." Detova spoke in unaccented English.

Fermen turned to the last of the women. "Riva Thompson, NSA."

"My pleasure."

Sheila followed Fermen to the front of the room. *KGB? Red Army? IDF? Why?* She took the seat Fermen indicated, juggling the data. *Commanding officer? Me? What do I have that they need?*

Fermen stood at the head of the table and cleared his throat. Sheila settled back, brow furrowed. An aide slipped a blessed cup of tea into her fingers.

Fermen seemed at a loss for words as he looked up. "You are all wondering why you are here."

She barely heard a faint, "Understatement of the year," but couldn't spot the speaker.

Sheila looked around, hearing a slight whispering, realizing the sound came from instantaneous translation of Fermen's words into Russian and Hebrew.

"The circumstances," Fermen continued, "well, they're somewhat extraordinary. Suffice it to say, President Atwood, General Secretary Golovanov, General Kutsov, and myself are the only people who know at least some of the facts.

"We've had, well, a unique communication from . . ." He swallowed, appearing lost as he tried to find the right words. "Ladies and gentlemen, you've been called here at the behest of a species called the Ahimsa—at least they say that's the closest translation of what they call themselves. I believe the term in vogue is either extraterrestrial or, if you're of a slightly different mind-set, alien."

Sheila sat in a stunned silence.

"A what?" Daniels asked softly, uneasy eyes on Fermen.

Fermen raised his hands in a pleading motion. "It sounds crazy, but . . . but . . . Captain, it appears we've been contacted by a life-form from outside of our solar system. A species which . . . oh, damn, I sound like a lunatic."

Daniels raised an eyebrow, shooting a quick glance at the Russian whose controlled expression looked like it might crack his face in two.

"Colonel Fermen, perhaps I can explain better than

you." The voice spoke from thin air above the table. "I am called Wide."

The image which formed didn't appear to be a projection. It just grew out of nothingness over the conference table. Sheila's first impression was of a large white balloon perhaps five feet in diameter. On closer inspection, she could make out low lumps and knobs around the circumference. Two thin stalks extended on either side of the ball and terminated in black spheres perhaps an inch in diameter. Eyes? So it seemed since they immediately swiveled, searching each face in the room. At the base of each eyestalk she could make out a puckered sphincter and a breathing spicule.

"You see me in one to one scale," the apparition calling itself Wide continued. "If you will watch, you will observe some of the primary characteristics of Ahimsa physiology."

The white beach ball rolled neatly through the air the length of the conference table, easily backed, and suddenly stretched all out of shape into a square, a pincushion, a long rod, and then protruded various branches of arms and other unidentified appendages. With these the Ahimsa performed various examples of dexterity.

From the darkness, a voice asked. "So, where'd you catch this critter? What does it have to do with us?"

Fermen continued to stare at the apparition with awed eyes. "We didn't catch it . . . it caught us."

Sheila could see the speaker, Daniels again. He lounged back in his chair, a tall long-limbed, broad-shouldered man. His face displayed a series of deep lines forming a perpetual squint around knowing eyes, broad nose, and wide mouth. The uniform appeared to be stretched smooth over solid muscle. His eyes carried a hint of threat. He had a pencil between his dark fingers, tapping it absently on the tabletop.

"Caught how?" Daniels demanded, head cocked so the steel wool of his short-cropped hair glistened. Sheila sipped her tea and watched, curious at the animal magnetism in the captain's posture, the skepticism in his expression.

No more skeptical than I am. She shot a quick glance at

the Russian, surprised to see a glint of amusement had formed in his blue eyes. The KGB major glanced warily around the room, as if searching for projectors. The Israeli leaned forward, a grin giving his face a gnomish look.

The projection turned in midair, an eyestalk shifting to stare at Daniels. "If you will allow me, Colonel Fermen, perhaps I could answer Captain Daniels' questions."

"Go ahead." Fermen's voice couldn't hide the irritation and the . . . what? Fear?

The Ahimsa spun and looked Captain Daniels in the eyes with his two stalks. "Our appearance out of the sky would have caused considerable consternation. The shock would have set off riots, warfare, perhaps nuclear holocaust. We therefore opted to simply obtain your superiors' attention and convince them we had arrived. To do so, we selectively drained your defense networks and placed your nuclear arsenals in a state you would call stasis. The American President ran for a computer where we communicated our wishes. The Soviet General Secretary tried to escape Moscow and we were forced to transport him to a terminal where he could learn our wishes. Subsequently, contact between our species has been attained without the confusion, uproar, or calamity which might have followed a less circumspect approach."

A staccato of Russian translated instantly into, "This is an American Walt Disney trick?"

The Ahimsa turned and answered, also in Russian. The translation never faltered. "Not at all, Major Staka. My people come from beyond your solar system. Our actual evolution began in a different galaxy—the one you call Sculptor. We expect skepticism and encourage it. What you chose to believe at this point in time is of no importance. By the time your belief and cooperation are necessary, all doubt will have been removed."

Major Staka ran a tanned hand through his close-clipped blond hair. She would have called him beautiful, were it not for that steel in his expression, the insolence that bespoke calculated violence. He, too, had those keen, knowing eyes and a raptor's expression. He moved gracefully, nothing wasted as he leaned back, muscled shoulders slantwise in the chair. His expression remained controlled. Only the threatening eyes, bracketing his straight nose, stared flintlike and alert.

"To convince me that you are from another star will take a miracle."

"I shall remedy that in time, Major." The Ahimsa rolled forward. "For the moment, you only need this preliminary briefing. You are under orders to accede to my demands for the time being. That is sufficient for now."

Sheila bit her lip, trying to understand it all. *Why me? This can't be real! Aliens? They woke up the Prime Minister to get me here? Is this really happening? Can this . . . thing really be a space monster? Why all the subterfuge? Does the story* it *gives make sense? Why did they put me in command? What do I know about commanding combat veterans like these? How do we know any of this is true?*

"Colonel Fermen," Sheila cupped her tea as she frowned. "The alternative to assuming this, uh, holograph we're seeing is real is that we are undergoing some sort of stress test. Is that indeed the case?"

The Ahimsa wheeled in place to stare at her. A chill ran down her spine. The projection was very very good. "Excellent reasoning, Major. You determined that most rapidly given the data at your disposal. Very well, let's assume you are right for the moment. Will you play along? Go ahead, consider this to be an evaluation of some sort—a test of your abilities. Our purposes do not require that you believe any of this—so long as you function as if it were indeed the case. Can you do so?"

"I can."

They flew her here—the only passenger—on the Concorde. An Air Force tactical bomber brought her north—alone. The implications shuffled through her mind. Her heart began to bang against her chest. Why? What was the game? The alternative was that an alien hovered in thin air before her eyes. And that had to be completely impossible.

Impossible? This rubbery beach ball *couldn't* be an alien!

Why conduct this test in a buried Arctic military base? How much did it cost to charter the Concorde? The American bomber had been waiting just for her. What kind of coordination did that take? Presidential order? Chief-of-Staff?

So why here?

Assume a spaceship showed up one day hovering over Trafalgar Square. What then? Panic? Military response from frightened officials? Religious fervor? Economic paralysis? Stock Market crash? Rioting? Millenarians shouting in the streets? Fear? Anxiety? Mass hysteria? End of the world syndrome. Governments toppling.

Assume the aliens had a thorough understanding of who we are as a species. How would they proceed to make contact? She swallowed dryly, her tongue suddenly thick. *Just like the Ahimsa said.*

Gut hollow, she looked up at the harmless appearing beach ball. One of the black eyes centered on her.

"That explains the chartering of the Concorde for one person. An Air Force jet all my own. There would be no press leaks in a place like this. What happens here can't get out."

The Ahimsa seemed to suck its sides in, to thin. "That still does not disprove the elaborate hoax hypothesis."

"No, but it becomes less and less plausible, doesn't it?" Her voice sounded distant as her mind hacked the alternatives away from the conceptual core.

"Indeed," the Ahimsa agreed.

"Oh, my God!"

CHAPTER IV

The short Israeli sat with his elbow propped, chin cupped in the palm of his hand. He studied the Ahimsa before shifting his glance back to Sheila. He looked like a stereotypical Israeli tank officer. Broad shoulders filled a somewhat mussed uniform that looked like it had come straight out of the field. A deep tan had burned his face. An amused expression lined his features, gaze sober but spirited. His nose had been mashed into a stubby thing that looked like it had been broken a time or two. His sandy hair needed cutting, having grown almost too long for a military man. His cheeks sprouted a four-day stubble.

"I don't understand." His Hebrew translated automatically. "This would seem to be the responsibility of Prime Ministers, Presidents, and generals. I was brought here by order of the Prime Minister of my country. Major Dunbar was sent by her Prime Minister. Where are they? What am I, a tank officer, doing here?" He bit off his next words before he articulated them, smiling at his thoughts.

Wide turned to center an eyestalk on Moshe Gabi's weathered face. "Your Prime Minister does not know why you are here. He simply complied with a request from President Atwood. I have already told you. Outside of those in this room, only the President, the General Secretary and KGB head know of the Ahimsa."

Moshe's face screwed up and he lifted a finger but thought better of it, leaning back in his chair, looking perplexed.

"How long have the Ahimsa been involved in this dialogue with the Americans and Soviets?" Sheila asked, seeing that no one else had much to say.

"Less than forty-eight hours," Wide replied in his perfect voice.

Sheila articulated a question which had been bothering her. At first it hadn't sunk in, now it begged to be asked. "I notice that we are all military personnel. Is there a specific reason for that, Colonel Fermen?"

"There is," the Ahimsa answered in his place.

"I assume, then, that our relationship is to be of a military nature. May I ask if this is a future reflection of Ahimsa-human relations?" She cocked her head with growing tension. Around the table, she noted that Gabi, Staka, and Daniels were leaning forward, interest shining in their eyes—like stalking tigers. Detova, the KGB woman, sat with crossed arms, expression pinched.

The Ahimsa rolled back and forth in the air. His form seemed to deflate and flatten for a moment. Almost immediately, he sucked his sides in to the point where he almost became a wheel. His modulated voice echoed slightly. "In a way, yes. We, the Ahimsa, need the services of each individual in this room." At the stir, he added. "I wish to set your minds at rest. The Ahimsa do not have any plans for conquest. We have screened the movies you call *War Of The Worlds, Footfall, The Invaders, V,* and many others. Had we wanted your world, we would have already taken it. I assure you it is well within our power. That should be sufficient to allay your fears."

Sheila felt something slip into place. "You do, however, need mercenaries." She half-rose out of her chair. The Ahimsa flattened again then straightened as Sheila continued, "Captain Daniels, what is your specialization?"

His gaze shot meaningfully toward the Russian and then to Colonel Fermen, his jaw clenched tight, expression harder than nails.

"Special Operations Department, United States Army," Fermen's wooden voice supplied. "To follow up. Major Staka commands a Long-Range SPETSNAZ unit in the Red Army. Colonel Gabi's command is the special Assaf Assault Tank Company." He gestured to the KGB officer. "Major Detova is the Resident Head for KGB operations in the Pacific Rim. Everyone else in the room is either an intelligence specialist, such as yourself, or has some other skill the Ahimsa require for their, uh, operation."

"And who and where are we supposed to fight?" Viktor Staka asked softly, gaze sweeping the room.

Wide's voice didn't change inflection when he said, "If I told you, it would be meaningless at this time."

"Space!" Captain Sam Daniels chuckled hollowly. "And Ronald Reagan thought he'd be the first to initiate Star Wars!"

"And if we decide we don't want to go?" Moshe asked, lips twisted with amusement.

The Ahimsa spun to face him. "Do you wish to remain behind?"

Moshe fingered his bristly chin. "Defense Minister Natke tells me I must obey any of the American's orders. I will do so. I am a colonel of the Israeli Defense Forces. I would ask you one question, however. If I go, can you, with your superior technology which can blank American and Soviet defense nets, assure me that my country will not be Arab when I come back from these stars?"

Wide's eyes extended from the sides of his body, stretching until they stopped inches from Moshe's. His voice sounded flat as he answered, "Your Israel will be safe in your absence. I will pay your price for loyalty."

Moshe looked around, leaning back as Wide's eyes retreated. He winked at Sheila and smiled. "So I have saved God's chosen by agreeing to fight on a star? Ben-Gurion and Dyan should have had it so good. Who would have thought my country's safety could be bought by subordination to an English commander?"

Sheila remembered the distrust the Israelis had for the British. "Before we go further, why am I in command? Why not the Colonel? Or Captain Daniels, or Major Staka? These men have seen combat. Why me, a simple analyst?"

Wide turned again. "Major Dunbar, we searched the records of every man and woman in the military forces of your world. Some, of course, have no electronic records so we can't be sure we have the best in you. On the other hand, you are familiar with sophisticated technology and its adaptation and utilization. A Mujahadin strategist wouldn't necessarily have those skills. Further, your advanced study in game theory makes you most desirable. Your talents will maximize the efforts of your command. You have the ability to produce the most effective fighting force ever created."

"Couldn't your computers do that? Manipulate your technology?"

"We don't need human computer specialists. We need military personnel," Wide insisted, flattening slightly.

From the corner of her eye, Sheila noticed that Svetlana Detova had gone ashen. The KGB major lowered her eyes. Significant? Sheila studied her hands, now turning the teacup on the table. For years she had cursed her ability with games. More than one potential relationship had been broken irretrievably when a handsome young man couldn't win a game of chess, a hand of gin, or even croquet. That same skill had given her such an incredible edge during the Falklands war. Her brilliant analysis had shot her through the ranks from lieutenant to major.

"And now we go to the stars?" she asked, looking up as she came to a resolution. "I suppose it is poor morale for the troops, but perhaps you will give us an idea of what we are facing. I assume you have the best Earth has to offer when it comes to soldiers?"

Wide turned in the still room, searching each of the faces that stared sullenly up at him. "We have made a careful study. As in any situation, there are compromises to be made. Major Staka, for example, understands that the Afghans are the finest fighters in the world." Viktor's face went stiff. "They, however, are a superstitious lot. Taken away from their land, tribes, and religion, they would be worthless. Nevertheless, his SPETSNAZ unit has picked up a great number of their traits. Captain Daniels and his trained command have other skills and a certain ruthlessness we appreciate on an academic level. Colonel Gabi will provide the necessary expertise with heavy equipment as the IDF has produced the finest mechanized warriors ever—and he is the best of them." Wide's eye turned toward Sheila. "Yes, we do have the best."

* * *

Wide used three manipulators to refine the image. In the bridge monitor, the figure of another Ahimsa formed. The hide could have been sun-bleached leather, streaked here and there as if by age. Glaring black eyes took Wide's measure, as the image gained resolution.

"Greetings and health, Overone." Wide flattened slightly.

"Greetings and health, Wide. I had almost come to the conclusion that you'd gone on to other studies."

"Respected Tan, I have simply taken prudent measures to ensure that no mistakes would be made." Wide flattened even more, his foot tread beginning to crinkle.

"Then you have defied the Overones? Broken the quarantine?"

At the strain in Tan's voice, Wide drew his sides in, thinning. "You know what I fear. When I met with you a ten thousandth ago, I shared my concerns—which were yours. I expected to have heard from you had you decided a more circumspect approach was warranted."

"I am well aware of that. I take it your Nav-Pilot is elsewhere?"

"He is in meditation stasis. I didn't feel he needed to hear this conversation. The transmission through singularity is tightly focused."

Tan's sides fluttered slightly. "Why did you come to me, Wide? What did you do to me when we shared molecules?"

"I . . . Do to you?"

Tan rocked slightly, a mellow whistling piping from his spicules. "You came to me for a reason. What did we exchange that day? Who are you?"

"I am only Wide. Nothing more, nothing less. I went to you because you were the first to come to this galaxy. Among all Ahimsa, you restrict yourself from sharing thought molecules. Many have speculated on your reclusiveness, and I was no different. I assumed you wished to remain pure, to keep the old values that led you to make the crossing to this galaxy in the first place. As the galaxy has turned, we've changed, lost so many of the old values. How long since anyone has journeyed back to our home? Immortality had just been perfected when you left—but Ahimsa still reproduced. Yet none have followed after Hurt's migration. Where are they? Lost to the traps of the minds like the rest of our fellows? Are they, too, satisfied to allow insane species like the Pashti to slowly gain control of their lives and destinies? I am not. I will not."

Tan's spicules chimed with a harmonious exhale. "Whatever you gave me in that sharing of molecules has changed me. Yes, Wide, you spoke correctly. I see the failings of the Ahimsa. I feel the concern you filled me with. Were you not Ahimsa, I could almost believe you tainted me with something alien, something insane."

"You know why I have taken the risks I have. I'm not driven by insanity, but the need to preserve our species. Ahimsa must recover their heritage. We must not fade, lost in our minds, in the Shithti trap of disassociation."

Tan thinned. "Beware, Wide. The realm of the mind—like space—is endless, larger than the universe, more powerful than a multigalactic singularity. In an existence of such wonder, the mundane can pall with incredible rapidity. Do not seek, or expect, to lure the Ahimsa away from that singing intoxication."

"I would not; however, we must balance our existence, respected Tan. The loss of ambition is a sin, inexcusable, especially for Ahimsa. Praise the Shithti for their intellects, but existence is more than probing at the boundaries of reality."

Tan stared at him. "They have often wondered if I were crazy for avoiding the Overones, for taking no new Nav-Pilot."

"I have shared. I know the feelings which are yours."

"Do you? I wonder, for you have no idea of how your sharing affected me. Would that I had thrown you out that time. You have brought me . . . brought me . . ."

"What?" Wide found himself flattening despite his efforts at control. *If I have alienated Tan, I would do just as well to bare my unshielded body to humans. Have I destroyed myself?*

"Anxiety, Wide. Disquiet with myself. Displeasure with

my kind and what we have become. Whatever you shared with me shattered my complacency. You have stirred depths of ancestral memories I barely remember. You've made me hurt. Made me fear. I am angered, dismayed. How did you lead me to that?"

"You know only what I have come to feel after studying the humans. Perhaps that is the reason for their interdiction. They can teach us too much about ourselves. I intend to force our stagnating Ahimsa to deal with real things again, to regain the control which has atrophied and wasted. I will light a new fire in this galaxy, and perhaps we'll yearn to see the stars again, Tan. Not just think about them."

"What have you finally decided?"

"I will take the humans to TaHaAk at the height of the cycles. The humans I have chosen have talents for destruction and anger. Yes, Tan, they are insane, violent, hideous in their own wonderful way. I shall unleash that on the Pashti. And when the cycles are over, the cry of terror will shudder the very dimensions of space."

"You don't intend to let these creatures loose?"

"Of course not. I shall keep a supply of them so long as they serve some useful purpose. In the event anything goes wrong, or if they become threatening, they will be quickly and quietly disposed of. No one shall know that I broke quarantine. You see, I shall leave the blame for the Pashti destruction of TaHaAk on their own decompressed carapaces."

"I shall say nothing, Wide, since I agree with your motives, if not your methods. Perhaps you *have* tainted me, infected me with something I do not understand, but I think something must be done." Tan thinned, tread foot becoming pale. "One last thing. If you fail, I will do everything in my power to protect the Ahimsa from blame."

Wide piped and thinned, a warm feeling churning within. "That is an acceptable risk."

"Risk?" Tan chirped. "You stir me to speculate, Wide. I could almost convince myself you have developed a fascination with death. But to do that you'd have to be . . ."

"Insane?" Wide clicked with Ahimsa laughter. "No, Tan.

I am quite sane—and I know exactly what I'm doing. After TaHaAk, nothing will be the same."

"Be careful. I have warned you. I will destroy all trace of your activities if you fail. I will deny that you confided your scheme and brand you insane. The humans, of course, will have to be destroyed."

"No one will know." Wide reached up and cut the connection.

* * *

The communication might not have plagued Chee'ee'la's study of teleological mathematical inversions of reality space change had the transmission not been concentrated on such a narrow singularity beam. As it was, his crystal body pulsed as the Ahimsa transmission shivered his perception of the subspace and disrupted his theoretical manipulations. The contemplation of the phase shift from primordial nothingness, along with its corollary that nothingness was inherently unstable, took long and careful deliberation as well as rigorous discipline and a critique that would brook no interruption.

Chee'ee'la analyzed the content of the Ahimsa coding and considered Wide's actions. Chee'ee'la's crystalline body pulsed with spectral emissions as he ran statistical predictions modifying the parameters of the future. And if Wide's claim that " . . . *the cry of terror will shudder the very dimensions of space,*" were true, interdimensional teleological phase change data might be hopelessly compromised.

Any such interference simply could not be countenanced.

CHAPTER V

Mika Gubanya laced his fingers together and flexed his muscles in an isometric exercise. His pale skin rippled and bulged as he worked his powerful arms. Looking up, he squinted out the triple-glassed window to the blowing snow beyond.

Why did they bring us here? Why are we in the middle of an American military base? What does this mean?

He turned, catching his reflection in the mirror. He stood in fatigues, a white T-shirt stretched and molded to his bulging chest. His thick black hair had been cut close to his scalp. The angular bones of his face reflected the Oriental influence of his mother's people—a mark against him in the eyes of the Great Russians. His black eyes glared at the image as he narrowed his thin lips.

"What now, Viktor?" he repeated the question that had been burning within ever since their transport had dropped them. "What is this all about?"

He waved at the small conference room attached to the barracks they'd been housed in. A coffee table contained American magazines. The chairs looked suitably comfortable and cushiony, the sort of thing he'd expect a soft American to sit in. The place didn't have the feel of a military establishment, but rather of a night club. "I tell you, I don't like this, Viktor. It feels like a trap. This isn't the place for us. I trust none of this. We should be . . . well, anywhere but here, in the midst of Americans."

"Patience, Mika." Staka walked over to stand beside him and stare out at the white bleakness. "I don't know what to tell you."

"Aliens? Creatures from another planet? We're expected to believe this? What is it? What? Some American lie that they bought in the Kremlin? Viktor, I don't like it. I don't know what this is about, but I *don't* like it."

"So you've said. Easy, Mika." Staka raised a calming hand. "We're soldiers of the Red Army—the best of the army. We do our duty. For the moment, the duty is here, for whatever reasons. I remind you, the General Secretary himself gave us our orders."

Mika flared his nostrils as he inhaled. "Viktor, you know better than that. Of all people, I don't question my duty. Still, a soldier has the right to question the circumstances. For me, to be in this situation, surrounded by an American base . . . well, it's difficult. I don't trust Americans. How many times have they smiled, extending their hands to the Soviet Union while at the same time slipping knives into our backs from behind? Didn't Gorbachev learn? All that time seeking better relations with the west while American stingers, arms, and ammunition were traveling to the Uzbeks?"

Viktor reached up, slapping a hand to Gubanya's shoulder, a wry smile on his lips. "We haven't been shot at yet. Not only that, KGB is here. If anything should reassure you, that should."

"And if it all goes sour, Viktor?"

Staka's eyes hardened. "Then we'll deal with it. They wouldn't let us bring rifles, but we've still got our knives and our bodies."

Mika shifted his gaze to the window. "And escape to that?"

Staka shrugged. "Don't worry. You're seeing trouble before it visits us. Relax and enjoy yourself. It's better than Afghanistan, my friend."

Mika shook his head, pacing irritably, smacking a blocky fist into his palm. "There we fought a cancer—a creeping disease that could corrupt and destroy us all. Here? What do we fight? Stories of space creatures? In an American base? I'll take Afghans and Uzbeks any day. At least with them, I can strike back. Kill before they get me. But here?"

The muscles in Staka's face pinched. "Just follow orders. For the moment, our duty is to obey."

Mika thumped a finger hard into Viktor's chest. "We obeyed when we withdrew from Afghanistan. Look what that got us."

Viktor met his angry gaze. "And what did that get us? Another rebellion when the Uzbeks saw Afghan success and Gorbachev's promise of a better future?"

Mika's heart constricted. "Viktor, what's happened to you? In the last couple of months, I've watched you close yourself off from the world, changing. That hardness in your eyes, I respected that, thinking the anger was directed at the enemy. Now, I'm not so sure."

Viktor smiled wearily, rubbing the back of his neck before stepping over to one of the overstuffed couches and dropping loosely down. "Mika, don't you wonder what's happened to us? I was a boy when Brezhnev invaded Afghanistan. As a young lieutenant, I thought I'd burst when I received orders to report to Kabul. Two years later I cried when we received orders to withdraw—but from relief, Mika. From relief." His unfocused eyes stared at some place hidden in memory.

"Withdrawing proved to be a mistake." Gubanya crossed his arms, looking down at the scars that crisscrossed his forearms. Combat wounds—like those on his legs and chest—they told of his commitment to the cause.

"Was it?" Staka was lost in his own mind. "I watched the finest army in the world grind itself apart in the Kush. I watched young men blown apart by little boys with hand grenades in broad daylight on Kabul streets. I watched an entire people blasted, booby-trapped, starved, machine-gunned, bombed and terrorized—and yet they endured."

"We could have won."

Viktor blinked wearily before rubbing his eyes. "How? Invade Pakistan? Do you think the Americans would have let us? Would the Chinese? Even India would have turned against us—and they *hate* Pakistan . . . but I lose my point. The fact is, we're still in Afghanistan. Suka died there, his blood soaking the ground. Like Ivan Makarenko, and Mikhail Lomonosov, and Stepan Baktin, and so many others we've known, laughed with, and watched die. Now young Soviet soldiers are blown up by little boys with hand grenades on the streets of Dushanbe and Tashkent and Samarkand. As we increase the pressure, bring in more troops, they become more dedicated, the resistance spreads through the southern Republics."

"And what would you do, Comrade Major?" Mika raised an eyebrow.

Viktor chuckled hollowly. "I don't know, Mika. I honestly don't know. But, I wonder, can we go on this way? Outside of you and me, how many are left of our original unit? Only the two of us. Ten years of warfare—with a two year respite in Zossen-Wunsdorf—and we're still fighting, being chewed up and digested, first by Afghans, and now by our own southern Republics. We're dead men, Mika, waiting for our opportunity to fall. That's all."

"You sound defeated, Viktor." A cold fist knotted in Mika's belly. *And if Viktor believes this? What then? What do I do?*

Staka shook his head, smiling grimly. "Never that, old friend. Only . . . only tired. Exhausted by the dead whose souls have marched past us in a dusty, parade goose step. But what about you? You always seem so invincible. Doesn't it bother you that the war gets bigger, that your chances for survival lessen each day, that we're fighting our own people now?"

Mika lifted his chin the way the Party officers had taught him. "My duty, Viktor, is to the Party, to the country which has given me everything. What's my life worth compared to that? How can you question? We have a great cause, that of justice, of universal brotherhood."

"And the dead that we leave in the wake?"

"We've always had to pay in blood! Twenty million of our people paid that price to stop Hitler! The way to world liberation won't come easily. Look at the challenges we face. We *must* keep our faith, overcome the lies and . . . and . . ."

"Yes, yes, Mika, I know. And don't look at me that way. I still have my loyalty to the Party and the state." He laughed, slapping a hand to his leg. "I'm not about to defect, to entertain Capitalist heresy. My country means too much to me. My duty remains a sacred trust, but I wonder about who we are. Where we're going. That's all."

"Good Party members never question," Mika whispered, eyes narrowing as he studied his major. *Never question! How well I know. How much I've paid.*

Staka cocked his head. "I know how you feel, Mika. You've more than made up for your parents by your—"

"Don't mention them again, Viktor. I never want to hear it. Not even from you, who I owe my life to." Mika's blood rose, hot and pounding. "They betrayed the Party . . . betrayed me. From the day I . . . Well, just forget they ever lived." *As I have forced myself to forget.*

An image of his father's face tried to form and he shoved it brutally away, drowning it in other things, memories of Party officials, of Political Training sessions, of combat and terror as tracers cut the night and rockets streaked the skies while men cried out and died amid the rocks and sand.

Viktor nodded. "I'm sorry. Forgive me. It's a measure of how tired I am." He stood, lips bent in a crooked smile like the old Viktor. "In the meantime, don't worry. Enjoy yourself—despite being surrounded by Americans. Learn what you can about their base, about their manners and habits. Look at it as an intelligence mission. Whatever this is about, the Kremlin chose us because we are the best. That's our duty now—to be the best—and to obey our orders, even if it means cooperating with Americans."

"No one has ever accused me of failing in my duty, Viktor." And the memory of his parents goaded him, like a thistle spine under a fingernail.

"No, my friend." Staka slapped him on the back and walked out, leaving Mika to stare out at the snow, memories of his parents sour in the back of his mind.

"With so much of the Soviet Union eroding away, I can't lose you, too, Viktor." He swallowed hard, remembering the look in Staka's eyes before each mission. And if Staka had begun to break? "Impossible!"

Doubts gnawed at him.

* * *

As he claimed he'd been instructed, President Atwood stepped out five paces into the Oval Office and turned, looking nervously at Howard Milfred, his Chief of Staff.

What do I do now? Milfred wondered. Jim didn't look off his rocker . . . but aliens? The Secretary of Defense had already been frying the phone wires to find out what had happened to his missiles. Every military base in the country stood on alert, jets patrolling the skies. With the whole country about to go berserk did Jim have to pick now to start acting weird? *Aliens, for God's sake?*

"Jim, are you sure you're all right?"

"Howard, we've been together for a long time. I know the whole thing sounds like the ravings of a lunatic. You know the warheads are dead. The Pentagon knows. Congress is going crazy and the media's finally getting wind. The aliens are here."

Milfred narrowed his eyes, fingering his chin as he stared at his old friend. "Look, maybe you ought to talk to someone. Vietnam did strange things to a lot of people."

Atwood swallowed. "I *have* talked to someone—you. My instructions are that I will be transported to White Base by the aliens. Ahimsa, they're called. I had to fill you in. There's going to be a lot of shit coming down and you're going to have to help me keep the lid on."

The lid's already off! "Jim, maybe it's the stress. I mean, well, just where *are* your aliens? Look, I don't know what the Russians did to the missiles, but this insane story about little green men. . . ."

"They're not green." Atwood shook his head, licking his lips. "Fermen called. He says they're round . . . and white . . . sort of."

"And you're going to be teleported out of the Oval Office to someplace in the Arctic?"

"That's right." Atwood looked at the clocks that studded one wall, each with a different time zone displayed. "In just thirty seconds."

And what am I going to do when it doesn't happen? He winced. *We'll have to remove him—put the Vice President in. Burt Cook's a good man. What will this do to us?*

Damn it, why now, when the Soviets have done whatever they've done to the missiles?

Milfred turned to stare out the bullet-proof windows for a moment, organizing his thoughts. "Look, Jim, I . . ." He gaped and ran forward, staring at the spot where Atwood had stood. A faint heat remained.

"Jesus." He pressed his foot into the carpet, feeling for a false floor. Then, slowly, he inspected the room for mirrors.

"Jim, damn it! Quit playing games!" He looked around, an anguished expression on his face. "Jim? *Damn it!* You're forcing my hand. We can't afford this. *Not now!*"

James Atwood stared at his friend's worried expression. He caught the second hand of the clock sweeping toward the twelve. The sudden lurch of his stomach barely gave him warning. Vertigo caused him to blink.

Grayness dropped around him, blanketing the world.

He stumbled, caught his balance, and shook his head to clear the fogginess. He stood in a paneled conference room under fluorescent lights. The acoustically tiled ceiling looked like any other and the blue carpet cushioned his feet reassuringly. He blinked hard and felt his gut settling again. Tremors of fear worked up and down his legs.

This was too damn much! Teleportation? Jesus! What had they gotten into? Worse, what could they do about it? Concede? Send all those men and women out for what? Three companies of the world's finest assault troops and intelligence personnel slated for some madness beyond the stars? Lunacy! The whole thing was incomprehensible! No wonder Howard looked at him like he'd lost his mind.

Shivering slightly, he wobbled toward the table and leaned against it, comforted by the wood-grained formica top and chrome steel legs. He took a deep breath, hand to his heart, staring at the blue carpet. Fake walnut wainscoting went halfway up the walls where painted white cinder block took over to the paneled ceiling. Plastic chairs lined the table and a coffee dispenser stood on a counter in the rear. A faint stirring of the air and a low hum caused him to look behind.

There, where he had just appeared, Uri Golovanov flickered into existence. Atwood reached a hand out to steady the green-faced Golovanov as he almost toppled.

"Easy," Atwood said as he led the General Secretary to the conference table and pulled out a chair. Golovanov nodded and pulled a handkerchief from his pocket to wipe his face while his mouth worked nervously. The Russian's dark brown eyes looked fearfully out from an ashen face. The General Secretary wore a dark suit—Italian, if Atwood had any eye for clothing. The man's worry reflected in his complexion, gray-cast in this light. A gleam of scalp penetrated through Golovanov's thinning gray hair.

Atwood stepped to the coffee dispenser and plucked a couple of cups from the row stacked on the counter. He poured and handed one to Golovanov before seating himself and sighing heavily.

"I will never get used to that," the General Secretary muttered under his breath. Atwood started as the Secretary's voice translated magically, just as Fermen had said it would.

He studied the room. Well, why not? How difficult could translation be if they could whisk people from one part of the globe to another? Curious, he looked around for a projector or some sort of translator as he said, "It is a different world today, Mr. Secretary." He could hear his own voice speaking Russian. "Feeling better?" Who could feel better? The whole universe had flip-flopped!

Uri Golovanov filled his lungs and nodded, eyes somber. "It is nothing. Stomach ulcers—so my doctor tells me. I take it we are at your 'hidden' Arctic base?" The Secretary's eyes went vacant as he added, "We had two agents here before you pulled all of your regular staff out."

Atwood lifted an eyebrow. "Does it matter anymore?"

Golovanov took the coffee cup and sniffed it before drinking. "I don't know. Perhaps we will wait and see. Suddenly, Comrade President, the liberation of the world from the chains of Capitalism is not of such pressing urgency. The survival of my country. . . . Who knows what is at stake?"

Atwood checked his watch, figured the time difference from Washington and sipped his coffee. "A lot of things—once you think about them—aren't important any more." He settled himself in the seat and leaned on an elbow, feeling exhaustion running through his veins. The posture looked most unpresidential, but at that moment he didn't feel important.

"Listen," Atwood began, butterflies in his stomach, "Uri, we'd better level with each other. I think the whole world's about to come apart. You and I, we've got to come to some sort of grips with this. We're on the same side now. The human side. I think, despite our differences, we've got to work together."

The General Secretary's eyes blinked dully, bloodshot—fully as hot and exhausted as Atwood's own. He came to a sudden decision. "I think, Mister President, that our troubles with each other are temporarily on hold. My people still cannot regain control of our Strategic Rocket Forces. No matter how they bypass and rewire, they cannot get electricity to the rockets. My KGB tells me your ICBMs are the same."

Atwood nodded, dimly aware that Golovanov had just betrayed "Eyes Only" secrets. The JCS had gone mad trying to understand what had gone wrong. And how could he, the President, tell them that aliens had done the impossible? If they believed him, the news would leak. The public would go berserk. The engineers had become the next thing to blubbering idiots as they tried to figure out why thousands of volts poured into one end of a cable didn't appear at the other. Damn it, conductivity couldn't just stop—not like that! Physics—at least for missiles—had ceased to work.

Golovanov snorted wryly, seeing his discomfort. "So, we are to order our people to go to the stars. My SPETSNAZ commander will go. What will the reaction be of your oppressed black war hero?"

Atwood slammed a fist onto the table. "Damn it, Uri! It's all happening so fast. They show up and we're jumping to their tune! How do we know what we're sending those people into? Haven't you ever questioned that?"

"I have thought, Mr. President." The General Secretary absently waved a hand. "Unlike your country, we order people into many situations which we do not like. Unlike your West, my Soviet Union cannot afford the attitude that life is sacred. Major Staka will take his unit and they will do whatever the Aliens want of them."

"But what if—"

They both looked up as Sheila Dunbar entered. She stopped, eyes wide as she recognized the men, muttered a weak "Excuse me," turned, and rushed from the room.

"So that is the commander of Earth's extraterrestrial strike force." Atwood looked bleakly at Golovanov. "Seriously, Uri, what are we in for? They completely blanked our net. Five minutes ago, I was standing in the Oval Office. I presume you were at the Kremlin. They're translating everything we say—or I assume it's another one of their tricks. How can we. . . . I mean, what could we—"

Golovanov raised a hand, his expression warning Atwood. "You don't have an innate caution, Mr. President. As in the spiderweb of Soviet politics, you must learn to say no more than you must."

Atwood nodded numbly. "I suppose an endless supply of KGB and Party commissars instill such behavior." *Damn! Did I have to add that?* In a small voice he added, "No matter what, our people must go. They're a small price to pay."

"We do not know these Ahimsa are hostile. Perhaps they are the salvation of mankind?" Uri chuckled, one eye narrowing. "Perhaps one was whispering into Karl Marx's ear while he wrote? Perhaps one rode with Lenin on that fateful train from Switzerland? Perhaps they're the true Communists?"

Atwood laughed along with Golovanov while his insides tightened. Was that the way it would be? Golovanov and the Soviets becoming patsies to any Ahimsa wish in order to curry alien favors and technology? *Damn it! I've got to survive in my own nest of political vipers! I can't worry about the Soviets sucking up to the Ahimsa to gain hegemony, too!*

James Atwood studied his Soviet counterpart. No, it was not over. The East and West were still at each others throats. There could be no trust—even now. An advantage could still be gained. One power would rise out of this to become supreme. But which one? How could he communicate the importance of that quest to Captain Sam Daniels? Would that rogue officer understand the importance? Would he know what to do? Would anyone?

* * *

Colonel Moshe Gabi smiled at the sight of his officers staring out the insulated windows at the snow piling up and shifting outside of the Israeli Defense Forces barracks. Sure they had all seen the thin crust of white that shaded the Golan and occasionally left the faintest mark on Jerusalem. Nothing had ever prepared them for this!

The barracks held most of Assaf Company. They lounged on bunks, some smoking, others playing a card game. The room heater had been dialed up to a comfortable eighty-five. Soft music played out of the wall speakers. Here and there, bits of uniforms hung on chair backs while the television showed news people interviewing suited politicians. A ring of his men watched with interest as some manicured Washington political dandy explained that no truth lay in the rumors circulating Washington that the military had suffered some terrible blow. And, yes, the missiles worked fine. There was no danger.

Moshe sniffed from a sinus condition—his own personal plague—and took one last look at his uniform. Still not the preening perfection the Soviet major enjoyed. No, Moshe still looked like what he was, a crack tank commander. The IDF didn't have room for fancy strutting uniforms.

"Aliens?" Ben Yar repeated, shaking his head. "And did the Tanach foretell this?"

Arya shrugged, walking over to the coffee machine with his slight limp. "The Prophets didn't foretell coffee so weak it runs like water either. Why do you worry? Think of where we will go, what we will see!" Arya looked gangly, a tall bony man with thinning hair on the top of his long head. A beaklike nose jutted prominently between two hawkish black eyes. More than once, Arya's tank had covered Moshe's rear—kept him alive.

"And what is the purpose of all this?" Shmulik asked, arm in a sling to immobilize the shoulder where it had been ripped by a fragment of Saggar missile. Shmulik's eyes shifted curiously to Moshe's.

"I don't know," he told them. "The Ahimsa didn't say. He only mentioned that we will go to the stars. You can bet it won't be easy, whatever they want." Then his expression fell. "I suppose it won't be news to any of you, but we may not come back. The stars could be like Lebanon."

Arya lowered his eyes to his scuffed boots. Into the silence, he added, "According to Jewish law, a man cannot be declared dead unless two witnesses see his body."

Moshe patted his belt where the stubby tongue stuck out from the buckle—not quite long enough to fit the nearest loop. He sighed and dropped into one of the overstuffed chairs. "Does it matter in the end? The Ahimsa have promised that Israel will be spared at least until we return." His eyes sought theirs. "Has anyone ever bought so much for so little?"

Ben Yar chuckled hollowly. "But aliens? Yes, I've seen the tapes and films of the meeting you had with that white beach ball. I don't believe it, Moshe. No, tomorrow, in a few days, next week, or sometime, we will be home again smelling diesel as we raid more PLO rocket bases. This isn't real. It can't be." His voice went up an octave. "I should be in a rabbinical!"

"We should be so lucky," Arya countered, eyes dancing. "One day at a time, my friends."

Shmulik's mouth twisted. "The men are worried. Many have wives and sweethearts they will not see on leave."

Moshe cocked his head, thinking about that. How long since Anna had been buried? Five years now. Time passed so quickly. He had always thought his bones would lie next to hers someday—God, missiles, and high explosives permitting.

"Wait. Be patient. We don't have all the answers yet. I've only been to one meeting." He checked his watch. "I'm almost late to another."

He stood, noting their measuring eyes. "I'll find out

what I can. Meanwhile, enjoy the view." He pointed at the window and headed for the door. Down the hall, he could hear the soldiers singing a song Yaffa Yarkoni had made popular during and after the 1967 war. Moshe stopped for a second, listening to the harmonious tones of male voices. How much were they leaving behind? The mystery deepened.

* * *

"I don't like it!" Murphy muttered under his breath. "This is weird shit to start with! Man, we're flying to the moon with a bunch of puffballs? And with Russians? C'mon!" Murphy leaned back on the bunk and pillowed his head on his duffel bag.

"Hey, we've seen some weird crap come down the tubes. But this, man, this takes the cake." Mason chuckled, honing his Randall fighting knife to a keen edge. "Aliens? Jesus! Hollywood, where are you when I need you?"

"Cool it!" Sam barked, tightening his tie. He hated having to horse out in dress uniform. Not only that, but any time his people had to sit around idle, trouble always followed. If his unit couldn't find any, they'd make their own.

"Look!" he said, turning, leveling a finger, staring down his subordinates. "I don't know what kind of shit we're in for, but you guys think of one thing." He sniffed a deep breath. "We got chosen because we're the best! Got that? You meatballs think about that!"

"Yeah, but, Captain, aliens? Man, they're talking about us going to space. You saw what they did to the shuttle? Man, this gets into some real weirdness," Murphy protested, reaching to put another cassette into Mason's prize stereo tape player.

Mason raised his hands and shook his head. "So think of the duty pay, buddy boy! Not only that, man, but we go up and clean up whatever the puffball wants cleaned and we come back heroes. Think of the chicks, man! They'll fall all over you. Take your pick. Movie stars, celebrity dames, hey, the girl next door!"

Murphy shook his head as Madonna's violent musical

expression exploded from his bunk. "I don't know, man. I ain't into getting wasted between the stars by no bug-eyed monsters—not with no damn Ivans." He punched the bunk bottom over his head with a knotted fist. "We gotta trust them bastards?"

Sam checked his appearance and pulled his hat over his bushy hair. "Okay, listen, crud. I'm off to another meeting. Keep cool and don't go bustin' up the Commies, hear? I want you goons to keep your brains engaged and your mouths closed. I don't want any reports of, uh, 'incidents,' you hear? I promise I'll clean the floor with the first one of you nuts who gives me grief."

Sam swung around on his heels to look at Murphy. "Listen. This time we're in deep. Got it? There's stuff coming down that none of us has any idea about. This ain't like no ordinary mission, maggot breath. Keep your nose clean like you've never kept it clean before."

"Aw, Cap—"

"Cut it, Murph!" Sam bellowed, hot eyes pinning his lieutenant. "Yeah, I know we got away with a lot because we were the best. We're here because we're the best. But you *think*, man. This time, we're not waiting for the mission. This *is* the mission and it's like nothing we've ever done! So no tricks, huh? Don't you go messin' with the computers, or sneaking into the women's john. Don't blow this, because sure as shit's brown and sticky, your ass will hang!" He straightened and smiled into Murphy's suddenly sober eyes. In a softer voice, he added, "Besides, Murph, it's an order."

Murphy laughed lightly. "Yeah, Captain. I got it. Mason and me'll keep the boys in line. We won't put no rotten eggs in that fancy SPETSNAZ unit's omelet till this is all over."

"Keep the faith, baby," Sam said, slapping their hands as he stepped to the door. He winced, looking back into the room, seeing Murphy, who smiled innocently. *Man, do I* have *to turn my back on them?*

A shiver ran down his spine on cold mouse feet.

CHAPTER VI

"It is like we are in the lion's den," Mika Gubanya added nervously as he poured another cup of the surprisingly good coffee from the pot.

Viktor flinched mentally at the ominous sound in Gubanya's voice. *He's not meant for this. Mika's a tiger, a predator not meant for a cage—especially one built by the enemy.* There would be trouble before this was all over. Viktor could feel it hanging like the thin film of cigarette smoke that left the air bluish.

Lieutenant Nicholai Malenkov laughed as he flipped through the channels on the stereo and found a classical station. "Mika, my old Comrade, enjoy this Capitalist experience. Think. One day soon we will rid the world of this tyranny! The Americans are struggling horribly to wade through this thick carpet. Consider the pain they feel as they listen to this wretched music coming so fine in digital stereo. It's barbaric to have to exist in these plush decadent quarters. Take some time to pity them for their excesses." Malenkov twirled lightly on his feet. "Pity them!"

Viktor checked the polish on his boots as he reminded, "You are not free of the KGB yet, Nicholai."

Malenkov's face fell. "And after all these years and so many battles where our lives hung in the balance, do you now confide that *you* are their ears in this unit? I knew that we had worked for them before—praise the Party for its wisdom—but to learn now that you are the man who has had my head beneath his glorious boot. I'm cowed, Comrade Major!" Nicholai raised a hand to his forehead in defeat.

Even sober, Mika chuckled at the dramatic assessment. He poured half a glass of vodka into the coffee and looked suspiciously about the room. "Nicholai, I'm glad you can be less than serious when we're surrounded by enemies. I hope you're still smiling when we leave here . . . if we leave here. What if all this comes apart? Where do we go? Providing you can win your way free of their clutches with only your fighting knife and your wits, have you secreted arctic gear away in your duffel?"

"I'm not going to worry about escape." Nicholai shrugged it off, padding to stare at the color television in the corner.

"You'll just surrender to the Americans?" Mika crossed his arms, an inquiring eyebrow lifted.

"Not at all. You see, we're not the only ones," Malenkov grinned as he paced back, expression changing to one of mild interest as he accepted a second glass Gubanya poured and inspected the wainscoting closely. "Such fine workmanship. But, as I was saying, I know who to surrender to. I saw Svetlana Detova about an hour ago. I met her once during a joint KGB maneuver. Where there is KGB—"

"—a good Soviet citizen need never fear," Viktor finished as he checked his image in the mirror and deftly plucked the glass of vodka from Nicholai's hand. He took a small swallow and handed it back.

"So, how do you feel about all this, Viktor? What is going on? Are we to be cosmonauts? Does any of this make sense?" Malenkov glanced around nervously, doubts about the security of the room in his expression. He'd already checked the obvious places were a bug could have been hidden by the crafty Americans.

Viktor swirled the liquid around his mouth, grimaced, and swallowed. Surely the Americans had better than that! No wonder they all drank bourbon or scotch.

He shifted his feet and thought. "I don't know what to think. Space?" Viktor threw up his arms. "We are asked to believe this Ahimsa is a real alien. Why not? It's very difficult to change the way we think, is it not, friends? So, say it's true? Just act like we're supposed to go and fight a war for this round white alien. We'll do that."

"Beats flying into Afghanistan every night," Malenkov added with a sigh.

Viktor caught the tensing of Gubanya's face, the narrowing of his eyes as he fingered his chin and stared speculatively at Malenkov.

"Just play the game. We'll probably be back climbing mountains in the dark while Mujahadin shoot at us before we know it. And, friends, when that day comes, we'll wish we were back here surrounded by safe snow and subzero temperatures instead of surrounded by maniac Afghans carrying Kalishnikov rifles. So enjoy it while you've got the chance."

"With pleasure!" Malenkov cried and flipped himself into the couch to stare at the television, vodka in hand.

Viktor smiled at the sight. *And Sheila Dunbar had made sense with her argument.* "Myself, I think it's some kind of test. Perhaps to study our reactions. But think about this. Whatever this is all about, we're SPETSNAZ, the best. Our duty now is to act it. Got that, Mika? No trouble. None. I know you're strong. You don't need to prove it by pulling some American's head off his neck just to hear the pop."

Nicholai chuckled gleefully as he figured out the remote control, eyes locked in rapture on the TV where it flickered soundlessly from one American commercial to another with each press of the button. How did they get such incredible color with an impossibly sharp picture? The image depicted houses too spotless and too well equipped with improbable electric gadgets.

"Don't you wonder?" Malenkov asked. "I mean, what if it's true? Let your imagination drift. Think, we might be engaged on a mission to the stars—the first men to be chosen by aliens for such a task. What a wonder, what a . . . a . . ." He shook his head, a curious glow in his eyes.

"I think Viktor's right," Gubanya insisted. "It's some test. I'm just trying to understand why the Party is cooperating with Americans. And what is the KGB role? What purpose could misdirection through something as absurd as aliens serve?"

"And I'm to serve as a subordinate to an English

woman?" Viktor screwed his face into a distasteful frown. "We're outnumbered two to one by an Israeli tank company and an American SOD unit—who are to work with us. I've met several women from KGB, women pulled in from all over the world—including deep agents, illegals KGB would rather kill than have exposed. What does this mean in the end, Comrades? And another thing, if someone must be sacrificed on a battlefield, who do you suppose they would leave behind?" Viktor cocked his head, seeing the impact of his words.

Gubanya's expression narrowed as he stared silently into his drink, huge muscles flexing as he tightened his fingers around the glass.

Malenkov added in a cunning tone. "Then Comrade Major, we must surrender to reality, join their ranks, convince them we are good Capitalists!"

Gubanya made a strangled sound, staring.

"Look there!" Malenkov cried, oblivious, pointing to a woman luxuriating in a huge tub with mountains of bubble bath covering her female charms. "I'm ready and able to tell the Americans I'll gladly join their ranks and jump into the same tub as their Capitalist women!"

"Ah, Nicholai," Viktor sighed as he opened the door, "sometimes I regret not being KGB. There are times I would love to condemn you to the penal battalions. Were you not so good a weapons officer, I'd do so."

As he closed the door behind him, he saw Nicholai's rapt expression as an American male in a flimsy sweater and a stupid hat gaped at a talking toilet seat and watched it flush blue water. Pray the aliens didn't have American TV!

* * *

Sheila Dunbar checked her watch. The time had come. She could see the sawed-off, banty IDF Colonel, Gabi, coming down the corridor. He looked like a man headed for battle, walking in a no-nonsense manner. Taking a deep breath, she entered the room where the two leaders sat at the head of the table talking earnestly and headed for the coffee dispenser.

Filling a cup, she left them as much privacy as remained. Her eyes caught Gabi's double take as he entered. The little Israeli's expression tensed before a thin smile crossed his lips. He flashed her a look, shrugged it off, and walked over, pulling a cup of coffee from the silver urn.

"In all of my days, I've been many places and seen many things. I never thought I'd be in the same room with the two most powerful men in the world." Moshe grinned like a gnome and sipped at his coffee, a look of disgust replacing the grin as he grimaced at the weak brew. Over the rim of the cup he glanced surreptitiously at the General Secretary and the American President.

"Indeed, Colonel, I sympathize. I hadn't any idea we were meeting with *them*."

"There may be many surprises yet, Major Dunbar. Don't tell me you expected to be placed in command of the first human extraterrestrial military force?"

"No, Colonel Gabi. I had no idea." Was that challenge in his eyes? "Does it bother you that you are under the command of a woman—a woman with no combat experience?"

The Israeli looked up at her, amusement twinkling in his soft brown eyes. "No, Major. As a boy, I served during the Yom Kippur war under a woman Prime Minister. I was present when Golda Meir was briefed on the planned destruction of the Egyptian Third Army. Her questions and her grasp of the field conditions was perhaps only second to General Avraham Adan's. Please, do not forget, in 1948 our Sabra fought side by side with the men. They bought our land with their blood, too."

"I think I understand, Colonel Gabi. I would imagine. . ."

He raised a hand and shook his head slightly. "Major, please, I come from an army where titles and proper behavior differ somewhat from anything you have been used to. Call me Moshe. In the IDF a command structure works like a family—well, not like a real family. You know what I mean? To win a war, there must be communication among individuals who know each other's needs and weaknesses. I'm used to obtaining results, not memorizing ranks."

She stared into his honest eyes. "And, pray tell, what

sort of results do you expect to obtain in our present unusual situation?"

He laughed. Sheila could see the President and Secretary look up, startled.

"Who knows?" Moshe said expressively. "These Ahimsa tell me my country's safety has been bought by my service in their army. I know the Ahimsa are powerful enough to get me and my men out of a war of attrition and here to the Arctic. Should one minor tank commander question power like that? It's cheap insurance. Perhaps the Ahimsa know something about the Arabs we do not?"

"Then you think the Ahimsa are real?"

The crow's feet tightened around his eyes. "Consider, if the Ahimsa are real, Israel is safe. If they're not, what have I lost?"

Captain Sam Daniels swung through the door, took two steps, and stopped to stare, mouth coming open. He pulled himself to attention and snapped out a salute, body rigid.

"At ease, Captain," came President Atwood's voice. "Go on about your duty. Just pretend the General Secretary and I aren't here."

"Yes, sir!" Sam beat a hasty retreat to Sheila's group. "Jesus!" he whispered as he poured. "'Pretend I'm not here,' he says. Sure! Shoulda handcuffed Murphy and Mason to the wall! Lord, keep them outta trouble."

"Your leftenants?" Sheila asked, head cocked.

"Yeah, good men so long as they're in the field. Try and pen 'em up with nothing to do but shine shoes and you got trouble. Nobody in the world I'd rather have at my back in the dark in enemy terrain—but locked up in that little room?"

She studied his dark skin and considered the faint scars that ran across his cheeks. Combat wounds? She'd read his personnel file. Quite a colorful career. Not many black American officers graduated first in their class from West Point. Not many rose among the ranks of Special Operations Department either.

"It seems that I have had the cream of the crop placed

under my command, Captain." Sheila gave him a challenging smile.

"Thank you, ma'am." He gave her a wary appraisal, expression blank.

Sheila crossed her arms and fingered her chin. "It has been suggested by Moshe that for the present we dispense with formal titles, Captain. Would that bother you?"

"No, ma'am."

"Then call me Sheila," she phrased it as an order and could see the distrust in his eyes.

"Uh, Sheila, did the Ruski go along with that, too?"

"You mean Major Staka? I don't know." Ruski? His voice carried the threat. Lord, don't tell me, not political division between the ranks. "Sam, how do your men feel about serving with the Russians?"

"They don't like it, ma'am."

Moshe watched them quietly, expression speculative.

"You say they're good soldiers." She paused, thinking hard. "I'm not sure that old enmities apply anymore, Sam. It's safe to assume that when we leave Earth, there will be no one but us. We're all we've got. I think the first order of business is to ensure that your troops and Major Staka's don't run into disagreements we simply can't afford. Is that within your abilities?"

For what seemed to be minutes, their stares locked, neither giving and Sheila felt him probe the very depths of her soul. His eyes had locked with those of men he'd killed. Death lay behind them. Sam Daniels reeked of a brutal strength, untamed, untrammeled. She faced intelligence and deadly competency. Her mouth went dry. *God, why did I question* his *ability?*

She steeled herself and a toughness rose within. *Sheila, this man will kill you as soon as look at you. If you don't win now, you'll be a mockery.* A bitter anger swelled as she fought to hold her own against his conquering glare.

Slowly, the corners of his lips crept upward. "Yeah," he breathed. "I can take care of my monsters. They're professional, Major. We'll do what we need to."

"Just so we understand each other." *Damn! Did he know how scared I was?*

He opened his mouth slightly, jaw cocked and eyes gleaming. "Yeah, I think we do."

A victory—slight to be sure—but still a victory. Nor had anything been decided. Sam Daniels would test her constantly to make sure she merited respect. Did he do that to all of his commanding officers?

"I'm curious, Sam, how many women commanders have you had?" She turned to fill the cup again. The coffee had grown cold in her fingers.

"Counting you . . .one."

"I see."

His eyes fixed on hers, as if to say, *Do you?*

* * *

Svetlana Detova ran a brush through her hair. Thank God that Barbara Dix had a spare. She looked at her suit in the mirror, patting at the wrinkles, hating the thought of appearing twice in the same outfit.

"No help for it," she added under her breath.

The redheaded American woman, Riva Thompson looked up from the magazine she had been reading.

Easy Svetlana, watch yourself. A sheep has more friends among Siberian wolves. She studied the lounge. Did the men divide like that? Soviet on one side, American and Israeli on the other? Of course, they'd only been together for one night. Still, she would have thought her comrades would have immediately integrated with the Americans, seeking to learn all they could, to take advantage of the situation.

Time to go. She took the brush back, smiling graciously. "Thank you, Barbara." The automatic translation still bothered her.

"Any time." The tall woman smiled crookedly. "As fast as they pulled everyone, I guess I have the only kit. I learned years ago. Don't take anything for granted."

"Looks like a flight bag."

"It is. Nice and compact." She smiled again, but those brown eyes indicated no more information would be forthcoming. "Let us know what happens."

"I will."

Svetlana turned and headed for the door, wishing she

had a different pair of shoes. The spiked heels snagged in the rich carpet.

Why did the Ahimsa need women? That question played over and over in her mind. *And what do they know about my computer abilities? There were no electronic records. I deleted them all.*

The thought sent a shiver down her spine.

She closed the door behind her, and stood for a moment, lost in thought. *I've started to assume the Ahimsa story is correct. But is it? Or could this be some curious game?*

"Meeting time."

She looked up to see Viktor Staka striding toward her.

"Good day, Major."

She fell in beside him, aware of the keen inspection he gave her. She could feel the animal magnetism of the man. She forced herself to walk with back straight. She smiled at him, taking his measure. He showed an interest—but what? Did the curtain he hung over his emotions have no holes? The deadly blue eyes betrayed little.

"You looked worried back there."

She lifted a shoulder. "Considering our present circumstances, a little worry would seem prudent, Major."

"Yes, we are quite a way from Hong Kong."

How did he know that? "I don't remember seeing you before, Major."

He smiled, the effort forced. "One of my men recognized you." The look went deadly again. "My unit . . . well, we've received replacements in the last years. The man who worked with you before is one of those."

"I thought your unit had done very well in Afghanistan."

Those cold blue eyes slitted. "We did."

"But even the best lose some, don't they?"

Jaw muscles bunched and rippled. "Even the best."

They walked in silence. What pricked her to goad him? If she ended up needing him, she'd have to have his complete loyalty.

He surprised her, saying, "How does it feel to be under the authority of MI6?"

For how long, Major? Aloud she said, "About the same as it feels for you."

The glance he cast her way would have frozen ice. "And tell me, Major Detova, what is your assessment of this situation? Is this Ahimsa situation real?"

In English, she said, "I think so," hearing it translated immediately to Russian.

Staka's eyes narrowed and he gave her a slight nod, understanding her warning. Yes, even here they were monitored. And what did it mean? Whatever program was being used, it immediately made a translation, even when two Russians talked to each other. That implied a certain weakness. Now, how could she exploit it?

* * *

Major Staka walked fluidly into the room and stopped cold at the sight of the General Secretary of the Soviet Union. Svetlana Detova followed, a thoughtful look on her face. She recognized Golovanov and smiled secretly to herself, not a crack in her armor. Major Staka, on the other hand, threw out a salute, face stiff and expressionless.

Sheila kept her eyes on Svetlana Detova. In complete control, the KGB agent poured a cup of coffee, meeting Sheila's gaze for the briefest instant.

"Thank you, Major Staka. Please, join your colleagues," Uri Golovanov's translated voice rumbled as the General Secretary caught sight of Staka, who still stood at attention.

"That will not be necessary, gentlemen, ladies."

Sheila turned to see that the Ahimsa had formed in the air at the end of the room.

Wide continued, "It is promptly 1400 hours. Let us get to work. If you will all be seated, I believe you have had time enough to come to grips with the situation and should have formed some questions. It is now time for my response to your concerns."

Sheila took a deep breath and settled herself, totally unsure of the protocol.

"If I may," Atwood began, "in view of the extraordinary nature of this meeting, could I request a secretary to record the proceedings? What we are about to do here is to conclude an agree—"

"I assure you," the Ahimsa responded, cutting him

short, "all this is being recorded. Yes, Mr. Secretary, I can see your concern. Do feel free to be blunt."

Uri Golovanov looked uncomfortably at Atwood and began. "Certain of our military systems have been affected by your activities. May I ask how you have neutralized our weapons and when we can anticipate their return to normal?"

The Ahimsa seemed to pull itself upright. "Your ICBMs will remain deactivated forever, Mr. Secretary. This is the dawning of a new age. I assure you that you no longer need them."

"But what about our common defense?" President Atwood cried, half out of his chair.

"You are commonly defended," the Ahimsa informed calmly. "Has it not been your intention, endlessly expounded upon by all, to rid yourselves of the scourge of nuclear war? I have done that for you. Consider it part of my payment for the services of your brave military forces." The Ahimsa spun and sent both eyestalks toward Moshe, ignoring the sputtering leaders. "Yes, Colonel?"

Moshe looked nervously at the Secretary and President before he cleared his throat and asked, "First, may I ask who we are to attack, or defend, and what weapons we should requisition to do so?"

"Excellent question," the Ahimsa chortled with what sounded like glee. "You are attacking a species called the Pashti. You are defending us—that is, both the Ahimsa and humanity. As to weapons, we have been studying you for some time. I assure you, we will supply you with everything you will need and our war material will be considerably superior to anything you are used to using. Training will take place during our journey to the Pashti home worlds."

"Who are the Pashti?" Sheila asked as she seated herself.

"That will come later," the Ahimsa told her. His eyestalk swung to Moshe again. "I believe you had a second question?"

"Uh, yes. Can you give me an idea as to how long the mission will take? What are the projected casualties?

And last, I do take it that there are satisfactory medical facilities aboard your vessel, correct?"

Wide thinned his sides. "You will be in space for roughly five years Earth time. To you, it will seem something like a year in space as a result of what you call relativity. Projected casualties are as high as two or three percent. Indeed, we suspect that our medical facilities will be most remarkable and effective. Major Staka?" The Ahimsa turned.

"My men and I have noticed KGB personnel here at the station. Can you tell me their purpose?" Staka made a tent out of his fingers, looking uneasily at Golovanov, never meeting the General Secretary's eyes.

Svetlana Detova's expression seemed to sharpen.

"The analytical teams you have noticed are present to assist you in the planning and conduct of your mission against the Pashti. You will receive the plans we have gathered and, along with your intelligence officers, you will begin strategic and tactical studies as soon as you board the Ahimsa spacecraft." Wide rolled easily through the air in his holographic projection.

"How soon are we leaving on this . . . mission?" Sam Daniels asked.

"Ten hundred hours, tomorrow, Captain Daniels." The Ahimsa spun effortlessly, eyestalks peering at the captain. "I suggest you brief your men that they will ride up into the sky inside a huge transparent bubble. I'm sure it will be disconcerting for them."

"Why not the instantaneous teleportation?" Uri Golovanov asked, face contorting with distaste.

One Ahimsa eye turned toward the General Secretary. "There are certain restrictions as a result of the gravity well you live in. To be sure, we could transport your people up like that—only it would kill a human. You do not have the body to withstand the sudden change in kinetic energy."

"How do we know we can trust you?" Daniels asked suddenly, leaning forward, eyes narrowed. Everyone stiffened attentively. Sheila felt her chest constrict. There it was—the question she had been too nervous to ask.

Daniels pressed on, finger pointed at the Ahimsa. "How

do we know you have Earth's best interest at heart? How do we know that you haven't come to take this planet over? How do we know you're right and these Pashti are wrong? I mean, there's a lot we've had to take at face value."

"Captain . . ." Atwood had paled.

"No, the question is reasonable." The Ahimsa rolled through the air and looked down at Daniels.

"To put it simply, Captain Daniels, we're the only choice you have. We've known about your planet for over two billion years. Until recently you were a minor curiosity to us. After your species began to evolve and expand, we were faced with a dilemma. You see, Captain, every species has a certain talent. Yours is war. Would it surprise you to know that yours is the only intelligent species which makes a ritual of killing others of its kind? No other intelligent species in the known universe wars with itself like yours does. No other species places its members in death camps, or tortures and starves its fellows. Think about it, Captain. Your species rushes headlong to kill fellow human beings at the whim and suggestion of your governments. Correct?"

Daniels glared hotly at the Ahimsa.

"You call it a patriotic duty to cross your national borders to maim and kill people you don't know and might cherish and love under different circumstances. People like yourselves . . . just because your leaders say so. Is that sane behavior, Captain?"

"It's a little more complicated than that," Golovanov began, raising a finger.

"Is it?" Wide wheeled. "You may believe what you like. That is your prerogative as a giver of insane orders. Nor do I fault you for attempting to maintain the myth which keeps you in power. Meanwhile, learn how true civilization dealt with your unique aberration. The Overones, as a result of this most remarkable and irrational behavior of yours, interdicted your planet in a landmark decision over one hundred thousand of your years ago."

The white beach ball moved slowly back and forth, flattening slightly. "So, you see, not only do we have no use for your planet, but you are stuck here within your system forever . . . unless you have friends on the outside."

President Atwood opened his mouth to speak.

The Ahimsa's voice rose. "And what we are about requires delicacy. Should any of you get caught, you will leave the Overones no other option but the destruction of your species and planet." Silence filled the room. "Oh, yes, I can see your reactions; but I warn you now and with all sincerity, they can destroy your world to keep their peace—*and they will.*"

CHAPTER VII

Howard Milfred looked up as the door burst open. He sat in the President's chair, leaning back with elbows propped. He might have felt some embarrassment, had his mind not been so preoccupied.

Admiral Bates, Head of the Joint Chiefs of Staff, charged in despite the protests of security personnel. Bates pulled up, recognizing Milfred. "Where is he?"

Howard's gut sank. "Tim, I think you and I had better talk." He looked at the aides trailing in Bates' wake. "Alone."

Bates jerked a nod, pulling at his uniform coat. "All right. Everybody out."

Milfred watched as the nervous staff members retreated uneasily through the double doors. The security personnel, looking unsettled and jumpy, pulled the door closed behind them. Well, being Chief of Staff did have some benefits. The thought of having to cut Jim Atwood's throat here—in this room—soured his belly.

"Where's the President?" Bates walked forward, his anger obvious. "I've been on the phone for the last three hours and every time, they say the President is unavailable. I've had it! I'm sick and tired of it. Now, in case you guys here don't understand the situation, we're sitting ducks. The whole damn country's gone nuts. People from Des Moines to Brownsville are scared stiff of the stories the press—"

"I know."

"Then, damn it, where's the President? Look, I've got my tail in a crack and something funny's happened to my warheads. I damn well want some answers!"

Howard shook his head slowly. "Tim, I don't have any."

"Well, you'd better damn well start thinking of some—"

"We may have to remove Jim from office."

Bates stopped short, a pointing finger half raised. His mouth went slack as he stared.

Forgive me, Jim. I'm sorry, but the country comes first. Howard stood, strolling over to the flag, feeling the texture of the material, wondering what loyalty meant. That funny vanishing act he'd pulled had been the last straw.

"You want to elaborate?"

Howard swallowed. "I think we'd better call the Vice President. Burt's—"

"Been going crazy, too. He's been on the hill saying the President's working on it!"

"Shut up!" Milfred spun on his heel. "Do you think this is easy? Listen, I've been with him ever since Vietnam. Jim Atwood . . ." The words choked in his throat. "He carried me out of a rice paddy one time. I . . . I guess you just had to be there."

Bates' face hardened. "I was."

Milfred's smile strained. "I mean in the jungle, Tim. Bleeding, not knowing where you could put your feet. Counting days until . . . Oh, never mind."

"Yeah, well, the Secretary of Defense is acting like a chicken with his head cut off. Every warhead we've got is useless, and my guys can't make heads or tails of what the Russians did. Those mirrors are . . . well, one of the boys says they're a stasis field."

"I know, I know."

"Then you know we haven't had a military crisis like this since Pearl Harbor!"

"Speaker of the House has been calling all night."

"*Then where's Atwood?*"

Howard Milfred worked his jaws against the tears that tried to form at the corners of his eyes. "Tim, he's flipped out. Disappeared." He stared into Bates' disbelieving eyes. "That's right. Listen. I'm going to call a meeting. I'll need the Vice President, the Speaker of the House, and the Cabinet. We . . . we've got to remove James Atwood from office."

"You're serious."

Milfred winced. "Jim says everything that's happening is because of aliens. Beings from outer space."

Bates' jaw dropped. "Aliens? Jesus!"

* * *

Viktor's heart bumped against his chest. *What are you, that you can threaten us so? How powerful are you, really?*

"Destroy the world?" Secretary Golovanov stared, hands gripping the table. "Impossible!"

Is it? Isn't this all impossible? Viktor scrutinized the alien, wondering where a bullet could be placed to kill it immediately.

Wide thinned. "And your silly little nuclear arsenal wouldn't? I placed your primitive nuclear warheads in a stasis. I would remind you, you live on a delicate planet. Suppose we dropped your moon in the middle of the Pacific Ocean?"

"No one can move the moon!" Golovanov reddened.

"You have no understanding of our power. But then, would one of your Chukchi aboriginals understand the power of a thermonuclear bomb? I assure you, human, our powers defy even that comparison."

"Uri," Atwood reached across. "He teleported you from Moscow. He drained our entire defense net. How could we resist?"

Golovanov's cheek muscles jumped as he clamped his teeth.

"With all respect, General Secretary," Viktor spoke carefully. "I, and my unit, will do our best for the alien. If this . . . apparition is truly an alien. If it destroyed our Strategic Rocket Forces like it says, we have no choice. Instead we will bargain our services for our world."

Svetlana Detova studied him through narrowed eyes. He sat back in the seat, a curious fear in his gut. How many lives would this cost him? Did the Ahimsa lead him to another, more terrifying Afghanistan?

"I have a question." Svetlana steepled her fingers. "Most of us came with what was on our backs. We are in need of clothing, personal items, communications links to our subordinates in the field. Will such things be allowed to us?"

Wide swiveled an eyestalk in her direction. "All supplies you request will be provided. You will have no further need for communications to your subordinates. I believe the President and General Secretary will confirm your new position and status. Any loose ends regarding your professional duties will be attended to by their offices. If you would like, you may also have promotions to any rank you wish."

"What about our families?" Moshe asked.

"A suitable explanation for your absence will be provided by the President and the General Secretary." The alien rolled forward. "I think you can understand the problems it would cause if you sent a . . . how do you call it, postcard, from Pashti?"

Viktor considered, realizing he tapped his fingers on the tabletop. His mother and father, both waiting in Tula, would be frantic. "It could have morale implications."

"I will see to it," Golovanov offered. "Major Staka, you do the Soviet Union a great honor. As do you, Major Detova."

"We have another problem," the President said uneasily. "I've already got my military and intelligence services up in arms. The Congress is aware that something's gone wrong. Wide, how do you expect to break this information to the public? I mean, the whole country is about to come apart."

"That will be handled at the appropriate time."

"When?"

Viktor noticed the strained look on Golovanov's face. Yes, the Kremlin wolves would be sniffing around, too.

"We'll work that out when the time comes." Wide seemed to flatten. "No matter what, the skeptics will be countered when we are visible in your skies. I suggest in the meantime, you prepare your populations."

"Prepare? How? No one's ever done this before."

"You have experts. Many of your scientists have been looking for life in the universe. My expertise is not in human propaganda—yours is."

"You have dropped a terrible problem in our laps." The General Secretary pushed back in his chair.

Wide rotated on his rump. "But who made the problem, Mr. Secretary? Only the misguided and short of sight could have looked up at the stars and not come to the realization that other forms of life could only be the grossest of statistical improbabilities."

"And I vetoed funding for SETI?" Atwood started to shake his head and stopped. "Wait. Why didn't we hear you? Pick you up with our radar and radio receivers?"

"Your listening stations monitor for electromagnetic spectral emissions bound by light speed. I won't even attempt to describe the physics we employ. Suffice it to say that what you would call a null singularity is dependent on neither time nor space."

"Null singularity? What the hell is that?"

"Precisely my point." Wide swiveled his eyes. "I have nothing more to say. I will begin transporting your people at 10:00 hours tomorrow morning. Please have your personnel ready. They will advance by twos onto the landing strip carrying their personal possessions only. What will appear to you as a transparent bubble will form around them. From there, they will be raised to my ship. Prepare them for the experience, please."

"What about us?" President Atwood asked.

"If you have no further need to communicate with your people, I will return you to your offices."

The President looked around nervously. "I'd like to say good-bye."

"Very well. Call when you're ready." And the Ahimsa disappeared.

Viktor took a deep breath. "Then, I suppose at 10:00 tomorrow, we will discover if this is all a hoax."

Golovanov stared at him miserably. "I greatly fear, Major, that this is no hoax."

* * *

Marshal of the Soviet Union, Gregori Kulikov, stepped into the room and nodded to the officers around the table. He took off his hat and went to sit at the head of the table. He looked at the grim faces, finally meeting Marshal Sergei Rastinyevski's measuring eyes.

The room had been finished in crushed velvet—the

color a bright scarlet. An oak table filled the center of the room. The ceiling arched above, plastered and painted white. Light reflected from golden filigree along the ornate curves and arches.

Gregori poured a cup of tea from the jeweled samovar beside him and composed his thoughts. "The situation is this, gentlemen. General Secretary Golovanov will not return my calls. I contacted General Kutsov, expecting some sort of cooperation with KGB during this terrible trial. What I got from Andre consisted only of misdirection and evasion. Either he, too, is frightened and unsure, awaiting some synthesis of KGB data—or he's involved with Uri in some way which we can only speculate."

"And the Strategic Rocket Forces?" General Pashka asked.

"Whatever the Americans did, however they did it, the rockets remain useless. Some of the physicists say they've never seen anything like it. Nothing they have attempted has put so much as a dent in the mirror balls."

"Then our only defense lies with the army." Grushenko closed his eyes. "We're in the same position we were at the end of the Great War."

"Militarily, yes." Kulikov lifted his tea. "Politically, we don't have a Stalin to stand up to the American President."

"And your decision, Comrade Marshal?"

Rastinyevski looked around the table. "In retrospect, Gorbachev made a critical mistake by not retaining the Brezhnev Doctrine. As Supreme Commander of the Red Army, I firmly believe we must reestablish our control of Eastern Europe."

"And if the Politburo disagrees?" Pashka asked.

"We have the guns, General." Kulikov looked around the table. "In the last ten years, we have been emasculated by budget cuts, by Perestroika and the Afghan debacle. Perhaps the time has come to reverse that trend?"

"Kutsov won't like it," Ivanov stated, fingers laced before him.

Rastinyevski filled his lungs and sighed, resignation reflected in the thin smile he gave them. "KGB must fend for itself. The time has come to cut the Party off at the knees. In the past twenty-four hours, I have placed two divisions of Siberian troops in Moscow."

"You are talking . . ." Pashka couldn't finish.

Kulikov chose his words carefully. "I think the peril has become too great for us to continue under Golovanov's leadership. We must seize the initiative before the Americans rebuild their nuclear threat."

"I must agree with the commander of the Strategic Rocket Forces. The time has come to reassert the power of the Red Army. First we will crush the Uzbeks and roll through the southern Republics—then we will retake Eastern Europe. The gamble, of course, will be whether the Americans will retaliate with their nuclear weapons."

"We take an awful risk," Grushenko said soberly, looking from man to man.

"Risk?" Rastinyevski asked, spreading his hands wide. "If the missiles are truly down, this might be our last chance to save the Soviet Union from disintegration . . . and obtain all of Europe as well.

"And who disabled the missiles? Their scientists? Surely not ours—the brightest scientific minds in the country are baffled." Kulikov rubbed his face nervously.

"Perhaps they conducted some bizarre physics experiment that went wrong?" Ivanov gestured his confusion.

"Then the time to act is now." Kulikov thumped the table with the heel of his hand.

"Gentlemen, what choice is left to us?" Rastinyevski lifted a challenging eyebrow.

* * *

Sheila stared at the ceiling. Everything seemed to be happening so fast. Why? If the Ahimsa faced a threat half a galaxy away, why did they need to hurry so?

She got up from the bunk in her room and walked to the table, picking up a note pad and pen. One by one, she listed the things Wide had said. Then she diagrammed the political systems of both the United States and the Soviet Union.

Frustrated, she stared at the papers she'd marked up. Not enough data. What would the political reaction be? What sort of fallout would come from the announcement that aliens had meddled with national security? How could either Atwood or Golovanov survive? No matter how she mixed the variables, she couldn't come up with a workable solution.

Unless Wide's magical technology could blunt the effect of the stasis protected weapons. NATO must be going mad . . . along with China, India, Pakistan, and Israel.

The situation in the Soviet Union had to be worse. They'd been teetering ever since Gorbachev's removal. The conservatives had watched appalled as Poland, Hungary, Czechoslovakia, East Germany and the Baltic states slipped away. They'd suffered severely from world opinion when they ruthlessly crushed the Georgians, Armenians and Azerbaidzhanis after the ferment of the Gorbachev years. For the moment, the Soviet Union seethed from within, the East bloc smoldering, the Uzbeks fighting a desperate guerrilla campaign that bled the Red Army a drop at a time. In such a period, could they afford another change of leadership?

The Americans staggered under problems of their own. The crushing depression caused by the national debt had gutted the world's most powerful nation, leaving Japan and Western Europe reeling in turn. Helpless to do more than condemn the Soviet outrages, the United States suffered under its collapsed economy. The people surged restlessly, looking for an answer. Atwood's election had been by the barest thread—two electoral college votes—with the Libertarians taking a whopping percentage of the popular vote. Since the beginning, Atwood's administration had stumbled like a drunken sailor from one crisis to another.

She filled her lungs and puffed her cheeks out. Politics carried so many random factors, so many unknowns.

She paced the little room, lost in thought. Her own situation prickled with just as many booby traps. And poor Tips, he'd be going half berserk now. Only she couldn't bring herself to ask Wide about her cat when all the rest of the world had been thrown into chaos.

She shivered at the memory of that look in Daniels' and Staka's eyes. *And I have to order men like those around?*

Nervously rubbing her hands up and down her arms, she considered them. Each was a trained commando, each had faced death hundreds of times—and dealt it. The Israeli, Moshe Gabi, came from a different culture. An Israeli could smile and sigh as he shot you dead in the most efficient manner possible. Worse, what baggage did the Israeli carry from the days before 1948? England had denied visas to European Jews—even during the Holocaust. Part of the responsibility for those six million people gassed by the Nazis rested squarely on England's shoulders. Lord Moyne's refusal of Adolf Eichmann's "blood for trucks" deal rang in her ears. Moyne's very words, "What shall I do with those million Hungarian Jews? Where shall I put them?" Nor had England made amends prior to the "48" settlement when they left the guns and fortifications in Palestine to the Arabs.

"And I have to command these men?" She closed her eyes. *You've got to do it. You must.*

She took a deep breath. "But where do I start?"

* * *

Murphy moved as soundlessly as smoke, bare feet placed just so. At the door, he carefully turned the knob, slipping into the hall. How long since dinner? Four hours? Five? Worse, he couldn't sleep in the room. It felt stuffy and close. Even through the insulation, he could hear the Arctic wind moaning outside.

He padded softly down the hall, stopping at the corner. "Let's see, kitchen's this way."

He dropped low to peek around the corner. Wouldn't do to run into anyone. They'd probably march him right back to Daniels and he'd be cleaning floors with toothbrushes or something equally beneath his dignity.

Murphy stood an inch shy of six feet. Years of vigorous training had left his muscular body whip-thin. He kept his reddish-blond hair close-cropped. Blue eyes looked out at the world around a pug nose meant for trouble and bent this way and that from past mishaps. A square jaw framed a mouth suited for grinning. Once he'd tried to be the archetypical Irishman, tough, brawling, and loud. SOD had taken that out of him, honing his instincts—but he still couldn't resist doing things, often just to see what would happen.

As he peered around the corner, he caught a glimpse of a man sneaking quietly. He knew that style of fatigue—Red Army!

Murphy's grim smile curled his lips. *And what would a Russian be up to in the middle of the night in an American base?*

Murphy tensed his muscles to loosen them. Not as good as a real warm-up, but it might make the difference.

He drifted along behind, each step placed perfectly. Just what destination would draw a Russian? The files in the main office? The communications room? Maybe the radar or the restricted monitoring facilities?

The Russian looked fit, spare, and he moved like a tiger. Black hair had been shaved close to his skull and he stood maybe five-eight. Murphy guessed his weight at one-seventy— and every ounce of it deadly.

East meets West. Now we'll see.

Murphy ducked behind a soda machine as the Russian slowed and glanced up and down the hall, arms out, ready for anything. Then, satisfied, he bent down, taking a small kit from his pocket.

Lock pick! Murphy's heart began to beat faster. The Russian worked with skill, using no more than thirty seconds before he replaced the lock pick and opened the door the barest of cracks to peek inside. Like a specter, he vanished into the room.

Murphy frowned. But wasn't that the kitchen? Then his gut tightened. Poison! The damn Ruski was going to poison the food!

Murphy approached the door, seeing a bit of plastic slipped between the strike plate and bolt. He paused for a second, wondering if it would be better to get the

Captain, to call the base to alert, and—being Murphy—promptly decided against it.

Concentrating, he kept the firm plastic in place as he opened the door a hair to stare through the slit. A few lights were on in the area he could see. Murphy ducked into the room, settling the door silently in place behind him.

The air carried that distinctive odor like a kitchen anywhere—that sort of soapy, fresh food smell. Around him were polished stainless steel sinks, cutting benches, and cabinets. He scuttled across the tiled floor, spying over the nearest cutting table.

The Russian had crossed the room, stopping before the walk-in cooler, looking around in puzzlement. He cocked his head, shrugged, and opened the heavy insulated door. Groping fingers found the light switch before he stepped inside.

Murphy licked his lips, darted to the knife rack, and plucked a French chef's knife from its holder. On cat feet, he approached the walk-in.

With careful fingers, he eased the latch back, knife held low.

* * *

Svetlana Detova checked the hall as she stepped out of her room. In stocking feet, she walked down the corridor. Where to first? Her initial plan had been to see if the computer room was guarded. The aerosol in her purse would put a guard to sleep for about half an hour and leave his short-term memory fuzzy. Assuming they changed the guard here at 24:00 hours, she should be able to crack the computer system and get to the bottom of all this.

She hesitated at the ladies' room and entered. It could be a long night. Besides, adrenaline had that effect on her. She had just stepped out of the stall when the door opened. Svetlana smiled as Sheila Dunbar came in.

"Good evening. You're up rather late." The Englishwoman's greeting translated perfectly into Russian.

Svetlana bit off her frustration. So, she'd been monitored anyway by their damned system. So much for the computer room.

"Biology works full time." *Do I look as haggard and*

worried as she does? She cataloged the redness of the Englishwoman's eyes, noted the strain around her mouth.

"I suppose."

If not the computer room, then perhaps she could pry some bit of data from the Englishwoman? "Major, if you have a moment, could I ask you some questions?"

Dunbar paused and nodded. "Of course."

Svetlana gestured to the stall. "At your leisure."

When Dunbar was ready, she said, "Why not my quarters. It's a little more private."

"You have your own room?" *Then I'll be under observation there, too. But then, where wouldn't a person?*

Sheila offered no comment.

Dunbar's room turned out to be Spartan and measured perhaps four by five meters. The walls here had been wainscoted to obscure the familiar cinder block. A cot—with the blankets rumpled—a couple of chairs, and a table composed the remaining furniture. A series of notes lay spread over the tabletop. A temptation that, could she use the spray on Dunbar and get away with it?

"Please, do be seated." Sheila took a chair opposite hers, leaning back, an exhausted slump to her shoulders. "Bloody strange, if you ask me."

"I *was* going to ask you."

Sheila chuckled dryly. "I suppose I could expect no less from a KGB Resident Head."

Svetlana steepled her fingers. "And that bothers you?"

Sheila rubbed her eyes. "This whole bloody thing bothers me. I mean, I can't convince myself that we're going to ride up to the stars in a transparent bubble. It all seems so impossible. Aliens that look like Ahimsa look? The thought that they could neutralize our entire strategic forces?" She shook her head. "I can accept it intellectually, and proceed from there, but my gut instinct? Well, that's another thing."

She seems to be telling the truth. But then, they'd put experts into a situation like this. "And why are you in command, Major?"

"Quite honestly, I don't have sufficient data to answer that. I assume they have something in mind tailored to my skills."

"And those are?"

Sheila smiled. "I think that's classified."

Svetlana nodded. *Maybe I'm more tired than I think, too.* "Point taken." If only she could get to her Cray, she'd have the whole of this in no time.

Sheila lifted a shoulder. "You know, if this isn't some crazy scheme cooked up by the UN or some other powerful group, we're going to have to depend upon each other. Major Detova, if we really do leave here in transparent bubbles tomorrow, I think all we'll have is each other."

Svetlana let her body sag. "Let us wait and see."

Sheila frowned, staring at the floor. "Assuming this *is* some sort of exercise, who would be behind it? Who would have the leverage to force the Americans and the Soviets into cooperating?"

Svetlana considered her answer. "Academically, Major, the international banks, any combination of multinational corporations, various energy cartels, perhaps the Japanese. Since the overthrow of Gorbachev, the world has become a dangerous place. The Soviet Union is being rent from within. The Baltic rebellions and the crushing of Georgia and the Armenians have frightened the rest of the world. Only, why not simply put pressure on the leaders? Why this simple charade?"

Sheila looked up at the ceiling. "I'd hardly call instantaneous translation simple. I still wonder how they do that."

"One of the KGB women trained in such matters has already searched the ceiling of the women's quarters. From a visual inspection, without her specialized equipment, she's found nothing. No projector, no devices of any kind."

"And the President and General Secretary? Were they actors?"

"If they were, they were very good."

Sheila crossed her legs at the ankles. "Something Wide said keeps sticking in my mind: that bit about only dolts looking up at the sky with all those billions of stars and galaxies and thinking we were alone. You know, he's right. Only a fool could still maintain we were the only intelligent life in the universe."

"But why now?" Svetlana demanded. "Why would they pick this particular moment to come to us?"

Sheila lifted her hands. "If we assume the Ahimsa story is correct, then perhaps they knew something we didn't. Perhaps we had finally moved too close to the edge? Perhaps they had to move when they did?" Dunbar gave her a haunted look. "Perhaps they just kept us from annihilating ourselves?"

* * *

When he growled, "Gotcha, Commie!" two unexpected things happened to Murphy. First his voice translated into Russian. Second, the Soviet soldier gagged and coughed, blowing the orange juice he'd been chugging all over the refrigeration compartment.

Murphy stood ready, knife lowered. After all, the security of the Western Alliance didn't teeter on a quart of orange juice—no matter how fast it disappeared down a Russian throat.

Still coughing, the Russian glared at him. "You practically scared my soul from my body!"

"Well, what are you doing, sneaking around in the middle of the night?"

The man grinned, wiping a callused hand across his mouth and shaking orange juice from his fingers. "I could ask you the same, American."

Murphy grinned wickedly. "I got this problem with my stomach. It goes empty a lot."

The Russian stared at the orange juice that dribbled down milk cartons and plastic containers. "Me too."

How did they do that? Translate everything in midair?

The Russian frowned, looking around. "Can't take my demobilization away."

"What?"

He waved his finger around, pointing up. "I don't understand. I just said something we used to write on the barracks wall. It sounds to me like it comes out in English."

"Yeah, weird shit, man."

The Russian coughed again and swatted at a dribble of orange juice on his chin. "You going to try and use that knife?"

"Huh? Uh, no, I guess not." He looked down at the blade in his hand. "Uh, at least not if you're only after orange juice."

"And maybe a sandwich or two. What did you think?"

"That you might be going to poison the food."

The Russian blinked, then grinned. "You know, for an American, you're not very smart. I have to eat the food here, too, you know. You've looked out the window? Think there's any forage there?"

Murphy considered. "Yeah, well, you've got a point there."

The Russian still didn't relax. "As much as I'd like to take that knife away from you and discover the arrangements of your insides, Major Staka has given us orders not to spank you Americans. But if it's self-defense?"

Murphy grinned. "As much as I'd like that, I got orders, too."

The Russian shrugged. "Then, if we're both under orders, and your stomach is giving you problems, why don't you go put the knife away and we'll raid this Capitalist heaven together?"

Murphy's grin extended to a smile. "You know, Ivan, I like your style."

"My name's Malenkov. Lieutenant Nicholai Malenkov."

"Lieutenant Ben Murphy." He turned, stuck his tongue out as he tested the balance of the knife, and tossed it. The tip thunked into the wainscoting, hit the cement underneath and bent, the knife hanging limply.

"What's this?" Malenkov held up a can.

"Piss water American beer. Drink it, and you'll find out why. Let's see what we got here." Murphy kept a careful distance, checking the shelves. "Here, catch. Ham. Black rye. Maggot eggs."

"What?"

"Uh, mayonnaise. Sorry, the translators can't handle that, I guess. Hey, wow! Guinness!"

"What?"

"Stout, man. Good beer. It's Irish. Somebody in this iceberg knows how to live."

"That's enough, besides, my feet are freezing in here."

Arms filled, they carted the booty out to one of the cutting tables.

"Uh, one of us has to cut this. Which one of us trusts the other with a knife?" Murphy glanced from the Russian to the food and back again. Malenkov ripped off a piece of bread.

"Well, I suppose if we kill each other, we'll both be sent to the penal battalions."

"How can they do that after we're dead?"

"Knowing Major Staka, he'd find a way."

"Sounds like Daniels."

Malenkov laughed through a mouth full of food. "So, maybe officers are the same in every army. Go ahead, cut the food. You started with the knife and I'm still in one piece."

They sat on the counter, eating, staring surreptitiously at each other.

"If I tell you I'm not a member of GRU, will you tell me why we're here? I mean, they pulled us out of combat, flew us to Moscow, and then here. What's this all about? Viktor keeps telling us it has something to do with aliens."

"Daniels tells us the same thing."

"You believe that?"

Murphy lifted a shoulder. "Hell, I don't know. Sounds pretty weird to me. We talked it all over and I don't think anyone really believes it's aliens. But, hey, if they tell us to believe we're flying into the sun with a bunch of puffballs, that's fine so long as the pay keeps coming."

"We think it's some sort of test. Maybe psychological warfare of some kind."

"Sounds good to me." Murphy chewed thoughtfully. "So, where you from?"

"Volgograd. You?"

"Boston."

"This piss water beer isn't so bad."

"Yeah, well, if it's psychological warfare, that stuff will do it to you."

"And your stout won't?"

"Try it."

Malenkov lifted the bottle, throat working. He grinned, wiping at his mouth and smacking his lips. "Definitely Capitalist excess. Perhaps we should save you from such excesses and take it for ourselves. Sacrifice in the name of world revolution and emancipation. Tell me, do all toilets in America talk?"

"Talk? Man, you've been around some different toilets!"

"I was watching television. The toilet talked and flushed blue water."

Murphy frowned and thought about it. "You're right, it is psychological warfare."

CHAPTER VIII

Chee'ee'la would have been surprised at the human reaction to his form. Or, perhaps not, since Chee'ee'la wouldn't have cared in the slightest how something as unpredictable, unstable, and ephemeral as a human being would have reacted to the oldest intelligence in the universe. The fact is, the average unenlightened human would have placed Chee'ee'la in a geological museum. His crystalline body radiated every color of the rainbow as chemoelectrical reactions carried on his thought and metabolic processes. His very size would have awed a human—making him even more in demand. The topmost of the array of geometric spikes that composed Chee'ee'la rose fully three meters off the floor.

Until he had become alarmed, Chee'ee'la had been drifting randomly through the endless black between stars. As a result, his color had turned a deep purple merging to a yellow-red at the crystal tips. His ultraviolet and infrared emissions would have impressed an observer as spectacular, too—only the humans would never have noticed without the help of their machines.

Chee'ee'la radiated several shades of magenta to indicate his displeasure as his spherical ship drifted close to TaHaAk, the massive Pashti governmental center that hung in L-5 orbit around the Pashti primary, SkaHa. Chee'ee'la manipulated the time-space around the vessel, guiding it with unerring precision to the Pashti lock. Barely pausing to transmute the material of his hull, Chee'ee'la created a lock to match the Pashti design.

Chee'ee'la's species, Shithti—as they were called by the Ahimsa—had never needed spaceships or rapid transportation until they encountered the Ahimsa so many star lives ago. Instead, Shithti had enjoyed floating serenely through the depths of space, thinking. Sharing ideas through the radio emissions, they exchanged thoughts across the light-years, riding the solar winds and intergravitational fields. Occasionally, some mishap would shatter a mature Shitht and the angular fragments would begin the slow process of regrowth as they collected raw elements from interstellar dust and gas. The long process methodically regenerated new crystals while the new organism remained haunted by vague memories of the progenitor.

The spaceship shivered as Pashti grapples and electromagnets bound the craft to the dock. Chee'ee'la fluxed space around him and rose, accessing information on the Pashti. Given their current understanding of engineering and materials synthesis, a gravity flux would have disrupted the entire station. He'd have to use the antigrav. The thin sheet of metal levitated, repelling itself from the deck plating below. Chee'ee'la manipulated the molecular density of the liquid hydrogen around him, pushed forward by the differential and onto the antigrav. The lock opened in a cold wisp of gases as Chee'ee'la entered. The system strained and wheezed, attempting to purge the near absolute zero of the atmosphere and replace it with a nitrogen-oxygen mix. A thick fur of frost grew over everything—including Chee'ee'la—as the air reacted with the deep cold.

To Chee'ee'la the transition into the glaringly hot oxygen atmosphere proved only mildly annoying as his body began to expand. Through careful manipulation of internal fluids he kept his hard exterior from cracking as it warmed.

The Pashti appeared to be scattered here and there around the dock. They ceased shuffling loads of cargo to watch, major eyes radiating excitement as their pincer-manipulators tensed on the bundles, crates, and packages hovering before them on antigravs. Shithti were uncommon on TaHaAk—or anywhere for that matter.

Pashti hadn't changed since the last time Chee'ee'la had inspected one. They measured three and a half meters in length. The eight bilaterally located multijointed legs terminated in flexible manipulators of soft tissue backed by a hard ridge of tissue which provided incredible traction. Rows of hairs along the legs acted as vibrassae. Their normally thick leathery skins had begun to slough off and harden for the cycles. Two major eyes and four lesser ones bounded the turretlike dorsal extension raised on their backs. Rising anterior and medially, two powerful pincers extended which allowed them to efficiently manipulate and exploit their material world.

Chee'ee'la noted that his body had warmed beyond the threshold of shattering into a thousand pieces and turned his attention to directing himself through the incredible maze Pashti wove out of their environment: compartment after compartment, all attended by various corridors. The whole thing seemed scarcely less complicated than manipulating a star into supernova. Then again, oxygen breathers tended to such irrational constructions.

Chee'ee'la stiffened the crystals he would use to support himself as micro-fracturing from the sudden gravity began to take its toll. Lost in thought about the motives of the Ahimsa, he didn't notice the guards at the door of the Pashti Central Council Chambers. Their eyes expanded while their legs shortened and Chee'ee'la passed into the brain center of Pashti space without a whisper of protest. Only the oxidizing mists boiled along behind his still deep-space cold body.

* * *

The cycles loomed just over the future's horizon. Try as he might, Councilor RashTak couldn't ignore the inevitable. Already his body had begun to change. His skin had shed only two days ago and a tough armor chiton had formed and begun to harden. At the same time, his normally keen brain had begun to slow in some ways, while in others he remained acutely aware and found problem solving easier. His appetite couldn't be sated, and, while attending to that need, the comsat on his ear orifice chirped.

"RashTak," he signaled, feeling the vibrations through the sensitive hairs along his limbs.

The comsat buzzed out, "Councillor. A Shitht has just

arrived at the docks. Currently it is winding its way through the central access corridors and is apparently headed for the Council Chambers. Request your orders, Councillor?"

Typical! The inferiors had begun the process of sucking up to the dominant ones, suddenly unsure, incapable of functioning on their own. Curse the cycles! Curse the Shitht! What was it doing here now?

"Let him go where he wishes," Rashtak decided, mandibles and teeth clicking while his vibrators strummed into the comsat. "Shithti do not realize others live by schedules. Inform the rest of the Council that he is here. Tell—"

"Councillor, the Shitht has arrived at the Central Council doors. Should we deny it entrance?" The guard's fright transmitted as a humming vibration.

The crazy idiot wouldn't try and stop a Shitht! The cycles couldn't have clouded his sense enough for that!

"No! Allow him in! Allow him anything he wants! He's a Shitht! Listen . . . relax." RashTak purred, sounding loud vibrations of reassurance. Violet Heavens! The cycles affected Pashti differently. Some, rising in status—like a guard—might turn aggressive.

RashTak signaled a frantic meeting call as he turned, cursing the inflexible shape of his body. Then he felt a subtle thrill. Violet Curses on the cycles and what they did to intelligent beings. He fought down the urge to utter a territorial challenge and clicked his way through the door and into the corridor. Despicable atavism, this.

Pashti scampered this way and that, subservient, obedient to his authoritative signal and the vibrations he thrummed into the deck below him.

The Shitht had settled down, mottled purple slowly lightening into lavender as it picked up energy from the hot strobe lights. A puddle of water had started to grow on the floor where condensation dripped from the huge creature. Frost patterns still formed hoary patches on the larger crystals. RashTak entered and slowed, conscious that several other Councillors had preceded him. True, they were inferiors but with the cycles coming on who knew how stable they would be?

A vigorous flush of emotion surged up from the vibrafeelers along RashTak's limbs. Territorial challenge! It tingled around his brain and rushed back down his spine alongside his reproductive organs and around his stomach before flaring out into his limbs again. With all his might, he stifled the surges of emotion.

"Not now," he rumbled, swallowing the vibrations. Shithti did not come to SkaHa system under normal conditions. They found too much activity here to disturb their Shithtish concentration. The constant comings and goings, the vibrations of machinery, the endless chatter of Pashti all bothered their thought patterns. Now, with the cycles coming on, this Shitht's presence could only mean something had gone seriously amiss somewhere in civilized space. Or had it? A Shitht might show up simply to inform of an anticipated scientific phenomenon which Pashti might or might not be able to observe given their inferior instruments. Shitht had been known to arrive out of the blue in an incredible hurry, excited, glowing every conceivable color, jamming radio and almost peeling paint with UV—and all that for the express purpose of communicating a mathematical formula no Pashti could understand—let alone apply—oblivious to the fact that the theory lay beyond ordinary intelligences.

RashTak reached the podium and lowered his body into the now unsuitable grooves. Violet Curses upon the cycles. He settled his feet and resonators into the comsat and accessed the translation patterns which would attempt to communicate with the Shitht.

"Greetings, Old One," Rashtak tried, watching the colors radiate on the spiky mass of crystalline intelligence.

The comsat remained silent as it began learning this Shitht's means of communication. Each of the huge crystal beings communicated differently, each devising a mathematical language mutually intelligible to other Shithti; but Pashti and Ahimsa systems took time breaking subtle and complex digital logs and precise mathematical formulas, spectral emissions, and heat changes into language. The process never functioned one hundred percent. RashTak couldn't help but wonder what slipped through the cracks. How much more would they know if Shithti could communicate everything they thought about? Would Pashti even now be able to beat the Violet Curse of the cycles?

The comsat crackled.

“Come>mark< Come>mark>Pashti< Name <me<Chee’ee’-la<sound<star<wave<make> Chee’ee’-la>hear>Ahimsa>call>Ahimsa< Ahimsa<worried<Pashti<cycles<come> Interrogative<?>Know>planet>species>called >human>interrogative<?><Interdicted< planet<human<one<is<currently><Thus> Ahimsa>want>bring>human>Pashti>space> purpose>of>interrupting>Pashti>cycles< Human<species<insane<species>Make>Pashti >insane<Violent<times<come<Pashti<result <of<Ahimsa<interference> Not>good>for> future>of>civilization<Much<turbulence<may <come<space >Chee’ee’la>come>warn> Pashti< Pashti<make<safe<space>”

RashTak studied the subtle speech of the Shitht who called himself Chee’ee’la, after the background sound the stars made. How many translations had Chee’ee’la’s message gone through to become this intelligible? How much nuance had been missed? Humans? Ahimsa fooling with interdicted space and species? RashTak could feel the growing anxiety of the other Councillors.

RashTak thoughtfully composed a response. “We thank Chee’ee’la. Not know Humans. Difficult time for us to study problem since the cycles are coming. Why do Ahimsa break rules of interdiction? Ahimsa dislike violent species! Such action on their part does not make sense.”

“<Violent<species<humans>Ahimsa>currently>fear>Pashti>too>much< Shithti<no <want<human<in<space> Too>noisy< Too <violent>Cause>too>many>problems< Take >too>much>time>from >thought<Disrupt< civilization<and<ruin<civilized<society > Exclamation<!>Ahimsa>not>know>what> they>deal>with>!<”

RashTak caught the final emphasis. The Shitht was worried! A sudden tingle burned through his hormonally disrupted body. Shithti blew up stars for fun. What could worry them about some primitive interdicted species the Ahimsa were fooling with? A portion of his hind brain wondered if Shithti went crazy all of a sudden. But who knew about Shithti? A lot could have happened in the thirteen billion years the Shithti had been floating through space. Pashti had only been among the stars for a few million years. Ahimsa would know, they'd been in space so long they'd lost their original shapes and become exclusively space creatures suited only to very light gravity or zero g. That fact partially accounted for the reason they'd lifted the Pashti out of their eternal trap in the first place. RashTak chuckled. They'd done it to save the Pashti from the very cycles whose results Chee'ee'la now said they feared.

He paused. Why would the Ahimsa mess with an unstable species? Where did the sense in that lie? Ahimsa enjoyed being sensible—it led to long life; and Ahimsa cherished their longevity above everything. How else had Pashti taken over so many critical Ahimsa industries and occupations? The only periodic interruptions in that Pashti process were the 760 year cycles.

"How do Ahimsa intend to use humans?" RashTak queried.

"Not>know<" Chee'ee'la responded. "Ahimsa <not<acting <rational>"

"What do you recommend?" Ee!Tak, Second Councillor, asked, having assimilated enough data to make observations. RashTak fought his irritation. Curse the cycles! They messed with everyone, causing emotional outbursts, getting in the way of refined thought.

"Chee'ee'la>does>not>know<Humans<Pashti<problem<now<too>Interrogative<?>What>will>you>do>?<"

"Think about it first," RashTak answered. Cutting out the Shitht, he accessed all of his colleagues. "You have heard. This is most distressing. I am having trouble separating emotions from rational thought."

"Agreed!" came a rumble throughout the Central Council Chambers.

"Councillors," RashTak began. "We have a serious

problem. There is much work to do. The cycles are upon us and this could not have come at a worse time. I—"

"Can we believe the Shitht?" AraTak demanded emotionally.

A chorus of vibrations canceled each other out in a loud shaking din.

"Stop this! *Think!*" RashTak roared, bringing some order back to the assembly. "First!" he continued, using all the volume and concentration he could muster, "We must know what sort of creature this 'human' is." His digitals accessed the comsat for humans. The screen showed up blank. He cross-referenced and found more blankness. Must be an extremely small or insignificant species.

"Violet Curses!" he gritted. He could tell already that a long night awaited him.

* * *

"Despite my misgivings, I will enjoy this." Spotted rolled down the control room, checking each of the monitors. The humans had filled the halls, joking. "Even now they don't believe they will rise into the sky. This will be fun."

Wide formed a manipulator, one eyestalk monitoring his field generation parameters while the other swiveled to Spotted. "Did you really think they would believe?"

Spotted piped a shrill note. "No. And I have looked forward to this demonstration. The ones who are the most arrogant and self-assured will be the most entertaining."

"Do not harm them. We must raise them carefully. Their bodies are delicate. You must remember that. Dead humans will prove worthless."

Spotted piped an acknowledgment and turned an eye to the monitor which depicted the main hallway of the human compound below. "A Soviet and an American have volunteered to go first."

"It is almost 10:00 hours. Are you ready?"

* * *

"Okay, meathead, you be cool, huh?"

Murphy grinned at Daniels. "Look, what's to it? We walk out there for a couple of seconds and when nothing happens, we walk back in."

Daniels squinted hard at Murphy. "Yeah, well, you two jerkoffs get what you deserve. I don't like it, Murphy. It's bad enough a Ruski gets caught raiding the kitchen against orders. But the two of you together?"

"Detente, Sam. East-West relations. Hey, Malenkov's a nice guy."

"You better hope the aliens are real, pal, 'cause I ain't done with you yet."

Murphy glanced over to where Staka engaged in a conversation with Malenkov. He couldn't hear the words, but from Nicholai's stiff face, he could guess the topic.

"Uh, it's almost 10:00, Cap. We better go do our thing."

"You better hope you freeze out there, Murph." Daniels tapped an unforgiving finger into Murphy's chest. His guts sank.

He shot a quick glance at the clock and then looked down the packed hallway. Babble drowned the place, people looking back and forth speculatively.

Murphy swallowed, swung his duffel over his shoulder, and walked up to the door. Malenkov disengaged from Staka and nodded to Murphy. "Looks like we've done it, Comrade American."

"Yeah, well, coulda been worse."

"Oh?"

"We coulda killed each other and been doing KP in hell."

Murphy reached for the door. "How long you suppose we've got to stand out there, dressed like this, before they let us back in?"

"Considering what's in store for me, thirty years."

"Yeah, well, it's time. Let's go play penguin." Murphy opened the door. A blast of chill sent slivers of ice through his fatigues. Snow crunched under his feet as he stepped out into the full blast of the Arctic winds. Malenkov trotted along behind, kit over his shoulder.

"Okay, my Red buddy, here's the landing mat. Now what?"

"We stand and huddle." Malenkov turned his shoulder to the wind. "And now a bubble comes and surrounds us?"

"Hey, you notice something? We're still being translated. Weird shit, man. What kind of equipment they got, anyway?"

"Hopefully heaters."

"Yeah, right."

Murphy looked up at the sky. Nothing. "Bubble, my ass."

"Your ass is a bubble?"

Murphy glanced at his watch. "Thirty seconds. Jesus! It's damn cold out here!"

Malenkov had tucked his arms tightly over his chest, squinting against the bite of the wind. "How long do we wait?"

Murphy looked back at the entrance where Daniels had stepped out in a parka to watch. Staka came right behind him. "Uh, until they say we can go back . . . or hell freezes over."

"It has!"

Murphy slitted his eyes against the wind, looking at the frozen wastes around them. "To be honest, I could leave . . . *Yaiii Shiiit!*"

The wind stopped as Murphy fought to catch his balance. He and Malenkov steadied themselves, the footing beneath them cushioned and firm.

"Blessed mother of God!" Malenkov's voice echoed.

Murphy gaped, heart thumping as they rose from the ground, no sensation of g, nothing. Even the air warmed.

Malenkov's rasping intake of breath matched Murphy's own as he looked down to see the Earth dropping away. "Hey, man, this ain't real! I tell you, *IT AIN'T REAL!*"

* * *

"God damn!" Sam stared, the terrible cold forgotten. "God . . . damn." Murphy and Malenkov rose into the sky. The sphere could barely be made out, a shimmering in the faint Arctic dawn.

"What *is* this?" Staka wondered beside him.

"Captain?" Mason called. "What's happening?"

"Murphy just got carried away."

"Uh, this schedule says two people every thirty seconds."

"Then move it, hamburger brain! Get out there!"

Sam barely realized when Mason and Cruz trotted past, hardly acknowledged their questioning stares as they jogged out to the landing strip. His eyes remained glued to the disappearing dot that had been his lieutenant.

He missed the bubble that formed around Mason and Cruz, catching it only as it rose into the gray heavens.

"So it's real," Staka said humbly.

"Yeah, guess it is." The implications began to sink in. "Holy Christ. What are we in for?"

* * *

Sheila shot a quick look at Viktor Staka, noting the Russian's cool control. Around them the wind whipped and gusted, icy crystals of snow battering the bubble noiselessly and falling, only to be caught and whirled around the sphere. She could have been standing in a huge fishbowl.

Sheila bit her lip and almost cried out as they rose from the ground. Around her the snow and wind thrashed in a convoluted dance of Arctic cold. Below her, the crusted snow fell away. She closed her eyes, experiencing no sensation of motion.

The walk to the landing mat had taken all of her will power. Nor would she ever forget the sight of Sam Daniels and Moshe Gabi rising into the heavens.

"Impossible," Viktor whispered under his breath.

She blinked her eyes open to stare at him. His cheek muscles bunched against clamped jaws, his stare as cold as the knives of frozen air around them. Sheila shot him a quick measuring glance and caught his curious expression assessing her reaction. She fought the desire to close her eyes again and looked down in horror at the land dropping away below them.

Acceleration should have been pushing them downward. Her mind struggled with that in a detached manner. Misty gray fluffs of clouds shot past as they rose ever upward.

"Frightened?"

"I suppose I'd be lying if I said I wasn't," she tried to keep her voice calm but it held a giggly note. Her heart pounded like the London Symphony's kettle drum when they did Wagner. Her bladder, emptied not so long ago, demanded relief. A queasy sensation stirred in her guts. *Yes, damned scared!*

"Myself, I'd rather drop into the middle of Kabul in bright daylight."

"Let's change the subject."

"Very well, we still don't know where we're going. Why us? What's the alien's purpose?" Staka actually shifted his feet defiantly against the curved bottom of the bubble. He clasped his hands behind his back.

Despite the act, every muscle in the man's body had knotted—like her own.

"Insufficient data, Major." *Blessed God, what if this thing bursts wide open?*

"So." Staka mused, "We're mercenaries for our world. No one declined the call of destiny. How did they know we'd do that? How could they pick the ones who would go simply for the opportunity? How did they know us so well?"

"If they can do . . . this, I suppose examining every computer file wouldn't stretch their abilities."

"They were very good. Have you noticed? Our group of intelligence specialists—all women—are the perfect complement for the soldiers. My intelligence liaison unit is composed of high ranking KGB. The American company is accompanied by female CIA case officers."

"I've noticed. I don't think bringing it up right away would be good for morale."

"Do they intend to breed us like rats? Are we caged?" His hand absently indicated the bubble around them. They lifted through the clouds now. Rushing up soundlessly, effortlessly. "Is it only coincidence that we are unevenly balanced male and female? What is the ratio? Two to one? Are women to be a scarce resource?"

The sky here deepened to an incredible blue, white clouds glistened below them as rays from the southern sun lit the peaks of white tufts.

"We're the ransom of our world, Major." It took all

her effort to fight the vertigo and look at Staka. "You know the Ahimsa must be monitoring all of our conversations. The translation still works."

He shrugged. "Every unit in the Red Army has its own KGB as well as a Party Commissar. I'm used to being monitored."

Sheila looked up at the deepening navy blue of the sky. The vertigo decreased. The fear of falling diminished if she couldn't see the clouds speeding away below them.

Forcing her mind to think helped. "It is, I would imagine, difficult to tell someone with the fantastic power of the Ahimsa to simply go away. Put in the place of our respective governments, would you tell them to take a jolly hike?"

"No, I suppose I wouldn't. For the moment, I'm a soldier of the Soviet Union. My duty is the protection of my people." A wary look formed in his eyes as the stars brightened in the darkening sky.

"Propaganda? You don't strike me as a martinet."

"Training helps define the situation, however. A Soviet soldier simply needs to know which way to go; how to shoot; to go without sleep for three days; and how to survive in the snow in only his greatcoat. We don't even train the rank and file to use a map."

If the bubble burst here, she'd be dead long before she hit the ground. She wouldn't even remember the fall. That made it easier. "I doubt they will give you a greatcoat out here—or a map."

His smile looked forced. "No . . . probably not."

Sheila studied the blackness above, waiting. Did a real alien spaceship lurk up there somewhere? Would this bubble take them beyond the realms of science fiction? With regret, she realized the only movie like that she had seen had been the second *Star Wars* film. It had bored her and seemed so trite at the time. She shivered and felt Staka's arm around her shoulder.

Another time, she would have given him an icy stare and distastefully removed it. Now she relished the sensation of touch in that eternal primate need to be held.

"It isn't a new concept, you know. Askaris were utilized by every major power in our history. The Ahimsa, from what I can discern, have made an in-depth study of who and what we are."

She realized she had pulled closer to him. "The curious part is that this entire operation is covert. That has implications. Someone, or some*thing,* out there is more powerful than Wide. If the Ahimsa is cowed, where does that put the Earth's ability to bargain if this all comes apart?"

He nodded, staring soberly at the starry splendor that began to unfold around them. "Maybe we're to be gladiators. Tell me, what do fighting cocks find when they're crated up and packed halfway across a continent?"

"Gladiators or surgical strike team. No matter what, our transportation is illegal. To someone . . . somewhere. Wide was specific that we couldn't be caught. Delicate, that was his word."

She made herself look down to see the ball of Earth falling farther away. How high? Odd to think she'd lived on that gleaming, bright planet. Tips waited for her down there. How desperately she wished she were home in her boring flat. Looking up, a gleaming sliver of silver could barely be made out.

"You know, if I could convince myself this was real, I'd be so terrified I couldn't stand."

His arm tightened around her shoulder. "That's one of the advantages of remaining ignorant."

"There it is."

Viktor Staka followed her pointing finger, swallowing hard.

The sliver of silver grew larger to become a long wedge. Odd looking spires thrust out the back. A spike bristling with various devices looked like a chrome Christmas tree on the needle thin nose. The craft looked about like she'd expected a spaceship would look.

The Ahimsa spacecraft continued to grow. With the lack of sensation, it appeared to be falling down upon them. Still it fell—ever larger and larger.

"My God!" Staka gasped. "How could our radar have missed this? This is huge! It's. . . ."

She felt him shiver for once and grasped his hand to reassure him—and herself.

A black dot grew in the bottom of the fantastic vessel. Sheila's perception changed. No longer did it appear to fall toward them; instead, from the change in scale, they were rising at an incredible rate, flying straight for the dull gray bottom of the vessel, racing for the black dot. Above them, the universe turned gray. Only to the sides could they see stars. Below, the round ball of the Earth fell away, warm and friendly and forever distant.

Like smashing into a wide plain, they dropped toward the black gap. Sheila closed her eyes. "I don't believe this!"

"Neither do I," Viktor whispered. "The mass of this thing! It's huge."

The voice startled them. "The actual dimensions of the vessel you are entering are: Maximum length, three hundred and twenty-six Earth kilometers; maximum breadth, ninety one kilometers. The vessel is powered by a device we translate loosely as a null singularity generator. The physics, unfortunately, Major Staka, go considerably beyond anything you might conceive."

"I . . . I suppose so."

She looked curiously at him, noting his wide eyes and the unmasked fear there. They slipped into the black gap in the bottom of the ship. He swallowed nervously, cowed by the scale of the alien ship.

She shot one last glance at the fluffy blue-white ball so far below them and wished again that she could go home. Would she ever enjoy a half-pint of Guinness in the local pub? Would she ever see the incredible green of the rolling hills in spring? Would she ever see the white forms of spring sheep in the dells? *Oh, Tips, I'm so sorry.*

Then the floor went solidly opaque beneath their feet. Sheila stumbled awkwardly as their bubble burst soundlessly. She sniffed—virtually odorless—and stared around, suddenly aware of Staka's arm about her shoulder. She disengaged it, flushing, and noticed the hallways which spread before her. Where she would have expected steel and darkness, light airy corridors stretched endlessly.

"This way," Wide's voice called. A little yellow light blinked before them and began retreating down a featureless pastel corridor.

"No way out now," Viktor muttered ominously.

She stood on an alien spaceship. Where there should have been a sense of wonder, only terror remained. She forced herself to step forward, following the light into the unknown.

CHAPTER IX

Viktor stared at the orange hallway that glowed before him. Sheila started off after a blinking light that hovered in midair. Numb, bereft of thought, he followed in a devastated haze.

How does a man cope when his soul has been uprooted, looted away from everything that's real? Viktor shivered, his mind reeling and jumbled. The anchors had been ripped from firm bedding to leave his soul adrift. In all his life, nothing had affected Viktor as that trip in the alien bubble had. The realities of his life, death, blood and combat, gut-wringing fear and premonition, the ecstasy of walking away from a dead enemy—knowing you had lived and he had died—nothing had prepared him for the sight of the Ahimsa ship . . . for impossibility becoming reality.

More than any other human being, a combat soldier deals with the fundamental truths of existence, with life and its meaning, and with death. Having followed the capricious dancing steps of death, few illusions remained to Viktor. Among them, the understanding that he knew his place in the world, that he'd faced realities others hadn't, that within him the spark of survival burned. He, Viktor Staka, controlled the power to take any human life. No man, not even the General Secretary himself could survive five seconds at the hands of Viktor Staka. Knowing he had power over life and death had kept him going, the one little truth—the one little lie that gave him a mythos of power and purpose in a hellish world of dancing illogical death.

And now the linchpin of the myth had been brutally crushed, the fragments fleeing in the unconscious flaying of his soul. The arrogant pride in his personal strength, in his association with the power of the state, had been shredded with the finality of a direct hit by field artillery. All that remained was the ringing silence, the stunned loss within.

Even the might of the Soviet Union becomes a mockery compared to the power of the Aliens. We're . . . powerless. Viktor shivered, baffled by sudden undeniable fear.

"Major?" Sheila Dunbar asked, realizing he'd stopped in the orange-lit hallway. "Are you all right?"

He swallowed against the dryness in his mouth, staring at her as if seeing her for the first time. How did she manage? How did she keep her composure when he felt like falling to the floor and crying out in terror?

"I'm . . . fine."

She smiled bravely. "Disconcerting, isn't it? To think this is really real?" She shook her head. "Maybe we have to act like it's a dream, Viktor." She waved around. "I didn't expect hallways like this. The place doesn't exactly look alien."

Wide's voice caused Viktor to jump as it sounded from the air overhead. "The portion of the ship you occupy has been specifically tailored to human needs, Major Dunbar. Environmental stimuli necessary for human comfort and health have been attended to. I can provide further data at your request. For the moment, please follow the directional light." The little light which guided them began to blink with greater intensity.

Viktor forced his rubbery muscles to work as he followed Dunbar down the hall and into a large auditorium.

For the number of people present, the room remained remarkably silent. Viktor entered with Sheila at his side. He stared at them, noting the pale faces, the strained expressions. Yes, it had all turned too real. They, too, had been shaken by the sight of the Ahimsa ship stretching across the stars. No building, no weapon on Earth, offered any parallel.

If only he could retreat to a quiet place, perhaps that little drinking establishment on Vanya Street, where he could sit back in the corner and drown himself in vodka while he repaired the damage to his shattered defenses.

Once, before those chilling moments in the bubble, he would have quietly despised the ignorant louts who boasted and cursed the Party, the economy, and all the fools running the government.

He took a deep breath, trying to still the bleat of fear that echoed along his spine. If only he could go back, surround himself with those simple-minded peasants, hear their vulgar jokes and drunken curses. If only he could take himself back to Tula and listen to his mother complain about the quality of the cabbages, he'd never set foot beyond the limits of the town again.

He shivered, realizing just how much the ordinary things in life could mean.

He had stopped short, the haunted stares of his troops locked hopefully on him.

Come on, Viktor. The men will be counting on you. You can't let them down. Shaken to the point of trembling, he forced his back straight, glancing around the big room—yes, just like an auditorium.

His SPETSNAZ unit stood uncomfortably, mixed with KGB women in a knot filling one side of the room. The Israelis clustered in the middle while the Americans surrounded the area closest to the entrance. No one talked above a somber whisper.

Wide appeared on the raised central dais. "Please, be seated."

They stood, staring, lost.

"C'mon, people," Sam Daniels called from where he stood. "Are you bumps on a log, or what?"

The SOD started to find seats. One by one, they filled the tiers, settling uncomfortably, staring at the alien. The IDF followed.

"Viktor?" Sheila prodded him.

His mouth felt cottony. He steeled himself, walking across the open area beneath the round alien. To have marched before the eyes of the Politburo after being convicted of treason couldn't have been so awful.

It's real! It's all so terribly real! Fighting shock, he took a breath and ordered, "Sit down. It's all right."

Gubanya, pale-faced, nodded too quickly, shoving people along, gesturing them into their seats. Even buoyant

Malenkov looked shaken, a pleading in his eyes as he looked to Viktor for some explanation.

Viktor started to take the first seat he came to. For a brief moment, he met Svetlana Detova's measuring eyes. Damn her, didn't anything faze her? She stared at him, as if seeing through his shattered armor. Viktor ground his teeth, forcing himself to nod to this man and that, and retraced his steps to sit in the very front—the proper place for an officer.

At the same time, the thought that Sam Daniels had found his voice first rankled.

Viktor, pull yourself together. You have no one to depend on but yourself. You can't fail now. A flashback of that terrible night outside Baraki returned to haunt him. He stumbled, the faint odor of gasoline and water catching in the back of his throat. He blinked, shaking his head, forcing the memory away, and seated himself. He looked up at the alien and tried to swallow—the result like choking down a knotted sock. He broke out in a cold sweat.

"Welcome aboard." Wide rolled forward in his queer and unsettling way. "First, you will each be provided with a separate cabin. There you will find every accommodation you need, including clothing, food and drink from the dispensers, bed, and computer access. If you have any questions, simply access the computer and ask; it will respond to voice commands or a headset, which you will find racked next to the computer. Your clothing should be placed on the floor at the foot of the bed each night.

"Major Dunbar will be your commanding officer. Immediately under her command—and coequal in rank—are Daniels, Detova, Gabi, and Staka. Whatever you work out beyond that is not my concern.

"We will only have the Earth equivalent of six months time to develop an assault plan and to train you in the use of our equipment. I understand the shock you must be experiencing as a result of your transportation to this vessel. Therefore, today will be for your orientation and familiarization with the ship. How you organize your activities is up to you. Since you are the finest professionals your planet has to offer, I don't expect more than the usual problems. Keep in mind, your commanding officers are a law unto themselves and discipline is up to them—I will support *any* decision they make.

"I would suggest that you acquaint yourselves with the ship, explore the routes you will need to take to find exercise rooms, weapons training rooms, flight simulators, armored vehicle simulators, the gymnasium, and the common mess. Again, if you have any questions, use any computer terminal and an answer, or direction light, will be provided.

"Your access is, of course, limited. You will be unable to pass certain hatches into restricted portions of the ship. A direction light will lead you to the personal quarters at the end of this meeting. Access can be gained by placing your palm to the illuminated hand on the door. Each will key to your body chemistry. Other than that, I wish you good day."

Wide disappeared.

For long moments, silence lay heavy in the room.

"Weird shit, man."

"Shut up, Murphy," Daniels growled.

Sheila Dunbar stood and walked out to the dais. "I think that's all for now. I suggest we take Wide's advice and inspect our quarters." She cleared her throat. "I would like to see my officers by . . ." She looked at her watch. "Well, let's make it 15:00 in my quarters."

A light appeared in the air over her head and retreated back the way they had come.

Sam Daniels hollered out, I want to see all of my people right now!"

Viktor bit his lip and stood with the rest, following along as they filed out of the auditorium. His legs remained shaky, his gut in turmoil. Damn! He wiped a nervous hand over his face.

Mika Gubanya appeared at his elbow. "Major? Are you all right? You look ill."

Viktor sighed, steeling himself to meet Gubanya's penetrating gaze. Damn it, how could Mika be so calm? "I'm fine, Mika. But I'll tell you what, I'd rather turn my back on fifteen Afghans than ride that bubble up into the sky again."

Mika nodded, a reservation in his eyes as he walked on ahead.

Viktor studied his lieutenant's muscular back. Had it been that apparent? He'd seen that look in Gubanya's eyes before. It meant trouble.

* * *

Sam rose on his toes, feeling the muscles of his legs tense and flex. He took a deep breath and worked the muscles across his chest, knotting his belly against the churning emotions that possessed him. *It's all goddamned real!* His thoughts whirled as he looked at the faces of his men. They stood in a cluster in the center of the auditorium, waiting anxiously.

"You all look pretty pale," Sam began dryly, and got a rustle of subdued laughter. "I guess I look a little white myself—but don't tell anyone."

"Cap?" Slap Watson asked hesitantly. "I didn't dream that . . . that soap bubble ride, did I?"

"No. I pinched myself a couple of times to be sure." He looked around, noting the worry in their eyes. "Look, I wanted a couple of minutes to talk to you. I mean . . . well, I don't know what's going to be expected of us. I don't know where we're going, or what we're going to do when we get there. I don't know how many of us will come back."

Sam paused to catch his breath, practically bouncing on his toes as he tried to shed the excess energy that pumped through his body. "Now, we're into something new. No one's ever done what we're about to. Look, I've never given you guys any shit you didn't deserve. Every time we went into action I gave it to you straight, figuring that you'd do the job no matter what. This time I don't know what to tell you. I don't know what to expect, but I want you to remember something—we're the best, the pick of the Special Forces. Let's act like it. Got that? No trouble with SPETSNAZ, or the aliens, or anything."

"And we're supposed to work with Russians?" Slap Watson asked as he raised his hand.

Sam spread his own hands wide. "Do the words, multinational force mean anything to you? Remember the joint exercises we've conducted with NATO, the IDF, the Canadians? This is the same theory; you muscle bones just have to make it work."

Kearney raised his hand. "Cap, what if they don't want to play?"

Sam squinted, nerves tickling the middle of his back. "They're SPETSNAZ, Bill. They were plucked out of combat and sent here; they know their business. Beyond that, all I can say is that Major Staka doesn't strike me as the kind who puts up with any kind of shit. He's got a crack team—probably the cream of the crop like we are—and his unit is a *combat* unit, got that? For every hundred hours of action we've had, they've probably got a thousand."

"That don't mean they're better than we are," Ted Mason insisted.

"No, it doesn't, but respect them for it."

"What about command?" Anderson asked from where he leaned against the wall in the rear. "We really under Major Dunbar's thumb?"

"Guess so."

Gene shook his head. "I don't want to sound like bad whiskey in an empty belly, but what's she got that makes her so hot? Why her?"

"I don't know, Gene. I guess we just assume the Ahimsa knows what he's doing. Until she proves herself incompetent, you treat her like any other commanding officer you've ever had."

"Never had a C.O. that pretty," Simpson added with a grin. "Just hope she don't worry more about her makeup than the grunts who're gonna bite it when she fucks up."

"You corral that crap, Simpson!" Sam leveled a thick finger. "Sheila Dunbar gets a fair start."

"And Staka?" Anderson crossed his arms.

Sam's gut tightened. "The Major and I are going to have to work that out. Wide says the rank is co-equal." *And it damn well better work out that way in the end.*

"And if some Ivan puts the moves on one of the CIA chicks?" Mason asked. "We supposed to just sit there?"

Sam chuckled to himself. "Ted, from what I've been able to put together, you'd be better off to throw yourself on the mercy of the SPETSNAZ than piss off one of those chicks. They're CIA, man. Case officers. I think they can handle themselves."

"Hey, Ted? You want to sell tickets when you pull this stunt?" Murphy laughed.

Ted lifted a suggestive finger and made a kissing sound with his lips.

"All right, that's about it. How you guys gonna act?"

"Professional!" came the chimed response.

"Damn straight. We're SOD and the whole universe is going to know it. Now, beat feet, people. Check out your quarters and settle in. Hey! Hey! *Hey!* One last thing. Okay? Remember, we're on our own. There ain't no leave, no relief, no nuthin'. So if any of you guys start to flip out, you come see me. You get to feeling weird, you come tell me! Got that?"

He met their eyes, one by one, as they walked out, following the corridor the others had taken. Murphy managed to sneak out first, avoiding Sam's attention.

"Damn, it could all come apart. Just one flip out and we're all dead."

* * *

Spotted's eyes remained intent on the main monitor. The solar system passed slowly to the rear as the big Ahimsa ship accelerated out of the gravity well. The monitors began the countdown, measuring the system's pull. Some time would pass until they reached the point where they could safely engage the ship's null singularity and bore a hole through the space-time continuum. Spotted checked the monitors, acutely aware of the gravity waves of the guardian beacons. They grated through his system as if his soft body could feel each pulsation as he manipulated the null singularity, balancing gravities just enough to cancel the effect without causing structural damage to the ship.

"To destiny!" Wide blurted suddenly, spicules hissing. "After this cycle, the Pashti will be tame once more!

Once again, Spotted, we shall control our own destiny, no longer relying on Pashti to supply our needs."

Spotted kept his peace, manipulators caressing the knobs which let his thoughts flow into the navigation system. "The political situation on Earth will deteriorate into chaos. Our presence has unsettled the system."

"That is precisely why we acted with such haste." Wide whistled and thinned. "I wonder what we will find when we return? The monitors we left will provide most fascinating records of their behavior as a result of our tampering with their warheads."

"I suspect they will fall on each other like the insane beasts they are."

"I anticipate that, too. They are, after all, animals. I would be surprised if either the American or Soviet leadership survives."

"And if the humans aboard find out?"

"They won't. How could they?"

"I feel an unusual disturbance, Overone. It is an unpleasant feeling."

"Disturbance? Is it the ship?" Wide rolled easily around the inspection track, checking the readouts.

"No, Overone." Spotted's thought patterns shimmered and his sides dropped against his will. *What have we done? Humans are aboard this vessel. When we pass the gravity buoys, we will have defied the interdiction.*

Wide rolled over and extended a feeler, sharing the thought processes. "Ah, I know that emotion. You have forgotten much over the centuries, my little friend. What bothers you is a primitive response: fear."

* * *

"Aliens?" Vice President Burt Cook shook his head. "Jesus, Jim. Why didn't you get help? We could have covered."

Beyond the white-framed French windows of the White House, the lawn looked tawny, patched here and there by grayish snow. The trees and shrubs waited, skeletons to the memory of summer, and warmer days. The Washington skyline looked dull under charcoal-streaked clouds. For a brief moment, he wished he could be out there, beyond the walls, beyond this too well lit conference room.

The men at the long table stared with hard eyes as they waited for Atwood's response. Heart thudding, he swallowed hard. "Look, I know it sounds crazy, but it's true. They put our weapons in stasis." He looked at the Director of Central Intelligence. "Matt, your agents know it's the same in the Soviet Union."

Matt Brown coughed softly. "According to reports, yes. But it could be another Ogarkov smoke screen. Maybe that's what they want us to think—and we're sitting ducks."

The President lifted his hands, getting to his feet. "Look, we've put some of the best minds in the country to work on those stasis balls, and what have they found? Nothing, that's what!" He turned, pointing a finger. "How about it, Tim? You've got the records. The balls appeared at exactly the same time. All over the world." Atwood slapped a hand on the table. "Come on, people, wake up! This isn't Soviet physics we're dealing with here. Electrical cable has ceased to work. Every nuclear plant in the country is shut down while the engineers scratch their heads and wonder what in hell is shining back from their reactors. The bomb plants, the breeder reactors, everything is useless—either electrically dead or in stasis."

Atwood glared from face to face. "You tell me, people. Whose technology is this? Soviet? Ours? Those stasis balls defy even the best of theories."

"Jim?" Howard Milfred said gently. "We've got your diaries. Rather than have this thing out in public, rather than make a circus out of it, why don't you simply . . ."

"Resign?"

"Well, I didn't . . ."

"Damn right, you didn't!"

"Then where are your aliens?" Cook demanded. "I mean, all they've got to do is step out of the woodwork and this is all cleared up."

Atwood chuckled, rubbing the bridge of his nose. "They won't be back for another five years, gentlemen. They've spaced with one of our SOD units. Tim, you can check the records. See if you can find Sam Daniels any place on this Earth."

"They just picked up a SOD team and left?" Cook lifted a skeptical eyebrow.

"They took Israelis and Russians, along with some of Matt's case officers. It's all in Fermen's report. He's in the air from White Base as we speak. Debrief him the second he sets foot on the ground."

Bill Birch, the Speaker of the House, filled his lungs and turned to stare out at the Capitol. "Do you know how ludicrous this sounds?"

Atwood stared soberly at the carpet underfoot "Yes, I'm well aware. The fact is that no power on Earth could shut down our defense net that quickly. I only wonder if the Ahimsa knew what they'd unleash with their little trick." He rubbed his hands together, pacing slowly across the room, aware they watched him warily. "You know, they took almost four hundred people. Now, I wonder if they didn't play us for the biggest suckers to come down the block in years."

"We've got to do something." Brown propped his elbows, looking around. "The press is digging like mad. Rumors are spreading all over the country."

"The people are already on the verge of panic," Birch added wearily. "Do you want to tear this country apart? Me? I can't believe little green men came down and neutralized our missiles. How in hell can I tell that to my constituents? Look, they've got to believe in Washington. With the press scooping the missile story, we can't put a spin on it that will cover the reality. It's going out. Maybe today. We can't afford the trouble. Not now. Our very survival is at stake."

Atwood glared at him. "Bill, maybe you'd better give our situation some thought." He turned. "Matt, as Director of Central Intelligence, how do you think the Soviets are going to handle this? Only Golovanov and Kutsov know the truth. If we've been set up, left holding the bag by the Ahimsa . . ."

"Rastinyevski will go berserk." Brown didn't even hesitate. "They'll figure it's some super secret NATO technology."

"And can we keep them from knowing about our missiles?"

Brown shook his head and swallowed. "We can't even keep the public from knowing."

"My God," Birch whispered. "For the first time since World War II we don't have a nuclear shield."

Atwood rubbed a knuckle along his cheek, feeling stubble. "I think we'd better give some immediate thought to rebuilding our defenses. Start from scratch, rebuild the nuclear capacity. It's not like we have to remake the Manhattan Project. If the economy just weren't dead in the water . . ."

"You're assuming your aliens didn't screw with uranium," Birch added, staring over the tops of his glasses.

"If they didn't, we're in for a real rough ride, people." Tim Bates stared sullenly at the light panels. "All right, Mr. President, I'll buy the alien story for the time being—and feel like a damn fool when someone comes up with a rational explanation."

"Would to God that were true," Atwood added into the silence. "Meanwhile, keep the Air Force on twenty-four hour alert. I don't want Backfire bombers appearing out of nowhere."

Bates squinted, noting the ashen looks of the others. "You got it, Mr. President."

* * *

Riva Thompson stepped into a well-lit hallway as she followed Sheila Dunbar. The direction light had led them down a long corridor from the auditorium. What had at first seemed like pastel walls turned out to be light panels. The main corridors, she found, glowed a pervasive orange. The personal quarters lay along a hall marked by white walls. Doors lined the way, each with a blinking hand imprint on the center.

Sheila stopped, frowning. "Do you think there's a reason for the hand flickering?"

"Wide said they'd be illuminated." Riva steeled herself and pressed her hand to one. The door opened immediately and the handprint ceased to flicker. "I guess I'm home."

Dunbar did the same, and walked into a room across the hall. The others, men and women, walked past, each one pressing a hand to a door as they came to it. Riva watched for a moment, noting that the divisions had begun to break down. SOD took rooms with KGB on one side and SPETSNAZ on the other. She turned to inspect her new quarters.

To Riva's practiced eye, the room measured eight by ten paces. Two beds, nothing more than platforms, stood next to each other. The computer—or so she assumed—consisted of a huge monitor that covered one wall. The headset Wide had spoken of seemed to be an affair of golden wires that resembled a diadem and rested on a head-sized dome. A device that could have been a plush recliner stood next to it. A low table of decidedly unearthly design sat in one corner, four rakish-looking chairs beside it. A shower stall, without curtain, created a niche in the other corner. A boxy looking toilet stood in another niche. Closets with standard metal knobs filled another wall, while a mirror surface covered the other wall and added to the spacious feeling of the room. A light panel composed the entire ceiling. The walls looked like plastic and the floor, well, that was something else entirely. It appeared translucent and shimmered a metallic gray in color, but gave under weight like cushioned carpet.

Riva ran tired fingers through her red hair and exhaled. In all her life, she'd never had an experience like the trip up in the bubble. To watch the Earth drop away like that had been frightening and sobering. For the first time, it had all become real. How could she ever tell Pete and Linda at NSA about this?

Emotionally exhausted, she lowered herself onto the bed, found it surprisingly comfortable, and took a moment to try and compose her thoughts.

I'm in space. Aboard an alien spaceship. And I'm not a lunatic! She patted the comfortable support beneath her. *Ari, you just wouldn't believe it!*

"And I'm not sure I do, either." She had only to open her eyes to see the reality around her. Thoughts cartwheeled through the confusion and disbelief in her mind.

Some minutes later, Barbara Dix's voice intruded. "Riva? You home?"

She sat up, looking around. "Yes. Where are you?"

"Outside the door."

"Well, come in."

"I can't. . . Holy cow!" The door swung open, leaving a startled Dix staring at the hand she held up to the print. Barbara's face had a funny look. "You said . . . and it did."

"Must be the fancy computers."

Dix stepped in and looked around. "Just like mine."

"Are we here? I mean really?"

Dix shrugged and walked over to drop down on the other bed. "I keep waiting to come out of the dream. It just keeps going on with that sick feeling you get in your gut that something terrible has happened."

Riva leaned forward to cradle her head in her hands. "You know, I've been a lot of places and done a lot of things. If I hadn't had a gun to my head more than once, been trained to keep my wits while my guts turned to water, I think they'd have had to scrape me off the inside of the bubble."

Dix exhaled and nodded. "Yeah. You know, most people are walking around in a state of shock. Me included. I saw one of the SPETSNAZ guys bawling when he walked into the auditorium. I guess it didn't get to me as bad. Too much time jumping out of airplanes skydiving. I did okay until this spaceship started to drop out of the sky."

"You know, when they picked us, they didn't choose a single powder puff. Somehow, I've got the feeling that despite what Wide says, we're going to be hanging by a thread. Barbara, are you ready to look death in the eye?"

"You know, I took a lot of risks with the Company. I flew into Tehran, Beirut, Tripoli, and even Kabul more times than I care to remember. Looking death in the eye is nothing new." Dix pointed a slim finger. "What about Detova? She strikes me as a cold fish."

"I don't know. She must have been good to make it to a Residency. You know how the Soviets are about women."

"I wonder if the alien knows how hard it is to get women to obey another woman?"

"Almost one hundred and thirty of us? And we still haven't heard what our role is?" Riva stood nervously. "Makes you suspicious, doesn't it?" A cold chill ran up her spine. "What is the alien *really* after?"

* * *

"Wide?" Sheila stood before the computer terminal. "Computer?"

The terminal flickered to life. She pursed her lips. "I would like to speak to Wide, please."

The Ahimsa formed in the monitor. "Yes, Major?"

"Very well, what's next? What's this all about? What are your instructions. I need something to plan with. What precisely are we supposed to do now that you've got us?"

Wide rolled back and forth in the monitor, eyes pinning her from the odd stalks on both sides of his body. "I will give your officers a briefing tomorrow at 08:00."

"But I need to begin putting this together now. I need your cooperation, Wide. Is this a military operation? Or are we some sort of specimens for your zoo?"

Wide made a squeaking sound she'd never heard before, his body thinning. "Very good, Major. Yes, this is to be a military operation. Everything you've been told to date is true. Your females will pilot torpedoes which will make the initial penetration of the target . . . which you call a space station. Once the walls have been breached, the assault will consist of the SOD and SPETSNAZ in support of Assaf's armor. When the Pashti have been crushed, all units will withdraw to the torpedoes and I will transport you back to your world."

"I need more details."

"You will receive them when the time comes." Wide's staring eyes seemed to gleam in the lights. "For the moment, that information should be sufficient to allow you to formulate a command structure. Tomorrow, I will give you more specific information during the briefing."

"What about special training? What about—"

"Major. Please. Do not rush ahead of yourself. Presumptions may only lead you to confusion and frustration. Trust me."

She crossed her arms. "Why should I?"

"Because you have no choice. Good day." And the monitor flicked off.

Sheila stared at the blank screen and bit the knuckle of her thumb. *My God, how am I going to handle this? What am I going to do? They'll want answers I don't have.*

Grimly, she returned to her notepad, the sheets before her accusingly blank. She stared up at the computer. "Computer? What time is it?"

"13:45.36"

"Do you have the files on Colonel Gabi, Major Staka, Major Detova, and Captain Daniels?"

"Yes."

"Do you have printout capabilities?"

"Yes."

"Please print them."

She took the flimsies and settled herself in one of the chairs. Wide had taken special care in selecting the best. Perhaps a pattern would emerge. "It better," she whispered, her nerves grinding like sand.

CHAPTER X

Nicholai Malenkov walked down the hallway, lost in his own head as images of the improbable day's events whirled through his mind. Not more than forty-eight hours ago, he'd been pinned behind a rock while an Afghan machine gun pocked the other side with 7.62 AP rounds. He retraced his path from the time Gubanya's rockets blasted the machine gun into silence: from the firefight, to the helicopters, to a cargo jet in Dushanbe, to a military transport in Moscow, to the American White Base in the Arctic, to trouble with Murphy in the kitchen, to the bubble ride and the auditorium.

"And I'm supposed to believe I'm on a spaceship?" He cocked his head, squinting down the orange-lit hallway. Nothing on Earth could have prepared him for that terrifying ascent he and Murphy had survived. Together, clinging to each other, they'd risen up above the clouds—all sense of nationality and politics vanished like night frost on a late spring morning. Shivering and trembling, they'd watched the Ahimsa ship grow out of the star-grayed sky. He and Murphy had collapsed when the bubble burst, hanging on to each other as they stared around. Even now Nicholai couldn't find shame in his reaction to the experience.

The personal quarters at the American base had shocked him, but nothing could compare with the luxury of the Ahimsa room—and it was all his! Yes, he walked down a hallway on a spaceship. A *real* spaceship. He stamped his foot to feel the solidity and rapped knuckles on the glowing orange walls. Real!

A sudden springy lightness come to his steps, the feeling of joy similar to that enjoyed by a senior soldier on the day of his demobilization. "I'm in space. I'll go places the cosmonaut corps could only dream of. Me, a simple Soviet soldier." He chuckled, slightly giddy at the thought.

The corridor emptied into a large cafeteria. Moskvin, Dontsovietski, and Gubanya sat at a table sipping something from cups. Nicholai walked over and sighed, settling himself into one of the curious chairs. The material might have been plastic—but not quite. The table looked rooted to the floor and had been constructed from some dark smooth stuff that defied description.

"Are we really here, Nicholai? Or is this a dream? We were just talking about it. Wondering what's happened." Moskvin's face lit, excited and flushed like a man who'd just received a promotion after surviving a hellish battle.

"We're here," Nicholai admitted, noting the same bundled excitement in Dontsovietski's expression. "How do you get something to drink? Dontsovietski, go get me something. Earn your worth as a corporal for once."

"Officers. Even in space." Dontsovietski jumped to his feet. "Vodka? Just like the rest of us?"

"Fine."

Gubanya had been sitting leaned back in his chair, curious eyes on Nicholai. Mika alone seemed nonplussed by the events of the last couple of days. His look remained penetrating, almost reserved. "We're going to wake up and realize it's all a dream."

Nicholai rubbed his face, looking around. Three women, wearing what had to be American clothes, sat at the end of one table, talking earnestly. A clump of Israeli tankers lifted bottles of beer, peering nervously toward Nicholai's group. "I'm not sure that wouldn't be better in the end. No, I didn't mean that. Anything's better than Afghanistan."

"Maybe we're dead," Dontsovietski offered as he set a cup down before Nicholai and settled next to Gubanya. "We all died that last night outside of Kabul. We're only ghosts."

"If I'd known, I'd have killed myself long ago." Moskvin lifted his vodka. "To death."

"You may be right." Gubanya rubbed the back of his neck, staring at Nicholai. "We may be as good as dead.

We're going to be gone from our homes for five years. Perhaps, faithful Comrades, the effect will be the same."

"But think of the adventure, the honor of being the first Soviets beyond this solar system."

Gubanya smiled thinly. "Perhaps that's because you have less to leave behind."

Nicholai lifted his hands, palms up. "Perhaps. But maybe I don't have anything to come back to either, hmm? Perhaps the rest of you are luckier than I am. You have families. You, Mika, have a wife. When Mama died last spring, that was the last of my people. Oh, I can't count on those cousins—scum all of them. Lazy parasites in the flesh of Ural Motor Works. They put in their time and collect their rations. I won't miss them."

"I'll miss my family," Moskvin said sadly. "I told Anna I'd marry her after I got back from . . . if I got back from Dushanbe. My parents are both still alive. I hope the General Secretary remembers his promise to tell them, to ease their worry."

"And we'll be gone for five years?"

"If you survive," Gubanya reminded, his sharp black gaze moving from face to face.

"Enough pessimism," Nicholai put forth, staring at the vodka. Remarkably good, he thought. How did aliens know how to make vodka?

Nedelin walked into the room followed by Konstantin, Nikita, Pietre and Pashka Popov. Nedelin smiled like a scum who'd just liberated an officer's private liquor reserve. "We're going to see the simulators. There's a whole new universe to discover." He waved around. "Think of it. A starship—run by space creatures! And we're here! Want to come?"

Gubanya smiled like a tiger. "Nicholai and I were going to talk about some things. Moskvin and Dontsovietski will go with you."

Of course, they took the hint, both men rising, saluting, and following their friends out.

Nicholai tossed off the last of his vodka. "Perhaps we should walk down to the personal quarters? I don't think you'd want to say what's on your mind in a place like this."

"You make a very good lieutenant, Nicholai." Gubanya stood and paced across the room for the corridor.

Like a caged tiger, Malenkov thought. *He's nervous, as tense as when a mission goes sour and falls apart.*

"What's bothering you?" Nicholai asked as Gubanya palmed his door and led the way in. The room looked like a carbon copy of Nicholai's.

"Viktor."

"Anything in particular?" Nicholai stepped over to the dispenser. "How do you get anything out of this? Machine, I want a glass of vodka." He lifted an eyebrow, shooting an inquiring look at Gubanya. "Two."

Two glasses full of clear liquid appeared in the cavity at the bottom of the device. Nicholai lifted and tasted, grunting approval as he handed one to Gubanya and settled in one of the chairs.

"What about Viktor?"

Gubanya gave him a hard stare, black eyes burning. Then he turned away, the thick slabs of muscle in his back tensing and rippling as he worked his hands. "I'm not sure he's well."

Nicholai frowned, cradling the vodka between his fingers. "Maybe you might want to explain?"

Gubanya shook his head absently, rubbing a callused hand over his close-cropped bristly hair. "He's . . . changed, Nicholai. I don't know. It started after Baraki. Then, during the time at Zossen-Wunsdorf he seemed to get better. When we were transferred to Dushanbe, he seemed to get worse again. Preoccupied. Lost in his head."

"Being in a combat zone does that."

"No, this is something more."

"What are you talking about? Viktor seems like he always has. I don't see it."

Gubanya turned, jaw thrust out as he glared at Nicholai. "I think his nerve is breaking. He's losing it, Nicholai."

"Mika, you're sure you're not overreacting? This is a little hard to take . . . I mean this ship. The thought of being in space. That bubble ride up. You're not under some deep stress? Some disorientation that—"

"Nicholai, don't push it. You and I have drunk together, killed together. I carried you out of that disaster at Khost. You shot that Afghan in Beghez before he could finish me off. We owe each other a lot of blood, but think. The old Viktor would have broken you into little pieces over what you did last night."

Malenkov laughed. "Is that what's really bothering you? That I drank beer with an American? Or that I got caught?"

Gubanya's expression strained. "You know I can't approve. I think Viktor should have taken harsher measures. As an officer of the Red Army and a representative of our unit, I expected better of you. That's all I'll say. You know how I feel about orders and responsibility. It was a fool trick—like you'd expect from a recruit in training, not a SPETSNAZ Senior Lieutenant."

Nicholai laughed and slapped his knee. "Mika, my friend, you try too hard. Relax. This attitude of yours, it causes you more trouble than good. How many times have you been turned down for promotion—"

"I don't want to hear the same old tired speech from you, Nicholai." Gubanya stepped over to stare at himself in the reflective mirror surface of the wall.

"I worry about you, Mika."

"I'm not the topic of conversation. It's Viktor. If he's losing his nerve, responsibility falls on my shoulders—and yours. This is a dangerous time. We're trapped in this ship with Americans and Israelis. You've seen the look in the men's eyes, all wonder and no reality. We're in danger here, Nicholai. Terrible, deep danger. I don't sleep easier wondering about Viktor's commitment to the service—or about your fraternizing with Americans."

"Perhaps if you fraternized more often, you'd find a way of dealing with them besides over a gun barrel."

Gubanya tilted his head to give Malenkov a disgusted glance. "Really? And what did you learn from your American friend besides disobedience of a direct order?"

"Murphy would be a good one to sit around and drink with. He's a tough man, an ingenious man—self-reliant."

"Unpredictable."

"Absolutely." Nicholai frowned. "That may be their only strength in the end. That and their technology."

"Oh? Irresponsible rabble can have a strength? A disciplined force will cut them apart time after time."

"Like we did to the Afghans?"

"Surely you can't equate Americans with Afghans. Afghans have guts, courage, and the stupidity to never know when they're beaten."

"True, and I agree that Americans are basically soft and gutless, but they have the ability to adapt. That's what I learned from Murphy last night."

"Go on."

Nicholai frowned. "It's hard to put into words, but I expected an American to be different. You know, arrogant, pushy, all breezy talk and no . . . no steel to the soul. He wasn't that way. I guess you'd say he treated me as an automatic equal. Wary, to be sure, but there was a respect there."

"And you couldn't wait to show him your own respect?" Gubanya crossed his arms.

"Hardly! He had me dead to rights. All he needed to do was shout for the guard and I'd have been in deep. Instead, I put on my most innocent, fun-loving face, and . . . well, it worked out."

"Getting caught isn't what I'd call worked out."

"No, but I have a friend among the Americans, Mika."

"Not something to brag about. You have a duty to the Mother Land, Senior Lieutenant. The Party would take a very dim—"

"Damn it, Mika!" Nicholai jumped up, facing his friend. "Use your head for more than calculating missile trajectories and target vectors. Think about where we're at! Think about what we might have to do! You rode that bubble up the same as I did! Tell me, didn't you look down and see the Earth? That's who *we* are. The people of *that* planet and we're all we've got up here—or wherever we're going. My life, *and yours*, might depend on an American someday soon."

"I find that thought as reassuring as dead batteries in a night scope. Nicholai, you can't trust an American—no more than a German, or an Uzbek, or an Afghan. They have no honor, no sense of right or responsibility to mankind. Look at what they've done! And I can't trust Viktor not to knuckle under to their pressure either."

"Of course you can trust Viktor."

Mika's face hardened. "If it happens, Nicholai, if Viktor breaks, will you back me up?"

Malenkov took a deep breath. "I don't know how to answer that. I'll watch him, keep my eyes open. In the end, Mika, I'll do what I think is right. But please, my hopes aren't just for Viktor. They're also for you. We're in a new reality now. The old hates and fears may not have a place in this new world of aliens and star travel. Please, Mika, after all we've been through, give the future a chance."

Gubanya dropped his stare to the translucent floor, a frown lining his forehead. "I hope it will all be as simple as your faith would make it, Nicholai. Because, you see, I agree with you. We can only rely on ourselves and our beliefs. In guarding those beliefs, I will do my duty, Comrade Senior Lieutenant."

* * *

Moshe walked beside Chaim and Yeled, running his fingers down the orange walls that illuminated the corridor. His fatigues and his beard looked worse. If he hadn't been so familiar with the odor of his own sweat, he might have worried about the pungency.

The thought that as they walked, they rode miles above the earth in an alien starship didn't seem real. Still, curiosity over the armored simulators had drawn them to that training room immediately after exploring the incredible capabilities of their quarters.

"So what do you think of alien armor?" Moshe asked.

Chaim gave him a shrug that ended by slapping callused hands against his thighs. "No matter that it looks like a chrome turtle from the outside, the controls remind me of an M1. They seem to have kept as much the same as they could."

"But until they make it operational I won't know what the gun will do." Yeled pinched his long face into a frown. "I wonder, Moshe. It's one thing to design a tank from theory, another from having been shot at in one."

"Well, let's hope these Pashti don't have Saggars, huh?"

"Or antitank capabilities," Chaim amended.

Moshe glanced at his watch. "I've got a meeting at 15:00. You two go relax. I'll meet you in the mess when this is all over."

"So what's going to happen when this Englishwoman takes command? Do we expect her to duck RPG7 fire with us?" Chaim made a face. "My grandmother almost drowned because of the British. The ship she was in was sinking and they wouldn't let it into Haifa. I don't trust them."

"Remember, Moshe, the British have never done us any favors." Yeled's sour expression went bitter. "Remember who they left the guns with in '48'?"

Moshe stopped, raising his arms. "Okay, listen. Sheila Dunbar wasn't in charge of Palestine before independence. Let's give her a chance. I don't want you Matzos creating any problems in the meantime. Keep away from trouble. You know what happens, it comes looking before you're ready."

"Okay."

"And another thing," Moshe lifted a warning finger. "I don't want slogans scribbled on the wall—assuming this stuff will take scribbles."

"Got it."

"And keep the rest of Assaf out of trouble."

"Yes. We know. We know."

"Good. See that you do." Moshe stopped uncertainly. "Wonder where I'm supposed to go?"

"Try the computer."

"Oh, yeah." He walked down to the next terminal. The things seemed to be spaced along the wall at one hundred meter intervals. "Uh. Computer? I've got a meeting with Major Dunbar at 15:00. Where do I go?"

A light appeared overhead, blinking yellow. Moshe started after it, calling over his shoulder. "Out of trouble, right?"

"Right!" Chaim called back.

Thoughtfully, he followed the light, marveling at the

idea that he walked the corridors of an alien starship. And did the Ahimsa use these same corridors? Or had their marvelous technology created this just for humans?

"Anna, if you could only be here. If you could only see." The old familiar welling of pain stitched his heart. So much of his life had been ripped away by violence, by the grim reality of the Middle East. How much baggage of hate did they carry to the stars? And if the Ahimsa hadn't lied, if a peaceful civilization lay out there, did Wide carry a plague to the other intelligent species?

In his imagination, he could foresee Pashti recruiting PLO, other strange species exporting Dinka while their antagonists took Sudanese Arabs. God alone knew who'd take Syrians.

Moshe . . . Moshe . . . you've become a hard-bitten cynic.

The light led him down two orange corridors and stopped before a door in the personal quarters. A display read "MAJOR SHEILA DUNBAR."

"Now what?" Moshe wondered. He raised his hand and knocked. The panel seemed to absorb the blows.

Moshe scratched his head. He grimaced at the thought of just bursting in, but put his palm to the handprint like he'd done to his own door. Nothing. "How am I supposed to have a staff meeting if I can't get in?"

The voice startled him. "Colonel Gabi?"

Moshe looked around, searching for a speaker, a button, anything. "Here."

"Just push on the handprint."

"I did."

"Push again."

He sighed and raised his hand. The door opened noiselessly.

Moshe walked in to find Sheila Dunbar seated at the table, a notepad already covered with script.

"This place takes getting used to."

Sheila's smile wavered weakly. "A lot will take getting used to. Please, help yourself to the dispenser and make yourself comfortable. I've been making notes as to scheduling. How are your men taking it?"

Moshe walked to the curious unit in the wall, and frowned. "You've used this?"

"Tell it what you want. A cup appears in the recess with your choice."

"Coffee. Real Israeli coffee."

The cup appeared, filled with thick black brew. He tasted it, smiled, and seated himself across from Sheila. "I don't know how to read the reaction of the men. For the moment, they're awestruck. I think they're grappling with the impossible by ignoring it, joking, bolstering their courage."

She stared absently at her notepad. "So much is so . . . different."

A voice announced out of the air, "Major Dunbar? This is Captain Daniels."

"Come in, Captain."

Sam Daniels entered, nodded to Moshe, and went straight to the dispenser. He took the seat next to Moshe's and sipped at the insipid brew the Americans called coffee. "Jesus Holy Christ, man. It's true." He shot an uneasy look at Sheila. "That or I'm so drugged up this is one hell of a trip."

"Then I fear I'm on it, too." Sheila gave him a somber stare.

"Yeah, as much as I'd like to think I was stoned, I got a feeling it's actually happening."

Moshe studied Daniels, seeing the strained lines around the man's eyes. Perhaps it was harder on Daniels who came from a more sophisticated technological culture. Maybe it weighed more heavily on his mind and spirit, was more frighteningly real than it was to the Israelis, who dealt with it all as fantasy. Americans had gone to the moon. The Russians had learned to live in space in the Mir station. To Israel, space lay beyond reach, an impossibility.

Staka arrived next, Svetlana Detova following within seconds.

When they were all seated, Sheila leaned back and steepled her fingers. "First, are there any problems?"

"Outside of the obvious?" Daniels chuckled humorlessly. "My mind went blank when that bubble picked me up."

Staka smiled weakly, lowering his eyes.

"I think we're all a little shocked and confused," Moshe added with a grin. "None of this is real yet."

"It's real to me." Detova lifted her hands. "But I have no idea what my responsibilities will be. Major, what am I supposed to do?"

Sheila's jaws clamped momentarily, frustration glinting in her eyes. "Major, I tried to pry more information out of Wide. He told me that we were indeed to make a military strike against the Pashti. Insofar as you are involved, he says the intelligence personnel will fly some sort of assault craft, torpedoes, he calls them. They will pierce the Pashti space station wall. After that, Moshe's armor will advance, supported by Viktor's and Sam's people. He refused to answer any further questions at that point. He did, however, promise more information at the briefing tomorrow at 08:00."

"That's it?" Sam asked, crossing his arms.

Sheila tensed. "That's all he'd say."

In the silence that followed, Moshe studied her, watching her determination rise as she met the American's challenging stare.

"Very well," she began. "If we have a command briefing tomorrow at 08:00, I want everyone up at 06:00. Each of you has two hours to get your people to the mess. They can eat while we're in the briefing. As soon as that's over, we can fill them in in the auditorium. I think that unless we all keep to a rigorous schedule, the truth of the situation will sink in. People will start thinking about five years out of their lives, about relatives and loved ones, about home. I don't think we can afford homesickness, or the concurrent problems in morale."

"Like boot camp," Sam added, a thawing in his expression.

"I have another question." Svetlana's face had hardened. "We have a political problem. The Soviet conscripts are outnumbered nearly two to one by Americans and their allies. You, a major in MI6, are in command."

Sheila tapped her pen on the tabletop. "Major Detova, when you rode up in the bubble, did you look down?"

"I did."

"What did you see?"

"The Earth."

Sheila nodded. "Yes, the Earth. One little planet without any lines, any divisions or politics. It looked vulnerable, fragile, from so high up. Just one planet. Major, we're all here together. We are all that we've got. Every human life aboard this ship is precious—since for all intent and purpose, it can't be replaced. No matter what our ultimate fate is with the Ahimsa, we're all together in this . . . or we're dead."

"And what about justice?" Viktor asked. "How do you intend to enforce that?"

Sheila filled her lungs and sighed. "Discipline is up to you. Viktor, if one of your men scuffles with one of Sam's, the two of you work it out. Your men are the best. They should be able to understand orders. I don't think you'd be here otherwise. But make one thing clear, we can't afford any political divisions. Either we survive out here *together*—or we die."

* * *

Svetlana stood to leave as the meeting broke up. Worry ate at her. For the first time in her life, she had no hint of the rules, of what was expected, or even possible. *I'm lost . . . and I don't know how to find my way.* She swallowed against the sudden fear.

"Major Detova? Could you spare a minute?" Sheila Dunbar asked.

Svetlana smiled, pulling the old familiar mask of deception into place. "For the moment, time is all I have."

Sheila watched as the door closed behind Sam's broad back. She walked to the dispenser. "Scotch, please." She lifted an eyebrow. "Anything?"

"I take it this isn't official? Scotch would be fine." A breath of relief stirred. Perhaps now she would discover some of the threads that made up the weaving of this insane situation.

Sheila ordered and offered the glass.

Svetlana watched as the tall Englishwoman walked over

and settled in the chair. She still looked worried and tired. *As I do.*

Sheila gestured to the other chair. "Please, sit down and relax. I think we need to talk."

Svetlana lowered herself and sipped the scotch, waiting.

"You've got quite a file," Sheila noted. "Resident Head for the Pacific Rim, the highest ranking KGB official in Hong Kong. You've accumulated quite a list of accomplishments."

Svetlana's heart skipped. "I wasn't aware that MI6 had access to that sort of information."

"It doesn't. It appears, however, that all of our personal files are available to the Ahimsa."

Svetlana's eyes narrowed. "I see."

Sheila waved it away. "I wouldn't worry about it. Those days are gone. By the way, your mascara needs a touch-up. Here's my compact." She tossed it across the table. "Now, about your record. . . ."

Svetlana opened the case. IT DOESN'T ADD UP had been written across the glass.

"Your mirror is a little dusty." She wiped it on the hem of her suit. She picked up the brush and made a swipe at her eyelashes. "Thank you."

What do you mean? What do you want?

Sheila glanced meaningfully up at the ceiling. Then she smiled. "Well, it's an outstanding career you've had. Too bad you didn't get into computers."

Svetlana fought to keep her face blank, smiling as she lifted a shoulder. *Damn! If she found out, where did I make my mistake? What could it have been?*

"My own training is in game theory. MI6 found that skill useful for testing strategy and tactics. I assume that's why I'm here. They used me to pick apart battle plans, to look for holes the generals might have missed. There's an intuitive grasp you develop, the ability to see all the details while you study the whole. Sometimes a strategy will come across my desk where they forgot the little things, like the setbacks, the common mistakes that everyone makes."

Svetlana nodded slowly, a chill feeling like Siberian wind blowing through her soul. "I see."

"Only someone with my background could pick it up."

"But what does that mean for this situation?" *Here is a worthy opponent. Why tell me she knows? What does this mean for the future?*

Sheila's smile had turned crafty. "It means I want to use every resource I have. Given your deficiency in computer training, I'd like you to augment your skills. Who knows what the Pashti have in store for us? This must be handled most delicately. I think, given your perfect record, and your successes in Hong Kong—too bad about that stock market crash they had, another example of the power of computers in the modern world—that you understand the critical nature of your duties."

Svetlana gulped her scotch to loosen her choked throat. Her mind raced, seeking the snare. *She knows I triggered the stock market crash. What else does she know or suspect?*

"I'll already have a full schedule with the women and their training. Unlike the men who have already worked together as units, the female corps will have to be welded out of individual pieces."

"I'll find someone qualified to handle part of that load." Sheila's eyes refused to waver.

Everything. She suspects everything! Slowly Svetlana nodded. "And what else, Major?"

Sheila shrugged, catching the double meaning. "Just do your best . . . and don't take any unnecessary chances with our lives. The past is behind us. It's the future, and simple survival, that we face now."

"I think we understand each other." Svetlana knocked back the rest of her scotch. "Then perhaps I had better begin my studies."

Sheila stood. "That would be fine. I'll work with you in any way I can. Oh, and feel free to borrow my compact any time."

Shaken, Svetlana stepped into the hall and walked toward her quarters. She entered her room, taking a deep breath, feeling her heart race. *Damn it! How far do I trust Sheila Dunbar?*

Throwing off her jacket, she walked to the computer and sat down. *This time, I can't afford any mistakes.*

Every nerve in her body quivering, she placed the headset over her brown hair.

* * *

"So, that's the way of things, huh?" Sam asked as they walked out of Sheila's room.

"Give her a chance," Moshe said, arms expressively wide. "How would you feel if you were put in charge of an intelligence operation made up of Mossad, CIA, and KGB and had no orders or battle plan to work from?"

Sam thrust his jaw out. "Yeah, I guess. Well, how about seeing what kind of trouble our monkeys are into?"

Moshe laughed. "I already have an appointment with my crew. But later, perhaps we should talk."

"See you around."

"Captain?" Staka stood, thumbs in his belt. "If you have a moment, I think you and I should have a serious talk about the situation we find ourselves in."

Sam stopped, meeting Staka's gaze. That moment might have been eternal, though it only lasted for seconds. Each took the other's measure, sensing strength and proficiency. Blooded warriors, they silently exchanged the ritual challenges, and in a single glance bridged the gap between two professional killers.

Staka's smile barely twitched his lips.

Daniels took a deep breath, the hard squint in his eyes relaxing. "Yeah, if we don't do something, my boys will be trying yours."

"I'd suggest the common mess, where we can be seen."

"A stabilizing influence?"

Staka's predatory smile grew. "Well put."

Damn Commie. Why'd he have to look like such a perfect God damned white man. Tall, blond, muscular . . . and God alone knew what went on in that mind of his. Russians had their own brand of racism. Just ask the Uzbeks. *Easy, Sam, don't let the past dictate the future. You got a lotta demons hidden away. Wait and see what comes. Keep the faith, baby.*

They walked along, passing the doors of the personal quarters, each aware of the other, steps light and balanced as they traversed this minefield of personalities with the caution of two veteran fighters.

Staka broke the silence. "You know, all my life, I've trained with the knowledge in the back of my mind that I'd fight Americans one day. I doubt your system is any different."

"Yeah, we've been waiting to lay into you guys."

"Together we must overcome our training. If SOD and SPETSNAZ meet in this ship, who knows what we'll let start—or where it could end up."

"Yes, I suppose the rules have changed on us. Having aliens around . . . well, everything's different. I wonder if it will be for better, or worse?"

Damn it, and to make matters worse, Staka had to be a major, wearing them damn shoulder boards so the whole world would know. Sam tried to swallow the rankle. For a man who'd graduated at the top of his class, he'd had to fight for every damn inch. No matter how many decorations he'd received, the advancements had always seemed to slip by—generally to white men who fought from behind desks!

"You know, Major, it ain't gonna be easy."

Staka smiled. "No, Captain, it won't. But then, we could start by following Major Dunbar's suggestion."

They walked into the common mess. It looked like a mess anywhere. Tables in long rows had been placed in the middle. The ceiling consisted of a solid light panel. Food evidently came out of the dispensers along the wall. Mason had a knot of people around his sacred tape player where it banged and clashed with some awful modern music. The Israelis already clustered in a group at the far end. The Russians sat here and there in little gatherings, generally around KGB women. And nobody had squared off with anybody else that he could see.

"Dunbar's suggestion?"

Staka smiled, the action stiff and expressionless. "That we dispense with this business of rank. Let me tell you a little bit about the Red Army. The man you click your heels to isn't always the highest ranking officer present. For example, I had a general and several colonels under my command at Zossen-Wunsdorf."

"Huh?"

Staka shrugged uneasily. "It's a complicated system of promotions that originated in the Great War. Appointment is more important than rank. I remained a major to keep my active status in SPETSNAZ. In the Soviet system, a captain cannot command a platoon. A colonel cannot command my type of SPETSNAZ unit—but a major can command an army or even an army group. At the same time, I understand the inflexible system of rank utilized by the West. In your position, I would not like to address a command equal as 'Major.' "

Sam stopped, giving the major another inspection. *Damn it, Staka isn't going to turn out to be a decent human being, is he?* The barest flicker of warmth lit in Sam's belly. "All right, in that case, I'm buying."

They sat across from each other at the head of a table. Staka laid his hat to one side, sniffing the vodka before chancing a swallow. "As good as you can get."

Sam sipped the bourbon. "Yeah, not bad."

They stared at each other, aware that everyone in the room kept glancing their way. Where did they begin in the search for equal ground? Sam made a throwing away gesture. "If you were in command of generals at Zossen-Wunsdorf, how'd you end up back in Uzbekistan?"

Staka's gaze iced blue. He hesitated, locked eyes with Sam and nodded curtly. "I suppose under the circumstances a few trusts must be given. Strictly between us, Sam, the Red Army isn't perfect. That system of promotion I mentioned is perfect for darlings, bootlickers, and sycophants. When I took command I'd come straight from Afghanistan, from the thick of it." He tapped his fingers in a quick staccato. "In Pakistan, or Iran, or the other places we operated, you only got one mistake. I expected to find the same mentality in GSFG headquarters. Perhaps they weren't ready for reality."

Sam chuckled. "I hear you. Sounds like your army is as botched up as mine." Sam tapped his captain's bars. "See these? Been there a long time. Desk officers seem to get new shoulder hardware all the time. But field people? Who wants to promote a man who's got blood under his fingernails? A combat soldier might tell a bird colonel that his latest weapons program is a man-killing pile of shit. Worse, news of what a real soldier thinks might get out to the press."

"But you must get something out of commanding such an elite force."

"Yeah, just like you keeping your rank as major. You know, it's a little thing, a tiny way of getting back at the bureaucrats who command file clerks and accountants and shuffle stacks of paper back and forth. Those guys sit safe and sound in their office buildings on the holy Potomac and worry about late reports. They haven't heard a bullet whistle over their heads since boot camp. But you know, when I walk in a room and say SOD, the myth just pops like a bubble and the bullshit's gone weak in the knees. Like when a scarred pit bull walks into a room full of clipped and perfumed poodles."

Viktor sipped his drink, turning the cup slowly. "Perhaps it's a good thing we haven't had to fight. We've saved ourselves embarrassments."

Sam leaned back, relaxing slightly. "Oh, we've had them. Generally the screwup came from bad intelligence. That or some silly-assed politician stuck his nose in the middle of it and fucked it up royally."

Viktor's grin grew. "An advantage to living with *Pravda*, our mistakes were never reported."

"Maybe we could send you the *Washington Post* or the *Baltimore Sun*. One skewed reality for another."

"Better not. We seem to do all right with our own version of the 'facts.' If we tried something new we might make a real mess of it."

Sam met Staka's grin with one of his own. "So, what do you make of Sheila? She going to make the cut in the end?"

"We'll see. This is all too new yet." Staka waved around the room. "When the newness wears off, then we'll have to see what happens. I think she was right about one thing. We've got to keep the men busy, keep their minds off what's happening."

"I don't have any choice."

Staka lifted an eyebrow.

"Hell, yes. If there's trouble around, my guys will find

it. If there's no trouble—like last night—they'll make it. Murphy's the worst."

"Malcontent?"

"No. He's just got to see how far he can go. He's the kind you can give a box to. You can show him there's a scorpion on the inside and tell him to keep his fingers out of it, and he'll still reach in just to see if he can do it and not get bit."

Staka laughed. "Speaking about Murphy, you handled that very well. You could be an officer in the Red Army. You think like we do."

"I noticed Malenkov, uh, volunteered just as quickly."

"Nicholai's a good man. He has enough medals to cover a wall. Like your Murphy, he also has an insatiable curiosity." Staka paused. "What should we do about their little escapade last night?"

Sam pushed back in his chair. "I'd say nothing. You'll notice Murphy's stayed out of sight since we got here. He's taking time to think on his sins—and hoping that in all the confusion I'll forget about it. I don't know. When I found them last night, they were laughing and talking, having a good old time drinking White Base's beer stock down to nothing. I think maybe that's all right in the present situation."

Staka frowned, wiggling his jaw. "And if, one day, we have to face each other again? That can't be discounted."

Sam stared into the amber fluid in his glass. "Yeah, well, I guess that's the real problem, isn't it? But then, if we don't make a team out of these meatheads, and these Pashti kill us, it won't make a hell of a lot of difference down the road."

Staka narrowed his eyes. "I think, Sam, we understand each other. Perhaps the sooner we start working together, the better. I would suggest that we integrate the training. Group PT—"

"Physical Training? Good idea. Let's start them at 07:00 tomorrow. Maybe mix the teams. I'll bet Gabi will go for it. Who knows, we may have a lot to teach each other."

"He's over there talking to his Israelis, let's go ask."

"To your health, Viktor." He raised his cup and touched it to Staka's. "You may need it."

* * *

"Mr. General Secretary," Bill Fermen wiped nervously at his face as the satellite linkup stabilized. His translator repeated the greeting in Russian.

Golovanov spoke, the translator supplying, "Good day, Colonel. I take it there is a reason for such a dangerous communication at such a critical time?"

Fermen licked his lips, feeling the sweat bead on his balding head. "Mr. General Secretary, this morning Jim Atwood was almost forced to resign the Presidency of the United States. It was a combination of events. CIA and military intelligence aren't sure what the truth is about the weapons. They think it might be some sort of disinformation trick like the ABM thing. The Secret Service recovered Jim's diaries. All the information about the Ahimsa . . . well, they think he's gone off the deep end. Insane, I mean. Look, this is all about to come apart. Can you do something? Can you tell them about the arrival of the aliens?"

"Why would I do that?"

"Because, Mr. General Secretary, they're scared to death that you'll be toppled and a hard-line government installed. With the missiles out, well, there's nothing to stop the Red Army from—"

"You think I would save your Atwood?" Golovanov smiled wearily.

"The whole world is about to come apart! The press broke the story about the missiles at noon today. We've got a hell of a mess brewing. We're in the middle of a damn depression here. People are slightly berserk anyway. Damn it, if we can't defuse this thing, it could blow up in our faces." Fermen waited, almost panting as he wiped his face with a handkerchief.

Golovanov frowned. "Colonel Fermen, I think I am too late to even do anything for myself." The transmission flickered and went dead.

"Damn it!" Fermen pounded the table with a knotted fist.

The translator stared at him, shocked. "Aliens?"

Uri Golovanov studied the monitor, aware the connection had been cut from the other side. His heart, like a mallet in his chest, pounded a slow cadence.

"So," Marshal Rastinyevski said slowly, "did you talk to the Americans often?"

Uri stared at the GRU officers who surrounded him. The black bores of the pistols and machine guns centered on him, as if they had a malevolent life of their own. *Is this how Gorbachev felt? Is this some divinely ironic justice?* "I think . . . anything I say will be considered fantasy. But, yes, I did." Uri smiled uneasily. "I just don't know what went wrong. Where is Andre?"

"Under observation. I think, Uri, the time has come for another . . ."

The pounding of his heart became a stitch of pain that crippled his left side. Uri felt his balance go as he sagged in the chair. The pain stabbed, causing him to vomit.

He could feel hands on him, voices in the background. The pain in his chest blinded him to anything else. He barely heard himself moan, "I think . . . you're . . . too late, Sergei."

Consciousness slipped away like the Moscow fog on a spring morning.

CHAPTER XI

Sheila woke in a fantasy land. She stretched lithely on the large bed, feeling more rested than at any time in her life. Then gravity returned, making her limbs heavy. She blinked and sat up. Was that the difference? The beds did something with gravity?

She stepped into the shower facilities and studied the single button. She sighed, pushed it, and water jetted. Normal looking soap appeared in a tray, and she scrubbed herself from one end to the other. The water shot out at perfect body temperature as the lather washed down her long legs and drained into the solid floor without a trace.

"How do they do that?" The next surprise came as she stepped out of the shower. Her foot met resistance and she would have pulled back except for her momentum. The water squeegeed off by some invisible pressure. Startled, she froze, watching drops of the liquid coursing down the invisible field. Hesitant, she put her hand through, then the other, and felt them. Dry!

Taking a deep breath, she stepped through, aware of the sensations as her breasts passed the invisible field. Her head pulled and she realized each strand of hair was passing through separately, water cascading down in ripples as her blonde tresses emerged.

"Blessed be!" she marveled. "I could make a bloody fortune if I could market that in New York or Paris." She fluffed her clean, dry hair and laughed. "Space might not be so bad for an old girl like me."

Her uniform had vanished from where she'd dropped it—as per instructions—at the foot of the bed. Only her possessions remained. She frowned and went to the closets, opening them to a complete wardrobe. The clothing had been cut differently and came in various colors. Her uniform didn't hang from the rack. She felt the fabric. Incredibly soft. Having no choice, she donned the exotic space garb. To her surprise, it conformed remarkably well. Too well, she decided, looking in the reflective wall of her room.

While she stared, the door announced, "Svetlana Detova to see you, Major."

She hesitated. "Come in." Looking at the computer, she noted that an hour remained until the briefing.

Detova entered, dressed in a similar skintight suit.

"Blessed be, yours, too?"

Svetlana nodded, blue eyes pensive. "From what I can tell, the same happened to everyone. We only have these," she gestured at her skintight suit. "Evidently, our old clothing sank through the floor. Only the materials in the pockets were left behind."

Sheila bent down and picked up the keys to her Austin, her pencil, fifty pounds and six shillings, her wallet, and assorted other bits and pieces. "Remarkable," she murmured, testing the floor with her feet.

"Major, I think we should discuss this—and the implications."

Without her sophisticated business suit, Svetlana looked less imposing. Her figure was a little on the heavy side with large breasts, wide hips, and a thin waist. The form-fitting space clothing she had adopted obviously made her nervous—and with reason. She'd be the target of every male eye on the ship.

Sheila checked her own appearance. Nervous, indeed. Did she want a man to see her looking like this?

"And what do you think it means?"

Svetlana's mouth curled up slightly. "Do the Ahimsa *really* want us for pilots?"

* * *

Murphy groaned, stumbling over to the dispenser. "Uh, got anything for a hangover?"

He glanced at the computer. It read: "06:30." Another

note stated, "PT IN GYM 07:00 BREAKFAST 08:00 AUDITORIUM 09:00."

A whole hour for breakfast? Maybe space wouldn't be so bad after all.

A glass of something popped out the bottom. Murphy stared at it. The stuff looked like coconut milk . . . or Alka-Seltzer®. He tossed it down, gasping at the taste. Then he ducked into the shower. Oddly, he felt better by the time he stepped out, but not good enough to realize what had happened. He stuck his hand back into the cubicle, felt nothing, and looked down at his body. Dry. He sniffed under his armpits—maybe he really *had* taken a shower—and looked at the spot where he'd tossed his uniform. All his possessions lay there in little piles. No uniform.

"Christ, Mason! You're gonna get it for this!"

He checked the closets, and found clothing. He yanked one of the fine fabrics off the rack and tugged it on. He caught a glimpse of himself in the mirror, bulged his muscles and posed like Mr. Universe. He grunted at the image, and sprinted for the door. If he didn't find his uniform before Daniels saw him, he'd be as good as dead. Daniels might have forgotten the kitchen raid, but another incident would be unthinkable.

He pounded down the hall, palming Mason's door. "Damn it, let me in!"

"Murphy! I was just on my way to kill you!"

Murphy pushed the door open in time to see Mason standing in the middle of the room, buck naked, trembling with rage.

"Where is it?"

"Huh?"

"My uniform, you dirt-ball maggot-breath son of a bitch!"

Murphy gulped, looking at the pile of keys, coins, billfold, and rabbit's foot.

"You didn't take *my* uniform?"

"Hell, no! Now, where's mine! Cough it up or I'm gonna take you apart right here!" Mason advanced, red-faced, fists clenched as his biceps swelled.

"Hey! Back off, man! Mine's gone, too!"

Mason stopped, brows beetling. "Yours, too?"

"Yeah!"

Mason's cheeks twitched. "If not you . . . *God damn COMMIE BASTARDS!*"

Murphy cocked his head. Who else? "Get dressed. Grab one of these things out of the closet. This time, by God, there's gonna be war!"

"Oh, damn!" Mason winced. "But do we have to when I'm feeling like this?"

"Ask the dispenser for hangover stuff."

Murphy burst out into the white corridor, and stopped dead as Gubanya stepped out from across the hall. "This your idea of a joke?"

Mika Gubanya, fitted out in the skintight suit, grinned. "Where are our uniforms? This time, American, you've gone too far."

Murphy dropped to a crouch, waiting. Damn! Gubanya was big! *Got to stay clear of those hands. He gets a hold on you, and he'll snap your spine like a twig.*

Gubanya balanced on the balls of his feet, the ugly grin spreading across his face. "I will enjoy breaking every bone in your body, American. Now, you feel the might of the Red Army."

"Not today, pal. Cause I enjoy taking meat piles like you apart."

"What the hell . . .*Murphy!*" Daniels' voice thundered in the hall.

"He took our clothes, Sam!" Murphy didn't shift his eyes, seeing Gubanya's sudden hesitation.

"Two of you?" the big Russian asked. "All the better."

Daniels slapped a hand on Murphy's shoulder, pulling him back, stepping between Murphy and the Russian.

"Look, meatbrains, I don't know what this is about, but it's over."

Murphy caught a glimpse of Daniels, seeing the same shiny garb on the captain's muscular body. "But they took our uniforms!"

"Who took *whose* uniforms?" Gubanya turned red with anger, stepping forward, jaw thrust out.

Daniels lifted his eyes, shaking his head. "Lord, give

me strength! Damn it, Murphy, did you see what he's wearing? Huh? Did you take time to look, Gubanya? Did either one of you assholes look around? *Everybody's goddamned uniform is gone!* I was just on the comm to Staka about it."

Murphy grimaced as Mason came charging into the hall, face contorted—and pulled up at the sight of Daniels.

The captain glared at all of them. "You in on this, too, Mason?"

"I. . . . Someone stole my uniform, sir!" Ted slapped a salute, standing stiffly at attention.

"Jesus Holy Mary," Daniels groaned. "All right, hare brains, hit the deck. Give me thirty . . . *now!*" Daniels turned on his heel "You, too, Gubanya. Thirty! Or do you want me taking this to Viktor?"

"You have no authority over me, American."

Sam seemed to swell. "Did I hear you right, Lieutenant? Did you hear something different from the General Secretary than I did? Did you attend a different meeting with Wide than I did yesterday? One the floor, mister. Now!"

Murphy caught a glimpse of the big Russian's face. Not nice! Then he stared at the floor as he pressed out thirty as fast as he could. Whatever had been in Daniels' eyes—and Murphy'd seen it more times than he cared to remember—had made an impact. Gubanya slapped palms to the floor and started bobbing like an oil well pump jack.

"All right, people," Daniels added to the grunting cadence. "It stops here. Murphy, Mason, if Major Staka or Gabi, or any other staff officer gives you an order, you do it. Not later, not after you check with me, but on the spot, you hear, pus brains?"

"Yes, sir!" they cried in unison.

"Gubanya, the same goes for you. Viktor and I decided it all last night. We're one unit now. I expect the Major and I will be having a word with you people during PT. In fact, we'll all do it at the same time just so there's no misunderstandings."

How did Daniels get that kindly tone in his voice just before he ordered you to cut your throat?

"Nice work, Mika. Good form." Staka's voice came from somewhere behind Murphy's bouncing buttocks. "I heard the end of Sam's little speech. It would have hurt me to have learned you disobeyed him after whatever caused your joyful morning exercise."

"Yes, sir!" Gubanya shouted.

"All right, meatballs, hit it. You've got ten minutes before PT," Daniels called.

Murphy jumped to his feet. "PT?"

Gubanya rose, glaring his hatred as he wiped his hands.

"Physical training, cripple brain. Cal to us Western types. And, yes, children, we're all going to do it together. *Now, move!*"

"This isn't over," Gubanya whispered under his breath.

* * *

Wide—as usual—appeared as a hologram at precisely 08:00. He hovered in midair to one side of their table while a second display flashed into existence. What looked to be a steel wheel hung in the air, a starry background behind it.

"We seem to have a problem," Sheila stated. "Our uniforms are gone." *Let's get to the bottom of* that *first!*

"I have supplied much better clothing for your requirements." Wide rolled back and forth. Enjoyment? "A uniform, Major, does two things. It symbolizes a common identity—and, at the same time, signifies divisions between peoples or classes. You now have a more serviceable uniform and you all look the same. For humans, we have noted, that serves a purpose."

"What if we want the old ones back?" Gabi raised his hands.

"Outside of the perpetuation of your nationalities, why would you? The material is nowhere near the quality you now wear. This material is more durable and will resist abrasion and tearing. Further, this dress provides protection against radiation which is harmful to humans. With several additions, it also serves in vacuum as what you would call a spacesuit. The material thermally regulates itself to maintain optimum body temperature and can be worn for years prior to replacing."

"And the fit?" Svetlana asked. "These are . . . well, too tight. Too . . ."

"I can assure you they are most elastic and will give in any situation, thereby creating no restriction to inhibit movement."

"I didn't mean that." Svetlana glared at the alien.

"Ah . . . you mean they reveal too much of the body's shape? We sought to make them practical. In these suits, you have the best of two worlds. Dress which will protect you from radiation, vacuum, temperature extremes, and still accommodate freedom of movement.

"Now that that subject is closed, perhaps we can get on with meaningful discussions?"

"Kiss the uniforms good-bye, I guess." Sam looked down at his sleeves, a frown lining his forehead.

"Meaningful discussions? Like what this is all about," Viktor muttered under his breath.

"What you see here," Wide ignored them, "is the Pashti station. They call it—in as close an approximation as I can get to human tongue—TaHaAk. It means Star Home in Pashti. They, like so many species, have little originality when it comes to naming their properties and stations."

"I take it that's the target?" Daniels had both feet kicked out in front of him, the notepad before him already covered with doodles. Quite a few props—like the notepad—had been provided. The workmanship, quality of paper, all exceeded the Earthly originals.

"Correct. This is a space station. It is situated in the L-5 position in relationship to their primary. It—"

"El what?" Moshe looked up, perplexed.

Sheila tried to explain. "The fifth LaGrange point, Moshe. It was named after the French mathematician. That's the intersection where the orbital planes of two bodies. . . ." She stopped at his blank look. "Let's just say it's a stable orbit—one which doesn't take much adjustment, if any, to keep the station from straying."

Wide spun so both eyestalks could study the humans. "We have anticipated many of your problems. In order to save time and effort, any questions you may have on orbits, life-forms, Pashti history, or space travel will be easily accessible on your private computer consoles. Similarly, your headsets can access that same body of data from anywhere on the ship."

Moshe frowned, reached for the headset next to the terminal, and whispered the question. A miniature holo formed before his nose, showing a white star, circling planets, and a blinking light.

"Moving on," Wide continued, rolling back and forth in the air. "We expect you to have your forces totally familiar with the structure and composition of this space station by the time we arrive. The timing of your assault will be critical. You must deploy, gain entry, and destroy the station within a day's time. Thereafter, you will reassemble, making sure to leave no physical trace of your presence, and withdraw to the space vessels we will provide you with. Those vessels will return you to this ship and we will transport you back to Earth and your families."

"How are we supposed to break into the Pashti station? You called it TaHaAk?" Viktor asked, frowning as he studied the spinning disk.

The top layer of steel peeled away in the display, showing a scale model of the walls, corridors, pipes, and tubing that made up the structure.

Wide seemed to deflate a little. "We are leaving that up to you. Your expertise is war."

"Tell us about these Pashti," Sheila prompted. "What are they like? Are they aggressive? Do they pose a serious threat? What are their characteristics?"

"This is a Pashti."

A monstrous-looking beast, half scorpion, half tailless lizard, appeared next to TaHaAk. A rich reddish brown in color, eight limbs supported it. Two forward arms ended in multijointed pincers that jutted out from under the sturdy mound that housed the eyes.

I'll never eat crab again. Sheila licked her lips. "Is that actual size?"

"Half-scale. You will practice against full-scale models to become familiar with their appearance and nature." Wide rolled around the figure. A light danced as he spoke, illustrating his words. "What you see here is analogous to a carapace. Normally it is penetrable to anything sharp. When you encounter these creatures, however, this carapace, along with the rest of the body, will be incredibly tough. The vital points are located here, here, and here." The pointer light darted about the creature. "A blast from any of the projectile weapons we will supply you with will not only penetrate the armor, but should kill a Pashti if you are close enough to any of those sensitive areas."

"So these things will attempt to resist," Viktor said softly, blue eyes narrowing as he studied the creature.

"What will my men be called upon to do?" Moshe asked, subdued as he looked at the Pashti now being dissected by the holo projector.

Sheila fought the urge to squirm. None of the internal organs looked like anything familiar, clear down to the hairy looking legs and the peculiar mouth.

Wide rolled around, body expanding and contracting as he answered. "You and your Assaf Company will be provided with armored vehicles which will function within the station. Your purpose is to spearhead the attack and break up any resistance. Your superior protection and mobility will also allow you to paralyze Pashti communications and logistical systems while the infantry mops up behind you."

"So you've planned this the same way we would a human ground action?" Sheila chewed the end of her pencil. *And what else have you planned, Wide? The more we learn, the less I like this. Where are the holes in your little scheme?*

"That is an accurate analog. The details will be up to you."

"How about defenses? What sort of heavy artillery, missiles, antitank . . . er, anti-lander weaponry do we have to neutralize before we even set foot in that station?" Moshe squinted at the turning wheel, the humor gone from his eyes.

"None."

"What?" Sam Daniels straightened.

"That is right, Captain." Wide sucked in his sides. "Please, remember, you are dealing with *civilized* space. Your attack will come as a complete surprise. The Pashti are not armed. Who would they fear? Violence, you see, is an aberration, barbaric, associated with only backward, developing planets."

"Let me get this straight," Sheila interjected. "You want us to go murder an intelligent species of pacifists? Are these creatures harmless?"

"Hardly harmless, they've taken ever greater portions of Ahimsa resources over the last million years. They are a vigorous and aggressive species. The action I am now undertaking will simply return balance to the system."

"With the blood on our hands." Sheila crossed her arms, glaring at Wide through slitted eyes.

Wide thinned. "I hardly expected to hear humans objecting to the murder of innocents—unless, of course, you are engaging in a ritual of negotiation similar to the disseminations of your politicians. Is that your intent? What would you negotiate?"

Sheila felt herself begin to bristle and Sam Daniels looked like someone had snuffed a cigar in his pizza. *A shouting match now might kill us all. We're still prisoners, like it or not. Play for time, Sheila. Play for all the time you can get.*

"What have we got to bargain with? Arguing ethics won't get us anywhere if you've made up your mind. Have you already mapped out the moves each unit will make once we gain entry to TaHaAk?" She hurried to change the subject, making a "desist" signal with the flat of her hand which Daniels caught. The look he gave her would have melted ice.

Wide seemed to become a little paler. "I can help you define the objectives and the computer will give you technical advice. What you do with that information is your decision. Your lives are at risk, Major Dunbar. We only make suggestions when it comes to the tactical aspects of your operation. Since it is your risk, you make the final decisions as to the tactics you wish to employ. That is, after all, your expertise."

"And what is the overall strategy?" Daniels asked, expression veiled. "You don't want anyone to know who's kicking the hell out of these Pashti. Why? What do you gain out of this?"

Wide deflated slightly, black eyes swiveling to Sam. When he spoke, his sides crinkled around the eyestalks. "We do this for the obvious reasons, Captain Daniels.

Pashti pose a threat. They continue to encroach on our space—take our resources. We have tried diplomatic efforts, but they cannot counter the Pashti cycles. It is a biological flaw, you see. We intend to neutralize that threat."

"With no risk to yourselves," Sheila added.

"Can you think of a better strategy?" Wide asked in turn.

Ah! At last, that makes a lot of things fit into place. Ahimsa not only want their cake, they don't want a trail of crumbs leading back to the eaters. "No, I suppose I couldn't. Assuming, that is, that other methods have been tried which didn't involve damage and destruction. Are the lives worth the gains?"

Wide thinned himself, which Sheila had come to translate as confidence—or bluff. "They are. Consider your own interests. The Pashti were among the species who interdicted your planet. Suppose you managed to keep from turning your planet into radioactive waste? Suppose you managed to colonize your solar system? Do you know that you would never have passed beyond your Van Oort regions? Indeed, ships which might have ventured there would have mysteriously disappeared. They—"

"What?" Daniels exploded. He had taken the headset from Moshe. A holo model of the solar system hovered where he'd been referencing the Van Oort clouds.

"To be sure, Captain." Wide sounded smug. Had he picked up so many human characteristics? "A system of gravity beacons have been placed out there where your comets reside. Six in fact. A vessel which did not have the capability of null singularity to neutralize the distortion would be destroyed by a localized projected tidal effect.

"Please, you can all look that up later. For the moment, let us concentrate on the issues. The fact remains that your participation in this mission frees your species for the stars and forever negates the potential for nuclear holocaust." Wide's voice became smooth. "We offer you survival—and space!"

At the price of a little innocent blood! Sheila thought to herself, mind already locked on that slowly spinning wheel that represented TaHaAk station—and human freedom.

Wide thinned, eyestalks scanning the room. "For the

near future, training will begin with weapons familiarization. We have designed the equipment to closely simulate terrestrial arms. Upon familiarization, your personnel will be able to conduct mock exercises inside a full-scale model of TaHaAk station which we have constructed for your use. You and your people will practice against robot Pashti which will react to a lethal or debilitating hit. I believe you will find the simulations remarkable. You can fight and refight the operation in a way you've never before experienced. Let us call it the ultimate military training ever devised. You may begin your exercises as soon as you feel ready."

"And the female intelligence personnel?" Svetlana asked. "They are to pilot the torpedoes?"

"That is correct. I made the decisions based on flying experience as well as exposure to personal risk in case they need to cover the rear areas. You will find that information in the manuals which will be provided after this meeting. Feel free to modify our suggestions any way you wish."

"And this is the only reason you chose *female* pilots?" Svetlana leaned forward, fire in her eyes.

"No. I also wanted to balance the human contingent." Wide made a whistling sound as he watched Svetlana's expression tense. "Yes, Major Detova, I did have another reason. Your men are going someplace no human has gone before. You are clever enough to know that I wouldn't waste an opportunity to study your species in as many dimensions as possible. Fortunately, the present crisis came after your technology has freed the female of your species from being a decorative piece of reproductive chattel. As in hunter-gatherer societies, your industrial age has lifted females from the bondage of the agricultural age. I will be able to study your behavior as male equals. And evaluate your potential for induction into civilization."

"And that's all?"

Wide's piping whistle shrilled. "One never knows where research will lead, but, yes, for the moment, that's all. I can guess your fears, Major. You will not be used for breeding specimens . . . or for prostitutes."

Sheila bit her lip. *And you can just damned well bet on that, Wide, old chap! This whole thing is rotten—a dirty underhanded deal.*

* * *

"I could come to enjoy this." Malenkov sighed as two of the CIA women walked past, turned into the next aisle, and found seats in the third row.

The auditorium had begun to fill. Murphy craned his neck to see. The first time he'd been here, the shock of the bubble ride had paralyzed his ability to think. Now, as the air crackled with a feeling of excitement and adventure, he took note of his new companions. Of the roughly four hundred people present, maybe a third were women. Two to one, not bad odds compared to most places he'd been stationed.

Murphy tried to take their measure, and came to a realization. Each looked like a knockout. The second thing he noticed was that they looked back—and there was none of the giggly self-conscious insecurity he was used to in those hard measuring glances. *CIA? KGB? Damn it, Murph, why do you get the feeling they ain't none of them secretaries? Watch your ass, boy. You go getting any too friendly with these chicks, they'll cut your throat and feed you your nuts for dinner.*

"You know," Malenkov speculated, "they almost seem to have been picked for their, uh, feminine charms. And I've heard of American women. They have a reputation."

"So do Russian women—but I don't want to get into that. I almost cooked my ass once this morning. I don't want to be doing push-ups with you, too."

Malenkov grunted. "Mika . . . well, he has an attitude problem. Something that happened when he was a boy. I don't know all the details. But he's one of those who can't see beyond the Party. Right or wrong."

"Yeah, well, I was a little out of control this morning. Tell him it was just the situation. I mean, hell, to lose your uniform like that."

"I will." Nicholai made a clicking with his tongue. "Mika and I have been friends for a long time. He's covered my back, saved my life a few times. Give him, how do you say, the benefit of the doubt? This is all new. I think, for Mika, not finding aliens to be faithful members of the Party . . . well, it hurts."

"Yeah, I've known some guys like that. America, love it or leave it types. Any sin, covered and draped in the flag, is a good sin."

"And Captain Daniels? Is he one?"

"No. He's a damn fine officer."

"Does he play a banjo and eat watermelon?"

Murphy choked. "Jeezus! Don't *ever* say that in front of him! You'll be picking teeth out of the back of your skull!"

Malenkov frowned, honestly baffled. "I don't understand."

"Hey, look. You don't joke about that and . . . and I won't joke about Russian women, all right?"

Malenkov spread his hands. "I've never *seen* a black man before. Well, Afghans are kind of dark. I've only seen black men on the television, and once, in a movie. The men in the movie played banjos and ate watermelon."

Murphy groaned. "Yeah, well, we've come a long way from those times. I mean, race doesn't matter anymore. I mean, well, it does . . . but it doesn't. You see?"

"Is that like Perestroika doesn't matter anymore . . . but it does? I understand. Like Party propaganda."

"Yeah, maybe."

"Attention!"

Murphy snapped to his feet. Sheila Dunbar, followed by Staka, Detova, Daniels, and Gabi walked into the room. Sheila stepped up on the platform and looked around. "Be seated, please."

Murphy lowered himself into the seat, glancing nervously at Malenkov. The damned aliens had a load of human dynamite aboard. First the uniform thing, then Malenkov's innocent remarks. They'd be lucky if they made it three days before someone killed someone else through a silly misunderstanding.

"Gentlemen, ladies, we've just had a briefing from Wide, the Ahimsa commander of this ship. Beginning immediately after this meeting, each of you will break into your training groups to begin familiarization with Ahimsa weaponry."

Major Dunbar looked around. "No one here has been in this situation before. I understand there was some confusion over the change in uniforms this morning. An incident almost occurred as a result."

"Oh, man!" Murphy groaned to himself, sinking into the chair. Malenkov snickered.

"People, we are the first humans to represent our kind among the Ahimsa. While they've studied our planet for the last two billion years, we haven't been a very good example of 'civilized' beings. That will change on this ship. I will *not* tolerate any incidents.

"Our position is rather precarious—and dangerous. We have been given the objective. Our mission is to attack and neutralize a Pashti space station. We will brief you on the details as soon as you've become proficient with the weapons systems we've been provided with.

"At that time, we will begin maneuvers to hone our skills. If you have any questions, please refer them to your officers. Assaf Company will assemble at the armored simulators. Intelligence personnel at the torpedo simulators. SPETSNAZ and SOD on the rifle range. Tonight, there will be mandatory training at your computers which will familiarize you with Pashti anatomy and general information you will need for this operation.

"Let me repeat what you've already been told. We're in space for a year, people. That's how long it will seem to take us. Six months out, hit the station, and six months back. During that time, you will have to come to grips with each other. A lot of political water has passed under the bridge since 1945, but I will remind you, Americans and Soviets and Jewish partisans worked together then. There's no reason why we can't again. I will have no political eruptions on this mission. Is that understood?

"One final thing, I would like to see Riva Thompson immediately after this meeting."

She looked around the room. "Dismissed."

"She sounds like a tough one." Malenkov shook his head.

"But I never had an officer so good looking," Murphy grinned. "I wonder . . ."

"You like suicide, don't you?"

CHAPTER XII

Riva stopped before Major Dunbar. "You asked to see me? Riva Thompson?"

Sheila Dunbar smiled and extended her hand. "I read your file. You served in Europe as well as the Middle East. You also have a specialization in languages. Given our current problems, I need two things. First, I need someone to take over as second in command for Major Detova. From your file, I noted that you coordinated covert operations first in Vienna and then in Lebanon after Buckley was killed. Subsequently you worked with Mossad in Israel. In all cases, you were most capable in the handling of your networks and personnel. You rank high in administrative skills and management."

Riva's heart skipped. Could she do that again? Could she step into the lion's jaws? The last time had cost so very much. She'd sworn never to let it happen again.

Sheila studied her reaction. "The second thing I need is coordination of a Pashti language team for intelligence purposes. I have only one question before offering you the position. Why did you transfer from a field position in Central Intelligence to a desk at NSA?"

The hollow place inside cried out. She steeled herself. "Personal reasons, Major."

Dunbar lifted an eyebrow, waiting for more, then said, "I can't afford to take chances with this. I need someone to assume responsibility for one hundred and twenty-eight women who need to be turned into a combat unit in less than six months despite their various backgrounds. Your file indicates that you have a particular competence. I think you know what I'm talking about—and why I have to have a straight answer."

Riva took a deep breath, meeting those penetrating eyes. "During the time I was in Israel, I fell in love with a man. He died at the hands of the PLO. I didn't feel I could balance my assessments of the political and military situation in an objective and professional manner. I took the position with NSA because . . ." *How do I tell her?*

"Go on. I'm not trying to be difficult. I need an honest answer."

Riva smiled wistfully, surrendering against her natural hesitation. "I made it because I didn't want to get involved with someone else who might be killed like that. I couldn't stand the loss twice in one lifetime. Then I saw a young Palestinian girl shot down in front of me. The lines blurred and I didn't know what was right anymore."

Sheila nodded, staring absently at the empty auditorium. "Do you want the assignment?"

Riva cocked her head. "Damn right, I want it!"

"Now tell me why you can do the job and someone else can't?"

"Because I'm the best. If you've read the file, you know that had Washington listened to my reports, a lot of lives would have been saved. My predictions came out on the money each time. And I have a top proficiency ranking in language skills. I'd love a crack at alien communication. I knew what I was doing when I asked for the transfer, and I took that option with the understanding that I'd never get a field position again. I lived with the choice because it was right at the time. Now I'm ready for another round—and if I can't do my job, you'll get my resignation before the fat's in the fire."

Sheila nodded, "Then we'd better get down to the torpedo simulators and I'll introduce you as their commander. Supposedly, everything we learned in the briefing is in the manuals supplied with the simulators. You should be able to access the Pashti language tapes from your room terminal. Good luck. If you find you need anything, ring me up."

They started down the orange hall.

"Major?"

"Hmm?" Dunbar turned.

"Thank you."

"In six months, if we're still alive after TaHaAk—we'll see just how much thanks you think it's worth."

* * *

Marshal Sergei Rastinyevski contemplated the logs burning in his giant fireplace. In the corner of the long room a string quartet played Mozart. Antique gas lamps lit the length of the room, giving it a mellow comfortable cast. The Persian rugs lay four deep across the floor and the arched ceiling stretched a good two meters over his head. Bookcases lined the walls, the volumes reflecting in the light of the lamps. An Irish wolfhound slept by the side of his velvet upholstered chair. He'd crossed his legs at the ankles, the firelight gleaming off his boots where they rested on the footstool.

One of the logs popped, sparks whirling as they shot up the chimney.

Marshal Rastinyevski reached for the glass of Irish whiskey that gleamed a deep amber through the cut crystal of the Waterford goblet. Sipping, he looked across at the heavy, white-haired man who sat opposite him, pale blue eyes studying the fire. Yevgeny Karpov had laced stubby fingers across his stomach. Perhaps sixty years of age, his bulldog approach toward politics had increased his power during the Gorbachev days. Under Golovanov, he'd advanced further, but managed to avoid the taint of the American scandal.

"I think you should take the job. As to what will come, we think alike." Rastinyevski placed his whiskey back on the table, reaching down to scratch the dog's ears. The wolfhound stretched out its legs, grunting happily.

Karpov filled his lungs and exhaled. "You think it will reunite the country?" His attention shifted from the fire to Rastinyevski's face. "What about the southern Republics?"

Rastinyevski steepled his fingers, watching the red-yellow flames lick around the big logs. "We buy them off. The same with the Armenians and Georgians. A lot of wealth can be had from Europe. What Hitler did to us, we will do to them."

"Hitler robbed the peasants and created the Partisans."

Rastinyevski pulled at his earlobe. "The difference, my dear Yevgeny, is that Hitler had a small army invading giant Russia. We will have a large army invading small Europe. I think you have to keep in mind that most Soviet citizens will settle down when we give them Renault, Mercedes, and BMW automobiles and appliances and fine clothes and all the luxuries of the West. If we strike rapidly, we can paralyze all of Europe. NATO can't make a calculated response without their nuclear shield. KGB has infiltrated most of their high command. If, for example, we dropped SPETSNAZ on Brussels, Paris, London, Bonn, and the rest of the major nerve centers in the dead of night, we could decapitate most of their top command. Assassinate General Willis in his own home. The same for the others. Our heavy lift aircraft can settle two divisions, one armor, one a motor-rifle, at a major airport every four hours until they're shot down. The chances of that depend on how many NATO aircraft are destroyed on the ground. We should be able to get most of them by using Aeroflot commercial craft as suicide bombers in a first strike. Immediately afterward, the entire forces of the Western Strategic Direction will roll across the borders. I estimate Europe will be ours within four weeks."

"And the Americans?"

"That will be your specific problem. They know our Strategic Rocket Forces are paralyzed. We've already mobilized. They've mobilized. If you're the new General Secretary, you can stall them, tell them that it's better to let the Soviet Union build its forces on the borders, that it will pacify the old conservatives, allay fears of another World War II. By the time we strike, they'll be too far behind. It will take them a while to decide the defense of Europe is worth it. Not only that, they're stretched too thin. They can't afford to withdraw from the Pacific, from Central America, the Indian Ocean, or the other places they've made commitments to. We might make a move on Japan, or drive through Afghanistan again and threaten them with their warm water port myth by invading Baluchistan. In fact, a feint in any of those directions would probably be beneficial. When they realize the extent of our advance, it will be too little, too late, and Europe will be ours. At that point, you sue for peace."

Karpov stroked his chin, frown lines deepening in his forehead as he stared at the fire. "And our nuclear program?"

"It takes time to rebuild from the ground up. Whatever the mirror balls are, they still defy the best brains in the Academy of Sciences. We're racing with the Americans again. This time it's to build new bomb factories. Fortunately, their depression leaves them staggered. Despite their advantages, taking money from the recovery to build bomb plants has to be done judiciously. At the same time, the effort has drawn resources away from NATO and the rest of their worldwide army."

"So our time is now or never?"

Rastinyevski cocked an eyebrow. "Think of it like this. You will be the ruler of all lands and peoples in the east from the Chukchi Peninsula to Dingle Bay on the west."

"And the internal stabilization of the Soviet Union?"

Rastinyevski lifted a shoulder in a shrug. "I honestly believe we can take most of Western Europe's industrial centers with minimal damage. I also predict we'll be able to keep those skilled workers at their jobs. The output will be channeled to Soviet citizens. Once the lines are gone and fine Western products are on the shelves, I imagine dissent will drain away to nothingness. How can people complain when they're fed, warm, and have new toys to play with?"

"And the Europeans?"

"To the victor goes the spoils. They'll have to be pacified, of course. But then, who is better at pacification than KGB? Look at the hold Hitler had on them. Look at the work camps, the labor gangs he used to fortify the entire coastline. Surely we can improve on that."

Yevgeny chuckled softly to himself. "Very well, Sergei, I will be your new General Secretary."

Rastinyevski nodded soberly. "I knew you would. I've already had my staff type up your first speech. It will be on your desk first thing in the morning. See what you think and make any additions or deletions you feel necessary. For the moment, the time has come to mollify the Americans."

* * *

Svetlana Detova had immediately fallen in love with her headset. Scarcely had she learned to use it before she turned her attentions to the Ahimsa. If only she had her Cray! Painstakingly, she explored her access. With care she'd never exercised before, she began the process. Where she might trip alarms, she laid false trails, slow going, but a check would reveal the fumbling attempts of a novice trying to learn the system. After breaking the locks and security of the Bank of Hong Kong, Mitsubishi, or the Subic Bay Naval security data banks, how much more trouble would she have with the Ahimsa? It took a delicate hand to keep her activity undetected, and to do so was further complicated by the need to learn and utilize Ahimsa, a very, very old and structured language of whistles, peeps, and shrill notes.

Svetlana Detova hadn't been anybody's fool on her meteoric rise through the KGB. Clamping her lips tightly, she settled onto her couch, concentrating on both the Ahimsa dictionary that flashed before her eyes, and the mental links which led to the ship's brain center. One by one, ever so slowly, she gained access to bits and pieces of data. On a notepad, she drew idle pictures of animals, geometric figures, abstract art, anything which would serve as a mnemonic for her own system. By the end of the first night, bleary-eyed, she had a faint glimmer of a vague pattern emerging from the fragments.

The shower barely relaxed her tired body—as ideas for programs continued to flicker through her head. She forced herself to bed, trying to still her active mind. She couldn't chance a mistake overlooked in a haze of fatigue.

Sleep would refresh her, perhaps tap some hidden clue buried in the subconscious. The headset, the key to another little sliver of the Ahimsa puzzle, gleamed as the lights lowered.

Am I smart enough? Dunbar picked up the clues, somehow, through some slip. Can I fool the aliens? And if I can't. . . .

* * *

Nicholai nodded to himself. Murphy had a definite style as he recovered from the weapon's awesome discharge.

"Sheee-it!" Murphy cried. He looked up from the sights of the odd rifle the Ahimsa had given them to train with. The shredded remains of a half-inch thick steel plate clattered loudly across the intervening hundred yards. Fragments smoked in the cool air.

"I thought you'd be impressed." Nicholai gestured at the range. "I've shot just about everything—or had it shot at me. These, well, if we had rifles like these to use against Afghans, I'd be a younger man today."

"Sure pasted the hell out of that steel plate. Doesn't feel like it's that powerful." Murphy looked at the weapon with wide eyes, then stared at the target. "You'd expect that kind of performance with fifty caliber SLAP ammo, not from a dinky little rifle like this."

Malenkov braced himself and stepped on the target trigger. A second steel plate shot up out of the floor. A one-to-one scale picture of a charging Pashti had been drawn on the thick plate. Finding his sight picture, Malenkov tightened on the trigger.

RAAAAPPPPPP! The blast of the weapon deafened. Spatters of steel erupted out of the center of the Pashti drawing. The Ahimsa weapon barely shook in his arms. With the recoil no more than a low frequency buzz, the image in the sights didn't even blur. The entire burst remained controllable with no tendency for muzzle climb.

"Nice shooting, Nicky," Murphy grunted, seeing the smoking outline disappear. He pressed the magazine release and slapped a new mag into his gun.

"Not bad," Malenkov agreed. "What I would have given to have had one of these on patrol outside of Jalalabad!"

"Yeah, wonder what makes these babies rock and roll?"

Nicholai inspected the weapon. Maybe ten pounds, the material it had been constructed from defied him. Nor did the sealed magazine give any clues. The weapon had selective fire, semi-auto, tri-burst, and full automatic feed functions. The rifle looked similar to the Heckler & Koch

G11. The bore, however, appeared to be .25 caliber and, from the compact size of the one hundred and fifty round capacity magazine, there wasn't room for much more than bullets. Even better, the sights consisted of a field that bent light, magnified, and penetrated even total darkness. With a flick of a switch, it could pick up infrared.

Mika Gubanya entered the range area, wearing one of the skintight spacesuits. He stopped short at the sight of Murphy and Malenkov. *Oh, no. I know that look. Just like that time Oleg got crazy and snuck out to see his girl. Mika, don't do this.*

"Mika! Come show us your style!" Malenkov gave him a friendly grin, hoping against hope. Gubanya's look turned nasty and Nicholai's guts twisted.

"Lieutenant, I thought you checked out on range facilities already." Gubanya had stiffened, hands behind his back, thick neck taut, while his expression was one of sullen dislike.

The back of Nicholai's neck prickled.

"Come shoot with us, Mika. These are wonderful. Think what we could have done that time we were pinned down outside of Zibak."

"Yeah, I could have used one of these that time we hit Medellin." Murphy patted the stock paternally, apparently at ease.

"I think, Nicholai, that your time on the range is up." Gubanya crossed his arms.

Murphy spoke before Malenkov could respond.

"Look, Lieutenant, I was sort of out of line yesterday." Murphy raised a placating hand. "Come on and shoot with us. Hell, we got enough troubles as it is without making more."

"This isn't your concern, American."

Nicholai shook his head, making a face. "Come on, Mika. You and I have watched each other's backs too many times for this. We've seen too much, carried too many of our friends out of bad situations. What is this? Why are you—"

"Comrade Senior Lieutenant, I think recalling the times we did our sacred duty and upheld the policies of the Party should remind you of your duty now . . . and of *who* you do it with."

Nicholai settled the butt of the weapon on the deck, straightening. So it would be that way? "Mika, please, you can only push so far. After all we've been through, this is—"

"I think maybe it is."

"Viktor said—"

"Viktor hasn't been himself recently."

Malenkov stiffened, a charge of adrenaline hyping his muscles. "I think he has. Mika, since you're the one who's pushing, you've set the tone. When I practice is of no concern to you, Comrade Lieutenant."

Gubanya's muscles rippled, eyes going to Murphy where he lounged to one side, assault weapon resting haphazardly in his hands. "It is *who* you practice with, Nicholai."

"It's a free country," Murphy added softly. "Besides, I might have him at my back someday. I like to know how a man shoots when he's covering my back."

Mika nodded, a slow grin coming to his face. "I have heard Americans are generally shot in the back."

Murphy's expression tightened. "Do you want to come a little closer and say that, pal? I'd hate to blow you and that wall all to pieces. Might be somebody I like on the other side."

"Wait!" Nicholai cried, panicking. He stepped between them, hands up, calming. "We're acting like fools! Mika, do not forget, we are fighting together now! Us, the Americans, the Israelis, we are allies! On the same side against the Pashti!"

Murphy stood easily, the muzzle wavering insolently in the air.

Mika's lips twitched slightly, eyes gleaming. "Allies. Yes, for now. But politics, like the wind, always seem to shift in the end." He turned on his heel, spine stiff, and marched angrily back the way he'd come.

Nicholai exhaled slowly, feeling his heart thump hollowly in his chest.

Murphy's jaws clamped, eyes smoldering as he studied the corridor where Gubanya had disappeared. "Hey, I tried."

"I know." Nicholai vented an exasperated sigh. "Don't hold it against him, Comrade Murphy. It is. . . . Oh, I don't know. Too much old blood. We train our officers well. Mika graduated from Frunze Military Academy. He has won several citations. He's a good soldier. He . . . he . . ."

"Yeah," Murphy mumbled, still angry. "I know. Look, Nicky, forget it. C'mon, this sky wagon the puffballs fly around in has some great scotch in it. Neat stuff, all you do is punch a glass in, say 'scotch' and glory be. C'mon! I'll buy—and to hell with Gubanya!"

Nicholai smiled and laughed, taking Murphy's arm, but he couldn't shake the memory of that look which had passed between his friends. He knew that look, a fighting dog look—a killing look. *And I had to call him lieutenant—to rub it in. This will lead to no good.*

* * *

The contoured seat seemed to fold around her as g force pulled Riva down. The curious transparent foam that immersed her supported her arms against the building g as she made the turn. The little meter that measured such things flashed that she'd just powered through a 16g maneuver—and 9 was about the best an F16 could produce without blacking out the pilot.

She stabilized and pulled the throttle back, her body squashed into the seat as the torpedo shot forward at a 10g acceleration. On the screen before her, the curve of a huge red planet grew. As her speed increased, she swept down, watching the ground surface flash past.

The system went dead.

"You have just destroyed yourself," the computer told her. "Your craft is not capable of entering atmosphere with a velocity of one thousand seven hundred and sixty-two kilometers per second. Vaporization of the hull has exposed your torpedo to destruction. Please reset."

Riva pushed the button, resetting to the view of the docking berth.

"Hey! Riva! You in there?" Something that sounded suspiciously like a gloved hand thumped on the hatch.

"Barb? That you?"

"Yeah, Katrina and I are logged out. We did our bit. You want to come get something to eat? We've got fifteen different files to study yet tonight, and 06:00's coming early tomorrow morning."

"Be right out." She pushed the cancel button on the simulator and the curious clear foam began to withdraw, sucked from the space around the command chair. Riva unbuckled from her seat, raising and locking the controls according to the manual.

As the last of the foam was vacuumed from the floor, she opened the hatch and stepped out, unfastening the helmet and setting it on the holder outside the simulator. "Wow!" she breathed.

Barbara Dix grinned where she stood next to a petite blonde woman, Katrina. "Damn, I never flew anything like that in my life! I paid a guy two hundred bucks one time to pilot a Tomcat, but I never thought I'd get to handle anything like that. How do they simulate the g that way?"

"Gravity control," Katrina added, a baffled expression on her face. "And if we could do that, Comrades, think of the possibilities."

"You said something about food?"

"Yeah, come on. My party. You know, I'm going to hate the damn mess hall. I feel like a side of beef in this outfit. If I'd wanted to be a *Playboy* foldout, I'd have gone the route my little sister did and become a model. Besides, I don't have the tits for it." Barbara grimaced.

"Playboy foldout?" Katrina asked, looking up at the taller women.

"Uh, for a girly magazine. You know, the pictures of nude women the men always drool over," Riva supplied.

"Ah, yes, they show up in Soviet barracks, too. Usually smuggled in from France, or some other Capitalist country bent on corrupting the morals of solid Soviet youth."

"You believe that crap? About corrupting young men, I mean?" Barbara asked.

"Of course not!" Katrina cried. "Corrupt young men? That's like . . ." she looked around, "corrupting the Party Commissar. They come pre-corrupted. I think it starts within hours of leaving their mother's wombs."

Riva grinned. "You know, the more I meet and know you stalwart Communists, the more I think you're all malcontents."

Katrina shrugged, a wry smile on her lips. "I don't know. Maybe. But then, I hear a lot of jokes from the women about politicians in your own country. Most of us don't like the Soviet system, the corruption, the constant shortages and mismanagement, but, you know, it's our country. The system, such as it is, is better than what came before. Think of it as Communism the idea and Communism the reality. The men who climb the Party ranks, do so for power. Is it so different than your American system?"

Memories of the reports she'd sent out of Beirut drifted through Riva's mind. "No, I suppose not. Washington, on the sacred Potomac, is the same sort of insular greedy snake pit. You know, here, away from it all, it sure makes you wonder, doesn't it?"

Riva winced as they walked into the mess, feeling the strain in her joints. The Ahimsa machine might counter the effects of g forces, but her muscles and joints were sure complaining. Self-consciously, she walked to the dispenser and considered the magical gadget. Out of the side of her mouth, she said, "Let's see what this thing will do." To the dispenser she called, "Maine lobster with a falafal on the side."

Grinning, she winked at Barb and Katrina. Her mouth dropped open when a steaming lobster appeared on a plate, a falafal resting neatly beside it.

Stunned, she walked over to a table. She was still staring as Barb settled in beside her with filet mignon. Katrina had something Russian on her plate.

"Is it real?" Dix asked.

Riva tapped the hard shell with a fingernail and looked up. "Sure looks like it. But I was only joking!"

"Don't ask for a live crocodile," Katrina added as she dug into her noodle dish.

If the lobster was synthetic, Riva couldn't tell as she opened the shell. The meat looked perfect, all the gooey green stuff was just like it should be.

"So you're the commanding officer now? What happened to Major Detova?" Katrina asked, chewing thoughtfully.

"I don't know. All Major Dunbar said was that she

was doing something with the computers. I'm also supposed to coordinate a language team to learn Pashti."

"I'll probably be working with you," Katrina added. "My training was in language before I got transferred to Khabarovsk."

"Jesus!" Barbara gasped. "That's way out east, isn't it?"

Katrina flushed. "China needs constant watching."

Riva dropped it. "Well, glad to have you. You know, we're on double duty. Flight simulators by day. Pashti language by night. Khabarovsk might not have been so bad."

"I don't know," Barbara stared into space. "I could spend the rest of my life in that simulator. If the real thing's better than that, I think I just found something better than sex."

"My meters showed me doing a 16g turn. I wonder how accurate that is?" Riva stared thoughtfully. Yes, it tasted just like lobster.

"Honey," Dix answered, "I've done high g maneuvers in birds the CIA has tampered with. "You did it. Something about the foam and the seat and the cockpit all make it possible. Did you notice, the cockpit's gimballed. You change attitude as the simulator accelerates. It all works to keep blood flow going to your brain. Not only that, but however they control gravity to the simulator, it can be used to counter g forces. You know, pull you the other way."

Riva noticed Mason and Cruz and two others approaching, eyes on them. She studied her plate as they went by, feeling their stares burning into her back.

"You're right, like a piece of meat." Katrina made a face.

Dix laughed. "But it works both ways. Some of those guys have dynamite bodies. You definitely know what you're getting. No padded shoulders, no girdles to keep their sagging bellies in."

Riva stared at the falafal, lost in thought.

"You still with us, Riva?"

She blinked, returning to the present. "Yes. I was just remembering some of the things I saw in Lebanon, that's all." She lifted the falafal, looking at it, remembering the taste. *Ari, the last one of these I ate was with you.*

* * *

RashTak shivered slightly as he struggled to keep his thoughts off his rebellious body and on the images forming on the screen before him. It had taken days to shuffle through the interdicted planets to find the Humans. They were listed under Homosapiens—a word taken from one of their own languages. Worse, they were a Class I interdiction, indicating a species to be left alone; not because they were developing without interference; not because they were part of someone's study project. No, indeed, Class I meant these beings were considered insane, violent, and aggressive.

RashTak studied the reports. An Ahimsa Overone had gone to Earth—their isolated planet—a galactic ten thousandth ago to study the self-destruction of the Homosapiens. His name translated as Wide. Wide belonged to the Council of Overones. He appeared to be old, even for an Ahimsa. If that were the case, Wide had watched stars born and seen them die. Rashtak thrummed nervously to himself. Ancestral Pashti hadn't even crawled out of SkaTaAk's muddy waters when this Wide was born. How much would an elder like that know? How much had he seen? How did the mind of a creature that old work?

RashTak pulled up a picture of a Homosapiens. They had two sexes, male and female. He felt his guts quiver with sudden interest. What? The records claimed the female to be intelligent? Could this be? He settled the hormones leading to his reproductive organs. Violet Curses on the cycles! His thrumming became louder as he began to think about the implications.

Among Pashti, the mindless females existed to be inseminated and the young, as they developed, killed the mother, eating her flesh. Finally, the immature males ate each other until only the strongest remained inside—along with the smaller sacred females. Subsequently, the little male chewed through the mother's hull and escaped into the world. The tiny females followed to be nurtured, fed, and raised to adulthood where the process was repeated.

Females existed only to bear young. Males cared for every aspect of their lives. Without males, the females didn't have the intelligence to find food, to keep themselves safe. They had to be guarded constantly to keep them out of trouble they couldn't understand—like out of the way of machinery, or from falling off things.

The thought of intelligent females couldn't be taken seriously! RashTak heard his vibrators rumbling with amusement.

He stopped the fine feeling of humor and won the battle to get his mind back to the problem. How would Wide make use of these Homosapiens? Give them ships? Neutralize the gravity mines at the Solar System border? Would the humans create a diversion? If so, how would that affect the cycles? Could soft-tissued aliens stop a biological fact?

Chee'ee'la warned that the Ahimsa would bring humans to Pashti space. Where? Which of the industrial worlds scattered for light-years along their arm of the galaxy would the humans be dropped on? How could they counter or affect the Pashti cycles? No matter which way RashTak looked at it, it didn't make sense!

RashTak studied the holos of the Homosapiens. Ugly things. They looked soft and fragile with no evidence of external armor but lots of sensorial fibers on their heads. They must have incredible hearing! That much fine hair should pick up any kind of vibration no matter how small. They had no real teeth, no stingers, no poison sacs, nothing offensive or defensive.

And the females are intelligent? How could they possibly make rational decisions regarding their actions? No wonder they'd been interdicted. With intelligent females to run around and pester them all the time, they *had* to be insane!

He checked their intelligence performance and found it to be little different from the Pashti's—or even the Ahimsa's, for that matter. True, the Ahimsa mind was larger and stored more. Scanning the data, he couldn't see much difference in problem solving capabilities, although the approaches each species took to reach a solution diverged.

RashTak's mind kept straying to his rumbling belly. Too bad he didn't have access to more information on these Homosapiens. Why not? He looked through the file, noting that they fought wars among themselves, often while riding on large flora-consuming four-legged animals. They killed by shooting slivers of wood from staves under torsion, and augmented that with sharp metal on the ends of poles. By far their preferred method of dispatching each other consisted of hacking opponents apart by means of sharp metal tools, often from the back of the four-legged creatures.

Barbaric beasties! From the holos, they wouldn't tolerate zero g well. What possible use could Wide have for these . . . *things!*

Humph! RashTak's stomach made a frantic appeal. Violet Curses on the cycles! How could a Pashti think with his body going crazy?

Let Wide make his human diversion. If the Homosapiens showed up, a swift kick should be sufficient to damage them into submission. Soft tissue? During the cycles? Pashti, armored by nature, managed—in times of extreme stress—to kill each other during the cycles. If Homosapiens came with their slivers of wood and sharp metal implements. . . . No, the whole idea smacked of the ludicrous! He battled with his desire to laugh again.

The real problem would be how to discipline Wide if the Overones refused to sanction one of their own for fooling with the interdictions and allowing vermin like Homosapiens loose. Perhaps Chee'ee'la could be manipulated to that use—as if a Shitht could ever be manipulated!

RashTak shut down the comsat. His belly rumbled, consuming itself. Who knew, perhaps, if they weren't full of strange chemicals, Homosapiens might be good to eat? His vibrators rumbled with unstemmable laughter as he rushed to kill his blinding hunger.

CHAPTER XIII

"Pashti is different than anything we've dealt with," Riva Thompson explained. "Of course, Ahimsa and Pashti communicate very well, but going through that channel, you go from English to Ahimsa to Pashti, and God alone knows what we're losing."

Sheila nodded. "And cutting Ahimsa out of the loop?"

Thompson shook her head wearily. "We may not have time."

Sheila paced back and forth, aware the others were watching her. *Another gamble. Do I dare rely on Ahimsa translation? And if we can't communicate by the time the attack is launched? What, then? More options lost, less flexibility in the system.*

She turned. "Riva, put all you've got into making that translation work without the Ahimsa loop."

To her credit, Riva nodded. "You've got it. Uh, I may miss some of the training. In the meantime, I'd like to pull Katrina from the flight simulators and let her use her full concentration on the Pashti translation."

"Very well. Let me know what that will do to the—"

"I've already checked. The Ahimsa have ten more pilots than they need. I suppose that was to make up for illness, lack of proficiency, or any number of other possibilities."

Sheila's instinct had just proved correct. Riva *had* been the person to advance.

"And the armor, Moshe?"

The Israeli looked up from his notepad, scratching behind one ear. "From the overall performance on the simulators, we're at one hundred percent. My people in Assaf have one common concern. It's one thing to drive a simulator—even one as sophisticated as this. It's another to use the actual vehicle, to find out what the true performance parameters are. As I like to recall, the Americans used computers one time to design an armored personnel carrier. The computer decided the top hatch should meet certain specifications. The hatch they got—based on that computer model—weighed two hundred and fifty pounds. Once the people were in, they couldn't get out.

"We want field trials before our necks are stuck in the noose."

"Sam? Viktor?" She turned. "Are your people ready for mock attacks?"

Viktor smiled at her, a gleam in his dazzling blue eyes. "We're familiar with the gear. On the whole, the men are shooting ninety to one hundred on the range. I think the novelty of the weapons has worn off. Like Moshe, we're ready for field exercises."

Sheila chewed the end of her pencil. "Then I'll inform Wide. If he has no objections, we'll begin exercises tomorrow. Anything else?"

Riva cleared her throat. "The women are getting used to the uniforms, but there is still some concern."

Sheila nodded. *And bloody well there might be.* "My thoughts on the matter are that any harassment will be dealt with accordingly. Riva, if you get any complaints, notify Sam, Victor, or Moshe." She turned to them. "I'll leave discipline to you."

"You got it." Sam nodded, grinning at Viktor.

"And I expect it to be swift and adequate."

Sam's eyes narrowed. "Major, my outfit knows their business. I think any reported incident will be dealt with completely—and to the satisfaction of all parties involved. So far, nothing's happened. I can't do anything about stares, but the first guy that lays a hand on one of the pilots will wish he'd never been born."

Viktor nodded and looked up, bracing his elbows and lacing his fingers together. "And now is a good time to bring up something else. What is our policy on friendly . . . I think you have a euphemism for it?"

"Fraternization? Considering the Latin roots, a poor euphemism." Sheila raised her arms. "What consenting adults do with their spare time is none of my concern—so long as it doesn't affect the unit's performance, efficiency, or morale."

Moshe raised an eyebrow.

Sheila sighed explosively, meeting Moshe's questioning gaze. "Well, what do you expect? Our command consists of healthy young men and women. They're not bloody priests. I'm surprised we haven't already had people pairing off. You don't put men and women together in a situation like this and expect biology to simply stop. Let's face it, any rule to the contrary would be folly in the face of the situation. Force, however, is another thing, and I won't have it."

No one said anything.

"Anything else?"

"One thing." Viktor looked up. "Gubanya pointed out something this morning during weapons drill. We've had no information about Earth. No newscasts, nothing. Some of the men are worrying. Given the Ahimsa technoloy, why aren't we hearing what's happening at home? Even with the time dilation, we'd expect something."

And I've been so busy, I never even thought about it. She stepped to the terminal. "Computer, I need to speak to Wide."

Seconds passed before the screen came to life, Wide's rotund shape rocking back and forth against a background of multicolored monitors. A manipulator did something to a recess behind the alien as both eyestalks swiveled her way. "Yes, Major?"

Absorbed in watching Wide's manipulator as it retracted slowly into the Ahimsa's foot tread, it took Sheila several seconds to recall the purpose of her call. "Wide, people have begun to wonder why we're not getting any communications from Earth. Could you address that?"

The alien whistled and thinned. "Major, we've passed the gravity buoys which guard your planet. Given our current situation under null singularity drive, your planet is now 2,765 light-years behind us. Any transmissions we could pick up, provided we could interpret the signal, would be almost three years old. I would presume your personnel would know what happened three years ago."

"But what about your technology? Didn't you say that same null singularity could—"

"Yes, yes, with a transmitter on the other end. Major, your planet—given its primitive state—has no such transmitter."

"But the buoys?"

"Do the buoys you place to mark navigational routes have microwave communications towers on them? How about the naval mines you use to blockade harbors? The purpose of the buoys is to keep humans in, not to talk to them."

"Since we can't receive, can we at least send? Can we send messages home through that means? Look, the relativity aspect of this is sinking in. We're going to have trouble with people—"

"That can be arranged. I can send communications through singularity effect."

"But not the reverse?" Svetlana asked.

Wide's surface crinkled. "Major Detova, most of the domiciles in your country contain a radio or television receiver, correct? Those devices can receive transmissions from a broadcasting station. They are receivers, not broadcasters. The same is true with the Ahimsa system around your planet. It can receive but not send. The reasons are a little difficult to describe, but suffice it to say a quantum singularity—a tiny black hole—must be placed in stasis and manipulated. In a crude way, you do the same with electromagnetism for your radio signals. We placed no such quantum singularity in orbit around your planet to begin with. Second, your planet is moving at roughly two hundred and thirty kilometers per second in your relativity. Communications in subsingularity must be directional or the signal disperses over distance and all of subspace would be a chaos of mixed signals. A very sophisticated physics must be manipulated and incredibly precise control is needed to match the signal with the target at the same time transmitter and receiver are moving. To do that takes a specialized computer network—not the sort of thing which is left unattended."

Sheila winced. "So, we're cut off from news about our planet until we return, but we can get messages out?"

"That is correct." Wide deflated slightly. "At the same time—for reasons I just explained—to make such a communication absorbs a great deal of energy and computer capacity. To restrict so many of the ship's functions for nonessential transmissions would—"

"How about one a week?" Moshe asked. "Perhaps the information could be compressed? Maybe one page per person? My Israelis will perform better knowing their families will hear from them."

"Is this crucial?"

Sheila said soberly, "I think it is."

"One page every two weeks," Wide acquiesced.

A feeling of loss welled within her. *Damn, Tips, I hope someone is taking care of you.* "Then my next question concerns training exercises. I believe we are ready to begin training against TaHaAk station. You mentioned that joint maneuvers could be conducted. We would like to start as soon as convenient. Say, tomorrow?"

"Very good." Wide rolled back and forth. "That is excellent. Manuals on the layout and uses of the mock station will be provided tonight for your study."

"Thank you, Wide. That takes care of our current concerns."

The screen went dead.

Sheila turned. "You heard him. We're cut off."

"Until we return home." Viktor cupped his chin in a palm and stared at his reflection, a grim set to his mouth.

"It's just us," Sam added.

Riva frowned, twisting a loop of red hair around her finger. "I wasn't present at the first meeting, but when you've spent as many years as I have in covert operations, you develop a sense for these things." Her gaze went from person to person, warningly.

Sheila sighed, nodding. "I think we all understand. Meanwhile, I want you to give serious consideration to our circumstances. The survival of every human aboard this ship—and possibly of our very planet—depends on Wide's good will." She pinned her attention on Daniels.

"I'll keep my wits, Major." Sam's fingers curled into

fists, tendons standing out from the backs of his hands. "And I remember my history lessons, too. All the details about how slavers dealt with cargo problems."

* * *

Spotted bent an eyestalk to watch the Overone. "You have become almost as adept at lying as the humans."

Wide whistled and thinned. "I have my reasons. And I will be fascinated to see what they write in their letters. Think of it, I have my own population to study."

"The transmitters we left behind indicate that Earth is about to plunge into war. Without their nuclear deterrent, they've panicked. Atwood is struggling for survival, Golovanov died of heart failure. Andre Kutsov is under arrest in the Lubyanka. The Kremlin monitors report that Rastinyevski is considering an invasion of Eastern Europe now that NATO can't reply with nuclear warheads. Do you fear the reaction of the humans on board to that news? Is that why you lie?"

Wide formed a manipulator and readjusted the gravity compensators. "You are becoming good at this game we play, Spotted."

"Then you will recall that I told you that neutralizing their nuclear weapons would destabilize their balance of power."

Wide hooted and piped, "The results were exactly what I had anticipated. Nav-Pilot, you will notice that each of my projects has developed according to plan. Just as I foresaw the collapse of the humans' fragile peace, so have I foreseen the impact the human raid will have on the Pashti. You will see."

"And have you anticipated the humans exterminating themselves? This war you expect could do that. They may not have their atomic warheads, but they have biological and chemical agents which would kill them all."

Wide thinned. "That may well happen. Again, I have anticipated such a development. If they manage to destroy themselves, I shall have the means of reintroducing their descendants to the planet. And this time, Spotted, they shall repopulate the planet under my direction. If they are not destroyed, but only in demoralized chaos, the humans we carry will restore them to the right path. Under my direction, of course. You see, humans have become my passion. I will civilize them yet—one way, or another."

* * *

Sheila sat back in the chair, the notepad open before her, a reminder of work undone. Ankles crossed, her legs rested on the table. *What have I missed?*

Too much. She didn't have all the details yet—but enough of what she'd learned pointed to a disturbing pattern. Daniels' mention of slave ships clung to her thoughts like cobwebs in a dark passage, an ill omen of something unpleasant around the bend of the future. Her skin prickled.

No matter what, we're prisoners. He treats us like children, lying like a parent does to a child. But what option do I have? What leveraqe? How can I use our helplessness against him? How much of what Wide has told us is a lie? The Pashti? She stared off into space, considering every permutation of the Pashti data she'd had the chance to skim. From what she'd read, the Pashti appeared to be basically likable sorts. Suppose that mentally the Pashti didn't have the behavioral traits their crab bodies suggested to the human mind?

You don't have that data. And if you did, what could you do about it? If they refused to fight, Wide might do something rash, like open an air lock, or poison them, or. . . . The possibilities could be infinite.

"Damned if we do, damned if we don't. We can't win . . . only survive. Damn you, Wide." And for once she didn't care if he was monitoring her room.

Wide *had* bragged that he wanted to study every dimension of human behavior in his little space-faring laboratory. He'd openly declared that he couldn't predict the direction his research would take. Therefore, if they crushed the Pashti, killed them to the last individual, they had no guarantee that Wide would stand by his word and take them home.

Sheila stared soberly at her uniform, still uncomfortable with the way it fit. The simple fact remained that

Wide had a captive population of humans: breeding stock for any kind of experiments he might think up in his little round brain.

And what can I do about it? We have no idea of what we're up against. We can't even locate him—or escape the human part of the ship, for that matter.

She glared at the neatly penned notes on the page before her. Svetlana hadn't been in contact, remaining locked in her room. Sheila tapped the pencil against her chin, raising her eyes thoughtfully to the light panel overhead. Had she been wrong? Had Detova really been deficient in computer skills? That look the day of the conference in White Base had clued her in. When placed against the events in the Pacific Rim, the catastrophic failures of stock markets, and too many policy blunders, Detova fit the missing piece of the puzzle that had left MI6 reeling in Hong Kong and Singapore. Too many computer viruses had appeared out of nowhere, untraceable, inexplicable.

Further, Detova's reaction to the accusation had been exactly what Sheila would have expected. The woman had been too professional. But without her KGB resources, could she crack an alien system? Did the Ahimsa computers follow a different logic?

Sheila's stomach churned. Like apes turned loose to run an aircraft plant, were they just fooling themselves, thinking they could counter the Ahimsa hold over their future?

How can I at least manage to gain an even break if we can't even talk without the constant threat of being monitored? And monitored they were, despite Wide's dissembling remarks. The translators still worked magically, projecting the speaker's voice in an almost instantaneous overlay. All of that had to be computer monitored, all of the conversations undoubtedly reviewed by some main computer for Ahimsa security purposes.

We can't plan a revolution on the mirror of a makeup compact. She frowned again at the outline she'd drawn on the note pad. Break the Pashti? Then what? Assuming Wide put just enough truth into what he told them, the Pashti were taking too big a bite out of Ahimsa resources.

She stopped short, remembering parallels from terrestrial history. How many times had older powers employed the skills of barbarians to free the aristocracy—only to find the vigorous barbarians gobbling up the important functions of the empire. Rome did so with her conquered peoples until classic Roman values had eroded to the point where the barbarians controlled the society. Jews had stepped into that role through most of the history of Christendom, handling the finances, gaining power despite Inquisitions, pogroms, and ghettos. India had gone that way under British rule.

And throughout all that time, Wide had been observing. Didn't he see the parallel? She sat for a moment, heart racing. Sure, the technology consisted of weaponry perfectly adapted to human styles—like handing a stubby rifle to a man used to aiming a crossbow. But did Wide truly understand the depths of human intrigue and complicity?

Sheila chewed at her lip, rubbing the back of her neck. A tension headache began to build in her knotted brain. The responsibility had been placed on *her* shoulders. The fate of every man and woman aboard—and her entire planet—might hinge on her decisions.

And what if I'm wrong, and Wide not only expects but anticipates a double cross. What if we are like some sort of trained apes compared to his intelligence?

Her gut wrenched.

I could condemn us all.

The more she looked at the notes, fleshing out the emerging pattern, the less choice she seemed to have.

* * *

Vitali Lunin threw himself on his belly in the ditch, heedless of the cold water. He splashed and wiggled into the tall grass, queasy at the shriek-hissing of bullets over his back.

Someone else splashed into the ditch beyond him and cursed quietly in Russian.

Vitali checked his rifle, making sure he hadn't jammed

mud into the bore. Bullets ripped the air just above him, searching. Icy water seeped into Vitali's uniform, creeping down around his foot wrappings and into his boots.

He blinked, fought the urge to shiver, and wiggled slowly forward, easing the grass to one side to peer out over the field. A motorway lay no more than sixty meters across the grassy park. Behind it, a grove of trees stretched in uniform rows. Behind him the Zaventem airport smoldered and smoked in the gray fog.

Everything had gone wrong. No matter how GRU had planned the attack, fog rolling in from the English channel did what NATO aircraft hadn't been able to—protected Brussels from Soviet reinforcements. Everything had gone wrong, the weather, the reinforcements, even the Belgian resistance. Now the Hammer Division of the Airborne Force attempted to hang on to their little corner of Brussels, cut off, guarding the airport where reinforcements would land if the fog would only clear.

Where is the rest of the army? Where are the reinforcements?

Vitali watched as Yezhov and Ryleyev sprinted for the roadway. The machine gun chattered angrily as it cut both assailants apart. He winced, staring across the drizzle-screened grassy patch.

"So this is World War III?"

Ryleyev kicked once and went still. The Belgians had begun to fight back.

* * *

Svetlana took a deep breath, trying to still her sudden excitement. The file poured across the screen in Ahimsa figures. She ran a hard copy, feeling sweat trickle down the side of her face. She'd broken the data file on an Ahimsa Overone called Tan. The information might be useless, but it had been sealed—unavailable to humans.

The hard copy stopped, resting in the tray. Svetlana swallowed dryly, looking up, seeing nothing on the monitor but the Ahimsa character for further instructions. No warning flashed across the screen. No alarm wailed within her hearing.

She blinked, wishing she could stop the racing of her heart. Adrenaline flooded her veins as she stared down at her mnemonic notes. She canceled the tag on the file, slowly backing out of the system, initiating the processes which she hoped would hide her access.

Minutes later, she shut the terminal down, having double-checked the security routes. Heart still pounding, she lifted the headset and wiped at her sweaty face. Had something triggered? Did Wide even now wonder who had tampered with his file? Or had she broken the first of many barriers?

* * *

Viktor hit the ground running, feeling the chill of the Afghan night, his breath condensing before him. The helicopter chattered behind him as his men followed. Cleared, the chopper rose, circling as it played spotlights over the surrounding area. In the darkness, other engines murmured and groaned as the BMPs drew the net tight around the town. So far, so good. No resistance stabbed gunfire into the night. The village remained quiet, only chickens and dogs announcing their presence.

A night of anger, a night of retribution, he stared, trying to penetrate the blackness. Pasha lay dead along with his squad. A brother shouldn't die that way. Not shot down and cut apart to be scavenged by the pigs and dogs. Not Pasha, not wide-eyed fun-loving Pasha.

Baraki waited for him, waited for the anger, no lights in the doorways, no sounds of men calling questions in Pushtu. Behind him, feet pounded, the muffled banging sounding as booted feet crashed into the rickety doors of the stone and mud huts.

Viktor pulled up, lifting his radio. "Mika? What's happening?"

The radio's crackle bit the night. "Only women and young children. No men."

No men? They'd known, somehow. Dirty Afghan bastards.

Lights shot brilliance as the BMPs switched on their floods. Viktor stared around, squinting, seeing just one more pathetic Afghan town, such as it was. Donkeys stared from over wobbling fences of sticks and rock. Pottery lined low mud-plastered rock walls. Roof supports protruded to make hangers for sacks of grain, rope, goatskin bags of curdling milk, and occasional tools. Under his feet, the uneven paths that passed for streets were rocky, shadows here and there making footing among the potholes a chancy thing.

The place smelled—like all Afghan villages smelled—of manure, human feces, chickens, and acrid grease.

The translator's voice boomed on the night, amplified by the loudspeakers. Through the melodic tones, Viktor knew the message by heart. ALL MEN, WOMEN, AND CHILDREN MUST ASSEMBLE AND BE COUNTED.

Shouts rose on the night as he peered around, that familiar tension in his breast, a strangling constriction in his throat. How could they resist? How could they defy the might of the Red Army? People hurried past now, women in *chadri*, little children, wide-eyed and frightened, crying as they clutched their mothers' hands.

These? These pitiful ragged specimens were the only ones here? Viktor chewed his lips, staring around in the darkness. Where were the men? Where? Pasha had been killed here, just outside the village limits, shot in the back and disemboweled.

Where were the men?

He followed, watching his unit search houses, flushing the women and the malnourished children as well as prized chickens and goats. Dogs barked and nipped and growled through the squawking of the chickens and bleating of sheep and goats. He approached the collection point, the hardness in his heart barely dented by the pleading eyes that stared up at him. The women and children of Baraki huddled against a stone wall that separated the nearest field from the town. He stared at them as they squinted into the spotlights, blinded, eyes narrowed into slits of fear. Most clutched their cotton-padded blankets tightly, as if these rags would provide armor against Soviet wrath.

Pasha, you're paid back. Terror for terror. Watch them, little brother, watch your retribution.

"Viktor?" the call came crackling over the radio. "We've found the men. They're hiding in the tunnels they use for irrigation. Just like they did at Ghazni."

"You know the drill." He spoke coldly, formally. *Terror for terror.* Turning his back on the fear-stricken women, he strode into the night, following the heavy vehicles. He hardly flinched as Mika's machine guns spat behind him. How many women? How many children? *Mujahadin. Murderers. They killed Pasha.*

He closed his soul to the screams and the sound of bullets smacking flesh and bone. Terror must be used to fight terror. Or how many more young men like Pasha would be found sprawled on their backs, their stomachs sliced open and their guts yanked out of their dying bodies? The scene burned in his mind: Pasha's bloody crotch, fly-packed and blood-soaked where the penis and testicles had been cut away. The gaping sockets of the orbits where the eyes had been gouged out—washed by dried pools of Afghan urine.

The machine guns stitched his soul with each shot, each impact of a bullet like a needle in his humanity. A helicopter hovered over the main irrigation tunnel, the lights playing weirdly as the BMPs surrounded the hive-shaped ditch heads. Afghans did it that way, piped the scarce water from an underground system to their pitiful grain fields.

Oleg and Pyotr stood at the top, each emptying gasoline cans into the flow. Even from where he stood, Viktor could hear worried Afghan voices echoing in the tunnels where they hid.

The heavy machine gun erupted on the BMP that covered one of the heads. No escape—not for the Mujahadin who'd killed Pasha. The callus around Viktor's heart thickened. A scream sounded weirdly from the rock-lined irrigation tunnel. Yes, they knew now.

Viktor clamped his jaws, walking up to where Oleg shook out the last of the gas cans. The private shot a worried gaze at Viktor, licking his lips, swallowing hard. A cold sweat stood out on the youth's face, his eyes bright and nervous.

Viktor pulled a flare from his pouch. "Stand back, Oleg."

"Major? There must be a hundred men and—"

"Stand back, Oleg."

"But to burn them like . . . like . . ."

"I gave you an order."

Oleg closed his eyes, stepping back, tripping over his heels. He scrambled away on hands and knees before bolting off into the dark. The odor of gasoline hung in the cold air. Afghan voices rose from below, questioning. Some coughed.

Terror to fight terror. Pasha . . . Pasha . . . come back. Viktor twisted the flare, tossing it into the hole as he heard a young woman cry out. The air erupted with a *Poof!* as the gasoline caught. Screams of horror and pain twisted with the roar of burning fumes. Shots echoed from deep in the tunnels as Afghans discharged weapons—perhaps in suicide.

Pasha, my brother, they've paid. . . .

The figure rose from the hole, wavering like a worm from a burning cocoon. Viktor's breath strangled in his chest as a young woman climbed from the burning inferno, her *chadri* in flames. She flopped out of the hole, writhing, peeling out of her burning robes, her hair crackling and curling in the flames.

He stared into her eyes, lit by the bonfire spouting high from the hole, meeting her pain-glazed stare for that one terrified moment. His soul locked, frozen timelessly as he watched her exhale, fumes burning all the way down her throat and into her lungs, searing them. Amid the flames, her face, so beautiful, contorted in a ghastly rictus and stilled. He stared into her glassy eyes, his gaze still locked with hers. Her eyelashes had singed away, the hair on her head looking like melted plastic.

How old? Seventeen? Sixteen? The night breeze flipped bits of charred cloth from her body, exposing full breasts, blistered now from the fire. The lines of her figure lay before him, provocative, sensual in death as the dancing yellow-orange flames traced her seared skin.

Screams from the tunnel had lessened, the machine guns pattering every now and then as some unfortunate tried to climb out of the trap. Blinded, burned, lungs on fire and charred, they scrambled in madness, heedless of the waiting gunners.

A vile odor coughed from the opening, carried by sickening black smoke. It plugged Viktor's nose, poisoning his soul as he stared at the dead girl. A glowing spark caught in her pubic hair, fanned by the breeze. The flames crackled and leapt, only to die as quickly as they came.

Viktor's fear deepened as his vision blurred unaccountably. Only when he blinked, did he realize the shimmer came from tears leaking past his eyelids.

"They hide like that to avoid rape, you know," Sergeant Yakubovich's voice intruded. "The men hide to avoid conscription and murder. The young women to avoid rape. Only the old women and the children remain outside. Who would bother old women and little children? Not even Soviets, they think. Only this time, Comrade Major, we showed them. Maybe they'll think differently before they ambush a patrol again."

Viktor still stared as Yakubovich's boots crunched into the night. The flames had died as well, extinct with the life in the tunnel—suffocated, burned out.

In the darkness, Viktor stood, rooted, the last memory of a beautiful young girl rising out of the conflagration replaying over and over. Her eyes pinned his, the oval features of her face lit by the flickers of yellow and orange. She rose gracefully in a twist of flame and stepped toward him, fiery arms reaching, seeking to wind herself around him, breasts rising and falling as flame played about her nostrils, dancing to her breath. She reached for him, fingers caressed by tongues of fire. From between her legs, sparks shot to light her pubic hair with a swirl of fire that curled around the flatness of her belly and molded to her navel.

"Come to me," she called in a melodious voice. "Burn with me. . . ." Viktor swallowed, feeling his erection, fear beating in time with the flames that leapt to surround him.

"NO!" he screamed, jerking bolt upright.

The light panel overhead glowed brighter, illuminating the room. Viktor blinked, wiping a hand over his sweaty face. In the silence, he gasped.

He rose from the bed and walked to the shower on trembling legs, slapping the button, reveling in the water that cascaded over his body. Heart still battering his chest, he stepped out, heedless of the Ahimsa field and demanded vodka from the dispenser.

Choking down the liquor, he dropped on the edge of the bed, head cradled in his hands.

"You're here, on the Ahimsa spaceship. Afghanistan is far, far away. You're safe, Viktor. Safe. It's all over."

He sniffed and filled his lungs, forcing his breathing to slow. No matter how far he got from Baraki, he could still smell the odor of gasoline, the curious oily stench of burning human flesh. Viktor shivered, eyes closed.

"What are we taking to the stars?" he asked the silent room. "What sort of madness?"

CHAPTER XIV

"Gentlemen, ladies, good morning." Sheila looked out over the auditorium. "I would like to congratulate all of you. Last night I checked your proficiency ratings on the Ahimsa weapons systems. The results, with credit to Ahimsa engineering and your own diligence and hard work, are more than satisfactory. Given that proficiency, the command staff and I have deemed it time to move on to the next step: integrating your proficiency into tactical simulations.

She triggered her headset and watched TaHaAk station appear in large scale before them. "As most of you know by now this is our destination and target: the Pashti station called TaHaAk. The station serves as the seat of their government, commerce, and space industry. Our duty is to take this station, destroy its capabilities, and render it useless to the Pashti."

She looked out at her command, sitting in tier on tier of seats, each with a desk and a cup of coffee or tea in a little container. The Ahimsa seemed to have thought of everything—revealing in itself. So far, no detail had been overlooked by their hosts.

But it's only technology! We could make a superior gladius *to arm a Roman legionnaire. We could make the weapon out of alloys that would dazzle an armorer of his day. We could put a sponge rubber grip on so his fingers never slipped and the handle never rotted. We could equip him with a* scutum *impervious to any substance known to the Romans—impenetrable even to modern weapons. We could give him technology that seemed like magic. But does that mean we're smarter than a legionnaire? Or only more technologically sophisticated?*

"Very well, people, the time to buckle down and get to serious work has come." She went on, lining out the tactical moves she, Moshe, Sam, and Viktor had put together. At each stage of the operation, lights indicated the routes and objectives of the advance through the station. Even more impressive, she could show them details of how the various corridors looked, the effect as if they were proceeding down them at that very moment.

"Major Svetlana Detova, my intelligence second, has been integrating the information we have on Pashti. Her language personnel have been madly learning Pashti for the purposes of monitoring their communications. At the same time we're making our own translations, the Ahimsa will be feeding raw data to us with their interpretations. This should allow us to have a thorough picture of TaHaAk throughout the operational and tactical phases; and with good communications we should minimize any surprises."

She scanned their faces, suddenly cognizant of the demands of command. Their eyes had a physical impact; she could feel her responsibility growing. If she failed them, real people—these people—would pay the price. She wagered their blood, their lives. She'd been so busy with the planning, study, and simulations, she hadn't really seen them as human beings.

"Last, and perhaps most important for us as individuals, there must be nothing left to identify us when we pull out. Any casualties *must* be evacuated—including the dead. There can be no prisoners—no corpses left behind to finger us as the culprits. Any blood or tissue must be torched. Any proof of who the raiders are may lead the Pashti to come down on Earth. I think you can all understand what that would mean." *Pray to God they did!*

"If you have observations, please feel free to pass them to your commanders. We don't have many channels to go through here. The entire expedition consists of less than four hundred people. I'll expect to address you all weekly unless circumstances intervene. That is all."

She watched them stand and hold a salute. It dawned on her suddenly that they were waiting for her to respond. Her hand felt light as she snapped off a quick salute. Slowly they trickled out of the room, talking animatedly to each other.

She caught Viktor Staka staring at her. His complexion seemed to have paled, the tension in his face drawn and dangerous. A bit of a shiver traced her spine as she met his glittering eyes. Then he turned, walking quickly away, spring steel in every movement.

She took a breath, trying to still the racing of her heart. If only she could penetrate that invincible armor and see the man underneath—know who and what he was. Of them all, Viktor appeared the most frightening. Daniels would always try her, see how far he could push. Detova remained dangerous, capable of anything to achieve her own ends. Moshe, genial and affable, remained predictable—dedicated to his duty. But Staka?

She shook her head, running nervous fingers through her long hair.

So many lives—all hers! Picking up her notes, she stepped down from the podium and headed for her quarters. Staka's eyes burned in her memory, eyes like those of a man possessed.

* * *

Bill Fermen looked up from the situation board as President Atwood entered the Strategic Command room in the White House basement.

"What's the latest?" Atwood asked.

Fermen scratched at his thinning hair, feeling the perspiration on his scalp. He stared up from bloodshot eyes. "Chaos, Jim."

Atwood stiffened. "We're . . . losing?"

Fermen slumped into a chair and reached for a cup of coffee, chugging the cold brew. "Wish to God I knew." He pointed to the map behind him. Different colored lights blinked everywhere. "The red lights are Soviet positions. White are NATO."

Atwood cocked his head, seeing no pattern to the dots. "I don't understand. Where's the front at? What's happening?"

Fermen glared angrily at the board. "Jim, no one expected this. The Soviets hit Bonn, Paris, London, Hamburg, Munich, Vienna, Oslo, Brussels, and Amsterdam. They bombed Weisbaden and Bremen before dropping troops. We've got more than five salients into Germany, Austria, and Switzerland. The English shot down most of a Soviet rescue or reinforcement of the two divisions cut off west of Heathrow. Meanwhile, the Poles are evidently refusing conscription and we've got unconfirmed reports of rioting in Warsaw. Hungary has declared neutrality but satellite information indicates at least two Soviet army groups are rolling westward for Austria. Czechoslovakia has been ominously silent although the Soviets are staging a frantic buildup west of Prague, perhaps to shore up the Hungarian side or to swing into the GDR since the East Germans aren't wild about warring with West Germany. It's the damnedest snarled mess you've ever seen.

"On our front, we've intercepted and shot down six Backfire bombers trying to hit New York, Washington, and Boston. Portland was bombed this morning. Not much damage, just a couple of blocks leveled with maybe three hundred dead. We've got sub wars all over the Atlantic.

"Jim, we don't have any fronts. It's a whirlwind. Radar is overwhelmed by so many aircraft and there's no way to tell who's who. Hell, I got a report of Soviet helicopters setting fuel tanks down for our tanks!"

Atwood gaped, color draining from his face. "No fronts? Like Vietnam."

"Worse. Nobody's ever fought a war like this." Fermen licked his lips, shaking his head. "World War I sprang new tactics on the world. World War II advanced blitzkrieg. But this? Yeah, it's like Nam, all right. The Soviets can go anywhere, and so can we. Bates called. He wants to drop a Marine division in Warsaw to buck up the Poles."

"Can we do that?"

Fermen nodded. "If things go right, they'll tear hell out of the Soviet rear. Tim seems to think we can resupply them from Norway—providing the Swedes and Finns hold off the Soviet army group headed that way."

"And if things go wrong?"

"They'll be as stuck as the Soviet Airborne division surrounded outside of Brussels."

"I'll take anything we can get for the moment. We need something like a Doolittle raid to take the heat off. If it would buy us some confusion behind their lines, go for it. Maybe we learned something from the Tet offensive after all, Bill."

Fermen took a deep breath and sighed. "We're one day closer to the end of the world."

* * *

Murphy ducked out of the tunnellike hatch, pulling up at the junction of two corridors. His heart raced as he panted in the cool air. Damn! This was *too* real!

He ducked his head around the corner, checking the silent hall. The Pashti built their stations with rounded ceilings for some sort of structural support; the exact way it worked hadn't stuck in his mind during the study sessions. Murphy caught his breath, wondering where the curious looking vehicle Arya called a tank had disappeared to. He took a quick look around the corner again and charged down the empty corridor.

Something made a chittering noise behind him.

Murphy dove for the floor, somersaulting and coming into a squatting position, assault rifle ready. The Pashti came at an ungodly speed. Murphy shot from instinct, lacing his fire across the animal's front, blowing off most of the legs—stopping the rush. He scrambled back, ejecting the old mag, slapping a new one in place. Changing the fire selector, he aimed carefully and took out the crab.

He stared at the blasted robot, trying to stop the shiver in his tensed muscles. *Huge!* The damn things were bigger than four-wheel drive trucks! He shook his head, trying to imagine an M16 with its puny .223 trying to stop a nightmare monster like that. Thank god for Ahimsa firepower.

He scrambled back and got to his feet, hating the typewriter pace of his heartbeat.

"Too damn real," he gulped. "And I'm goddamned lost in here." Getting to his feet, he charged on, trying to remember which of the spokes led to the center. "Just how big is this place anyhow? And it's all inside this damned spaceship?" He shook his head. "Mama, I wanna go home!"

Murphy pulled up at the next intersection. He peeked around the corner, seeing blown crabs strewn around in bits and pieces. Shot up, you could tell they were robots, but man, charging down on you, they goddamned scared holy hell out of a person.

He followed along the route of carnage, sure now that he headed toward the Council Chambers that had been targeted as his objective.

Ahead, a rifle rapped out a tri-burst. Murphy slowed, checking cautiously before he crossed the intersections. Each of the portals—curious arches, really—had been closed off.

"Murph?" A voice whispered in his headset. "Where you at, buddy?"

"Cruz? I ain't got the foggiest idea, but somebody's been through here busting things up. I think I'm headed in. Lost Arya's tank in a firefight back there."

"Keep cool, amigo."

"Ten-four, pal. Watch your ass."

He pressed on, climbing over a pile of blasted crab bodies that blocked the hall. Some sort of door had been blown open by heavy stuff, probably the tank.

Murphy sidled up to the blasted plate and peeked in. Humans stood around a weirdly constructed series of machines. Hell, not the Council Chambers. He'd missed the objective—and then Gubanya stepped into sight, staring up at the huge machinery.

"Oh, man." Murphy grimaced and started to back away when he saw the door slide up behind the Russian.

Murphy didn't have time for a warning. Instead, he slapped the rifle to his shoulder, sighting on the crab coming up behind Gubanya. The Russian caught his movement, looking up, eyes wide as Murphy triggered the weapon.

Instincts in trained people—especially soldiers—keep them alive. Gubanya pitched to the side as Murphy triggered the gun again, and again, lacing the Pashti. The robot stopped cold, legs collapsing, falling almost on top of Gubanya as he tried to bring his rifle to bear on Murphy.

"*Hold it, man!*" Murphy yelled, hand out.

Gubanya stared at him over the sights, as Murphy swallowed. *And we gotta train with live ammo?* He dropped the rifle, the weapon clattering loudly in the silence.

"I had no choice! You'd a been *dead!*"

Gubanya considered, glancing at the fallen robot. Slowly the Russian's grim expression turned into a smile. "Shoot a little wider next time, American. Now, pick up your gun and get out of here. The power plant isn't your objective."

Murphy gaped. "I just saved your ass."

"Thank you."

"Uh-huh, watch the doors next time, pal." He bent down, snaring up the rifle, knowing if he hadn't dropped it when he did, he'd have been dead.

Slowly, Murphy backed from the room, stepping over the door, and pelting down the hall as fast as his feet would take him.

* * *

The observation blister seemed like a miracle to Sheila Dunbar. She stepped into it, staring with awe at the stars that moved slowly past. Out there, beyond the glass—or whatever the transparent alien material was that surrounded her—the whole of the universe passed, patterns of stars like frost amid the twinkling of unfamiliar constellations.

She seated herself on the edge of the blister, thinking of the other alien miracle, the remarkable space clothing that neither stained, nor picked up body odor, nor tore. Nor did it chafe. Wonderful stuff, it insulated when the temperature went chilly and radiated during exercise to keep the body cool.

She pulled her knees close to her chin and leaned back against the polished bulkhead, feeling the clothing respond to the cold. The last days spun through her memories like a whirl as she looked out at the stars slipping along.

In her mind, she reviewed the pathways Moshe would take toward the Central Council chambers. She could see Ben Yar's armor breaking off, smashing the communications section while Arya entered from the other side, ripping through the station's computer centers and blasting the atmosphere plant. From a third direction came Shmulik destroying their stores, ripping apart bulkheads as the SPETSNAZ followed in three units detailed to mop up, disrupt, and support. Daniels' men would drop ahead of the tanks at the center of the station, paralyzing any resistance that formed, working behind the lines.

Again and again she went over it, seeing Thompson's team training to fly the oddly shaped torpedoes which would breach the outer portions of the station.

Sheila's mind picked at any possible flaw, seeing the entire action unfolding in her mind. At the same time, she watched the stars and wondered what little detail they might have missed.

"They shouldn't do that, you know." The soft, soothing voice came from behind.

"What?" Sheila turned. Sam Daniels stood there, a drink in one hand, face almost hidden in the shadows.

"The stars," he said, pointing, one finger extended from the glass. He moved and sat opposite her. "See how they're passing the window? We're supposedly moving faster than light. If we could—and I assume the Ahimsa can—we still wouldn't see stars like that. If we could see anything, it would come as a brilliant pinpoint of light from straight ahead. It's called red shift. Something to do with relativity and the speed of light. E equals MC^2."

"Einstein," she noted, looking out again. "So what happened to the red shift?"

"Ask the Ahimsa." Sam looked up. "Well, Wide? What happened to the red shift?"

Silence. Sam accessed his headset, the little jeweled diadem they had all taken to wearing. His frown deepened. "Huh, no answer."

Sheila tried hers, forming the question mentally as they had become so adept at doing. "It's dead."

Sam stepped back into the hallway. "I've got it. The ship's monitors recreate the actual path of the stars as if we were in regular space." He stepped forward into the blister. "But I'm not getting anything now."

Sheila cocked her head. "This is the only place where we're not monitored, then?" *My God, could it be?*

Sam settled opposite her. The wide smile made his teeth shine white against the deep tones of his skin. "Oh, mercy be! I've been going nuts in there."

"Like being in a bottle."

"So why the sad look?"

"Sad look?"

"When I came out, I stopped for a moment and watched the expression on your face. You looked like your grandmother had died." He lifted his drink and sipped at it.

"Do you think they really can't hear us here?" A pause. "Wide, is there anything new on TaHaAk?"

Silence.

Sheila rubbed hands along her arms and tucked her knees tighter against her breasts, blonde tresses falling over her elbows. "Sam, it's scary. Have you thought about what we're doing? Have you seen the data on the Pashti?"

He studied her, face a dark mask. "Yeah, we're going in to kick the shit out of a bunch of crabs whose only fault is that they get a little crazy once every seven hundred and sixty years. At the same time, the Ahimsa are slowly eroding away, spending more and more time in their own minds and less and less running their worlds. So they brought Pashti in to run their industries, make their ships and robots and mining equipment. Now they've adapted their bodies for free-fall and they're at the mercy of the Pashti. Some, like Wide, are scared of the trend. Enter us. We're supposed to stomp the Pashti—and win emancipation and the stars. Now, I'm a good old black boy from the streets of Detroit who's fought all his life for a fair shake. So why does the promise of pie in the sky bother me?"

Sheila took a deep breath, feeling alone and vulnerable. "You're good, Captain Daniels. That's exactly the scenario I think Svetlana has been putting together. Communication of that fact, however, is touchy with all the monitoring the Ahimsa are doing. She has experience with constant observation and monitoring. Clever people, the Soviets."

Sam nodded to himself. "Maybe I'll invite Svetlana out here to see the stars. I've met her a couple of times for brief moments. She seemed real friendly and interested in me." He grinned. "I don't think it's 'cause I was a football player at West Point either."

"Once an agent, always an agent?"

Sam motioned it away. "Yeah, something like that. Besides, all of a sudden the future is a chancy thing. Somebody as sharp as Svetlana will recruit when and where she can. In her business, you never know where you need to be able to plug into the network."

"You sound like a cynic."

"Comes from having to stare reality in the eyeball once every month or so." His expression twisted. "You know, after a while you quit caring. Some sag-belly politician gets a great idea in Washington—or he owes a campaign contributor a favor—and he makes an insane policy that enrages somebody in a mud hut someplace. The guy in the mud hut rants and raves and somebody from the other side gives him a gun—which he uses to blow away an official who probably deserves what he gets. Washington panics and Sam Daniels' SOD unit goes in to wipe out the angry little man who's waving the AK around. Meanwhile, the asshole who started it in Washington is appointed to a higher position in the administration—or reelected for wrapping himself in the flag. Great system we got, making the world safe for democracy and corporations that don't have any fiscal sense. All it takes is the will to kill angry little men who live in mud huts every so often."

"You weren't always that way. At least, your record doesn't show it."

"Major, I know how to play the game. I know when to shut up and when to lip off. Here, on this ship, I can lip off because I . . . well, I got a hunch I'm never going to see the Earth again. Just a feeling you get, you know?"

"Sixth sense?"

"Something like that."

"And you don't think being honest about your true feelings will prejudice me?"

"Nope. So far as I'm concerned you've passed the test." He grinned at her. "I think you'll make it, Major. You impressed hell out of me with the planning on that exercise."

"Earned your respect?"

"For the time being. Since you're a team player and not a martinet, I'll trust you with the knowledge of my cynicism. I don't think you'd use it against me, and knowing might keep some people alive."

Her heart leapt. *Victory!* "So where did it come from? What made you so bitter?"

His face went blank, eyes neutral as he pulled his legs up to mimic her position. "Yeah, well, my attitude got adjusted the first time when I was a kid in Detroit. They called it 'Black day in July.' I was out to save the world, man. I'd heard Doctor King on TV. I'd listened to Malcolm X tell us if we couldn't eat at the table, then we had to knock the effing legs off."

He leaned his head back and took a deep breath. "The first scar I ever got was given to me by a black man. That one runs down my back. One of the brothers smashed a plate glass window. They'd pick up the glass fragments and sail them like frisbees at the police, you see, only I got in the way.

"The second scar you can't see. It's in my mind. I couldn't get up cause my whole back was laid open and when I tried to stand, I got dizzy and vomited. Then the tear gas came and landed all around me. Couldn't run—couldn't do anything but lay there and cough and cry and die. And each time I coughed, the blood ran out of my back. I was lying there in the street in all the broken glass when the police pushed by. I passed out just as I heard one say, 'Bleed to death, you damn nigger!'

"Man's life oughta be worth more than that. I woke up in a hospital on the other side of town. My little brother had found me. Still don't know how he got me out of there. Told the people in the emergency room that . . ." he laughed softly, "that I got hit by a train! Man, can you believe that?"

He shook his head, voice turning rough as he swallowed. "You know, I'll never forget him. Never forget the tears in his eyes as he stood there by that hospital bed lying like a fool to keep me outa trouble. He . . . he died in a little village outside of Dakto. Turned his back on a young woman. She was pregnant. Had just told him her husband worked at the base. I heard that he'd grinned at her, and nodded, and she shot him in the back as he walked away." He paused, lost in his thoughts. "Yeah, I'm a cynic. I don't know what any of it means anymore."

"But you stay in SOD?"

He lifted a muscular shoulder in an empty shrug. "I've seen both sides. We ain't angels—but the other side's worse. You didn't see the bodies they hauled out of Hue during the Tet offensive. The list grows. We kill one innocent, they kill two. Communism doesn't work. Gorbachev damn well knew it. Economic disaster. It's a hard sell for them. The only thing that helps is that our side is so stupid when it comes to foreign policy, we play into their hands more often than not. Naw, I'm no starry-eyed, jingo spouting hero for Uncle Sam. I'm just a professional who does his job and tries not to think about it beyond keeping my guys alive."

Sheila shook her head. "And you went from the Detroit riots to head of the class at West Point?"

Sam hunched his shoulders. "Hey, the army was a way out. Them riots made a difference, you know. They needed a token . . . and I got to be it. Then when I got there, I couldn't let myself be no damn token! I busted ass for four years to learn everything I didn't know. Thank holy God for the mind I got!"

Sheila nodded, thinking of his impressive record. "So why did you volunteer for first Vietnam and then Cambodia? It would seem all the apples were stacked on your plate."

"I don't know. I've never been able to figure that out myself. Man, maybe it was just Detroit in a different place, you know what I mean?"

"You don't talk like a West Point man, Sam." Who was this man, really? What drove one black man in America to excel and another to try and destroy himself? Was Sam Daniels driven to both?

"Major Dunbar, West Point martinets don't survive in places like Vietnam, Cambodia, Nicaragua, Lebanon—or Detroit."

She frowned, shifting to stare at him from the corner of her eyes. "And what do you make of Viktor Staka?"

Sam leaned his head back, taking a breath. "The man's a professional. The Red Army doesn't put the commissar's favorite nephew in charge of a SPETSNAZ unit. Viktor's got that look about him, too."

"He and Gubanya survived a lot of Afghanistan." She pursed her lips. "There is a look about him. Dangerous and incredibly capable but . . . well, I don't know how to say it. A—a glass look. Do you know what I mean?"

Daniels studied her thoughtfully. The pause lengthened before he said, "Yeah, I know that look of his. He spent a lot of time in Afghanistan. He copes most of the time. Like I do. Like most vets of modern wars do. That glittering look, Major? Used to have it myself. When that wall is up between Staka and the rest of the world, when he looks at you like his eyes are shards of broken glass, that's just the ghosts of the people he damned looking back."

"You make it sound so terrible."

He laughed—the sound dry, rattly, without humor. "It is, Major. Washington doesn't have a monopoly when it comes to pissing off little men in mud huts. Somebody in the Kremlin had a great idea, throw a coup to give the Khalq Communist party control of Afghanistan—balance against Iran, right? Then they found out the Saur Revolution didn't go over too big with Afghans. Somebody in the Kremlin decided it would look bad if the Afghans shot all the Communists so they had to go in and bail out the revolution. Problem is, the guy in the mud hut got real mad then. Maybe the decision was Brezhnev's, maybe the decision was Eisenhower's, or Andropov's, or Dulles'. It doesn't matter. They never had to live with the consequences. But Viktor? He's still living with it."

"And that wall he puts up. It's to keep himself safe from the rest of the world?"

Sam nodded. "Yeah. You know, you were right when you said it was a glass look. That's a good analogy. Glass is hard, sharp, capable of cutting neatly and efficiently."

"But it's also brittle. Bend it too far, and it'll shatter."

Sam shifted, eyes taking her measure. "Yeah, well that's the problem, isn't it? You're still dealing with a human being under all the armor. You can train a soldier, make him strong and tough, and you can even fool with his mind until he'll kill a gook or a Sandy or a chink without batting an eye. But somewhere, there's still a human being locked in there."

Viktor's face hung in her memory as she remembered the haunted look she'd seen in his eyes after the trip up in the bubble. That vulnerability touched something deep within. Did that cold-steel Russian hurt on the inside? Did he ever wake in the night lonely and in need of human companionship?

"You know," Daniels continued. "I'd hate to think we'd exchanged some silly policymaking asshole for a puffball. Wide may not wear a tie, but I can't help wondering if maybe the Pashti don't live in the equivalent of a mud hut."

She thought about that. Would he survive whatever was coming at TaHaAk? Would any of them? "You and I think a lot alike, Sam. The only question is, what are we going to do about it? We've got to keep Wide thinking that we're cowed. At the first sign that we're not under his thumb, not playing his game, we're as good as dead—along with Earth."

And the image of Viktor Staka's haunted eyes stared into her subconscious. *Will I look like that? Is that how the ghosts of the Pashti will reflect from my eyes?*

* * *

Viktor placed a palm against Gubanya's door. "Mika? It's Viktor. Do you have a minute?"

"Come in."

The door opened magically as Viktor stepped inside. Gubanya lay on the bed, hands behind his head as he stared at the featureless ceiling. Even flat on his back, Gubanya looked dangerous. The formfitting Ahimsa uniform accented his powerful chest, the bulge of thick biceps and ripples of flat, muscular belly.

Viktor settled into one of the chairs, kicking his feet out, crossing his ankles and leaning back. He looked over, seeing the stony expression, the fixed eyes that stared vacantly at the light panel. "You all right?"

Gubanya's lips twitched. "I am fine, Viktor."

"I've had several of the men come and tell me—"

"Malenkov?"

"Among others."

"I find his concern curious, or have his American friends already turned their backs on him?"

Viktor hated the constriction in his heart. "Mika, things have changed. We've got to work together in this. You heard the General Secretary. We are to follow orders and do our sacred duty for the Motherland."

"Since when is our duty defined by an Englishwoman?" Gubanya laughed. "Viktor, we're under the command of a *woman?*"

Staka exhaled, rubbing the back of his neck. "Mika, have you looked around? Does this look like Afghanistan? Like Tashkent, or Dushanbe? Everything is changed. The world is turned upside down and we're all we've got. I know it's crazy. I know everything is different and strange and unbelievable—but we're *here*! We have to deal with it until the end. You can't go back, Mika. You can't have things the way they were."

Gubanya swung his feet over the edge of the bed, hunching there like some giant Siberian bear. "Five years, Viktor. That's how long we must survive in exile."

Five years . . . exile? Viktor sighed to himself. Yes, it all came clear now. "I see."

"Do you?" Mika lifted an eyebrow. "Then think back, Viktor. Remember where we were, and why? The Soviet Union is splitting apart at the seams. The Party is reeling from one defeat after another. Tell me what our duty is? To fool around among the stars with space creatures who could care less? Or to save our country? And what about my wife? Five years? What does Irina think?" Mika closed his eyes, shaking his head slowly back and forth.

"She does her duty, Mika. Just like you. You used the word exile. We're not exiled. We're SPETSNAZ, and we're doing what we must—just like Russians have done all through our history."

"With Capitalists?"

Viktor gestured aimlessly. "Have you forgotten that side by side with Capitalists we crushed Hitler in the Great War."

Mika glared at him, eyes hot. "Yes, Comrade Major, you said that very well. We crushed Hitler. Twenty million of our people died in the crushing. And the Americans? I've read the figures. They lost one million people to the Nazis—and the Japanese. Where were they while we were bleeding ourselves dry at Stalingrad, at Moscow, at Kursk and so many other places? Not ready. Not ready. I've read the history as thoroughly as you, Comrade Major."

Viktor avoided the burning resentment in Mika's eyes. Instead he studied the palms of his hands. "I don't like this hostility. You didn't used to be . . ." But he did. He always had been.

"You were saying, Viktor?"

Staka shook his head, a curious premonition in his gut. "It just struck me that you've always had trouble adjusting. You're trying too hard, Mika. The Party gave you everything, and unless you're in the front lines, fighting with everything you've got, you're lost."

Gubanya said nothing, hard black eyes slitted, tension in his face.

Yes, he'd seen it through the years. As long as they were killing Afghans and Uzbeks, Mika had been a perfect warrior. Buy what would happen now that the lines had blurred? Soberly he studied his old friend. "Mika, we've got to adapt."

"By fraternizing with the enemy? You should have broken Nicholai in two for that, you know."

Viktor shook his head slowly. "We don't have to compromise who and what we are, Mika. But we must learn, adjust. This impossible situation, well, for the moment it seems new and wonderful and frightening, but it too will change. Like the first time in combat, when you think you'll never learn to deal with it. We'll learn to deal with space, too, but it takes a different strategy, different tactics."

"And in five years? Will we go home to a Soviet Union? Or will we find anarchy?"

"I don't know, Mika. I really don't. But I have to remind you, our unit wouldn't make the difference. You and I couldn't hold the Soviet Union together if it comes apart at the seams. The Party, like you or me, must survive by its own means. You and I can die in the discharge of our duty, but the Party has to assume responsibility for its own survival."

Mika shrugged and stood up, pacing slowly across the room. "Just so we don't lose ourselves, Viktor. That's what I'm afraid of. Irina . . . well, in five years I don't . . ." He lowered his head and smacked a hand into the wall. "She'll think I'm dead, you know."

"The General Secretary—"

"Will *what?* You know the situation as well as I do, Viktor! Damn it, she'll think I'm dead! Or worse, arrested and sent to the camps! You know how that is. You think Irina, the Commissar's daughter, will wait around for a man who's been stained by arrest?"

Viktor winced at the pain expressed by the pinched words. "Mika, don't take it so hard. You're going to come back a hero, greater than Gagarin, greater than Romanenko and Laviekin in the *Mir*."

"If there's a Soviet Union to come back to."

"There will be, Mika. There will be."

"But will we recognize it?"

Viktor chuckled, standing and clapping the big lieutenant on the shoulder. "I doubt Golovanov will let anything happen to it. What else is bothering you? I've heard rumors that you've begun to doubt my ability as a commander—that you're saying my nerve's broken."

Gubanya's gaze wavered and fell. "I've been worried about you, Viktor. About your dedication to your sacred duty. You haven't been the same for the last couple of years. Not since coming back from Zossen-Wunsdorf."

Has it been that obvious? "I suppose." Viktor laughed with more vigor than he felt. "If I never see another camel, I'll be a very happy—"

"Viktor, you weren't the same."

He stiffened, a chill around his heart. "No. I wasn't the same. I have a right to the scars. But Mika, they're *my* scars. I've always done my duty to the best of my ability—and I always will. No matter what I think. I'm a professional—just like you are. I obey orders."

Mika's hard look softened. "I'm glad to hear that,

Viktor. I'd begun to fear you'd broken. Then, when I saw you here, looking so shaken, I worried you'd failed, that you'd turn us over to our enemies."

"No, I didn't break." He cocked his head. "But tell me, don't you ever think about where we've been? Don't you ever wake up in the night shivering, afraid, reliving the fear and the horror of places like Ghazni and Baraki? Don't you see the rockets flaring on the hills around Khost? See the women and children you've gunned down? Don't their faces haunt your sleep?"

Mika shook his head slowly, dark eyes measuring. "No, Viktor. They were enemies—a threat to the Party."

Viktor dropped his hands to his sides, stepping away. "They were people, Mika. Human beings like you and me. They loved, they feared, they hungered and—"

"Viktor, does this have a point?"

Staka turned on his heel, a hand half lifted to Gubanya. "Mika, you and I, we've seen a lot of miles pass beneath us. Recently, a file crossed my desk. I noticed an old report. I was wondering . . ." Could he ask? Should he?

"Yes?"

"Nothing, Mika. I'll be going now. But promise me one thing. You'll work with me, won't you? I know how difficult this is for you. I know what you feel when the Americans are around, but will you consider this as a tactical situation? These are joint maneuvers—just like we conducted with the GDR troops around Erfurt."

Mika nodded. "I think I understand, Viktor. I, too, take my duty—and my orders—seriously."

"I thought so." Viktor hesitated at the door. "And Mika, if you get depressed or worried, come and we'll talk about it."

"Yes, Comrade Major."

As Viktor closed the door and walked down the hall, anxiety ate around the inside of him like a hungry rat.

CHAPTER XV

Spotted shifted one eyestalk in Wide's direction as the Overone rolled into the control room. He kept his other eye on the monitor which followed the humans as they conducted yet another exercise. Did they never tire of killing robot Pashti?

"Exquisite, aren't they?" Wide asked, rocking back and forth. "Ultimate killing machines."

Spotted's sides weakened as he started to go flat. With all of his concentration, he pulled himself up straight, manipulators strengthening to maintain touch with the controls.

"My fears, Overone, are becoming stronger and stronger. My concentration ebbs and it becomes difficult to think. Idle unconnected thoughts form and I wonder if humans are loose in our portion of the ship. What if they come here, Overone?"

One of Wide's eyes shifted from the exercise to Spotted's blotched bulk. "You have nothing to fear. They're sealed off from this portion of the ship, Nav-Pilot. They cannot get to you. Besides, they dare not. Their world is choked by our manipulators. Their families and homes, their memories, even their very futures hinge on *our* good will—and *our* power."

Spotted's outer surface crinkled at the words. "You no longer speak like an Ahimsa, Overone. Your words are—"

"Different?" Wide twirled. "Perhaps. Have you thought, Nav-Pilot, that another phase of Ahimsa power and domination is overdue? Have you considered that our Overones are less and less involved with the future of our species?"

"What about our past? We must keep in mind who and what we are. All these many years of evolution, of learning how to prolong our lives and purge our bodies of poisons and radiation damage must count for something. We live forever—to think. Remember? That's who we are, who we have changed to become. Only Shithti live longer than Ahimsa. Once, Overone, we aspired to be like them. To seek to know the foundations of the universe, to solve the problems of—"

"To become slaves of our own creations?"

"No. You've lost your perspective. You—"

"*I* have rediscovered my perspective, Nav-Pilot." Wide's eyes centered on the screen where the humans in their simulators rampaged through the mockup of TaHaAk. "Observe the vigor! See the acumen and vitality they display! They know this is a drill, but they have such passion! Where has that spirit gone in our lives, my friend?"

"But, Overone, the laws are clear. The other Overones—"

"Have become disengaged, isolated from the universe around them . . . and from the future!" Wide expounded, air spicules hissing. He rocked back and forth and his tone softened. "Oh, I've seen it coming. What have we done to ourselves over all these star lives? What has become of our kind? I see us becoming more and more like Shithti, thinkers with no purpose. There must be *purpose* beyond the contemplation of the infinities. I will return it to our kind."

"By turning these humans loose on the Pashti?" Spotted fought to keep the creeping panic out of his voice. He could feel his outer surface expanding as color mottled his foot tread. "I have given it careful study. Listen to me, Overone, I have thought this through in great detail."

"Very well, I will listen."

"Your worry is that the Pashti, who are a kind and gentle species, are slowly eroding Ahimsa control over the administration of manufacturing and resource utilization. This has been accepted as good by the Overones since it will free them to pursue their separate investigations of the nature of the universe, of thought itself, and the mysteries of creation."

"That quest has already harmed us, Nav-Pilot. Look at the decline of our brains! We have come to rely too much on computers for the storage of knowledge. What was once kept in our heads is now kept in machines. We've become lazy, slothful."

"That is not my point. You agreed to listen to my thoughts on the Pashti."

"I did. Proceed."

"We agree that the cycles are unsettling. We agree that the Pashti are taking ever greater control of Ahimsa resources, but they do not do so to exclude Ahimsa. In no instance have they ever sought to deprive Ahimsa of the products or resources produced by industries they have begun to manage. I do not find that characteristic among the humans. Humans are possessive, aggressive, and will seek to dominate."

"They will do none of those things under my control. What precisely are you trying to say?"

"That by seeking to subvert the Pashti with humans, we may well be trading the minor annoyance of the Pashti cycles for a human plague."

Wide thinned. "You make one assumption which negates your entire argument. You assume I will let them escape my control. I remind you that in all the universe, no one knows humans like I do. No one has studied them as thoroughly as I have."

"They have studied themselves."

"And been blinded by their own humanity. I can see by your response that you disbelieve. I will prove my point. Humans blind themselves through their emotions. We can learn a great deal about them by studying their last world war. The German leader, Hitler, is a classic example. Had he followed his original agenda, the world would have been united within twenty years of—"

"He was insane!"

"Precisely. That is the curse of emotion. That emotion destroyed him. First, he blinded himself to the power of the Soviets—despite warnings by his generals. Second, he failed to take England—which provided a staging base for superior air power. Third, he blinded himself to the reaction of the Russian peasantry to his looting policy and turned people who greeted him as a liberator into a partisan force which wrecked his supply lines. You see, that is the weakness which will always destroy humans. They lose the ability to remain abstracted and objective."

"Then why don't we simply dispose of these humans and—"

"Because, Nav-Pilot, they can be useful given the proper direction. Do you sincerely think they can challenge me? They are condemned by their other fatal flaw."

"And that is?"

"Death, Nav-Pilot. Death lurks constantly in the shadows of their emotional and unstable minds. The problem which goaded Hitler into his foolish and prideful actions was death. Humans can't see goals beyond their microscopic lifetimes. They feel compelled to rush ahead, full tilt into the impossible because death awaits them all. Had Hitler been able to plan in decades instead of years, he would have controlled the world within twenty years. You see, death feeds their insanity and goads their insecurities. Listen to human students of Hitler. They miss the entire point. His mistakes, the madness that blinded him to reality and spurred him to act imprudently, were all motivated by death. Do you see that understanding in their histories? Of course not. They remain oblivious to its power because they live with it, accept it as part of their reality.

"That has been the bane of all their leaders. The thought of death drives them all, and because of that, I have no fear of them, for Ahimsa never die. Ahimsa can remain aloof, dealing only with the exigencies of the future whether it be a galactic year or a thousandth away."

Wide extended a manipulator on which a clear bead of molecular information—reflections of his thoughts and feelings of confidence—formed and glistened. Seeking the remedy to his fright and worry, Spotted made a receptacle and greedily sucked the fluid off Wide's manipulator. Courage and reassurance flooded his system and expanded as the molecules replicated.

"Just as long as they don't get loose," Spotted muttered. He quickly fell silent, fascinated as he caught a glimpse of Wide's plan. His own minds reintegrated and began to see the logic.

Wide's acoustic box made the clicking sound of Ahimsa amusement. "Please, do not worry, my friend. They are simply phantoms among the stars. They will not break free . . . and, if they do, we shall simply destroy them. Surely, you don't think I went to all this work just to let wild vermin loose in our civilization? I have planned for the whole of the future, not just the moment as humans do. These phantoms we carry will become nothing more. Tools which will be molded to our use or discarded when they have served their purpose."

Nevertheless, deep in a section of Spotted's preoccupied mind, he couldn't help but wonder if the Overone hadn't spent too much time studying these wretched humans. One eye managed to catch a glimpse of the Israeli tanks squashing robot Pashti in the corridors of the simulator. One eye studied the monitor which showed the humans; the other bent to stare at the Overone. *Who do I fear most? These violent humans—or Wide, who has learned so many of their traits?*

* * *

Svetlana bit her lip and initiated the translation program she'd compromised. In stealing it, she'd eased into the system, countered the Ahimsa security program, and then reprogrammed her copy of the translation, adding the most sophisticated security she had. Now she watched the program on Tan run. The Ahimsa Overone's biography spilled out in English.

Svetlana frowned. The Ahimsa had compromised some of the most complicated computer security systems in the world to obtain data for their conscription of shock troops to crush the Pashti. Breaking the security of the ship's computer system hadn't exactly been easy so far, but compared to what she had expected, none of the systems seemed particularly well guarded. Why? Considering the ease with which they'd rifled the files in Moscow, London, and, most of all, the United States, why didn't their security—like their technology—supersede anything she could crack?

But Dunbar—who had picked out Svetlana's complicity with such apparent ease—might know. That left only one substantive problem. How far could she trust Dunbar?

She remembered the cool-eyed look the English major had given her. That mutual respect had touched something Svetlana had kept buried for years. Why? And why now, when everything had changed like some dream gone crazy? Sheila Dunbar knew everything, had pieced together the missing elements that not even the careful scrutiny of Special Service II, the internal KGB watchdog, had suspected. Nor had Dunbar threatened, she'd simply asked for compliance. *And I gave it. Why?* The memory of those clear blue eyes, so honest, so penetrating, hovered in the back of Svetlana's mind.

She got to her feet, pacing back and forth. All her life, she'd been on her own. Unable to place confidence in anyone, she'd given her full concentration to her career. The KGB didn't foster trusting relationships. So how could she trust Sheila Dunbar?

She fingered her chin, noticing her reflection. Had she really grown into that attractive woman? Was that image a reflection of the real Svetlana Detova?

Fragments of scenes from her youth formed in a collage of sights, sounds, and smells. Her mother had been tall, proud, full-busted with a severe and dour face that never cracked, never wavered to reveal the woman beneath. *And I lived alone—even surrounded by them.*

Her father's image had continued to fade. Even during her youth, he'd been a shadow man. While she played on the thick Armenian rugs before the fire, he'd sit, reading, periodically looking over the tops of his books and pamphlets to watch her. She could still see him, sitting in the big chair, silhouetted by the gray light of the window behind him. Beyond that thin pane, fluffy snowflakes tumbled out of the dull Moscow skies—a perpetual winter of the soul. Every morning he would pat her on the top of the head and bundle up in his coat. The black car would come and take him to the Lubyanka. Years later, she learned about the Lubyanka, the terrible KGB prison on Dzerzhinsky Square.

Her mother would leave later, spending time piling her hair just so, doing her makeup exactly right and dabbing perfume behind her ears, on her wrists and at the hollow of her throat. Only years later had Svetlana learned how privileged her mother had been to have perfume. But then, perfume played an important part of her mother's role.

She'd seen her mother once, years later, in her professional mode. She'd been in the presence of two well-dressed handsome men—lesser officials of the Swedish embassy. The mother she'd always known, strict and forbidding, had been laughing, a curious light in her eyes as she flirted, walking gaily down the street holding hands with the men.

I learned why, Mother. No wonder you kept yourself in such control at home. You must have been very, very good. They let you have your house, your daughter, and a husband—your full-time watchdog. You knew, didn't you? No wonder you never laughed inside the walls of our apartment. No wonder you never allowed yourself to love me, to hold me like other mothers did. You couldn't. Not with him *watching, noting, reporting to the others within the walls of the Lubyanka. You couldn't have let them have that knowledge, couldn't have allowed them to use me against you.*

She filled her lungs, feeling the ache in her chest. "What did you give up for me, Mother? How did you feel having to bed him after bedding the others day in and day out?" Her expression hardened as she studied herself. "And what did it feel like to see me every day, knowing I was your salvation and damnation rolled into one?"

How many long years since her mother had disappeared? Seven now? Despite Svetlana's manipulations, she'd never been able to uncover the truth. Now, aboard an alien starship, headed for someplace beyond the night sky, she clenched her fists. "I hope you're in Paris, Mother. Or perhaps in Washington, or Winscombe or someplace safe. I hope they've given you a new name and enough of a pension so you can sit back by the fire on cold nights and sip warm tea . . . and remember the little girl you sacrificed so much for."

She couldn't stand the thought of the other alternative,

of the rickety barracks surrounded by barbed wire and wind-sculpted drifts of the Siberian landscape.

Her father had informed her that she'd be going away for school. The KGB took care of its own. Nor had the endless succession of housekeepers and maids been for naught. Tutors had been supplied to augment her academy training. "And through it all, I never had a friend." She could remember seeing the other girls playing outside on the spring days. A child of the KGB never interacted, never had the chance to compromise her parents.

She stopped short. *And what have I missed in life? How many times have I turned down invitations to sit around and talk to other humans? What do I know about people, besides how to manipulate them for my own ends?*

And Sheila Dunbar wanted her trust and cooperation? Curiously uneasy, she walked closer to the reflective wall and stared at herself, seeking to see past the pools of her blue eyes into the bottom of her soul.

* * *

"I never dreamed it would be like this." General Secretary Karpov stared at the wreckage where the American cruise missile had impacted on the Kremlin wall.

Marshal Rastinyevski chuckled with wry humor as he rubbed his hands together. "They came very close, Yevgeny. I think from now on, we're better off operating out of the dacha."

"It didn't explode."

Sergei shrugged expressively. "One of the problems with very expensive weaponry is that you can't afford to use it for practice. If you can't bear the cost of shooting your sophisticated missiles, how do you ever learn if they are flawed, or how to fix them?"

"Like our Western strategic direction?" Karpov stared from under lowered brows. "Four weeks, you told me. It's been four months—and no end in sight. The entire Western strategic direction is snarled and hopelessly chaotic. NATO seems to grow stronger as we stumble. Nor are we safe here. This is the third time the Kremlin's been hit with a cruise missile."

"But none have detonated." Rastinyevski waved at the wreckage. "And besides, we might get something useful out of this one."

"It took an entire army to destroy the NATO forces around Warsaw. The Poles took a great deal of courage from that." Karpov turned, walking back toward the gate. "Are you sure you want to reinforce what's left of the Hammer Division? Every time we try we lose two out of every three heavy air transports."

Rastinyevski sniffed in the cool air. "I think it's worth it. Every time we reinforce the Belgian bridgehead, we eat up more of their resources. I can't believe they've held on while the division we dropped on Bonn surrendered. The English crushed the London drop—but only at great cost."

Karpov shook his head. "It's madness, a gulag war—islands of battle all across Europe and we can't tie them together. We can barely supply them and evacuate our wounded."

Rastinyevski spread his arms wide. "Comrade General Secretary, the situation defies logic. In the beginning, the strategy made sense. Now? I don't know anymore. It's as if events control us instead of we them."

"Almost a half million men have died, Sergei. The Polish situation is critical. Opinion is rising against us. Eastern Europe sees a chance to break us once and for all. The Uzbeks are worse than ever. They killed over one hundred men last night in Dushanbe. Where once we operated on the offensive, now we struggle to simply defend the bases."

"We managed to bomb Washington last week," Sergei countered. "Because of the fighter cover, we only blew up some Department of Interior buildings, but it was a start—a serious blow to their morale."

"At least our bombs go off." Karpov kicked a piece of aluminum shrouding from the cruise missile. "And how is the nuclear bomb program?"

"We're working round the clock to manufacture new reactors. If we can beat the Americans into production—assuming no more mirror balls appear as we complete the warheads—and blast Washington with a hydrogen weapon first, the war will be over."

"Then you had best hope this is one race we can win, Sergei." Karpov stared up at the gray sky, sighing. The heavy air mocked his soul.

* * *

Riva moved the controls with a new confidence as her torpedo shot for the edge of the Pashti space station. Like a huge wheel against the stars, the giant station turned, flickers of light appearing here and there, towers, curious antennae and knobby protrusions prickling the whitish-gray surface. The disk glinted in the light of the yellow sun while behind it a wealth of stars sparkled and gleamed against a fogging smoke of distant galaxies. To her right, a bright lozenge of stars shot yellow-white light in a slant across her monitor.

She fired the reaction rockets that combined to soften the metal-graphite sides of the Pashti structure and killed her velocity. Almost six gs strained her forward as the long craft's laser sliced the already bulging metal-fiber composition of the station wall. The nose of the torpedo slipped through, bringing the craft to a complete stop. Gravity shifted as Riva initiated the grapple locks in the hull that anchored them against angular acceleration and kept the torpedo from sliding out of the breach.

Riva palmed the assault hatch switch, watching as the forward observation camera showed the nose of her torpedo blossoming like a skinny lotus. "Go for it!"

The torpedo shivered as Moshe's tanks and Viktor's troops bailed out. From her position, she could see the insides of TaHaAk. Pashti came scuttling out of the corridors as Moshe's tanks wasted them right and left. Viktor's troops formed up, pouring fire into the disintegrating alien forms.

Riva immediately started down her checklist to assure herself that the torpedo had sealed the station wall. She reran the power checks and disengagement sequence until satisfied, and then settled back to wait.

How incredible. Here she sat, surrounded by the simulator, while almost a quarter of a mile away, Staka's commandos ran through a full-scale mock-up. She shook her head, unwilling to believe that all she had to do was lift the hatch cover and look out to see several rows of gleaming silver capsules just like hers bathed in the soft glow of the overhead light panels. Yet as long as she remained inside, surrounded by the curious foam, she experienced the sensations of true flight. How did the Ahimsa do it? How could they fake the sensations with such perfection?

A Pashti rushed out, staring around the room. Riva flipped the weapons override into play, targeted the creature on the main monitor, and coolly blew it apart with the forward guns. For a long moment, she stared at the ripped remains. *Just a robot*, she reminded herself. Only one day, it would be an alien life she'd snuff.

And what did that mean? For her personally? For humanity in general? The first human presence among alien life-forms would be that of mercenaries—killers for hire. The image that conjured in her mind soured, festering into a slow burning unease.

"As if we've been left a choice." *Damn you, Wide. Damn your little round hide all to hell and back.*

She watched the blasted robot, snatches of Pashti language flitting through her head. Pashti spoke and vibrated their speech. What would it be like to *feel* your language? Granted, vocal chords vibrated the air, but not the floor under your feet. How did a creature who communicated like that think?

"Maybe we'll never know." The uneasiness stirred further, a growling resentment gnawing at her conscience. *Wide, you're just like those assholes in Washington. You made the policy, and to hell with the ethics of it all. Sure, wipe out a Pashti space station. How's that any different than bombing a Suni villaqe just because it's there—and the people happen to be Suni?*

Twenty minutes later, Major Dunbar's voice echoed through her headset, "Mission complete. Station destroyed. Pull out!"

Fifteen minutes after that, Riva initiated the disengagement and throttled her torpedo for the Ahimsa mother ship. Even during the exercise, fragments of thought centered on the Pashti language. And what if the Ahimsa decided to use humans to wipe out all the Pashti? Assuming Wide had been correct, the Pashti would offer no resistance. If that were the case, what difference would there be between the human raid on TaHaAk and the National Front for the Liberation of Palestine bombing of an innocent 747? Or any of the endless terrorist actions she'd given so much of herself to stop?

An ill feeling began to creep through her stomach—a feeling she hadn't felt since Nablus.

* * *

"Major, I've come to return your compact. Thank you for the use of it."

Sheila looked up from the piles of paper she'd scattered across the table. "Any time." Accepting the compact, Sheila said, "If you don't mind, I think I'll touch up."

She opened the case to read, "PROGRESS. WE NEED TO TALK."

Sheila made a few swipes at her eyelashes and yawned, stretching. "Been a long day. How about a stroll?"

Svetlana nodded warily. "I've been so busy with the computer, I could stand the exercise. If nothing else, this journey, no matter how improbable, has opened my eyes. I didn't realize there was such a *deficiency* in my training."

Sheila caught the emphasis. *What has she found?* "Well, since you've been cooped up, how about a look at the stars?"

"Stars?"

"This is a spaceship after all. Come, I'll show you."

They made small talk, discussing the training sessions, the way the people were adapting.

As Sheila stepped into the bubble, she swept her arm to indicate the vista of stars. "Look at that!" She didn't hear a translation.

Svetlana stepped out, eyes searching the swirls of light.

Sheila accessed her headset, asking for a display of the torpedo simulator room. Nothing. Then she tried accessing Viktor's headset. Still nothing.

In a low voice, she added, "I think we can talk here. I

know from your file you're fluent in English. What's up?"

Svetlana continued to stare at the passing heavens. "You're sure?"

"As sure as we can be. Whatever their monitoring system, it doesn't seem to work here. There's no headset access, no instantaneous translation."

"I suppose a risk must be taken somewhere. Have you checked this out? Tried to trap them?"

"Yes. We don't seem to get a reaction." Sheila sat in her accustomed spot.

Svetlana turned, pacing uncomfortably. "I broke into a file . . . I think I can compromise their entire system. But I'm leery of a trap."

Sheila read her hesitation. "Go on."

Svetlana stopped, studying her, as if to decide what to say.

Sheila waved her hand. "Look, we're all in this together. Any scrap of information could be the key to what saves us in the end."

"And afterward?"

"Afterward?" Sheila chuckled. "Major, whatever happens as a result of this, the Earth will never be the same. Every rule in the book will be changed. The very way we think about ourselves and our planet will be forever altered. Tell me, how do you suppose the average man and woman will feel when they find out we were caged by creatures who believe us to be vilely barbaric? Wide gloated over the fact that we kill each other and have devoted large amounts of our resources to mass murder. Imagine how scenes of the Second World War play in places like TaHaAk station. When you think about it, it's a wonder they didn't drop something on us in the very beginning. The point is, however, that we can't go back. Our adolescence as a species is over. It has to be—or eventually the Pashti or Wide will wipe us out."

"All the more reason for me to wonder what will happen to the Soviet Union."

Sheila crossed her arms, introspection softening her face. "Our concerns must go beyond our respective countries. I don't think we have any choice. We act for the planet now, not England, or France, or the USSR."

"And you'd sacrifice your country?"

Sheila sighed. "I remember a story about Dutch spies during the Second World War. The Germans had put rocket launchers in the town. The intelligence people smuggled the information out to the Allies, knowing their town, their neighbors and relatives would be killed in the subsequent bombing. Of course, they could give no warning; the Germans would have known something was coming."

"And this has a point?"

Sheila nodded, meeting the woman's stare. "The point is our planet, Major. Considering Wide's undoubted double cross in the end, if I have to sacrifice to save the world, I will. Like those Dutch spies, I've no choice but to look to the future. If it means I have to give up England, I will."

Svetlana raised an eyebrow.

Sheila lifted her hands. "Let me ask you a question, Major. It's an ethical dilemma. You have a choice. You are locked in a building with a man holding a lit stick of dynamite. He's going to throw the dynamite no matter what. Before you are two rooms which contain the remains of the human race, the last eleven people alive on Earth. In one room is a Soviet citizen. In the other room are ten people of different nationalities. Knowing the man is going to throw the dynamite, which room do you order him to throw the dynamite into?"

Svetlana's gaze didn't waver. "And you think that is our current dilemma?"

"I had a most curious experience riding up in that bubble. I saw the Earth. Not as England, or East versus West, but as one tiny place which is everything we're made of. If we fail at this, not just London, but Moscow, Ulan Bator, Nairobi, Los Angeles, the rain forests, the oceans, all of it is at risk. What Wide is doing is illegal. He's breaking interdiction to further his own ends. How many times have our respective governments used mercenaries—and then destroyed them to cover their activities?"

"And you suspect the Ahimsa will do the same?"

"Wide says there are a lot of species out there in their galactic civilization. Wide is ambitious. If we seem acceptable tools, he'll find some sort of future use for us—but on *his* terms. And, if I can appeal to one of your concerns, he has breeding stock—he doesn't need the planet. He can't just let us go. Eventually it will all come out. I wonder what the 'civilized' species will do to his supply of humans once they find out we're the ones doing his dirty work? How will the creatures who placed those gravitational buoys respond?"

Svetlana nodded soberly, walking to the transparency, staring out at the stars. "I've never trusted anyone, Major. I grew up in a KGB household. All my life, I've only had myself to depend on."

Sheila nodded. "Funny how that happens. My father worked as a claims investigator for an insurance company. I saw him twice a week. The rest of the time I spent with my grandfather."

"And your mother?"

Sheila twirled one of her blonde locks around a long finger. "She left when I was five. Ran off with a pilot who flew for British Air. For a while I got an occasional postcard from Bombay, or Tokyo, or Sydney. I used to love the pictures of all those places. Then the cards stopped coming. I didn't learn until later that my father had put a stop to it. Now, looking back, I can understand why. It must have hurt to know that the woman he'd lost had found such a wonderful life."

"You don't see your mother anymore?"

"No. I don't know where to find her, actually." Sheila stared out at the stars. "With the perspective of time and distance, I guess I never really took the time. Perhaps it would have hurt too much. My father is a sour man, bitter and set in his ways—a lonely man. Maybe I never wanted to find out what really happened. Maybe it would have become too uncomfortable, a reflection of where I was going in my own life."

"You were unhappy with MI6?"

"Not at all. The work fascinates me and I'm always pressed to surpass my limits." She paused, pursing her lips. "You know, there's always a flaw somewhere. The trick is to find it—like a treasure hunt. No, if I were to be honest, I'd say I was becoming too much like my father, carried away with work to the exclusion of all else. I just wouldn't want to end up like him, looking back at the wreckage of my life, wondering why my mate had left with someone exciting, wondering if I'd ever lived."

"And your grandfather?"

Sheila laughed, sadness modeling her features. "He treated me very well, became my best friend after a curious fashion. He smoked himself to death. Died horribly of lung cancer. I got my love of puzzles from him. He was a grand old gentleman who'd lived beyond his time. He would have made a delightful colonial governor in someplace like Madras. He never really knew what to do with me. Had I been a boy, he could have filled me full of the mythology and traditions of the Empire. But we found a common ground in puzzles and mind games. He'd bring me Chinese puzzle boxes, interlocked bent nails, anything that took thought. I got the bug through him, caught his obsession for games."

Sheila rubbed her shin, staring out at the stars. "We used to play chess by the hour. He'd been a member of chess clubs for years—even competed internationally. Finally, my ability developed to the point where I had to let him win."

"Returning to your ethical dilemma, do you think we're really in the building? That we must throw dynamite into one of the rooms?"

Sheila glanced up at the woman. "No, I don't. Our job is to see that we're not placed in that situation, but we're being pushed into the building, Svetlana. The dynamite's lit and Wide is ready to throw it if the door slams shut behind us. Somehow, we've got to find a way to blow out the fuse, or toss the explosive out the front door. Meanwhile, we have to determine where our loyalties lie, to the Soviet citizen, or to the world. Myself, I choose humanity. How about you?"

Svetlana turned, her decision made. "I've broken their security in several files and guarded my own programs with much more sophisticated protection. Nothing I did drew a response. Tags and traps I set remain undisturbed. That I can enter their secure files so easily, makes me nervous. That they're so poorly guarded makes me even more nervous—especially in light of their ability to read top secret documents in Washington, London, and Moscow."

Sheila pursed her lips, frowning. "What do you mean by entering their files easily?"

Svetlana paused, steeling herself. "If I had my Cray, with its programs, I could be inside in a matter of seconds. Compared to the Bank of Hong Kong, the Ahimsa have only rudimentary security. Why? Is it a trap?"

Sheila nodded, another piece falling into place in the pattern that had started to emerge. "I don't think so." *Damn! What a gamble I'm taking!*

Svetlana stood before her, arms crossed, expression demanding.

Sheila looked up, head tilted. "It's the trained chimp syndrome."

"The what?"

"You don't put a trained chimpanzee in a maximum security prison. You put him in a chain-link enclosure with a simple combination lock on the door." Pieces rearranged in her mind, information correlating. "Wide thought he'd eliminated any threat to his computers by his selection of personnel. You hid your skills—even from your superiors. I think I understand your reasons for that. But Wide didn't have the time to look for patterns, to see what was missing. No, he picked carefully, excluding people with extensive computer backgrounds. Your superiors have no idea you have that Cray, do they?"

Svetlana struggled with herself for a moment. "Let's just say the Soviet hierarchy guards its power jealously. Threats from outside are eliminated as carefully as possible—but so are threats from below."

Sheila lifted her hands, palms up, a weary smile on her lips. "The fact that you hid your talent so brilliantly may have saved us all—even your Soviet superiors."

"Oh? The Ahimsa still retrieved that same file out of a system—"

"They didn't break the security."

"Then how did they compromise the systems?"

Sheila smiled and gestured around her. "Their technology did it for them. I mean, their machines translated our speech on Earth. They transported Golovanov from Moscow to the Arctic. I suspect that whatever their resources, they simply scanned the data from . . .well, outside. What I mean is that they didn't have to access the programs. Didn't have to run them."

"And the security on their current systems?"

"It's a human oriented security, isn't it?"

Svetlana's face lit. "Maybe Ahimsa don't need security against other Ahimsa? This might be new to them."

"Exactly. They thought they had chimpanzees in the cage—not a competent locksmith. Wide feels safe. He's tailored his defenses to defy people with my computer skills—not a master who cracked the finest security in the world. Tell me, could anyone without your experience have broken the system? Despite your Cray, *you* had to write the programs to break the Bank of Hong Kong."

Svetlana's eyes narrowed as she thought, nodding slowly. "No, but then we're still working on assumptions, aren't we?"

"We damn well don't have anything else. Nevertheless, I think it makes sense." Sheila pulled her knees up as she stared at the stars. "Wide has counted on his machines for too long. They've become a crutch for him. From my study, he's no smarter than we are, only his technology gives him the edge. Now all we need to do is determine how to neutralize it."

"And hope we don't make a mistake."

CHAPTER XVI

President Atwood rubbed his eyes, hating the feel of his stomach as it knotted and growled. "It's like the whole world has gone crazy."

The air in the planning room had a stuffy odor. The fan overhead whirred silently while bleary-eyed staff people murmured back and forth, some tapping computer keys as they ran simulations. The walls had been plastered with maps, reports, and diagrams.

Pat Hixon, the Secretary of Defense, slumped in a chair at the cluttered main table, a weary look in his eyes. "Who would have thought we ever would? Under every scenario we planned, we'd have gone nuclear by now and the radiation would be settling. How's DOE doing on the bomb plants?"

"They estimate another seven months. The physics teams we put to work on the stasis spheres are still baffled. If we could break those damn mirror bubbles, we could free up the ICBMs and have an end to this whole thing."

"If the bombs are still functional," Hixon reminded. "God alone knows what those mirror things did to them."

"Anything new on Philadelphia?"

"No. Looks like we've got about twelve hundred casualties. Who would've thought they'd be able to feint like that and draw our air cover out of the way? You know, if we could divert resources from conventional weapons and put them into bomb plants, we could speed—"

"Sure! And I've got a country full of screaming civilians who are crying for defense. No one has ever bombed the United States before. All of a sudden all those comfortable housewives are realizing their cities are targets—and they see it when the local Kmart is turned into a crater. They don't like the thought that their bodies might be filling emergency stretchers. They don't like the power going off, or the water mains being ruptured by Soviet bombs. The latest poll shows that I've got a fifteen percent approval rating. Birch's cry for a recall petition is gaining ground." Atwood looked up. "Am I really that incompetent?"

Hixon spread his hands, shaking his head. "No, Jim. We just didn't understand how this would line out. It's like fighting a war in a blender. No front is unturnable. Nothing can be protected because we're spread too damn thin! The cuts during the Gorbachev years, the deficit and the depression, all left us with a reduced military spread around the world like a patchwork. As soon as we lost the satellites, we couldn't tell what was going to happen where."

"How about the Crimean invasion? Any word on that?"

"General Mack reports that we're still fighting from house to house in Odessa. The problem is going to be maintaining supplies. Rastinyevski hasn't withdrawn troops from Pakistan like we expected. Instead, they keep activating ghost divisions, calling up the old men and handing them rifles from mothball storage. We're cutting them apart like chaff, taking one casualty for every ten of theirs, but they keep coming."

Atwood took a deep breath and exhaled. "The Turks are moving along the coast. Maybe they can provide some relief."

"Not if the Armenians have any say in it. It's a toss-up who they hate worse. Moscow or the Turks, and for the moment as long as Moscow provides them with arms, they'll fight Turks. The Greeks won't help since the Turks are already involved and, well, I don't blame them, but they figure the way to survival is keeping their heads down and talking neutrality."

"And the Rumanians?"

"Still waffling. But if the conservatives come out on top, they'll hit the Crimean front from the west. And if they do . . ."

"That'll break our back in the south. Pat, we won't be able to evacuate those troops."

Hixon said nothing.

"And Poland?"

"Not good. Hell, they're just ordinary people. The Russians rolled ten army groups into Poland. How do you expect them to stand up to that?"

"But it saved Germany?"

"For the moment. Poland destabilized enough of the Soviet rear that with the French and English, we've cleaned up most of the German salient. We can't do anything about Belgium. If we pull units back to strike at the Soviet forces around Brussels, the German front will fall apart. That or Rastinyevski will land a couple of divisions back of our lines again. We've got to keep that air cover in the north intact—even if it means the Russians can reinforce and resupply their Belgian bridgehead."

Atwood rubbed his ulcerous stomach. "The whole world's gone crazy."

Hixon grunted and leaned forward. "And I want to make it crazier.

"Good luck. What have you got in mind?"

"I was talking to the JCS. Without pulling anything away from critical situations, I think we can take Vladivostok—and hold it. If it works, we can open up an entire new front."

* * *

Moshe paused, feeling the stubble on his chin. As usual, he'd forgotten to shave. Hesitantly, he placed his palm on the door. "Yeled? It's Moshe."

He waited, calling again, "Yeled?" The door finally opened and Moshe stepped in. Nothing seemed amiss, this room like every other one.

Yeled sat propped on the bed, staring emptily at the holo that spun before him: Earth.

Moshe's sense of premonition grew. This wasn't going to be good. He walked over to the dispenser and asked for Israeli coffee. Cup in hand, he pulled out the chair next to Yeled and sat, leaning back and sighing as he closed his eyes. "You want to talk about it?"

Silence.

"Yeled, I just want to hear your voice." Moshe turned the cup nervously, frowning down into the black liquid. "Talk to me. Tell me what you're feeling. You and I, we've seen a lot. Remember me? Remember the guy who pulled you out of the M60 that time they poured gasoline all over us in Jenin? We wouldn't have made it if you hadn't driven like a madman."

Silence.

Moshe winced. *Is Yeled only the first? Is this what will happen to everyone? Is it shock over this impossible situation, or just homesickness? Or, what if it's space? What if God never meant us to leave our planet? What if we sicken and die—like a bird taken from its nest?*

"Yeled. I *need* to know what's bothering you. Not just as a commander, but as someone who's lived with you, fought with you, and . . . and cried on your shoulder."

Yeled's mouth worked, glittering eyes glued to the holo. "I . . ."

"Yes, go on."

"Five years, Moshe. Do you know how long that is? My daughter . . . she'll be ten. And my wife . . . well, a lot can happen in five years. Will my son even recognize me? He's an infant, Moshe. Just a little tiny baby in diapers."

Just homesick. Thank God. Moshe stared into the coffee, the ceiling panel reflected whitely in the black brew. "We bought their safety for those five years."

Yeled turned tortured eyes to Moshe. "Did we?"

"The Ahimsa promised."

Yeled blinked, numb. "We've had guarantees before. Sadat made us a guarantee. Even the Americans made guarantees. How many guarantees have ever been worth anything, Moshe? Our only guarantees are backed by our armor, by the Mossad and their covert operations. That's another thing. The Ahimsa tell us Israel will be safe. But does that mean my wife? My daughter? My son? Does that include bombs? Infiltration and terrorist attacks?"

"We all do the best we—"

"My son is growinq up without me!" Yeled balled his fists. "That's the worst. I thought we'd get news."

How did he answer that? What could he say?

"Five long years. She's going to live through five years of hell, Moshe. She won't even know I'm alive. Five years of worry and . . ." Yeled's red eyes returned to the holo of the planet, a blue and brown jewel wrapped in a froth of white clouds.

"She'll get your letter. The American President will see to it." *Five long years.* For the first time, Moshe could sigh with relief that Anna was no longer there to fret about his safety. But the others? Yeled would simply be the first.

"But will she believe I was the one who wrote it? We don't know what they told people. What would you believe? That someone you loved had flown off with space creatures? If you weren't here, if you hadn't seen, would you believe?"

"Old friend, I don't have an answer for those things. What I want you to think about is this, we're a practical and pragmatic people. Unlike the Americans who can sit safely separated from danger by their oceans, we have to live with a stark reality. We're alone—Ahimsa prisoners. In this circumstance, you can do two things. Do your best and give everything you've got to keep us all alive—or give up."

Yeled continued to stare at the holo.

"I'm sorry, Yeled, but space, like Israel, isn't safe. The Pashti will be just as deadly as the Arabs. I'll handle the main gun while you decide what you're going to do. In the meantime, Chaim and I, we'll tell them you're ill."

Moshe stood. "I guess that's the nice thing about being a Jew. You never have the luxury of choice. Only the option of sacrificing what you love . . . or dying."

He didn't look back as he stepped out and walked down the hall. *I can't blame him. Who will be next? Reality has invaded their minds—and it, instead of Pashti resistance, will most likely damn us all.*

* * *

Sam rubbed a hand over his face. The skin felt like a mask as he walked into the mess. He'd forced himself to reawaken the old proficiency in physics and astronomy, forgotten during these years of training and war. Study helped to alleviate the worry, the knowledge that his people would begin to dwell on the reality of their situation—and their dependency on aliens whose intent remained clouded.

At this time of night—01:30 hours—the place should have been empty. Instead, a lone woman sat hunched over a tray, eating.

Sam ordered a ham and cheese sandwich from the dispenser and a large cola. From this angle, he could recognize Svetlana Detova. He walked over, plate in hand. "Excuse me, this seat taken?"

She looked up, meeting his gaze with eyes as weary as his own. "Sit, Captain. I'd welcome the company. It's been too long since I've spoken to a human. Computers, as I am learning, have a logic all their own."

"How's it going?"

She shrugged, cradling a cup of coffee. "Long, and hard, but I never would have guessed I could have made so much progress so fast. It's curious how not having a choice can speed a person's ability to learn, don't you think?"

"But it's coming along?"

She shrugged, staring at him through those knowing blue eyes. "If Wide is watching, he's probably been amused by my fumbling attempts. Given my performance, we're lucky he hasn't returned us all to Earth as total idiots."

Sam nodded. "Yeah."

She smiled wryly. "From your expression, I see you have no interest in my computer follies."

"You look a little worn out."

She shifted on her elbow staring at him, the front obviously dropped. "So do you."

He yawned. "Yeah, well, I noticed the boys are drinking a little heavier. I caught a couple of pointed comments. They're getting jittery. When that happens, I perk up because I don't want trouble coming down. I know my meatheads. In between patrols to keep my merry band of assassins in line, I've been catching up on a little astrophysics and galactic geography."

"Meatheads? Assassins?" She laughed, apparently genuinely amused. "But you like them."

He nodded, relaxing a little. "Yeah, I like them. I don't know, over the years I served with a lot of people. Sometimes, a unit just comes together. You know, like teachers will tell you about a class. Or a coach will tell you about a softball team. You just get the right personalities and everything clicks. These guys are like that."

"But they're getting nervous?"

Sam winced, taking a swig of his soda. "Viktor and I have been pushing them as hard as we can without overcooking. A unit can train too hard and you lose that edge. Just like an athlete peaking too early for a competition. Anyhow, Viktor and I have to back off a little or we'll run them too ragged. But backing off gives them time to think. So what if it seems like a year to us? They've got five years Earth time away from home—and no way of knowing what's happening. Maybe someone's father hasn't been feeling good. Maybe has a heart condition. Is he going to be alive when we finally get back? You know, we left in such a hurry, a lot of loose ends were left dangling. It's going to start seeping into their busy little skulls that the world's going to be a different place—provided we ever get home."

"Like the POWs?"

Sam nodded. "Yeah, just like that. And if you get to thinking about being MIA in outer space, hey, that will really mess with your mind."

"And your own family, Captain?"

He considered for a moment and lifted a shoulder, chewing thoughtfully on his sandwich. "Never knew my father. My mother, well, she's in a nursing home in Detroit. My sister . . . let's say we lost touch. It's easier that way—and almost the truth. My little brother got killed in Nam. Both of my grandparents are dead. Outside of memories, I left nothing behind."

She lifted her eyebrows. "Thank you, Captain. Until now, I haven't had the time to depress myself with thoughts like those."

Sam rubbed at his eyes. "Yeah, well, that goes to show

you how tired I am. Normally, I think before I put my foot in my mouth."

She laughed. "I learned from second nature that you never talk when you're tired. Too many ways to make a slip."

He cocked his head. "Yeah, but I mean, how does that make you feel? I mean, is it worth it to always live on the edge like that? When can you ever be yourself?"

"Maybe that's who I am. Major Svetlana Detova: competent, capable—and alive."

"Alive? Maybe, but you're not free." He let his gaze trace the delicate lines of her face. Her blue eyes had a depth, unveiled for the moment, the hard calculation he'd been accustomed to, missing.

She pulled the lustrous mass of hair over her shoulder. "Freedom, Captain, is a relative thing. How about yourself? Tell me, you, too, have to survive by being better, more cunning, more ruthless, don't you? Wait, hear me out! If you blow a mission, you're twice as likely to be discounted in the future, aren't you? Yes, I know how it is. You're black in America. I'm female in the Soviet Union. In either system, you get one chance to fail, while all around you, white men get several."

He met her level gaze, nodding slightly. "Yeah, maybe. But I ain't screwed up yet." *Do you really know what it's like, woman? Can you understand?*

"And that's why you're up when everyone else is asleep." She nodded to herself. "Yes, Captain, I understand you better than you think."

"And why's that?"

"Because you'll notice I'm also up."

He chuckled. "So, is this a butter up to recruit me to the KGB?"

She lifted an eyebrow. "And what do you think my chances are?"

He drank down the last of his cola. "Not very good."

"You know, we could offer you a—"

"Not interested in the slightest."

"You haven't heard my terms yet."

Sam leaned forward, pointing a finger. "Major, in America Dr. King at least got the chance to walk down the road with his marchers. Now, you can sit there and spout all that brotherhood of man bullshit the Communist Party likes to parade through the slogan factories, but, sister, you and I been around the block and we both *know* better!"

"Dr. King wouldn't have been shot down by a lunatic in my country, Captain."

"Hell, no! 'Cause they'd a sent him so far north he'd a been the first black icicle to form in history. Your Party woulda had to build a new gulag on the tip of the Taymyr peninsula just for King."

Tapping her fingernails, she leaned back in the chair. "Well, if ideology won't work, how about money?"

"Now you're talking my language. I can be had for . . . well, a hundred million will do for starters." He squinted at her. "This could be a long dry negotiation. I'm gonna go get a bourbon. You want anything?"

"Go get me a scotch. You might be worth ten bucks a month."

"Well, fifty million . . . and not a penny less." They walked to the dispenser together. "So, how does a good kid like you get sucked up by the KGB?"

She shot him a quick glance, measuring. She started to say something and stifled her cynical laughter. "You know, it doesn't make any difference anymore. No one is here but you and the Ahimsa. Funny, isn't it? I've lived with lies for so long, even the opportunity to be truthful leaves me nervous."

"I don't want you nervous, so kick back and relax. Lie to me. I don't care."

She looked up at him, a pinch of suspicion in her eyes. "Why *did* you want to know?"

He handed her a scotch, shrugging. "So I'd learn something about who you are, where you came from, what makes you you. I'm not after anything classified, just interested in you as a person."

She sipped her scotch, lifting an eyebrow. "You know, I've heard that line before."

"Yeah, well, take it or leave it. Look, I don't really care about what you did in Hong Kong, who you doubled, or what your operation was. It's just that there's no one but us out here, Major. I don't know what's going to happen in the end. My life might be in your hands someday soon. Works the same way the other way around. To build a team you got to start at the bottom with a handshake and a howdy-do."

She shook her head, filling her lungs. "I'm sorry. It's all the old training, all the years of living in the game. Intelligence is a lonely business. You can only trust yourself. I suppose I'll never be like . . . like . . ."

"Like real people?"

"Yes, like real people."

"Well don't go asking a black SOD antiterrorist squad leader what real people are like."

"You're not real?"

He gave her a reprimanding squint. "People who drop out of airplanes to kill other people aren't real. Or maybe we are and the rest of the world is unreal. Hell, I don't know. How'd we get on this, anyway?"

"You asked how I got into the KGB."

"I said I was sorry."

She took a deep breath and locked her elbows. "I'm going to be brave, daring, and scared stiff, but here goes. I was born into the KGB. My mother worked for the Foreign Embassies Department of the Second Chief Directorate. My father worked for Special Service II." She waited, lips slightly parted, an expectant look in her eyes. "Well, tell me something, for God's sake!"

"You mean like a trade? A secret for a secret?"

"Yes."

"I stole a car when I was sixteen. I never got caught. I stole another one when I was twenty. Didn't get caught that time either. If I had, they would've drummed me out of West Point."

She crossed her arms. "That's not quite the same."

Sam shook his head and rubbed a hand over his mat of hair. "No, I guess not. I guess I'm just not as exciting as you are. Mom never did anything important but try and raise us kids."

"Any women? A girlfriend waiting for you to come home?"

He chuckled at that. "No. I don't think I'll find any on

TaHaAk either. Mostly it's the job, you know. Women, at least, American women, get a little nervous when you tell them you kill people for a living. I suppose it's the same if you're KGB?"

She laughed at the image that conjured. "My job description called for associating with men. I used to date very important ones. I found it delightfully amusing that they'd be so condescending, pumped up with their masculine power, while I could have snuffed them like candle flame with at least seventeen different poisons, six different projectile weapons—or my bare hands. Images of power are relative, you see. What are you laughing at?"

He grinned at the narrowing of her eyes. "Oh, I was just picturing it in my mind. Seeing those fat cats, rolling in dough and million dollar deals, strutting high and mighty like a bunch of goddamned kings, and here's pretty, petite Svetlana with her troika in her pocket trying to keep from laughing in their faces." He shook his head. "You know, the only thing that surprises me is that you didn't waste 'em just on principle."

She seemed to relax. "It amused me even more when they'd propose, telling me how I'd never have to worry again. You see, they'd protect me, see to my needs. Keep me from the wolves and jackals prowling the corridors of the embassies and stock exchanges."

"Keep *you* safe? Man, that's good." He sighed. "Too bad you couldn't tell them every now and then."

She smiled, lips curling, predatory. "Oh, on occasion I did. Unlike your CIA, KGB doesn't worry itself over anything so petty as morality when it comes to assassination."

"I would have loved to have seen their faces."

She sniffed, spreading her hands expressively. "Most simply blubbered and collapsed. Like I said, power is relative." She cocked her head. "But hearing that doesn't bother you? Doesn't make you think differently of me?"

Sam tossed off the last of his bourbon. "Nope. Not in the slightest. Like I said earlier, you and me've been around the block, sister. I know how both sides of the street work. You're just like me, a professional with no illusions about life, or what it means."

"You say that like you mean it."

"I do. I hate bullshit—especially when a decision you make might mean the difference between me or some of my guys not making it home. I've been around a lot of death, Major. It's real permanent."

She met his gaze, held it, and slowly nodded. "I like the way you think, Captain. And, yes, you're right. I don't have many illusions about life. Or about this mission either. I'll work with you, Captain. We've got a lot to deal with in the coming months. I just hope you're as good as I think you are."

"We better hope we're all as good as we think we are, Major."

Her challenging eyes bored into his, as if to reach his soul.

CHAPTER XVII

Marshal Sergei Rastinyevski rapped a fist off the wall paneling as he paced back and forth. The operations room had gone quiet as the reports began to trickle in from the Far East. His staff watched him worriedly as he turned and started the fifteen steps to the other end of the room.

"Get me Stavka on the line." As soon as he spoke, a lieutenant-colonel handed him a field telephone.

"Sergei?" Pashka's voice came through. "Have you been updated?"

"About Vladivostok? Yes. How bad is it?"

A pause. "Bad, Sergei. I talked to Ustinov in Khabarovsk. From his sources and from aerial reconnaissance, it appears the Americans landed most of the Tenth Army. Reinforcements can be expected any day now."

"Did they get the aircraft carrier? The *Kiev*?"

"No, thank God. The *Kiev* managed to slip through Tatar Straight into the Sea of Okhotsk. But the naval shipyards there are firmly in American hands."

"And the situation on the ground?"

"Not good. American armor has taken Ussuriysk and Arsen'yev. Ustinov expects them to be threatening Khabarovsk within a week and has scrambled everything he's got, trying to slow the advance until we can rush him reinforcements. For the moment, we've acceded to his requests, but it's frightening. If he takes too many of the KGB Border Guards, what kind of an invitation will that be for China?"

Rastinyevski bit his lip, a premonition eating at his gut. "For the moment, Pashka, American tanks are moving on Khabarovsk. They've taken our western port. I think we can worry about the Chinese later. Let me think for a bit and I'll get back to you."

He handed the phone to the lieutenant-colonel and stepped to the map, staring at the Soviet Union. How had the Americans—Japan, of course. Somehow they'd managed to get their troops concentrated and shipped out of Japan without KGB or GRU catching wind of it. Now what? Where could he pull units from? As quickly as divisions were mobilized and shipped off to Europe to free veteran combat units from holding Poland, Czechoslovakia, and Hungary, something happened. Each time he readied a final overwhelming push against Western Europe, some viperous hydra lifted its ugly head from the stewing chaos to threaten from another direction.

"We're reeling from the blows," he whispered. "There's no time to plan, no time to prepare. Each action is a reflex to crisis." Where had the plan gone? Four weeks to crush Western Europe? How blithely he'd promised that. No one could have guessed the fog would roll in over Brussels that day. No one had known that three motor-rifle divisions would be shot out of the sky because they couldn't land at Zaventem. Now, after a year of war, five million Soviets had died—and no end was in sight. If only there was a way to take the war to the Americans.

He glared at the map. "Get me Stavka."

The lieutenant-colonel handed him the phone. "Pashka?"

"Here, Sergei."

"How is the situation in the Odessa District? We've retaken the city, but is there any progress routing the NATO forces out of the Crimea?"

"Not yet. They're weakened but they've fortified Sevastopol and established an airlift to resupply from Turkish bases. If we had another three divisions, we could—"

"We don't. And Kolnov's Army group in Pakistan?"

"Nikita's bogged down. It's Afghanistan all over again—but without the air support we could provide. GRU reports more and more pressure from his west. Afghans and Iranians are showing up in greater frequency."

Sergei clicked his tongue against the roof of his mouth.

"Pashka, we've got fifteen divisions in final training outside Minsk. I want them shipped east immediately. Commandeer any transportation you can—"

"*Minsk!* But Sergei, without those divisions, the chances of breaking the Hammer Division out of Belgium . . ."

"They'll just have to wait. They've held on this long, they can last a while longer as long as we can keep NATO spread thin enough to allow air drops."

Silence weighed heavily on the line.

"Pashka? You there?"

"I'm here, Sergei. Are you sure you need that much strength to throw the Americans out of Vladivostok?"

"No, Pashka. I want the *Kiev* to steam north. With her air power, we should be able to keep the Bering Strait open. I don't care how you do it, but get me enough air transports and ships to carry fifteen divisions across the Bering Strait. Americans might have a toehold in Vladivostok, but we'll have our own in Nome."

"Sergei, are you sure you—"

"Do it!"

* * *

The lump in her throat felt as big as a knotted sock as Sheila walked into the observation blister. They waited there, her top echelon. She took her place, heart triphammering her sternum. One by one, she met their eyes. *Damn it, no one ever let on that intrigue could be so frightening. To plan is one thing. To initiate an action is somethinq entirely different. And if I fail? I could be killing us all—perhaps destroying our planet.* Sheila forced her back straight. "People, I don't know how long we can get away with this. For the moment, I think we're all right."

"I don't get any translation talking to Moshe or Viktor," Sam added.

Sheila licked her lips, wishing her breathing would ease. "This place appears, from all the tests we've made, to be unmonitored. If we come here too often, Wide might get suspicious. So this will be short and sweet—Top Secret! I think we've all had a little experience with that."

Riva Thompson translated Sheila's words to Hebrew for Moshe while Svetlana translated to Russian for Viktor.

She studied Moshe, Sam, Viktor, Svetlana, and Riva where they sat looking out at the stars. "From now on, we're the fifth column. We don't have much time so let's make it fast, people. Major Detova, have you anything to add?"

"*Da,* I have proven beyond a doubt that we are breaking the law. The Ahimsa have a council called the Overones. Currently—though Wide is an Overone—he is acting outside their agreement with the Pashti and yet another intelligent species known as the Shithti. Of the Shithti, we know nothing at this time other than that they appear to be very old and never die."

"And, of course," Viktor added, eyes meeting Sheila's with that piercing quality, "that is why we were pulled so secretly from Earth. No one monitoring space frequencies would know Wide had been there. No news bulletins would fly to the stars and alert either the Pashti or these . . . what?"

"Shithti," Svetlana supplied.

Sheila's gut turned. *So we've caught Wide in another lie. Radio waves travel at the speed of light.* The implications staggered her. *Wide never meant to expose himself to the Earth. He's covered his tracks. How? My God, Sheila, don't think about it—not now.*

Moshe had listened intently as Riva translated. "So what do we do? They have our whole planet hostage. Can we accept for a moment that their power is limited only to deactivating missiles?"

"Man, we take the only option we've got." Sam shrugged. "Either we cream these Pashti, or the Ahimsa do something funny to our world."

Sheila kept silent, waiting to see where they would take things. *Are they willing to take the risks? Do they understand?*

"That's the problem." Moshe waited until Riva got the translation across. Then his expression hardened as he looked at each of the other commanders. "All of you have been lucky. You've never watched your . . . your son and daughter borne off, bloody and broken." His jaw muscles rippled. "Having lived with threats that my people would be driven into the sea, having lived with Metzada, the symbol of despair and death, we have taken the stand of 'Never again.'

"Comrade Staka, Major Dunbar, Captain Daniels, we must face the fact that we confront two enemies. First we must strike a preemptive blow against the Pashti, eliminating whatever threat this TaHaAk station poses. Then, swiftly, we must turn after stabilizing that front, and deal with the Ahimsa."

"Like you dealt with the Syrians first and then the Egyptians during the Yom Kippur war?" Viktor asked.

"A good analogy but a poor application," Moshe smiled, gnomelike features twisting good-naturedly to belie the flinty look in his eyes.

Svetlana pursed her lips. "We don't know the true power of the Ahimsa. Have any of you ever seen one? I mean, outside of the holos, have any of you ever seen one alive . . . in the flesh?" She glanced from face to face. "No? Then it is as I—"

"Damn!" Daniels exploded. "They could all be robots! Or maybe—"

"Maybe they are little puffballs as your Murphy calls them, eh?" Staka asked. "Sam, we must accept that whatever their physical form, they are like KGB—dangerous."

"I'll take the circumstances into consideration," Svetlana added wryly as she translated.

"My apology, Comrade Detova."

Sheila added, "Similarly, we must not forget that our very survival here hinges on their good will. We'll get one chance—and one alone. If we so much as hint that we're not under their thumb, they'll jolly well spank us good and heave us out the lock to survive out there." She pointed at the stars on the other side of the blister. "And that's only one option in their bailiwick. Consider the fragility of the human body. Could they poison us through the food and drink spigots? Can they gas us? How many ways could a clever and knowledgeable alien use to kill four hundred recalcitrant human beings in a ship this size with the incredible resources we've seen at their disposal?"

"So we'd best play along, no matter what." Riva squinted at the stars, lost in thought. "I'm starting to develop an aversion to Ahimsa tactics. I don't like being used as a tool. I got my fill of that in Lebanon."

"But you'll play?" Sheila asked.

Riva narrowed her green eyes. "You damn betcha, and I'll do it so well you won't even know how I feel—despite having been told, Major."

Detova sighed. "Then I take it we're going to resist? You have something in mind, Sheila?"

"I do. At least, it's starting to flesh out. I'll fill you in on the details as soon as I get more information from Svetlana and Riva's translations of Pashti. As long as we can come here to talk, we can put it all together. People, it's a risk—and a damn scary one. If we fail . . ."

"We're used to risk," Moshe added, "and to coming out ahead despite the odds."

"Count me in," Sam said, face expressionless.

"We must be very careful. More careful than the Jews in Treblinka, or Sobibor. A single hint that we're not reliable, and Wide might just open the doors to vacuum," Moshe cautioned.

Sam frowned, steepling his fingers. "Speaking of which, this TaHaAk station is surrounded by vacuum, right? Would the Ahimsa see it as an unreasonable request if we asked for vacuum training?"

Viktor smiled, nodding. "Good point, Sam. What would our fate be if the Pashti opened their station and let all the air flow out? Not only that, but cosmonauts train for several things. There is vacuum to worry about, but what happens if the gravity fails? We'd be flopping like fish. Let us train for both of those situations. Additionally, it will be another novelty to keep the men's minds off Earth—off home." Staka fingered his chin, mind working. "Of course, our weapons will have to be functional in vacuum."

"And where did you get such a devious mind?" Sheila asked, propping her chin on her knees. The light glinted in Staka's golden hair. Something in the way he smiled touched her, left her off balance.

"Performing parachute jumps outside of London as

part of the Central Army Sports Club," he gave her a wicked smile. "Be glad that I was never called upon to jump into London on other business."

Sheila's mind clicked as the piece fell into place. "Bloody foolish of me . . . of *course!*"

"What is this?" Svetlana demanded.

"It just might work if . . ." She waved their curiosity away, explaining, "Viktor just cued a thought. Let me have a couple of days to think about it, firm it up. Svetlana, see what you can pry out of the Ahimsa system regarding the potential for a Pashti counterattack. Not on TaHaAk—though we had better give that item consideration—but against *this* ship as well. Do you see? I want background information regarding the actions we would have to take to secure this ship—"

"—In the event the Pashti came and took it!" Sam cried, eyes dancing as he slapped his hands in a hollow smack. "Svetlana, as soon as you get that, dig me up and we'll come here and discuss it. Maybe with your prying and my tactics, we can put together a threat nasty enough to scare Wide into buying it."

"*Da,* good, Sam." Did her smile seem warmer when directed toward Daniels? "And I get another chance to haggle price. Together we'll see who is the most cunning."

He grinned and winked at her.

"Price?" Sheila asked.

"Private joke," Sam replied.

Moshe cleared his throat, shifting in his space wear. No matter what garb he wore, he still looked like a tank commander fresh from the desert. "In the meantime—skulduggery aside—I'll work on holding TaHaAk station against a counterattack by the Pashti. I'll need some sort of coordination with the torpedo pilots. Perhaps we can take action to increase the range and firepower to the point where we can have a mobile attack and defense capability. Some sort of hull-down ability for anti-ship warfare."

"Riva will handle that. That will also mean resealing the station after the torpedoes pull out," Sheila reminded.

Daniels nodded. "I've got just the guy, Moshe. I'll send you Ted Mason; he's pretty good at improvising.

It'll give us a handle on how much we can squeeze out of Wide, too. We're going to have to be cagey though. The puffball can't realize that we're extending our capability."

Viktor Staka laughed. "Work closely with Svetlana, my friend, and thank your lucky stars you have Soviets with you. How do you think we got the ABM treaty signed? Ogarkov and his Ministry of Disinformation convinced the whole Western world that we had ABM capability. It's a Soviet textbook example. Now we use the same principles to hide our other skills."

"I think that's enough for now," Sheila added. "Too many minutes talking in here will draw suspicion. Meanwhile, I'd like to see how all this comes together—what we can get away with."

"We will find ways to report," Moshe said softly.

"Carefully, Moshe. One mistake will kill us all."

* * *

"Overone?" Spotted bent an eyestalk to stare.

"Yes, Nav-Pilot?"

"I think the humans are up to something."

Wide rolled easily down the inspection track. "And what do you suspect they're up to?"

"Some disobedience. I just checked the records. I think we may have overlooked something. The observation bubble has no monitoring devices."

"And they found it?"

"Yes, Overone. The monitoring computer just tagged an anomaly. In the standard cross-reference for communication monitoring it noted that Dunbar's staff all occupied the observation bubble at the same time. For twenty minutes we were unable to observe or record their behavior. I fear they're up to something."

"Of course, they are, they're human. But consider, Nav-Pilot. How could they dare challenge me? What could they do?" Wide thinned, minds integrating at the intriguing possibilities. "Fix the recorders, Nav-Pilot."

"And if the humans rebel?"

"Oh, I'm sure they'll try something. You have to remember, they *are* wild animals. Like all wild animals, they will have to test the bars of their cage. Learning to be civilized and obedient takes time."

"Then you will immediately punish them?"

"Nav-Pilot, you have a lot to learn. Were I to immediately punish them, they might do something utterly stupid. Perhaps refuse to attack the Pashti in the futile belief that they have bargaining leverage. Humans always tend to overrate themselves. By pandering to that, by flattering, I'll keep their morale up. The last thing I want is resentment on their part."

"There already is. The morale has been falling." Spotted formed a manipulator and adjusted the magnetic reflex field around the thermofax towers. "Many are homesick."

"That will pass. No doubt Sheila Dunbar will think up things for them to do to keep their minds off their homesickness. Bizarre quirk they have, don't you think? When she asks, I'll grant an occasional wish."

"But won't they come to expect that?"

Wide clicked his amusement. "Let them. You've heard the tapes. They have an inherent understanding of their situation. They know they are captives and that their planet is hostage. For the moment, they suckle every drop of hope they can from the notion that good behavior on their part will be rewarded, but they don't forget their planet is collateral.

"I will play their game, Nav-Pilot. I want them to strike the Pashti with resolve and vigor, not under duress. Mistakes happen when humans feel desperate. They become emotional, liable to accidents. I want their hearts and souls committed to the destruction of the Pashti; but afterward, well, as soon as TaHaAk is wreckage, my real studies can begin."

"What will you do with them?"

Wide piped happily. "Anything I want, Nav-Pilot. *Anything!*"

* * *

Murphy studied the release system for the emergency escape hatch, trying to figure out how human fingers could undo the latch. Assaf had raised the possibility of being trapped inside. SOD and SPETSNAZ had to know how to conduct a rescue. That meant Murphy and his people had to figure out how to open the hatches. Now he squinted and scratched his head before yanking vigorously on the emergency hatch.

They worked in what had come to be called the weapons bay, a large room lit by wall and ceiling panels. Lines of Ahimsa-made tanks gleamed in the light. The vehicles reminded him of turtles, or roly-poly bugs, the ones with the rounded half-shell. Unlike the armor Murphy had known, these tanks reflected a pearlescent gray, the material almost translucent and like nothing he'd ever seen. They'd shot one up for Moshe's benefit. Assaf had watched nervously as the vehicle absorbed magazine after magazine from the deadly Ahimsa rifles. When they blasted it with grenades, they peeled back deck plate, destroyed the ceiling light panels and scattered shrapnel all around the room. Yet when they walked up to check, they found the opalescent surface of the tank smudged and pockmarked here and there; the interior remained sacrosanct.

"That's some armor," Arya had whispered in awe. "With one of these, we could drive through Damascus every Friday of the month!"

Murphy growled at the hatch, fingering the latches. "Phil? Hand me that manual." Murphy threw his weight against the hatch. The damn thing had to open some way. Everybody else had figured it out.

He looked up, aware Phil had ignored him. "Hey, you all right? Yo! Phil! Good morning!"

Phil shivered and looked down from where he sat on top of Shmulik's tank. "Huh?"

"I asked for that tac manual up there," Murphy repeated, pointing at the thick Ahimsa book.

"Oh, sorry." Cruz stepped around and handed the book down.

Murphy fingered through the curious pages, found the hatch schematic and slipped the latch sideways. The hatch swung open easily. Placing the manual on the skirting for the odd-looking treads, he squinted nervously up at his friend. "Uh, you're not all here today. C'mon, let's take five and go get a cup of coffee."

Cruz looked at him, nodding absently as he dropped to the floor.

"So what's bugging you? You've been getting weird the last couple of days. Don't this thing make tacos with jalapenos, or what?"

Cruz glared, raising a finger. "Hey, man, do I make jokes about corned beef?"

"Whoa!" Murphy raised his hands, backing off. "Bit touchy today for a guy who used to joke that he was the company tacobender."

"Yeah, well, maybe them days are over."

Murphy shrugged loosely. "Whatever turns your crank, man. I'm easy."

Cruz seemed to wilt all of a sudden. "Aw, hell, Murph, I don't know what's wrong with me. I've just been touchy, that's all. I don't know. Thinking about Trinidad, how I'll probably never see it again. Thinking about Dolores. Five years, man. Hey, she ain't gonna wait no five years for me. And Mom? Pop? Maria? Hey, wow, they're gonna be five years older! Maria, jeez, my little sis, man. She'll probably be married to some *pendejo* jerkoff I could'a been around to kill. And, hell, Luis? He'll be graduated from high school and I won't see it, man. He'll be married—unless he screws up and gets busted or something stupid."

They strolled down the long hall, Cruz talking, head down, gesturing with his hands. "Five years? So what if it's not that long for us? I mean, man, the whole world changes in five years. And what are they gonna think, huh? I mean, Mama's gonna be worried sick."

Murphy nodded, getting two cups of coffee from the mess. Cruz's words bothered him, set something inside on edge. What a reflection on life that he'd missed the feeling. The old anger yawned within—until he strangled it, putting it away like he always did.

"Hey, you know what I miss the most?" Cruz continued, taking the coffee, sitting down. "It's hunting season in the fall. Man, the frost settles on the ground, making the sagebrush all white. The aspens have just changed—leaves gone all yellow and red and falling around like a shower of gold. And the high country, it smells so clean and crisp, piñon and juniper like perfume mixed with sage. The air's cleaner then, the sky bluer. And, you know, you can feel the soul in the rocks, in the dry grass. The eyes of the Santos are on you, man. Hell, I don't even care if I shoot a deer. It's just being out there, walking around, hearing the birds and letting your soul move with the land.

"Then, at night, you walk back to the truck, and you drive the dirt roads, coming down the mountain. While you do, the sunset lights the whole sky on fire. Yellow-orange, red and pink, the clouds look laser-lit, like the colors in a Navajo painting. The headlights show you the way around the rocks and potholes and you play this game to keep from falling in the ruts and high-centering. You wind down the mountain to the blacktop and it's eight miles into town. By that time, it's full dark and you see all the motel signs, the Seven-Eleven and Sanchez's IGA. You stop at Herb's and get a six-pack of cheap beer and joke with Rosa about all the big bucks you missed that day and how if you hadn't hit that skinny little aspen tree and blown the shot, you'd have this monster Boone and Crockett deer in the back of the pickup right now. Rosa laughs and wishes you better luck tomorrow."

Cruz stopped, a wistful smile on his lips. His dark eyes saddened as he became lost in his thoughts. Murphy realized he'd sunk his teeth into his lower lip. Why didn't he have any memories like that? Something more to miss than just a good drunk and maybe a fight or two? He swallowed hard, whispering, "Go on, Phil. Then what?"

Cruz sighed, a curious glow lighting his dark face, as if his soul shone from within. "Then you pop a top on a can of beer and drive through town, honking at old man Montoya, and Filipe and Ramon, and calling jokes out the window. When you get home, the lights are on, all yellow-looking, and the dogs come out to bark at you. Sis opens the door and asks, 'Did you get anything? Or miss again?' And then, as you walk up to the door, man, the smell of the tamales rolls out fit to knock you over. Mom always made tamales when we went hunting. I don't know, just sort of a family tradition. Then, it's warm inside and Pop tells about the time he shot the six-point buck up on Las Cruces Peak and left the horns behind.

It's an old story, one he's told since I was too little to understand it." Cruz's lips twitched. "Wonder if I'll ever hear it again?"

Murphy nodded, hearing the longing. "Look, take me with you when we get back, huh?"

Cruz cocked his head. "You want to go hunting? After all the . . . Why, man?"

Murphy lifted a shoulder, looking away, afraid to meet Cruz's eyes. "I don't know. I'd . . . well, it sounds pretty wonderful. Just the way you described it. About just walking around and sniffing the air and then coming back and knowing all those people. And going home . . . to tamales, and your family. Hey, look, pal. I never knew my father. My mother, well, she . . . she . . . Aw, I don't want to talk about it.

"But you've got something, Phil. Something precious. Next time you get all homesick, you look over at me. Cause when this is all over, I don't have nothing to go back to." Murphy grinned. "Except maybe a hunting trip someplace up above Trinidad."

Cruz smiled, reaching over to slap Murphy on the shoulder. "Right on, man!" He hesitated, unsure. "Uh, you want to talk about it? I mean I just unloaded on you, you oughta—"

"No." Murphy grimaced as he tossed his coffee off. "Just leave me with a sliver of your dream. That's too good to waste."

"Someday?" Cruz lifted his coffee cup.

"Someday." Murphy toasted him. *If we don't end up as the first human corpses among the stars, old buddy.*

* * *

Moshe looked curiously around Riva's small quarters. Why did they all have to look the same? Only the soldiers, with their duffel bags, had any possessions.

"Make yourself at home. Want a beer?" Riva asked, reverting to English.

Moshe immediately accessed his headset ordering a holo of the now so terribly familiar TaHaAk station to appear.

"Please," he called, standing, walking around the station, noting once again how the major corridors ran. But this time suppose his tanks were filling the cracks left by the withdrawing "air force" torpedoes? What field of fire would he have? His cannon had limited capability—considering that too much explosive would split the station open like a can.

"Gold Star," she said, placing the cold bottle in his hand. "I don't know if it's quite the same as they serve at the Jerusalem Hilton, but it'll have to do."

"I can't tell the difference. The Ahimsa are quite good at making us feel at home." He frowned, eyes still on the station. "We need to improve our cannon and our tracking and targeting."

Riva cocked her head, spilling red hair over one shoulder. "The torpedoes shoot lasers line of sight. No leading since we're talking light speed."

"Comm access," Moshe requested. "I need to see a model of each class of Pashti spaceship. Search function, which would appear adequate or capable of assault capabilities?"

Holos of three different kinds of craft appeared beside the turning wheel of the Pashti station. "Are these to scale with the station?" Moshe asked. Immediately they shrank.

"Comm access," Riva ordered. "Graph the comparison of performance between these craft and our assault torpedoes." She scanned the numbers and bars which indicated relative capabilities of the various vessels. "Not good."

"Comm access, assuming the potential speed of the Pashti craft displayed, what is our effective kill zone with tank cannon exposed to vacuum. With yellow light, please impose those data in flat trajectory fire from the breach points where the torpedoes will withdraw at recall." Moshe took a slug of beer as the bars of yellow shot out like spokes. "No, Miss Thompson, not good at all."

She made a face at him. "Miss Thompson? Who's that? Call me Riva."

Moshe grinned at her. "Very well, Riva, how are we going to create a tactical kill zone with what we've got?"

"Let's start playing with numbers and capacities, and see what works."

Hours later, Moshe watched yet another empty bottle of Gold Star sink into the floor. He blinked and looked up from where he sat next to Riva. The wretched station still spun; only different bars of yellow light stuck out at different angles.

"Maybe if you moved Ben Yar's number 2 into that blind zone underneath," Riva suggested.

"Then we've got twice as big a gap between Ytzak and Shmulik." He raised a hand and let it fall lifelessly.

Silence stretched as Moshe fought the cobwebs that muddled his mind. "We've simply got to lever more cannon and targeting potential out of Wide."

"And if he doesn't give it to us?"

"It's 1948 all over again, I suppose."

"You're too young to remember that."

"So are you. But I remember the tense days during the Yom Kippur war when we ran desperately short of material. Maybe Wide is our current version of Richard Nixon."

Riva ran fingers through her hair. "Maybe it would have been better to chuck all this and go sit on the beach at Ashqelon and drink beer while we watch the surf."

Moshe shifted uneasily, remembering the last time he'd been there. He and Anna had just been married. How curious that they'd never gone back.

"You've got a funny look on your face."

"It was the mention of Ashqelon. I just lost myself in memories of the time we were there." He shook his head. "Another time, another place. Looking back from here, in the bowels of Wide's starship, I could almost wonder if those days . . . well, all of life is a fantasy. Sometimes it terrifies, others it bores."

"We? You mean you and your wife?"

"Anna." He smiled, remembering her slim body, the twinkle in her eyes, and the secret smile she always reserved for him.

"Did you really have to bury your son and daughter?" Riva's voice changed tone.

Moshe looked at her, seeing the vulnerability in her green eyes. How long had it been since that day? He could remember Anna's grief as she waved the picture of their son, Chaim. It had been hot, the sun beating down on the stifling streets. The funeral—as all funerals in Israel—had been loud with grief and screams of anguish. Flies had been a damn nuisance. And there had been an odd hollowness, a feeling of impossible loss and unreality. It hadn't changed—even when his friend and commander, Avraham Adan, had showed up. The prayer shawls had been bright that day.

"Yes," his voice sounded far away. The death of his daughter had been worse. A PLO mortar had torn her body apart. The medical people had assured him all the pieces in the casket were hers. It had been cloudy. A light cold rain had fallen. The hollowness had grown then. Adan hadn't come that time. The prayer shawls had not been so bright—and some part of his soul had broken.

"Your wife must be worried sick about you," Riva observed quietly.

"She's . . . dead." Anna hadn't suffered. . . . *No, don't dwell on it, my memories, my friends. I do not want to remember the prayer shawls that day.* He stood and walked over to the dispenser, asking for another Gold Star. She watched him as he walked back and settled himself, staring at TaHaAk with empty eyes.

"So, what did you do, Moshe? How did you make yourself go on?"

He shrugged and granted her a crooked smile. "I went back to my tanks. Avraham got me back in. There wasn't much else for me then, I suppose. I collected the hard cases and we put together a good unit. Maybe I taunted the odds. I don't know. Why do you ask?"

The green eyes misted slightly as she lifted the fake bottle of Gold Star and stared at it, rolling the bottle between nervous fingers. "I had more trouble than you did. Maybe I wasn't as strong, didn't have the chance to go back and taunt the odds without jeopardizing my entire Section. I liked the Middle East—something warped in my personality, I guess. Washington was curious about certain KGB activities which were funding the political resistance against the occupation of Lebanon and pipelining money to the Intefada. One thing led to another. I met a young lieutenant. The Hesballah got him in a little place called Qana in Lebanon." She paused, the corners of her mouth twitching. "He was . . . was. . . ." She raised a shoulder and looked up at the station turning above them. "After that, I couldn't. . . . Well, I went back to Washington. That's why I asked how you kept going."

Silence stretched.

"It's late," Moshe offered, hating the tender feel of poorly-scabbed wounds.

"Cup of coffee before you go?" Riva asked.

Then, embarrassed, she added too quickly, "It's just a thought."

"A good thought, unless you're as tired as I am. You're sure you don't want to go to sleep? Morning isn't that far away." He stood, feeling an odd reluctance.

"With so much to think about I won't sleep anyway, just toss and turn while the brain spins out different places to stick tanks out of space stations. Besides, it's been a long time since I've had the luxury of being able to simply talk with someone. Especially someone who's been shot at in Lebanon."

"I don't understand—talking's easy. The world's full of it."

Her expression mellowed. "Not when you're an agent for the CIA, Moshe. A person doesn't have friends then. At least, not in the sections I worked in. The need to maintain a cover, keep your wits . . . well, you know. You couldn't relax with anyone. There were always suspicions that—"

"Except with certain Israeli lieutenants," he guessed.

The smile flashed—a fleeting, delicate thing. "Yes, I suppose so. Washington disappointed me. It's the people there. They're not real. They walk around projecting images of power, superiority, and sophistication, but they're fakes, artificial facades to hide insecure people. God help them if they ever have to deal with the real world where people shoot each other and die and stare death in the eye day after day. I mean the most important thing to them is whether the Broncos or the Redskins will go to the Superbowl."

Riva clenched and shook her fists in frustration. "God, the most terrible night I ever spent after I got back to Washington was one where I went with my sister to a god damn baby shower. I spent five hours, *five hours*, listening to women babbling endlessly about whose kid could walk. How amazing it was that little Johnny could crawl and how angelic Samantha was. They couldn't bear to discuss anything difficult. I don't think they believe anything truly terrible exits. I wanted to slit my wrists!"

Moshe nodded, frowning, trying to understand a society so protected it could allow itself such delusions. "But they get the news, don't they? They see the wars on television."

Riva gave him a hollow-eyed stare. "It's not real, Moshe. Vietnam was real. They could make that connection when a beloved son came home in a body bag. But living in America today is living in a surreal fantasy. They can't even find it in their souls to execute mass murderers. These are the people who voted to ban their right to own guns for self-protection. Sure, they see blood on TV. They see people shot, stop and stare for a moment, and then go back to talking about babies and football. It's not real blood they see on the news program. It's not a real human being who just died before their eyes."

"No wonder you need someone to talk to. Fix me that cup of coffee. But only one. I still have to check on how my people did on the exercise today."

CHAPTER XVIII

RashTak thrummed uncomfortably to himself as he looked at the three Ahimsa Overones. Their images formed one by one on the large Council Chamber holo monitor as the sophisticated communications system integrated interdimensional parallax from Ahimsa sources scattered over half the galaxy.

Dealing with Ahimsa made RashTak nervous. Ahimsa weren't dangerous, but to the Pashti way of thinking, they'd assumed the same sort of venerable mantle humans tended to wrap around their more benevolent gods. From the beginning Ahimsa-Pashti relations had been colored by the constant Pashti preoccupation with inferiority. The feeling persisted, even after so many generations, that Pashti hadn't quite overcome their barbarian roots—although the Ahimsa never mentioned it. RashTak now suffered through the same awkward self-consciousness that had plagued his people for so long. Valiantly, he tightened his vibrators and attempted to deaden his tingling nervous system—none of which was made any easier by the approach of the cycles.

"Greetings, Overones. Forgive this interruption; however, a Shitht, the great Chee'ee'la, recently arrived with most disturbing news. . . ." He went on to delineate the whole of Chee'ee'la's message and explain Pashti concerns. When he finished, he clicked his pincers and folded them before his multi-mandibled jaws.

"There is nothing we can tell you," Hurt answered summarily, thinning himself. Two brown-red eyes stared out from his extended eyestalks. His foot tread exhibited a jagged area—an ancient scar from some mishap beyond any Pashti's memory—the healed wound from whence he gained his name.

Sees added, "We have seen nothing of Wide for over half of your planet, SkaTaAk's, orbit around SkaHa. We knew he went off to study primitives and that he was preoccupied with some odd obsession."

RashTak heard his vibrators clicking. "Odd obsession?"

"Some atavistic thing about Ahimsa reverting and retaking control of the physical world," Low supplied. "Wide, unlike most Ahimsa, never seemed to notice the mystery of existence. He was too dogmatic about physical things. For example, he *wanted* to expose himself to alien atmospheres. Imagine, placing yourself at risk among strange savage life-forms! The very thought is incomprehensible."

RashTak felt himself start to shiver and fought it, strangling the urge by using a mental scream to center his thoughts. With all the concern, his body had—in a metabolic sense—turned upside down and inside out. The cycles waited inexorably for him to slip, to relax for only a moment. Tentacles of their presence crept along his organs, only to be beaten back as he kept his mind on the Ahimsa and Homosapiens problem.

"Did Wide go off to study an interdicted species known as Homosapiens? Sometimes called human?" There, he'd laid it out in the open; RashTak centered his main eyes on the Ahimsa, watching their reactions.

"He did," Hurt announced, leathery sides hardly falling. "I didn't pay much attention. One moment, please, First Councillor." Hurt quickly formed a manipulator and touched a comm console half visible in the holo. Seconds passed while RashTak reviewed the Ahimsa reaction. Whatever Wide had managed to get into, the rest of the Overones appeared oblivious, uninvolved.

"Ah," Hurt's spicules puffed. "Wide has been watching the humans for quite some time. Yes, here are the reports. He begins with a resurvey of the planet prior to the most recent cycles of glaciation about a galactic ten-thousandth ago. At that time we have notes of an indigenous life-form that demonstrated considerable intellectual potential. The creature was bipedal, possessed adequate manual dexterity, scavenged and collected as a primary subsistence pattern, and periodically hunted smaller animals. We have rudimentary social organization in a band state with serial mating patterns. Wait. Yes, here. I've just cross-indexed. These are ancestral forms of Homosapiens."

"But those reports are old." RashTak clacked his multiple mandibles together nervously. *Obsession? That was the word they used.* He shifted, thrumming nervously into the sounding floor.

Hurt continued, "I'm running through on fast forward, using a subject tag on the file. Yes, here's another. Wide had a definite interest in the developing Homosapiens. Here and there along the way, he took specimens for study, finding their mental powers leveling off through the early portions of their planet's glaciation. Finally, we've had a burst of evolution on their part—almost astounding, it would seem." Hurt thinned, his eyestalks starting forward, the sign of intense Ahimsa interest.

"Fascinating. Such a vigorous and brutal species. They're not all bad. In their band societies, they care for each other—even those who are deformed, crippled by accident, or sickened by internal parasites. Beyond that, I really shouldn't think you need worry, Councillor. They're rather dirty beasts, dressed in hides, having only fire and stone-tipped sticks for weapons."

"Allow me to suggest that more recent data indicates they've developed a primitive metallurgy and have domesticated other beasts for their use."

Hurt thinned. "And *that* frightens you? Forgive me, First Councillor, but it's not the same as if they'd harnessed mass distortion or gravitational fluxing."

Rashtak raised his pincers. "I will agree. My first inclination is that Homosapiens poses no threat. Buffering that is the fact that I have a Shitht sitting in my Council Chambers—and Chee'ee'la is concerned. Nor do I need to remind you the cycles are upon us."

RashTak waited, beginning to feel ignored and a bit silly as Hurt perused the files on Homosapiens. Impatiently, he thrummed and clicked.

Hurt's sides sagged slightly as he added, "Odd, Wide's

reports ceased soon after he arrived for this latest fieldwork. Homosapiens seems to have domesticated plant as well as animal foods, established a series of warring multinational tyrannies and engaged in the most fascinating mutilation of each other. *Nasty* creatures, these humans."

"If you would be so kind, could you—"

"Fascinating!" Hurt piped, interrupting. "What could possess them? They *kill their own kind!* Literally, they organize large groups for the purpose of killing each other over ideals, policy, their various concepts of God, resources, almost anything. Curious behavior for a species whose evolution has been toward cooperation, don't you think?"

RashTak caught a glimpse of the other Ahimsa where they filled different monitors. Sees started to thin, adding, "No wonder they were interdicted. Imagine what they would allow themselves to become out here!"

"You're assuming they possess the intelligence to get off their planet—an assumption which appears remarkably optimistic on your part, I believe." Hurt thinned, piping cynicism.

Low had accessed his own comm, following Hurt's study. "I see. Yes, I remember these animals. We ordered them interdicted quite some time ago. Here's the case, Councillor RashTak. I'm sending it."

RashTak's screen flashed. He placed a foot on the tactile sensor and followed the arguments back and forth as he watched the visual imagery. The scene which formed consisted of a collage of visuals depicting an alien world. A huge continental ice sheet slowly melted toward the polar caps, retreating, leaving an awkward-looking big-headed Homosapiens type in newly green meadows. The Homosapiens, armed with stone tipped tools, methodically killed large hairy beasts, lived in open camps, and raised their young.

At the same time, others, smaller-headed, more agile with more varied tools, slowly moved north, encroaching on the awkward ones. These looked very much like the specimens in the Pashti records; only their dress appeared more primitive. When competition for resources became acute, the southern humans killed the northern ones, took their females and food, and moved in.

"Disgraceful!" RashTak chittered to himself. He worked his muscles and settled his suddenly emotionally charged organs. "We have always been somewhat bashful about our reaction to the cycles. At the same time, it's a biological fact beyond our control—but irrational savagery such as this! I cannot see what Wide—"

"Neither do we," Low piped a shrill note of irritation from his spicules. "Still, Councillor RashTak, consider that Wide—eccentric though he may be—is several average star lives old. He has seen many things, studied many phenomena. While his surface actions often appear to be without justification, he has never, in the end, proven to be irrational. Everything he has done has always been for someone's benefit and never harmful."

Sees quickly followed up. "Whatever Wide is doing with humans, he would have had to have gone insane to have broken an interdiction! Ahimsa haven't suffered that illness for. . . . Let me see. Hurt, had this galaxy formed when Red attempted to prove gravity nothing more than a metaphysical extension of imagination? How long ago did he attempt to roll across the surface of that neutron star?"

RashTak thrummed nervously, getting the Ahimsa's attention. "The fact remains that the Shitht, Chee'ee'la, is sitting in our Council Chambers thinking about humans. We're not used to Shitht showing up. With the cycles coming, it is very difficult to maintain sanity around here with a Shitht occupying Council Chambers!"

Hurt's sides fluttered in and out. "And you say Chee'ee'la is certain that Wide is *interfering* in the cycles? Or did he perhaps mean Wide is doing something to *change* the cycles. You see, there is a distinct difference in interpretation and given your current sensitive—"

"I realize there are problems with translation. Not even Ahimsa can understand Shithti with any guarantee of accuracy. Yes . . . yes, those are possibilities." RashTak's stomach tried to curl around itself. *Could that be it? The translation got botched and Wide's struggling to do all Pashti a favor?* He winced to himself. *If that's the case, and I push this, I'll look stupid. They're already blaming it on the cycles, but are too polite to mention it. Violet and Double Violet Curses on the cycles!*

Hurt speculated, "You don't suppose he's found some biochemical agent do you? He may have—"

"Why not simply access his transducer and send us a template?" RashTak asked, vibrators pounding out sarcasm as he tried to analyze every angle rationally, fearful that he couldn't. "That wouldn't bring a Shitht out of deep space for a chat, now would it?"

Sees thinned himself slightly, spicules harmonizing a low chime. "Councillor, your species often considers us Ahimsa to be, shall we say, detached? Shithti, on the other hand, engage in thought processes that we can only speculate about. Would that we had the capability of grasping the concepts they—"

"I can only tell you what the Shitht said! I have been informed that Wide has broken interdiction and may be bringing humans out into space for the purpose of influencing something concerning the cycles. The cycles are touchy enough with Pashti. You know that! We're worried here. What is Wide—"

"First Councillor," Hurt sounded sympathetic. "You keep referring to the cycles. We can see the changes in your body. In view of the considerable turmoil you undergo, don't you think perhaps you are overreacting?"

RashTak froze on the dais. *They did it. They finally admitted it. What now? Anything else would be a reflection of Pashti paranoia. The cycles. Always the cycles.* He filled his long lungs and forced the air out, tickling the sensorial fibers along his legs.

Each of the Overones slowly began to thin as they explored this new hypothesis. RashTak beat an angry response out of his quivering nervous system, knowing it would only be the damning proof of his loss of control to the cycles. What other logical conclusion could they make—especially if you had thousands of years of previous examples at your manipu-tip?

RashTak thrummed his under parts in dismay. "Anything I say now would automatically be suspect. But, please, stay in touch. If the Shitht is right, Wide will do whatever he intends to do soon. If not, we are only days away from the cycles. If we're really all crazy right now, it is a very unique manifestation of the cycles and we'll want good data to review after this is all over. Will you, therefore, monitor the coming events so we will have a record? We may all learn that way."

Hurt flattened himself in acquiescence. "We will do that, First Councillor. In the meantime, we will try and reach Wide. During this conversation Sees has sent several queries over different subsingularity spectra. Wide does not answer. When he does, we will ask him for an explanation. If he is involved in something, we will let you know immediately."

"Thank you," RashTak responded. "That is very kind, Overone. Now, if you will excuse me." He went through the formal good-byes, adhering to each of the multiple steps of protocol. He didn't need them accusing him of being rude on top of everything else.

The screen dead, RashTak slapped the floor angrily, sending several of his females scurrying.

CHAPTER XIX

Sam sat on the table, legs swinging. Viktor smiled at the image it conjured in his mind and leaned against the wall of the room, staring down at the holographic model of TaHaAk station. The top had been omitted, allowing them to watch the action unfold inside as their troops rushed through the halls, shooting down Pashti.

Curious how he and Sam had come to grips with their situation. They worked well together, each an expert who valued the other's opinion. Two separate tactical approaches had melded into something else, something new and exciting. Had Wide understood that? Had his selection process looked for compatible personalities?

"I think Malenkov should be a little closer to his tanks. When they hit the second junction, they're spread out. If Pashti were to counter here, they could separate Malenkov's people from Ben Yar's armor." Sam pointed at the holo record as he talked.

"I'll have a word with Nicholai." Viktor stepped through the holo and settled in a chair, legs crossed at the ankles. He made a note on his pad. "Anything else?"

Sam shook his head. "Nothing that's come to my attention. You see anything?"

Viktor gave a command to the headset, replaying the initial assault. He flipped through the various monitors to one specific scene where a torpedo slipped through the station wall, the landing ramp dropping. "Here. I think Ytzak is coming out fine, his armor is racing as the ramp drops, but Nedelin and Watson aren't following him out fast enough. Here, see? Watch, they're sloppy, laughing even. Granted it's a training exercise, but . . ."

"But they oughta have their asses chewed on for a while."

Sam pursed his lips, making a mental note through his comm. "Anything else?"

Viktor shook his head, shutting the system down. "No. Well, yes." He cocked his head, considering how to broach the subject.

Sam rubbed the back of his neck, dropping into one of the chairs. "Speak, Comrade Major."

Viktor braced himself on his elbows. "I'm getting a feeling that something's about to happen. Just that itch that says if you don't scratch, you'll regret it."

"Morale?"

He nodded, giving Daniels a calculated look. "I've had three people out. Sick, supposedly. I sent Mika down after the exercise this afternoon to remind them of their duty to the Party and their suffering fellows on Earth."

"Then why do you look worried?"

Viktor lifted an eyebrow. *Do I tell him? Yes, he's earned the right to know. He may have to make a decision, issue an order one day. Knowing your command can be critical.* "Because it was a gamble to send Mika. He takes his duty very seriously. Sometimes it blinds him to command flexibility. At the same time, I think the morale problem deserves Mika's charming personality.

"Sam, there are some things you should know. Mika has been with me a long time. He joined my command as a junior lieutenant just after he graduated from Frunze Military Academy. While he was there, he turned in his best friend for sneaking out one night to see his girl. The penalty for that was two years in a penal battalion. Mika places duty above friendship. That inflexibility I was talking about has cost him a lot—especially advancement. He should be a captain by now—but he's still only a lieutenant. He hasn't even made senior lieutenant. He doesn't have that ability to adapt, to understand the subtle nature of command."

Sam crossed his arms, nodding slightly. "Yeah, I think I know. He's the perfect lieutenant."

"No, he's the perfect sergeant." Viktor smiled. "And then, only so long as he's doing the Party's work. In Afghanistan, there is no other man I would like to have at my back. Mika might have been born specifically for that war. He would have been perfect in combat against Nazis. But to be quite honest, he makes me uncomfortable here. Every other man in my unit can adapt, deal with the situation. Mika, well, his imagination is limited. His life is devoted to a very narrow definition of Communism. There's a reason for that, but it's personal and I won't get into it. I thought however that I should let you know. I'll try and keep him under my supervision. I know him, and how to deal with his problems."

"Like for morale purposes?"

"Exactly. Shall we deal with that next?"

Sam nodded. "Yeah, I've noticed it, too. Among my guys, the erosion is a little more subtle. I think Murphy's been talking to them. I noticed Cruz looking pretty bad the other day. Then Mason started to mope. Probably worried about whether he'll still be married to Pam when he gets back. Murphy's been keeping his thumb on the pulse of the unit."

"We're going to have to do something," Viktor pointed out.

"You got that right, that five years is starting to sink in now that we've grown accustomed to the routine."

"My people, well, many are starting to think about their demobilization—and how the world will have changed by the time they get back." Viktor sighed. "And here we are in an Ahimsa Gulag."

"Oh, wow, man, don't even *think* that around the men. That's the last thing we need."

Viktor smiled grimly, his own thoughts on Tula. *Will you even care, Father? Would it matter to you? Have I become a real soldier now?* "No, I'll keep it to myself. Besides, they'll think it up on their own soon."

"Any married?"

"Only Pietre and Mika. Most are too young to have married. Then, once they're in, the army would like them to stay celibate as priests. The Party would like them to marry and do their duty by providing Mother Russia with new babies for the next generation. The KGB would like to have them married so they can 'stabilize' the proclivities of wild youth—and maybe have another means of keeping their thumb on the heartbeat of a potential career officer."

"And Mika, being a good Party boy, married immediately?"

"Of course. The daughter of one of the Commissars. A . . . well, she'd been something of a problem to her father. Marrying her off to Gubanya solved a problem for the Party. As for Mika, I don't know that he did himself any favors. I think, for reasons of his own, he loves her a great deal." Viktor grinned. "And, of all of us, Mika might end up the best off for the five years away."

"She's still a problem, huh?"

Viktor swallowed the urge to chuckle. "Strictly between you and me, Sam, she's the ultimate Capitalist when it comes to men."

"Hey, man. I hear you. I almost got involved with a gal like that. I think I was perfect for her. She could set up in style, buy a nice house, get a great check every month—all that hazardous duty pay adds up, you know—I'd be gone so I wouldn't cramp her style, and most likely I'd get knocked off so she'd get the pension."

"And you saw through her?"

Sam grinned. "Yeah, she got compromised. A little fifth column action on the part of some bacteria that infiltrated one time when she exposed her rear to friendly forces. How about you? You never married?"

Viktor forced images of a burning Afghan girl's face from his memory. "No—and I think you know why. For me, a wife would be a fallacy. I could marry, sure, and produce my strong sons for the benefit of the Motherland. But that's all I'd have in common with her." He shook his head. *And live the rest of my life with the nightmare of Baraki.* "I guess I'd rather live alone than live a half-existence with a woman. How could I talk to her? How could I tell her how I feel after a raid? I've never met a woman who could deal with me, with what I have to do. Therefore, it's better to simply avoid it—and keep the Army happy at the same time."

Sam lifted an eyebrow. "There's Svetlana."

He appreciated Sam's sly wink. "No, my friend. Svetlana is a major of the KGB. We know too much about each other. Tell me, have you ever watched scorions mate? The male deposits the semen on a rock and plays a very careful game with the female. He must lock pincers, and maneuver her over the semen since she will not allow him to couple with her like other species do. I fear that Svetlana and I would be too much like those scorpions."

Sam nodded. "She's a beautiful woman."

"And dangerous."

"I'll keep that in mind. She seems to think there's a way of putting me on the KGB payroll when we get back."

"And you're considering it?" Viktor kept his relaxed posture while his insides prickled with sudden interest. *And if you'd betray your country, Sam. What would you do to those of us who depend on you?*

Sam's slow shake of head reassured—and partially disappointed. "I see that look in your eyes, Viktor. Sorry. Not me. I don't know, if the Soviets really had a better system, maybe I could be recruited. Facts are, they don't. There's too many abuses in the Party, too many folks sent to Siberia. Hey, Stalin almost killed more of his own people than Hitler did!"

"Stalin's been gone a long time."

"Yeah, and the world's a better place. But getting back to the point, I know too much about both sides. The CIA's allowed itself to sink to the same muck and filth tactics as the KGB. Ends justify the means, baby, and don't look back if you're serving the noble and glorious cause. Anything goes—so long as you don't get caught."

"Knowing that, why did you stay with it?"

Sam's smile went sad. "Got trapped, I guess. The job gets in your blood—and you can't go back. Like you were talking about earlier, who'd you talk to? Hey, middle America is full of people who've never been hungry, never been scared, never seen a dead human being, let alone killed anybody. They think the death penalty is cruel and unusual punishment for rapists and murderers. And do you think I could sit down with some guy from the suburbs who thinks banning guns will stop crime and milk comes from Safeway or Piggly Wiggly and have any kind of a meaningful conversation? Shit! If he knew I'd killed anybody, he'd crap all over himself and puke on the spot."

"So why protect them if they're unwilling to protect themselves? Svetlana's offer would seem even better. The Russian people are stronger. They live with more reality in their daily lives."

Sam made a face. "Because I don't think Communism works. It breeds Uncle Toms. People who don't have to hustle. There's no incentive or discipline for the individual—no reward for busting your ass. The Soviet system's stagnant and crumbling. So, in the first place, I can't see any ethical advantages to your rotten system over my crummy one. In the second place—and probably the most important of all—I gave my word I'd take care of the U.S. of A. They pay me pretty well for it, too. So long as that's my job, I'll do it. And I'll do it to the best of my ability." Sam sighed. "Sorry, Svetlana."

"In a way, I'm relieved."

Sam cocked an eyebrow.

"We understand each other."

Sam nodded, crossing his muscular arms. "And you know, Viktor, for being both a Commie, and a blond white guy on top of it, I think you're probably just all right. So what did you leave behind? Family?"

Viktor pursed his lips. Daniels' expression reflected an honest interest. "You're not the only one who doesn't have anyone to talk to. I haven't been home in six years. The last time was a disaster. What the people at home thought and what the soldiers in the field lived were two different things. My parents were both so terribly proud of me. I was fighting for Communism, for the liberation of the oppressed masses of Afghans. Only when you were there, well, it was different."

"Like Nam, I guess."

"Worse." Viktor sighed, trying to keep the ghosts at rest. "In Vietnam, you had a fervent minority who supported Americans, another fervent minority supported the Communists. The vast majority of the people feared your side and ours. In Afghanistan, everyone hated us.

A Soviet soldier had no friends outside of his fellow Soviet soldiers."

"You didn't lose as many as we did."

"We didn't have the same kind of war. They couldn't sneak unseen through the jungles. A band of guerrillas crossing a stretch of barren desert shows up fairly well on night goggles. We didn't fight anything resembling what you did in the Tet offensive. Had we, our casualties would have been higher than you suffered in Vietnam."

He waved it away. "Anyhow, I'm losing my point. That last time I went home I hadn't been there for three hours before I was in a fight with my father. As a youth he marched across most of Eastern Europe with the 24th Iron Division. He was so proud when I graduated and went to Afghanistan." The image of the old man's smile remained, untarnished. Ah, what pride had been in his eyes. "His son had taken up the flag, marching off to do his sacred duty. Only I doubt he'll ever understand. Killing Germans in Poland is one thing. Machine-gunning a village full of women is another. The worst of all were the toy bombs. You heard of those?"

Sam nodded.

Viktor clasped powerful hands over his knee and pulled it up. "Terror to fight terror. I wonder. I watched a little girl—no more than five years old—pick one of those little mines up. I started to shout, but it came too late. Fragments caught her in both eyes. Normally they just blew off the hand. This one not only took off her hand but blinded her." He sighed, the ghosts stirring. "Why the children? They're the perfect Communists. The Party line was that we were fighting for the future. If children aren't the future, what is? Why did we have to maim and kill them?"

"And did you tell your father?"

Viktor nodded, wincing, remembering. "I should have known better. I know what they used to get through Tass. I should have known they wouldn't believe me. Not only that, but like you were talking about in America, they just didn't understand. My father knew a little about the horror, but the Great War was different. He couldn't imagine the might of the Red Army unable to crush the resistance in Afghanistan. How could the mighty military that trampled Hitler beneath its booted feet fail over a bunch of rag-wrapped goat herders? He said I fought better with family than I did with Afghans."

"And now it's another five years before you can go back and mend fences."

"If then." Viktor sighed and leaned his head back, staring at the light panel overhead. "How about you?"

"For me it's all free and clear. I just wish it was for all the troops."

Viktor rubbed his tired eyes. Yes, that was the next major problem. "Then you will no doubt agree that we need to change the exercises to keep our people from going crazy."

The terminal beeped, Mika Gubanya's face forming. "Comrade Major, I wish to inform you that Private Kuzentsov is wounded. Further, I am filing charges against him for attempting to strike a superior officer."

Viktor looked across at Sam. "I fear it's started." *And what will I do now? Is this the first spark of the fire that will consume us whole?* Flickers of Baraki hovered in the back of his mind.

* * *

Hurt filled his breathing sacks and whistled irritation in a long exhale. "Wide does not answer. Such behavior is unlike him."

Sees thinned, sides pulsing where he filled the monitor. "I can think of many reasons. Perhaps he is involved in some meditation and does not wish to be disturbed."

"Perhaps, but his Nav-Pilot should have reacted. That's what Nav-Pilots are for. They should be learning from their betters, studying the ways of the Overones, seeking to improve their abilities to think abstractly while freeing the Overone from routine duties and allowing him to perfect his thoughts."

"Which is what we should be doing instead of worrying about Wide." Sees grunted through rasping spicules.

Hurt thinned, his surface taking on a crinkled appearance. "I undertook the responsibility of finding Wide only because a Shitht may be involved. I have other studies to conduct. This is not a lark for me."

"And the Pashti? How seriously can we take them with the cycles coming on?" Sees thinned even more. "My inclination is to let it be. Wide hasn't shown tendencies toward trouble. How serious can Homosapiens be? I accessed the records of the interdiction. They don't lead me to suspect that Homosapiens could be much of a threat to Pashti."

"They are violent, considered insane."

"Honestly, I can't see what harm they'd be to Pashti—except that they're terribly dirty and wild mannered."

"They use weapons. In fact, they've evolved a dependence on weapons."

"Which Pashti can easily resist during the cycles. Homosapiens, from the latest records, use only crude metal weapons which would barely mar a Pashti shell. A swift kick would disable one of the vile creatures and probably kill it."

"Then why were they interdicted?"

"Mostly to keep Ahimsa—or Pashti—from meddling with them. Certain chemicals in their brains are similar to ours. There is a faint potential for contamination. Beyond that, we could see no possible use for a self-destructive species. Even if they could be trained for menial jobs, they have no ability for higher communication, for advanced technical skills, or contributions to civilization. The decided opinion of the interdicting council was that Homosapiens would most likely fall on others of their kind at some time in the future and create havoc. Who wants a creature around who might turn violent from one moment to the next? At the same time, they are incredibly self-oriented. They demonstrate aggressive behavior toward superiors, or anything which they perceive as threatening to their goals. Would *you* want to have some animal around who might think you were a threat?"

Hurt had begun to sag. "The universe is dangerous enough without wild beasts loose among us. In the event Wide has broken interdiction, we'll be forced to take measures."

"Are you thinking of pursuing this?"

"After what you just told me, yes. If Wide has gone insane, we'll have to excommunicate him, isolate him someplace where he can't contaminate the rest of us. As to the humans, perhaps the kindest course would be to simply exterminate them now that they know civilization exists."

"You don't think maintaining interdiction would be sufficient?"

"Would you want to live confined to a planet, knowing that others lived among the stars?"

"They're animals, but you may be right."

* * *

Sheila paced the length of her room, fingers laced behind her back. She stared at the floor, oddly aware of Viktor and the way his hair shone golden in the light. With a firm resolve, she forced her mind to the problem at hand. "And what do you propose we do, Viktor? *How am I supposed to keep them from dreaming of home?*"

Staka lifted his arms. "For the moment, Sam has everyone running and sweating, based on the assumption that if they run in their spare time, they'll be so exhausted they'll simply fall over and sleep instead of worrying about home.

"And the computer training? I've read the marks, we seem to be most adept at picking up the information Wide has requested we learn."

Viktor frowned. "The Ahimsa headsets seem to react with the human brain. I've noticed that information imparted seems to stay . . . that a person doesn't have to memorize. It's just there, on file, as if planted in the brain."

Sheila turned. "Then we'll learn more. I want every individual to spend at least four hours a day at the terminals. I want them studying physics, galactic history, Ahimsa science, you name it." *And perhaps it will pay off in the end. Education usually does.*

She stepped to the dispenser, drawing a cup of tea. "Viktor, give me an honest answer. Will you and your people follow my orders?" She held her breath. So much would depend on this quiet, deadly man.

He caught the undertones in her voice. She turned to stare at him, refusing to give, a slight rise to one eyebrow.

"That would depend on the order. I doubt we'd be willing to storm the Politburo at your request."

Her gaze didn't waver. "What I want to know is, will you obey *any* order I give you here, now, on this mission? I need to have absolute obedience—to the letter. Will you give it to me? Trust me?" She held her breath.

Staka's eyes narrowed to slits. "Those were my orders from the General Secretary. But beyond that, why should I trust you?"

She crossed her arms, pacing to stand before him, meeting those ice-blue eyes. "If I could walk down and show you the stars in the observation bubble, you'd probably understand. There's a whole universe out there which will be denied to humanity. And this time, I can't tell you about it. Wide *extended the translator to the observation bubble.*"

His eyes bored into hers, probing, seeking her weaknesses. A slow smile grew on his lips; an acknowledgment flickered in his eyes. For that brief moment, their souls touched and Sheila's heart seemed to swell. She let herself be captured by his gaze, awed by the vulnerability, buoyed by the strength. The hurt and the pain unbalanced her. Her lips parted as if she'd seen him for the first time.

"I will follow your orders, Major. Yes, I will trust you with our lives.

"Thank you, Viktor."

You're gambling everything, aren't you? The look in his eyes couldn't be mistaken.

Sheila steeled herself. "We'll begin new exercises tomorrow. That might help with the morale situation. At the same time, we've got to prepare for the inevitable Pashti counterattack."

He turned, a burning curiosity in his eyes. "Pashti counterattack? But I thought . . ."

She winked conspiratorally. "Tell me, if you were a Pashti whose station had just been invaded, what would your first reaction be?"

A slow grin spread across his lips, a genuine admiration in his eyes. "Counterattack, of course."

* * *

Katya Illych swept her ash-blonde hair over her shoulder as she stepped into Gubanya's room. She leaned against his thick arm, body light against his. He studied her in the reflective wall of his room. She seemed so small compared to his big body.

"You look nervous, Mika." She stepped away, dropping her small bag of personal items on the table, running her fingers along the back of one of his chairs. The way she did it looked almost . . . well, professional. Her knowing eyes teased his as she looked up, a veil of blonde hair hiding half her face.

Despite the quaking of his heart, he kept his calm expression. "Anticipation." He winked at her, walking to the dispenser, asking for two glasses of vodka. He'd already downed four doubles, seeking to bolster his courage.

Memories of Irina flooded his mind, adding to his guilt. Katya took the drink, studying him from lowered lids, a slight teasing to the cant of her hips. Cool green eyes watched him, predatory eyes.

"Worried about your wife?"

He swallowed. "How did you know?"

She laughed, exposing her throat, white teeth flashing. "I've watched men wrestle with themselves for years, knowing they're going to do what they're going to do and preparing themselves for the suffering afterward. Mostly, I help them along. With you, I don't care."

He refilled his vodka, letting his eyes trace her perfect features. Katya's high breasts pressed against her uniform. Her flat belly and small waist emphasized the swell of her hips. She stood before him, smiling at his appraisal, sensuous, defiant. No dumpy Irina, Katya had a professional courtesan's look about her.

"Why me?" Mika asked suddenly, goaded by that wary part of his brain that kept him alive.

She walked up, inspecting him before running her hands down his chest, tracing fingers over the ridges of his muscles. "Honestly, I've never had a man like you. Most are powerful bankers, politicians, generals—influential people who know something KGB wishes to know. Let's say I'm curious about what a man like you feels like." She smiled over the rim of her glass. "Interested?"

Mika grinned.

She sipped at the vodka and set it on the table. Like a lazy tiger, she walked up to him, reaching up to kiss him, the touch of her lips delicate and promising on his. Her tongue moved against his. He barely realized it as she peeled the uniform from his body, letting her hands trace down his hot flesh.

She worked lower, her warm breath playing across the ripples of his belly muscles. He moaned as she reached for his hardening penis.

"Lie down," she told him, voice like honey on a warm morning.

As he settled on the bed, she began to slip the uniform from her body. His heart hammered at the sight of her. She stood before him, reading the look in his eyes, a triumphant smile on her perfect face.

The image of a predator flashed again in his mind as she leaned over him, kissing him passionately.

Gubanya stared at the light panel overhead. "So, five years from now, when I come back from space, I'll see what Irina has done." He looked over at Katya. "What will you bet that I have two more children with a third on the way?"

Katya shrugged. "I think it's foolish to worry about. For one thing, I don't think you care that much for her."

Gubanya frowned. "She's my wife."

"You can't trust her. How can you really care about someone you can't trust?"

Mika lifted a shoulder. I guess I . . . Maybe I haven't thought about it."

She smiled and stood up, winking at him. "I'm going to shower and go back to my place."

"You don't want to stay? Maybe . . ."

She placed fingers to his lips, the predatory look now guarding her emotions. "Mika, I'm *not* a surrogate wife.

I'm an officer in the KGB. You're not the only person who's worried about what they'll come back to in a world five years different. But thank you. Take care of yourself and give me a call sometime. If you're not busy, and if I'm not busy, well, we'll see what happens. But no guarantees."

She hesitated for a moment, glancing over her shoulder. Mika's soul shivered. Then she stepped into the shower and punched the spray.

He stared at her superb figure, remembering. In all his life, he'd never had sex like that. He'd bought women, taken them on the battlefield, and Irina and he had shared a night whenever he could get away, but Katya's use of muscles and movements had left him a whimpering wreck, physically drained.

"How did you do what you did?" he asked softly. "Never, in all of my life, has a woman brought me to—"

"Professional secret." She grinned, pulling on her uniform. "It works on Capitalists, too."

And then she was gone.

Mika lay back, feeling the room spin. Too much vodka. He blinked, remembering the sensations she'd aroused from his flesh. He couldn't help but think about Irina, and how she lay there, unmoving while he reached climax.

Maybe five years wouldn't be so bad after all.

* * *

Moshe hopped lightly up the side of his tank, staring down the line of deadly vehicles as Assaf Company climbed up and prepared their tanks for the exercise. The rounded shapes of the vehicles gleamed in the white light of the tank bay. He undogged the hatch and powered up as Arya climbed in with Mikael.

"And Yeled?" Arya called, slipping into his driving seat, fingers flicking switches.

"I think Yeled . . ." Moshe waved it off. "Well, I guess in all honesty I don't know what he's . . . I just don't know."

"I'll miss him," Arya stared at the systems lights as they came up.

The net crackled in Moshe's ears. "Assaf?"

One by one they called off as they backed into the torpedo simulators.

"Here are the new orders. You will take the station as in previous exercises. As soon as you have secured your objective, leave infantry and return to the torpedoes. There, you will run your tank into the gap created by the torpedo's withdrawal. If you advance too far, you will be blown out of the station by decompression and therefore, dead. A special tactics unit will seal the breach and anchor your tank. Thereafter you will fire through the breach in the attempt to disable counterattacking Pashti spacecraft."

He heard the shouts of appreciation through the net.

"Something new? Great!" Arya cried. "I'm tired of crushing Pashti."

Moshe nodded. "Well, we'll see if I can function as antiaircraft." *And we'll see what reaction we get out of Wide when the simulators go berserk.*

"I wish Yeled were here," Mikael said.

CHAPTER XX

"Overone!" Spotted's screech filled the narrow control center.

Consciousness came slowly as Wide disengaged from his stasis field. His minds had been sorting methodically through the lists of his peers, remembering the political leanings of Sees, Low, and Hurt. They would need to be swayed—all of them—as soon as Wide had attended to the proper disposition of his humans.

He extruded a manipulator and lowered the field, rolling out lethargically as he re-formed neurons. Spotted's cry echoed through the command chambers.

"I heard you call, Nav-Pilot." Wide balanced one manipulator with another and pulled a concentrated food stick from the dispenser, opening the sphincter to one side of his eyestalk. His stomach protruded like a gray balloon and enveloped the concentrate.

"Overone, you must come see what the humans have been requesting! They tripped a warning circuit. *They're up to something!*"

Wide concentrated on pulling his digestive sac into his body again and got his stomach centered, relocating portions of his brain so his body balanced. The rush of nutrients refreshed, stimulating his partially depleted mind. He would have to produce another shot of courage for Spotted. Partitioning part of his brain, he began formulating the proper chemicals. Couldn't his underling maintain some notion of Ahimsa superiority, if only for a little while?

"Easy, Nav-Pilot, I'm here. You're fine. The ignorant humans haven't broken into the command module. None of their guns are pointed at your little round body." He kept his tone reassuring and used his still extended manipulator to excrete the calming molecules. Spotted formed a receptacle and greedily sucked the thin mucus off Wide's manipulator before the Overone pulled it back and let it merge with his tissue reserve.

At the same time, Wide had taken some of Spotted's memory in the exchange. He sorted through the fear and anxiety and found a trace memory which led him to the main computer boards. He extended the remaining manipulator and accessed the human requests.

"Space suits? They're training for both vacuum and zero g? Most interesting. In association, what have they accessed?" Wide rocked back and forth. Fascinating! They'd taken a completely different initiative than he had anticipated. Delightful! Of course, he couldn't keep track of everything they asked for, but the data from this expedition would keep him occupied for several Earth millennia as he studied their thought patterns from the trail of requests they made off the immense comm system.

The monitor flashed through permutations which might suggest the humans' direction of inquiry. "Hmm," Wide mused, both eyes glued to the screen. "This counterattack, is that what triggered your fear response, Nav-Pilot?"

"Yes, Overone. They're also requesting more powerful cannon and materials which could be used to augment the potential of the assault torpedoes. I have not allowed the processors to provide them with the supplies they request. I am afraid they will obtain the means to assault us! We cannot—"

"Give them the material, Nav-Pilot." Wide felt himself starting to tense as part of his mind tried to flatten for having overlooked the fact the Pashti might counterattack. At the same time, another portion of his mind tightened his sides at the incredible cunning his humans exhibited. They overlooked nothing! Zero g? Of course! He searched for and found an exploration of combat probabilities should the Pashti evacuate the station or should it be decompressed accidentally. Such smart animals! But what else were they plotting?

He searched the files which had been created for Pashti counterattacks and whistled. He stared at the simulations they were running. File after file formed of strategies and the subsequent development of tactics. Some had been immediately discarded while others evolved, tactical permutation overlays being fitted to the given strategy.

Wide piped satisfaction to himself. *In their brains they're already battling harmless circling Pashti mining, cargo, and jump vessels! What vitality! Oh, what a delightful study in savagery this is!*

Engrossed, he looked at their technical requests. Files had been cross-referenced to tech specs on the assault torpedoes and how their range and firepower could be augmented to function with . . . *tanks?* Wide forced air through his spicules, shrilling curiosity. His eyes read two files simultaneously. "Of course," he chortled. "They want to shoot at the Pashti with the tanks in case the station gets cut off. Delightful! No wonder you were frightened Nav-Pilot. Ahimsa are not used to such dynamic innovation and anticipation."

"I did not see that file, Overone." Spotted sounded cowed. "I was frightened at the file they have begun preparing on the Pashti counterattack on *our* ship!" Spotted began to deflate again.

"This . . . ship?"*This ship? MY ship? IMPOSSIBLE!*

"I'm sending the file now, Overone." Spotted had a manipulator on the computer controls.

The monitor filled as Wide took it up, scanning the contents, feeling a dull blurring of his concentration. The humans had broken new ground, creating contingencies to defend the Ahimsa ship from a swarm of angry Pashti craft.

Wide struggled to keep himself round. *PASHTI WOULDN'T DARE ATTACK AN AHIMSA VESSEL!* The idea represented lunacy—unthinkable! Ahimsa were civilized beings! Ahimsa had brought Pashti to space! Besides, the Ahimsa weren't attacking the Pashti—humans were! That much would be readily apparent, wouldn't it? Any Pashti could see that, couldn't they?

"Give them the data they request," Wide announced. "Inform the factory to produce the materials the humans think they need."

Wide swung away from the computer monitors and

rolled to the holographic console. Instantly he accessed a holo of Sheila Dunbar's room. The major lay on her side, asleep, eyelids wiggling with that reaction their psychologists called REM. Wide studied the phenomena closely, rolling forward until his eyes almost touched the laser image. What would dreaming be like? Sleep itself had fascinated him. Only terrestrial species slept. Dull to watch, to be sure. But the implications it had for human inferiority couldn't be discounted. After all, how could a species that spent one third of its life in a stupor hope to be competitive?

Wide idly scanned the different personal compartments. Most of the humans slept. He found one couple copulating—Gubanya and Katya Illych, he decided. He studied the reactions, his monitors picking up GSR, blood pressure, brain wave activity, and finally the whimpering sounds they made. He backtracked the pickup and listened to the incredibly inane things they whispered to each other before and during the stimulation prior to copulation. That was love poetry? How idiotic! Why didn't he charm her with an exhibit of his mental prowess? Perhaps flash a quick mathematical formula? Offer an insight into astrophysics, or the nature of parallel universe existences? Why would an obviously intelligent female choose to mate with a man whose conversation hinged around how he could consume her like an obscure Latvian pudding covered with ice cream and sticky syrup? Irrational!

Four hours later, his scan informed him that Sheila Dunbar had awakened. He accessed her room, watching as she stepped out of her shower. She lingered, passing her body through the water trap. Despite her closed eyes, she had a most peculiar expression on her face.

"Major Dunbar?" Wide asked as his pickup formed his image in her room. "Good morning. I have some questions regarding—"

She screamed!

Wide bounced off the floor and landed, quivering, sides dropping as he felt himself color and random manipulators began appearing around his body, making it impossible to carry on coherent thought. Fragments of ideas ran through his separating brains as he struggled to re-form himself. His brain, divided into mutually exclusive sections, attempted to identify the strange molecules his quivering thoughts produced at random. One memory noticed the similarity between the molecules and Spotted's fear.

She continued to stare at him with wide, shocked eyes, after jumping back into the shower. Her head protruded around the corner of the stall. Thankfully, she began to speak and her voice provided a centering point as he fought to put his disparate thoughts into order again.

"Do you *mind,* Mr. Wide? Granted you are an alien, *but it's bloody rude to intrude into a lady's bath!*" Dunbar's ringing English accent stirred still more strings of thought and Wide managed to shut the imagery off so his holo disappeared from her view.

Her body had turned a deeper shade of red as she stepped out, hurried across the room to pull a new uniform from the closet, and climbed into it. She pulled the blouse over her bust and tightened the fasteners. Then she checked herself in the mirror, muttering under her breath about "Bloody nosy aliens" before she picked up her headset and asked for his presence.

Wide tried to make sure he was all together before his image re-formed in her room. "Accept my apologies," he began. "I was totally aware of your privacy taboos. It was my fault."

She shook her head, spilling the loose hair over her shoulders, eyes flashing almost violet. "Very well, Mr. Wide, you are forgiven." Then she laughed, "As if I should be modest before a . . . creature with no interest in. . . . Never mind. How may I help you?"

Wide struggled to remember why he'd called. The fear molecule tied it all together and it came clear in his still muddled mind. "I, uh, oh, yes, you have built a file on counterattacks against this ship by the Pashti."

A strange glow—totally unfamiliar to him—suddenly shone in her eyes. "But of course. No doubt as we gain familiarity with defensive measures, we can integrate our observations with yours. Given the nature of our task we would like to know if our contingencies are compatible with your current defensive systems."

Current defensive systems? Incredible! They really believed the Pashti would attack an Ahimsa ship!"

"Major Dunbar, this ship is Ahimsa. Do you not understand? The Pashti wouldn't *dare* attack an Ahimsa ship!"

Sheila Dunbar walked easily to her dispenser and pulled a cup of tea. She turned, face pinched with an expression television had taught him other humans perceived to be relief. "Splendid! We can assume then that should the Pashti counterattack the station, your Ahimsa ship will be able to blast them out of space as they arrive! At the same time—"

"No! No! No!" Wide rocked back and forth, spicules wheezing. "Let me try again. This is an *Ahimsa* ship! Pashti do not attack Ahimsa."

Sheila frowned and cocked her head. "Why not, Mr. Wide?"

Wide's spicules began to sing as he relaxed his brains and thought. "Pashti don't attack Ahimsa just as Ahimsa don't attack Pashti. We are *civilized* . . .and Pashti are civilized. Ahimsa are nonviolent. For that reason alone, the Pashti wouldn't attack this ship. It would be illogical for one nonviolent species to attack another. Don't you see?"

Sheila Dunbar leaned against her wall and studied Wide as she sipped her tea. "Mr. Wide, correct me if I'm wrong, but aren't we, I mean humans, here to counter a Pashti threat to your Ahimsa?"

"Correct."

"Then have not the Pashti already acted against your people in one fashion or another?" She raised an eyebrow.

"Yes, but to attack an Ahimsa ship is—"

"Totally within the bounds of expectation, is it not? May I remind you, you canvased an entire world for the best military genius a military species had to offer. I dare say, Mr. Wide, you're quite competent at jamming our missiles, but were I Pashti, I would have your ship blown out of space within minutes of the launch of the torpedoes. That—Mr. Wide—is simple defensive strategy. Correct?"

"But nonviolent intelligent beings do not attack other intelligent beings!"

"And what is your role in the destruction of TaHaAk station and the Pashti there, Mr. Wide?"

"Ahimsa do not attack the Pashti station! No Ahimsa will be involved! It will be *humans* who attack the Pashti!"

"Extraordinary logic, Mr. Wide. I'm not sure the Pashti would agree. I would imagine they, too, have a philosophy of responsibility." She lifted a finger, eyes lighting. "Ah! Yes! Let's try this. If Pashti are civilized, they'd never attack an Ahimsa ship. Rather, their machines, rockets, explosives, and lasers actually do the attacking. That way no Pashti has killed an Ahimsa in self-defense. Logical, don't you think? And eminently . . . civilized."

Wide's thoughts began to disintegrate again, his sides going rubbery.

She lifted her hands, obviously seeing he was upset. In a different voice, she asked, "Can I strike a deal with you?"

Wide rocked back and forth, feeling that new and interesting fear molecule in his mind. "What deal?"

Sheila Dunbar took another drink of her tea. "It's my inclination to make a smashing success out this operation. Do you object to that?"

"Of course not."

"Then here's my deal. I won't take up dictating Ahimsa foreign policy—nor the flying of Ahimsa starships—if you'll let me apply my expertise to conducting warfare: both offensive and defensive. Fair enough?"

"You were chosen for exactly those qualities, Major Dunbar."

"Splendid," Sheila Dunbar gave him a wide smile. "Now, may I please have the requisite plans and specifications so I can competently go about planning the protection of this vessel in the event of a Pashti counterattack?"

Wide hesitated, awed by the feeling of fear. *What could this silly female do with* . . . "Yes. Yes. Your access is cleared. But I warn you, don't threaten me. Don't make me regret your presence."

Her face lost some of its color, a curious tension in the set of her mouth. "I'm well aware of our vulnerabilities—and the extent of your power."

"See that you don't forget."

He cut the monitor, aware that Spotted stared at him—a sagging puddle of flesh.

"Yes, Nav-Pilot? Why are you looking at me that way."

"You'd exterminate them if they crossed you?"

"Absolutely."

"They'll try, you know."

"They know what they risk."

* * *

Sheila's gut twisted like a wounded snake. She clutched the cup of tea with both hands, knowing she'd slop it over the rim if she let go. Using all of her willpower, she forced her expression to remain calm despite the fear-bright blood racing in her veins and the trembling in her muscles.

How did a human read an Ahimsa? How could she tell if she'd pushed him too close to the edge? For the first time, he'd overtly threatened her.

The beginnings of a plan had begun to form. The rudimentary idea had taken on flesh. Elements were still shaping up. She *had* to get more out of Wide. If he balked, the whole thing would collapse. So many ifs, and not all of them related to the Ahimsa.

"I must be mad, insane."

And I've got to keep pushing; get all I can out of him. She gulped at the hot tea, hardly noticing that it burned her mouth. *We have no privacy;, no peace. If we're to stay out of that fatal room I told Svetlana about, I've got to jimmy the door, give us an out.* She shivered at the thought. *Grandfather? Where are you now? This game is so very frightening. And there is no one but me to play for our side.*

She tossed off the last of the tea, crumpling the cup before she futilely smacked the wall with the heel of one fist.

* * *

Svetlana Detova moved through the Ahimsa files with growing skill as the new information appeared. She cross-filed, noting the new patterns, adding programming information to her "secure" files. One by one, she inspected the security clearances that passed through the newly unrestricted files.

She paused, rubbing thumb and forefinger over her tired eyes. She looked around, feeling stifled. The features of her room had become too familiar. Despite the airy appearance and the illusion of added dimensions created by the reflective wall, the place seemed more and more like a cell in the Lubyanka.

She nibbled at her lower lip. No cell in the Lubyanka had ever held so critical a prisoner. An idea of what Sheila Dunbar had in mind had begun to tease at the corners of Svetlana's mind. With the observation blister compromised, she could only guess—and trust blindly. Never in all her life had she been forced to trust. But then, so much had turned around.

She stared at the terminal screen, irritated by the glowing Ahimsa symbols. People like Sam Daniels were depending on her.

"He's an American," she reminded herself.

Vigorously, she shook her head, clearing the image away. Before her, the symbols mocked. On a hunch, she added a new sequence of commands and instantly regretted her rash approach. New information flooded the screen. A command menu. She recognized the logical sequence.

She stared for a moment before a slow smile crossed her lips.

"Maybe this time, Wide, I've got you by your little eyestalks," she whispered under her breath. Practically trembling, she traced her mnemonic in an artistic doodle that resembled the command menu tree. Using all she'd learned, Svetlana called up a restricted file. She smiled as the data flickered up on the screen.

* * *

Spotted struggled to keep his sides firm as Wide watched the message comm flickering. This time Hurt requested that Wide return his communication. Wide formed a manipulator and canceled the request.

Spotted piped quietly to himself. Why? How could the

Overone refuse to even answer a communications request from his peers?

Wide, are you insane? Nothing you do makes sense anymore. Worse, if you've gone mad, what will happen to me? I'll be cast loose. Tainted by your actions. It's the humans. It must be. They've done something to you, but what? How?

Spotted hissed through his spicules as he studied the monitors. Somewhere there had to be a clue. If not, what could he do? How could he, a simple Nav-Pilot escape from a mad Overone? It had never been done before.

* * *

"I think I'm making progress. I don't seem to have as much trouble writing programs, but I'm sure they're nothing a first year university student couldn't do."

Sheila nodded, aware of the tension in Svetlana's eyes, in the set of her shoulders. She sat across the table, rubbing her hands together. *What is it, Svetlana? You're normally cool as a November breeze.*

"Nevertheless, I've tapped new resources, things I didn't know I could do. But learning is always a journey, it leads you to challenges you never knew existed. And sometimes you find frightening things."

"I see." *Damn it, if only we could talk!* Sheila stood and paced the length of her room, aware of her reflection mocking her step by step. Why had Wide put that damn reflecting wall in the rooms? What did it hide? Monitoring equipment?

"If you can take a moment, I thought you'd like to see the notes I've made. Not much, really, but I wanted you to be aware that I didn't spend all my time locked away sleeping."

Sheila forced a fake smile and took the sheaf of papers from Svetlana's hands, scanning the notes. Nothing made sense.

Seeing the look on her face, Svetlana added, "Learning programming from an Ahimsa system has little resemblance to human systems. If a KGB analyst saw those, he'd think they were misdirection."

Sheila flashed a quick look at the Russian, catching the undertones. "I suppose he would. It's that different?"

"And that much harder than human systems. I may never make heads or tails of it, but I wanted you to know I'm trying."

Sheila swallowed against the tension in her throat. "I want you to know how much I appreciate your efforts. Even if it looks futile, keep trying."

Svetlana took the papers, placing them on the table again. "The training is going well?"

"We're making progress. For the moment, we're working on possible counterattacks."

Svetlana's expression eased a little. "Well, then I won't keep you from your work. I just wanted to check in."

"Thank you, Major." She watched Svetlana pick up her notes and walk to the door. "I do appreciate your dedication."

"Good day." Svetlana let herself out.

Sheila frowned, picking up her pen. Then she noticed the single sheet of paper Svetlana had left from the bottom of the pile.

She stood, walked to the dispenser for a fresh cup of tea and settled in Svetlana's chair, plucking a couple of sheets from her side of the table. In the process she snatched Svetlana's. One by one she worked through her notes, hoping Wide had lost interest—if he'd even been watching! Damn it, the tension never eased.

She fingered through, coming to the single sheet—apparently a group of random doodles. She studied the drawings for a bit and her heart chilled. The first consisted of a human eye, the second a cracked egg, and then a crosshatched flat thing with a tang. The next proved to be a highly stylized rendition of the word "subject" complete with spikes and scrolls followed by a colon. The last doodle consisted of a caricature of a man's face. He wore a peaked military hat with a swastika. The scowl and the mustache left no doubt as to who.

I cracked a file. Subject: Hitler.

CHAPTER XXI

Ted Mason gestured with his hands as he talked. Murphy watched him as they walked out of the mess. Ted looked like the same happy-go-lucky inquisitive sort he'd always been despite his depression over his wife Pam. Cruz seemed on the right track, too. But since talking with them, he'd had to deal with Slap Watson and Bill Kearney. *Yeah, and before long they're going to call me Grandma Murphy.* He winced at the thought.

Murphy glanced across at a dynamite-looking ash-blonde. She met his curious gaze with one of her own—and smiled. Invitation? Murphy hesitated for a brief instant, and shot an evaluative look at Mason and Malenkov. Nope. Duty first. He grinned an apology and shrugged, letting his gaze mix with hers for a moment. She nodded slightly, and lifted an eyebrow.

By the time Murphy got his heart slowed, he'd lost most of Mason's explanation but caught, ". . . I think we can work something out. The problem is that the torpedo measures four meters in cross section. The tank is only three. That turns into a lot of area we've got to seal. Not only is there a lot of area, the patch has to withstand maybe twenty pounds per square inch of atmospheric pressure."

"Thought atmospheric pressure was about fourteen pounds." Murphy added, taking one last glance over his shoulder at the blonde as they left the mess and started down the long orange hallway toward the bay where the tanks were stored.

Who was she? One of the KGB women as he recalled, but they'd all been so busy with training, exercises, PT, and computer studies, he hadn't seen her. Then, too, with all the Mother Hubbarding he'd been doing, there'd been no time for women. That cool green-eyed look haunted him as he followed along behind Malenkov and Mason.

"Yeah, for Earth." Mason corrected. "For safety we'd better be thinking in terms of twenty pounds per square inch, more if we can get it."

"And SkaTaAk is not Earth." Lieutenant Malenkov shook his head. "Nothing that looks like a Pashti could grow on Earth."

"You've never seen the New York sewer system," Murphy replied. "You'd be surprised what will grow down in that . . . Hey!"

They stopped short. Where the hall had once bent left and emptied into the tank bay, now it bent right. Murphy swallowed and looked back and forth at his companions.

Mason mumbled, "Uh, you guys see what I see?"

"The halls have changed." Malenkov nodded.

"Weird shit, man." Murphy walked over, pressing his hand to the firm wall that had once emptied into the tank bay.

"Well, let's see what's down this way." Malenkov stared down the new hall, stopping for a moment to inspect the unbroken floor and ceiling.

Murphy swallowed hard, thinking, *If they can switch walls around like this, it wouldn't take a hell of a lot for them to isolate us any way they wanted.* "Great, Murph, scare the hell out of yourself, why don't you?"

"Murph? You coming?" Ted called.

"Yeah." He stared back at the way they'd come, suddenly uneasy. "Yeah, I'm coming." *And I wish to hell I had my rifle.* The orange corridor extended another one hundred meters and opened out into a carbon copy of the old tank bay. Murphy practically ran over Mason, who'd stopped short.

"Wow."

Lines of tanks sat, squat and gleaming, in the light of the ceiling panels. The huge room bristled with vehicles of a different design. Murphy walked out, running his hand along the skirt of one of the vehicles. The armor consisted of that same lustrous translucent gray stuff, but the gun had been changed, moved forward and lowered, as if the entire nose of the tank became a turret. What had been one gun now looked like three in a triangular mount with curious sighting mechanisms all molded into the front of the vehicle.

"Tracks are farther back," Mason observed. "I think my patching problems just took a turn for the better."

Malenkov walked around, pointing at the sleek hull. "There's no hatch. The tread design on the tracks is all new, all different. This is a completely new vehicle."

"Sure as hell is," Mason added. "Like going from a Cessna to a Ferrari."

Murphy spun on his heel, looking around, searching the walls and ceiling. He dropped to his knee, placing an ear against the padded stuff of the floor—and heard nothing.

"What's wrong?" Malenkov asked.

"How come we never hear anything? No machinery making this stuff? No clangs or bangs or . . . I mean, look around you. Sheila changed the tactics a week ago. Last night we had the old tanks. In those couple of hours, all this appeared and all that disappeared. And we didn't even hear a sound. That's enough to spook the crap out of you."

"Huh?" Mason looked up from where he was inspecting the bottom of the tank.

"They completely remanufacture." Murphy didn't miss the entrance of the ash-blonde. She looked around, green eyes taking it all in, head slightly tilted to spill the tumble of her hair across one shoulder.

"You want to elaborate?" Mason reminded insistently, straightening and wiping his hands.

Murphy tore his eyes away from the blonde, acutely aware of her approach. He filled his lungs, trying to reorder his thoughts. "Look, we changed the game plan. I mean, think about it. The tanks the Ahimsa gave us were fine for a quick assault, right? The torpedoes penetrate the station, the tanks rip it apart and everybody loads up to go home. Now Major Dunbar wants us to be able to stop a counterattack. Ted, you're working on patching the holes if the torpedoes have to withdraw to fight off Pashti spacecraft. And just like that"—he snapped his fingers—"we've got new tanks designed specifically for that task."

The blonde spoke, her voice a sultry contralto. "Which means they have incredible manufacturing capabilities."

"That we never see." Malenkov waved his arm around. "The old tank bay is gone. A new one is here—practically overnight. They didn't modify the old tanks, they simply made new ones."

"Yeah." The problem absorbed Murphy so that he even ignored the green-eyed beauty. "You know, I wonder . . ."

"Spill it, pal." Mason slapped a nervous palm on the tank's side, the sound loud in the quiet room.

Murphy hesitated, chasing the idea around his mind. "I'm not sure there's anything to it—and I could be all wrong—but I think there's a difference in approach here. I mean, on a basic level."

Malenkov crossed his arms, frowning. "You mind being a little more specific?"

Murphy beetled his brows, trying to find the words. "Think about the way we manufacture. I mean, first you make a prototype, right? Work out the bugs, refine the design through several models. Then you mass produce the . . . well, let's say an automobile. When you go to the next model you don't scrap everything you've got and make an entirely new automobile. You keep things from the first design, use the same frame, the same axles, the same radiator and so on, only refining the design. When the evolution of the vehicle reaches a certain point, you build on everything you learned from the first model and make something new. But you can still see the similarities. A World War I Spad and a Boeing 747 have traits in common. You can see the ancestry."

"Katya? You've got that KGB look," Malenkov said nervously.

She turned to him. "Nicholai, it could be a psychological ploy, a way of keeping us subdued, in our places and appropriately awed by Ahimsa power."

"Or it's an example of different thought processes entirely." Murphy ran his fingertips across the smooth surface of the armor. The stuff almost felt like plastic. "Almost . . ."

"Yes?" Katya asked.

"Mechanical," Murphy whispered, frowning to himself. "I wonder. Like maybe the computers do it all. Computers think differently than we do."

"We're not Ahimsa," Nicholai pointed out.

"Yeah, but I think I'll mention it to Sheila." He gave the tank a sour look. "Like suppose Wide told his machines to make new tanks to fit the following criteria. A computer would sort through the options and simply pick the best for the job."

"Assuming unlimited manufacturing resources," Ted added, his own gaze slipping surreptitiously to stare at Katya.

"Or else there's a million Ahimsa workers hidden away in the rest of this ship." Murphy stamped on the floor. "I mean, think about it, this thing is over three hundred clicks long. We use up a square kilometer in personal quarters, weapons bay, simulator bay, tank bay and torpedo bay, firing range and the mess. The mock-up of TaHaAk takes up maybe thirty cubic kilometers. How many cubic kilometers of space are there inside this thing?"

Mason screwed his face up as he thought. "Uh, I'd guess somewhere around seven hundred and thirty thousand square kilometers from the dimension we've been told and the shape of the vessel, but that could be off by a couple of—"

"So we're taking no more than a gnat's whisker's worth of space in an empty refrigerator," Murphy added, slapping a fist into his hand.

Katya scuffed a toe on the floor, head down, arms crossed. "I would remind you that a gnat constitutes a minor threat to a refrigerator. That's an admonition to keep in mind."

Voices echoed down the corridor. Moshe Gabi stepped into the room, gaze lighting on the new tanks, a puzzled look on his face. Sheila walked beside him, her expression haggard, as if she'd been working and worrying too hard. Murphy caught himself making sly comparisons between her and Katya. Katya had the beauty contest, hands down.

"They're all Wide said they'd be." Moshe's face glowed as he walked up, placing his hand on the tank.

"They're totally different so far as we can see," Murphy added.

Sheila nodded. "I got one of the manuals last night, Leftenant."

Murphy lowered his voice. "You know, Mason and I were here around midnight last night. It's just after six hundred hours now. We were working on the old tanks. None of this was here. When we found it, well, we were talking about the differences in the way they make things. Like from the ground up instead of . . ."

She raised a hand, cutting him off, measuring him with her wary stare. Murphy suffered a distinct unease. *Damn it, she's changed—she's turned into a commander.* He realized he'd straightened under her inspection, chin going up, shoulders back.

Sheila nodded, as if to herself. "Yes, Leftenant. Curious, isn't it? They do things . . . well, rapidly."

"Yes, ma'am."

"If you wouldn't mind, could you write down your observations? I would appreciate the opportunity to review your thoughts on the matter." She glanced around. "I assume you've all talked about it?"

"Yes, ma'am."

One by one, she pinned them with steel-blue eyes. "You are excused from duty today. I'll inform your commanders. Please prepare your reports with as much detail as you can. Feel free to speculate—no matter how incredible it may seem." Her voice changed, the tone leaving no doubt as to her intent. "Beyond that, I'm sure you'll understand this is an amusement, a mental exercise. I'm sure you'll *forget it* as soon as you've put your reports together."

"We understand perfectly, Major," Katya responded professionally.

Murphy snapped a salute. "Permission to be excused, Major?"

She smiled slightly with a trace of warmth breaking through her weariness. "Excused, Leftenant."

Murphy swallowed hard, aware that Mason, Malenkov and Katya followed.

Mason noted caustically, "I thought you made it a policy never to salute an officer if there was any way around it."

Murphy scratched the back of his neck, frowning. "You know, I learned long ago that you don't trust lawyers, used-car salesmen, or commanding officers. But something about her . . ."

Malenkov laughed. "I know. But who was it that sat in the auditorium the first day and thought about seducing her?"

"No!" Mason's jaw dropped.

Murphy winced, shooting a sly glance at Katya. She watched him pensively. "You have ambitious tastes, Lieutenant. I congratulate you."

"Uh, we haven't really met. Call me Murphy."

"I know who you are."

"You do?"

"Of course she does, idiot American friend of mine. She's KGB." Malenkov said it neutrally, eyes on the corridor ahead of them.

"Katya Illych," she added, giving Malenkov a quick glance. "And I know all about you, too, Lieutenant Mason."

Seeing Mason's interest warming, Murphy cut him off, saying, "Hey, look, sorry to get you involved in all this report stuff."

"I'm sure I'll survive it." He could hear the challenge in her words.

"Yeah, well, let's see where it goes."

She nodded, a cunning smile on her lips. "Yes, let's."

"I guess my room is as good as any," Mason suggested.

Malenkov managed a surreptitious gesture to draw Murphy back. He didn't mind. Watching the sensual undulations of Katya's perfect bottom in the tight Ahimsa uniform had his hormones running headlong into each other with each beat of his heart. "I ain't dead."

"Murphy?"

"If something like that can walk in front of me and I don't react, I'm dead."

"Murphy!" Malenkov hissed. "About Katya, she's—"

"Hey, man! I *know* what I'm doing."

At that point she turned to look back, the lights shimmering gold and amber in the wealth of her hair. The promise in her green eyes curled the edges of his soul.

Murphy took longer steps, catching up with her. "So, how did a nice girl like you end up with a bunch of lunatics like us?"

She smiled at him, flashing white teeth.

Murphy barely heard Nicholai mutter "suicide" under his breath.

* * *

RashTak shivered as he studied the holo of the dirty, greasy Homosapiens clustered around a small fire in a forest clearing. No matter how improbable the Shitlit's story, he couldn't shake the foreboding feeling of impending disaster.

"Violet Curses on the cycles! They leave me half insane when I would normally shrug off anything this silly."

RashTak looked closely, rerunning parts of the Ahimsa recording. The southerners looked smaller, not as muscular as the big-headed ones. They had finer features and darker skin. Rashtak watched the record, the big black orbs of his major eyes expanding as the victors took the females of those they killed. Perhaps the Ahimsa were mistaken. Maybe these females were not intelligent. Crazy idea! He studied the differences, seeing the curves of breast and hips. The males—like Pashti—had spikes. He ran the holo until he could see a raider copulating with a captured female. Indeed! Just like Pashti!

RashTak trembled as his reproductive organs begin to throb. Bodily fluids surged, his internal temperature rising. A rhythmic pulsation of muscles extended his spike, tingles of the action running through his reproductive organs. The burning tendrils of excitement began to radiate through his brain.

He inhaled, opening his olfactory senses to search for those trace molecules. Yes, he could pick out the female scent. The cycles had arrived. The time had come. He let his sensitive feet touch the floor. The delicate song of the females could be felt through his sensorial hairs. Could he do it without losing his senses to the cycles? If only he could maintain control! He trembled, muscles spasming. No one had ever tried to maintain control before—no one had ever *had* to!

Using all the willpower at his disposal, RashTak cornered a female and jumped, pinning her in the corner. She chittered and clicked mindlessly as he positioned himself. There, just right! He jabbed and felt his spike sink home. Under him, the female wiggled, squealed, and thrummed her panic at the fiery sting that ripped her flesh.

RashTak experienced the ecstatic pain as his eggs passed through the tight sphincter. The sacs tore as they encountered the barbs of his spike, spilling the young into her body.

"Careful," he gritted to himself, keeping his main eyes on the holo across the room. "Don't lose yourself, RashTak! You are . . . First . . . Councillor! First . . . First . . ." He screamed and clicked his mandibles, body raging with the flood of released sexual molecules. Fever burned hot along his circulatory system.

"I am . . . First . . . First Councillor!" He glared at the holo image of the wretched looking Homosapiens. No matter that that very same filthy fragile looking creature might be coming to disrupt their lives—another generation of Pashti *had* to be born.

The last of the eggs passed, the pain diminishing as the ovipositor sphincter and spike contracted. The female continued to shift and quiver under him, jumping frantically as he withdrew his spike. She shot away as he slid off her.

"I am *First Councillor!*" RashTak thundered to the quiet room, feeling his mind wavering to the honey thoughts of the cycles. "Control! I *must* control!" He squeaked from the agony of effort—a paean to the combat raging in his soul and shivering body.

The female—a trickle of body fluid leaking down her back—cringed in the far corner. A second female extended a foot, the sensorial fibers inspecting the fluid. Together, they keened.

RashTak started across the room. He shrieked, tortured within, as he forced himself to stop. Foot by individual foot, he fought the battle to turn and face the holo. He advanced to study the scene frozen forever by Ahimsa monitors. A dead human sprawled spread-eagled on the ground, a gaping red wound in his chest. RashTak watched as a victor leaned over the body, reaching inside with one of its upper manipulators. The grasping digits closed on something inside, lifting out a red organ, raising it overhead, shrieking loudly. Others stood, mouths open as they whooped in some sort of approbation, shaking their stone-tipped weapons. The victor stepped over and squatted by the fire, using a sharp stone to slice at the organ in his hand. Red fluid dripped to color the Homosapiens' hand. He handed the strips of flesh to his fellows who squatted to join him. Together, they roasted the pieces, devouring them one by one.

In the background, one of the southern men had corralled a circle of the frightened, muscular northern females.

RashTak studied the second of the females in his room. The trauma she'd sensed in the impregnated one had already been forgotten. For the moment she sniffed curiously at a food dispenser.

Trembling, he moved, battling with himself. He crooned to her, drawing her close. She clicked and pawed at him, searching for food. He stroked her tenderly, a terrible sadness yawning within. "I know, little one. It's not your fault that you were born female. What a terrible fate nature has given you. You understand, don't you? Another generation of Pashti must be born. Little mother, you are the salvation of us all."

She uttered the soft noises of a worried female.

With his heightened senses, the tragedy of their situation struck him. Without impregnation, there would be no more Pashti and perhaps the females got the best of it after all. All the female young would survive, but only one male.

"It's not fair." RashTak turned to stare at the holo. Was that the Homosapiens' secret? They could reproduce without killing their females? Is that what Wide had found? Some sort of hope hidden locked away in Homo-sapiens' biology?

He froze, struck with revelation. I *am thinking rationally. In control.* RashTak savored the feeling. Never before had Pashti mated without falling heir to the madness of the cycles. Could he do it again?

"Forgive me, little one." He cornered the second female, keeping his eyes on the holo, centering on the unknown threat Wide was about to spring on his species. The female cried out as RashTak spiked her. A melancholy feeling spread through him as he impregnated the female, condemning her to the future. The pain wasn't as bad this time.

"And humans take females as booty, too," he whispered to himself and the heedless, frightened female. She trembled beneath him as the last egg slipped into her body.

RashTak's shivering body went limp, the female silent under his weight. "Perhaps Pashti and humans are not so different after all?" But that was absurd!

* * *

Murphy gasped as she trembled beneath him. Her legs locked tightly around his hips. Her pubis pressed into his as he tensed, breath exploding in a ragged cry. He lifted his head to watch her expression, the quivering of her eyes, the parted lips and sexual flush. His body went limp, Katya silent under his weight as they both lay panting. *Jesus Holy Mary, she was good! Every nerve in my body's fried and I think my skull collapsed.*

A freak thought burst through his mind. Did Pashti have this same rush?

Katya sighed and blinked, eyes pools of green as she reached up to run a fingertip down his chin. "My compliments, Murphy. There are very few men who could do what you just did."

"Takes two to tangle." Murphy gave her his lopsided grin. "You could be a pro."

"I am."

He rolled off and flopped on his back, sighing. She

laughed, throwing her wealth of ash-blonde hair over a shoulder. She trotted athletically to the shower stall as Murphy sat up and looked around the room. He pulled himself to his feet and followed her.

Bodies and water mingled.

Dressed, he accepted a cup of coffee from the dispenser and admired her long legs as she seated herself.

Murphy grinned and motioned at the room around them. "Be honest, does it bother you that that little fat puffball might be peeking in right when you hit high C?"

Katya raised an eyebrow in amusement. "Are all Americans so naive?" She leaned back, hair swinging. "Intelligence work has varied needs, Murphy. If I worried about who had bugged my room, I would never have fun. Spies are always watched. Our superiors must make sure we're not being compromised. Who are we talking to? Has CIA or MI6 doubled us? Could we be working as moles? And if the other side can identify us, they press their eyes against the other side of the goldfish bowl to watch."

"Sounds real crummy."

She shrugged. "It's the job. You might say, it comes with the territory, if I got the metaphor right. When I was working Vienna, we took turns. You see, we kept it, as you would say, in the family. I monitored the rest of my team, they monitored me. That made us a very good team. We knew each other's secrets and, if he said something in the heat of passion, it went straight into the recorder." She smiled wickedly. "No way for me to forget his unit maneuvers while I'm involved in others, eh?"

"Are all spies saucy dishes like you?"

"Depends. Am I Tartar perhaps?"

"Don't they have black hair and ride horses?"

She got to her feet and stretched, each movement catlike, lithe, and exciting. Murphy couldn't pull his gaze away. *Damn! I could get used to havinq her around. Women shouldn't oughta be that pretty. They screw up a man's mind.*

"You know, they make sculptures of women like you."

"Come, we will be late. Exercises are supposed to begin in five minutes." She slipped into a suit.

"What about breakfast?" Murphy cried.

She arched an eyebrow, posture teasing, chin lowered, "Did you not just have that? Are all Americans so decadent?"

Murphy worked his mouth as he gave her his most threatening glare. "C'mon. Let's go. More free-fall today. Every time the gravity drops, I want to puke anyway. Be easier on an empty stomach."

They passed the door and headed for the armory. Nicholai Malenkov waved and winked lasciviously. He and Mason were clipping thin golden wires on over their clothing. Space suits hadn't looked anything like what Murphy just knew a space suit had to look like. The Ahimsa models weren't white. They weren't bulky; and suited, he had no resemblance at all to Neil Armstrong stepping off *Eagle*'s ladder. Instead, the "space suit" consisted of a thin film of golden-colored net and the "helmet" consisted of a wire affair that extended up from a metallic choker and curved around the saggital suture from a power pack at the back of the neck. It generated some sort of energy field that held air in. A second pack that looked like sponge rested at the collar converting CO_2 to oxygen.

Katya drew her suit and joined the little group as Murphy began slipping the flexible netting over his Ahimsa clothes.

"Missed you at lights out last night," Mason greeted dryly.

Malenkov's eyes twinkled. "Forget it, Comrade American. Your friend was in the capable hands of the KGB. I can vouch for Comrade Katya, she is loyal Party member. She was no doubt pumping Murphy for everything he was worth last night."

Mason snorted with good humor. "Somebody was pumping somebody for sure."

Murphy bit his lip, shooting a quick glance at Katya. She appeared unaffected as she clipped her hair back, settling the "helmet" wire over her skull.

"Duty, Comrade Mason," Katya remarked casually, "comes in many forms. Should we live to return to our homes, Comrade Murphy will make an excellent addition to the intelligence forces of the Soviet world revolution."

"That true?" Mason demanded while Malenkov laughed. "You done sold out over a piece of tail?"

Katya parried, "Perhaps the 'piece' was enough, but I get the impression Comrade Murphy wanted all of the tail. He certainly used every bit of it."

"Some have it, some don't." Murphy added flippantly. "I'm doing my duty for East-West relations." He snugged Katya's arm into his and pulled her close, a satisfied grin on his face. "Oh, Lordy! The sacrifices the troops in the field make!"

"Indeed sacrifice! I'm ready to sacrifice myself to one of these CIA women who . . . Whoops." Malenkov's voice lowered, eyes going wary as Mika Gubanya entered the room—saw Murphy and Katya—and stopped. His mouth worked while his eyes glazed. His fists knotted at his sides, muscles bulging along his arms and chest. Turning on his heel, he almost ran two Israelis over as he stormed from the room.

Murphy felt his heart bump around in his chest. To cover it, he let himself slouch.

Nicholai groaned. "I think there will be trouble soon."

Mason saw the tension as he belted his Randall fighting knife around his lean hips. "Why? What's Gubanya's problem?"

Katya's voice had gone flat, professional, deadly. "I was seeing him before Murphy decided to initiate detente. Where Murphy is fun and exciting, Mika Gubanya is . . . preoccupied with his career and politics. Such things may no longer be reasonable when our lives all hang from the same thread."

Murphy ground his teeth loudly. "Besides, as I see it, Katya isn't his property." Then he winked at her and grinned. "Like Abraham Lincoln, I read Katya the Emancipation Proclamation."

"And I am liberating Murphy from Capitalist tyranny. Equitable, *nyet*?"

Sam Daniels' voice exploded from the doorway. "All right, people, let's move it! The universe isn't waiting for any of you slobs! Hustle your asses! Move!"

"Delightful man," Murphy noted. "Wish I'd fragged his ass years ago."

"He could be sergeant in Red Army," Malenkov agreed. "He has the same silver tongue, the same limited, how you say, perspective?"

Murphy trotted out the door, pulling one of the assault rifles from the rack on the way. As in all exercises where robot Pashti weren't involved, the guns carried laser blanks that marked hits or misses for the computer simulation. He slung a belt full of magazines over his shoulder and took off on Katya's heels.

The mission this time centered on finding ways to capture a Pashti jumpship, the fastest, most maneuverable of the Pashti vessel types.

Mason and Malenkov both managed to get themselves killed during the boarding exercise, Pashti having flanked their assault where Phil Cruz forgot to post a picket. As a result, they "bought" that night.

"I think we fight better with women in the ranks," Malenkov noted, belching loudly where he leaned on the table, hands cupping a can of Budweiser. He winked at a CIA torpedo pilot on the other side of the room. "Upon my return to Mother Russia after throwing the Capitalist Imperial yoke off the stars, I will order Stavka to attach a female battalion to every division. It will serve as the exact opposite of the penal battalion. Those who deserve reward will get to fight side by side with the women."

"Bullshit!" Murphy muttered. "What makes you think Pashti are Capitalist?"

Katya giggled as she leaned against Murphy. "If they are not, Comrade Murphy, *Tass* will make sure *Izvestia, Pravda* and *Bremia* correct that fact immediately. For what other reason are we fighting among the stars?"

Mason was twirling his Randall fighting knife between his fingers, the razor point failing to even mar the Ahimsa material that composed the surface. "I bet they don't even know we're here. I bet the letters to Pam aren't getting through, that it's a morale setup. It's like we disappeared into thin air back there. No announcements, folks. Washington and Moscow didn't tell anyone. I know them bastards." Mason raised his eyes. "Whatever happens out here, it's for keeps. Remember that."

"You about to go over the deep end again?" Murphy asked, twisting his mouth into a sour expression.

"Naw." Mason lifted the Randall, staring at the finely polished steel. "That first time, well, it was just the way it all sank in at once."

"Captain Sam'll keep our butts in one piece," Murphy muttered softly. "He's got our asses in and out of more than one mess."

"But the stars, Comrade?" Nicholai tilted his beer back and chugged it. "Viktor Staka kept us mostly alive in Afghanistan, too—but who are Afghans compared to Pashti? We will find out at TaHaAk."

Murphy slapped the table, grin lopsided. "Afghans, hell! Who got you into that mess, man? Jesus! You guys were dumber than manhole covers. Of all the people on Earth, first you don't pick on no Afghans! Man, them people fight for fun! Before you went in, every village had a local gunsmith copying SMLE rifles the friggin' British left behind when they got their butts kicked eighty years ago. Now you went and left them with AKs. And we sent 'em a bunch of Stinger missiles. How many helicopters did you guys lose there? What kind of shit's gonna come rolling out of them little village smithies now, for Christ's sake?"

"Maybe we ought to send them our asshole gun control lobby. Pay 'em back but royal for having the nerve to win the war." Mason grinned, a twinkle in his eyes.

Nicholai stood and pulled another Bud from the dispenser. "Don't worry. Having been there, I can tell you, it's not a national security problem. When Afghans don't have Soviets to kill, they kill each other."

"Yeah, fight for fun," Mason agreed. "That's why you don't pick on Afghans first—and Turks second. Loony bastards, all of 'em."

Katya ran her fingers down Murphy's arms while Mason turned to grab his pouch full of cassettes for music.

"Play Twisted Sister!" Nicholai demanded, belching again. "I want to hear the song about 'We Ain't Gonna Take It.' "

"Jesus!" Murphy groaned, shaking his head. "Thought you guys only listened to classical stuff and danced ballet.

Weird shit's going on here. We didn't need a trillion dollar budget to pervert the Soviet system. Send 'em punk rock and the whole USSR falls flat on its nose."

Nicholai waggled his finger. "Shostakovich and Tchaikovski came before Gorbachev. We're reformed now."

As the loud jangling music blasted from Mason's boom box, Nicholai torpedoed yet another can of beer. "No, Comrade Murphy, we only fall flat on our noses after a case or two of this decadent piss water beer." He uurrppped loudly and stood, gyrating with the music, shaking his fist in the air defiantly as they laughed.

No one saw Mika Gubanya where he watched, chewing his lip, eyes slitted as he fingered his knife.

* * *

Spotted kept one eyestalk swiveled behind him, carefully monitoring the stasis field that masked Wide's blurred body with its shimmering. The other eye watched the monitor as he accessed files with three of his manipulators. The whole process would have gone faster had he been able to use both of his eyes to scan the menus he searched.

HOMOSAPIENS—NEUROPHYSIOLOGY TDK-GM 6.086956522 GALACTIC

Spotted piped victory despite himself. Text formed along with illustrations. Spotted stared, scanning information. Humans, he knew, had two brains locked away in their heads—nothing to really excite an Ahimsa with rabid curiosity, outside of a mild pity that humans couldn't integrate the whole, or, conversely, divide their brains further.

Perusing the file didn't offer much in the way of enlightenment. Spotted studied the structure down through neurons to the molecular transmitters and receptors. The chemical basis for emotion as channeled through the hypothalamus, to the cingulate gyrus, to the hippocampus, then through the midbrain reticular formation and subsequent autonomic results occupied him for a moment. Perhaps human insanity and emotion could be controlled? Perhaps their preoccupation with death could be ameliorated?

Spotted formed a manipulator to cancel the file and caught the notation for the methodology. He flattened slightly, anxious at the reaction should Wide drop the stasis and question him about his activities. With furtive manipulators, Spotted accessed the file.

The image formed, the actual record of Wide's dissection of a demobilized human. The specimen consisted of a living young male disrobed of his animal skins and sterilized of all bacterial, viral, and fungal parasites. Delicate machinery moved around the specimen, removing hair, scalp and skull to expose the brain. Wide moved close, peering at the organ as he dictated to the recorder and the monitor reflected the accumulation of data. Imaging holography represented the brain morphology as probes activated various parts, tracing the neural pathways.

The specimen twitched as individual motor circuits were mapped. Fuzzy images appeared on the monitor—fragments of memories. The dissection machinery blocked blood flow and removed each section of the brain as it completed mapping. From the previous tape, Spotted recognized the emotional centers. The probe touched the hypothalamus and the subject reacted violently enough to rupture the delicate tissue on the probe. The sequence jumped to another specimen, a young woman dissected to the same degree. A windowed inset noted that the spinal column had been severed to avoid physical reaction by the specimen. Wide continued to narrate as he inspected the hypothalamus. The probe moved around, while another of the monitors displayed the specimen's reaction.

"This structure," Wide was saying, "appears to be the root of emotional response in most terrestrial species. By triggering chemo-electric activity, a variety of emotional responses can be initiated."

Perhaps if the hypothalamus could be removed, humans could be made sane. The idea would bear closer inspection in the future.

Spotted stopped short, watching Wide roll closer to the specimen, staring as the probe moved.

"The possibility cannot be discounted that such behaviors could be bred out of the species," Wide said.

The probe stimulated the organ which caused a series of displays to flash through various emotional states. "I have studied the molecular transmitters which such stimulation produces, having found them very similar to molecules in the Ahimsa nervous system.

A footnote indicated another file. Spotted immediately accessed. Wide studied a human brain which lay on a support before him, saying, "I will now secrete what I believe will act as a neural inhibitor."

A manipulator formed, a clear drop of fluid on the end.

"No!" Spotted piped in horror as Wide reached for the exposed human tissue. "No, Overone, not with your . . ."

Wide touched the tissue, one eyestalk swerving to the monitor. "Now, the previous series of stimulations will be rerun to show . . ."

Spotted lost the rest, both of his eyestalks glued to the monitor. "How could you do that, Overone? How could you risk contamination with human brain chemicals? How? How? How?"

Perspective changed as Spotted began to deflate, fear running brightly through his body. He canceled the program, staring at the blank monitor.

A single thought continued to loop through his segmenting minds. *I have shared thought molecules with Wide! Am I infected with human insanity, too?*

CHAPTER XXII

Lin Xiao stamped his feet and lifted numb hands to his lips, blowing softly to warm his fingers. The biting cold ate into the flesh, leaving an ache in fingers and a throbbing in the feet. Snow crunched loudly underfoot. No more than twenty meters from his forward observation post, the Heilong Jiang—the river the Russians called the Amur—flowed slowly, holes of black water visible through the snow-covered ice.

Xiao had seen tanks moving at dusk the night before and had reported to his superiors. Who but a foolish Russian would move in weather like this? He stamped his feet again, remembering the mists on the Xi far to the south where he'd grown up. Now, as dawn's light grayed, he lifted his frosty binoculars to peer across at the Soviet side. Something different there, but he couldn't tell what. It looked like a huge tent had been set up in the night.

"May the souls of their ancestors freeze in darkness." He puffed foggy breath. "Like me."

A half kilometer behind him, his camp would be waking, hot food steaming on the tables. Talk would be subdued the way it always was now. The Americans had taken Khabarovsk and dug into Vladivostok despite furious Soviet bombings. Only three days ago, Xiao had watched Soviet and American aircraft tangle high overhead, bits of wreckage and machine gun brass raining from the sky.

Behind his forward observation post, the tanks waited, camouflaged, their crews huddled around charcoal fires. The infantry dug in farther back. The generals in Beijing worried that the Russians might attempt to cross the Heilong Jiang. If they did, Soviet armor could race from

Hegang to Jixi, launching a lightning flanking attack on Vladivostok.

Xiao shook his head. "They been staring at the moon too long. No Russian is that stupid. Cross the river, and China is in the war. Not even the Russians are that stupid."

A low roar grew out of the north and he looked up, squinting at the thick clouds. The thunder couldn't be mistaken: jets. American or Soviet? They knew where the border was. Only they didn't stop. They flew on over.

"Somebody's going to get it." Lin shook his head and beat his snow-frosted arms against his heavy coat. While he fought to keep from freezing to death, his mother and father would be walking out to tend the rice, wading through the warm water, black mud squeezing up between their toes.

Muffled thuds sounded from behind him—the sound explosives made when they hit the ground. Knowing he couldn't see anything, he turned, bending to gawk back at the leafless skeletons of the trees. Nothing, only grayness.

When he looked back at the river, something stirred. He lifted the glasses, seeing the tent thing on the Soviet side moving forward. On the still air, he could hear diesels.

As his heart started to accelerate, he picked up his radio, snapping the switch on. The light remained dead. Pulling off his glove, he blew to warm his fingers again and used a thumbnail to pry the back off. Frost coated the batteries. Artillery *kumphed!* in the distance, shells shrieking in the chilled air.

He glanced up, seeing the tent thing fold out, camouflaging dropping away as motors roared louder. "Pontoon bridge."

Desperately, he cleaned the contacts, snapping the batteries back in place. The light flickered as he powered up his radio. "Lookout point twenty-seven reporting. There is activity on the other side of the—"

The bullet caught him in the shoulder, making a smacking sound like he'd been slapped. The ground seemed to spin, rising to meet him, the whole world turning. He barely felt the impact. Gasping, he blinked at the snow, feeling it against the side of his face. His entire left side had gone numb, the feeling like a bad wasp sting.

He fell back when he tried to sit up, and stared at the red stain growing under his chest.

"What? What?" He lay paralyzed, hearing the roar of the motors, the snapping of brush. Voices sounded. He tried to move again, cold eating into him, his strength gone. Through blurry vision, he made out the two soldiers who stepped up and kicked his forgotten SKS away. He cried out as one of the Russians centered rifle sights on his forehead.

Ustinov's desperate flanking maneuver to retake Vladivostok had begun. China had entered the war.

* * *

"Come in, Viktor." She looked up as he entered, noting the curiosity in his eyes. A flicker of excitement expressed itself in the smile that warmed her lips. She stood, aware of the sense of anticipation he aroused in her.

"Did you ask for batteries?" Staka asked.

"I did. I take it Wide delivered?"

Viktor rubbed the back of his neck, looking at her uncertainly. "A room appeared. Just a little alcove off the armory. It was full of batteries."

"Magic." Sheila asserted. "Cup of tea?"

"No, thank you. About the batteries, would you like to "

"Later, Viktor."

He studied her for a moment, the trace of a crafty smile on his lips. "You looked like you were busy. I won't take your time."

"Sit, please." She massaged the back of her neck. "I'm about half mad. It seems like there's never any time lately. I spend hour after hour in here running one plan after another. As soon as I devise a battle plan, I go through a dry run on holographic simulation. When I refine that, I call you for a planning session. We work out more bugs and I send you on your way. The next day we run a simulation with the troops. It just goes on and on."

"You look like you haven't slept well."

She smiled at that, noting his concern. "Is it that apparent."

He nodded. "It is. I hate to see you look that miserable. Can I help?"

"You already are." Did that sound awkward? "I'm bloody well ready to just hear a human voice. God, what I'd give to be able to sit in my flat and scratch my cat's ears. Poor Tips, I wonder how he's doing."

"You have a nice place?"

"It's not Buckingham Palace. Just a three room flat. I suppose the nicest part of it is the window. I set a table up there so I could sit and drink my tea while I watched the sun come up over the park. Tips would curl up in my lap and try to get cat fur all over my uniform. Periodically he'd actually manage to snag the fabric with a claw and do terminal damage."

"And your friends? Did you go out much?"

She smiled at the thought of it. "No, Viktor. Somehow I never seemed to have the time."

He pursed his lips, frowning. "I'm surprised. You're an attractive woman. I would have thought you'd be surrounded by interested men, laughing women who went to the theater, that sort of thing."

She puffed her cheeks out as she exhaled. "I think I was too dangerous for that sort of thing. Especially for the men. Holding a sensitive position in MI6 isn't conducive to an active social life, either. How about yourself?"

He glanced away, a humorless smile on his lips. "I don't know how to answer you. Since I left home I've lived in barracks. Compared to someone from the West, I suppose I'd be classified as a social cripple."

Her voice went wistful. "You don't need to be in the Red Army to be like that. It happens everywhere—a by-product of the world we've built. I just wonder why. I'd like to blame it on the politicians, but being here, so far away, you see that it's each and every one of us. The more I look back—having the perspective of being here, on an alien's starship—I wonder just how right the Ahimsa are. We *are* crazy, Viktor."

He crossed his arm, chin on his chest. "Are we? Really? Or is that just the way the entire universe works? Universality?"

She searched for the answer. "I don't know. Maybe it's the baseline assumptions—the myths we just naturally absorb as being fundamentally true."

He gestured to the papers spread around. "More tactical permutations?"

"Pashti information. Know your enemy. These cycles," Sheila picked up the notes, grateful for his understanding, "come upon the Pashti the equivalent of every seven hundred and sixty years. Their planet is in a highly elliptical orbit about their primary, SkaHa, an F-type star high in iron and calcium. At perihelion, their planet, SkaTaAk, becomes a hot nasty place. The Pashti used to migrate to the polar caps of their world. In fact, all their lives, they moved, herding their females from the poles at perihelion to the equator after aphelion when the planet almost froze. That effect was cushioned by the tectonic activity tidal effects initiated at perihelion. Crustal movements, vulcanism, and atmospheric effects ameliorated the climate until well past aphelion."

Viktor laced his fingers together, watching as his headset holo portrayed a working model of the system. "How did civilization arise among wandering peoples?"

"Well, that seems to be the problem. The Pashti were able to leave enough information stored so that after the cycles the few dominant males and their subordinates who survived could put it all back together; but they could never maintain enough population to survive the killing cold at aphelion or the blistering drought at perihelion to exploit the resources which would let them modify their environment. That's when the Ahimsa took pity on them and gave them a leg-up to space."

Viktor nodded, considering the data. "And why are these cycles so important?"

Sheila cocked her head as she pulled another cup of

tea from the dispenser. "It seems they go quite daft. It's a biological thing—internally timed, actually. Every seven hundred and sixty years, the dominant males begin stockpiling food, females, and subordinates. They become territorial, based on how much they can control. Unlike a human response—which would be violent—they can only control through their ability to provide."

"Say that again?" Viktor leaned forward, propping his chin on his hands.

She settled herself on the bench and cradled her teacup. "It's an alien idea. To us it won't make much sense, but the leader who stockpiles the largest supply of food and the biggest herd of females will have the largest number of followers—that is, subordinate males, the ones not strong enough to compete on their own. It actually makes excellent sense from the standpoint of their ecology. Too many stock-stockpilers would lead to everyone starving. The weak, by swearing fealty, drain only the stockpiles of their particular masters—not the carrying capacity of the species as a whole."

"And the leaders who can keep their liveries alive are the ones who inherit their world every time they pass the sun?" Viktor shook his head. "It's madness!"

"Perfectly—when you look at it from our perspective. It becomes utter lunacy as the supplies run out—subordinates abandon masters and begin running about frantically trying to find acceptance among successful masters who are surviving."

"They don't riot?"

"Indeed not." Sheila sipped her tea. "That was the characteristic which the Ahimsa thought so bloody admirable. They couldn't bear the thought of the poor Pashti grinding themselves so nobly to bits each time their planet reached perihelion."

"How about the females? Being smaller, they must not eat as much." Viktor asked for, and received, a glass of cognac from the dispenser.

Sheila's face went grim and she dropped her eyes. "They don't eat at all. Every female is bred by the dominant males who own them. Oh, to be sure, they're not intelligent—that is, they don't think and participate in the society. When the male impregnates them, for all purposes they cease to be a factor. They cease to eat. The young, being parasitic, are like larvae and are hatched by the ovipositor as they are injected into the female. As they grow, they eat the mother, ingesting her flesh and integrating her genetic material. She dies and they clean out the inside of the carcass, eventually breaking through to the world. The interesting thing is that the only active aggression in the Pashti lifetime occurs inside the mother's body. The males won't touch a female—they all survive; but the males battle among themselves, eating their rivals until only one is left. He is the one who chews his way out of his mother's body."

"Delightful creatures! They sound like the Politburo."

She laughed with him. Their eyes met. The steel wall dropped for a moment and she could see his soul. Forcing her eyes away, she settled herself in the chair, wondering about the uneasy silence.

"If they're so harmless in effect, why do the Ahimsa want us to destroy them?" Staka shook his head, swirling the cognac as he thought.

"It would seem that the very craziness of the cycles is working against the Ahimsa. Remember, Pashti stockpile goods and grab all the economic control they can lay their pincers on. Each time the cycles come, the Pashti take control of something new. Not overt aggression mind you, they are—you might say—the ultimate Capitalists; and they never give it back. Never really seem to remember taking it actually."

"Wouldn't it make sense for the Ahimsa to demand it back? Surely the Pashti would turn it over."

She frowned and gestured. "That isn't cricket among Ahimsa. Viktor, we've got to keep in mind that we're dealing with *alien* thought processes here. They *think* differently than we do—have different underlying assumptions about the nature of reality: Their own mythology of fundamental truths that seem just as crazy from the perspective of an outsider. Of course we'd demand the property back. But remember what the Pashti—and the

Ahimsa—think about our preoccupation with violence to achieve our ends. If you abstract yourself from the system, rise above the reality of our distinctly human culture, the idea of killing each other to achieve an end isn't any crazier than the fact that Pashti stockpile, or Ahimsa don't ask for things."

"Except Wide."

"Except for Wide. Naturally, we'd demand our property back first thing, with the troops counting ammunition as they loaded in the transports. The Ahimsa Overones would never allow themselves to breach etiquette in such a disgustingly rude manner. It would be unthinkable. They'd rather forget the entire incident than embarrass the Pashti or demonstrate their own possessive nature. According to them, it simply isn't done. Uncivilized. Barbaric."

"Yet we are here."

"Indeed, we are." She shook her head. "I don't know why we're surprised. Look at all the intricate logic our own governments go through to support the current situational ethics. The Falklands war took Britain to the height of hypocrisy. The Americans support Mobutu in Zaire. Who overthrew the democratically oriented Dr. Mossadegh to install the Shah? The Americans at least got to sleep in their Iranian bed—and found it full of nails. Soviets supported the Chinese, and what happened? Brotherhood of man, Viktor? Should I mention the MPLA in Angola? The invasion of Afghanistan stands out, for one, but think of the hypocrisy your own government perpetrates on the people. The dictatorship of the Proletariat becomes a nasty pun, doesn't it?"

"So we shouldn't fling too much manure on the Ahimsa."

"I wouldn't."

They were silent for several seconds. She studied her notes, acutely aware of Viktor's scrutiny. He said softly, "We may have a problem."

"Which one," Sheila asked dryly, delicate fingers turning her cup of tea. His body reeked—almost insolently—of maleness as he reclined in the chair. His mind was a match for her own, challenging, refreshing. How would he react to losing a game of chess?

His lips twitched. "It may be a problem resulting from fraternization."

"Oh?" She lifted an eyebrow.

Viktor shrugged slightly, showing his irritation. "There is an American, one of Daniels' lieutenants. Murphy is his name."

"I know him. I think he's got more potential than he ever realized. Go on."

"Among my officers is one Mika Gubanya. Between them is one Katya Illych. Several of Riva's women noticed the problem. It appears that Katya, a rather physical young woman, has been sleeping with Gubanya. Mika and Murphy had rubbed each other the wrong way before, but never to the point of striking sparks. Now Katya is sleeping with Murphy and making no uncertain terms of her preference."

Sheila closed her eyes and nodded, feeling worry build. Yes, it had to have happened sometime.

Viktor continued, "Our problem is that Sam's lieutenants and my lieutenants are all directly or indirectly involved. When it comes to a boil, it will split command efficiency right down the middle. Politics will become an issue; personalities will become an issue; names will be called; threats issued—and two groups of very proud, very talented men will find a very efficient outlet for their passions."

Sheila's mind began to turn the problem around, picking at the dilemma. "It seems that Pashti are not the only ones fouled up by biology."

"No. Sex is a problem for all of us."

She caught the undercurrent. Had he meant to say that much? She tapped her cup with a nervous finger, noticing that this time, he was the one who looked away, a faint flush visible along his neckline. *Is that the deep vulnerability he hides so well? What happened to him? Something in his childhood? Something in Afghanistan?*

She made her decision. "Viktor, Lieutenant Gubanya's behavior is your responsibility. Murphy is Daniels'. At the same time—as in any military organization—Riva is responsible for Katya. It can be no other way. You've already had Kuzentsov cleaning torpedoes and carrying trays back in the mess for taking a swing at Gubanya."

She took a deep breath, seeing his amused smile. He thought she would leave it at that—pass the buck. Hardly! "Viktor, we're dealing with adult men and women. They are all professionals. I expect discretion and I expect them to keep their private affairs private. Make it clear to Gubanya, Murphy, and Illych that any, and I mean *any* disturbance which affects the functioning of this command will result in immediate court-martial. The penalty upon conviction will be death to all parties concerned."

"All parties?" He straightened, blue eyes animated with interest.

She nodded, feeling the challenge, refusing to back down. "I insist on discipline, Viktor. Too much is at stake. No matter what physical drives our people have, I will not endanger this command—for anyone."

He chuckled softly to himself. "You don't look like the nervous woman I remember from White Base."

"No, I suppose not. Responsibility does that, changes a person. And there's so much at stake. I can't fail." She ran her fingers through her hair, looking at him. "If I do, I've failed everyone . . . everything."

He smiled at her then, with warmth and understanding. "And you can't share the responsibility?"

She shook her head, eyes rising suggestively to the ceiling. "My English still translates into Russian. No, Viktor, this is on my shoulders. I know how Atlas felt—how all the heroes suffered. Unlike them, I'm not heroic, only a lonely frightened woman. In the legends, the heroes never question, are never burdened by their own insecurities. Gilgamesh just goes out and saves the world.

"But Sheila Dunbar? All I have to do is make one little mistake, a slight miscalculation, and we'll lose everything. Do you know how that eats at me? The safety of every man, woman, and child on Earth lies in my hands. People I'll never know. A young boy in India, a little girl in Argentina. A whole bloody damn planet—my planet—could die if I err. God, I can't sleep. My stomach burns. I feel like I'm a thousand years old." She closed her eyes, the admission ringing in her ears as she wavered on her feet.

He stepped close, as if by impulse, and hugged her. For a second she tensed, then she pushed back, staring up into his blue eyes.

He said gently, "Just relax. Only for a minute. Trust me."

She did, feeling the warmth of his body, the reassurance of his arms around her. She closed her eyes, thoughts fragmenting and drifting as her breathing settled. "Why does this feel so good?"

"Because you know you're not alone."

"How do you . . . I mean, of all people, Viktor, you seem so invincible, so . . ."

"Terrible?"

"I didn't use that word."

He took a deep breath, hugging her once more before pushing her back, staring into her eyes, the steel veil wavering. She added, "Tell me, Viktor."

"Maybe just now, when you were telling me how you felt . . . well, I know that feeling. I've lived with it." A trace of red crept up around his neck, flushing his cheeks. "I . . ."

"Go on. I'll keep your secret."

He shrugged, turning away. "In Afghanistan . . . Damn it, there were times when I wished I could have held someone. Just felt the presence of another caring human body."

"But a cold calculating SPETSNAZ major can't be that vulnerable? That human?"

"Ours isn't a very human system." He waved it away. "Forget it happened, Sheila. Chalk it up to a moment of lunacy."

She stepped closer, putting a hand on his shoulder, feeling him tremble at her touch. "I won't forget. We're a curious bunch of creatures, we humans. A simple touch can be as great a gift as diamonds or gold." She smiled up at his embarrassment. "Thank you. I don't feel so alone anymore."

His smile died on his lips, as he battled with panic. "I'd better be leaving."

"Please. Stay. Just talk to me." She noted his hesitation, and spread her hands. "Perhaps it's your turn to trust me?"

His lips compressed as he frowned, then nodded. "All right. But I'm not sure it's a good idea."

On a hunch, she asked, "Why? Because I scare you?"

He nodded. "And you confuse me."

"Then we're even. You confuse me, fascinate me, in fact. I catch myself wondering who you really are. Are you the cold-blooded, deadly SPETSNAZ commander, or the fragile, caring man who could hold me with such self-assurance?"

He stepped nervously to the dispenser, the muscles in his arms bunching as he rubbed his hands together. "Neither, I suppose."

"Why do I scare you?"

He turned, a sadness in his eyes. "Because I catch myself thinking about you. And when that happens, I don't know what to do with myself. I don't know what it is. You're an attractive woman, a woman worthy of respect and I haven't been around women much in the last ten years. That leaves me suspecting my own motives." He caught her shocked look and added hastily. "I shouldn't have said anything."

"No, I asked you to. The problem with honesty is that it opens you to all sorts of vulnerabilities. I just, well, I'm not that familiar with . . ." She felt her skin heating. "I'm afraid it's my turn to blush. You see, my relationships with men aren't the sort of thing romance novelists write about. They've been rather abysmal failures if I were to be downright honest." She took a deep breath. "There, we have secrets to share."

He rubbed the back of his neck. "I've never talked about things like this. It's unsettling. What do we do now? I mean, everything's changed. I don't . . . I mean, you're not just another . . ."

She paced to burn off some of the adrenaline that insecurity pumped into her system. Turning on her heel, she cocked her head. "You know, I think we've just become friends." She laughed. "Not only that, but I think it would be difficult to go back."

He leaned his head back, staring at the ceiling "And what comes next?"

She shook her head, seeing his worry return. "Tomorrow, Viktor. And then the day after that. I don't know what that panic is in your eyes, but I don't want any more from you than just your trust."

He swallowed hard, unsure what to do with his nervous hands. "I just. Well . . ." He wheeled around. "I don't think I could be more than that even if things . . ."

She seated herself. "I didn't ask that, did I?"

"Well, Western women, they have this reputation for . . . I've seen the magazines, the movies. It seems like a man meets a woman and they're in bed together."

She thought about it. "I suppose it would seem that way. Just come and talk to me, Viktor. I want nothing more than to share your time—and maybe to be held when it all seems to be falling apart and my fears take over."

"I think I can uphold my end." He gave her a genuine smile.

She stared into her tea. "I'd probably be a rotten lover anyway."

He sat down, tension draining out of his shoulders. "Me, too. I have my own ghosts. Things that creep out of my mind. Things I keep hidden and strangled most of the time. I don't think I'd be very good to live around."

"Do you want to tell me? Perhaps I can help." *Look who's talking? I must be out of my mind!*

"Can you find me a new mind? A new set of memories?"

"Bastard!"

He stiffened.

She waved it away. "Not you. Sorry, I was thinking about something Daniels said about Brezhnev, about the people who have to live with the guilt. He was the bastard—just like all the filthy politicians who send decent human beings into places like Afghanistan—or perhaps, TaHaAk. Do you think Brezhnev ever lost a night's sleep over Czechoslovakia? Vietnam? Afghanistan? Do you ever see politicians with missing arms or flashbacks?"

"Guilt." He closed his eyes. "Do you know how many times I've wondered? Sought some sort of reason for the things . . ." He shook his head as if to rid his mind of the memories. He blinked, staring into her eyes, as if to see into her soul. "And what about the Pashti? What if they're innocent, too? Do I want another black mark on my soul? Will I spend the rest of my life reliving TaHaAk like I do Ghazni . . . and Baraki? Sometimes I wonder if I'm nothing more than the Devil's tool. A creature like a demon sent to make others suffer and die."

"One day at a time." She propped her elbow and studied the light panel ceiling. "If only I could prop the door . . ."

"What?"

"Oh, lost in my head. Thinking."

"Mika thinks I'm falling apart. He thinks I've lost my nerve."

"Have you?"

He raised his eyebrows as he stared at his reflection. "Only around you."

"When you let that steel curtain down."

"Yes. A curious analogy, don't you think? Is that what we've done to ourselves? Each of us as our own Iron Curtain locked away inside to keep us strong."

"Viktor, what about when we take TaHaAk?"

"You mean can I do it? Can I kill the Pashti?" He leaned his head back, staring at the light panel with weary eyes. "Yes. I can kill them if that's my duty. In the meantime, I'm not going to think about it. That's what makes a good soldier, you see. It's not the discipline or the drills. It's the ability to do what has to be done, no matter how it tortures you and tears your soul. A soldier just has to live with it afterward—because that's the way it is."

* * *

Sees formed in the monitor, hide stretched to indicate his displeasure. "My Nav-Pilot interrupted a detailed analysis of the reality of mathematics at your insistence. I hope this has merit."

Hurt thinned, uttering a bristling piping at Sees' attitude. "I assure you, I'm no fonder of this irregular affair than you are. At the same time, I have information which I believe it's necessary to share. I cannot see any advantage to maintaining a single perspective on a matter which may involve us all."

"Very well," Sees relented, flattening as a bit of color returned to his tread foot. "What has come to your attention?"

"I think Wide may indeed be worth some concern. He has, for all intents and purposes, disappeared. I have attempted to locate his vessel, searching the Homosapiens' system by means of our gravitational buoys in high solar orbit there. No indications of his vessel could be discerned."

"Hardly worthy of disturbing meditation."

"Perhaps, but I also ran a history on Wide's activities. Did you know that he hasn't met face to face with an Ahimsa but once within the last galactic revolution? With one exception, he hasn't shared molecules with anyone during that time."

Sees' sides began to quiver. "That's not significant in itself. You say he did share with another Overone?"

"I did. Wide met with Tan prior to this last research expedition."

Sees lost the battle with his sides and his tread foot turned a shade darker. "Tan? That's still nothing conclusive. I suppose you've tried to contact him?"

"Tan, as usual, refuses to answer. His Nav-Pilot, however, did respond and confirms that Wide had met with the Overone and spent some time in discussion. The Nav-Pilot has no idea what they discussed. When I asked about any Shitht involvement, he said he knew nothing about Chee'ee'la, or any other Shitht for that matter, that Tan hadn't mentioned a Shitht in thousandths."

"Anything else?"

"The Nav-Pilot is relatively sure Wide and Tan exchanged molecular information."

"Tan." Sees sagged slightly, eyestalks rising as his tread foot crinkled.

"You know his history."

"Red served as Nav-Pilot when Tan first came to this galaxy. And now Wide—who perhaps we should be concerned about—has met with Tan? And has exchanged molecular information? Tan hasn't exchanged molecular information in . . . how long?"

"Two galactic years? Maybe more? Four quarters ago, Low and some others tried to get him to exchange, to share the mind whole. Tan refused rather succinctly."

"Is there a chance Tan might be doing something? Perhaps teaching Wide? Sharing some mind reality?"

"I don't know," Hurt admitted. "Had it been anyone else who Wide had seen, I simply wouldn't bother with it."

"Tan." Sees, sagged a little more. "I would hate to anger him."

"I would enjoy dropping this, but as you can see, something curious is developing out of it all."

"Red was Tan's Nav-Pilot. That fact sticks in my mind."

"And Red went insane."

* * *

RashTak growled and thrummed to himself, studying the Council reports, scanning screen after screen of information. He accessed his fellow Councillor, HakBar, seeing the features of a subordinate male form on the monitor.

"This system is closed. Second Councillor HakBar refuses supplicants. Our resources are closed!" The subordinate rose to his full height, major eyes deepening in refusal.

RashTak clicked in shock for a second before it hit him. "Quit that! I am RashTak, First Councillor for TaHaAk. Get HakBar. Now! This is a matter of the utmost urgency. I need information on—"

"Our resources are closed!" the subordinate insisted. "Go elsewhere!" The monitor went dead.

RashTak thrummed nervously to himself. He tried the manufacturing world of TalEek!Ak and felt no surprise when the system remained silent.

"Violet Curses on the cycles!" RashTak slapped his resonators on the floor, weaving back and forth on his feet as he glared at the screen with his major eyes. "Homosapiens might be loose among the stars and they pick now to barricade themselves away?"

But at least the systems he'd tapped hadn't had any

information on Wide or his filthy beasties prior to shutdown.

"But what does it all mean?" RashTak darted to the food dispenser on nervous feet, slapping a pincer to the Bak!Gil button. Nothing. He punched the button again and again.

"Violet Curses! Now what?" The main door opened as he approached to expose a packed hallway. Subordinate males, some bearing packages—actually gifts with which to curry favor—jammed the wide corridor, spilling in the door as it groaned under their weight. They poured forward in a mass of clicking, whining bodies. A cardamom odor of supplication rolled over him like an intoxicating wave.

RashTak wavered, his olfactory glands responding to the plea. He rose to his full height, the subordinate males keening their need, singing their flattery for his greatness.

For a second he capitulated, the power of their call growing, blocking his brain, erasing the memory of his purpose for leaving the room in such an insane manner. One of his lesser eyes happened to catch sight of the holo of Homosapiens ripping the red organ from the dead body of his vanquished fellow. He'd left that image dominating one wall. Now, it recalled him from the edge of the abyss. Biology struggled with imagination, slowly giving way to a greater fear.

Homosapiens! Wide's threat! Chee'ee'la!

The subordinates came crowding into his quarters, a sea of hard bodies rubbing and clicking with gratitude. The din of their pleas drowned out any ability to reason.

"No!" RashTak rose high again, trying to sort out the confusion of emotions and thoughts. "No! It's not time for the cycles! GET OUT OF HERE!"

But they didn't listen. That's why the Bak!Gil dispenser had ceased to work. The cycles had come.

The cycles? Then AraTak, EE!Tak . . . "Oh, Violet curses! No! Not here!"

Desperately, RashTak charged forward, actually climbing over the bodies of his moaning supplicants, careening into the corridor on scrambling feet.

He raced for AraTak's rooms, heedless of the whimpering subordinates he passed. Behind him, his supplicants followed in a clicking and keening wash of bodies, pleading for his protection.

"Madness!" RashTak wailed to himself as he ran. "Homosapiens is someplace, doing something, *and we've all gone insane!*"

* * *

Riva studied Katrina's notes, tapping her pen against her chin. She shuffled in the seat, drawing one leg up to change the circulation in her bottom. Behind her, the terminal monitor glowed with Ahimsa characters and what were supposed to be Pashti analogs.

"It doesn't make sense. Where's the key?" Riva sighed and replaced the notes on the table, leaning back to massage the bridge of her nose with thumb and forefinger.

"Reminds me of a cross between Greek and Chinese." Katrina stood and walked to the dispenser, ordering another cup of coffee.

"You didn't used to drink coffee."

"I had my reasons." Katrina smiled, her expression weary. "I hadn't tried to translate alien languages into English, but probably more importantly, we couldn't get it in Khabarovsk."

"Greek and Chinese, huh?" Riva returned her attention to the cryptic characters on the monitor. "Greek and Chinese with more accent marks. Greek and Chinese crossed with cuneiform, you mean."

"We need a linguist, not just a couple of translators." Mary Dak stepped out of the toilet cubicle. Her appearance contrasted with petite Katrina's, black-haired where Katrina's blonde almost smacked of platinum. Dak had been recalled from her post in the U.S. Embassy in San Salvador where she conducted operations against the Cubans. The weary look had etched into Dak's face as well. They all looked that way, drawn, tired, frustrated by the incomprehensible wall they'd run into when it came to deciphering the Pashti language.

Riva shook her head. "You know, humans don't have a very good record when it comes to talking to other intelligences."

"We don't do so well talking to ourselves," Mary pointed out.

"Got that right." Riva chewed the end of her pencil as she frowned at the inscrutable characters on the screen. "But what I was thinking of is this. We can't even talk to dolphins who use a sophisticated digital language. We had to teach apes sign language or the arbitrary use of symbols."

"So? We're looking at symbols." Dak pointed at the monitor.

"But what if we're missing something? Like Katrina said, it's got all those accent marks. What are they? Some complex pronunciation? Pashti consists of one hundred and thirty-five separate characters all modified by the accent marks. That sort of eliminates ideographs—we think—but what about the accent marks? Is that some way of developing the Rebus Principle? Are they diacritics? Stress, tone, or pitch? Are they even related to verbalizations? Maybe they're a reflection of body language? Given the number of characters, maybe it's all syllabic?"

"You assume it's phoneticized." Katrina shifted uncomfortably. "It might not even have any relationship to a phonemic system we can begin to comprehend. What if it's like bee language, a reconstruction of a dance, or posturing, or, who knows, color, or infrared emissions, or . . ."

". . . Or any of the whole universe of symbols." Riva raised her hands, letting them slap angrily to the table.

The room went silent. *That's the whole problem.* Riva told herself. *Pashti could be anything, any combination of symbols which might have to do with the entire spectra of communication, not just speech as we know it.*

"You look horrible," Katrina stated, tension in the set of her mouth.

"Yeah," Riva exhaled her frustration. "I'm just trying to figure out a way to tell Major Dunbar that we're stopped cold. If we only had a linguist!"

"We don't." Mary Dak reminded. "We don't even have access to the references that would break this open. I never thought I'd miss a library."

"And Wide won't give Sheila any information on Ahimsa." Katrina glared up at the light panel overhead. "But then, Soviet troops from Latvia are stationed in Khabarovsk."

"Meaning?"

Katrina smiled grimly. "Meaning if the troops can't speak the local language, they can't develop a sympathy for the plight of the locals—they can't understand the appeals shouted at them by the people they might be ordered to shoot down."

"That makes me feel wonderful." Riva battled back the image of a dying girl on a dusty Nablus street.

CHAPTER XXIII

"I'm telling you, meatball, any trouble and I lock you and me into a small room! You got that?" Sam felt his temper rise as he glared wickedly into Murphy's steely eyes. The lieutenant stood stiffly at attention, eyes forward, jaw clenched.

"Further, Lieutenant Gubanya," Staka's cool voice added from one side, "the penalty for any misbehavior on your part will be immediate death. That will go for you, for Katya Illych, and for Lieutenant Murphy. You had better understand, Mika, that this is a military operation. I remind you we are completely within the control of the enemy. Any, and I mean *any* insubordination could kill this entire command—every man and woman aboard—and possibly our planet."

"Any insubordination, Major? Is this a new policy?" Sam tensed at Gubanya's tone.

"Mika, don't force me. I won't take it. Not even after what we shared and survived in Afghanistan." Viktor's voice had dropped to a deadly whisper. "You asked me once if I'd do my duty. I want you to know that I will. If Major Dunbar issues an order for your execution because of trouble with Murphy, it will wound my soul, but I will carry it out."

Sam shot a quick glance at Gubanya where he stood like a statue. Viktor stepped easily around his target like a circling shark, and continued, "Should any one of the three of you die in combat from mysterious causes, Major Dunbar has informed me that the death penalty will be carried out. No one will be shot in the back! *Understood?*"

"That's the word," Riva added, voice toneless. She looked at Katya, the only one of the miscreants who stared back. "Major Dunbar believes that your personal lives are up to you. It is our conclusion that her approach is correct. It is my understanding, Katya, that you wish to share quarters with Lieutenant Murphy. Is that correct?"

Katya said a flat, "I do. If, however, it will interfere with my duties or my ability to work in a professional manner with Lieutenant Gubanya, I will not."

Staka asked softly, "Lieutenant Gubanya, the lady seems to be reasonable. Do you have an objection to that?"

"*Nyet!*" he answered crisply.

Sam stepped up to Murphy, nose to nose, squinting into those steely eyes. "Meatball, you got any objection to being Gubanya's good friend?"

"No, sir!" Murphy shouted, not a twitch of a muscle anywhere.

"Good," Sam grunted. "That being the case, you three are assigned to cleaning torpedoes three, four, and five. Couple people got sick in zero g today. Majors Staka and Thompson and I want that duty attended to before exercises tomorrow. Now, people, do I hear an objection?"

The only sign of resistance Sam noted was the pronounced stiffness of Katya's expression.

His voice sounded pleasant, almost musical. "No? Well, that's nice and friendly. I'm so glad we could iron out this little misunderstanding, *without blowing your fucking heads off! NOW, MOVE!*" Sam got the satisfaction of seeing Katya jump at his explosion.

Gubanya and Murphy saluted before trotting stiffly out. Katya followed hot on their heels.

"Let's hope that is that," Viktor added, crossing his arms as he leaned up against a dispenser, a frown etching his brow.

"Yeah," Sam agreed.

Riva made a clicking sound with her tongue. "I'll see to it that there's no more friction. I have several people working on the problem. If anyone so much as whispers a threat, my people will inform me immediately." She grinned. "See, there's an advantage to having a ship full of spies."

Viktor nodded, "Good. If I can be of help, call." He

pushed off the wall and gave Sam a weary smile. "At least it wasn't politics."

"Right on, man!" He reached up, slapping Viktor's hand before the major exited.

"There's something about Gubanya," Riva added, eyes narrowing. "Call it a feeling. He's a very dangerous man, a killer biding his time."

* * *

Svetlana looked up as Sheila stepped into the room. She nodded, and waved, looking up to check her monitor.

"I got a message over my terminal that you wished to see me?"

Svetlana gave her a grim smile, pointing at the monitor. *"Da, tovarisch."*

"No translation?" Sheila lifted an eyebrow.

The warm surge of victory rose in Svetlana's chest as she grinned and said in English. "You wanted a locksmith, Major."

Sheila's relief filled the room. "Then we can plan in secrecy again!"

"It doesn't come free."

Sheila's expression frosted. "Would you like to elaborate on that?"

Svetlana pointed at the monitor, watching as Sheila craned to stare. The image showed Svetlana in her recliner, head back, eyes closed as if asleep. "That's what Wide will see on the bridge. The monitor for your room shows the same. I have no idea how long I can maintain it without discovery—and I don't think we can afford that. Nor can I accomplish this with more than two people without betraying my access to the system."

Sheila chewed her lip, frown lines deepening. "And I suppose each time you do, it's a risk?"

"*Da,* and then some." Svetlana laced her fingers together, swiveling in the chair to face Sheila. "Major, I placed a lot of trust in you based on our discussion that day. I take it you've put some plan together to keep us from throwing dynamite?"

Sheila nodded, sinking into one the chairs. "It's risky."

"Everything in life is. Quickly, we have very little time."

Sheila nodded, taking a second to order her thoughts. "I'm gambling everything, Svetlana, but here's what I've put together so far."

Svetlana leaned forward, one watchful eye on the monitor, a constriction around her heart as she listened to Dunbar and waited for discovery.

* * *

Murphy's heart continued to pound as he slipped along the long cable, that tickling feeling of falling mixed with his berserk inner ear to leave him feeling nauseous and disoriented. A carabiner on his belt circled the line that ran along the deck of the Ahimsa ship and kept him from floating off into the stars. *I don't goddamned believe this.*

Daniels had sprung it at the meeting that morning. "People, the Ahimsa are stringing a cable along the hull outside of the ship. Major Dunbar thought you were all looking a little peaked, so she arranged to give you some time off. Consider it as a chance to get a little exercise outdoors.

"That's right, boys and girls, we're gonna kick each and every one of you out the hatch in a space suit to break you in to the excitement of life in space. We've done zero g and vacuum maneuvers inside. Now let's see how you all react to the real thing."

There'd been silence in the room, men and women looking back and forth.

"And may the Force be with you," Murphy had blurted in a stentorian voice. Daniels had stared at him from lowered brows with his "I'll get you for that" look, and Murphy's gut had dropped down around his ankles.

Below him, the hull plating of the Ahimsa ship slipped slowly past in the white splash of his shoulder-mounted suit lights. The silver-gray plating appeared hexagonal, maybe two meters across. The border on each section interlocked, like a piece of jigsaw puzzle. Here and there a pockmark indicated some sort of impact, like a rifle bullet hitting a thick steel plate—or the surface of the moon.

Murphy swallowed hard, taking a deep breath. Reality crashed down on him like a case-hardened hammer head. *I'm floating in fucking outer space, man!* "Holy shit."

His insides tensed and twisted like a wounded snake. His breath came in ragged gasps as his mind began to scream. "Easy, Murph. Hang in there. It's okay, man. You're alive. You're breathing. You're warm." *And I'm falling . . . FALLING!*

"You're supposed to be falling. It's space, man. Free-fall, like all the drugs in the world."

"Murph?" Sam's voice came through the headset.

"Huh?"

"You're talking to yourself. You all right?"

"Huh?"

He bent his neck, looking out over his shoulder, watching a shimmering black haze that rippled like a piece of translucent light sculpture. How could anything so incredibly black have a sensation of illumination? "Black light, man. What a rock song that would make." He shivered.

"Murphy?" Daniels' voice came through the headset. "You all right? Talk to me, Murph."

Murphy grinned, hearing Sam's concern. "I'm fine, Captain. This is weird shit, man. I'm just coasting along. Thought I'd see stars out here."

"Can't. We're going faster than light."

"Null singularity. Yeah, falling through the backside of the universe. Riding on the bottom of a gravity bullet."

"You've been studying."

The constriction in his dry throat threatened to choke him. The line seemed to go on forever as he fell headfirst through darkness. "Cap? How many guys have flipped out doing this?"

"We don't know, Murph."

"What do you mean? You told me half the unit made this trip!"

"Hey, well, I lied. Somebody had to be first."

"Huh?"

"Yeah. Thought you'd appreciate the opportunity to get a little fresh air after you and Gubanya cleaned the torpedoes all night. Oh, by the way, he's here at the hatch, waiting to go out and rescue you if you flip out or go crazy or die or something."

Oh, shit! "Hey, I'm fine, Sam. Doing just peachy as a matter of fact." There were worse things in life than a little free-fall in shimmering blackness outside an alien spaceship that had fallen through a hole in reality and dropped outside the universe.

"Great." Sam sounded so cheerful. "That means there's no reason any of the rest of these goons in here can't do just what you did. Oh, by the way, we're watching on the monitors. You might want to turn around so you hit the other end feet first. You've still got all the inertia you jumped with. Since your legs imparted that much energy, they ought to be able to absorb it. On the other hand, if you hit that steel post headfirst. . . . Aw, hell, it's okay, Murph, I forgot."

"Forgot what?"

"It's *your* head we're talking about. Doubt you could hurt it, thick as it is."

Murphy growled to himself as he flipped this way and that, trying to employ the zero g tricks they'd been learning. "Space war," he grumbled. *But I'll be goddamned dead before I let Gubanya come out and rescue me!*

* * *

Moshe walked along the tank, running his fingers over the curious material that composed the armor. Some sort of ceramic lattice mixed with metal, Mason had said. Whatever it was, the stuff had proven infernally tough.

"You ready?" Arya called down from where he sat in the hatch.

Moshe chuckled. "No. Would that make any difference?"

"Don't sweat it," Cruz slapped a callused hand on Moshe's shoulder.

"Easy for you to say." Moshe shook his head, looking at the long torpedo where its nose splayed open like a perverted crocodile.

Phil grinned, double-checking his oxygen pad. "Ah, I don't think there'll be anything to it."

"You don't?" Arya asked, leaning out of the top hatch. "Personally, I'm scared to death."

Cruz spread his hands, anticipation in his eyes. "Figure it like this. I've jumped out of airplanes. I've jumped out of helicopters. I've jumped out of gliders. I've jumped out of boats. I've jumped out of trucks. I've swum out of submarines. What's jumping out of a spaceship after that?"

"I've only jumped out of bed," Moshe protested, seeing his pilot walking up the ramp into the torpedo. "Almost time."

Cruz followed his gaze. "Yeah. I still can't believe we're going to do this."

"Sure you're not nervous?"

Phil chuckled. "Yeah, I'm nervous. You always are before an exercise—even if it's jumping out of an airplane. There's always something that can go wrong. Chute might not open. You might land wrong—or in the wrong place. Knew a guy who wasn't watching what was coming up and hit some high tension lines. Training's dangerous."

Moshe straightened, filling his lungs. "Well, it's time. Good luck, Corporal Cruz. Hope we can buy you a beer tonight."

"Hey, you Matzos take care. Hope your tank don't spring a leak."

"A leak?" Arya asked.

Cruz grinned. "Yeah, like the kind where all the air runs out."

"And we hope your safety line doesn't snap," Moshe returned. "You've never checked the tensile strength of that Ahimsa cord, have you?"

Cruz glanced warily at the cord hanging at his waist, swallowing hard. "Uh, no."

"Have a good day," Moshe added over his shoulder as he climbed up on the tank.

Cruz waved farewell and gave an arm signal to his unit to form up for a final equipment check.

"Start us up," Moshe ordered as he swung his legs into the hatch. He took one last look around the torpedo bay. A corridor had opened which allowed them access to the torpedoes. Down the entire line, men and tanks waited before the gaping jaws of the torpedoes.

"Moshe? What if something does break out there? What if the torpedo malfunctions? What if one of the other torpedoes can't get to us?" Arya called up.

Moshe laughed, checking the systems monitors. "What's this? You've started to worry now? No one is even going to shoot at us this time. After all those trips into Lebanon where death lay in wait everywhere, now I hear you're afraid of a little vacuum?"

Arya craned his neck to look over his shoulder and replied with a flat, "Yes."

Moshe reached forward to push his shoulder. "Go on."

"It's about dirt," Arya added philosophically. "A person can die on dirt. It's right, you know? People have been dying on dirt for a long time."

"What about sailors?"

"They get to the dirt eventually. I mean, the ship sinks to the bottom and finally hits dirt. Same thing with fighter pilots. Even when a SAM takes out an F16, the pieces of the pilot still land on dirt."

"Arya, God will see to you. Dead is dead. Only your soul needs to worry you—and what will become of it."

"Still wish there was a little dirt out there."

"Stardust. That's dirt. The Earth was formed of star dust—so it's got to be dirt."

Arya scowled at the monitors, nervous hands resting on the controls. Finally he jerked his head in an emphatic nod. "Yeah, I suppose so, huh? I guess I can die out there, then. I can become a piece of stardust."

"Cruz is waiting for us. You might want to—"

"Hey!"

Moshe turned, seeing Yeled walking across the deck. He wore space gear, helmet and oxygen sponge on his neck. Sheepishly he jumped up, swinging onto the tank. Lower lip pinched in his teeth, he avoided Moshe's eyes. "Uh, maybe you'd better move over. I can't have you going around shooting things up. You're a commander, not a gunner. You wouldn't know PLO from a settler."

Moshe grinned, making room so Yeled could crawl into the gunner's seat. "You know how to work this new gun?"

"Schematics are available on the computer in the rooms. I think I can make it talk." Yeled competently flipped the switches that checked the laser circuitry and cycled the automatic feed for the cannon.

"Glad to see you," Moshe said softly.

Yeled turned in the seat, blinking as he swallowed. "I heard you were going out into space today, that if something went wrong. . . . Well, Sword wouldn't be coming to bail you out. I . . . I guess I can't walk home to Israel, but maybe I can help get us there." He paused, dropping his gaze, fingers tracking the target sights and triggers. "Moshe, Arya, I'm sorry."

"It's a different kind of war." Moshe slapped him on the back and sat in his usual seat in the hatch. "Well, what are we waiting for? Arafat to enter a rabbinical? Let's go. Cruz is waiting."

Arya backed the tank around, watching his periscopes as the treads bit in and hauled them into the narrow confines of the torpedo. Moshe ducked and slammed the hatch down, securing it.

"Well, now we see if the oxygen unit in this thing works." Arya locked his treads and settled back in the seat. "Wish I had a thermos full of coffee."

Moshe watched Cruz form his squad up in front of the tank. Then the sections of the nose closed.

For long seconds, Moshe listened to his heart beat.

"Prepare for lock down," the pilot's voice sounded through the net. The tank shivered as grapples secured it. "Thirty seconds to launch, people. Welcome aboard. We're going out to see the stars for real this time."

The torpedo lurched and Moshe's gut twisted. G force pushed him back into the command seat. He didn't realize until later that he'd closed his eyes.

* * *

Spotted struggled to keep his brains from splitting into fragments as he watched the monitor. The frantic response to form manipulators overwhelmed him and proved impossible to entirely suppress. His sides and foot tread lumped, and turned into a knobby mess. His reddish-pink splotches had darkened over the last month. Fear—so long absent from his life—had become a constant.

He shifted an eyestalk to catch a glimpse of Wide. The Overone rocked happily back and forth, watching the monitor. Awed by Wide's control, Spotted stared back at a monitor. Characters flashed across the screen.

Maybe I'm not insane. Only the insane could watch the humans without collapsing and lysing. I'm terrified, therefore, I am *sane!*

Fluids on the inside of his body rushed randomly from compartment to compartment. Panic vied with fear and lost. Despite the raging turmoil inside, Spotted managed to integrate two of his brains and call, "Overone, I am receiving yet another appeal from the transduction net. Sees, Hurt, Low, Pale, and the others firmly request you contact them."

Spotted realized his perspective had changed as his sides started going. He made a conscious effort to pull himself round again.

"Do not acknowledge," Wide piped irritably. One eye remained on the monitors displaying the humans who slowly advanced up the length of the ship as part of their first EVA exercise. The other eye studied the list of materials they had been requisitioning from the ship's production facilities. "Double-strand insulated wire? Fifty-five miles of it? Why did they need that?"

Spotted's mind quivered at the sight of the humans dropping down toward the access ports.

Sheila Dunbar's voice cackled through the comm. "We've made the hatches in excellent style, Wide. I say, perfect execution!"

Comm showed him individual humans dropping from the locks on the torpedoes. They settled lightly to the hull, silver threads of lifelines hooking them to the hovering craft.

Sheila's voice came through the comm. "Assuming your computer-generated model is accurate, Moshe's gunners are one hundred percent on approaching Pashti jumpships. What? Superb! Wide, we have planted the dummy charges and the hatches would have been blown open. Please allow us access."

Spotted didn't even ask as he opened the hatches. Instead, he struggled to keep his brains integrated into a functioning whole.

* * *

Wide rocked back and forth, whistling and piping to himself as he watched. His minds staggered at the implications. Until this very moment, he'd never considered the possibility of humans as space beings. The original concept had been to transport them to TaHaAk and get them inside. Once in the station, their raid would have been no different than one carried out in a large building on Earth. But to see them actually so well adapted and functioning in a space environment? The American and Soviet space programs had demonstrated humans could manage in space, but they'd trained their people for years to reach that primitive ability. Here, Sheila Dunbar had orchestrated a perfectly executed deep space maneuver on the first try.

The possibilities unfolded exponentially. Humans could be used for all kinds of things, mining, retrieving scientific specimens, hazardous duty which robots couldn't perform for one reason or another—even raiding Pashti shipping if he felt like it!

"Pirate Wide!" he whistled and tooted. Spotted swiveled one eye in his direction and began to prickle with half-formed manipulators.

Sheila's disembodied voice continued with the progress report as the torpedoes dropped inside. Monitors followed them as their torpedoes raced through the access tubes and companionways toward vital sections of the null singularity generator, the computer central, the atmosphere plant, the field generators, the stasis drive, the reaction control, the maneuvering substation. And, *his bridge?*

Wide felt a shiver of fear as one human ship broke off and shot in the direction of the bridge. His minds began to compartmentalize as he struggled to maintain his shape. Rocking back and forth, he felt the stubby protrusions of manipulators forming randomly as frightened glands produced structural molecules.

"Major Dunbar, there is a ship *attacking my central control room!*" Wide squealed into the system. Spotted looked like a pancake, one shaking eyestalk horror-locked on the monitor.

"Correct, Wide. Keep in mind, this is only a drill. We're doing it for your safety. What if Pashti were in the ship? Wouldn't they have the same priorities as we do? They would attempt to take the strategic portions—that includes making you hostage and controlling your center of operations. My people, however, will not pass your security off-limits. In the event of a Pashti attack, a guard will be placed immediately to protect both you and your subordinate. Spotted is his name, isn't it?"

Wide swiveled an eye and saw the attacking torpedo begin to slow, its bulk filling the corridor, leaving no passage out. True to Dunbar's words, they stopped at the security seal and immediately began to retreat. Wide felt a surge of relief as his sides began to tighten.

Spotted's voice barely made an impression. "How did they get the central control location?"

"What?" Wide shot both eyes toward Spotted where the lumpy Ahimsa attempted valiantly to pull himself thin again.

"They know where the central control is," Spotted repeated. "That was restricted data, security coded!"

"Check and see if there has been tampering in the comm." He felt himself going flat again.

Spotted tried three times to form a manipulator. Finally, he touched the control, piping his command to the system pickup. Wide had a great deal of difficulty rolling his flattened body over to where an eye could monitor the display.

"None of the safeguards have been tripped, Overone." Spotted straightened a little. "They have not breached the comm security. None of the safeguards are compromised."

Wide felt his minds knit together. "Where could we have failed to safeguard? Did we leave that information in any other file? I thought comm searched the whole system—made it foolproof!"

Spotted snaked an eye toward his superior. "The Overones are calling again. This time they have left off any of the polite applications. They want to know where we are and what we are doing with the humans."

Wide puffed a snort of disgust. "How could they know we have humans?" *Tan? Had Tan slipped? No, impossible!*

One part of his mind screamed a warning, frantically trying to assimilate and analyze the data. Such alarms had come so often lately, they had become a regular nuisance. He dismissed the echoes of Pashti and Ahimsa collusion and quashed the thought, wearily pulling himself to the dispenser. He forced his abused stomach through his side to grasp another nutrient bar.

At his station, Spotted slumped to one side as another manipulator began to form under his foot tread. He stifled the growth and reabsorbed it. It was all getting out of control!

* * *

Riva looked up as Major Detova stepped into the room. Like the rest of them, Svetlana had a strained look about her. The KGB woman smiled, and nodded, walking forward. Riva noticed the sheaf of papers under Svetlana's arm.

"Hello, Major Thompson. I hear you're working hard. I couldn't have done as good a job as you when it comes to training our fliers."

"A gross understatement, I'm sure, Major." *What does Detova want here?* Riva laced her fingers together, searching for some sign, some meaning for the woman's presence. "Sit down. What can I do for you?"

Svetlana sat, staring thoughtfully at the papers. "I heard that you'd run into a dead end with the Pashti translations."

Riva forced her expression to remain neutral while her temper rose. *My entire career was spent in mortal combat with people like you, Detova. Don't get me started now.* "We're not beaten yet, Major."

"But it looks a little grim." Svetlana's eyelids narrowed as her voice dropped. "I also understand Sheila asked Wide for information on the Pashti. He refused to provide it. According to him, he'll handle all the translations during the attack. He feels there's no need for us to communicate with a species we're simply going to destroy."

"He does, does he?" Riva stiffened, meeting Detova's measuring stare.

"Sheila and I agree," Svetlana added, leaning forward. "After all, Wide's point is well taken. As a result, you can enjoy a little relaxation, if you'd like. The Pashti language program is no longer a priority."

"I see."

"Do you?" Svetlana raised an eyebrow. "Sheila isn't heartless. She's not disbanding your team. If you'd like to work on it—in your spare time, of course—feel free. Everyone should have a hobby."

Riva realized her jaws had started to grind, the muscles in her cheeks giving her away. *Too damned long in the Middle East. Success only comes to the brassy hard asses.* She did one of the hardest things she'd ever had to do. She relaxed and smiled, making a trite gesture with her hand. "Well, I'm glad the pressure's off in that quarter then."

Svetlana nodded. "Yes, we're all getting close to the end. I realize how much effort you and your team have put into the language program. I really have a great deal of respect for you. We crossed swords a time or two on Earth—very indirectly."

Riva nodded slowly, the simmering anger stirring in her breast. Which corpses could she lay at Detova's feet? Which brutal murders, disappearances, and maimings had come from her minions? "I guess it was just a small world."

Svetlana lowered her gaze then and her posture slumped slightly. "Yes, a small world. Buckley trained you, didn't he?"

Riva controlled herself with steel reins. "Among others."

"I admire you. You were quite capable, given the area you were working in. You had a sense for the Middle East most officers in that part of the world never develop."

"And we never crossed swords directly?" Riva raised an eyebrow.

Svetlana's lips twitched, a ghost of a smile. "No. My area was the Pacific Rim. I worked out of Hong Kong."

"Then you had something to do with the Sudan?"

"A lot of people had something to do with that—all the way up to General Kutsov." Svetlana cocked her head, dark stare trying to bore into Riva's defenses. "I think, however, that now is not the time to discuss the past, and who did what. Perhaps, someday, if you'd like."

"I'll keep that offer in mind."

Svetlana stood, indicating the stack of papers. "Just so there are no misunderstandings, Sheila had me print out a hard copy of your orders to terminate the Pashti language program. You might want to take a look so you know the orders are official. But, just on the side, good luck with your . . . hobby."

"Thank you, Major."

Svetlana stopped at the door and turned. "You know, we put a lot of effort into keeping the PLO supplied. Between your office and the resources of the Mossad, we paid way too much for the results achieved. After meeting you, I think I know why."

Riva stood, nerves like iron. "Thank you for the compliment, Major."

Detova turned and left, the door snicking quietly shut behind her.

Riva stood for a moment, rooted to the spot, anger twining with frustration. *Sheila canceled the language program? Just like that?* She clenched her fists.

Damn! I hate having to face facts. "But we'd never have broken it before the attack."

She reached for the papers, lifting the cover page and staring. The note had been written in a neat hand:

Dear Major Thompson:
Sheila said you'd hit a snag on Pashti communications. Hope the enclosed breaks it all open. Project TOP PRIORITY—but keep cover. If direction can be provided for addit. info. contact Sheila.
Msd
NORFORN

Riva stared at the text that followed and sucked at her

lower lip. A giddy joy rose to replace the anger and frustration. She stared at the NOFORN at the bottom of the page—the CIA code for top secret. "Damn you, Detova, rub it in. But I think you just saved my ass on this."

Riva took the cover note and crumpled it, dropping the curious Ahimsa paper into the toilet, flipping it about with her pen as the paper disintegrated. Then she walked back to the precious report—written in English!—and stared at the title:

AN AHIMSA REPORT ON PASHTI COMMUNICATION AS NECESSITATED BY THEIR PHYSIOLOGY.

CHAPTER XXIV

"Seriously, Wide, you've monitored enough of our conversations, strategy meetings, and what do the Americans call them. . . . ah, yes, bull sessions, to know that we're worried. We can't afford a mistake. Our whole bloody *world* is at stake here along with the very future of our *species!*"

"But you are going *too* far!" Wide rocked back and forth, surface lumpy, laboring sides going in and out. "Don't threaten me! I could destroy you all!"

Sheila crossed her arms and didn't budge. "You could always take us back. We're not wild about kicking the Pashti, you know, but we'll do it because we have to."

Wide pulled his sides in, thinning himself. "No, I think you must raid TaHaAk. The cycles are upon them. Your action will cause consternation among the Pashti all through space. The Ahimsa will reestablish control over all they have lost, fearing to leave Pashti passions to chance during the cycles. We're talking about the *future* of civilization! My species is at stake—along with yours!"

"Absolutely," Sheila agreed. "That is why we'll do your job for you. Why do you think you've had such perfect compliance? I bloody well didn't come on this jaunt for my health—and neither did the rest of the troops. We expect reward and at the same time, we want you happy with us. Lord knows, we're aware of the power you have over our planet. We *need* your good will!"

"But these exercises!" Wide's surface colored to a light pink as his foot tread dimpled with emotion. "Pashti will not attack this ship! They simply wouldn't dare! It's—"

"Haven't we had this conversation before?" She shook

her head. "Look, abstract yourself and try and see it from *our* perspective. Suppose the Pashti took your ship? How would we get home? All my people would be at their mercy, wouldn't they?"

"But you're not supposed to be caught! You're phantoms, Major Dunbar. If anyone recognizes you're human, everything is lost. Disaster! For me . . . you . . . the Ahimsa! You can't leave any trace behind! You must act as if you were never—"

"Precisely!" Sheila agreed. "And no one can trap or capture any of us as long as we evacuate. That's the key word, *evacuate!* As long as we can get away, no one will be the wiser. We're doing everything in our power and imagination to guard against having that evacuation cut off! Consider, would you want the Pashti to take your ship? They'll be in the cycles, remember? Unstable, Wide. You can't count on what their actions will be—nor will they remember what they've done after the mating and the hormonal imbalances. They could go berserk at the notion you're destroying their stockpiles. Maybe kill you in their madness." She noted how he deflated and manipulators began forming, "They'd blame it all on us! We *must* have you and your ship safe and secure! There is no other insurance that you won't get left holding the bag in any future investigation of the Pashti suicide on TaHaAk!"

Wide slowly pulled himself together. "Pashti could kill me?" he muttered, quivering. "Pashti could *kill* me?"

Sheila soothed, "Easy, Wide. Easy. Think. Now you've seen our boys in the exercises. Can the Pashti stand up to that? We're behind you, Wide. As long as you are under our protection, no one in the entire universe will harm you. Not even the other Overones have a bodyguard like yours."

Wide sucked his sides in as her words soaked into his segmenting brains. She watched his color fade to a normal white and saw his skin smooth out as the manipulators reabsorbed. Victory!

"You're right, of course." Wide rolled confidently back and forth. "Who could touch me?"

Sheila pressed her advantage. "Now do you see why we had to cover all the bases?" She smiled and waved her hand in a throwing away motion. "Dear Wide, you've told us that you studied our world intensively for three hundred years. You've seen and followed every war we've ever fought. Think of the number of times surprise attacks have gone awry. You've heard the adage that battle plans are perfect until the first shot is fired? In so many military instances, it has been the adaptable ones who carried the day and won the field.

"Consider Sherman in Georgia. Think of Konstantin Rokossovsky against the Nazis. Remember the brilliant generalship of Moshe Dyan or Elazar in the Israeli wars. So much is gained by flexibility. How else did Vietnam fight America to a standstill? How else did the Mujahadin bleed the Red Army into defeat? Flexibility is the key to success, Wide. That is truly our only weapon. That is our strategy to keep you safe, stop Pashti aggression, and rescue our world from interdiction."

"Yes, and abstraction. Abstraction. I must remember to abstract. To avoid the mistakes of . . . of the past." Wide continued rolling back and forth, so thin he looked almost like a motorcycle wheel with a bent eyestalk axle protruding through either side. His color now gleamed a deep white.

"I'm trying to think this out as logically as I can, and you're right, I have to live with total abstraction."

Boy, is that a lie!

"Excellent! Excellent! Excellent!" he kept repeating over and over. "No one will stand before us. We will save the Ahimsa. What is rightfully ours will be returned. Even the Shithti will make way before the Ahimsa. Excellent! Excellent!"

Sheila nodded, feeling her satisfaction grow. Flexibility—it meant so much in a military situation, or in politics, and perhaps in interstellar affairs, too.

* * *

Murphy listened intently as Major Dunbar explained what she wanted to Ted Mason.

"The idea is that the box should be able to produce certain sounds. Clicks, thumps, strumming noises, and sounds within the range we normally consider audible.

The boxes will be battery powered, capable of sending and receiving. Sam tells me you used to build radios. Can you make this device?"

Ted scratched behind his ear, nodding. "Sure, Major, but I don't have the things I need here. I mean you've got to have—"

"I believe you'll find everything you need in the weapons room. I just came from there and an entire inventory of parts suitable for constructing the device I've described is at your disposal."

"Pardon me, Major," Murphy straightened under her penetrating gaze.

"Yes, Leftenant?"

"Well, uh, why didn't we just have Wide build it to spec like he's done the tanks and everything?"

She crossed her arms, a faint frown on her forehead. Under her inspection, Murphy felt like squirming. He noticed that the worry lines, the haunted weariness in her eyes, had deepened. Damn it, didn't she get any rest?

"Morale, Leftenant. We can't come to depend on the Ahimsa for everything. Besides, primitive though this will be, it's *our* technology. We know what's gone into it. Leftenant Mason will know how to fix it if something happens in TaHaAk station. Does that answer your question?"

"Yes, ma'am." Murphy nodded respectfully—and realized he didn't quite buy it.

"If you don't mind, ma'am," Ted looked up from where he'd been staring at his toes, lost in thought, "why the thumps and clicks and stuff? And why all the sending and receiving?"

She fixed Ted with that strained look of hers and Murphy enjoyed seeing his friend shift and stiffen under that appraisal.

"Leftenant, have you given consideration as to what would happen if the Pashti could jam our communications net?"

"No, ma'am."

She smiled then, a delicate fleeting thing. "Well, I have. That's the secret of the boxes—nothing arcane or terribly sophisticated about it. You can't jam a telephone line unless you tap into it—but Radio Free Europe can be jammed quite effectively. Unless the Pashti cut our wire, we'll be able to maintain some element of communication, and I doubt the Pashti will be expecting such a primitive device as this."

"And the thumps and clicks and stuff you were talking about?" Murphy frowned, trying to imagine what Sheila had up her sleeve.

"I see that look, Leftenant," she warned, pointing a slim finger at him. "You can drop the speculation right now. Yes, the box has a second function. In the event we suffer some setback, the box can be left behind. Given our data on Pashti physiology, it appears they have quite delicate hearing. A random burst of white noise through the box might act to distract them in the event of a counterattack. Battles have been won and lost on less."

"Uh, Major, begging your pardon, ma'am, but—"

She raised a hand, and Murphy stopped short, mesmerized by the commanding look she gave him. "Trust me, Leftenant. Leave the speculations to the Pashti."

Murphy gave her a quick smile of support. "Yes, ma'am. If you'll excuse us, ma'am, Ted here has a battlefield communications system to build for you."

"Thank you, Leftenant," she nodded briefly and turned away, walking down the hallway.

Murphy watched her, a nibble of worry eating at the edges of his mind. "Damn, she looks worn out. Pushing too hard, if you ask me."

"All that stuff about a diversion? I know bullshit when I—"

Murphy clapped a hand over Mason's mouth, dragging him backward. "Nobody's asking you. Come on, loose lips, let's go build the lady a squawk box."

* * *

"We may indeed have a serious problem," Hurt announced, swiveling his eyestalks to inspect the holographic images of Sees and Low. "None of us have been able to get Wide to respond to our transmissions although we've sent queries on wide dispersal. Had Wide heard, we should have received some response as a result of having accused him of carrying an interdicted species."

Sees wheezed and flattened. "Before I make my report, I must remind everyone that we still have no proof that Wide broke quarantine. We must operate under that assumption until such time as data are presented to indicate otherwise.

"I must report, however, that another irregularity has appeared. I have run a complete analysis of the monitors of the human world. I fear we have been working under a false assumption. Humans are not the rude primitives we have assumed them to be. Rather, the last one hundred thousandth has seen a quantum growth in their cultural development. Overones, the humans have spaceflight."

A chorus of whistles and shrieks filled the monitors as Hurt and Low piped and stared.

"Spaceflight? Wide broke the interdiction and taught them. . . . I can't believe it! No Ahimsa would *dare* such an affront to the Overones!" Low rasped from juddering spicules.

"I remind you, there is no evidence that Wide broke the interdiction. I can find no record of tampering, no trace of Ahimsa representations in their art. Further, their speculations about space life appear to be markedly terrestrial in nature. The vast majority of star creatures, or spacemen as they are known in the popular literature, look like them."

"Impossible!" Hurt chirped. "Their form is singularly unsuited to zero g environments."

"You say you find no evidence of Wide tampering?" Low asked, sides beginning to bulge.

"None. I think, however, that we know exactly what Wide's fascination with humans has been for the last thousandth. They are truly an aberration. If Tan would reply to our requests for information, perhaps this entire thing could be cleared up. If they *have* been dealing with humans, as the Shitht, Chee'ee'la, insists, perhaps they have reasons for their silence. We must assume, however, that for the moment, they are not in violation of the interdiction."

Hurt filled his breathing organs and asked, "Should we inform the Pashti that they may not be crazy after all?

Perhaps the First Councillor should take some action? Prepare to exterminate vermin?"

"I would not advise that for the moment. I remind you, we have no proof." Sees thinned slightly, his foot tread losing some of the flaccid appearance.

Low swiveled his eyes from one to the other, preferring binocular vision for some reason of his own. "We must be willing to anticipate the worst. If Wide has broken the interdiction and gone insane, we will have to repair the situation. What is the current status of the humans? Are their space capabilities a potential threat?"

Sees thinned, his hide stretching tighter. "Their space capabilities were never a threat. Whatever Wide did, the buoys have not been tampered with and humans appear to remain ignorant of their presence. One small robot spacecraft will approach their field of influence in another ten of their years. Meanwhile, the humans are are in the process of taking care of themselves."

"Then they've begun to civilize?" Low asked, sides sucking up and thinning. "I knew Wide wouldn't engage in anything foolish! He's an Overone. He—"

"I beg to differ, Overone," Sees interrupted. "As we speak, the humans are killing each other by the millions. Their entire planet is engulfed in war. Nothing has changed. They are as insane as ever."

Hurt sagged, insides going weak. "And if Wide really has brought humans past the buoys?"

"We will have to destroy them, of course."

* * *

"Major? Are you in?"

Svetlana blinked awake, sitting up. The lights came up, illuminating the room.

"Sheila? That you?"

"If you have a minute."

Svetlana stood and dressed, glancing at the time displayed on the comm monitor. "What in hell is she doing up at this time of night anyway?"

Sheila looked like hell, bags under her eyes, hollows under her cheeks. A woman might look like that if her only child were dying of cancer.

"Have you eaten recently?" Svetlana asked, frowning.

"This morning, I think. I hit the mess just before everyone else did."

"That was almost twenty-four hours ago. Come on." They passed down the silent halls, uneasiness beginning to twist the tail of Svetlana's thoughts.

They walked into the mess, the long tables stretching emptily in the gleaming light. Svetlana ordered Sheila a solid English breakfast of ham, eggs, scones with treacle, and Yorkshire pudding. She added a cup of cofee and a glass of milk.

"You want to burst me in two?" Sheila asked as Svetlana placed the tray before her.

"Fires, be they physical or mental, must be fueled. Starvation leads to mistakes."

Sheila smiled absently. "I suppose so." She picked up the fork and began eating while Svetlana returned for a plate of her own.

When the empties had been pushed aside, Sheila blinked and yawned. "I think I needed that. Maybe I ought to write a note to remind myself to eat every now and then."

"We're getting close, aren't we?"

"Yes." Sheila stared vacantly at the far wall. "Wide told me we've only got a couple of days. About fifty hours, as a matter of fact."

Svetlana's guts tightened. "It doesn't seem like six months have passed."

Sheila rubbed her face, as if to massage blood into the tired flesh. "I know. How have your studies been proceeding?"

"I think I'm beginning to get a handle on how things work."

"I'm glad to hear that." Sheila's expression sharpened. "I suppose computers could control everything, if they had the right programming. Do you think that could be the case? I mean, take the government, for example. Could a single skilled person take control at a critical moment and run his own programs?"

Svetlana's excitement increased. "I think that would depend on the system, Major. In Washington, for example, the computers aren't all linked together. In Moscow, the computers have a habit of going down at the most inopportune moments—or so I've been told. They aren't as sophisticated as the Ahimsa system where centralized programs run everything. There's a lot we could learn from them."

Sheila raised an eyebrow, the question achingly clear in her eyes.

Svetlana hesitated. "No one has ever had the nerve to try something like that with the government. It would be terribly risky. I thought you knew that from the past. If someone tried, and were caught . . . well, who knows what would happen. If you tried it in Moscow it might invite a firing squad. In Washington, they'd lock you up and throw away the key."

"Yes, well, desperation can drive people to take risks. But with the right system, you think it could be done?"

Svetlana's heart raced. "It's all hypothetical . . . and I'm certainly no expert, Major."

Sheila's hand trembled as she picked up her coffee, her burning, red-rimmed eyes never leaving Svetlana's. "What do you think an expert would say?"

Svetlana's palms had gone clammy. She gave the empty plate in front of her a hard stare, considering the extent of her knowledge of the system. "Assuming you had the best in the business, it could probably be done."

"Would someone with that amount of skill need a practice run? Or would past diversions, no matter how limited, be sufficient training?"

Svetlana took a deep breath, thinking her way through the tangle of access she'd so laboriously charted out in her mnemonic notes. How much did Sheila want her to tamper with? Providing cover for half an hour through a looped holo of a sleeping woman was one thing—and chancy enough. They'd only dared that once.

"That's hard to say without knowing the system or the extent of the project."

Sheila nodded, forcing herself to lean back in the chair, nervous fingers stroking her coffee cup. "Well, no matter. I reran the records of our training exercises from the first to the last. You'd be surprised at the improvement. I think we'll be all right when we hit TaHaAk." She lifted her gaze to pin Svetlana's again. "At least, that's what I hope Wide will see when he's watching his monitors up there. I want Wide to think we're magicians."

"Magicians?"

Sheila sighed and tipped her cup, a wistful smile on her face. "Didn't you see magic shows when you were little? You know, tricks like rabbits popping out of hats, card tricks, things like that. Sleight of hand. Misdirection. It happens in politics, too. Remember Ogarkov?"

You've thought up a new permutation to the plan! Damn it, Sheila! Do you know what you're asking? And I've only got fifty hours—or less? There's no way I can test my ability to compromise their control and still put together what I think you're getting at!

Sheila giggled nervously. "Bloody hell, listen to me! Talking about magicians and childhood. Can you tell I'm tired, or what? Next thing you know, I'll be relating tales out of fantasy books, magical battles where the evil king sees what his wizard wants him to. Meanwhile, his demons are turned into white knights as they ride down on the unsuspecting peasants at work in the fields. When the battle is over, the wizard waves his wand and the king is faced with reality."

Svetlana nodded slowly, the chill eating into her heart. *My god, Sheila. Is that the way of it? Is that what you've gambled our lives on? Magic and fantasy?* The pieces began to fall into place.

"You should get some rest. All this talk of computers and fantasy wars. You're tired, Sheila."

Dunbar stood, her expression steely. "I suppose. Sorry I woke you at such an ungodly hour. I've been so busy I just needed someone to talk to." She put a hand on Svetlana's shoulder. The fingers ate into her flesh, the grip one of desperation. "Are you with me?"

Svetlana hesitated. "I'm with you, Major." Her stomach dropped, as if she'd just condemned herself. "Go get some sleep. Dream of magicians and wizards and kings. Who the hell knows, maybe you'll get a miracle." *Provided I'm good enough—and that the Ahimsa haven't outlawed miracles!*

* * *

RashTak paced irritably, aware of the Pashti who crowded fearfully outside the doors of the Central Council Chambers. Lights gleamed off the orange-yellow crystals of Chee'ee'la's body where it rested motionless, seemingly inert. He'd literally dragged Ee!Tak and AraTak into the Council Chamber and slammed the door in the faces of the fawning subordinates.

Ee!Tak had lowered his flat body to the floor, major eyes on RashTak as he thrummed a moody vibration into the sounding tiles. AraTak shifted anxiously to one side, charging forward several meters before backing up to charge forward again. Nervous energy, all of it.

Violet Curses! We're perched on the edge of the abyss. How long can I hold them, keep them sane? Where is Wide? Where are the Homosapiens? RashTak lifted his pincers, clicking them loudly as he paced along the margins of the wall.

FeerTak had not been able to keep himself above the draw of the cycles. He had barricaded himself into one side of the station with all of his females and an ample food supply. A few hundred subordinates had gone with him, keeping that entire section and two jumpships effectively locked away.

"But it's only speculation," Ee!Tak insisted. "Simply because Wide is fooling with Homosapiens doesn't mean he's threatening us."

RashTak, his control as iron as that of his rivals, turned, maintaining his calm. "Be that as it may, he has affected us. Councillors, we have made history! Look about you! Each of your females has been bred—and we stand here, carrying on a sane conversation! That means—"

"That," AraTak reminded, "was precisely what the Ahimsa suspected. They mentioned the fact that Wide had never done anything except that which was to the benefit of others. Could it be that Wide leaked a meaningless threat to Chee'ee'la for precisely this purpose?"

RashTak thought it over. The idea made so much sense he had trouble trying to masticate, swallow, and digest it. He could have accepted that explanation, if

Wide had answered any Pashti communications requests. No Ahimsa Overones had called back with explanations as to Wide's behavior. No, indeed, the subspace remained uncharacteristically silent—and all the more ominous for it.

Worse, Chee'ee'la still sat before his eyes, rocklike—incommunicado despite Pashti appeals—in the middle of the Council Chambers. RashTak clicked and hummed to himself before whirling to face his peers. "How easy do you think it is to manipulate a Shitht?"

Ee!Tak shuffled nervously, thrumming slightly into the floor, savoring his own vibrations. AraTak pulled his sensorial fibers through his multiple jaws—a gesture of heightened anxiety coupled with the disruption of the cycles. Nevertheless, he kept his control, although his legs trembled and gurgling sounds of internal turmoil sounded through his carapace.

"Oh, very well!" RashTak grumbled. "Look at us! Suppose that Wide is just what the other Overones say he is. Suppose he's really working to beat the cycles. What if we accept that it's all a sham? What if we simply forget the Homosapiens threat as a fake and Wide is manipulating us for—"

"But you still have no *adequate* explanation of how Wide would use these Homosapiens against us!" AraTak interrupted passionately, skittering sideways to relieve the tension that ate at his organs.

"I *know* that!" RashTak thrummed his frustration into the floor, sending the resonance out over the room. Ee!Tak felt of it, sensorial fibers absorbing the power of the emotion.

RashTak continued, "Nothing makes sense unless Wide is mad—more insane than poor FeerTak back of his barricaded bulkheads!"

"This galaxy hadn't formed the last time an Ahimsa went crazy," Ee!Tak added, pincers snapping idly in the air. To add to the weight of his statement, his vibrators began making soft rhythms of authority.

"Red tried to roll across a neutron star," RashTak reminded. "I wouldn't exactly call that normal."

AraTak interjected, "The Ahimsa are slowly dwindling. One died a few hundred galactic years ago. It's in the histories. He suddenly ceased to be—simply went flat. Looked like a puddle of something wet." He paused, absently adding, "Imagine the sensations of placing a foot in that and getting the sticky stuff all over one's sensorial fibers!"

"Please, AraTak, not now! Wait, I was saying something. What was—"

"About what Wide was doing to us," Ee!Tak provided, searching the memory of the vibrations and replaying them. "You were supposing something about the Ahimsa, Wide."

"What? Yes, of course, it comes back now. Violet Curses on the cycles! They play cacophonous Violet Nothing with memory." RashTak paused, restructuring his memory. "Suppose Wide is misleading us about the threat. I was about to say that we have made history here!"

"You *said* that already," AraTak reminded, lowering his pincers.

"Well, we have," RashTak plunged on, irritated at the interruption. "We're standing here, functioning in a mostly logical manner—at least insofar as our memory and concentration permits. What benefit would accrue if we continued to assume Wide is bringing Homosapiens here to harm us? Will we not be able to maintain our senses, subverting the cycles with a greater fear? Namely, that of Homosapiens?"

"But you don't have any *proof* Wide is bringing Homosapiens here! It's just the word of a Shitht—"

"*That's just the point!*" RashTak thundered, drowning AraTak's protest. "It doesn't *hurt* us to believe that! We can still function! Can't you see? None of us has run off to cower over our horde of food! We're still thinking, talking to each other! As long as we can convince ourselves the Homosapiens are coming, we will continue to act rationally. Don't you see, *we will have beaten the cycles!*"

RashTak filled his lungs and tensed his vibrators, ready to roar another volley into the suddenly thunderous silence. He stopped, poised for stentorian magnificence and exhaled at the stillness. Never had Pashti been so quiet. The room felt eerie, spooky and unreal.

"What's wrong now?" he couldn't help but whisper.

A sign of severe shock, the response came so faintly that he almost missed the subtle vibrations. He couldn't even tell if AraTak or Ee!Tak authored the tiny vibrations. With each cycling they grew in intensity until RashTak could make out the subtle message, "We've beaten the cycles?"

RashTak froze, afraid to move, afraid he'd cover their slight, shocked sounds. He couldn't even force himself to refill his empty lungs. The hormones in his body—concurrent with the mood—seemed as still as the room. The finest of the sensorial fibers on his foot could make out the faint shivers of Pashti—subordinates hidden away in someone's rooms, or the chitter of the impregnated females, nervous at the feeling of new life within.

Ee!Tak's exclamation was only normal but it seemed to fill the room. "We've beaten the cycles."

AraTak thrummed happily, loudly, vigorously, *"WE'VE BEATEN THE CYCLES!"*

* * *

Marshal of the Soviet Union, Sergei Rastinyevski stared at the map, eyes hollow and sunken, a fever of frustration burning in his soul. He turned at the sound of the door, swinging around on his heel to see General Secretary Karpov entering.

"Sergei! It's good to see you again."

They embraced, Yevgeny holding him at arm's length. "You're not looking well, my friend."

Rastinyevski waved it away. "It's the darkest hour before dawn. What is the news?"

"Plenty." Yevgeny walked over to the Waterford crystal decanter and poured scotch into a glass. "First and foremost, the American President, James Atwood, has been defeated in his bid for reelection. His Vice President, Burt Cook, has won the Republican Party's primary election."

Sergei sighed. "Then we have a reprieve. Cook will pull back on the bombing raids. He's promised better defense of the continental United States, hasn't he?"

"He has, but what a man says to get elected, and what

he'll do in office are two very different things. I suspect, however, that the pressure will be off for a while."

"They just got lucky, you know." Rastinyevski turned to look at the map. "Damn Ustinov! He had to pull that fool stunt and cross the Amur."

"Spilt milk, Sergei. He paid for his foolish error."

"I shoot him every night in my dreams. He may have lost us the war. Do you know that? The Chinese invasion came so suddenly. We had promised them! Sworn to them that we'd leave them alone, that our fight was with the West—and Ustinov had to pull that crazy . . ." He ended with clenched fists, grunting in anger while the veins at his temples throbbed. "We'd have had the bomb, Yevgeny. We'd have had it—and the Americans would have lost."

Karpov shrugged, sighing. "No one could have foretold that the Chinese would advance as far as Krasnoyarsk and capture the reactor there. So what. We pushed them back."

"But at the cost of so much territory." Rastinyevski placed palms to the sides of his head, dull eyes on the map. "As we speak, for the first time since Hitler, NATO troops are fighting inside our borders. They are *in* the Ukraine."

"At the same time, we're making progress. The Alaskan port at Anchorage is under attack. We've diverted them. Not only that, our intelligence capabilities are better than theirs. They have no idea KGB has an agent in the NSC. Each time they complete a bomb plant, we take out the breeder reactors. I'm sure they're pulling their hair out over there."

Rastinyevski nodded. "Yes, yes, but at what cost. We've lost sixty-nine percent of our intercontinental bomber force in the last two years. Manufacturing is so slow. We made a mistake in the late seventies when we changed from producing lots of cheap simple aircraft to these engineering marvels which take so much sophistication. When Gorbachev switched the emphasis in manufacturing from heavy industry to consumer goods, he cut our throat militarily."

"The Americans are suffering just as much. We've

leveled their Lockheed, Boeing, and Northrup plants. Most of their fancy factories are rubble now."

Sergei shot Yevgeny a look. "Have you seen Moscow recently?"

Karpov lifted a hand and let it slap to his side. "Berlin looked like that at the end of the Second World War. It didn't take long to rebuild it. Besides, Boston, New York, Washington, Denver, Atlanta, San Francisco, Seattle . . . they all look the same as Moscow and Kiev and Kharkov."

"So. We've rolled the Chinese back by spilling a river of Soviet blood. Beijing says they will keep a cease-fire for the moment. Why? Because we blasted their Forbidden City into rubble? Or because T86 tanks are rolling through the Great Wall?"

"Maybe they didn't expect fifteen million casualties in the first seven months." Karpov raised an eyebrow.

"And in the middle of all this insanity, the Hammer Division still holds onto Brussels." Rastinyevski shook his head. "I can't imagine how they do it. Not with the supply lines so tenuous these days."

Karpov scratched the back of his head. "I wanted to talk to you about China. If we take the cease-fire offer, we can pull those units back, use them to force the Americans out of the Far Eastern District, or push the borders back on the west. What are your suggestions?"

Sergei filled his lungs, a weary sadness in his eyes. "They're fighting in the Ukraine. With the front in eastern Poland now, I say push them back. There are historical reasons, Yevgeny. Only when we beat back Hitler, the Poles and Czechs and Hungarians were with us. This time, they've greeted the NATO forces as heroes. It will take all of our national will, but we've barely unleashed the might of Mother Russia.

"Yes, take the Chinese peace, then let's see NATO stand against us."

* * *

Sheila Dunbar blinked against the gritty feeling in her eyes. Physically and emotionally exhausted, she reached for the cup and took another giant swallow of coffee. For days they had been preparing for this. Food had been set aside, hidden in packs and clothing off the floor—they had found the hard way that it ate anything discarded. Water had been stored in containers produced by the amazing Ahimsa factory. In the future their relations with Wide might not be so friendly.

Sheila felt the aches and pains in her body as she looked out at the faces of these people she'd come to know so well—and to depend on completely. Most were fresh, up and dressed after a night's sleep.

"Ladies, gentlemen, friends," she began, knowing her voice sounded hoarse—brittle from lack of sleep like the rest of her. "Some of you may have noticed the change in the ship. Some have seen through the observation blister that the stars have ceased to move. Wide has shut the null singularity generator off and we are in normal space. Ahead of us, some four hours away, is TaHaAk."

The only reaction she got consisted of tightening expressions and some shifting in the seats. She lifted her hands. "You've had the benefit of everything I can think of—all I can offer. We have prepared for a type of war no one has ever fought before. For the rest, you must rely on your instincts and reactions. Each and every one of you are the best our planet has produced. You've risen from Earth in an alien bubble, watched your homes and countries disappear. You've gone where no human being has ever been. You've trained to fight aliens and invade space stations. You've jumped out of torpedoes in deep space and watched the backside of the universe. People, this is the final challenge. If we don't pull this mission off perfectly, we could condemn our planet."

She leaned forward, searching their faces. "Do you understand? Think of your homes, of the faces of the children. What we do today directly affects every man, woman, child, plant, and animal on our Earth. If we make a mistake, if something goes wrong, the aliens will blame us, and Earth and humanity will pay the price."

Weary, so very, very weary. She straightened, drawing strength from the stories Moshe had told her about the Yom Kippur war when the Israelis fought for four days with no sleep.

"You will assault in four separate tactical wings. You all know the sequence—no doubt, in your dreams!" They laughed uneasily. "At the same time, we must be prepared for the worst. If you run into any setbacks, unexpected behavior by the Pashti, or unusual developments, call us immediately.

"Major Detova's intelligence center will be monitoring the Pashti station and comm. We'll apprise you the second that anything changes. Communication is the key here. If anyone gets into trouble, give a shout. We'll be right behind you and pry you out."

She wiped her nose, feeling so incredibly proud of these displaced humans, all so different, all so similar.

"Wide has half-jokingly requested that we become star phantoms. No one must know it was our little command which committed this raid. We must leave no one behind—no evidence of who we were. Star phantoms. A curious way for humans to finally travel to the stars. I suppose we ought to have some sort of designation. Phantom Brigade strikes me as appropriate.

"Very well, Phantoms, our time has come. I can only hope and pray you will obey every order to the letter. Remember, no matter what, you're professionals." She searched their eyes one more time, a numbness anesthetizing her soul. *It's all out of my hands now. Events will dominate from here on.* "Good luck, people. Come back alive."

CHAPTER XXV

RashTak enjoyed the sensation of his mandibles slicing the tender flesh of Bak!Gil as he stood stuffing himself at the food dispensers. The only other cycle he had lived through had been as a young one. He had attached himself to AakTak—and fortunately, chosen correctly. His faint memories of those times had been of extreme hunger, constant fright, and incredible sexual drives which he obviously couldn't have fulfilled—the females belonging to his master. Now, the only luxury of the cycles he could allow himself to fully enjoy was that of gluttony. That is, until the comm chattered, "Chee'ee'la is speaking!"

RashTak dropped his half eaten Bak!Gil on the floor and left at a run for the central Council Chambers. Ee!Tak and AraTak had beaten him there.

He mounted the podium and stared at the translation coming through the machine.

"Humans>have>now>arrived>in>your>system<

After<your<considerable<deliberations<->what>do>you>intend>to>do>about>them>interrogative>?<"

RashTak thrummed nervously. He settled his dominant eyes on his Second Councillor and raised his pincer-manipulators helplessly. "Most wise and noble Chee'ee'la, there are no Homosapiens in our system. What gives you the, ah, suggestion, that Homosapiens are here?"

"Humans<are<even<now<closing<on<your<system> They>come>from>the>direction>of>their >home>planet< Within<an<eighth<of<your< light<cycles<humans<will<arrive> Repetition> What>do>you>intend>to>do>about>them>interrogative<?>"

RashTak's organs wiggled and squirmed, the sensation

that of trying to digest rocks. “AraTak, please, go to comm central and check the scan toward the Homosapiens’ system. See if you can see anything coming in from that direction. If they were coming, one of the buoys should have chimed an alarm.”

AraTak left in a clatter of excitement as RashTak addressed the translator again. “There has been no alarm from the navigational buoys. Certainly—”

“Ahimsa<Wide<has<blanketed<your<navigation <buoys<with<a<localized<electron<absorption< field<effect> As>we>speak>the>humans>are> assembling>to>come>here>and>create>much> noise<”

“Why didn’t you tell us? Why did you let them come so close before speaking?” RashTak exploded. “How do you know all this? How can you be so sure that Homosapiens are coming here? Why—”

“To<answer<you<mark<first<interrogative<-> I>informed>[see ~record ~past ~conversation ~with ~ RashTak ~named ~Pashti ~dated ~356.7^{-69} ~uranium ~half ~life]you>humans>would>come>at>that>time <Second<Interrogative<answer<->Control>of> their>movement>is>not>within>my>capacity> as>it>involves>ballistic>transmutation>of> matter>while>subject>to>null>singularity> Ahimsa>drives< Continuation<->such>effects> require>complex>mathematics>with>N>geometric>vector>analyses<[See ~above ~comments ~ about ~when ~Chee’ee’la ~informed ~Pashti ~about ~ humans ~Illogical ~contradictory ~statement ~ See ~ above ~explanation] <Mindspace>continuum> expanded>personality>many>places[see ~N ~geometric ~above]at>once> <Note>||This>may>be>an> experience>beyond>intellectual>comprehension> and-or>experience>of>Pashti< Last<complete< interrogative<presented<before<conversation<terminated<as<spurious<->Chee’ee’la>notes>humans> already>here<->hence>interrogative>of>RashTak >meaningless<”

He chewed on that. A lot of thought had gone into how the Shithti could send their perceptions out among the stars. He'd known they couldn't interfere with null singularities as a result of the N dimensional difficulties of perception, structure, and location outside normal light space. He had to accept that Homosapiens were somewhere close. They must—

Comm didn't even warn him. Instead it exploded in AraTak's frantic, "Violet Curses! *An Ahimsa ship is right on top of us! It is splitting apart! I count at least fifty smaller craft of a type unknown! They refuse normal navigational hailing!*"

RashTak quivered. He turned. "Ee!Tak! Go! See if you can help him. Go! Now!"

The Third Councillor scrambled for the central communications center. RashTak settled a foot on the visual and watched a holo of the huge Ahimsa ship blocking the stars as the light of SkaHa reflected dully from the gray graphitic metal of the hull.

RashTak hissed a Violet insult at the huge glowing crystalline form of Chee'ee'la. The mistakes piled on top of each other, compounding. How could he have known Chee'ee'la's warning about the Homosapiens had been literal? Why had the Ahimsa defused the situation when he'd been so close to panic? How could any sane creature conceive that Homosapiens were coming in person to set foot on the station? Violet Curses! A Shitht statement could mean so many things!

"Ahimsa ship! Attention! Wide, we assume it is you we are speaking to, please answer. What is your purpose? You are in violation of the navigational regulations concerning the entry into the Pashti—" A whine indicated the powerful Ahimsa ship had completely damped his signal.

Frantic, RashTak thought, hitting the access channel to central communications. AraTak's hard features formed, the multiple mandibles of his mouth moving in a frenzy of chewing motions. "AraTak! This is important! Open a channel to the Overones. We will be jammed immediately by Wide's ship, but open it and leave it open. Do *not* shut that channel down for fear of the Violet Demons themselves! Do you understand? It might be our salvation! The worst is true! *Wide is insane!*"

Thank God we beat the cycles! What if he'd shown up

with us running around like lunatics? Violet Disaster! He opened a line to the whole station, hoping FeerTak would understand enough to keep himself alive. "Attention! This is an emergency! We are about to be infested with an insane alien life-form. They are unstable beings imported from an interdicted planet. They are violent when approached. Flee before them! Show no resistance! Stay away from them! I repeat, they are wild animals and extremely dangerous! Do not resist! Do anything they want you to! Just don't aggravate them! Keep your wits about you!"

His vibrators thrummed the essence of the message throughout the station. Violet Gods! How did this ever happen? How could Hurt and Sees accuse him of being crazy and paranoid from the cycles while Wide committed this foulest treachery even as the Overones spoke? His guts roiled and ached as he chittered softly to himself. Or had it been an Ahimsa plot all along? Could they all have been a part of this? Was it possible the Overones had lied? Even now, were humans raging through every Pashti settlement and station throughout the galaxy? Lost in the passion of the cycles, were they being butchered as TaHaAk was about to suffer?

RashTak shuddered with fear, his pincer-manipulators clacking in the air. "Pity the race of Pashti," he cried into the comm. "Pity! I cry for pity! What have you brought upon us, Wide? What horror do you let loose upon the females and the little ones? What do you invest upon the subordinates? *WHY ARE YOU DOING THIS?*"

* * *

"Sealed orders, gentlemen," Sheila told them as she handed the envelopes over. "Please peruse them as soon as you have embarked for TaHaAk station."

She knew what they saw, a thin woman who looked haunted with a drawn and haggard air about her. Her stomach burned and churned, paining her. From the way they felt, her muscles could have been made of lead. A headache knotted and wrung the nerves back of her eyes like a twisted washcloth. How many hours had she pored over those orders, making sure the translations were perfect?

She drilled them with her fevered gaze. "Flexibility,

gentlemen. I'm counting on the fact that our personnel are professionals. We've done a lot of improvising in the last month, starting a raid, pulling out. Often they've seemed like strange maneuvers. I've had my reasons. I think we're capable of instant adaptation to a situation. In fact, I've gambled everything on that."

They took the thin envelopes of odd plasticlike paper the Ahimsa machines had produced. She studied them: Moshe, his gnome features carefree; Sam, face long as he chewed his lower lip; Svetlana, casting furtive glances at Sam, a desperate efficiency in the set of her mouth and her posture; and lastly, Viktor, his eyes having taken on a shade of dynamite blue, his features strained, his thoughts, as always, so carefully guarded.

"Questions?" Sheila asked one last time.

There were none.

"Good luck, people. Fight smart—come back alive. We have a lot to do." With that, she dismissed them, fighting the urge to reach out to Viktor, seeing his eyes suddenly change—a devil-may-care glint in them.

Sam and Svetlana had walked off arm in arm, heads bent close. Moshe left at a dog-trot. Viktor stood, arms crossed, as he looked at her. A huge emotional fist clamped on her heart, making it difficult to breathe.

"I've never known a woman like you, Sheila." He spoke softly. "In view of what is about to happen, I think you have taken the universe upon your lovely shoulders. I will do what I can to help you hold it up."

She nodded, the muscles in her neck cramping. "Thank you, Viktor. I . . ." She hesitated, stepping close, reaching for him. He hugged her, his touch gentle. "I've done everything I can to keep this from being another Afghanistan for you. God help me if I've failed."

He pushed back, searching her eyes. Yes, he understood what she meant. He smiled, nodding his assurance. "I'll be back."

"Be careful, Viktor."

He smiled the wary smile of a soldier. "You, too. If it . . . well, you know."

"I know."

Little lines formed at the sides of his mouth and he

nodded, acknowledging her secrecy. "I do have one question, Major."

"Very well, Viktor?" She hoped he'd say nothing to give her away. God alone knew what or who Wide was watching at the moment. It had already been a gamble to give out the orders. She'd played a tight game writing those out—risking everything as she put the pieces together over the last couple of days. The Rubicon had been crossed.

"I'm going to ask for something I've never requested before an action." His eyes went serious, voice husky as he stepped close. "Kiss me."

Startled, the confusion must have shown in her face. "Viktor?"

His expression dropped at her hesitation and he was turning away, the eyes hardening as some resolve formed behind them. He got three steps before she caught him, turning him to stare into those icy eyes.

"You caught me by surprise." She met his lips with hers, feeling her blood race in her veins. A hunger and an emptiness built as she felt his warm mouth and seeking lips.

He pulled away, and she could see his pulse at the base of his neck, the oxygen and "helmet" packs barely obscuring it.

"My," she breathed. "I dare say—that was delightful!"

"Just a lark," he offered with a smile. "Every soldier should have at least one kiss before a mission. Maybe it will keep the ghosts away this time."

"Then it was worth it."

He nodded, hugging her one last time. "For luck."

Then he walked away, shoulders straight, while she stared after him.

* * *

Moshe held Riva tight, seeing the lights glistening in her red hair. "You'll be careful," he insisted, feeling his heart squeezed by some unknown pressure.

She kissed him passionately, firmly—as if she would never kiss again. "I won't be the one facing Pashti on their home ground, Moshe. Oh, for God's sake, I don't want to lose you, too!" Her arms tightened about him.

He separated her grip, aware of the grins and amusement the display caused his men. Here and there, others of Assaf Company were hugging sweethearts, getting last minute kisses, folding prayer shawls, and making a final check of their Ahimsa made space tanks. The vehicle sides were already "decorated" with Hebrew letters, slogans, and names. Most were lettered in the traditional, "Never Again!"

He valiantly tried to find the words. "I never thought I would care for another woman again. When I buried my Anna, I thought—"

She placed soft warm fingers on his lips. "I have come to care a great deal for you, Moshe Gabi. Just come back. We'll sort out the rest then."

"Coming up on time, people," Sheila's voice sounded in their comms.

"I've got to get this tank loaded. It's your torpedo—you take care of us, huh?" He kissed her one last time and crawled up, slipping easily into the restricted turret. Chaim had already checked the systems and Yeled had the laser as well as the projectile weapons on the long assault vehicle charged.

Riva ran up the ramp, feet thumping hollowly, and disappeared into the guts of her torpedo. Moshe looked around, seeing the motto Chaim had painted on their tank. L'CHAIM stood out in large white Hebrew letters.

He felt confused as he waited while two other tanks, Uzzi's and Kalman's, backed in behind him. What was he doing? Riva had to be at least ten years younger than he. Could Anna be replaced by another woman? But Riva? Could a CIA agent be right for him? God alone knew, she'd earned the right to be called Sabra—if not a Jewish one. What sort of life would be theirs? *First, Moshe*, you *must survive this space war. Do that and you can deal with the rest.*

"Only everything's in turmoil," he whispered to himself. *But when hasn't it been?*

A shrill whistle made Moshe look back. The second tank moved slowly up the ramp, its commander, Uzzi, ducking under the low hatch. He tapped Chaim on the shoulder and they purred silently back and up the ramp. As always, the silence of the machine bothered him.

What a shock to miss hearing the growling diesel and smelling the fumes he had so long associated with war.

Moshe ducked under the low hatch. Inside, he tapped Chaim again as they snugged up to Uzzi's tank. "We're in, Riva." His tank shivered as the grapples locked down. Motors whined as the ramp lifted and sealed.

"Assaf net, this is Moshe; report," he spoke into the headset.

"I've got you, L'chaim," Riva checked. "You're hooked into the Tin Tuna." How had she ever named her torpedo such a thing?

"Shmulik here." "Arya here." "Ben Yar here." One by one the rest checked in.

"Fifteen minutes to drop," Riva reported. "Moshe, I've got the command net. You're plugged in."

He could hear Sheila's patter of conversation to Svetlana Detova. To his crew he added, "And we thought the Syrians and PLO were odd people!" They laughed good-naturedly. To Yeled: "Remember, same tactics we used in Suez City. Keep moving, shoot whichever way you want to keep them off balance."

Yeled grinned up from his sophisticated visual and laser sights. "But of course, *ba'al*!"

Sheila's voice informed. "Phantom Battalion, five minutes to drop. Good luck, people."

Moshe's thoughts returned to Riva. What should he do? Assuming they both lived through this—was he ready for that kind of commitment? A pang built as his tumultuous thoughts returned to Anna. His hands ran nervously over the corners of Dunbar's secret orders. He twisted the edge of the indestructible alien paper.

Under his breath, he muttered, "If you must think first—don't act!" Was it true? Or, should he simply ask Riva to move in with him? It had been a trial on those long nights they had worked together. How often had he longed to reach over and pull her to him, to take her as his woman. He had seen the desire in her eyes. More than once, there had been an open invitation that he—with his old-fashioned values—had turned down. Now, with death no further than what lay beyond that hatch, had he been a fool for not accepting her love? He could hear his teeth grinding in his head.

"Five, four, three, two, one. Drop!" Sheila's voice announced, Moshe felt himself pushed back as the torpedo accelerated.

Sheila's voice added, "Operation Yom Kippur initiated."

Moshe strapped himself in and buttoned up the top. He slid a nail under the seam of the envelope and opened the thin sheets. The problem of Riva was now academic—pending God, luck, and Pashti artillery.

* * *

Murphy let his eyes feast as Katya walked up, hips swinging in the skintight Ahimsa cloth. Damn! Something about her just seemed to grow on him. The more he watched her, the more carried away he got. She just seemed to get sexier by the day. Not only that, but he'd never known a woman with her intelligence. What did she see in the likes of him?

He kissed her a resounding smack and swung her feet off the ground. "Glad to see you checked in before we took off. Gotta go kick the crabs in the chops. Makes a man horny!"

Her green eyes searched his. "You'll be back, Murph, promise me that."

"Hey, what happened to the old no-commitment, no-worries, Katya? Thought I was just convenient for the time being."

The corners of her lips twitched wryly. "I don't know. Maybe in the long term that's how it will be. For now . . . well, I've never had so much fun with a man."

He nodded, running his hands up and down her back. "Hey, look, we'll just see, all right?"

"You'll have to come back in order to find that out. Meanwhile, you'd better get to your squad . . . and I to mine."

"You got it, gal." He kissed her one last time and hugged her tight, feeling her body against his, refusing to imagine a Pashti standing over it.

Murphy turned and heaved a sigh as he caught sight of

Gubanya staring, eyes almost glowing with pent-up up frustration and rage. "Oh, boy."

Katya lounged beside him, poised and relaxed.

Mika advanced, walking fluidly, feet padding with the careful power of a stalking tiger, arms swinging easily. The muscles in his jaws knotted and jumped while the lines deepened around his mouth. "I have come to wish you luck, *friend.* I would not like to hear you died. I hope you remember what I told you about Americans and how they were usually shot."

Murphy throttled the hot blood surging through his body. The echoes of his heartbeat sounded a low roar in his ears. It had been a tough two nights cleaning puke spots in torpedoes with toothbrushes. First, there hadn't been that many toothbrushes around until Katya got the Ahimsa factory to produce a batch, and second, *he hadn't been that damn humiliated since boot camp!*

"Oh, I'll be minding my back with folks like you around, *good buddy!*" Murphy grinned, aware of the curious glances sent their way by observers. "You keep yourself in fine shape, Guby. Katya and me don't want nothing to do with being croaked if you're dumb enough to stick your head up when a crab's shooting."

Mika smiled thinly and replied softly, "One day, *dear friend,* we will be out of space . . . away from Viktor Staka. Then you and I will test our . . . friendship." He nodded curtly to Katya and backed away, slightly crouched, shoulders a yoke of muscle as his fingers slowly curled in the air at his sides. He turned and trotted for his torpedo, adrenaline-charged legs pumping like steel springs.

"You watch yourself around him." Katya squinted along the route Gubanya had taken. "He would love to kill you . . . only the risks are too great. Major Staka has issued his orders. If either of you is thought to have killed the other. . . ." She waved it away, pulling him tight against the curve of her hip.

"I don't give a crab's ass about him!" He smiled and hugged her. "Gotta go, but don't worry! Mika and I ain't gonna bump heads over there. There's plenty of crabs." He ran his fingers tenderly through her blonde hair. "Hey, I'm off to play Mr. Wizard!" He slapped her bottom and smothered her with a passionate kiss before he ran for the hatch on his torpedo. He could hear Phil Cruz calling roll as he passed the hatch—already closing—and climbed over the only tank his unit had gotten. He sat down, buckling into the crash gear as he heard Major Dunbar's launch announcement. A second later, gravity tried to pull him apart as his torpedo was shot at TaHaAk station and destiny.

* * *

Svetlana Detova tried to clear her mind as she entered her room. The incredible Ahimsa headset rested on the stand beside the monitor. The gold gleamed redly in the overhead light, gaudy, almost bloody. She approached, staring down at the delicate-looking metal, hands working nervously at her sides.

The whole plan smacked of the ludicrous. Everything had come too quickly. *How many mistakes did I make in the programs? What if Wide sees the fakery? What if he notices the Pashti? Recognizes a particular scene?*

With trembling hands, she reached for the headset, the chill of the metal biting into her flesh—burning despite being room temperature.

"I'm no magician, Sheila. I'm not even a low class wizard. What if I missed something?" *Too late now.*

She settled nervously in the contour conforming chair, vaguely aware of the blank monitor before her. The golden glow of the headset held her attention. *What if I'm not clever enough? What if I can't do it?*

Images of Sam's smile, his gentle touch and soft voice, echoed in her thoughts. No doubt but that they'd all be dead soon. Sheila had taken her shot at propping the door open at the last minute. Most likely, Wide would react, trigger the gravity buoys and pitch the Earth into cataclysm in his rage. Then he'd turn his wrath on them.

"The final battle," she whispered, lowering the headset in place. Ahimsa phrases appeared in a scattered fashion in her mind. She reached for her notes, thumbing through the mnemonics, tracing the roundabout way she would have employ to thread her way into the system.

Still, she hesitated to initiate the first program. Her

mouth went dry as she remembered that last vision of the Earth as her bubble had risen above the planet. That whole world, all those people, the plants, the birds, even the fish and insects that resided there became her responsibility now. No matter what Sam or Viktor accomplished, Svetlana Detova would determine each of their futures based on one desperate effort: Sheila Dunbar's master plan had to be perfectly plotted—and perfectly executed.

If only we'd had more time. But then, that's what people always say. If only . . . if only. . . .

She forced her fists to unclench and wiped her sweaty palms on the slick Ahimsa fabric.

Svetlana allowed herself one shiver before she purged her mind, took a deep breath, and ordered the computer to initiate the first of her programs. Committed, she had only her wits, her cunning and skill to pit against the power of the Ahimsa.

* * *

Sam ignored the chatter coming from his headset as he pulled Sheila's special orders from his pocket. The torpedo kicked him back into the soft padded seat as his eyes quickly scanned the thin fragile-looking pages.

The smile that began to crease his face slowly exposed his strong white teeth. "I'm a goddamned son of a bitch! Bless Sheila Dunbar's heart!" Then he realized the ramifications of failure and his heart almost stopped.

"Thirty seconds to impact!" the pilot's voice came through the net.

Six gravities pulled Sam's face like a mask as they curved and decelerated over TaHaAk station. At least he hadn't felt the torpedo take any evasive action. The bump felt a little rougher than during the practice sessions.

"We're in, boys!" came the excited call of the pilot. "Visual shows the other side swarming with crabs! It'll be tough!"

Sam had already hit the release. "All right, maggot meat, let's hit 'em!" Sam yelled. "Anderson, Watson, lay down a perimeter! Cover us—but don't shoot until my order! I repeat, *no shooting until my order!*"

The hatch dropped down and their tank plowed out,

fragrant air boiling in from the station. Sam followed right after the tank, assault rifle ready.

He stood in an odd-shaped room, not exactly round, and the gravity seemed a little light, not quite Earth normal. The air, however, made the greatest first impression as it ran over his skin—almost hot and particularly dry. The tank fired a bolt, blowing away what seemed to be an impromptu barricade at the end of the corridor.

"Ytzak! Hold your fire!"

The Israeli turned, hearing his name. He rattled off a staccato of Hebrew.

"Oh, shit!" Sam felt that tingling rush of panic surge up his spine. "Sheila?"

"Here, Sam."

"The damn translators don't work over here! Get Moshe's net to order his tanks to cease fire!"

"Riva? Did you copy that?"

"Yes, Major. I'm into Assaf's net."

What the hell else is going to go wrong? A rifle barked.

Sam ducked behind the armor of the vehicle, his men filing out after him. Anderson and Watson efficiently provided cover. At the other end of the room, the Pashti huddled, cowering against the wall. Watson's rifle was coming up.

"Hold your fire!" Sam screamed. "I repeat, HOLD YOUR FIRE! New orders! Shoot only when shot at! Major Dunbar wants minimal Pashti casualties. Push 'em toward that Council Chamber. Everyone got that? Sound off, you goofballs. Watson?"

"Understood."

"Anderson?"

"Understood."

He could see the confusion in his men's strained expressions. They'd arrived here expecting to fight tooth and nail, only to find cowering creatures climbing over each other to flee through the barrier the tank had blown open.

"Murph? Mason? You in?"

"Here!" they both chimed at the same time. "No resistance, the crabs are running before we can get a shot into 'em!"

"New orders from Major Dunbar! Hold your fire! Understand? No shooting unless *absolutely* necessary. Keep the bloodshed to a minimum! Repeat, to a minimum! Sheila doesn't want another Mylai, got that?"

"Roger! If Sheila wants it, she's got it." Murphy sounded bewildered. "Hold up!" Murphy bellowed into the headset, causing Sam to wince. *"SHEILA SAYS HOLD YOUR GODDAMN FIRE!"*

"Murphy?"

"Sir?"

"If you yell into the headset like that at full volume again, I'm gonna reach down your throat and rip your lungs out."

"Yes, sir. Sorry, sir."

Sam switched access, repeating the orders to each of his teams. "Take your objectives. Don't be afraid to defend yourselves if the crabs get nasty—but only if they're really nasty! I'll bust anybody that goes off his rocker shooting hoodoos!"

His unit stood, staring around, looking at the blasted barricade.

"All right, you pussy pukes, move it! We've got a communications center to take and control!"

Ytzak looked to Sam for instructions. Daniels waved the tank forward, pointing to his rifle and shaking his head a vigorous no. Ytzak made an okay with his fingers and grinned.

"God help us that that's the only friggin' screwup," Sam prayed under his breath, trotting down the hall with his team.

The Pashti melted away, their calls like cicadas on a warm summer evening crossed with bullfrog croaking and generator turbine whine.

"Why not waste 'em?" Peters asked, wary gaze creeping from side to side where the Pashti huddled, often packed on top of each other, their vibrations felt even through the floor.

"Strategy, puke brain!" Sam gave him a quick grin. "The Major doesn't want 'em to have any nasty beef with humans. Get the picture?"

"Huh?" Glen Peters watched the Pashti while he licked

his lips, assault rifle at the ready. "It don't make sense to—"

"Shuddup and soldier!"

"Shit!" Murphy's voice exploded through the net. "I ain't even seen a gun yet! Weird shit here! These things are all scared to death. Christ, it's like fighting sheep!"

Sam sprinted after the tank; the odd square doorway that led to the Pashti computer and communications center stood wide open. Two larger red-black crabs hovered over the strangely shaped equipment as Sam ducked in the door, the tank filling the hallway, covering the situation.

Anderson and Watson spread out to either side, stepping slowly, cautiously, assault rifles ready. Sam could see the sweat trickling down Gene's face as he swallowed nervously.

One of the crabs scuttled forward as Sam ordered, "Hold your fire!" He triggered three shots that blew holes in the deck in front of the Pashti. The creature immediately reversed directions in a wail of clicking, keening noise. It quivered and shook, a new odor like burning hair rising in the air.

"Status report, Sam?" Sheila's voice came through the net.

"We're in the communications room. Looks like we've got two big crabs here, darker in color, Major. They seem to be pretty smart. Bigwigs maybe. Dominant males."

"Very good. Any resistance?" Sheila's voice sounded coolly efficient over the net.

"None. Looks to me like they're scared to death of us. Hell, no one's even been shot at. Nothing. These things are passive."

"I had hoped so," Sheila sounded relieved. "I'm sending a translator in. Keep an eye out for her."

"Translator?" *Her?* Sam's eyes narrowed. "Shit! That's open territory clear back to the torpedo!"

He'd wondered what all those extra CIA gals had been for. But that had been outside of his sphere of influence—Svetlana's bailiwick.

Three minutes later, Mary Dak ducked past the tank and stopped, studying the Pashti. A large spindle hung from her hand, unrolling telephone wire—the stuff they'd been stockpiling. Quickly, she set up a small unit that Sam recalled Mason had worked on, something that had needed batteries.

Looking up at him, she added, "I'm ready to talk to them, Captain. Let's see if we can bring this to a rapid conclusion."

Sam swallowed, his rifle steady on the two Pashti. "Go ahead."

The machine hummed, vibrated and clicked and croaked, the Pashti immediately reacting, shuffling back and forth, clicking and warbling.

"I'm asking for their surrender. Their responses will go straight to Sheila's comm." She inserted a tape marked Moody Blues and the box chittered and throbbed in Pashti noises. The Pashti grunted, chittered, and clicked back.

Sam licked his lips, aware of the sweat forming and beading on his forehead. What in hell was Sheila up to?

* * *

Viktor Staka's expression took on a cunning look as his torpedo crashed through the side of the station. Gravity immediately changed and they were hanging downward, subject to angular acceleration now.

"Go!" he ordered. The three tanks clawed their way up and out, guns banging as they passed the hatch. "Armor, hold your fire! Group 1, form up in a defensive perimeter immediately upon exiting. I repeat, hold your fire! Await my orders!"

He could see Nedelin and Oganski looking at him soberly as he hustled up and out into the warm dry air of the station. The tanks had formed up in a triangle, guarding the breach. Somewhere, an assault rifle hammered away.

His SPETSNAZ began to line up to each side, covered by the bulk of the tanks. Viktor accessed the net. "Gubanya! Malenkov! Hold your fire! I repeat, HOLD YOUR FIRE! Herd the Pashti toward the center of the station. Do not—I repeat, do *not* shoot first! That is an order from highest authority. Confirm please!"

"Confirmed, do not shoot first!" Malenkov's voice came through.

"Understood, Major," Gubanya added.

A female voice broke into the system, speaking something incomprehensible. The voice sounded like Riva Thompson's. Viktor accessed his net. "Sheila? What was that? Sheila? Are you there?"

He picked a few words of English from the answer. *Blood and Fire! The translators!* "Attention, SPETSNAZ! The translators don't work. If you have any trouble—"

"Major Staka? Katrina, here. Major Dunbar would like you to know that everything is on schedule. Please advance as planned."

Viktor sighed, and called out, "Advance and concentrate the captives in the Council Chamber rooms. Do not take risks, gentlemen, but no unnecessary enemy casualties will be permitted. Consider it to be an exercise in detente, eh?"

"Da!"

"Move out!" Viktor followed his tanks as they ripped through bulkheads heading for the main corridors. The air filled his nostrils, spicy, almost having the odor of Arab coffee. Before them, the Pashti scattered, making their unique noises as they ran in a wild panic from the human advance.

"Katrina? What about Assaf? Can you talk to them?"

"Through Major Thompson, sir. I'll meet you at the Council Chambers. Currently I'm stringing wire behind Malenkov's advance."

"Affirmative." *And God help us if a crab gets you!* Botched communication? A last minute change of orders? Viktor started ticking things off on his fingers. A hell of a lot could go real wrong.

Viktor didn't look twice as the guards formed to protect the torpedo. The KGB agent who emerged after him unrolling electrical wire didn't surprise him either. Being a good Soviet officer, KGB activities were none of his business. Pray Sheila knew what she was doing!

CHAPTER XXVI

"First Councillor!" AraTak's voice thrummed fear and a chittering hysteria into the comm. "The Homosapiens have pierced the skin of the station! I can feel them ripping the walls! Violet Death! Will they spill the atmosphere? Do they intend to kill us all by decompression and cold? Do they wish us to die in blackness? My young! Violet Curses on the Homosapiens! *WHAT OF MY YOUNG?*"

"Control!" RashTak demanded, forgetting that only a moment ago he, too, had been bellowing fear into the comm net. "Keep your wits, AraTak! Think! Prepare to run for your pressure suit! Perhaps we may yet do something! Perhaps we—"

The sensory transmitters shook under RashTak's fibers. "Violet Heavens! What was that?"

"They are coming from all over!" AraTak looked up from the comm. "Feel the vibrations! They have machines inside! I can hear panic among the subordinates and the females! Pashti are running everywhere! Explosions are shaking the walls! *Homosapiens are all around us*!"

"Are they killing? Do you feel Pashti being killed?" RashTak couldn't make out the difference between what was real and communicated as his feet were tied up sensing the comm as well as the vibrations that trembled the floor under him.

"I can't—" AraTak spun away from the comm. Ee!Tak chirruped sheer terror.

RashTak widened the angle and saw his first Homosapiens. Violet Insanities, what could have spawned such horrid creatures? They wore pressure suits fitted to their soft bodies. AraTak and Ee!Tak both advanced on the Homosapiens who spread out from the door. One, radiating more light waves than the others, a southern one—if the Ahimsa holos could be trusted—lifted a bulky black tool and the floor before the Councillors exploded in a rain of hot metal.

Pashti screams of terror couldn't drown the thunder of the weapon. Violet Horrors! Violet Dismemberment! Violet Atrocities! What sort of creatures were these?

RashTak could hear the rustling. It took all of his concentration to tear his eyes from the horror in the comm central. The Council Chambers began filling with the furtive shapes of subordinates as they scuttled through the doors, clinging to the walls, fearing this place of Master power—fearing the blasphemy behind them more.

Lost females scampered in and out of the confusion, keening and calling, panicked. *No, not the females! They don't have the sense to stay away! Violet Insanities, don't let them be hurt.*

RashTak shivered as his organs began writhing in his body. They had beaten the cycles! The single curse of all Pashti existence had been banished, overcome by their evolution and . . . and . . . so swiftly upon the heels of such a magnificent victory came this *abomination!* The younger males continued to pile into the chambers. Here and there, a female, squeaking, out of her mind with fear, shot past the young males and darted wildly about.

Panic. Panic everywhere. Is this how we die? Is this how our species will end? Why? Violet Curses, why? What did we do to deserve this?

RashTak stared, his mind numb at the magnitude of the disaster. A male dragged himself into the chambers. Fluids ran from his side where Homosapiens had no doubt blasted him with one of their weapons. He made chittering noises—piteous cries of pain and death drowned by the general paean of fear. Still other stragglers came at a run, some struggling with gaping, leaking wounds. Others—mad with terror—clawed their way over the very bodies of their comrades to reach this last refuge.

The room filled from wall to wall, overrun with Pashti. Panic and fear thrummed in the air. RashTak's legs buckled under him. Too many. More in one place than he'd ever seen before. They plugged the doors, tumbling over each other, the floor shaking with the impacts of their bodies as they resonated on each other—the room a cacophony of vibrations and clattering. Impossible din crashed down on him. Above it all, a loud *Brrrrapppppp!* reverberated, overwhelming even the packed bodies. Pashti froze and an almost Violet silence followed.

A few last minute, panic-stricken Pashti ran through the doors, burrowing in a cowardly fashion under the bodies of the others, vainly trying to hide beneath the suddenly still mass.

And they waited, frozen, all of them; fear a pungent odor in the air. Vibrations came from every direction—alien vibrations that shook the halls, floors, and ceilings with a cacophony of meaningless sound and signals the likes of which no Pashti had ever heard.

RashTak, nerve fled, could feel Chee'ee'la's presence, see his shimmering glow at the edge of the room. Silence! Then a rumble shivered the floor and strange pattering vibrations disturbed his sensitive leg hairs.

Silence again.

Movement! RashTak tried to turn without moving, his circulatory pumps throbbing like vibrators. He looked. One of the doors filled as the rumble renewed. A metal object occupied it. Something alive moved at the top as a long tube and a big laser slowly scanned the room.

Homosapiens appeared behind the machine. They crouched, weapons ready. RashTak heard the scuffle as frantic Pashti scuttled away from the door.

More movement and a rumble. One by one, each of the few entrances filled with the horrid machines and the terrible humans. Pashti melted into a final knot of trembling terror before the podium.

Now we will die. I will watch the senseless murder of my people. When the last of my body is ripped and torn, only my soul will be left to cry among the stars. Why?

From the metal monster, a Homosapiens emerged. RashTak felt his organs convulse as he stood alone—the only Master—above the huddled remains of his kind. He forced his mind to think.

The Homosapiens was followed by another who strung out a wire from a box. The two didn't advance as far as the pile of fearful Pashti who crowded before him. The one with the box set the unit on the floor, checking the wires attached to it.

The box spoke and immediately the crowd whimpered and cried out in fear.

"Silence!" RashTak roared—and millennia of having the Master voice bred into their souls stilled them. Bless the cycles, if only for that! The box spoke again, in Pashti muted but intelligible.

"Greetings from the commander of the human forces. I am called ~~~~~~. I have come to discuss the surrender of TaHaAk. No one will be harmed if you will agree to abide by the Human authority. Those who resist will be killed. Do you surrender?"

RashTak pulled himself as high as he could so the sound and vibrations would reach. "I am First Councillor RashTak. We will do as you wish! Do not harm us! We will do anything you want! *We surrender!*"

Out on the floor, one Pashti—his side ripped open—thrummed softly in pain. His legs kicked weakly and he whimpered as he died. RashTak choked at the sight, his soul twisting with sorrow as he collapsed and shivered.

What have I done? What have I done?

* * *

Svetlana rerouted control of the bridge monitor, hardly aware of the pounding of her heart.

Her monitor flickered and showed two Ahimsa looking like swollen nerve cells with dendrites plugged into the control consoles. On the screen, torpedoes shot toward the rotating wheel of TaHaAk station.

Svetlana followed the transmissions Wide called up on his holo. She watched as the torpedoes darted into TaHaAk and as the Phantom Brigade rushed into the Pashti station.

Now! Without another thought, she overrode the master menu and initiated the file she had so painstakingly built, a melding of scenes lifted from the records of the training exercises.

She threw herself into a frantic battle to control the data as Wide constantly sought to change files and follow separate elements of the fighting. She didn't even feel the sweat that formed as a fine mist on her features and began to trace its way down her grimacing face.

* * *

"Now, it is done!" Wide hooted, rocking back and forth. He flashed from comm pickup to comm pickup, watching the humans as they huddled in the torpedoes. Changing to several screens at once, he watched as Sam, Staka, and Moshe read from sheets of film while his other eye kept the overall view from the ship, watching the lances of metal puncture the sides of the station.

For a second he eyed the ships latched to the docking facilities. Most were Pashti. One, of unknown design, bothered something deep within his mind. Action, as the humans punctured the vulnerable walls of TaHaAK, made it irrelevant.

"And now the battle is joined!" Wide crooned. "Two barbaric, uncivilized species are locked in the death struggle which will kill them all!" He felt himself thinning with triumph as his spicules shrilled.

A slight shimmering flickered on the monitors as the humans crowded out of the torpedoes.

"Overone," Spotted noted. "Something just caused—"

"Hush!" Wide grunted, following the scene through the tank mounted pickups.

The humans met waves of mad, circling Pashti who darted this way and that, charging the humans in a desperate rush as withering blasts of automatic fire exploded carcasses and the tanks churned ahead, crushing bodies, blowing out bulkheads, smashing through restrictive doorways.

Wide flattened slightly as a rushing Pashti, half-dead, grabbed the American lieutenant, Murphy, and pitched him headfirst into a bulkhead. Assault fire literally tore the Pashti in two as it chittered and thrummed in death throes. Fluids and Pashti body parts covered the floor as the screaming humans battered their way over piles of corpses.

Wide's brains began quivering ecstatically. "Marvelous!" he whistled to himself. He caught a vague impression of Spotted slowly flattening himself at the carnage on the screen. "Simply splendid!"

"What have we wrought?" Spotted asked through a hushed rush of air.

"The future of the Ahimsa," Wide chortled. "Look at them! Pashti in the midst of their cycles! Look at the death and bloodshed. Whoever comes to TaHaAk station will find . . . .this! This proof that Pashti are insane during the cycles. Ahimsa will demand the return of all the Pashti have stolen. Once again, *we* will be the power in the galaxy. Cowed, the Pashti will be submissive—tractable."

Spotted began to look lumpy as random manipulators started to form about his body.

On another monitor, a Pashti vessel broke away from the station, bits of the lock ripping loose in the jumpship's haste. Reaction glared against the gray background of stars in the galactic plane. The null singularity generator pods looked ominous where they stood out from the reduced-drag hull.

"What is that?" Wide asked, feeling his sides going. "What is that ship? Get me Major Dunbar!"

Sheila's careworn face filled a monitor. "Yes, Wide?"

"There is a Pashti ship! It has left the station! See it? See it? It's turning! It's *headed for us!*" Wide realized manipulators had begun forming as his tread foot turned lumpy and his brains began to compartmentalize.

"We've got it." Sheila looked up at her monitors. "Appears to be a jumpship, Wide. We'll try and take it out before it closes."

"Kill it!" Wide shrieked. "*Kill it!* Quickly!"

Sheila talked into her headset. Two needle-like torpedoes disengaged from TaHaAk and shot after the Pashti, streaks of light and projectiles seeking the bogey. The screen flashed and one of the pursuing torpedoes disappeared into a fireball of exploding gases and bits of metal. The second torpedo died in a similar spectacular display.

Dunbar's voice snapped like old wire as she cried,

"Damn you, Wide! *You didn't tell us they had ship-to-ship defensive capabilities!*" Her odd human eyes pinned his, angry, violent.

"I didn't know! *I didn't know!*" Wide's sides were dropping like sails, his features becoming more irregular as his terror increased. The Pashti ship braked to a stop, settling over a lock. "They are here! Kill them! *Kill them!*" His minds drifted into frightened discrete entities.

Sheila began to shout orders into her net as Wide kept his eyes glued to the monitors. In one, he could see the humans blasting Pashti to bits as they grimly advanced through the corridors, slinging grenades around corners with reckless abandon.

"Pashti are in the ship!" Sheila announced. "Intelligence teams, take positions. Shoot any Pashti on sight." She looked up. "I'm putting a guard on your central command there. Drop your defensive barriers so you don't fry my people."

To Spotted, he ordered, "Do it!"

One of the screens showed the Council Chambers, desperately defended by Pashti, explode in a thunderous crash of smoke and fire.

"Overone?" Spotted piped, so flat he could barely force air through his spicules. "That last scene. I'd swear—"

"We've got the station!" Viktor Staka announced.

"—I saw gears spill out."

"Hush, Spotted! We're about to die! You're crazy!"

"Withdraw, Viktor." Sheila ordered, a strain in her voice. "The ship is under attack."

"We've got a couple missing!" Sam Daniels called back. "We can't disengage until we find our people and blast or fry any blood they spilled!"

"Affirmative," Sheila responded. To Wide, she added. "Open the hatches and drop any protective measures, Wide. We're coming to clean this last bunch of Pashti out—then you can take us home." She took a deep breath, the effort forced. "I didn't know we'd lose so many, Wide. You said they wouldn't fight back."

Wide stared, minds fissioning. *I didn't know. Pashti wouldn't fight back. Pashti wouldn't fight. They were civilized. Once. I didn't know. I didn't . . . Oh, thank God for the humans. Thank God. Thank God.*

"Wide? Are you going to clear the security hatches?" Sheila's voice penetrated his confusion and fear.

"Drop . . . drop them, Spotted."

"Overone, something's not—"

"DROP THE SECURITY PROTECTION!"

Spotted sent a trembling manipulator to the master boards, canceling the system. With a shrill whistle, Spotted sagged across the deck plating, tiny whimpers mocking the disaster.

Paralyzed, Wide watched as human guards jumped from a torpedo, taking up stations outside his central command hatch. He recognized one of the women as Katya Illych. The assault rifles looked bulky in their arms. They settled themselves, placing spare magazines easily at hand, kneeling to face back down the corridor.

Wide checked another monitor and could follow the progress as the Pashti advanced slowly toward the central control. Another bit of himself succumbed as his body flattened even further. Spotted looked like a knobby puddle, eyes glued to the scene, spicules piping a hoarse, piteous whistle.

* * *

"Murphy! Mason! Malenkov!" Sheila's order came through the net. "Get to the nearest torpedo! That should be sector 15-A down the main corridor! Move it! Special orders are waiting there for you! Go!"

Murphy sniffed at the incredible odor of Pashti fear—burning saffron and anise—and turned gratefully, pounding down the corridor toward the torpedo. Anything to get away from the sight of all them ugly crabs crapping on each other!

"Wide's afraid of *them?* Damn! Sheep are more dangerous!"

All that training? Shit, man, they hadn't even fought back! He hadn't seen a single weapon looking thing in the whole station.

He almost killed himself as one of the little ones—female, he guessed—skittered from almost underfoot and squealed and hooted down the pastel hallway. Somehow he kept from blowing the Pashti and himself apart in fear-choked reaction. Seconds later, out of breath, he arrived to find Mason placing one of the atmosphere patches he and Malenkov had cooked up to seal the torpedo hole when they pulled out.

Booted feet echoed on metal and Nicholai Malenkov rounded the corner, grinning from ear to ear. "All that work! Not even a single serious fight!"

"C'mon! C'mon! Move it!" Barbara Dix called from inside the torpedo. "Pick up your new orders and belt in. We've got five minutes to have you inside the Ahimsa ship and in position. Read and gab on the way, damn it!"

Murphy got shoved ingloriously past the hatch by Malenkov as Mason put the last touches on the "flower-petal seal" and bailed in behind. The hatch snicked up tight.

Murphy barely had the harness buckled down before he was thrown sideways and forward by the torpedo's movement. He plucked up the special orders and began skimming the pages, all written neatly in Sheila Dunbar's fine Spenserian script.

"Holy Mother of God!" Mason, a quicker reader, exploded. "No wonder they called it operation Yom Kippur!"

Murphy experienced a sensation that felt like a plastic garbage sack full of water had fallen on his chest. He couldn't breath or think and his vision went gray; then, as suddenly, he was weightless and his stomach was stuffing itself up into his throat. He fought the urge to vomit. Malenkov wasn't victorious—a stream of globules shot across the compartment followed by Russian curses that lost power in their translation.

"Oh, man!" Murphy moaned. "Me, Katya and Gubanya ain't about to scrape that one up! That's your shit, Nicky, you clean it!"

"Better scam them orders, Murph!" Mason called, ducking a yellow-green globe of barf that smeared the wall next to him.

Murphy looked nervously at the stuff left in the air, tried to breathe through his nose, and ran his eyes down the orders.

"I'll be damned. Today is 'get the alien day.' Hey, I wonder what it would feel like to play volley ball with Wide's little round carcass?"

He pitched forward as the torpedo slowed, which threw the remaining gook hanging in the air onto the clamlike mouth of the hatch with a sick splat.

The pilot, Barbara Dix, called down. "We're dropping through the hatch nearest the bridge complex. Just like the exercises. Two of our female officers are at the hatch now, keeping Wide from triggering any of the defenses—we hope."

"Oh, shit!" Murphy moaned, wondering what sort of booby traps Wide might have up his sleeve. Word was, he shut down the entire missile systems for the US and USSR! *Shut down?* "Oh, man! How do we get in these messes?"

"We have atmosphere outside. Wide has repressurized. Get ready, boys." Dix's voice came down, controlled and unemotional.

"What in hell did you do before you flew spaceships?" Murphy called up.

"Flew a Lear jet for the CIA, buddy boy. Somebody had to hustle her tail around the international arms trade."

Murphy bit his lip, one hand on the quick release of the buckles.

She ran guns for the CIA? That was one tough broad! "Five, four, three, two,"—inertia threw his body forward then back as the craft stopped—"one! Go! And good luck!" The hatch almost blasted open.

Ahead, Katya and another woman knelt in the dim light, glaring steely-eyed down rifle sights. A metal doorway stood immediately behind them. The only problem was it looked kind of short, and worse—closed!

"Now what?" Nicholai asked.

"We go through there, Comrade!" Katya pointed at the doorway.

Murphy shrugged, "Get back." He lifted his assault rifle as people jumped to get out of the way. The backlash from the exploding projectiles frightened him. Incredible! Bits of hot steel spattered Murphy's body and burned on his face and hair.

Squinting, he looked through the smoke and smell of things burning to see the hatch, not looking healthy, but still intact.

"Major Dunbar?" Mason shouted into the system. "We're stymied!"

CHAPTER XXVII

Svetlana studied her image of the control room. She could see Wide slowly re-forming himself as she played a tape of the Pashti attack for all it was worth, the two KGB women heroically beating back assault after assault.

Wide almost had himself back to normal as he spun and formed a manipulator out of one side of his body. He accessed a different panel and called up a new display.

"What are you doing?" Spotted's voice sounded like it had been through an echo chamber as comm translated it through several channels leading to her headset.

"It is over, one way or another. The Pashti are broken. The time has come to clean up the loose details. I am exploding several of the nuclear warheads on Earth. Humans are incredibly valuable. The uses to which humans can be put is only limited by the imagination. Therefore, I will eliminate their current socio-cultural system and begin a new civilizing process. Most of the radiation will have dissipated by the time we return the humans we currently carry and under my guidance, we can begin to rebuild their society as I think it should be."

Svetlana's heart skipped as she gasped. Could he do that? The thought paralyzed her for a split second. She lost the image, her concentration broken as she dropped system after system, seeking the program which Wide even now called up on the screen.

"Something is wrong with comm!" Spotted cried.

In the bridge image she still controlled, Svetlana could see Spotted staring at a monitor. Outside the control room hatch, a torpedo jolted to a stop, Murphy's crew tumbling out. The jig was up.

Frantic, she culled one file after another, watching

with horror as Wide entered a series of odd figures onto the screen. Desperate, with nothing left to lose, Svetlana repeated the figures into her mindlink, looping the system. The headset formed an image before her nose, duplicating Wide's.

The manipulator touched one figure as a frightful jackhammer racket echoed through the bridge monitors. Wide's manipulator jerked away as his sides deflated with fear. Svetlana began groping through the security, mentally latching onto the override sequence, forced to bet that single binary data link could hold the program in stasis.

"Wide? This is Major Dunbar." Sheila's voice reverberated loudly through the systems, echoing in Svetlana's ears.

"What are you doing?" Wide swiveled to stare at the monitor, seeing the humans in the corridor. Behind him, the hatch looked pimpled and dented, slightly buckled, but it was holding. "That's Murphy! I saw him dead! I saw. . . ."

Sheila's face formed on the next monitor. She stood in a huge room that, from the angle, seemed filled with giant segmented worms.

"I'm dickering, Wide. On Earth, we call it diplomacy by force." She motioned at the tank rolling into place behind her. "We now control two critical things. We control your ship's null singularity generator here—and the Pashti station."

Wide's manipulator reached up again, wavering but touching the console, sending information clicking through the program. Svetlana watched it continuing to loop, not initiating complete activity. Somehow she maintained an electron's gap between Wide's fumbling and the death of her world. Sweat trickled down her nose as she gritted her teeth, refusing to let loose of that last override, forcing her mind to concentrate on blocking each of the accesses Wide continued to try.

"Do you know what this board controls?" Wide asked, his eyestalk indicating the console his manipulator fiddled with. At Sheila's negation, he added. "This is the link, through singularity transduction, to your nuclear arsenal on Earth. If you do not leave the generation room, I will trigger the whole system and your planet will become a radioactive cinder."

Svetlana's heart pounded. She couldn't back out. She couldn't shout a warning to Dunbar. Any break in her concentration and Wide would access a channel past her override. Even so, she barely managed to keep ahead as the Ahimsa brought up one string of numbers after another—Svetlana clued only by the visual images he conjured on the screen she monitored. She lived a nightmare, a hideous looping game of move and countermove—the fate of her world hanging by so delicate a thread.

Sheila surprised her.

"Don't do it, Wide. If you push the wrong button and destroy the Earth, *we'll kill you!*"

Wide flattened, losing his touch with the manipulator.

Sheila continued, "You have several options, Wide. You can open the hatch and surrender. You *will* live that way—and enjoy our protection. Another option is to stay locked away and take your chances when I order my pilot to blast your hatch with her tank cannon. I think you are familiar with the amount of firepower we've added to your basic equipment. *Spotted! Touch nothing!*"

Spotted resumed his imitation of a knobby blotchy puddle, his longest manipulator sinking into his mottled hide.

Sheila picked it up in the same tone of voice. "The last option you have is to initiate that destruct system—at which time we blast the door. I may add that if you survive—by any odd chance—human beings will cut you apart piece by piece." Her voice held a vicious knife edge of threat. "You know us, Wide. You've studied us at our best and worst. Kill our planet—and the horrors you saw at Dachau, Treblinka, and Auschwitz, will be the lot of the Ahimsa!"

Wide's manipulator slowly dropped, his sides losing that last final shape. His eyestalks dully stared into Sheila Dunbar's unforgiving eyes. "You say you control the Pashti station?"

Sheila looked at the monitors. It showed a crowded room, easily recognizable as TaHaAk's Council Chambers. RashTak perched on a dais above the crowded Pashti, looking into a monitor of his own. Around him, a cordon of humans—familiar faces all—stood with weapons at the ready. A huge crystalline structure rose behind them glittering in the light, shimmering in waves of red, blue, purple, and yellow.

"A huge crystalline . . . No, never that! Not that! NO!" Wide's fragmented personality wailed hideously as each of his brains sought to divide and divide until eternity. He began to run like pancake batter across the deck.

Sheila's jaw thrust out. "Wide, we might disable your ship by blasting the bridge, but we've got the Pashti for hostages. We've got them to teach us how to pilot the jumpships—and if you choose to go that way, we'll let the whole of civilization know what the Ahimsa tried to do at TaHaAk. All of civilization will know that you lied, lied with intent to kill innocent Pashti, and double-crossed humanity in the process. You want that legacy for the Ahimsa, Wide?"

Spotted spoke, "I am opening the doors, Major Dunbar. Do not hurt me! I am a subordinate! I didn't do this!"

"No!" Wide shrilled in a whistling explosion, pulling himself upright again, involuntary manipulator spikes beginning to give him the appearance of a sea urchin.

Spotted struggled to raise a manipulator as Wide piped and whistled. Unable to complete the formation, he caved in under Wide's pressure and orders.

"Barbara, prepare to fire your forward cannon." Sheila Dunbar's voice thundered with the impact of dropped tungsten steel.

Svetlana barely managed to keep her concentration as she held the already initiated program on hold—the pressure off as long as Wide didn't begin accessing again.

Sheila sounded eminently reasonable. "Wide, you have thirty seconds—after which, we'll blast that control room door apart. Murphy! Get your people out of there!"

On the monitor, Murphy's team threw themselves into the safest place—the torpedo.

Sheila's voice began the slow countdown. Wide's eyes, standing up from an ever widening pancake of himself, watched the hatch close and the two barrels of laser and projectile cannon center on the door.

Dunbar's voice droned on. "Five, four, three—"

"I give up!" Wide screeched! "Don't kill me! *Don't kill me!*"

"Hold your fire." Sheila's voice remained rock steady.

Svetlana swallowed hard, panting with effort. *Damn! How does she do it? I'm a wreck just sitting here listening to it.* She tackled the weapons program again, rerouting, initiating a search function from the main control menu. How long would that take? How long could she keep her mind sharp? How long before she lost that edge?

The front of the torpedo opened like a blossom as Murphy's crew jumped out again.

"Just a moment," Wide mumbled, wits obviously scattered. "It will take a while to become functional."

Spotted moaned over and over. "I am a subordinate! I am a subordinate! I am a . . .."

Slowly a manipulator rose, touched a console, and the battered hatch ground open with a squeal. At the same time, as Wide grew larger, his bulk hiding the panel he rolled against, another manipulator shot out to punch figures into the detonation program.

Unable to see, Svetlana fought to extend the overriding lock. Only the taste of blood in her mouth let her know she had bitten through her lip.

* * *

Murphy ducked through the hatch, seeing a live Ahimsa for the first time. He paused in the light gravity, startled. The things didn't look to be more than a couple of feet in diameter! He couldn't stand in the control room, so he crawled right up to Wide whose horrified eyes stared, the manipulators forgotten where they touched the boards behind him.

Murphy reached out with his Wind River fighting knife—a tool he knew Ahimsa understood—and let the sharp point dimple the alien's sides. "You want to pull them feet in, little buddy? If you don't let loose of them boards, I'll push a tiny bit and see if you blow all over the room like a kid's balloon."

Wide's manipulators retracted immediately and he began to sag.

The board behind the flattening alien continued to flicker, strange shapes and figures flashing back and forth on the holo derived screen.

"Lieutenant Murphy," Sheila's voice came louder through the net than in the tiny monitor. "It would be safer to get them out of there. I can't seem to raise Major Detova. She's been manipulating their comm. I assume they have her tangled up somehow. Please take Wide back to TaHaAk station. He will be placed under guard there—away from his ship."

Wide whistled with fear and flattened even further.

"Yes, ma'am," Murphy grinned, feeling his back knot up at the cramped position.

Spotted, eyes bulging at the end of rigid stalks, fixed his attention on Murphy. "What of me?" It came through the translators as a reedy weak expression.

Sheila replied, staring out from the tiny monitor. "Spotted, you are now *our* pilot and navigator. Where you once served Wide, you now serve us. No harm will come to you; on the contrary, you will be accorded every right and privilege as long as you cooperate in educating us on the running of this ship." To Murphy's shock, she even smiled at the thing!

Spotted slowly began to take shape, pulling himself round as Murphy, face twisting with disgust, put his knife away and ran his fingers nervously under Wide's flaccid bulk. To his surprise, the Overone must have weighed almost a hundred pounds. He grunted and lifted, awkward in the restricted space, trying not to push buttons with his elbows as he backed out. "Man, this is the same as carrying out a large dead jellyfish!"

Spotted hesitantly rolled out behind him, not round by any means. Murphy glanced nervously at the little globular being, hating the sensation of those curious black eyes on the end of each stalk boring into his back. He stood up, grateful to get his spine unkinked.

A series of whistles, peeps, tweets, and shrills erupted behind him.

"Up the ramp, dude," Murphy jerked his head at the torpedo.

Spotted started to flatten as he swiveled his eyes to that gaping maw.

"C'mon, man. We don't have all day. Hustle your tail. We're not going to hurt you and I'll be damned if I'll carry two dead jellyfish up that ramp."

Malenkov moved warily around behind Spotted, followed the whole way by an eyestalk.

Murphy watched with fascination as the alien rolled up the ramp, keeping clear of Katya.

* * *

Sheila leaned back against the tank, breathing a heavy sigh of relief. They had won this round. Both TaHaAk station and the Ahimsa ship were theirs.

"People, the war is over."

She craned her neck, aware of the cramped muscles and ran a hand through the tangled curls of her hair before leaning back to stare at the heavy piping—or whatever it was—over her head. She ran her palms over her face. *So this is what it's like to feel a thousand years old.*

She climbed onto the tank and added, "Let's get back to the auditorium. We need to set up some sort of interim occupational government."

Her legs swung limply as the tank pitched and shot back along the corridors to a torpedo which waited to fly them the couple hundred kilometers to the human section of the huge ship.

"Svetlana?" Sheila called out into her headset. Nothing. The net remained silent. Something ominous, like a quick growing fungus, crept around her heart.

"Viktor?" She tried another avenue.

"Here, Major." Katrina's translating voice filled her with relief.

"Tell Viktor to attach all the Councillors and any males which might be capable of rising in status. Transfer them here under guard. I want them away from TaHaAk. At the same time, have some of the women check out the Pashti ships. I'll need an estimate on how long it will take to learn how to space them. Oh, and, Viktor, be *very* careful. Think of our status as that of apes turned loose in a rocket assembly plant. We can't afford to push the wrong buttons. We might be overloading reactors or . . . or heaven knows what other bloody thing."

His laughter sounded dry and humorless as Katrina translated, "I think we understand. For exactly that reason, the military in the Soviet Union makes two forms of tank. One is complicated, with computers and high technology targeting. The other we call the monkey model. It is for export and easily learned by any idiot. We will be very careful."

She nodded. Blessed be. Thank heavens Wide had chosen his conscripts well.

"Sam?" she called.

"Here."

"How goes it at your end?"

"Just fine, Sheila. We're waiting for further orders."

"Turn your Pashti Councillors over to Viktor and the station is yours. Assist the pilots any way you can and see what you can accomplish with the Pashti remaining on the station. We need a collaborator."

"Roger, will do!" He hesitated. "Uh, I'm not sure, mind you, but it seems this communications center is active. Want me to try and shut it down?"

She realized she was shaking her head with no one to see it. "Negative. Did you hear the conversation with Viktor?"

"Yeah, I get the point. We'll just leave it run and put a guard on it."

"Svetlana?"

Still nothing.

So, now what? The tank purred its way into the torpedo and the hatch clanged shut. The trip didn't take more than twenty minutes of flight time, but she'd fallen asleep; the Israeli tank commander lightly rocked her shoulder.

"Major? We're here. Back in the torpedo bay."

She blinked, smiled, and tried to clear the cobwebs from her brain.

On sandpaper joints, she got wearily to her feet and

forced herself out the hatch, pushing her tired body to a trot on the way to Svetlana's quarters. She passed the doorway and stopped, seeing Svetlana's strained face. Her features shone with sweat, eyes closed, images blinking and flashing on the terminal monitor.

Svetlana raised a hand, aware of Sheila leaning down next to her. Sheila frowned, watching the woman's expression as her mind remained knotted with the computer.

Sheila took a deep breath, trying to oxygenate her own staggering brain. Something had gone deadly wrong. Svetlana struggled in silence, lips tensing and pursing as she waged her own war inside the Ahimsa computer system.

"Svetlana? If you can tell me . . ." She froze as the Russian's hand clenched into a fist.

A printout slipped out into the tray. Sheila picked it up, reading: SHUT DOWN DESTRUCTION PROGRAM OR EARTH IS DEAD!

Sheila crumpled the printout, accessing the net. "Lieutenant Murphy! Turn back! Get Spotted back to that control room. Wide did something to the comm system. He's got Svetlana locked into some sort of program." To herself, she breathed, "And who jolly well knows how it works?"

Her mind almost unhinged from fatigue and worry, she sank to her knees, chewing her lip as she waited. *Murphy get back there in time!*

* * *

"You want your fucking head blown off?" Murphy demanded, glaring at the flattening form of Spotted. His back knotted into a painful mass as Spotted's manipulators played with the board. Hell, they'd just left this goddamned rabbit hole! What had Wide done?

Malenkov sat in the torpedo beyond the cramped hatch, arms crossed in a guard position, his army knife held easy while Wide remained completely motionless. Katya speculated the Ahimsa might have gone catatonic—or dead.

Spotted whistled, piped, and puffed as his manipulators worked over the board, never quite managing to stop the dancing Ahimsa figures.

The little bridge monitor, built for Ahimsa size, stuttered. Murphy turned to look, wondering what new disaster was about to unfold.

"Mur-phee-note-fol-low-ing-in-nish-ee-ation-see-quence-from-comm-dee-struct-pro-gram," came the disjointed syllabic words in a monotone he'd never encountered before. One of the bridge monitors wavered and one by one, symbols began to emerge from the haze.

Spotted, one eye on each board, moved his manipulator. A light blinked off on the weapons board. Then another and another went dim. Spotted grew ever thinner as he progressed, the symbols coming faster.

"Jesus!" Murphy grunted, glaring at the happy Spotted, who rocked back and forth on his rounded bottom. "What in hell was that all about?"

Spotted whistled, chirped, and piped as the comm translated, "Svetlana Detova has just saved your world from blowing into little chunks of radioactive dust."

Murphy's cramped stomach turned a little queasy. "Yeah, sure," he breathed, slowly backing his oversized body from the undersized bridge. "Weird shit, man."

Spotted rolled along behind him, his spicules parroting, "Weerd shit, weerd shit, weerd shit!"

* * *

Sees studied the holo. Each of the Overones had linked into the system. How many stars had been born and died since such singular circumstances had brought each and every Overone together in one meeting? No one could remember the last time—if ever.

Hurt swelled up as he scanned the various images of Ahimsa intellectual might. "It is apparent that a disaster of unknown proportions has befallen civilization. Wide has brought us to the brink of ruin. We must do something."

Low tried to pull himself up to stature but didn't manage. "We made a mistake by not acting sooner after First Councillor RashTak contacted us. But his Second Councillor, AraTak left the transduction channel open. From the bits and pieces we can translate of the guards' conversation, the situation has deteriorated. The Pashti government center is in the hands of violent aliens. Wide is captive, as is his vessel and several Pashti jumpships. We do not understand the motives of the humans at this time."

Sees felt himself going flat as he added, "The worst is yet to come, my friends." He struggled to pull his sides up. "While these circumstances might be enough to send us all permantly flat—oh, how do I tell you this?" He pulled his minds together and thinned, trying to ignore the enormity of the thing. *"The humans also have a Shitht hostage!"*

Around him, the entire room seemed to widen and shrink as a bedlam of whistles, piping, and agonized lament rose.

"Please!" he called out plaintively. "We must do something! Come, think! What can we do?"

The Ahimsa who spoke into the stunned silence was old, his color a light tan indicative of the number of molecules he had accumulated through a long life. Eyestalks swiveled in his direction as his mellow spicules began, "From the gravity of Wide's actions, we have only the following options. First, we can allow nature to take its course and allow the humans to do as they wish with civilization." Gagging exclamations erupted. "Indeed, we are agreed on that option. Second, we can somehow manage to nullify the SkaHa situation, place the humans back in interdiction, and rescue the Shitht before he loses his patience." Whistles of approval sounded. The old Ahimsa spun slightly. "The third option is to remove the threat at SkaHa and, at the same time, ensure it never happens again. By that, I mean we must eliminate the humans. Obviously, they're dangerous, insane. From the files I have seen, they kill each other wantonly, often torturing others of their kind to death in the most painful and hideous ways. I think, given the nature of their behavioral patterns, they have no redeeming traits. The third option, therefore, is simply to sterilize their planet and let it start over."

Toot shrilled his upset. "You can't just destroy them!"

Tan turned on his bottom, an eyestalk seeking out Toot's slightly blue form. "And why can't we? Among the humans, they treat vermin in a similar fashion. Insects which invade their domiciles are poisoned. Rodents which compete for their foodstuffs are trapped and disposed of. Even excesses of their domestic pets are euthanatized. I must also note that in their insanity, they classify various races of their own kind as subspecies and exterminate them as pests. Are we wrong to utilize their own standards against them?"

Sees nodded to himself. The pestilence must be eliminated.

CHAPTER XXVIII

RashTak fastened his main eyes on the monitor that displayed the growing Ahimsa ship while he fought to stem the horror that wrung his internal organs. Despite himself, he couldn't stop his mandibles from clicking—fear charged nerves did that. With each exhale, his resonators thrummed despair and anxiety. His minor eyes kept the Homosapiens female under constant observation, wary of the dreadful weapon she carried.

What purpose could this have? Why would they take me from my people, from my home? The muscles in his digestive system pulled and cramped as he felt the torpedo change attitude. An unbidden tremble ran up his legs, causing his body to lower toward the deck, a sign of submission. "Shame. Shame, RashTak. Where is your pride? What has happened to you?"

I am in their hands, at their mercy—a prisoner of Homosapiens. We are ALL prisoners of Homosapiens. Where did I fail? Oh, my people, my people, forgive RashTak. Forgive your First Councillor. Who could have foreseen Wide's madness? Who could have known?

Did death lie in wait inside that ominous Ahimsa hull? Did Homosapiens wait to cut him, to grasp his vital organs in their fluid-soaked hands, lifting the flesh of RashTak to their toothed mouths? He chittered at the horrible images spinning in his mind.

"Pity? Is there no pity for RashTak who failed his people? Has sanity fled from the universe? Will they torture? Will they dismember?"

"They will do nothing of the sort." The statement, delivered so forthrightly from the box, gave him the shivers.

"And how do you know, whoever you are?"

"I'm Major Riva Thompson, commander of the Homosapiens information gathering forces. That's how I know. You're simply being transferred to the Ahimsa vessel for security reasons."

"You don't eat the organs out of your prisoners?"

"Eat the. . . . What?"

"We have tapes of Homosapiens eating the dead of their own kind."

"I think, First Councillor, that we'll be very interested in those tapes. No one will harm you unless you harm them first. We don't want to hurt you. We just risked everything to keep your people alive. Wide wanted us to kill you all. To make it look like the Pashti went insane during the cycles."

"Wide? An Ahimsa Overone? Make it look like the Pashti went insane? I don't understand." RashTak actually turned away so he could stare at the speaking box.

"He wanted to break your power, disgrace you. You've been taking over more and more Ahimsa manufacturing, haven't you? According to Wide, every time the cycles come, the Pashti grab all they can get and when the cycles pass and everything goes back to normal, Pashti retain their hold on usurped Ahimsa resources. In short, you never give back what you take."

"But . . .but . . ." *Was that true?* "They didn't need to destroy the Pashti! We would have given it back! We would have been shamed, terribly shamed. We would have given them *everything* back!"

"Easy, First Councillor. Relax. You're quivering. Easy. That's it. You and your people are alive. The humans have Wide stopped for the moment. You're safe."

"So much confusion. So much insanity. Was that a reason for the Ahimsa to kill? Because of the cycles? Couldn't they have done something else?" RashTak shifted to stare at the Ahimsa ship. It filled the monitor, immense. A deeper horror curdled RashTak's guts. "Was it more than Wide? Did the Ahimsa really know? Even when I called them? Were they all involved?"

A bit of his soul came unanchored—cast adrift with the

unshakable horror of the thought. *What if the Ahimsa have decided to destroy us? What then?*

His legs buckled under him as the torpedo slid into a gaping vacuum lock in the side of the hull. RashTak stared dully as the craft rose through a molecular curtain and into a well-lit hangar.

Why? Why would they do it? Because Pashti had taken over industry? Pashti like doing things. Ahimsa do not. "Or have we been wrong all these cycles?"

The box interrupted his observations. "First Councillor, you will need to step out of the hatch and proceed down the orange corridor. A room has been prepared for you. Major Dunbar will meet with you as soon as possible and deal with your questions then."

"And after that I will be killed?"

"No one will be killed. Please make no sudden movements or attempts to escape. Make no threatening actions or gestures in the direction of your guard or other humans since your actions might be interpreted as hostile. Do you understand?

"Yes. I think. But hostile? Why do you tell me this?"

"Quite honestly, you frighten us with your size and appearance. We don't want any chance of a mistake, of an accident."

"I? Frighten . . .*you?*" RashTak couldn't stop the reaction. His quivering muscles and the fear in his veins vented in hysterical laughter.

* * *

"That should restabilize the calibration," Spotted declared as he rolled back toward Murphy. "Even with the computer programs, we have to periodically adjust superfluid ring interferometers. Random action—the effect your scientists call chaos or turbulence—shows up in gravity waves, too."

Murphy shifted, hating the confined space of the Ahimsa bridge. "Uh, and what do those superfluid ring . . ."

"Interferometers."

"Right, interferometers. What do they do?"

Spotted shrilled and piped. "Murphy, you humans have a long way to go to become civilized. What does a pressure gauge do on a hydraulic system on your planet?"

"Keeps track of the pressure inside the line so you can estimate the amount of work a system can do, or get a second's notice to run before something ruptures and blows you away."

"Exactly. Ring interferometers are only one of several ways we have for monitoring null singularity generation. I will teach you the rest when we finally space. Humans aren't stupid. Just untrained.' "

"Yeah, well, you're going to need a bigger bridge first"

"That's already being constructed."

"It's . . . Huh? Who said you could . . ."

Spotted thinned slightly, both beady black eyes focused on Murphy. "It does have to be done, doesn't it? We will need it to space. I am now your Nav-Pilot. Major Dunbar said so. A Nav-Pilot has duties to perform in service. It's the way to becoming an Overone."

"Right. Yeah, we'll need a human-sized bridge. But maybe you'd better clear all that with Sheila, huh?"

Spotted piped and whistled, the translation coming through the system. "She has been meditating, hasn't she?"

Murphy chuckled. "Yeah. That's a good word for it. The Major was pretty fried. Hell, I don't know. Maybe taking all this was the easy part."

"And since I am Nav-Pilot, I will serve. Meanwhile, you will watch me—become *my* Nav-Pilot. You're my guard."

"That's right. So don't pull any funny shit."

"Until I am worthy of becoming an Overone, I will serve." Spotted swiveled an eye. "The monitor indicates that the fields are balanced again. Everything else looks fine. We should come back and recheck the system in another ten hours. Until then everything will remain stable."

Murphy crawled backward from the bridge, while Spotted rolled easily.

"You know, I got a question. You said you'd serve until you were worthy to be an Overone. So what happens if Wide wakes up one of these days? You gonna jump to his whistle again?"

Spotted chirped and tooted, "Murphy, he's hopelessly insane. There could be no advancement from study with an insane Overone. I have wondered about insanity. I should be mentally paralyzed like Wide, but I'm not. Yes, I've wondered a great deal about insanity. Tell me, do you think it's contagious, that the molecules are catching?"

"Catching? Naw. There's no molecules, but sometimes it's like flipping a lighted match into a powder magazine. What starts as a little insanity ends up like an explosion. You know, things build. Folks get angry and piss off other folks and everybody gets so wound up they can't see the explosion going up around them. People get too emotional to see straight."

"Like Hitler."

Murphy sucked at his lower lip, frowning. "Hitler was something else, little buddy. Hitler is like a nightmare come true. Brilliant, sick, and twisted. Let's hope we never see the likes of him again, huh?"

"Then you think someone like him could regain control of the Germans again?"

"Look, man, it's not just the Germans. They got a bum rap because Hitler happened to them at the wrong time under the right conditions. It's like a little myth we lay on ourselves. It's always the other guy, you know. It's easier to point the finger at the Germans. But, man, it could happen anywhere. You mix frustration, deprivation, and a lot of injustice together, and you get a Hitler or a Stalin."

"You could become Hitler, just go crazy?"

"Not that simple, I don't think." Murphy propped himself up on his elbows, bothered by the topic. "Hell, ask a shrink. I don't know. Maybe you don't want to ask a soldier, huh? Guys like me tend to get a weird impression of how the world works." Images came whirling out of his mind. Gunshots, bodies jerking under the impact of bullets as he targeted and triggered his rifle. *Why, Murph?* " 'Cause that was my job."

"What?" Spotted squeaked and chimed, pinning Murphy with his eyes.

"Insanity, puffball. That's what. Look, I don't want to have to worry about you, too. You're not going to do anything dumb, are you?"

"For the moment, you're my best hope and greatest challenge."

"Yeah, I guess." Murphy made a face as he scratched at his chin, feeling two days of stubble. "We'd better be getting back. The major wants to meet with you and the Pashti sometime. . . . Hey!"

Spotted had shrieked and gone soggy. "Pashti?"

"Look, I'm gonna be there. No Pashti's gonna be allowed to harm a hair on your. . . . Um, how about I just promise you'll be safe. I've got the rifle right here on the sling and I'll take care of any hard feelings."

"Thank you, Murphy." Spotted sucked his sides in again and rounded out, rolling for the ramp on the torpedo.

* * *

RashTak entered the room, anger, confusion, and terror vying with a burning curiosity. He found AraTak and Ee!Tak backed defensively into one corner. One of the Homosapiens' communication boxes sat in the middle of the floor, cables wiring it into the ship's computer system.

RashTak thrummed irritably. The floor had virtually no resonance whatsoever. How did these naive Homosapiens expect them to communicate properly in this kind of an environment?

AraTak lifted, raising his pincers. "Looks like they didn't eat you." It sounded muffled. "Are you all right?"

"Are any of us?" RashTak demanded, slapping the muting floor. "Everything is madness, like . . . like reality has been twisted inside out, pulled loose from the way it should be and bent."

"They say they won't kill us," Ee!Tak reminded, hope barely audible in his resonators.

"So they say." RashTak crossed, aware of the Homosapiens guard who stopped at the door, weapon ready. Behind him, a female Homosapiens followed a group of Homosapiens who lugged in a large pallet. This female, too, appeared to be in charge as she directed the males to place the platform. Did it never end?

"First Councillor?" the box emitted as the woman stepped forward. "I am Major Thompson. I'll be your liaison. We realize you need resonating boards to allow you to communicate more efficiently. Please try the device we've brought you."

"Patronizing effrontery!" AraTak erupted with a series of sarcastic clicks for accent. "They send a *female* to talk with us?"

"A *female* commands them! No wonder they're insane," Ee!Tak added, the floor eating most of his disgust.

RashTak watched the female Homosapiens turn a darker shade, crossing her arms as she stiffened. What did that mean? RashTak stepped onto the hollow surface, thrumming loudly. "Much better, but not like home."

"Major Dunbar would like to meet with you as soon as it is convenient." Thompson continued, the grating box rendering an abomination of Pashti speech. "If you would like to take a moment to confer with your Councillors, please do so."

Everything happened so quickly! RashTak turned, staring at AraTak. "What do we do?"

"Find out what they want from us," Ee!Tak clicked nervously. "Why are we here? Why did they take us from our station, from our people?"

"They say for security reasons. I'm just starting to realize what security means in their context. They fear us for some reason." RashTak smacked the floor. "All of a sudden *everyone* fears us! Homosapiens fear us! Ahimsa fear us! Why is everyone afraid? Are we all insane?"

"Perhaps." AraTak rapped against hard floor, watching as more Homosapiens brought in another sounding platform. He waited nervously until they left before scuttling onto it. "You say the Ahimsa fear us? What have you learned?"

"That perhaps the Overones lied. That they have become ever more worried about the cycles, about . . ." It hurt to say it. "About how we've taken so much of their industry into our control during the cycles. I don't know the history, but it might be true."

"So they decided to destroy us?"

"Yes. Or at least break our power by embarrassing us—by staging what would appear to be a mass suicide on TaHaAk."

"Why didn't they just say something? Come and take their possessions back?" Ee!Tak demanded, seeing Homosapiens bringing another sounding board.

"You know enough about Ahimsa to know how rude they would have thought that."

"And killing us isn't?"

RashTak fit the bits of data together in his reeling mind. "Not in the way Ahimsa think. This would have been tidy, polite, and no blame would have fallen on the Ahimsa. You must look at it through Ahimsa eyes and think as an Ahimsa would. There is a certain elegant logic here, insane, perhaps, but still elegant. In their eyes, Pashti caused the problem, therefore Pashti must solve it. To mention it to us would be an admission that Ahimsa care about the physical reality, about possessions and ownership—all of which would be unthinkable given their current preoccupation with meditation and transcendence. They do not wish to appear hypocritical to Galactic Civilization at large. Therefore a simple solution was devised which kept them disassociated. Our problem, our solution."

"Assuming all Ahimsa are involved," AraTak pointed out.

"Correct, but our assumptions about Ahimsa must be reevaluated. After all, we're here—imprisoned by Homosapiens. Today's reality is quantumly different than yesterday's."

"But what does it mean?" Ee!Tak asked, swaying nervously from side to side.

AraTak forced air through his breathing slits in a hiss of resignation. "I think it means we face a new reality in our relations with the Ahimsa. More pressing, however, what do we do about the Homosapiens? I would remind you that the Ahimsa will no doubt have some way of distancing themselves from Wide, but before we can worry about that, we may be dead."

"We don't know what the Homosapiens want," RashTak replied. "I have heard that they don't wish to harm us. The fact remains, or at least appears to, that they did take considerable risk to thwart Wide's plan. We at least owe them a hearing."

"If we refuse, they'll just kill us." Ee!Tak swayed from side to side with greater vigor.

"I think we'll die no matter what. They're animals." AraTak raised his pincers in acceptance. "Perhaps we should simply allow them to kill us. Everything is in chaos already anyway."

RashTak thrummed for attention. "You heard what they said, that we should study the records. Let us not be too hasty in rejecting them. Even if they do kill us in the end, let's have it be said that Pashti examined all the options."

"So how do we get these records?" AraTak asked.

"That's why I'm here," Thompson cut in. "I'll need to coordinate your requests through the central computer."

"How can a female communicate? Can't we deal with a male who knows something?" Ee!Tak wondered.

"She is supposed to be intelligent—or at least trainable," AraTak reminded.

RashTak turned to look at the Homosapiens, aware that her face had warmed and portions of the soft tissue had begun to quiver. The communications box, of which the Homosapiens seemed so proud, began to utter a nonsensical patter about bodily wastes, female spiking, and phrases regarding unknown siring of offspring—even of species RashTak had never heard of.

"Must be some sort of glitch in their software," he grumbled.

* * *

So how does a person set up a meeting like this? Sheila shook her head. Among humans, she would have known exactly how to place herself in relation to the others. She logically deduced, however, that as these were aliens seating probably had no correspondence to a terrestrial primate's concept of dominance. With that logical and rational conclusion in mind, she promptly set up the "interrogation session" so that her seat was higher and overlooked the others.

If Viktor minded, he didn't say anything. He entered, wearing a black uniform that set off his golden features.

Gubanya followed the Pashti in, his rifle slung, a stiff set to his expression.

RashTak turned out to be rather impressive. The top of his battery of eyes must have measured a good four feet from the floor. His carapace stretched a little over ten feet long and five wide. The armored legs added to the whole and those two fascinating pincer-manipulator "hands" were like nothing she had ever seen. Their design combined a power grip with a delicate precision grip. Not only that, but the chitinous shell gleamed and shimmered in the light, reflecting a dark red that ebbed into black along the edges of the shell.

RashTak picked a platform and slipped onto it sideways, the deep pools of his two major forward facing eyes never leaving her face. Sideways? But then, if you have eyes all around your, um, head, that sort of thing becomes infinitely more reasonable.

Spotted, to the contrary, rolled in on Murphy's heels, piping and whistling to himself, his sides more or less stable until he saw the Pashti. His spicules immediately shrilled in an ear-piercing squeal and he went flat. Murphy muttered something under his breath and toed the sagging Ahimsa toward the center, a look of disgust on his red face.

Sheila cleared her throat, talking into the comm, hoping the translation to the Pashti was adequate. "First Councillor RashTak, would you be so kind as to inform the Ahimsa, Spotted, that you mean him no harm?'"'

RashTak turned slightly, his main eyes on the now lumpy mass of tissue. He clicked, whined, and thrummed which in turn was translated to squeaks and musical notes, and Spotted began to round out again.

She noticed that Gubanya and Murphy exchanged guarded glances, each staring at the other's prisoner with unabashed curiosity.

"Very well, shall we be about it?" Sheila settled herself comfortably, aware that Svetlana's team of analysts sat in the auditorium seats watching and studying every detail. Damn it, if they only knew where they stood in the scheme of things.

RashTak sat silently while Spotted began piping softly, perhaps to reassure himself.

"To begin, First Councillor, let me extend our deepest apologies for the five Pashti who were killed during our assault on your space station. It was not our intention to do any more harm than necessary to achieve our objective."

"Five? No, Homosapiens, you killed four subordinate males and a pregnant female. You killed more than five, you killed part of the future. Why? What had we done to you?" RashTak asked, his response obviously directed to Viktor. "We would have received you without violence."

Sheila fingered her chin. "First Councillor let me lay the situation out to you in no uncertain terms. Wide didn't leave us with much choice in the matter. We managed the best we could, balancing our survival against that of the Pashti on your station. Had we rebelled against attacking TaHaAk, Wide would have simply exterminated us and all the living beings on our planet as an inconvenience. An experiment gone wrong.

"I don't ask you to take my word for it. The records are available for your inspection. Just like the Pashti, humans were victims of Wide's plot. We could have followed Wide's orders—which I'm sure you are now familiar with—and your station would have been laid waste. The Pashti would have been ruined, declared untrustworthy. My planet would be a radioactive desert—we barely avoided that as it is—and at this moment, Wide would no doubt have either killed us, or would be utilizing us as experimental animals for some sort of new plot. Am I right, Spotted?"

"Absolutely," the Ahimsa chimed. "Humans are insane. Dangerous."

"We get the point," Murphy growled, bending down. Spotted deflated.

Sheila glared at the Ahimsa. "No, we're not insane. First Councillor, if we'd been insane, we wouldn't have risked ourselves to save you and your people. If we were insane, we'd have killed Wide right off the bat in retaliation for what he tried to do to us—and you, for that matter. Instead, we'll turn him over to the Overones, to your government, or whoever will take responsibility for him. If no one will, we'll continue to care for him ourselves. We won't harm him."

RashTak was clicking, but she ignored it as her voice rose. "For the moment, however, we're interested in repairing the damage Wide has done." She accessed the net. "Sam? How are repairs coming along?"

Daniels' voice echoed through the room. "I think we're all right, Sheila. A couple of Mason's patches failed, but we got the doors closed before we lost too much atmosphere. I've got a group of AraTak's subordinates working on replacing the outer hull. Good thing they can do it, the machinery they're using is beyond us."

"You could repair the damage by simply leaving us in peace and returning to your planet. We don't want Homosapiens. Go back where you came from." RashTak raised his pincers and clicked them with emphasis as he stared at Viktor.

"Not an option," Viktor muttered from the side.

"Absolutely not," Sheila agreed, crossing her arms. "First Councillor, we're here to stay."

RashTak swayed from side to side on his jointed legs, the multiple mandibles of his mouth clacking like castanets. "Your planet has been interdicted. You have no right outside your solar system. I don't want you teaching young Pashti to eat the internal organs of other Pashti they've killed. I don't want you to teach young Pashti to steal other Pashti's females and spike them without regard to the Master voice. I have seen these things! Go back to your planet and shoot your slivers of wood into each other. Space is quiet and happy without you. Even Chee'ee'la wants you to go back and you had better listen to him."

"Wait! Hold it!" Sheila stood, leaning forward to stare at RashTak who continued to evade her glance and pin

Viktor with his main eyes. Sheila walked around to stand before him. "Look at me, RashTak."

The Pashti shifted, trying to avoid Sheila's angry glare. "I don't talk to females."

"Yes, you do. And you damn well will from now on."

"No wonder Homosapiens are insane."

"Let's back up to eating organs and stealing females. Where did you get that information?"

"It's in the files. Civilization has been aware of your planet for many thousands of cycles. We've watched you change through time. Homosapiens has been insane for a long time. The Ahimsa was right, you *are* dangerous. Go back now, while you have the chance. Chee'ee'la—"

"We're *not* going back!" She pointed a finger at him, standing defiantly within his reach, aware that Murphy had unslung his rifle to stand ready, eyes narrowed as he glared at RashTak. "Furthermore, First Councillor, your 'civilization' had effectively put us in a bottle! We have an old story about just that situation. Well, the genie is out now, and we don't intend on knuckling under to you or anyone else."

"There were reasons," RashTak purred and clicked, shifting to keep his main eyes on Viktor.

Sheila stepped closer, backing the Pashti to the edge of the platform. "Yes, perhaps there were, First Councillor. But we're out now. And if resisting being forced back means that we have to wreck your civilization and society, I swear, *we will!*"

RashTak thrummed to himself, clicking nervously. Spotted colored and flattened somewhat, his piping becoming almost inaudible.

The Pashti shifted in a darting motion Sheila had discovered betrayed nervousness. "You would kill? Destroy?"

Sheila nodded slowly. "If it meant our survival, yes, we would. But that's the final option, one we'll take only if that's the final choice we're left with. Extinction is a frightening thought. We think there's a better way. Consider, RashTak, in so many ways you are ahead of us. We're under no illusion when it comes to your incredible technological superiority." She waved at the ship around them. "You could do a thousand things beyond our conception to destroy us . . .and our planet, too, no doubt. To make our position comprehensible, First Councillor, *you scare bloody hell out of us*!"

"Then why don't you simply go back to your planet and leave us alone? We would have no reason to pursue you. It is not your fault Wide went insane. You have, in fact, showed admirable restraint. Your world would be safe; we would not retaliate." RashTak raised his pincers.

"And the Ahimsa? It's common knowledge now—Wide went insane. Humanity knows about your interstellar civilization. If we go back, we've effectively allowed ourselves to be imprisoned. No, the Ahimsa will retaliate, attempt to destroy us as they attempted to destroy the Pashti—by trickery and deceit, just as they tried to do to TaHaAk."

Sheila chuckled dryly. "You hope the genie will meekly return to his bottle so you can put the stopper on it and live happily ever after?"

"I do not understand this sound, this . . ." The translator failed.

"Genie, a mythical being with magical power to do good or evil depending on what is asked of it. Humans are in the same situation right now. We could enter space as partners with the Pashti. We have a lot we could contribute to your civilization if you'll let us. At the same time, you have a lot to teach us—perhaps even about ourselves and how we behave. We *need* the Pashti and want your help. Not as prison guards, but as partners to help us develop our potentials. Maybe we are a bit crazy, but that isn't always a curse. Innovations come out of crazy ideas, especially if they're balanced by experience like you have.

"But to meekly go back and let you trap us with your gravity buoys?" She sighed wearily. "That, First Councillor, is no longer one of your options. I and my Phantom Brigade have had a taste of the stars. Why should we have to settle for crawling in the mud when we can have this?"

"Survival!" RashTak cried, expounding to Viktor. "You have no idea of the power of the civilization you face. You know nothing of what is out here. Your world is safe. No one wants to go there! No one is interested!"

"My point exactly." Sheila snapped, disturbed by the Pashti's continued attention to Viktor. "Survival, you said. You're bloody right we're interested in survival! We have a planet about to reach carrying capacity. With your techology, we can find a way to feed and educate all those people—stop our diseases and wars. Look at the resources abounding around you. We'll not be choked until we suffocate in our own system, First Councillor. We'll not be held hostage by your gravitational buoys."

RashTak cried incredulously, "You would gamble the stars against survival?" He gestured to Viktor imploringly.

Sheila remained silent for a moment, then straightened to look him in his odd alien eyes. "Damned right!"

RashTak chittered and expelled a blast of air. "Male, why do you let this female chitter nervously? Will you listen to reason?"

Sheila snapped, "Take it, or leave it. I don't have to deal with you, RashTak. I can just as easily elevate AraTak to your position."

"Insane." RashTak thrummed softly into the deck, eyes still stubbornly on Viktor.

Staka added, "She is my commander, First Councillor. Nor would I challenge her intelligence or ability. I think you should keep in mind that she outsmarted Wide. Perhaps you had best consider that in your dealings with her."

Spotted twirled and squeaked, "Pashti have no idea what to do with you. Weerd shit. Weerd shit. They think weerd shit."

Sheila settled herself, aware that RashTak was going to be mulling the situation over for a while. "Spotted, does this ship currently have the potential to completely destroy TaHaAk station? I mean, can it function as a warship in the classic human sense?"

Spotted piped softly, thinning himself as his eyestalks twirled. "Quite possibly. I have watched human improvisation. I have learned. Most instructive. Wide paid no attention to you. He was an Overone. Overones don't always think about how to get things done. They think about other things, important things like the nature of reality. They just order. Others, who are less developed, get things done. I think we could possibly reverse the null singularity generator and possibly change the polarity of atoms. Most interesting idea, don't you think?"

RashTak's legs seemed to drop out from under him. "Mad!" he throbbed and thrummed. "They're all mad! Can it be some sort of Ahimsa cycles we've never observed?"

"And if we turned that effect on TaHaAk station?" Sheila suggested, watching RashTak out of the corner of her eye.

The First Councillor darted back and forth in distress. "Nothing would be left! You would make plasma! Insane! I tell you, you are all insane!" To Viktor, he added. "She's your female! *STOP HER!*"

Viktor simply laughed, eyes twinkling. "She's my commander, my First Councillor, RashTak."

"Enough," Sheila ordered, patience worn thin. "The fact remains, RashTak—no matter how distasteful it is to you—we are here to stay. Sure, we could do a lot of damage. That's the alternative that I want to avoid. We don't want to be forced into that. Please, let's find an alternative. The choice is yours. Will you help us? Join us in finding a mutually beneficial solution to the problem which allows us freedom in space and security for the survival of our species? If we really make you that nervous, simply ignore us. We'll do our own thing in space. It's big enough out here so we can avoid your territory, develop our own. We'd be happy to leave you in peace if you'll leave us in peace. Does that sound mad? Insane?"

RashTak hissed through his breathing slits, the sound of his thrumming growing louder.

"We'll work with you however we can. But it will mean violence if someone tries to force us back into our system."

RashTak could only respond, "Illogical actions. Insane options."

She rubbed her toe at the deck, frowning. "So tell me, First Councillor, if you're as intelligent as you claim to be, you should be able to abstract yourself, put yourself in our position. Let's say the situation were reversed and the Pashti were about to be forced back onto SkaTaAk. Would you go?"

"But *we're* not insane!"

"Oh? Wide thought so. But that's not my argument. What would *you* do in *my* position? Roll over and die? Think, damn you! It's not a wild fantasy. Wide almost did you in. What if he'd succeeded? What if the Overones found TaHaAk destroyed? What if *they* decided the Pashti had gone crazy in the cycles as Wide wanted them to think? They could *demand* that Pashti be restrained!" She pounded her fist on the desk, the vibrations causing RashTak to turn and stare at her for the first time.

The First Councillor clicked, then settled as his legs folded, a humming, chittering sound coming from his resonators. His mandibles worked nervously as the room stilled.

Sheila bowed her head. "And while you're thinking, I want you to consider another point. When Wide would have murdered you all—even the females—in his effort to destroy the Pashti, who acted with the most sanity? Who risked the death of their own world to save Pashti lives? Would wild animals have done that? Was that the work of the insane?"

RashTak turned his gaze back to Viktor. "I will need time to consider this. Do you promise you will not hurt my Pashti? You promise you will not interfere with our affairs?"

"We will not hurt Pashti unless we need you to bargain for our freedom," Sheila conceded. "It may take a while—but until we know you are not working to hurt us, we must meddle with your affairs. To do otherwise—considering our ignorance of your abilities—would be naive, don't you think?"

RashTak thrummed to himself, the floor vibrating slightly.

Viktor spread his hands. "Seriously, First Councillor, it can't hurt. Spotted has already given in to necessity. He is now one of us. Surely, if an Ahimsa can trust us, so can Pashti."

"You have more to gain with us than against us, RashTak. Think of the advantages in trade, exploration, science, and ambition." Sheila felt herself frowning. "Obviously, if the Ahimsa were not on the decline, Wide wouldn't have feared you. Think of the partnership between your ability and our ambition? How many benefits do you think would accrue for your young? And didn't I hear a translation of you saying you had beaten the cycles? According to your records, our coming played a part in that."

"We don't want to be your enemies," Viktor added. "We would both get more from cooperation than death."

RashTak lifted his pincer-manipulators in the age-old sign of accession. "Would you allow me to consult my Councillors? I would also like to review the records you spoke of. This is not something which can be decided lightly."

"That is a perfectly reasonable request. If we can be of further assistance, please feel free to ask."

Spotted rocked back and forth, his spicules piping, "Weerd shit. Weerd shit, man!"

Where had Spotted learned *that*?

CHAPTER XXIX

Phil Cruz called, "Sam? Got Major Detova on the line. You want to talk to her?"

Daniels grinned, turning away from the new wall section Pashti engineers were fitting to the breach. The stuff looked like old-fashioned asbestos board but must have weighed a couple of hundred pounds per square foot. "You damn betcha!"

"Access channel twenty," Phil called.

Sam retreated down the hall from the sudden wail of Pashti machinery, mentally changing his comm access. "Svetlana, you there?"

"Here, Sam. What's all that noise?" Her calm soothed something deep inside him. He sighed despite himself.

"We're not that far behind Pashti science when it comes to making construction loud. They don't have hammers, pneumatic nail guns, or gasoline powered compressors, but they can make just about as much noise with their thing-a-ma-jigets."

"How are the repairs going?"

"We're getting along. Hey, I hear you're the hero of the whole show. They're going to have to give you one of those hero of the Soviet Union stars when you get home. Maybe even four or five."

She laughed. "I don't feel like a hero. More than once we were closer to disaster than you could imagine. Most of the time I was scrambling like a commissar in a corruption investigation. I made mistakes, Sam. Spotted almost caught one where I didn't edit the gears out of a crushed Pashti robot."

"Uh-huh, the way I hear it, you kept the good old Earth from going up like a new sun."

"I am supposed to coordinate with you. Major Dunbar would like me to inspect the Pashti computer system. When would be convenient?"

"Depends. Right now I'm down on the rim." He looked up and down the corridor. "We're still getting things back to normal here, but I'd bet it will be settled down in a couple of days. Meanwhile, there's monitors in this joint—but I'm not Pashti enough yet to figure out how to work them."

"We're trying to get translation programs into the Pashti comm, but we need RashTak's approval first. Any change in Wide?"

"Naw, he's still looking like a squashed soccer ball."

"What are the Pashti like?"

Sam placed hands on hips, watching the engineers smoothing the last of the wall panel joinings while Mason watched. "Nice folks, I think. You know, they've been real decent considering what we came here to do. I don't know what it would be like with the Councillors here to stir things up, but the average joe Pashti seems to be perfectly content with the situation. We give the orders and they jump to help. Mason impressed the hell out of them by straw bossing our people to help them fix the holes. Once they get the idea across, people can do things Pashti can't. Like get into holes and hold stuff that's too awkward for their pincers."

"Then you think there's hope for future dealings?"

"How in hell would I know? I'm a soldier, not an anthropologist, but from what little I've seen, there hasn't been one iota of friction here."

"Sam, get someone to tape your people helping with the repairs. I want RashTak to see. Anything else that shows cooperation would be appreciated.

"You got it. How's Sheila?"

"Asleep. Just like I'm going to be in about ten minutes."

"So when you gonna come across with my fifty million to be a KGB agent?"

"You haven't forgotten that?"

"Yeah, I *never* forget what a beautiful woman offers."

"I think I said you'd be worth ten bucks a month."

"I look forward to dickering."

"Later." A pause. "You know, it just sank in. We've actually got a future."

"Yeah," Sam added neutrally. "Until the Overones find out what's happened."

* * *

Sheila accessed the dispenser for a cup of coffee and ordered a couple of BaK!Gil for RashTak to chew on. His multijawed mouth made an incredible crunching as it ground the wiggling food creature to death and digestion.

She kept her composure through the performance, and actually didn't find it nearly as disquieting as Spotted's stomach oozing out of his side to envelop a food bar.

"I hear you've inspected the records Wide made, First Councillor." Sheila walked over to sit across from RashTak, and smiled. "I'm glad. We need you, and extend our hands as friends."

The Pashti wavered for a moment, obviously battling to make himself look at her. "The records of Wide's insanity were of great interest to us. They played an important part in our decision. So did your actions in the attack. We came to the conclusion that you demonstrated responsibility for the safety of all parties concerned—including Wide, who had just attempted to kill your planet. But most of all, we saw what your Sam Daniels is doing on TaHaAk. He's a southern type, isn't he?"

"I beg your pardon?"

"A Homosapiens from the equatorial area of your planet. I refer to the tone of his skin which is adapted for increased exposure to your primary. He's one of the southern invaders."

Sheila looked at Viktor who lifted his shoulders in a shrug. "I suppose so. But as to being an invader . . ."

"He takes great care to see that all damage is repaired. He helps, and he works with Pashti. We know little about Homosapiens behavior, but he seems to like Pashti—and he hasn't eaten organ meat or stolen a Homosapiens female yet. Such behavior indicates that our conceptions about Homosapiens may be somewhat in error."

"Organ meat?" Viktor winced, shooting a quick glance

at Sheila. "Perhaps we'd better talk to Sam about this before the Pashti do."

"Good idea." Sheila chuckled. "First Councillor, on behalf of humanity, thank you for giving us this chance to work with you. Your suggestion that we allot a period of time to see if humans and Pashti can get along is an excellent idea. We welcome your prudence and your suggestions. You're right, of course, let's see what happens before we formalize our relationship."

"AraTak has offered to work with Major Thompson on the translation. He says it will be an opportunity to see if Homosapiens females are truly intelligent, or if she's just been cleverly trained."

Sheila's smile froze. "Tell the Councillor that his help is welcomed." Sheila tapped her fingers. RashTak watched the action raptly—like thrumming, she guessed. "I'm sure that Riva is more than just cleverly trained."

"AraTak states that he will treat her as worthwhile if she proves herself. You females will have that problem. I am sorry, but that's how we are by nature."

Sheila clicked her tongue off the roof of her mouth, and said dryly, "I suppose it wouldn't surprise you to hear we're used to that?"

"You are?"

"Never mind, some of us have outgrown the problem. Meanwhile, we still face serious questions. For instance, the Overones now have to be contacted and dealt with. I gather that you doubt they'll be as rational as Pashti."

RashTak swayed on his feet, clicking uncertainly. "I can add my appeal to yours in the event Homosapiens and Pashti continue to coexist peacefully. But, quite honestly, I don't know what to think of their motives anymore. They might consider me to be as insane as you—if they weren't involved with Wide from the beginning."

Viktor leaned forward, comm producing holos of two kinds of craft. "These are the Pashti jumpships. Our pilots have managed to fly each type and we're gaining proficiency as the Pashti navigators explain things. In fact, we've even flown one to your home planet to look over perihelion events. Yet we can't make any progress with this vessel—if that's what it is." A round globe appeared. "Sam said he'd asked what was inside and a Pashti told him probably liquid hydrogen. It is a fuel tank? Some sort of storage? We can't find it in any of the Pashti registries."

RashTak stopped chewing, eyes fastened on the dull round globe. "Violet Curses on the cycles! They make one forget so much! That is a Shitht craft. That belongs to Chee'ee'la!"

"Shitht," Sheila ran her tongue around the translation. "Yes, we've heard of them. When will this Chee'ee'la be back? We'd like to talk to him."

RashTak spun, looking directly at Sheila for the first time. "He is on TaHaAk at this very moment. You have him prisoner. He, too, is hostage—if a Shitht is ever hostage." RashTak slapped the floor with his vibrators, obviously agitated.

"What does that mean?" Viktor asked.

RashTak settled himself, drawing his legs up under him, thrumming. Sheila caught Spotted, slowly flattening out, his piping becoming shrill. All right, so not even human threats had brought about the fear which now gripped RashTak, what did *that* mean? A stellar-hot band constricted around her heart.

"RashTak? Should we be worried about the Shitht?"

"Chee'ee'la warned us to destroy you."

* * *

Murphy entered the Council Chambers, assault rifle in hand, and found Ted Mason backing across the room as he strung wire from the electrical generator to the funny translucent crystal statue. For the most part the huge sculpture had been used as a hat rack, weapons hanger, storage, or any other purpose for which the angular spikes could be put to use. Then Mason had discovered the thing carried an electrical charge and emitted radio waves among other things.

"Sam's not gonna throw a screaming shit fit about you playing with this thing, is he?"

"Naw." Ted looked up, grinning as he clipped the wire from the spool. "A couple of Pashti walked in a while ago, took one look, and sort of slunk out. They didn't look upset or anything."

"Yeah, but Daniels said—"

"No sweat, man. We've been sitting around here for a couple of days now with nothing happening but the paint aging. Cap ain't gonna make anything out of a little entertainment for the troops. I'm turning UFO into USO." Mason pulled his Randall from his belt and scratched vigorously, barely marring the surface of the hard crystal. "Odd stuff," he admitted. "Seems to be some sort of crust on the outside." As he spoke, multicolored lights seemed to twinkle inside of the sculpture.

Ted cocked a curious eyebrow as he peeled insulation from one of the wires. "You here on business or pleasure?"

"Business." Murphy climbed up on the sculpture and watched Mason attach a wire to the area he'd scraped. "Uh, Ted, you ain't seen an alien running around anywhere?"

Mason's face went deadpan, voice dry. "You gotta be kidding, right?"

Murphy kicked his feet up to recline on two of the big crystals, rifle across his belly. "Nope, not kidding at all." He swallowed a mouthful of air and belched loudly with good resonance. "Cap'n Daniels just got a frantic call from Dunbar. You know that funny round sphere the Cap can't figure out?"

"Yep. So what about it?"

"Belongs to something called a Shitht."

Mason squinted as he played with his wire, tongue out the side of his mouth. "So, what's a Shitht look like?"

"Beats me," Murphy yawned. "Let's see, Ahimsa look like puffballs and squeak and roll around like bowling balls unless they go flat. Pashti are like a cross between a crab and a bug during cycles and are like lizards when they're normal. How'n hell am I supposed to know what a Shitht looks like? You seen anything weird around here?"

Mason's face remained deadpan. "Oh, no! Nuthin' weird at all, man! Well, there have been a couple of spaceships, two flat puffballs, and a bunch of crabs that talk through their asses and listen through their feet. Hey, situation normal!"

Murphy sucked his lips as he frowned. "Nothing's been

skittering between your boots when you wake up in the morning? No puncture marks on your neck or nothing?"

"No bug-eyed monsters." Mason insisted, stringing another wire from the little electrical generator they'd used to power the phones during the invasion.

"I still don't know about this. Remember what they said about screwing with stuff we didn't understand?" Murphy asked, eyeing Mason's wires uncertainly.

Mason waved it away, mildly irritated. "Yeah, but me and Malenkov put an ohmmeter and voltmeter on this thing. It's just got enough juice to make lights and change color. We were thinking we could hook it to the stereo and invite the intelligence chicks to a dance. Neat effects, huh? Maybe I can make this thing sparkle to the tunes." He danced around singing, "Jang! Jang! Jang! Jang-jang-ja-jang Jang!" flashing his arms with the notes.

"Yeah, right, man," Murphy watched as Mason scraped the hard crystal and circled another of the hexagonal spikes with wire.

"All right, children, there's a closed circuit." Mason walked back to the generator and set his tape deck to one side, wires running from the speakers to a small box. "Amplifier," Mason declared. He bent over the compact generator and added, "You might want to get off, you'd get a better effect from back here. Besides, I'd feel bad if it blew up and you were on it."

"I wouldn't want you losing any sleep on my account," Murphy added solicitously as he hopped down. He peered over Mason's shoulder at the tape. "Whatcha got?"

"Old Waylon Jennings from back before he lost his voice. First song's 'Rainy Day Woman.' " Mason plopped the tape in and started the generator, watching the needles on his voltmeter.

As the song blared out, Murphy squinted at the statue. The lights slowly flickered around on the inside of it. The first Country and Western music among the stars didn't seem to be having an effect, then the lights danced, grew bright and pulsed.

"Ya-hoo!" Mason whooped, bouncing from foot to foot as he dialed up the power. "What a shit-for-fire-damn dance this'll be!"

He said that just before the generator whined, sparked, and began smoking. Then the tape deck crackled and popped, the speakers blasting a loud, *THRRRROOOOO-MMMMMM!* before blowing out. The amplifier box began to stink first, then the metal glowed red, red-orange, and white before the wires to it melted.

Sudden silence, thick enough to be touched, pressed down in the huge auditorium. Murphy watched a wreath of smoke curl in front of his nose.

Mason exploded with a violent, "Son of a bitch!" as he bent over, staring at the remains of his beloved tape deck.

Murphy had trouble swallowing. "Jesus! Ted, I ain't that smart when it comes to electronics, but that ain't supposed to happen!"

Mason straightened, he gave the statue a nasty glare, picked up his assault rifle and turned, weapon raised.

"Whoa! Shit! You crazy? You shoot that up and Daniels will have your ass for dinner!" Murphy sprang, jacking the barrel of Mason's weapon up, struggling, muscles bulging as they glared at each other.

"That gawddam thing ate my gawddam tape deck! *I'm gonna fuckin' kill it!*" Mason yelled, eyes glazed as he fought to lift the rifle.

"Yeah, and then Sam'll kick your silly ass so high you'll fart through your ears!" Murphy shook his head, straining to keep the rifle up. "Man, that might be some holy shrine or sumpthin. You want the Pashti to come lynch you?"

"It ate my . . .." Mason's voice trailed off. Then: "Holy shit!" His eyes went wide as he stared over Murphy's shoulder. Mason's mouth came open, gasping soundlessly.

Murphy turned, took one look, and muttered, "Weird shit, man! Let's get outta here! Lock the doors behind us and call the captain!"

* * *

When Chee'ee'la didn't really have time to concentrate, he amused himself by trying to prove the five hundred and first dimension of reality—a long-term problem that could be attacked in bits and pieces. He was thusly occupied when the Pashti came crowding around, chased by humans. After that, he'd barely noticed the humans as they came to look, scampered up and down his sides, and finally let him get back to his problem. Their talk proved nowhere near as disruptive as the intense vibrations of the Pashti.

Nor did he act, since the problem obviously affected the Pashti and they would deal with it in their own good time before Wide's promise to Tan became reality.

When the human had scraped him with the mildly charged metal, it had broken his concentration. His curiosity rose when the tiny metal wires were attached and run to several devices. Chee'ee'la felt them out and guessed at their purpose. Some sort of communications device? The primitive nature didn't bode well for that.

The stimulation supplied when the current began to flow proved a pleasant surprise. It did nothing for contemplation; however, the sensations provided a sort of refreshment completely frivolous in nature—if not remarkably sophisticated.

Chee'ee'la extended his conceptualization mode, attempting to understand the patterns and structures of the sensations. He employed a microwave, ultrasonic, light refraction, and particle probe—with disastrous results. Who would have thought the equipment could be so fragile? He ignored the two humans who had twined together over the remains of the electrical equipment. They made loud auditory noises as humans always did, moving around in a type of dance. Chee'ee'la powered up his transfer mat. As he floated toward the destroyed electrical equipment, the humans stopped their antics and left, feet pounding out a rhythm on the hollow-plated Pashti deck.

He hovered over the fragile box and probed it lightly. The remains of the magnetic tape interested him. Trouble! He'd probed with too much radiation and erased several of the careful arrangements. How incredibly primitive! At the same time, he traced the path and function of the wires and magnetized sensations.

Would it be possible to get the humans to make him

equipment durable enough for repeated stimulation? The obvious solution to such a simple problem would be to ask before the humans were destroyed.

* * *

Sam had placed his office in the major observation dome of the Pashti station. Overhead stretched an infinity of black vacuum, dotted here and there with a straggling star and the globular clusters. To the sides the sky shaded from blackness to a mottling of stars then to a light gray from the billions upon billions of stars that composed the Milky Way. He couldn't help but study the reddish-white lens of light that was the Galactic Core—visible from so high on the Cygnus arm. How far away was that? What would it be like to be there where no night could exist? According to Ahimsa data, a huge black hole lay at the center of all that light. Black hole? Racial equality among the stars, man!

"Cruz here, Captain. The Pashti say there's a Shitht on the station. Uh, we're having trouble with the translation. These guys are subordinates. The cycles affected them differently. Some are still real loony. Keep following us around begging for food. Others, well, I don't know, maybe as a result of the trauma of being taken prisoner, they're a little more lucid. Evidently, the only ones who really kept their wits were the Councillors."

"Yeah, and they're all over on the ship." With Svetlana. How was she doing? Still asleep probably. He'd heard through the grapevine that she'd been an incoherent mess after she got out of the Ahimsa comm system. He shook his head. Some woman. *Glad she's on our side.* "You guys get any idea of what this Shitht looks like?"

"Uh, like I said, the translation's tough to make out. Hard. Colors. Sharp-long. Glowing. That sort of the thing. We'll keep looking, sir," Cruz's voice sounded flat.

Where in hell could an alien be? Worse, what did it look like? How was a person to know? Damn! They needed to know more about the Pashti comm system. Hell, they needed to know more about everything.

"Moshe?" Sam accessed the net.

"Here, what's up?"

"How's the fort business?" Sam let his gaze roam the stars. They beckoned, drew him on. He'd stared at them from Earth, but they'd been forever beyond his comprehension. Now he stood among them, feeling the power, the urge to go and look for himself.

"Conventionally, we could hold off the American and Russian air forces. I'm not sure about Israel's, though. We train a little harder." The typical Moshe humor leaked past the serious report.

"Yeah, well, some are born with talent—the rest of us have to get by on brains, raw courage, and beauty. I'm one of the talented ones. Seen any Shitht recently?"

"No, still only Pashti here. They seem to be very amenable to helping fortify the station. We'll see what changes come after the cycles when they get their wits back."

"Captain!" Murphy's frantic voice broke into the net.

"Here!"

"We got something real weird in the Council Chambers! You better get down here pronto!"

"Is it that missing alien?" Sam was on his feet, grabbing for his rifle, wishing he knew if he needed it.

"Who knows what's what around here!" Murphy exploded. *"That damn statue is floating!"*

* * *

Sam Daniels had become a worried man. The flat planes of his face were creased by dark lines that radiated from his broad nose and curved around his square jaw. His eyes flickered nervously.

"I don't know *what* it is. It don't make sense for something that damn big to be *floating!*" His deep voice echoed his concern.

Sheila caught herself chewing the insides of her cheeks. *Nerves! Damn. I haven't done that since I was a child.* "Can you send me a comm picture of what it looks like? I know the Pashti there can't seem to help, but RashTak could tell us." She accessed a second channel to the First Councillor who had been going over stellar data with Viktor.

Sam shook his head. "Pat Dixon has been doing her

best with the Pashti comm. Until we have Svetlana to help link the two, we're still down to verbal communication. The vibrations the Pashti use are outside our experience."

"Getting back to the statue, Sam. I have RashTak on the line. He's listening and we get a good translation through this net." She could see RashTak's image produced by the headset holo before her face.

"Yeah, well in the Council Chambers there's this big purple crystal thing." Sam's hands were moving. "Mason tried to hook his stereo up to it and—"

"He what?" Sheila exploded.

Sam's jaw muscles rippled. "Uh, I'll see to it later, Major. Anyway, this big crystal statue floated off the ground. It's hovering over Mason's stereo now—doing nothing."

RashTak's legs had begun quivering as he battled the instinct to dart about. He said, "Chee'ee'la! Chee'ee'la!"

"That's a Shitht?" Sheila asked.

"You are all so stupid!" RashTak pronounced. "You will kill us all!"

Sheila looked at Sam's paling features.

"That *thing* is an alien?" Daniels sounded incredulous. "We've been hanging clothes, staking weapons . . .oh, crap!"

Sheila sucked a lungful of air. "Sam, keep away from it. I don't know what it is or how it acts, but I'm pulling everything we've got on Shitht in the system. I'm waking Svetlana and we'll be right over. Just keep it quiet!"

Sam stared nervously over his shoulder. "Yeah, well, on that one count, I think I can accommodate. It ain't made a lick of noise yet."

* * *

Sees didn't like the compact feeling. A great deal of stellar wind had passed along the hull since he'd needed to utilize so many manipulators at once. The complicated communications interface he employed to patch together a net to the Overones necessitated the segmentation and application of several of his brains. As he stared up at their images, an unease filled him, loosening his sides. "I have contacted three Shithti. They report that since Wide brought the humans into the picture, it is an Ahimsa responsibility to solve the problem."

The old one, Tan, never seemed o deflate with bad news. What made him that way? So much age that nothing was new anymore?

Hurt offered, "Perhaps the key is simply to contact the humans and ask them to go home."

Tan rolled in his holo image—the perceptual effect was that the floor slid past under him. "I suggest, before we create more trouble for ourselves, that we do just that. We know very little about them. Wide is the expert, and he has obviously fallen prey to these humans."

"Our only means of gathering intelligence at the moment is through the Pashti governmental center, TaHaAk," Low mused. "Contacting them there will compromise that ability."

Sees fiddled with his comm transducer. "Wide's ship still does not answer. It appears at this moment that TaHaAK is our only link."

Hurt added, "I think, however, to be on the safe side, we should turn the gravity buoys and refocus their beams. Reduce the power for the moment. It would not do to destroy their home world before they were within our grasp. Yet we could act within seconds should they refuse."

Tan's spicules, hardened with age, didn't carry the harmony he no doubt wished. "I wouldn't even go that far yet. If the gravitational harmonics were just right, tectonic activity would be the logical outcome. Their world is still too young and fragile. It would tip our hand before the appropriate moment."

"Must we destroy them?" Toot asked, thinning. "I recommend that we adopt a different approach. Perhaps we should investigate the possibility that they might be more than we suspect. Perhaps they have a purpose in the grander scheme of things."

"Toot, if you wish to live with vermin, go someplace and live with vermin. Do not force the rest of us to suffer in the process." Hurt puffed up and piped disgust.

"They haven't contacted their planet yet?" Low asked, shooting an irritated glance at Toot.

"They do not know the power at their disposal," Sees speculated. "We can only hope they do not learn immediately."

Tan asked, "How is Wide's condition?"

Sees checked a data bank. "At last report, he remained totally flat which indicates that his brains are divided into hundreds of parts. There is an increasing chance the division might continue until he is down to a cellular level. If that occurs, he will completely disassociate and lyse."

"How long has it been since an Ahimsa allowed himself to die?" Sees didn't see who said it.

"I think we must wait," Tan noted, getting back to the subject. "We cannot afford to contact them now through TaHaAK. Too much information is coming through the Pashti comm. That might prove to be our salvation."

"I ask you one last time to reconsider," Toot implored. "We don't have sufficient information on what we are dealing with. I've reviewed the tapes of their history. This dynamic evolution they've experienced during the last hundred thousandth has fascinating implications. If we simply exterminate them, we may be doing ourselves a grave disservice."

Tan spun on his tread foot. "And where were you when I first crossed the intergalactic void, Toot? Shuffling information crystals in the DatLib on the home world?"

More than one Overone clicked his amusement. Toot flattened. "Say what you will. I see the direction of Ahimsa will. I also see that we're making a mistake. Later, remember Toot disagreed." His holo flickered out.

Tan wheezed. "In the meantime, we will prepare a program whereby we can redirect the interdiction buoys and destroy the human planet. It shouldn't take more than a half light cycle to turn Earth from a planet to asteroids."

* * *

Sheila yawned, fighting to keep her concentration, as she slumped in a stiff backed chair pirated from Sam's office. The short period of sleep hadn't been enough to recharge her system. One worry piled on top of another. Every threat neutralized seemed to produce two more incipient disasters. Nor did any safe harbor seem imminent. Around her, her team perched on the Pashti platforms—the alien version of recliners—like larks on a billiard table. The platforms rose above the deck, allowing amplification, as if the things were huge resonators which augmented foot sensors and vibration sounding chambers.

Really, the first contact with the third intelligent alien species met by humanity deserved a more enthusiastic response. For that matter, any of their actions would have plugged Earth news services with an avalanche of press releases. Now all she wanted was ten more hours of good solid sleep. Not even Viktor's presence roused her interest anymore—evidence of her condition.

Svetlana, headset glowing, looked over. "I think we have it, Major."

Sheila glanced at the huge crystalline being now resting on the floor next to the dais. Pashti claimed this thing was almost as old as the universe? Fifteen billion years?

What did a person say? "Hello, Chee'ee'la. My name, in human syllables, is Sheila Dunbar. We didn't recognize you to start with. I hope you will forgive the oversight."

She waited while Svetlana frowned, listening to the comm generated translation.

Minutes passed. Then: "My>name>Chee'ee'la<-> the>sound>made>by>star>waves< Oversight< null<program[see ~look ~across ~for ~what ~purpose ~interrogative?]

"Why>are> you>here>interrogative>?<"

"We were ordered here by the Ahimsa, Wide. He threatened our species and planet with extinction if we refused. Wide wanted us to harm the Pashti. We had moral objections and found a different solution which saved the Pashti—and ourselves." Sheila frowned as she looked at the translation.

Svetlana shook her head. "The way that thing loads the nets, Major, it's pouring out fantastic sums of data. If I was to guess, the Shitht is the most incredible thinking machine in the universe."

"God?" Sheila asked dryly. "Chee'ee'la, are you God?"

The response came even before she'd ceased speaking. The holos formed tables of figures and images, pulses of light, a random sounding crackle of static . . .and the Pashti systems overloaded and shut themselves down, incapable of dealing with the flood of information.

Svetlana looked cowed, face ashen. "By my grandmother's skirts. That goes beyond belief. Have you any idea of the capacity these systems have? Chee'ee'la just dumped more information on God into the net than. . . ." Her head shook slowly. "Incomprehensible!"

"What does it mean, Svetlana?"

"Think of it like this. People who count on their fingers are using a basic digital computer. The Pashti system is to my Cray, what the Cray is to finger counting. Chee'ee'la just . . . just . . ." Detova's mouth dropped open.

The net had begun to power up again. A simple statement flickered into being on the holo. "System>Pashti >not>capable< Must<find<other<way<communicate<about<Human<name<God<-> Shitht< name . . . ." The system blanked again, overloaded.

Sheila swallowed nervously. "Why'd that happen?"

Svetlana wiped damp perspiration off her forehead and swallowed hard. "The Shitht name for God is too big for this machine. Major, what are we . . ."

The system recovered. Chee'ee'la continued, sending, "Study>machine>stimulator< Term>not>in>Pashti >system>Vocabulary< Wires<->electrical<->magnetic<->stimulation< Human<made<metal<carbon<polymer<surrounded<equipment>"

"Mason's tape player," Sam supplied looking at the pieces which had been laying before the Shitht when they entered.

"Tape player," Sheila supplied.

"Tape<player>-<term<integrated< Humans>produce>tape>player>for>Chee'eela>interrogative>? < Tape>player>insufficient>to>withstand>stimulation>feedback>from>Chee'ee'la< Humans<conditional<would<do<this<before<Ahimsa<destroy< Earth[home~planet~Humans<interrogative<?>"

Sheila sat up straight. "Ahimsa will destroy our planet?"

"Affirmative>humans>noisy<!> Destruction<of <humans<makes<civilization<quiet<so<Shithti< may<think> Ahimsa>Wide>has>brought>disruption<"

"What if the humans don't want to be destroyed?" Sheila felt her heart pounding.

"Interrogative>humans>have>reason>to>exist>? < Do<humans<exist<interrogative<?> Interrogative>why>should>humans>exist>?<"

"God almighty!" Sam breathed, eyes straying to Svetlana's. His lips worked and his swallow sounded dry.

"Do Shithti have a reason to exist?" Sheila asked.

"Shithti<. . . ." the net overloaded again—and remained down.

"Not only do they have enough reason," Svetlana whispered, "their reasons overload the system quicker than their concept of God."

"And the Ahimsa are planning to destroy our planet?" Sam smacked a callused fist into his hand. "Damn it! I'd thought we won!"

Sheila shook her head, overwhelmed by Chee'ee'la's intellectual power. The net came up again. "Chee'ee'la, would you destroy the humans?"

"Yes> Such<action<at<this<time<appears< logical> Is>there>some>logical>reason>not>to> interrogative>?<"

Sam's voice was soft. "Where's Socrates when we need him?"

Sheila whispered somberly, "Dead—maybe like us."

CHAPTER XXX

Moshe, a cup of coffee in hand, settled next to Riva. The knowledge that he'd been avoiding her ate at him. What did he say? How did he tell her that he'd fallen into a trap of his own devising? For her part, she'd accepted the situation, leaving him time to think—which earned her his eternal gratitude.

Sheila entered, notepad under her arm, comm humming. She set up at the little table, took a quick look to see if everyone was there, and checked the comm and translation to Spotted and RashTak.

"Very well," she began. "As we have all noted, taking territory in space is not especially difficult. Holding it is almost a pleasure. Our problems now revolve around the following: how to avoid having our species destroyed; how to keep from having our bluff called by the Ahimsa and the Shitht; and how to stabilize the situation so that every party can go his way in peace.

"Further conversations with Chee'ee'la have not proven particularly reassuring. We have informed him that as soon as we could compose a cogent reason for our continued existence, we would let him know. I called this think tank session to see if all our heads together might be better than mine alone. Immediately after this meeting, I am contacting the Ahimsa Overones to dicker for Earth's survival.

"Let me start by asking First Councillor RashTak if Chee'ee'la can destroy humankind? If so, what are the potential means at his disposal?"

RashTak sounded like twenty castanets. "To begin with, the Shithti, of all the intelligent life-forms, are the most difficult to deal with or describe. We do not understand them and we have dealt with them ever since the Ahimsa freed us from our planet ninety-eight cycles ago. Chee'ee'la can and will destroy your species. He would do it, I imagine, by traveling to your system and causing your sun to go supernova."

Svetlana Detova asked, "Isn't that unlikely? I mean, our sun isn't big enough. It doesn't have the mass, and our scientists estimate only half of the fusible hydrogen stored within the sun has been burned."

RashTak waved a pincer-manipulator. "Indeed, no one knows how Shithti modify physics to supernova smaller suns. Shithti do many things impossible to explain. They defy reality. To address your point, their reasons for inducing a supernova are explicit. They grow by the addition of exotic elements. Shithti do not die—ever. They are broken and even almost vaporized at times. Perhaps, if one allowed himself to be drawn too close to the star type you call neutron, he might become plasma. On the other hand, ancient Ahimsa sources report Shithti having established study stations on exactly those types of stars. From our understanding of atomic structure, tides should have stripped the charged cloud you call electron from their nuclei. Gravity should then have compacted their nuclear mass into the surface."

"So, in effect, we can determine them to be eternal and indestructible," Sheila concluded, brows knitting at the impossibility of the concept.

Moshe shifted uncomfortably. "Does it not take some sort of equipment to make a star go supernova? Perhaps we could damage or sabotage the equipment?"

RashTak quivered. "From all the information at our disposal, Shithti *think* stars into imploding. It is believed that is how they deal with gravity, radiation, atmosphere or any other trouble. They think it—and it happens. They make no artifacts—although Ahimsa provided them with ships once. They modify space by the power of their thoughts alone."

"Chee'ee'la wants us to build him a tape player before he destroys us." Svetlana tapped her pencil, brown eyes focused on someplace far away.

RashTak chittered while Spotted whistled as they discussed it, the conversation too fast for Moshe to sort out as it occurred. RashTak thrummed and said, "Don't build it!"

"How long can we get away with that?" Viktor asked.

RashTak slapped his hind end on the floor, "Probably about ten thousand years. Shithti have a very poor sense of time if they are occupied. Instead, find him a problem to think about. Something with an infinite solution. If it truly intrigues him, he may simply go away to think about it where he cannot be distracted. When he comes back with the answer, have another question to occupy him for another ten thousand years."

"You're kidding?" Sheila burst out. "That's hardly a pragmatic approach toward life. Considering the incredible mental ability of a Shitht—"

"They have been alive for so long time is dilated in their memory," Spotted reminded. "It is thought by some that Shithti formed when the universe exploded. One Ahimsa postulated a Shithti made the universe—caused your Big Bang, if you will. He postulated the Shithti existed prior to this phase change of existence."

The silence deepened.

Moshe hadn't realized he'd woven his fingers together with Riva's. Voice soft, he interjected, "For the present, our people face a greater threat from the Ahimsa than from Chee'ee'la. Sheila, your memo stated that the Shitht thought the Ahimsa were going to try and destroy our world. Our people are there. The Ahimsa speak in terms of genocide. Now, we are all Jews."

"Your assessment of the situation is correct, Colonel Gabi." Spotted spun to study Moshe with one eyestalk. "The Ahimsa Overones fear you. Wide has let a terror loose upon civilization. You are their responsibility because Wide, who was one of them, broke the interdiction."

Viktor cleared his throat. "Against the Ahimsa we probably have some leverage, then. They pride themselves on being so civilized, can we use guilt against them?"

Svetlana tossed silky hair over her shoulder, mouth pursed. "Having spent the most time on the study of the Ahimsa, I think we can bet they will respond to blackmail. The Pashti—who they would have wronged—may come over to our side." She studied RashTak. "They'll live and let live. The Ahimsa, driven by that very sense of guilt and responsibility, must act in some manner to repair the damage."

"Spotted, do you have an observation as to how they will respond? They are your people. What would you advise?" Sheila asked as all eyes turned to the little mottled alien.

Spotted whistled, thinning as he thought. "The Overones have many options. For now, they feel safe. Your world is hostage and you are here at TaHaAk while they are scattered all over the galaxy. You are concentrated. They are dispersed. From my new study of tactics and strategy, that is strength and weakness at the same time."

Spotted stopped, drawing himself full of air again. "Your planet, unprepared to begin with, is defenseless. You cannot counter an asteroid, a major solar flare, a gravitational disruption, subatomic manipulation of terrestrial fissionables, complex bio-phage infections, poisoning of the atmosphere, climatic disruptions, radiation from solar manipulation, or any of the other methods of extinction at the hands of the Overones."

Moshe felt himself tensing, thinking of the women and children, of the kibbutzim, of the young people with smiles on their faces and hopes for the future. "Which attack do you expect? Which is the most likely?"

Spotted hummed to himself before responding. "I doubt they will get close to your planet. They will seek to harm you and your world from a distance."

"Could they trigger the nuclear arsenals?" Sam asked, chin propped on knee.

Spotted considered, rocking back and forth. "I doubt it. Wide keyed that whole process to his own atomic, strong-reaction stasis fields. The Overones would have to break that stasis and initiate a reverse of the process. They might detonate the warheads one by one as they worked out the sequence. There would be a chance humans would escape. The Overones do not have the program Wide set up for his own equipment and I have erased this one so nothing can happen to your world. It would be cleaner to them if, say, they dropped a rock on you."

"Like happened to the dinosaurs," Riva offered.

"Exactly," Spotted agreed. "Dinosaurs were not as fragile as mammals. The effects would be catastrophic, causing—"

"How could we slow them down, Spotted?" Sheila tugged at her ear, lost in thought. "What could we do to delay them?"

Spotted piped, "You might ask them. They tried very hard to contact Wide before we reached TaHaAK."

"Yeah, right," Sam breathed. "Ask 'em! Hey, dudes, ya'll wanna lay off the home world? Man, screw with us, and we'll waste every frickin' Ahimsa we find! Dig, dude?"

Spotted chirped and hooted. "That is indeed the gist of the message I would offer, Sam. I'm not sure their comm could quite translate the rich vernacular, however."

"We've got to talk sometime." Sheila pronounced. "You can raise them from ship's comm?"

"Affirmative," Spotted asserted.

"Does anyone else have anything to offer?"

"Let me think about this business of dispersed Ahimsa," Viktor said quietly. "As Spotted says, a strength—and a weakness."

Sheila thought out loud. "In the meantime, we should assert control of Earth's solar system from a defensive standpoint. From a quick scan of the ship's records of the Sol system, they can't immediately dump a rock on us."

"Do not place too much faith in the orbital stability of the Greek asteroids," Spotted warned, thinning as he spoke. "A very slight energization of the gravity buoys could be arranged at any time. The results will not be immediate, but within two or three years. . . . The Ahimsa could always claim it had been an accident. An act of God, as you put it."

Moshe felt a dryness in his mouth. "I am ready, Sheila. We can leave as soon as possible. I volunteer Assaf to guard our planet."

RashTak offered, "Take a Pashti Councillor, his subordinates, and wives with you. They can advise on trade, and as long as they are near, no Ahimsa would attack you. It might be insurance—but, then, who would have thought Ahimsa would have attacked TaHaAK in the first place?"

Viktor twirled his pencil. "At the same time, we must hold TaHaAk, and maintain the fleet of Pashti jumpships. I have studied the accounts. As the cycles diminish, RashTak will begin spacing them again. I suggest we augment his crew to further disperse our forces. Concentrated targets invite attack. Aboard Pashti ships, we will reduce the risk to TaHaAk while increasing tactical advantage in case the Overones invite retaliation."

"Bloody mess, actually," Sheila sighed, "and in the meantime, all I have to do is keep Chee'ee'la occupied while we figure out if we deserve to live or not. Heigh ho! Perhaps I'll ask him how many possible ways there are to win a chess game, what?"

Svetlana coughed to get attention. "Another thing, Comrade Major. I do not fear the motives of the Pashti. They, like ourselves, are a young and ambitious species. Our goals appear on the surface to overlap. The Ahimsa, on the other hand, in almost classic Soviet doctrine, are old and corrupt bourgeois creatures. At least, so their Overones appear. In whatever way we deal with them we must expect Marxist doctrine, in that sense at least, to be correct. We cannot afford to trust them—as we could not have afforded to trust Wide."

Moshe whispered to himself, "The stars are Lebanon."

* * *

Each of the Overones monitored the conversation from their various locations. Sees had been surprised when the humans contacted them first. The surprise increased when the human female looked right at him and said, "We know you are planning to destroy our planet. Don't!"

"That is a singular statement for you to make. Have you a reason for so blatant an accusation? We consider you to be an . . . a being without civilized values or behavior. A—"

"Savage? Barbarian?" she supplied. "Those are all words from our vocabulary which no doubt fit this particular instance." She smiled. "Study our history, Overone.

Our past is replete with barbarians who came and supplied 'Civilization' with new blood, new ideals, and new vigor."

Sees wheezed and thinned. "You assume vigor—as you call it—is a desirable attribute. We, on the other hand, respect and profit by peaceful contemplation which—"

"Peaceful enough to destroy a world?" she demanded. Her face contorted in ways Sees did not understand. The change in tone, to his Ahimsa hearing, was a manifestation of an emotional charge. He tried to keep from flattening.

"Spurious detail, I'm sure—but returning to the issue, what makes you sure we would harm your world?" Sees felt himself regaining the advantage and thinned correspondingly.

Sheila Dunbar's mouth twisted with amusement. Sees felt his sides loosening.

"You Overones seem to have a great deal of trouble with the concepts of responsibility and guilt. First, responsibility for Wide's actions necessitates that you do something to compensate. Second, guilt for the harm done to the Pashti urges you to remove the memory—namely us." Her eyes glittered with an odd light Sees did not understand as she added, "And last, but definitely not least, our Shitht assures us you will at least attempt to destroy our home world."

Sees almost lost his nerve but caught himself, forcing his mind to maintain a strict control. He could see Tan watching from the rear and his fluster stabilized. "*Your* Shitht?" He piped amusement and thinned. "Ridiculous!"

She bobbed her head. "That is a human manner of speaking, but, yes, I suppose you might say that. He's ours, we're his—at least for the moment. Currently, we have given him a problem to solve. We thought the answer was infinite, but Chee'ee'la says there are a finite number of ways to win a chess game."

"Chess?" Sees asked.

"An absorbing human preoccupation, a diversion of strategy and tactics we employ to stimulate the mind."

Sees puffed and interjected, "Consider, human, you

have been brought here through a . . . miscalculation. What can you possibly gain by remaining so far from your roots and your world? Don't you think it would be better for all concerned if you allowed us to transport you and your kind back to your planet? This whole thing could be so easily—"

"No deal!"

"What? I was about to—"

"No deal!"

What now? Who would have thought the humans would simply refuse to. . . . "We would be more than happy to, how do you say, pay you for—"

"No!" She had crossed her arms.

What did that mean among humans?

"But, we—"

"Shut up and listen to me, Sees." Her eyes had taken on a narrowed look. Sees filed that into his store of human expressions. Her voice became a commanding monotone. "We're out to stay now. Were I inside your foot tread and planning to exterminate an entire species, I would follow the same strategy. Good plan! Get us located in one place and blast our planet. You know we're not capable of maintaining ourselves in space yet. We need that ecosphere down there."

"You have no proof we would—"

"You know, you're a lot like us. Just as piss-poor as liars. We're not going back. At least, not all of us, Overone. Now, before you decide to get too trigger-happy, listen to this. We're keeping Wide's ship. It's ours now. Anything happens to our planet and we come hunting. We have the Pashti fleet at our command and we have an Ahimsa with us who believes we are in the right."

Behind Sees, a chorus of whistles and piping grew. An Ahimsa? Impossible!

"That's right, an Ahimsa. We might even have Wide if he survives the metamorphosis he's undergoing." She seemed so sure of herself!

"Now, it is your turn to listen!" Sees fought to pull his sides up. "This threat of yours has two edges. Did I use that analogy correctly? Ah, I thought so! If you do not return to your planet immediately, we shall indeed destroy it. You have a choice to make. Life for you and your world—on that world—or immediate death for your planet and inevitable death for all of you—with the knowledge that you failed your kind."

She glared into his eyes and he locked his minds together, keeping his sides from sagging. Damned animal. Nothing had ever strained him like the battle to meet her deadly stare. This *beast* had killed with her own hands, no doubt.

"No." Her voice had that same solid sound. No wavering. "Overone, if you touch a single individual on that planet, we'll come after you. Worse, we'll come mad! Think, if you will, how many of the innocent will suffer. Can you get us all? Wide took the pick of a world and we're it—the cream of the crop of a race that breeds killers. How will you ever know? Did you get us all? Will the next Ahimsa to die be you? You kill our world, Sees, and you'll know that feeling. Each and every one of you. But it doesn't have to be that way.

"Think! You've got an out, Overone! Leave us alone. Wide studied us for three hundred of our years and he didn't know how to treat with us. Learn from that. Don't cross us or you'll have worse regrets than Wide. We're trained by our kind to kill. Do you understand? Death, Overone. Death and violence and blasted bodies and blown blackened space stations and planets hit with asteroids. That's your legacy if you kill our planet."

Sees hadn't noticed it when his sides had gone flat. His wavering cognition barely took note of the fact that Tan had displaced him in the holo. Tan—the recluse who had never been known to deflate.

"Then there might be a compromise, human?" Tan's aged spicules didn't have the resonance of other Ahima, his voice sounded flat.

Sees kept one eye on the exchange as he sought to pull himself together.

Sheila Dunbar nodded. "We become part of your so-called civilization. We'll make you the same deal we've made with the Pashti. We're a young species with—"

Tan's spicules piped in untranslatable laughter. "And would we let loose creatures who had just uttered such vile threats? Are we crazy-flat like Wide? Are we so foolish?"

Her head shook in human negation. "Not at all. If I truly thought you were foolish, we wouldn't be talking. I would have Wide's gutted body hung up beside me. I would be slowly but surely executing Pashti, one a minute, while you decided to leave our planet alone."

"Go back to your planet in peace, human." Tan thinned to the point of becoming a wheel. "We ask you to do this for the good of all. You have that concept among your kind, don't you? Save yourselves and all concerned the grief and the tragedy. All will be forgotten that way. Things shall be as if they never happened. Where does *your* responsibility lie? Don't you, too, have duty to those you seek to serve—human and nonhuman? Would you lay waste to the peace among the stars?"

"You ought to run for Prime Minister." she laughed. "The Conservatives would love the likes of you. No, Overone, you will only get us back into our gravity bottle again by killing us. We have reached an impasse. I have granted all I can. My terms are on the table, consider them—and consider the alternatives even more. Good day, gentlemen."

And she was gone.

Tan huffed and piped nervously. "Most thorny, I believe. The sooner we get about killing these escaped ones, the sooner we'll be able to safely turn our attentions to the home planet."

* * *

Moshe had watched the change of expressions, each face lined with thoughts, impressions, sadness or worry. The auditorium had filled for the last time, and even then, seats stood empty as critical personnel watched from monitors on TaHaAk.

Sheila Dunbar's voice had been low, husky. "It seems like it goes on forever. Everything has fallen on our shoulders. Each and every one of us has assumed the burden for the survival of our planet. Wide lied to us. The Ahimsa Overones can't be counted on for the truth.

The Pashti we have come to trust—and Chee'ee'la remains an unknown.

"Ladies and gentlemen, we have come face to face with a cold and brutal reality. It's not over yet. It may never be. We all knew there were no guarantees when we shipped up. We have a duty, ladies and gentlemen. I can only say that we'll all get home someday—if we do our jobs.

"Today I look out over this room, and see each of your faces. We're all so young, and so incredibly old at the same time. I've always thought the fate of worlds rested on the shoulders of elders who had learned responsibility and wisdom. Today, I look out at you and see that same responsibility, magnified tenfold, falling on your shoulders. We don't work to protect a nation, or an alliance, or even a hemisphere. We don't even act just to protect our species, or even just our world. Each and every one of us has assumed responsibility for our planet, true, but we've also assumed the burden of protecting the future, ladies and gentlemen. All of the future, for humanity and for the Pashti."

They waited, Soviet, American, and Israeli, CIA and KGB, the barriers eroded, vanished into a mist of memory. Each tense pair of eyes tightened in the silence, the set of their mouths hardened.

"First Councillor RashTak has offered to carry some of you to various locations in the galaxy in the event the Ahimsa move against our planet. People, we've got to act with haste. Communications gear are being placed in the Pashti jumpships. Ladies, I hate to tell you, but the burden falls on you. Most of you will be piloting in conjunction with the Pashti. You are the future of our species in space. If the *Phantom* is destroyed by the Ahimsa, you'll be the individuals who carry Earth's ambassadors to the rest of the galaxy. Learn your craft well.

"Assaf . . ." Sheila's brow lined, her mouth moving as if pained. "Assaf will be detailed out. One tank per jumpship. SPETSNAZ and SOD may volunteer for bunks as necessary. Certain other individuals will be required for the *Phantom*'s spacing home.

"I'll admit, deciding who would stay and who would go

is one of the hardest things I've ever done." She crossed her arms and leaned on the podium, searching their faces. "We have a long tradition in our literature. We remember Leonides and his three hundred Spartans standing at Thermopylae. Metzada never fell to the Seventh Legion. Travis and fewer than two hundred Texans gave themselves to the defense of the Alamo. I doubt that anyone who has seen the monument in Volgograd can doubt what the Russian people sacrificed at Stalingrad. None of us asked to be here, to be faced with what we must do, but with the legacy of Thermopylae, of Metzada and Stalingrad and the Alamo, we know our duty. History will know our names."

At that she collected her notes, heels clicking as she walked from the silent room. The moment lasted, her spell woven so completely none dared to break it.

Sheila's words echoed in Moshe's mind as he entered his quarters and plucked a bottle of Gold Star from the dispenser.

She had told him, "Moshe, we appreciate your volunteering to return to guard Earth. We understand it's in your blood, but you made a point we have all come to accept—we are all Jews now. Failure means holocaust for the entire planet."

So he would stay, prowling the stars. And, his world, the blue sea off Ashqelon, would he see it again? Assaf Company had nodded, like IDF anywhere, and set about doing their duty. Moshe's heart swelled with pride. Under their breath, they all muttered, "Never again!" their hearts breaking.

"Moshe, your Assaf Company will refit to Pashti specs. You and your men will be dispersed among the stars, our last stage of defense should the message come that the Ahimsa have succeeded in killing Earth or TaHaAk. You and your men will be our insurance."

Riva had been detailed to go back with the Ahimsa ship. They had named Wide's vessel now. They called her *Phantom*, and she'd carry the woman Moshe had come to love so very far away.

He sucked absently at the bottle, heart feeling like molten lead had been poured into it. The sadness spread, eating at his very being. *Anna, what should I do? Can I tie myself to the past? To the graves?* His soul tore at the thought of her gentle eyes, rebuking him.

Go, Moshe. A Jew knows that when God smiles, it's not an opportunity to be lost.

He chugged the beer with sudden resolution. His short blocky body left at a run. Time had grown so short now. How long did he have with her?

* * *

"I don't like *idiots* in my command, Mason!" Sam Daniels jabbed a thick finger into his lieutenant's chest, almost toppling Mason back a step. "I don't like people who can't think! Now, what do I do with you? This one's public! We don't have enough toothbrushes to go around for you to clean TaHaAK station. You know what would happen in the regular army, mister?"

Sam shook his head, pacing back and forth, glaring in disgust at Mason. "Murphy ought to be in this mess, too! Things happen around Murphy! You knew that, maggot brain! But no! You figured this one out all by your feeble-minded little self! But you and Murphy are saved for once, *because there ain't no gawddam replacements out here!*"

Mason stood ramrod stiff, eyes fixed on a distant point.

Svetlana Detova entered during a pause. "Excuse me," she apologized, turning to leave.

"No, hang on. This scum sucking maggot breath was just leaving to think long and hard on his sins. Ain't that right, mister?"

"Yes, sir!" Mason snapped out a perfect salute, spun on his heels and made the door with perfect square corners.

Sam sputtered a sigh and dropped into the chair—now his again—behind his desk. He gave Svetlana a boyish smile. "Discipline, you know. Gotta keep on top of these slug-brained pukes. One inch and they run all over you."

"I have two choices. I am supposed to return to Earth with the *Phantom*. Or, I could stay here, working on Pashti and Shitht communication, interfacing with the ship. Since you are going to be commanding the humans at TaHaAk, I was wondering what your thoughts on the matter were?"

"Maybe what I want isn't as important as what you want . . . and what's most advantageous for humanity." He looked up into those pools of blue.

She swayed her head in that sensuous way women use to swing a shining wealth of hair over their shoulders. "You and I would have to work together as a partnership. I need to know right now if that will be possible, or if we'll end up locking horns as we try and dominate each other."

"You willing to put up fifty million to recruit me?"

"I don't have it with me."

He smiled. "You know, Major, I like your style. Yeah, hell, I've learned a lot on this trip so far. Honestly, I'm going to miss Viktor. He and I put together a pretty good thing. You, well, I don't know about you. You're a dangerous woman."

"You're a dangerous man."

"But you're also pretty damn attractive. I find myself spending a lot of time thinking about you, and it bothers me."

"Oh?" She arched an eyebrow. "Sam, I'll be honest. I like you. You are the first person who ever knew me for what I was and didn't care. You just accepted, and met me halfway. No one's ever done that before." She looked away. "You know, I risked my life every day. I lived in constant danger of compromise, of assassination or torture by both sides. People paid as much as a million dollars to have me killed or captured. Living with that isn't as frightening as dealing with this new self of mine."

"Hey, look. It's a brave new world, huh? If it starts to get to you, if you feel like you're losing your way, come see me. We'll kick back with some good booze and talk about it."

She studied him thoughtfully. "I take it you want me to stay?"

He shrugged. "Yeah, I want you to stay for a couple of reasons. I like knowing I've got someone with your smarts on my team. I've enjoyed the little time we've spent together. And on top of that"—he smiled devilishly—"I'm getting used to having beautiful women around."

"Very well, Captain, I'll stay. Who knows where the future will take us." She hesitated. "You're special, you know."

He nodded. "Damn right. Takes one to know one."

* * *

"What do you wish to do with Wide?" Viktor asked, looking up from his list.

Sheila sipped her coffee—despicable habit to pick up, but tea didn't keep her awake anymore. "Transfer him here. Lock him up in a small room. He's still catatonic, isn't he?"

Viktor nodded. "Moshe would like to request that you leave Riva Thompson with him." Staka smiled. "He told me they've looked high and low and can't seem to find a rabbi. The matter is perplexing to a good Jew, but while you are not a rabbi, they would be interested in you, as commander, performing a marriage ceremony."

Sheila's hoarse laugh scared her. "Why not? I've done every other damn thing. But a marriage? Who'd have ever guessed?"

"Ee!Tak has most of his 'family' moved in. I have cleared him to make whatever additions to his quarters he feels suitable. At the same time, Sam's requests have dropped to almost nothing. He feels secure enough to defend TaHaAk. Moshe is refitting the Pashti ships for assault capabilities. In doing so, he's still consuming eighty percent of the ship's manufacturing capability and Spotted reports the fusion system is functioning at one hundred percent to meet those requirements."

She fought the yawn, realizing her brain was getting fuzzy. How long had it been since she'd slept? Two days? Three? How did the ship manage to make metal out of hydrogen gas? She didn't understand. They were soldiers, not scientists!

"What of Chee'ee'la?" she asked, trying to remember all the details.

"Still sitting in the Council Chambers. RashTak has built some sort of insulation around him to dampen some of the vibrations. He's evidently still working on the chess problem. No telling how soon he'll solve it." Viktor said pensivly.

"That's all?" Sheila asked, rubbing her hand over her face. Was there grit in the air or could just being tired make her eyes that way?

"No. I have a personal request."

"Who wants to come this time?"

"No one. It is *my* personal request. I simply want you to lie down and sleep for a couple of hours. There's nothing left for you to do. I have everything under control."

"Viktor, a thousand and one things could still go wrong. What are we forgetting? We can't afford to make mistakes. One little omitted detail could kill us all."

"And commanders, running on raw nerve, are infallible?" His stony blue eyes warmed slightly. He looked down at his hands. "I told you, it was personal. I . . . suppose I don't like seeing you this way. You're tired Sheila. Look, you've taken this whole thing onto your shoulders. You've done the impossible. Look at you. You've lost five kilos until you're nothing but bone. Your eyes have gone dull." He nodded as if to himself, and slapped his legs as he got to his feet. "Yes. I do care. And it frightens me to death."

"Viktor?" She sat up, looking after him. "I'm sorry. I really am. You know, I wish we could just take a couple of days off and . . . and go holiday somewhere. Have a nice candlelight dinner, see a play, walk along a sunny beach somewhere and talk, just the two of us. We could watch the clouds, drink coffee in a cafe. Anything that didn't have to do with this."

His shoulders dropped. "That does sound nice, doesn't it. Perhaps, one day, when this is all over. I know of a delightful stretch of beach on the Black Sea. The water's like turquoise crystal."

She smiled and walked close to him, reaching her arms around him. "Let's promise, Viktor. Let's do it. It's a symbol for us, you see. Not only are we fighting for the planet and everything on it, we're fighting for that beach, for the time to spend together."

"Then I promise."

She smiled at him, her tension lessening ever so slightly.

"And now you sleep," he told her.

She grunted. "I'll try. At least until the nightmares wake me up. I keep seeing everything on Earth destroyed. The whole landscape looks like something out of a Bakshi film. Ash floating in the rivers among the bloated bodies of dead fish, flesh like warm clay sagging off the bones of the dead. Houses crushed, doorways and windows black and gaping. The trees are splintered and leafless. Everywhere the air is muggy, lifeless and heavy. Bits and pieces of butterfly wings lie in the gray grass while the sunlight is blocked to a sickly yellow."

He tightened his hold on her. "We won't let that happen."

"Stay with me, Viktor. Will you do that? Stay with me? And hold me while I sleep?"

She heard and felt his hard swallow. "Yes. I'll stay and hold you if that will make you rest."

* * *

"Man, don't you ever sleep?" Murphy asked, looking over at Spotted.

"Only men sleep in all the universe," Spotted twitted and piped.

Murphy looked over to where Katya lay on her side asleep in one of the new command chairs. She'd finally dropped off, exhausted by the long watch they'd been keeping. With the chair fully reclined, she'd curled into a ball. He fought the urge to reach over and fondle that perfect body.

Murphy thought the new bridge had still been built on the small side. To Spotted, it must have seemed like a basketball court.

"And Ahimsa don't have sex?" Murphy wondered, awed by the idea.

"We never did," Spotted asserted, rocking back and forth, forming manipulators and checking the various status monitors of *Phantom*.

"Weird shit, man," Murphy shook his head. "I mean, how did you make new Ahimsa?"

"It happened on my home world's oceans, Murphy. When an Ahimsa decided to die, he went flat—like Wide. Then, if his brain decided there was no use to re-form, he let himself go, the cells floating free in the ocean. Then each cell would have the chance to grow into another Ahimsa. We changed through time, like in your evolution, by ingesting other Ahimsa cells and maybe they were changed by radiation, but it was a very slow process."

"So where's the Ahimsa home world? If we knew where it was, we could counter the Overones and their threat to Earth."

"That would be wonderful strategy, Murphy, but our home world is gone now. You have seen the big map of stars in the astrogation room? Our home galaxy is one of those. You call it Sculptor, almost 500,000 light-years from this Milky Way Galaxy. My star went nova before your galaxy formed."

Murphy looked nervously at Spotted. "Just how old are you, little buddy?"

Spotted hummed and piped, body thinning while he fed information into the comm. After a minute, he replied, "In your terms, about seven billion years old, but because of time dilation—"

"Holy shit, man!" Murphy choked out. Katya blinked groggily, mumfffed to herself, and rolled over. Murphy gaped. "I mean, don't you ever die?"

Spotted piped softly, "If I wanted, I could. Like Wide will probably do. Most wait until they go insane before they die."

"But. . . . But. . . ." Murphy struggled to form his thoughts. "How do you remember everything? You gotta be the smartest people around! I mean—Jesus!"

Spotted rocked back and forth. "I have forgotten many things. There is no other way. Damage occurs to memory molecules, so things are purged as inconsequential. The far distant past is forgotten. Do you think we are Shithti? No, memories are kept alive and traded back and forth so that all remember. We do that by exchanging body fluids. Some Ahimsa claim that one day we will become as the Shithti. That is the path the Overones have chosen—with the exception of Wide and a couple of others.

"That is why the Pashti take over. That is why humans will take over. I think it is an old process. To date, you have met three species, Ahimsa, Pashti, and Shithti. There are many many more. Some are interdicted. Some are older than we. Some are younger than you. Some are so different they cannot be communicated with."

Murphy frowned. "Well, you know humans better than any other aliens, what do you think of us?"

Spotted piped, flattened, and thinned. Time passed as Murphy's nerves began to fray. He was debating asking again—and would have had Spotted not blown his cool completely by claiming to be seven billion years old. How did you interrupt something that might be that frickin' old?

"I think you need time," Spotted chirped. "You are not bad—simply untrained. You have been wild for too long. No one has showed you how to get along with civilized beings. At the same time, you have never had to. Your misbehavior has always been reinforced and rewarded by other misbehavior. Had you killed the Pashti as Wide suggested, I would have already destroyed your world."

Murphy felt his heart begin to pound. This little harmless appearing Ahimsa wasn't so damned harmless! His hand had unconsciously crept to his knife.

"Yeah, well, what are you going to do with us?" Murphy asked, trying to make his voice casual.

Spotted thinned, rocked back and forth, and shot a gleaming dark eye his direction. "I am going to train you, Murphy! If I can civilize you, I will have proven my worth to be an Overone. You will have space and a future. It is only through proving the Overones wrong that an Ahimsa gets elevated."

"What if you fail?" Murphy wondered dully.

"Oh, then we will all die," Spotted chirped.

CHAPTER XXXI

"The Last Good-Bye Party," they called it. When they met again—if they met again—it would be in the shadow of a dead planet, or the light of a shining future. The dancing, drinking, feasting, laughing, and crying continued with desperation. Couples were seen pairing off, perhaps for a last taste of intimacy. Tears spilled along with the champagne and the final remains of KGB, IDF, SPETSNAZ, CIA, Mossad, and SOD collapsed irrevocably into the Phantom Battalion—the last defense of a species known as Homosapiens and a little out-of-the-way planet called Earth.

In the midst of the party Moshe Gabi and Riva Thompson were married with due pomp and ceremony—to the immense enjoyment of the Pashti, who, once informed of the significance, followed the happy couple in a parade, waiting for him to corner and spike her. The Pashti pursuit suffered a crushing disappointment when Moshe executed a rapid flanking maneuver and vanished with his bride.

Murphy, Mason, Katya, Barb Dix, and Malenkov, swaying, more than a little inebriated, even pulled Mika Gubanya off his rear and danced him around the cleared floor in a stumbling mixture of Cotton-eyed Joe and Bailekasch. If only for that one time, Gubanya's enmity faded in the desperate flourish of hope.

"Sheila?" She turned to find Sam Daniels standing there, a drink in one hand. "Got a minute."

"Sure, Sam." She followed him past a knot of chirruping, clicking Pashti and into one of the halls. They ended up in an observation room, the glow of the densely packed stars of the core casting an orange-tinged illumination through slanted oval windows.

Daniels stared at the scene for a moment, slowly shaking his head. "Who'd a believed it?"

She nodded slowly, feeling his awe and amazement. "We're really here."

"Yeah." He turned, a sheepish smile creeping across his lips. "Listen. I wanted to let you know that I . . . well, I shouldn't have pushed so hard at first. Chalk it up to a black guy with a chip on his shoulder. You're one hell of a fine commander, Major. Just for the record, I'll follow you through hell and back."

"You know, Sam. I owe you a lot. Back at White Base, it was that look you gave me that made it real. I never blamed you for testing me." The stars seemed to pulse with a life of their own. "Funny. We molded each other, grew to meet the challenges. More than once I caught myself wavering, losing my nerve, and I'd ask myself, what would Daniels say? Could I stand that look in his eyes? And I'd buck up and work twice as hard to make sure I had everything right."

He looked down at his hands as he rubbed them together, "I want you to know I couldn't have done what you did. I don't know what will happen when you get back home, what their reaction will be. But, well, if they give you any grief, if anything happens, we'll be coming to get you."

"Sam, don't endanger the mission over some foolish emotional response. No matter what, your duty—"

"With all respect to the Major's concern, we won't step into an Ahimsa trap, if we can help it. But no matter what we say to reassure the Pashti, people are assholes. Sure, the Ahimsa want to wipe us out, but you can't trust the folks back home not to slip a knife between your ribs when you're not looking, either. If they do anything, we'll be there, and God help them when we arrive. I'm not sure I could hold the troops back if I tried to stop them."

She felt a tightness in her chest, a warm flush at the base of her neck. "Thank you, Sam. But remember, keep everything in perspective—no matter what happens."

"You've earned a lot of respect, Major." He shook his head, a sour expression pinching his features. "You know, used to be, I practically had to use a cattle prod to get Murphy to salute a superior officer. For you, he'd not only stand at attention and salute, but say 'Yes, ma'am,' if you ordered him to slit my throat."

She laughed. "I think you overestimate your leftenant's capacity to be dazzled by success. He's smarter than he knows, and I think he's starting to realize it."

"Maybe. But I'll tell you what. I've just got a sense, a queasy feeling in my gut. Trouble's coming. Something we missed? God knows, but this all came too easy. We're gonna have to pay in the end."

"I think we share that feeling."

"Yeah, you may have a better idea than I do about the fix we're in. But I want you to keep something in mind. Might save the fort one of these days. Viktor's a damn fine officer. He's sharp, he's canny, and he's no one's fool. I've got a lot of respect for Viktor and a damn sight more admiration for him than I'd admit, but his brilliance is in adapting strategy and tactics to a situation. I want you to remember this, Major. 'Cause I know you're in love with Viktor—"

"Captain Daniels!"

"Hear me out. No matter what you think about Viktor, if you get in a situation that might be sticky, take Murphy with you. Sure, he's always in some sort of trouble, but where Viktor reorganizes his strategy, Murphy's already acting. He's visceral, intuitive. And for all the times we've been in combat, I've never seen him make a mistake. Trust him."

She took a breath, stilling the racing of her heart. "Very well. Thank you, Sam. I'll give your words a lot of thought." Time to change the subject. "How's RashTak adjusting?"

"About half and half—for someone who's just had the foundation of his reality cracked and crumbled to dust under his vibrators. He's coping, trying to feel his way through what's turned into a nightmare. He's overjoyed to find out we don't eat our dead. He's sorry we're here, but happy he's alive and that we don't grunt and defecate in halls. The good side is that humans and Pashti get along pretty good. But you can feel the tension around the Councillors. They genuinely like us, but we've brought the seeds of disaster with us."

"And that is?"

"We're putting killing machines on Pashti jumpships. RashTak understands why and can sympathize on a rational level, but emotionally, he's appalled." Sam kicked at the floor. "And quite honestly, I don't blame him. They had a hell of nice system until we came along. No war, no fighting, just a little harmless lunacy ever seven hundred and sixty years or so."

"If the Overones would relent. . . ."

"They won't. RashTak and I had a long talk about it. He can't think of any other alternative, but we've put him between a rock and hard place. Ethically, he can't order us out, or he'd be doing to us what Wide tried to do to him—only worse. The Ahimsa mean genocide, not just embarrassment and disgrace. On top of everything else, he's devastated by the thought that Ahimsa lie. Their ivory idol has been knocked off the pedestal—and when it hit the floor and broke, they found out it was full of sand."

She sucked at her lower lip, staring out at the stars. "Well, take care of them, Sam. Make it as easy for them as possible."

He nodded. "I don't envy you, either. What's gonna happen when the galaxy finds out just how crazy humans are? You sure you want to spring right-wing Moslem fundamentalists on the stars? How about greasy-assed politicians with their smiles and double-dealing? Used car salesmen? Then there're the slime-bag lawyers and TV evangelists looking for new schemes to line their pockets with gold. What a gift to the stars. The cream of the human crop. Everyone will know we're berserk then. How about all those people who buy those magazines that say, 'Human Baby Born with Chimpanzee Brain' at the grocery checkout. You want the Pashti to know we let people that stupid walk the streets?"

She lifted her arms and let them fall. "You know, when you think about it, you can understand why they want us locked up. It becomes difficult to argue with them in a rational sense."

"Speaking of catatonically crazy, anything from Wide?"

"No." She shot him a quick reproachful glance. "Did you have to send him over in a bucket?"

He grinned and chuckled. "Seemed the thing to do." After a long silence, he added, "Sorry about dropping that bit about Viktor on you."

"What makes you think . . ."

"Always play poker with white folks. They get a good hand and their ears get a little redder. You see, that's a problem you whites have. Skin's too pale, gives you away every time. Those blue eyes you make so much over contrast with the blackness of the pupil. You can read interest in skin tones, pupil dilation, blushes, other things. Now, aside from that initial disadvantage, you change posture around Viktor. Display, I think they call it. You spend more time looking at him, thinking to yourself. You worry about him."

She bit off the hot retort, admitting defeat. "You do seem to have all the data at hand."

Sam nodded, returning his gaze to the stars. "Yeah. He's pretty stuck on you, too, you know. I don't know what happened, but he's scared to death of you . . . of himself, actually."

She sighed and leaned next to him, eyes locked on the stars. "So what do I do?" Her laughter mocked. "I can plan military actions, overthrow star empires, and try to save the Earth, but when it comes to Viktor, I . . ."

"It's the ghosts, Major. Hell, I don't know but that Sees and the rest of the Overones aren't right. You know, maybe we are goddamned insane. Look what we do to each other for the sake of a little political heresy. Think Brezhnev ever worried an iota about what kind of scars his little war with the Afghans would leave? Bastard politicians, all of them."

"And Viktor?"

"You're going to have to dig out the ghosts, Major. He fought a nasty bastard war, one with even less justification than we had in Nam. They fought it even dirtier—and Viktor's a decent human being at heart. You need to listen, to believe, and to understand with all your soul. You need to help him forgive himself."

She nodded. "Providing the Ahimsa give me enough time."

Sam shivered slightly, as his eyes clouded. "Yeah, and there'll be hell to pay if we have to start hunting down Ahimsa Overones. Damn, Sheila, maybe we really are crazy. Psychotic killers loosed on the stars."

* * *

The silence deafened, pressing against the eardrums like some thick cotton. Aleksei Nasedkin swallowed, and thought everyone within meters could hear. If he concentrated, the blood in his veins seemed to beat like a pigskin drum. He could hear Boris Tomski's breathing. The man had always had a sinus condition.

Aleksei didn't see what happened. Ivan had turned, trying to resettle in the seat in an effort to find a more comfortable position. Whether his elbow bumped the table, or whether the wrench had just been carelessly set on the edge, no one would ever know. The heavy crescent wrench dropped, clanging on the deck plates with a ringing crash that might have echoed the gates of heaven being slammed shut.

For a shocked second no one moved, hearts racing as they froze in place. How much noise? Had it carried past the submarine's hull? Could the American killer sub have heard?

Aleksei swallowed hard again, heart pumping vigorously against his ribs as adrenaline shot through him.

Ivan flushed red, picking up the wrench, fear bright in his gaze as the lieutenant ducked through the hatch on silent feet, burning eyes pinning them both.

Ivan closed his eyes, shaking his head. When he opened them again, the lieutenant was pointing a finger that condemned like the wrath of God. Ivan began to tremble, gained control of himself, and rose unsteadily.

Aleksei kept his gaze lowered as his bunk mate passed in silence. Fear: it filled a man, thrived within his very soul in the submarine service. Fear of the American navy and their advanced antisubmarine warfare, fear of the officers, of the ever present death that left its acrid odor in the recycled air passing through his nostrils.

The Soviet land forces were striking back, rolling the NATO front back over Eastern Europe, throwing division after division against the overwhelmed allies in Rastinyevski's "Operation Napoleon." Casualty figures from the latest offensive claimed ten million NATO troops had been killed. Rumor said that in Vienna and Warsaw a man couldn't find two bricks stacked on top of each other.

In the oceans, the war intensified as American shipping struggled to resupply and reinforce the crumbling Western front. Aleksei's submarine, the *Onega* had already sunk three transports steaming for Europe with reinforcements. They'd sunk a merchanter full of explosives which had produced the most spectacular display Aleksei had ever seen against the night sky.

Now they were hunted. Here, in the silence of the North Atlantic at two hundred meters, they played a deadly game—they and the Americans, listening in the darkness, drifting on the currents, waiting for a signal that would identify the location of the enemy.

We haven't been doing well. He tried to slow his breathing, raising a careful hand to wipe at the sweat that beaded on his face. The fans had been shut down, the air going stale and heavy like the fortunes of the Soviet sub fleet. The last he'd heard, three fourths of his undersea comrades had been destroyed. Death struck in the silence, in the depths. What would it be like? A flash? Then that brief moment of realization before frigid black water crushed the life from him?

He worked his hands, knotting and unknotting his fists. The land forces at least had a better death. You carried your own gun—and the chance to kill before you were killed. Here, he waited, knowing that death lurked out there, silent, ominous.

He wouldn't know a hydrophone had detected the falling wrench. He wouldn't even have the brief moment of realization. The American torpedo detonated behind his head.

* * *

Murphy didn't care about the tears running out of his eyes. He hugged Cruz tightly, trying to crush him. "Take care, buddy. Keep your shit together and don't fill any puffball sights, huh?"

"*Vaya con Dios*, Murph. We got a hunting trip coming outside of Trinidad one of these days. You call Mom when you get home. Tell her I'm fine—and keep the tamales warm."

"You got it, man. I'll drop in and see her if I can."

"Do that. They'll treat you right."

Murphy nodded, turning to Mason, grabbing him in a clinch, feeling his own ribs groan as Ted's arms wrapped around him.

"Take care, Murph."

"Don't electrocute any Shithti while I'm gone, huh?"

"And don't you let Katya slip away."

"Not on your life, pal. Keep Cap from biting it, huh?"

"And don't forget my tape deck. Hell you ought to have enough back pay to afford a damn good one."

"Want me to call Pam?"

Ted shrugged, grin going sheepish. "Yeah, sure. She'll be divorced—but tell her I understand. That I don't blame her. Tell her, well, tell her I really wish her all the best in the world and to have a good life."

"Yeah, you got it."

Next came Malenkov. "Never thought I'd cry saying good-bye to a damn Commie."

"Commie-Capitalist, my friend. Stay out of kitchens—and watch out for Mika. He hasn't forgotten."

"I'll keep out of his way. I got your shopping list in my pocket. I'll hit the first mall I come to with a vengeance."

Malenkov winked. "Remember me every time you drink orange juice."

"Naw, I'll save it for Guinness."

"Looks like the torpedo's ready." Cruz pointed to where Barbara Dix waited in the hatch.

Murphy nodded. "God damn you all, take care. Stay alive, huh?"

And he turned and walked for the ramp.

* * *

Spotted rolled down the walkway around the new bridge He piped and whistled, happy with his new power. Forming manipulators, he ran diagnostics on each system, watching the levers on the human controls moving in mimicry of his commands. The headsets allowed for human input to the ship's computers. All that remained was to train his animals to the tasks at hand.

Spotted accessed a system. A monitor glowed to life, showing the General Secretary's office in Moscow. Nighttime. No one there. He switched to the White House and found activity in the situation room. With nimble manipulators, he dialed up the gain.

". . . Sixteen divisions supporting the Belgians at Liege. I don't know how they did it, but they're still holding. Any word from the Wermacht twenty-third armored? Did they get the fuel we dumped? Damn it, that cost us ten aircraft."

"They're moving, striking for Bonn, trying to crack the rear of the Russian lines wide enough to either get out, or divert enough attention that we can drive a salient."

One of the generals at the sand table straightened, rubbing the muscles of his back. "No one's ever fought a war like this! It's a damn chaos! Like a boxing match in a washing machine!"

A lieutenant looked up from where he sat monitoring headphones. "Alaska, sir. General Rodgers reports heavy fighting in the Talkeetna Mountains, but he thinks the Russian advance is stopped. Our antisub birds got another *Yankee* class boat off Sitka."

"Any word from Pakistan?"

"No sir. Karachi might have fallen. SATLINK says that Odessa is burning. It also looks like something's happened in Poland. They monitored a huge explosion outside of Warsaw. Probably munitions blown up by the Partisans."

Another lieutenant interrupted. "SoCom on the line, sir. Another offensive just launched on the Panama Canal. Got suicide bombers this time, sir. Don't know how they infiltrated, but Canal defenses are being pushed."

"And where the hell do they think I'm going to get people to back them up?"

Spotted caught sight of Murphy rounding the bridge hatch and canceled the access, fear flushing his brains as his sides loosened. Perhaps, if things worked out right, it would be better if the humans on Earth destroyed themselves. The future would be created by Spotted's whim.

I got some of your molecules, Wide. Only I will act with greater care than you did.

* * *

As the humans on TaHaAk stared with bloodshot eyes and winced at hangovers, *Phantom* departed for a distant blue, green, and brown planet covered by cloud patterns one thousand seven hundred and twenty light-years away: Earth.

Sam Daniels leaned on the railing next to Svetlana and suffered a curious hollowness of the soul. He experienced a pang as this last link to the world that had nurtured him disappeared.

"Comrade Captain, we are now on our own. Do you have first orders?" Svetlana tilted her head, bright strands falling to catch the light.

Sam swallowed, eyes straying to the reddish-white blaze of the galactic core—a sight humans had never seen until Wide brought them here. "No orders. We've got most everything taken care of for the moment." He tingled at the awareness, feeling the warmth of her body on his bare arm. "Moshe says we're all Jews now. Man, I thought it was rough just being black!"

"We were the lucky ones; the rest of humanity will not grow as easily as we did. It will be terribly difficult for them. So many of their precious beliefs will no longer be inviolable. How will the Party like hearing that Marxism is not the creed of the Shithti, the most powerful beings in the universe? How will the Western religions cope with the fact that those same Shithti can overload computers which dwarf Earth's simply with a definition of God? How will our military be told a simple alien technology stifled their biggest bombs? How do we tell the people of Earth that space is open to us and we will not come as masters, but as a trifling minority whose continued survival is precarious?"

Sam nodded, looking back to see the huge bulk of

Phantom sliding away at incredible speed. How did it keep from squashing everybody aboard? They had to be doing fifty gs for the big ship to shrink so fast! He thought of raspberry Jell-O being flung against a wall.

His voice came as a low rumble. "I guess my childhood ended that night on the streets of Detroit. I had to face it all then. It's the provincial ones down there gonna suffer the most. They're the ones who got truth! Man, it's gonna hurt when they find they ain't no bigger than gnats in the scheme of the universe."

"But we are here," she reminded. "We have the Pashti for friends. We have an Ahimsa who is on our side. There is Chee'ee'la, who we must yet win over. This is the toehold here. TaHaAk is mankind's first base among the stars."

"Never thought of it like that," Sam chuckled dryly. "How's that for a dumb street black from Detroit?"

"You are a symbol now. Yours is the first human command in deep space." She looked up at him and smiled bravely.

Sam's brow creased. "Tomorrow we start educating ourselves. We got a lot to learn here. West Point provided a great education in its day. Now, maybe with RashTak's help, we'll start learning again. The Ahimsa gotta root us out with sticks if they want to win. I ain't about to let that happen."

Phantom had shrunk to a tiny pinpoint of light. They watched until it flickered into nothingness. A shimmer occurred, nothing more than a wavering of a mist of stars. Engagement of the null singularity generator. *Phantom* was gone.

* * *

Moshe fought the cramp in his back. Sitting too long, he realized, and shuffled on the Pashti platform to regain circulation in his legs. Riva sat beside him, studying a monitor as information flickered across the screen in Pashti. Thank God, Riva could read the stuff; it still defied him. RashTak chittered and clicked, his vibrators making noises that Moshe, without his translator, had begun to develop a glimmering of comprehension for.

"There are two Ahimsa Overones at Frick!Teer. One

is Tan." RashTak turned to train his major eyes on Moshe. "Tan is among the oldest. His word is almost law."

Moshe looked at Riva and shrugged. "Why not? They are like the PLO, right? And, if Tan is important. . . . Let's take him. How long by jumpship to get there, and can we double the return with any cargo?"

RashTak checked the humming comm under his sensorial fibers. "Two and a half months. We can trade there. You must promise not to do unnecessary damage to Tan. He is venerable. According to the Ahimsa, he was the first of his kind to come to this galaxy when it was still new."

Moshe shook his head. "First Councillor, no one will be harmed. We can't afford that. I think our presence and a little conversation should be sufficient. Now, where can we send Arya and his crew? How about Low? Where is he? Anything there to mix business with profit?"

RashTak clicked and throbbed, pincer-manipulators raised in frustration. "Must *all* humans move so quickly?" His feet and vibrators sent more information into the system. "He's at KeeTaAkShee."

"What do they produce there?"

"Not much, only equipment that turns rock into water and basic elements."

"I can see it now. The Persian Gulf Arabs will buy them by the thousands. That takes care of Arya. Anyone else left?"

"There will be no ships left!" RashTak slapped his tail section against the deck.

"Sooner we are gone, the less desirable TaHaAk is as a target," Riva reminded, making notes on her pad and checking results on her headset.

Moshe grinned. "Unlike the Egyptian air force, you don't want to get caught sitting on the ground. Besides, each of those jumpships will be moving while the other Pashti are in the middle of the cycles. If you can show up on their doorstep with needed supplies the moment they come out of the cycles, you're ahead of the rest. Demand is the key to higher profit margins."

RashTak clicked to himself and slapped his tail again.

"True! In this case, haste will not only be safety—it will be profit, too. No one has ever had the advantage of trading through the cycles." RashTak thrummed excitedly. "There are advantages to working with the insane—even if they don't have enough feet!"

One by one, jumpships—refitted to carry not only tanks but cannon, too—slid out of TaHaAk and scattered to the major stars of civilization—stars with trade and Ahimsa Overones. Assaf Company was moving.

* * *

"The data are now conclusive. Some of the humans are foolishly returning to their home planet," Sees informed the assembled holos of the Overones.

Tan rocked back and forth, his darker tread foot moving smoothly over the surface. "Excellent. With such a high percentage in one place, the final sterilization will be that much more efficient. I sorrow. They have taken Wide's ship which means we will have to destroy it. I think, considering the stakes at play, such a loss, though regrettable, is only to be expected. Sterilization in times of plague is often necessary."

"But Wide is aboard!" Toot protested. "You can't mean to kill him? What sort of insane—"

"*Enough!*" Tan bellowed through his hardened spicules. "Wide placed *himself* in this position. *He* broke the interdiction. He may already be dead for all we know. Prompt sterilization is our only course. I wish no harm for Wide, but we cannot destroy ourselves to save him. A choice must be made."

"You no longer sound like an Ahimsa," Toot said softly. "You sound like Wide . . . like you've shared something with him, a bit of his insan—"

"*You DARE!* You dare use such an argument against me? I am *Tan*, who came here before any! I am Tan who crossed the intergalactic void! Where were you, Toot, when I dared the endless black? A Nav-Pilot seeking an Overone? When you have meditated the root of reality to the tenth power, then you may correct me!"

"The ship has many resources," Sees spoke into the sudden silence. "What chance is there that the humans or the mad Ahimsa, Spotted, would use those capacities as weapons?"

Pale demanded, "Do you sincerely think they are that smart? Indeed, how would they employ the devices aboard as weapons? It takes a certain ingenuity to make the quantum leap to weapons capable of warding off gravity waves or striking across timespace to endanger any of us."

"Then where have the modified Pashti jumpships gone?" Hurt thinned as he thought. "Curse the day RashTak returned to his station and thoughtlessly flicked the switch off on his comm! Is the insanity of the humans contagious?"

Tan's spicules carried their mellow deep hoot as he added, "If so, then indeed we must cleanse TaHaAk as well as the human planet. It would be regrettable, but contagious insanity cannot be allowed."

Low flattened slightly. "We can do that now. I believe sonic resonance, space warp, gravitational disjunction, mass transfer, or any of a series of solutions would sterilize quite satisfactorily."

"Wait!" Toot piped in anger. "What am I hearing? I made no major protest when the majority decided to exterminate the humans. I concede, they are violent vermin incapable of conducting their affairs in a civilized fashion. I can accept, but not condone their extermination. But now I hear that Pashti will be killed? And I ask, why? *They* were victimized by one of *us!* Because the humans did not accede to Wide's plan—which incidentally leads me to believe we might be compounding our—"

"Enough!" Tan thinned, gaining height as his tread foot smoothed. "Toot, you do nothing but add support to Wide's cause! You would have us do nothing, bear the consequences of insanity, when quick and decisive action could halt the process before it gets started. Overones, we can debate the ethics of our actions later. For the moment, we must preserve our civilization. We must act before we lose that opportunity. We can't *afford* to live in a galaxy where Ahimsa are suspect. That's the final line. I act for one reason and one reason alone: stability!

Stop the insanity now—to wait until later may doom us all. What is your will, Overones?"

"Stop it now," Hurt agreed. "A few Pashti are a small price to pay for peace. The other Pashti are locked in the cycles. They'll never know."

"I am not hearing this," Toot moaned. "I cannot be part of this." His image faded.

Sees called out, "Let's simply apply gravity flux in the area of TaHaAk. After the cycles, Pashti will arrive and assume a natural disaster."

Tan spun on his tread foot to stare with both eyes at Low. "And you expect Chee'ee'la to accept this kind of abuse? You would be the one to tell the noble Shitht it was your action which caused him discomfort? Perhaps disturbed his concentration? Perhaps cracked his body with temperature flux or gravitational tidal effects?"

Low flattened miserably.

Tan rocked slowly. "As I expected. The humans and Pashti at TaHaAk do not realize it, but so long as Chee'ee'la is among them, positive solutions will not be permissible. And you have forgotten yet one other factor."

"The humans who have disappeared," Hurt snorted through his spicules. "There are not very many. Only about one hundred men and perhaps seventy women the Pashti were teaching to pilot the jumpships."

Tan piped softly. "Yes, the missing humans. We may assume they are all in contact with each other. How do any of you suppose they would react if TaHaAk ceased to answer them? What do you suppose the humans would conclude?" His eyestalks swiveled, gauging their reaction. "For too long, my friends, we have been away from the realities of such problems. Unguided, I would have seen you make many mistakes. Have you truly forgotten so much of where we came from? Who we once were? Do these bodies we have adapted for so long color our perceptions of how we lived? In our oceans so long ago, *we were predators!* Think of that! Remember we killed for survival once. The roots are still there, hidden deep within us. Remember, once we, too, manipulated *things*—not abstract ideas."

"Immortality has changed us." Pale thinned himself.

"My memories of that long ago time are not complete. I can, however, see that we are not the ones we once were. Have other Ahimsa in other galaxies become as we? Are they soft, no longer in control of their own destinies? How many of us are left? Three, four million at the most? This galaxy will die in another ten billion galactic years. Will any of us be left to see it?"

Tan hooted. "This human problem Wide foisted upon us may not be the curse we currently perceive it to be. We have thoughtlessly consented to the fact that Wide was insane. Consider, was he? That question will not be answered immediately. It is to be pondered and tested from every dimension."

Sees piped, "Utilizing such information as is at hand, we must strike the humans at the same time—at least those who arrive at Earth and those at TaHaAk. The few scattered humans in the Pashti ships can then be dealt with one at a time. Surely they can be traced and their ships fluxed out of real space one by one, *and without the other humans knowing!*"

Tan swiveled and rested an eye on Sees as the others hooted and piped approval. "Now, my friends, you are beginning to think like Ahimsa again."

* * *

Murphy whistled to himself as he swung through the hatch to find Sheila Dunbar staring out the observation blister. He stopped, knowing she had to have heard him coming. It had taken three days of catch up sleep before she took calls. She had cocked her head when he mentioned meeting her here.

She turned, and he felt a sudden relief. She looked healthy again. Her skin flushed with color and the lines that had drawn so tightly about her mouth had disappeared.

"Leftenant," she nodded, reservation in her voice.

Murphy returned a subdued, "Ma'am," and saluted. All of a sudden his nerve lost its steadiness.

"And what's on your mind, Murphy? In trouble again?" An eyebrow raised suspiciously.

He chuckled uneasily and walked over, situating himself on the edge of the blister, to face her. "No, ma'am. I wanted to come down here where Spotted couldn't hear us."

"Spotted?" she asked, sinking down next to him. "And you don't think he can hear us here?"

His grin failed. "Uh, no, ma'am. You see, I shut the translators down in the blister. Took a while to find the right circuit, but I did it."

Murphy chewed his lip, meeting those probing blue eyes. How many men could have pulled off the things Sheila Dunbar had? She had worked miracles—this tall woman with sunlight-blonde hair and deep blue eyes. She had pulled the rug out from under *two* alien civilizations—so far.

"Yeah." Murphy got his mind back to business. "Spotted may be putting us in the position of being pawns again. Unlike Wide, his motives are to 'civilize' us. I don't know what that means. I don't know if it's good or bad. The way I was brought up, I don't trust anybody—and Spotted just isn't the cute bubbly alien we thought. He's got a lot of ambitions, Major. He wants to be an Overone—and we're his path to that position."

She leaned back, brow creased with a frown again as she laced her fingers around her knee, rocking back and forth like a thinking Ahimsa.

"We can't do without him," Sheila admitted. "We've begun making conversions so that we can control the ship. The problem is that he's had such an incredibly long time to learn how to space this vessel. We're learning astrogation from the ground up. Granted, Barbara flew jets for the CIA, but a starship is a bit different, don't you think?"

"Yes, ma'am. And I'm trying to be his star pupil." Murphy shifted as he crossed his arms. "You know how long he claims to have been around? Six or seven *billion* years!"

He wasn't used to Sheila looking shocked. "Good heavens! Jolly old little bugger, aye?"

"So he says. After meeting the Shiht, I don't question folks about age anymore."

"And what are your suggestions, Leftenant? You know him better than any of the rest of us. You seemed to have adopted the little whistler. How dangerous do you read him to be?"

He chewed his lip, frowning.

"Be honest with me, Murphy. Your thoughts on the Ahimsa manufacturing gave me an edge I needed. Sam says you're an intuitive type. I need that, too. I don't care if you think it's a whacky idea, tell me."

"I think it depends on how civilized we really are, Major. I think if we screw this up, we're in trouble. We need to maintain a show of strength. We need to be able to show an Earth ready to rise to the stars and function out here. We need to be just as smart as the Overones. We can't count them out yet. Hell, I don't know! I'm just a soldier."

Those cool blue eyes bored into his. "None of us are 'just soldiers' anymore, Leftenant. We're all strategists and specialists, every last one. They didn't choose you for special commando assignments for your sense of humor, God knows. I've already adopted the observations you mentioned and a few more to boot. I need all the help I can get. You are close to Spotted; keep his friendship at all costs. Katya is a very bright intelligence analyst, clue her in. At the same time, you don't discuss Spotted anywhere but here. That, Leftenant, is an order. We can't have him going off half-cocked, now can we?"

Murphy grinned. "Nope, guess not." He ran his tongue over his teeth. "Another thing is that Spotted is changing. He's not Wide's subordinate anymore. Have you noticed? I think they get submissive when an Overone's around. Hell, maybe they pattern their behavior. Maybe that's all an Overone is. Spotted is more sure of himself. He thinks and makes decisions. Remember when he followed everyone around all the time, piping and hooting, parroting anything anyone said? Well, he's becoming confident now, he's secure with us and with who he is."

"Becoming dominant. Good, I'm glad you confirm my suspicions on that account." She nodded to herself. "Anything else?"

He shook his head slowly. "No, I think that's about it. I'll tag along and keep an eye on him."

"And I shall rush the training for our people. We may

have to push a bit. No sense being caught with our bloomers about our ankles, is there?"

"No, ma'am." Murphy stood and saluted nervously.

"Oh, Leftenant?"

Murphy turned.

"How is the situation with Gubanya coming along? I notice there have been no incidents. I didn't want the two of you in this ship, but it was the only way."

Murphy ground his teeth. Level with her? Why not? "Major, we don't like each other. It's not the politics problem. That's a long way behind us. This is personal, one of those deep, grating sorts of things. In a regular outfit, one of us would transfer and the trouble would be over. Here we face each other every day, and it burns. We can work together. We don't like it; but we do our jobs."

"And in the long term, Leftenant?"

Murphy took a deep breath, standing at ease. "If we go our separate ways when we get to Earth, nothing will come of it. If we're stuck together forever, that's something else. A lot of things can still happen. He can be killed. I can be killed. One of us might end up on one side of the galaxy and the other in Andromeda, or someplace I never heard of. We might die of old age a million light-years apart. On the other hand, it's possible that when this is over, we'll meet and one of us won't walk away."

"Are you willing to forget it?"

"Yes, ma'am. It's Gubanya who's keeping it going. You have to understand that he survived Afghanistan day in and day out. In combat, especially that kind of combat, a man changes. Things that are important deep down in the soul get changed. I get the feeling Gubanya was a little weird to start with. The war just made him weirder—altered the way he expects the world and the people in it to work. Phil Cruz would say his mind has only one dimension."

"And that is?"

"To destroy the enemy. I think that fundamental truth motivates everything the man does. It's become his religion."

She nodded, glancing away toward the stars. "Please see that it doesn't interfere with your duties."

"Yes, ma'am," Murphy said, his voice soft. He left her staring out at the stars, an incredibly sad look on her pale face.

CHAPTER XXXII

Viktor cried out and sat up, blinking at the room as the lights came up. His owl-eyed image stared back from the reflective wall. His room. Aboard *Phantom*.

"You're all right, Viktor. This is the backside of space. Baraki doesn't exist."

Only it hadn't been Baraki. The dream had started there, like it always did, with the smell of gasoline and damp soil, of water and Afghan bodies. The flare in his hand had become a serpent when he twisted the cap. It had writhed away from his grasp, snaking its way into the Baraki aquifer to devour the souls of those hiding in the irrigation system.

The screams shredded his soul, clawing and tearing at the essence of him. Numb, he put his hands to his ears, as if he could stop it—knowing all the while the hideousness remained locked inside.

The beautiful young woman had risen from the flame-choked hole, reaching for him as her sensual body undulated with desire.

And when he'd turned to flee, Tula had spread before him, a city of fire and burning people. In the darkness, his father's commanding voice shouted, "You did this!"

Stumbling, he'd fallen to his knees, crying out. A soft sound behind him caused him to jerk around, staring in horror as the young woman reached for him with fingers of flame, her movements casting a sexual pall over him, stirring his desire, as always.

Whimpering, he tried to crawl away as she stood over him, the last of her garments burning away, flames caressing her skin like a lover's fingers. Fire burst from her pubic hair as she stepped over his prostrate body.

Viktor shrieked as she reached for his penis. Panicked, he stared into her face, watching her eyes change from burning black to piercing blue, fire sweeping the black locks into blonde.

"Sheila?"

His erection fled, the horror wrenching him from the dream's hold into wakefulness in his silent room.

His mouth tasted like goat bedding. A dull ache pounded behind his eyes. *Sheila? No, not Sheila. Not her. I can live with the dream, but not if Sheila. . . .*

He cursed and leaped to his feet, walking to the shower to follow the ritual of the dream. Then he dressed, padding out to walk the halls, ending, unconsciously at Sheila's door.

For a long moment, he stared dully, then placed a palm to the hand outline. "Sheila? It's Viktor. Are you up?"

He called softly, hoping she slept soundly, afraid she did.

"Viktor?" The voice sounded muzzy. "Is everything all right?"

"Fine. I was just up. Go back to sleep, I'll see you in morning."

"No. Wait."

He stood, shifting uncertainly. The door opened and Sheila beckoned him in, blinking sleep from her eyes. "My God, you look horrible."

He smiled weakly, stepping in, seeing the clutter on her table, the rumpled bedding where he'd held her that night, his body tortured. "Couldn't sleep."

She tilted her head, coming to inspect him critically. "Afghanistan?"

"No. We're . . . just not out of the woods yet."

The wry smile she gave him, the knowing look in her tired eyes, chastised. "Viktor, you really don't lie well at all, did you know? Come on in."

He walked past her, embarrassment burning bright. She waved him to a seat. "Sit. I'll fetch up two scotches."

"I shouldn't have come." He dropped into the chair, desperate to flee, craving to stay. The haunting images of the dream hung there in the back of his mind, tangible, waiting, bearing Sheila's features.

She settled across from him, placing the glass before him. “You know, you’re going to have to talk about it one of these days.”

“It?”

“Them, I suppose. Someone who suspects says it’s ghosts.”

“Ghosts.” Uttering the word sent a shiver down his spine. *Someone who suspects? Who?* He locked a blank stare on the glass of scotch, a single temporary point of shelter in a shifting infinity.

“If you could let it all out, give words to the—”

“How are you doing? What’s it like not to have to plan every moment? Are you feeling more rested? More worried?” He didn’t look at her, afraid of what he’d see in her eyes.

“For once, I can’t plan ahead.” Her voice held no censure. “With Wide’s scheme, I had data to deal with. Oh, sure, I was scared to death the whole time, afraid I’d made a mistake, misjudged the situation. But now? I don’t know, Viktor. I don’t know what to expect, how to plan ahead for something I have no experience with.”

He sneaked a quick glance, noting how her hair clumped as she ran worried fingers through it. Her expression appeared drained.

“One day at a time.”

Her exhale lengthened. “Perhaps. I feel like I’m walking down a dark alley with a blindfold on. As long as I touch the walls, I can find my way. Meanwhile, all around is danger. Thieves and hoodlums are lurking everywhere—and I can’t see them. Are they up above? Behind the trash can? I can’t turn back. I can’t do anything but stumble along and be afraid of what will finally happen.”

It was in a place called Baraki. . . . He bit his tongue, stifling the words that choked his throat. Why couldn’t he tell her? A blind alley? Yes, that was it.

“Is there anything I can do?”

The wry smile returned. “Can you see the future?”

He shook his head. “No. But if I could”

“You might keep an eye on Gubanya. Murphy says he still hasn’t let go of whatever’s bothering him.”

Viktor sighed. *No, Mika won’t let go. Is that why I*

keep him around? Because he was there? Because he's become a model? A source of strength? That night, Mika machine-gunned all those women and children. Why doesn't he ever wake in the night screaming? He rubbed his eyes with nervous fingers. *Is that it, Viktor? Do you depend on Gubanya's strength to maintain your own?*

"I'll talk to Mika," he agreed. *The women hide there to avoid being raped. . . .* "Pasha, did you. . . ."

"What? Did you say something? Who's Pasha?"

"My . . . brother." Viktor stood, tossing off the scotch as his heart raced, his pulse like fire pumping in constricted veins. "I've kept you too long already. Thank you, Sheila. I'll see Mika first thing and make sure he understands his duty." *Duty . . . duty. . . . Damn you, Pasha, you never could keep your hands off the women.*

"Viktor?"

He turned, halfway to the door.

"When the time is right. . . ."

He almost ran.

* * *

"It's like an unbreakable balloon," Spotted explained as he rolled along the bridge platform, one eye on Murphy and Barbara Dix, the other on the readouts.

"Why unbreakable?" Barbara asked.

"Because what we're doing is taking a section of time-space, the dimension of the universe we normally live in, and bending it around, squeezing it, and forcing it behind us from the inside out."

"Not a balloon," Murphy corrected. "You mean like a foam rubber mattress. That's time-space. What we do is create a singularity, like compressing a big gob of foam rubber and driving a pin through it. Then you anchor the pinpoint, and release the compression. Bingo! You're on the other side."

Spotted whistled and chirped. "Essentially accurate, only we use the singularity to penetrate into a different dimension, then compress the foam rubber."

Dix shook her head. "It's still hard to think about time and space being plastic, something you can deform and fall through."

"One hundred of your years ago, humans wondered if they could physically survive speeds of over thirty-five miles an hour." Spotted thinned. "Now your understanding of reality will grow by quantum leaps that not even your greatest physicists can appreciate."

"Great, they won't be able to appreciate it." Dix stood, pressing hands to the small of her back. "Meanwhile, I've been on duty for ten hours straight. I'm going to go feed myself and get some sleep."

"See ya, Barb. Katya's due in another four hours. Spotted and I will keep this thing from going up in a ball of fire." Murphy waved, waited until Barb got to the hatch, and raised his voice. "Okay, Spotted, old buddy, let's see if this thing can get scratch and wheelie! There's a drag strip in Pennsylvania that's ready for us!"

Barbara winced and shook her head.

Murphy watched her go.

"Get scratch? Wheelie? Drag Strip?"

Murphy chuckled and settled himself in the human pilot's seat. "That was a joke, Spotted. Humor."

"I don't understand jokes, Murphy."

"Yeah, I've noticed."

Murphy turned his attention to the holographic gauges that monitored the field charge around the null singularity. The idea of that power left him unnerved—an artificial density beyond his comprehension, it drew them forever through the underside of space. The readouts seemed stable.

"Murphy?"

"Huh?"

"How does it feel to know you're going to die?"

Murphy blinked at the non sequitur. "How does it feel to know. . . . What in hell are you talking about?" He shot a quick look at Spotted who watched with burning black eyes, rotund body slightly flattened.

"About death. The cessation of those biological functions which enable you to metabolize, cognate, oxygenate, and eliminate wastes. You will die in the next fifty human years or so. How does it feel to know that you'll die?"

Murphy leaned back, steepling his fingers. "Happens to everybody sometime, so I don't worry about it."

"It won't happen to me."

"Care to bet?"

"Very few Ahimsa have died, and then only because they went insane and wanted to. But humans die. Hitler died. So did Stalin. You'll die just the same."

Murphy thrust out his jaw. "You know, I'll bet Ahimsa will die one of these days. Accidents happen, don't they? Asteroids hit ships? Planets?"

"We have monitors to detect things like that."

"What about the end of the universe, Spotted?"

"The Shithti say the universe will never end, that giant singularities will form and everything in this universe will undergo a phase change into something else."

"Uh . . . right. Phase change into something else. When we die, human bodies turn into worm food. Is that a phase change to something else? I bet you'll die."

"Speculation on that remains spurious. How do *you* feel knowing that you *will* die within a very short period of time? That was my question."

Murphy frowned at the monitors. "I don't know how to answer. I guess you just go on about your business. I came real close to dying a lot of different times. You figure it's going to happen and keep doing what you have to. I guess it's easier knowing that it will happen sometime anyway. The saying is that the one guarantee you get in life is the one that says you won't get out of it alive."

"So you simply accept that you're condemned?"

"Yeah, I suppose so. I can't change it, and I'm not sure I'd want to." Murphy shifted, attention fixed on the monitor. "I've known a lot of old people who were ready to die. Most of them had lost loved ones, seen their world vanishing in all the changes. I've had good friends just get tired of all the bullshit and check out. I guess most of the ones who wanted to die got tired and wanted the rest."

"And you, Murphy? Would you take immortality if you could get it?"

"You offering?"

"I don't have the means yet. That will take some

study, some indepth research. That will be a worthwhile project after I've civilized you."

"Sure, I'd take it, but you know, I doubt I'd make it past a couple hundred years."

"You would get tired and check out?"

Murphy laughed. "Naw. But think about it, Spotted. They called Wide crazy, right? Said he'd gone insane to dare breaking our interdiction. Maybe he wasn't so insane after all. Maybe he'd lost purpose. You know, the Ahimsa might want to be like the Shithti, but I think they're wrong to do it. You don't grow by following in someone else's tracks. You grow by making your own. You know, dreaming, and then going hell-bent for leather to make that dream real. If Ahimsa want to be little Shithti, I think that's a cop-out, stagnation."

Spotted rolled closer, thinning, as he piped curiosity. "And you'd be dead in a couple hundred years from following your dreams?"

"Yeah," Murphy kicked back, lacing fingers behind his head. "Look out there. A whole universe is waiting for me to poke my nose into it. That's what I think you Ahimsa did wrong. You got the immortality, and that's become more precious to you than life."

"It is life."

"Bullshit! It's existence! Life's different. Life is dreaming, learning new things, seeing new stuff. Hell, yes, I'd probably be dead by now if Wide hadn't hijacked my ass to the stars, but I can damn sure tell you that if I hadn't been SOD, I wouldn't be here now. Give me a choice of being shot dead jumping into the some South American jungle or spending my life selling insurance in Brookline, I'll take the night jump every time."

"Even if the odds are that you'll die?"

Murphy smiled. "Even then. There's always the chance I won't. That's not to say I'm going to go out and *try* to get myself killed, but when I go, I want to have seen, smelled, tasted, felt, and heard everything I can."

"Even if it means dying before your time?"

"Even then. You see, when I do die, I'll have lived in all the ways a person can live. I'll have done as many things as possible. If I get taken out along the way, or busted up, well, that's the risk you take. Life ain't perfect—especially for dreamers."

"It's the risk that bothers me."

"No guts, no glory, pal."

Spotted whistled his curiosity. "And you don't think that compared to the other Ahimsa, Wide was all that insane?"

Murphy lifted a shoulder. "Spotted, sometimes you have to put your ass on the line to find yourself. Seems to me, the Ahimsa need to find themselves real bad."

"I will consider what you've told me. It puts insanity into an entirely different light."

"Yeah, right," Murphy continued, oblivious to Spotted as he began to thin. "Uh, what's this load resistance wobble on the monitor? I thought you said we had the magnetic lines frozen in the accretion disk and that they'd be matching angular velocity across the horizons."

"I will show you one more time, human." Murphy couldn't hear Spotted's barely audible, "No guts, no glory. No guts . . . no glory. . . ."

* * *

Viktor Staka found Mika Gubanya in the weapons room, carefully cleaning one of the Ahimsa rifles. He leaned over the rail which surrounded the armory and cocked his head. "What's this, Mika? I can imagine a private cleaning his weapon under orders. But a lieutenant? I would have thought you'd detail that to a scum."

Mika looked up, raising one eyebrow. "Do you see many scum around, Viktor? Part of the unit's flown off to the stars. Others are building a base at TaHaAk. We must clean our own rifles here."

"Yes, I suppose. We've come a long way from Afghanistan." He shook his head. "Half of the SPETSNAZ is among the stars working for an American captain. Half of the American SOD group is taking orders from a Russian major. Where will we go next?"

Mika shrugged, his laugh ironic. "Who knows, Comrade Major. Fate has done funny things to us, eh?" He settled the rifle on his lap and stared absently out at nothingness. His arms rested limply on the gun, the big biceps loose under his light skin.

Gubanya's voice softened, questioning. "What are we doing, Viktor? What's the real purpose behind all this? Where is our true direction? For me, anymore, it is lost."

Staka clasped his hands together and leaned forward. "I remember when our world was an incredibly complicated place. We asked, 'Did we do the right thing invading Afghanistan?' The Party changed positions, becoming lukewarm, leaving us wondering what we were to do? We sent guns to the Cubans, supporting the revolution and defense of the people while the Americans and the Arabs sent guns to the Afghans supporting the counter-revolution and the defense of the people."

"That was wrong?" Mika glanced up, eyes blank. "After what the state gave us, a little loyalty is not uncalled for, Viktor."

Staka shook his head. "I am not disloyal. I am simply thinking of how different we thought we were. Today I wonder who the people are. Capitalism was a hated enemy. Lenin, Stalin, Trotsky, none of them had met Shitht or Ahimsa. Now, Mika, the lines have changed again. Today, we no longer have the luxury of right and wrong. The question, my old friend, is will we survive—any of us?"

Gubanya lifted a shoulder. "I cannot believe the Party was wrong all those years."

"Because of your father, Mika?" Viktor asked gently.

"He was a traitor to the People!" Gubanya exploded vehemently, fist knotting and biceps rippling. "He betrayed the trust of all of us! His execution was only right. I myself would have pulled the trigger, Viktor."

Staka nodded. "It's not my business to ask, but did you ever hear from your mother after she was sent to internal exile?"

Mika's expression hardened. "No one writes letters from the Gulag, Comrade Major. Perhaps she has become a productive citizen of the State. Perhaps she has not. Perhaps she's dead—which is the same thing, is it not?"

Viktor took a deep breath and sighed. "I am sorry,

my friend. I shouldn't have mentioned it. I simply thought, perhaps, after all we have seen—"

Gubanya's response remained polite, not quite insolent. "Do not concern yourself over my personal life, Comrade Major. Your responsibility is the successful military performance of this unit and the protection of the State and the ideals of the Party. You do your duty, Viktor. I'll do mine."

Viktor smiled weakly. "Yes, Mika, I quite agree. Again, I apologize for stirring old memories. Excuse me." He straightened and walked slowly away, his mind a turmoil of what had been and what would be.

* * *

Svetlana looked up, meeting Sam's eyes as she bent over the comm. "There is no word from Moshe. Nothing. We can't raise any of Assaf out there."

Sam's eyes narrowed, jaws clenched tightly. "And *Phantom*? Can you get them?"

She manipulated some of the odd controls which had been partially adapted to human fingers. "Hello, *Phantom*, this is TaHaAk."

She nodded, relieved. "Right, *Phantom*, we hear you clearly. We called to report that Assaf has disappeared. We have no other information except that they are no longer answering transduction net calls. Of all the units dispersed, none answer. We assume this is the result of Ahimsa influence. We cannot comment at this time as to the safety of the vessels in question."

She listened for several minutes. "Roger, affirmative. In the event we lose contact with you, we will assume that we are on our own. We have had no evidence of Ahimsa communication or interference on this end either." A pause. "Roger. All our best to you. Good luck and God speed, *Phantom*." She frowned, shut the system down, and leaned back, gaze focused someplace beyond infinity.

"They tried contacting Moshe, too. Nothing, Sam. It's as if Assaf dropped out of space."

"What was the last thing we heard?" Sam racked his brains for any explanation that didn't include the obvious.

"Moshe was speaking," she said, "His exact words

were, 'Assaf, this just came to me. We are entering PLO territory. Remember, people, this is Lebanon. Obey the first and second law, and God keep you.' That was almost a month ago our time. Possibly a day at his relative speed?"

Sam closed his eyes, breathing deeply. "Nothing else? No SOS? Nothing?"

She shook her head. "There isn't any reason to think they were hit. Someone would have gotten something off. A warning, a Mayday, something."

Sam dropped wearily beside her, head in a whirling maze. "How many things have we pulled out of the Pashti comm? We're learning about gravity fluxing, plasma shifting, ergocentric gravisomatics, N-timeframe shifts, null singularity generation, and the list goes on. We can begin to grasp what they do, but to take it further and understand the concept, let alone how it works and how to manipulate it?" He muttered under his breath. "Using your imagination, how many ways could the Ahimsa track Assaf down and blip them a few light-millennia away—or even out of normal space?"

She put her arm around his shoulders and shook her head futilely. "I don't know. I used to think I was a pretty bright lady. The more we discover, the more I'm amazed we countered Wide. I can't help but think he didn't have his full mind on the problem." She leaned her head against his shoulder. "Face it, Sam. We simply got lucky. Sheila's strategy was perfect and Wide made his only real mistake by underestimating our capacity for double-dealing."

"Yeah," he breathed. "Well, baby, you got the stars if nothing else. Lord knows what we'll do with Mason and Malenkov's trick lasers and particle guns if the Ahimsa just take the easy route and slip a couple cubic meters of compacted plasma through a bent space continuum. In fact, I don't see why they ain't done it yet."

"They would have to kill the Pashti, too," she reminded.

"Yeah, RashTak makes a great hostage, doesn't he?" Sam chuckled softly. "But why are the Ahimsa keeping him alive when he's openly sided with us?"

She snuggled up next to him, eyes on the monitor.

"Unless it's that Chee'ee'la is here. Anything which did major damage to this station might offend the Shitht while he's inside—assuming, of course, that they have declared the Pashti to be expendable. And if they killed Assaf they've done exactly that."

Sam nodded wearily. "And there's no place to run. Space is getting real small real quick. Damn! We oughta be able to do something. What if Sheila is taking *Phantom* right into the middle of a trap? What if whatever got Assaf is about to get her, too?"

Svetlana's fingers laced with his. "Sam, all we can do is hang on here, hope that if Chee'ee'la solves the chess problem, RashTak or the rest of us can think up another one to tie him up. Other than that, we could load up on a ship and run for somewhere—but where?"

He nodded, feeling a thousand years old. "We only have you and three women. I've got twenty men here. Think we'd make a great colony? I ain't sure I'd want to share you."

"Hardly enough to restart the human race, is it?" she added soberly, burying her head against his shoulder.

"Yeah, well I'm not ready to play Adam and Eve yet. Meanwhile, we hang on and see what's happening. Not only that, I hated Cambodia. We made the promises that we'd back 'em up. Then, when the sky started to fall, we pulled out. Split. I can't just up and leave RashTak to take the shit. That would be Detroit all over again, and I'll die before I do that to anybody."

* * *

"You look almost as bad as you did at TaHaAk," Viktor remarked as they concluded the briefing. People shuffled out talking noisily—all, that is, but Mika Gubanya. He'd been preoccupied for days, his gaze resting on either Viktor, Murphy, or Katya. With everything else, she had to trust Viktor to keep his people in line.

She granted him a weak smile. "I suppose. I've been trying to come to some conclusions as to how to approach Earth."

"Buy you a drink?"

She let her eyes caress his perfect face and nodded.

"That would be jolly well accepted. I need to talk to someone besides a comm headset. Every time I run a simulation, I get deeper and deeper into the alternatives until I lose the original problem."

He led the way into the corridor. "Still in the dark alley?"

She walked slowly down the corridor, hands behind her back. "Yes, and it's making me crazy. I don't know what to try, what to expect. When it was only Wide, I could plot against an egotistical alien who didn't understand what he was playing with. Now Assaf is missing in action, Svetlana is constantly sending new scenarios the Ahimsa could use against us. Are we flying right into a bloody Overone trap? Did they track Moshe's people down and ray them or whatever they do? What is Spotted going to do when we get to Earth? What is Earth going to do? What are we going to do to break the news? I can't plan with so many unknowns!"

He nodded. "Is there any way I can help? You can always bounce ideas off me."

She laughed brittlely. "Do you know how to think a star into exploding? If we had that little trick up our collective sleeves, we'd be a sight more powerful, don't you think? That's the sort of operation we have to plan for. How do you anticipate some bloke popping your spaceship out of this time continuum? Did they teach you *that* at SPETSNAZ academy—or only how to parachute into London some foggy night and disturb honest Capitalists in their sleep?"

"Careful, some of my best friends are Capitalists."

She walked into her quarters and sighed. Viktor stepped to the dispenser. She'd had a davenport placed against one wall and now she dropped heavily onto it. "Just coffee, Viktor."

He handed her a rounded globe of cognac.

"Coffee? Hardly!" she said critically.

Nonplussed, he settled in next to her. "I told you I was buying. Consider it doctor's orders. It will do you good, loosen up your tense nerves, and possibly unwind your mind to the point where you can think reasonably again."

She gave in with a light laugh and sipped, leaning her head back and breathing deeply. "The training seems to be coming along quite nicely. Our people looked perfectly ghastly! I'm jolly glad someone else is missing their beauty sleep, too."

"You're beautiful enough. Any more and you would be doing the other women a disservice by taking away all the male attention."

"You're a jewel, Viktor." She looked at him, noting the hesitation in his eyes. "You're not the same man who came on board fresh from Afghanistan, you know. You've mellowed."

He lifted a shoulder. "Nor are you the same woman. We're all different now. The hard lines have softened . . . a little."

"You've been worried about something, Viktor. More than usual." She sipped at more of the cognac.

"Oh, it's nothing. Mika is simply being the person he always has been. I wonder. How different are we from what we'll find on Earth? Who are we now? How are they going to react when we show up in the sky and say, 'Greetings from the stars, forget the Party, forget the Red Threat. We're all one! Load your rifles and come aboard. To space! To space!' Mika is still living in that world. He thinks it's his sacred duty. It scares me."

She patted his hand and left her fingers on his. She hardly felt him increase his hold. It felt so natural, his fingers soft and warm on her palms.

"Blessed be, must we damned well fight ourselves as well as the bloody Ahimsa? If the Earth is too hostile, will Spotted. . . . Oh, dear, silly me. I'm tired, Viktor. Let's talk about something perfectly trite." She smiled and pulled her hair out of the way. God, he was still so handsome.

"I. . . ."

"Yes, Viktor?"

He looked away, lowering his eyes. "I haven't been sleeping well either. I almost came to your door last night."

"The ghosts?"

He sucked in his cheeks, eyes focused far away. "War

does that. War and command and the constant training to kill other men. Our system built the fear and the power into men like me. Sam is the same way. All of us were tough people, hard people who had seen death and felt warm blood run over our flesh as we knifed or shot or bombed. Life changes under those conditions."

"Yes," she agreed somberly, her mind on the fifty thousand things that could go so horribly wrong. "It does. Am I even human anymore, Viktor?"

"Yes, perhaps the most human of all of us. Do you still fear I would attempt to dominate you?"

"What if I beat you at a game of chess?"

"I'd expect it. Surprise would come the other way around."

"Want to tell me about the ghosts?"

He closed his eyes. "I'm afraid of what you'll think. Of what you'll learn."

She searched her mind, remembering other times, seeing the violent young predator he had once been. She remembered the respect she had seen grow in his eyes after TaHaAk. She remembered the way he had looked at her so long ago. Now, there was only concern and caring in those blue eyes.

"No, Viktor, you don't scare me anymore. Too much has changed for both of us. I think we have each proved ourselves, don't you?" She lifted his hand, looking at it, wondering about how much human blood really had run over it—not caring.

"You know I love you." His eyes were serious, vulnerable, and frightened.

"And I have loved you for a long time, Viktor." She smiled and kissed his hand.

He jumped to his feet, pacing violently, as if stamping on the haunting things around him. "I . . . I had a younger brother. His name was Pasha. They found his body outside of a place called Baraki. . . ." The muscles of his face twitched and quivered. "Baraki." He closed his eyes for a moment before looking at her pleadingly.

"Tell me, Viktor. I want to hear."

He nodded, taking a deep breath. "The ghosts? Yes, the ghosts. We . . . we surrounded the village in the middle of the night, closing the perimeter with BMPs and helicopters. I was enraged." He went on telling it all, each detail.

She listened, watching him bare his soul.

". . . And the worst part of the dreams is when she comes out of the flaming hole." He swallowed hard. "The last couple of weeks, when she reaches for me, it's your face."

"Guilt, Viktor. You killed her. Now you're afraid you're killing me, driving me away."

He stared at her, expression like carved granite. "Baraki wasn't the only place we did that."

"It doesn't matter."

"After that . . . when I think of a woman. . . ." He sat down next to her, dropping his head in his hands.

"Nothing happens?"

He shook his head, expression miserable. "I may be impotent for the rest of my life. I thought perhaps you should know."

She pulled him close and kissed him, feeling his lips warm, but hesitant. "I don't care."

She held him late into the night, feeling his deep breathing, as she stroked his head. The weight of his leg lay across her thighs as she stared at the darkened light panel overhead.

He jerked suddenly, crying out and coming awake.

"Shhh! It's all right. You're here, with Sheila."

He swallowed hard and exhaled. "I'm sorry. Perhaps I should go now."

"I'd rather you stayed."

"Even after what happened earlier?"

"Sleep, Viktor. There's always tomorrow, and tomorrow night, and the day after."

CHAPTER XXXIII

"Drop the magneto-gravitational fields slowly!" Spotted erupted, piping shrilly. "Don't you realize! That is the power of twenty of your suns you deal with! Imbecile!"

Barbara Dix bit her lip, face coloring as her teeth ground together, audible to all. She changed the setting under her control and carefully backed the dial out, the gauge indicating a gradual diminution of power, this time with no fluctuation.

Spotted rocked back and forth, manipulators monitoring all of the systems as the humans made the first transition from null singularity to space-time.

Murphy kept his thoughts to himself, eyes glued to his sensors, their readouts measuring the incredible fields that kept a two hundred and fifty thousand degree Kelvin temperature antimatter/matter reaction confined in a mystical magical electromagnetic bottle of Ahimsa design and sense.

To one side, Katya absently muttered under her breath at the autocratic tone that had crept so slowly into Spotted's voice over the months. Now, Earth waited out there, just beyond the scanners—behind a gravitational fence they had to open a gate through.

"Murphy, shed some of the temperature. We will be needing only a fraction to decelerate," Spotted ordered. Murphy's tongue crept out of his mouth as he began manipulating the fields to vent the heat outside space before they dropped back in.

"That is sufficient," Spotted added. "Thermal deceleration requirements increase by cubes of energy as you move out from the galactic core. There isn't as much radiation out here. Not as much gas or particles, 'solar wind' as you call it. We could shoot reaction straight into the sun to slow at the same time we employ radiation, magnetic, and gravity flux for braking purposes—"

Katya answered tartly, "But that would disrupt the entire system with the most incredible aurora ever seen and sterilize everything on Earth. We understand, Spotted."

"But do you understand that reaction can also be focused to move planets?" Spotted thinned. "No, you didn't see it, did you? Listen, humans. I will teach you much. You are like your young, without knowledge. You are, as you say, immature."

Katya closed her eyes for a split second, lips moving softly as she mouthed, "Give me strength."

Murphy completed his venting and studied his headset. He'd dropped to within five hundred degrees of the thermal retention necessary to decelerate. Not bad! That allowed a small but significant margin of error.

Sheila Dunbar's face formed on the monitor. "Spotted, have you scanned the system? Is there anything to indicate Ahimsa activity?"

Spotted twirled on his foot tread. "I have not. You may. Employ the subroutine you have become so proficient at using to contact TaHaAk. If you ask it to, that function will allow scanning at the same time it allows communication. Any Ahimsa energy source will be pinpointed. It is a redundancy built into our systems. To Ahimsa, it would be unthinkable not be able to locate another Ahimsa. Such an error could perceptibly subvert the process of a rescue mission or cause the actual loss of life in an extreme condition."

Sheila nodded, lips pursed, and her image faded out.

"Damn it, Spotted, why didn't you tell us?" Murphy demanded. "Maybe we could have masked our progress! Snuck in somehow! We're like sitting ducks out here!"

Spotted shot one eyestalk at him. "Murphy, there is nothing we could have done about the buoys. No matter if we had entered your system dead—it would have taken two hundred and fifty of your years that way, incidentally—the buoys would have registered the passage."

Murphy grunted and bit his lip.

Sheila's face reformed. "From what I can tell, there are no Ahimsa ships anywhere in the immediate vicinity. The only power readings I pick up correspond to the Van Oort gravity beacons."

Spotted twirled on his foot tread and rocked back and forth. "Very good. This is the most critical aspect of the entire journey. Katya, feed in the program for anti-interdiction. Murphy, Barbara, watch your screens. There should be no way the buoys can generate tides sufficiently strong enough to drain our null singularity effect."

Murphy swallowed dryly. He'd learned too much about gravity in the past months. He shivered as he watched the monitors begin to pick up fluctuations.

* * *

"Very good! *We have them!*" Tan's spicules broadcast a low note of satisfaction. His monitor showed the distortion of the interdiction zone. From the flux patterns, their comm generated images of *Phantom* sliding through the fields.

"They have an incredible amount of power available. We are lucky they did not destroy the buoys on the way in." Low piped with relief.

"Spotted is only a Nav-Pilot and has not perceived the nature of the threat," Tan reminded. "Nor are the humans that intelligent."

"But they could sustain the combined tides of all six interdiction buoys," Sees added. "We can kill the planets—but not the ship so long as it has null singularity."

Tan rocked slowly back and forth, his low-toned spicules humming softly. "They could but will they have their power up and ready? No, I think not. They will be wary for the moment, of course, but let them arrive at their planet. Close to their planet, can they employ null singularity to protect themselves?" He piped glee. "We will wait until monitors show their null singularity is completely shut down. At that moment, we shall contact this Sheila Dunbar. We shall allow her to watch the destruction of her world before we tear her and her ship into plasma."

* * *

Earth! The wondrous sphere of life! The planet, jewel among the stars, which had nurtured their lives. It hung below them, gleaming bright and glorious unlike the dull cloudy sphere of SkaTaAk they had seen suffering under perihelion.

Sheila watched as *Phantom* settled into geosynchronous orbit over the North Pole. She took a deep breath and looked to where Katya watched in the holo. "Very well, check the system. Are the holo generators Wide left still functional?"

Katya frowned, eyes half closed, as she focused her concentration on her headset and began sending signals to the system Wide had scattered to monitor Earth.

"We've got almost the entire net, Major. Only one, located in the Kremlin, appears to have been deactivated."

Sheila studied the terminator. It would be night in Moscow, mid-morning in America. She opted for President Atwood. The image of the Oval Office formed. The room was empty. "Now what?"

Spotted formed manipulators and touched his monitors. "We found that if you simply formed your holo, their security systems will pick it up."

She did. Within thirty seconds, security personnel poured into the room, pistols drawn. They spread out, surrounding her.

"Don't move. You are under arrest!" an eagle-eyed man ordered, pistol leveled.

Sheila smiled a greeting. "Please, fetch President Atwood. Tell him Major Sheila Dunbar has returned from the Ahimsa mission and would like to talk to him."

The man's expression hardened, his cheeks quivering. "You are in a secure area, ma'am. Don't make any rapid moves."

Two men approached from the sides, weapons ready, handcuffs out. The eagle-eyed one talked into his radio. Sheila couldn't help but laugh as they tried to grapple with her laser light image, grasping hands reaching through emptiness. Their faces reflected horror as they gaped at her apparition.

"It won't help to handcuff a holograph. Please, call

President Atwood. Tell him Sheila Dunbar would like to talk to him."

They were nervous now, shifting uneasily, worried, even a bit frightened.

"President Atwood?" The security chief asked, eyes wary. "What about President Atwood?"

Sheila crossed her arms. "Look, simply process the call, Mr . . . uh, what do I call you?"

"Major Robert Haxton."

"Very well, Major Haxton, call the President and inform him Major Sheila Dunbar has returned from the Ahimsa mission. We have quite a lot to fill him and General Secretary Golovanov in on. Oh, and by the way, what year is this?"

"Year?" Haxton swallowed. "Ma'am, Burt Cook is President. Atwood wasn't even capable of winning his party's nomination in the last election. *Who are you?*"

"Lost reelection?" Sheila asked suddenly, feeling an odd premonition. "What about the transmissions Wide sent? The letters we all wrote? What about. . . ."

The man's wary glance didn't hesitate. "Now, do you want to tell me what's going on here? Where are you?"

"Sheila!" Viktor's face formed on the bridge monitor. "There's a heavy band of radiation over most of Eastern Europe. Trying to refine the image, I've pinpointed radioactive hot spots not only in Europe, but Alaska, northern China, and Pakistan."

Murphy's face filled another of the monitors. "Major, they're testing ICBMs down there. I just followed a rocket from Vandenburgh. The thing went wild halfway over the Pacific. If I was a guessing man, I'd say it was headed for Kwajalein."

"Major!" Katya's frantic voice chimed in. "I am picking up Red Army military communication! They are talking about an assault on Liege, Belgium, to begin at dawn."

Other monitors began filling with data as Sheila turned to the holo, seeing the horrified eyes of the men watching her image in the Oval Office so far below. Mouths hung open—no doubt at the wealth of voices popping in the air about them. Possibly too at the strategic information bandied about so casually.

Sheila exploded, "*What in bloody hell is going on down there, Haxton?* Have you turned into a bunch of bloody raving lunatics? You're fighting a damn war! The missiles were disarmed when we left! Has the whole world gone mad?"

Haxton swallowed. "Who *are* you? Where are you?"

"Where's Colonel Bill Fermen?" she demanded hotly, feeling angry passion rising. "Bloody idiotic *imbeciles!*" A fragmented thought watched the total of her plans and aspirations teetering, cracking.

Haxton's face went tight, his lips thinned. "He's dead. Died in the one of the first bombings of Washington.'

Sheila braced herself, strength draining. *Washington? Bombed? And how many other places? How many dead?* "Viktor, have your holo imaged into the Kremlin—if it's still there. Talk to General Secretary Golovanov, find out what—"

"Golovanov's dead." Haxton added, words acid. "Heart attack took him years ago."

"And the KGB Head, Kutsov?" she asked, raising an eyebrow.

Haxton snapped, "We don't know. Disappeared just before their advance across Eastern Europe. Sources said he was shot. We didn't get anything else, and frankly, didn't give a damn."

Murphy's voice came through the system. "Weird shit, man! We go away and they all go fuckin' berserk down there!"

Haxton swallowed again, looking around nervously as his men shifted around Sheila's holo.

"Viktor?" she asked. "Are you in the Kremlin?"

"*Da!* I am talking to head of security. They are trying to take my image prisoner."

"As soon as you get through their thick Russian skulls and get the General Secretary we can bring this silly infantile war to an end." She sighed and turned back to Haxton. "Get your President. Now! Your quaint little war is jolly well over."

He took a step forward. "Look! You've got a lot of interesting tricks—but we'll find you!" He began to shout, fist shaking angrily.

Sheila crossed her arms, anger fueling the frosty smile she gave him. "Very well, Haxton, I'm not hard to find. I'm straight above the North Pole—roughly two hundred and eighty miles up. You can check if you like. We didn't come in masked. Your deep space radar, or any good telescope, for that matter, will pick us right out. *But do it on your own bloody time!* Get me your President."

* * *

"Damn you, Spotted! *Why didn't you tell us?*" Murphy thundered.

Sides shivering, Spotted held his ground. "Wide did that. What difference would it have made?"

"And all those letters?" Murphy asked.

"None were sent. Wide only did that to keep morale up."

"I ought to—"

"Leftenant." Sheila placed a restraining hand on Murphy's shoulder. Then she turned a stare capable of melting ice on the Ahimsa. "Why?"

"His plan was to break your arrogance. He wished to civilize you for his own ends. If your society was in ruins, he could help rebuild it by placing you in control. Through you, he could civilize—as results on your world certainly demonstrate the need for. You humans are—"

"And if they wiped themselves out?" Murphy interrupted. "Destroyed the whole environment? Left the place a waste?"

Spotted stared back, refusing to let his sides fall. "I don't know what the Overone planned then."

"I think you're lying!" Murphy slapped a hand to the deck, his face red and burning.

"I think I know," Sheila added. "He still had his captive breeding population. That's it, isn't it, Spotted? That was his plan."

Spotted whistled softly, refusing to budge.

"I wonder what else he's conveniently forgotten to tell us?" Viktor asked from the side, giving the Ahimsa a frigid stare.

"Murphy?" Sheila straightened. "Keep a close eye on him. If he touches anything you don't understand, tries to sell us out to the Overones, feel free to do as you wish with him."

"Yes, ma'am."

Murphy continued to glare as Dunbar and Staka walked out. "You heard. You want to come clean? All the way?"

Spotted piped angrily, and replied, "I *will* civilize all of you."

"Uh-huh. Over my dead body."

"I sincerely hope not, Murphy. I was becoming quite fond of you."

* * *

Mika Gubanya watched the bubbles rise from below. One by one they came. Each lifting through the permeable floor of the ship and bursting, the occupants staggering as they fought for balance. Wide-eyed, scared, they were led in groups to the auditorium.

With Viktor Staka, he greeted General Secretary Yevgeny Karpov and clicked his heels, leading the trembling Party Head to the auditorium, thinking of the honor of escorting the most powerful Party member to the greatest meeting ever. The proud remains of the SPETSNAZ saluted as Viktor led them in and indicated seats for the Soviet delegation. Feeling Karpov's eyes on him, Mika stood proudly, back stiff, assault rifle at present.

The Americans were led in by Lieutenant Murphy and Gubanya's jaws knotted. The American almost swaggered, a stupid grin on his face. And that was how they reacted to such important negotiations? Murphy disgraced all of his kind. To hell with Capitalism and what it bred! Order had returned.

Barbara Dix led the Europeans in, while China was brought by Pyotr Moskvin. One by one the chairs filled. By far and away, the majority of the Phantoms were Viktor's old SPETSNAZ. How fitting that Earth see the finest of the Soviet Red Army here at this of all meetings.

A hush fell over the room like a velvet blanket as Sheila Dunbar walked out onto the raised podium, Spotted rolling along on one side, Ee!Tak clicking along on the other.

The stunned silence continued as Sheila Dunbar introduced herself and the aliens. Mika swallowed dryly, the enormity of history weighing down upon him. A new reality faced the Party, and perhaps they'd have a place for him, perhaps a promotion to major, or colonel. He'd been to the stars, fought there. He could help carry the revolution out beyond the Earth.

"You have all experienced a change today which will leave your lives forever altered," Dunbar began. "The fact remains that the conflagration which we stopped yesterday was set off by our very departure and Ahimsa manipulations. Most of Europe is in ruins and ninety million people are dead as a result."

Someone coughed nervously.

"Well, that will never happen again on our planet," Sheila continued, leaning on the podium, looking around. "We can't afford it. At this very moment, the fate of this planet is at stake. On a space station in orbit around the Pashti star, SkaHa, the first human space colony currently exists. Out there," she waved randomly toward the stars, "the Ahimsa are even now planning a counterstrike, a starstrike of their own to eliminate us from the galaxy. You see, they believe we're insane. Incapable of civilized behavior. I'm loath to admit that what we stopped yesterday indicates they may not be wrong."

The hushed intake of breath sounded loudly in the room.

"Some of my command is missing in action. Composed of Israeli, Soviet, and American military and intelligence personnel, they may be the first humans to have died among the stars. Our plight is serious. At TaHaAk, American Captain Sam Daniels is frantically trying to keep the human presence in space and monitoring the Shitht, Chee'ee'la, who will ask us someday soon what reason we have for existence. If we can't solve that one, he will *think* our star into a supernova—a giant explosion.

"And what, you may ask, can we have to fear? The shiny mirrorlike globes which you found surrounding the detonators on your nuclear bombs were only minor stasis fields. You had to manufacture entirely new bombs from scratch. The subatomic interference in technical wiring which so frustrated your engineers was a simple trick which changed the nature of the atomic force. Null singularity generation, however, is neither simple, nor a trick. We know Ahimsa technology is capable of fluxing space, moving mass—like the insides of a sun—into any place in space—even Red Square or Times Square."

They moved nervously, looking around.

"Space, ladies and gentlemen, is ours. We will not go among the stars as conquerors or masters, only as a fragile, ignorant species, suffered to exist only by the grace of the Pashti, the Shithti, and possibly the Ahimsa—if we can win their trust."

Spotted rolled forward, piping loudly. "Further, as of this moment, you will become civilized! You can no longer behave as animals. You will call me Overone and I will be your teacher!"

Sheila smiled down at the thinning little alien and nodded. Ee!Tak began thrumming to himself in an untranslatable mutter.

Secretary Karpov stood. His troubled eyes locked on the aliens. "And how does this happen? How do we decide which governments obtain which benefits? Who will control who deals with these . . . aliens? Who will make sure that the needs of the world's people are met?"

A low chorus of voices rose in the dimly lit room. Mika shifted his feet as he began to think about the great Secretary's words.

The American President, Burt Cook, raised his voice. "However we do it, it'll take a committee to see that no one gets a raw deal out of this. Look, we just had an instance where the Soviets broke out and ran halfway across Europe! Now, there can't be any talk of—"

Sheila slapped a fist against the podium and glared out over the assembly. "We don't have time for committees, Mr. President. Mr. Secretary, we don't have time to worry about who gets what or who looks out for the benefits of the people. The Ahimsa might turn our planet into molten rubble at any moment." She paused, letting that sink in. "That, ladies and gentlemen, *is* reality."

As the Chinese delegate stood and took a breath,

Sheila continued with, "This ship will levy what it needs for the next journey to the stars. You might begin thinking about a trade delegation to the Pashti."

There was an instant ground swell of objection. Mika felt his mouth going dry. His heart began to thump in his chest. He could see the General Secretary's eyes studying Viktor Staka and him. It brought a sudden sureness. The strength of the Party must be maintained. If only his father. . . . No! Do not think it! The Party had no choice. The survival of the state was the duty of every citizen.

"I will have order." Dunbar raised her hands and silence returned.

"Is there no discipline among humans?" Spotted asked, his eyestalks looking up at Sheila Dunbar.

"Rarely, I'm afraid." She leaned over the podium, staring out at the hard faces staring back at her. "We didn't ask to go among the stars. We were drafted—shanghaied—by an Ahimsa named Wide. We left the Earth in peace. We return to find our planet in flames. In the words of my good friend, Moshe Gabi, *It will never happen again!*"

"And how will you do this? How will you make it this idyllic way?" General Secretary Karpov demanded, voice carrying a slightly insolent tone.

Mika studied him. This man had massed the troops and saved the Soviet Union from dissolution. He had seized the opportunity, aware that for the first time since the Second World War, no Western nuclear arsenal hung Damocles-like over the heart of the Motherland. This man had taken the World Revolution into the heart of Capitalism! Gubanya smiled his pride and experienced a warm rush of admiration for his people, for his government, for this General Secretary.

Sheila Dunbar worked her mouth, staring coldly at Karpov. "It was a long trip home from TaHaAk. I had plenty of time to think about that very problem. I had no idea I would find the bloody system in this much chaos, however. We have several options that I can see. One would be the formation of a multinational council which will take over administration of the Earth for—"

"The people of the Soviet Union refuse." Karpov stood

resolute, defiantly arrogant. "In a matter of months, the forces of Western aggression will be crushed. At that time, you will deal with us!"

Mika grinned despite himself.

"The hell she will!" Cook stood, glaring angrily at Karpov, face red with rage.

"The People's Republic of China will accept none of this. We are a sovereign nation and will not be bound by councils of outsiders. We will deal directly with these Ahimsa," Wan Dong Tao added his voice.

"So will the United States!" Cook bellowed, shaking a fist. "We've got more to offer the aliens than anyone! Why should we subject ourselves to you and *your* tyranny?"

A babble of shouted negations rose as Sheila's expression became strained. Mika could barely make out the slight shake of her head, as if she disbelieved what she heard. A pained look of desperation had grown in her eyes.

Viktor stepped up, giving Dunbar a worried look. Mika barely caught the words. "Considering conditions on the planet, Sheila, I think the time for diplomacy has gone. What we had to do through finesse and tact with the Pashti must be accomplished here with a hammer and anvil."

She gave him a bleak look before staring out over the bickering world leaders.

Viktor returned to his position as Sheila leaned slightly to one side, looking about the auditorium, raising her hands to gain attention. Her expression became grim, as if she were forced into something distasteful. "Is this the way you wish to go? Please, you have several options. We can work out something constructive. We can set up a world government which will function in whatever manner seems most appropriate. You can send for your best political brains to make contributions. I'm willing to work with you.

"If, on the other hand, you wish to continue the madness, I will be forced to take matters into my own hands. With so much at stake, ladies and gentlemen, I will have no choice but to place the Earth under martial law. I, and my staff, will see that no one misbehaves. We will sanction those who do by cutting off their electricity, by—"

"Ridiculous!" thundered the General Secretary. A loud roar rose from the seats as men and women stood. "The Soviet Union does not bow to threats!"

"Nor does the United States!" Cook followed with added bluster.

At a signal from Viktor Staka, assault rifles were leveled all around the room. The silence fell like a sheet, settling softly over the stricken expressions. Mika targeted the American President, the pad of his finger tracing the trigger with a lover's touch.

Sheila ran an anxious hand over her face, heartsick. She stared out at the room through haunted eyes. "Then, I have no choice. The planet and all humanity has become my responsibility. Very well. Wide conveniently shut down all the missiles. We have observed the American attempts to make new missiles. Those few bombs you manufactured in the interim are mostly expended upon yourselves. You have nothing in your arsenals this ship cannot handle. Our technology and our domination of space gives us the power to control our planet. I will make one last appeal. What can we do to work together to deal with this situation? Do we cooperate? Or do I declare martial law?"

Only one voice rose. Mika saw Yevgeny Karpov look Viktor Staka in the eye. "Comrade Major Staka! As General Secretary of the Soviet Union, I order you and your unit to immediately subdue this threat to the people and turn this vessel over to my authority."

Mika felt his heart jump. Here it would end. From this moment forward, the State, as Lenin intended, was the Party and the world. He felt a sigh of relief and almost missed Viktor's words.

"I am sorry, Mr. General Secretary. I cannot do that." Viktor's back had gone straight. "The stakes among the stars outweigh the cause of the Party. You will obey the orders of Major Sheila Dunbar. We can no longer allow ourselves to waste our—"

Mika's reaction came instinctively—built into muscle,

bone, and nerve by years of repetitious drill. His rifle buttstock easily crushed the back of Viktor's skull. He followed up with a a tri-burst to the head, making sure Staka was dead.

The moment froze in Mika's mind. The skull had snapped loudly under the impact of the bullets. Now the pale flesh mottled from the hydrostatic shock and bright blood ran in the golden blond hair. The eyes stared sightlessly where once upon a time they'd looked at him in friendship. The hands which had acted so many times in the past to save Mika's life twitched in last movements of violated nerves.

Viktor. It was duty. I'm sorry, my friend and Comrade. I had my duty.

Slowly he rose, eyes on the General Secretary's. "Comrade General Secretary! I, Mika Gubanya, Lieutenant of Long Range SPETSNAZ Unit—" He jerked, feeling the sting—the coolness lancing through his side. His reactions, catlike, still came too slowly. Turning to bring his rifle to bear, a strong arm, like an angular bar of steel, slid around his throat and choked off his air.

Mika kicked and thrashed as he felt the long blade efficiently loosening his insides, severing his organs as the sucking sound of his slashed diaphragm announced the certainty of his death. Still the iron arm that choked him refused to loosen. The knife moved tirelessly, a thing alive as it twisted and turned in his guts. Blood ran warmly down Gubanya's leg.

The room darkened slowly as Mika blinked his eyes. His father's voice came softly to his mind and he remembered the strong thick arms reaching down to pick him up. His mother smiled at him from the warm yellow glow of the kitchen light bulb, her broad face filled with love as his father spun him, giggling, in the air. Mika's tongue tried to work where the iron bar had forced it up so high in his mouth. He could see his father's loving eyes, fading now. . . . Fading. . . . Fading . . . into General Secretary Karpov's stunned gaze. And then haze and grayness wrapped around him. . . .

* * *

Murphy let Gubanya's body slip limply through his grasp, aware of the warmth of the blood staining his side. Quickly he looked around, seeing the shock. Moving, he bent over Viktor Staka's body. His trained eyes took it all in. Gubanya's bullets—if not the butt stroke—left no doubt.

"Don't anyone move!" Konstantine Nedelin's voice thundered in the silence of the room. "We are Phantom Battalion! We no longer owe allegiance to any government. We have seen beyond the stars."

Murphy eased Staka's exploded head to the floor and filled his lungs, feeling the futility of it. Then he looked up at Sheila Dunbar, who had stopped a hesitant step from the podium. Her face had gone flour-white, mouth partway open. Murphy could see her soul twisting itself in agony behind her glazing eyes.

Murphy stood, taking in the room, seeing the ashen faces of SPETSNAZ, CIA, and SOD. They were grim, biting their lips while they stared out over leveled assault rifles, braced to shoot.

"Yeah," Murphy's voice came hoarsely. "It's a new world, folks." Pulling himself straight, he looked into Sheila Dunbar's devastated eyes. "Major, he's dead. Skull's fractured, neck broken. Not even Ahimsa medical units can do anything for that kind of damage."

He could see the shock, paralyzing her usually swift mind. She stood there, horror and grief building, color continuing to drain from her face.

Oh, shit! She's gonna flake out on me! Murphy, in the best parade style he had, marched up, eyes locked on hers. He executed a letter perfect salute. "Lieutenant Murphy reporting, ma'am!" He heard his voice echoing in the chamber as he willed his strength into her. "How would you like the delegation from Earth disposed of, ma'am?" Under his breath he added a sibilant, "C'mon, Sheila, don't let us down now!"

Her eyes cleared and she nodded with a faint jerk of her head. "Quarter them in the personal section, Leftenant. Restricted access on my order only." Her voice sounded soft, wounded, and she couldn't hold his gaze.

"Phantom Battalion, Atten-*shun!*" Murphy snapped,

pulling himself up straight. He snapped out another salute as Sheila turned to leave the room, Ee!Tak following, chittering and thrumming to himself as he digested what he'd seen.

Murphy frowned, uneasy as he turned and strode to the podium. He put himself at ease, hands behind his back, legs spread. "Corporal Nedelin, you will assume the rank of Senior Lieutenant until promotion can be confirmed. With Corporals Oganski and Moskvin, you will attend to the visiting diplomats and arrange for their comfort in the barracks. They are restricted according to the Major's orders. If any disobedience is encountered, you are free to use whatever force you feel is necessary to maintain ship's security." Why did he feel so worried? *Damn it, what am I missing? Something important!* "Is that understood?"

"Yes, sir!" Nedelin snapped out a salute.

With military thoroughness, the room was cleared of diplomats.

"Somebody see to the bodies. Major Staka will lie in state," Murphy said. "As to Gubanya. . . . Treat him with care, too. The rest of you, let's get back to our stations. Oh, and try and lay off the major. I think she'll need some time to sort things out."

He saw their nods and felt a strange welling of pride. Not a goddamn man lost until they got home and the scumsucking politicians got to fucking with people's minds. They all knew what had to be done. He could see no anger at the deaths, felt none himself. They'd come an incredible distance in more ways than one. Their world lay exposed for what it was—good and bad. Right and wrong.

Why did he feel so disturbed? Something had been missing there at the end. He'd taken care of Sheila and. . . . He shook his head and looked around.

He wondered what Spotted would say. . . . Spotted was missing! "Oh, shit!" Murphy exploded. "Barbara! Katya! To the bridge! On the double! Move!" And he was running, leaving them far behind, pounding down the corridors, boots slapping the graphite steel underfoot.

* * *

Spotted had just formed another manipulator and was inserting it onto one of his consoles as Murphy charged through the hatch. Three of the thick stubby tendrils were already hooked to the system as Murphy slid to a stop, the door shutting behind him. Well, too bad.

One eyestalk turned toward the human. "I had hoped to have this done before you arrived. You are becoming most wise, Murphy. I congratulate you for your acumen."

"What are you doing, Spotted?" Murphy stopped as he noticed the null singularity monitors showing a rise of activity.

Spotted thinned slightly and piped to himself, one eyestalk on Murphy. Yes, the time had come. This is what Wide had experienced! Perhaps it was madness, but the euphoria of taking control spread through him, warm, rushing with excitement. Tainted, yes, the molecules *had* come from Wide. *I am insane!*

Murphy sucked a breath into his already heaving lungs and started forward.

"Stop!" Spotted piped. "If you come closer, Murphy, I will have to kill everyone on this ship."

Murphy pulled up, hands on his hips. "Why are you doing this, Spotted?" He could feel his leg cooling where moisture evaporated from Gubanya's blood. Already the dried blood was caking and cracking off around the edges.

Spotted piped and whistled softly. "Humans must be civilized if I am ever to benefit from all this, Murphy. I told them in the auditorium. I am now an Overone, a teacher. Humans will learn—including yourself."

"And if I refuse to learn what you're peddling?"

"Those who will not learn will be eliminated from the system, Murphy. There can be no other way. You see, humans have always reinforced their misbehaviors. From now on, right behavior will be rewarded. In no other way can I reach my due station in life. Incidentally, you *will* call me Overone from this time forward."

"Pretty cocky in your old age, aren't you, Spotted?"

"You will address me as Overone or I will evacuate the oxygen from the diplomats' quarters." Spotted moved his manipulators.

"Nope," Murphy said, stepping forward. "You won't do that, Spotted, little buddy."

"You will back up! When I open the bridge hatch, you will leave. And you will call me Overone. I know you are intelligent enough to learn *that* immediately. Go! You and your Phantom Battalion have taught me well, Murphy. Your people are now *my* hostages!"

Murphy nodded, feeling his heart pounding. "Don't you dare screw with anything, Spotted. Don't you hurt a single person! 'Cause you forgot one thing. I'm in here with you." And in one swift move, he had the blood-stained steel of his Wind River fighting knife poked against Spotted's fragile side. The little round alien piped frantically, sagging as he fought to keep his manipulators on the console.

"Don't do it!" Spotted whistled and squealed. "If you kill me, I'll engage the null singularity! This close to the planet, you know what effect it will have."

Murphy swallowed, mouth going dry. "We got a term for this on Earth, little buddy. It's called a Mexican standoff. So, you turn on the null singularity, you'll kill my world—and in the meantime, you'll die, Spotted! Man, I swear it! I'll rip you to pieces! There won't be enough for your med to save! *You hear me?*"

"So we are in a Mexican standoff!" Spotted whistled, sides sagging even more. "I won't lose! I won't! Won't! *Won't!* No guts, no glory, Murphy. I understand. Yes, you can kill me, but everyone will remember Spotted. I am an Overone!"

Bastard's gone as goddamned crazy as Gubanya! Murphy fought to swallow. Sweat traced trickling drips down the side of his face. *Shit! What to do now? Think! Damn you, Murphy? He's whacked out! Gone berserk!*

"Look, man, there ain't no winner if we kill each other. You've got how many years ahead of you? Aren't Ahimsa immortal? What good does it do you to die here?" He could hear himself pleading. "Let's work this out. We've got Earth taken care of. The major's in charge of it. There's no sense in you going and screwing it up."

"Humans cannot be trusted, Murphy. They are weird

shit, you know?" he piped in imitation. His sides were flatter and flatter. Knobs began to form on his hide as the anxiety spread. The piping voice grew fainter. "Wide was wrong when he first came here. It was a mistake to break the interdiction. Either humans come to space on my terms—or they die here." Spotted slowly sagged even more. "We all die here. . . . die. . . . segment into single cells, lyse . . . lyse . . . lyse. . . ."

"Hey! Spotted, damn you!" Murphy watched the manipulators loosening and stretching. He pulled his knife ever back to keep from puncturing the falling flaccid rubbery sides. "*Pull your Goddamned mind together puffball! Don't go flat on me you little son of a bitch!*"

Panic spread. If Spotted went catatonic and lost contact with the carefully balanced power flux, the null singularity would kick in and they'd all be gone. Murphy looked up at the monitors, seeing the continued power up. No, no way he could reach the human controls and shut it all down in time. Their fate hung by Spotted's thinning, wobbling manipulators.

With all his control, Murphy pulled the knife away and added, "All right! You win for now. I've put the knife away, I'm sorry, Overone."

Spotted began to reinflate, his touch on the monitors strengthening. "You see the necessity of my actions then?"

"Yeah," Murphy breathed, eyes darting from the monitors to the eyestalk Spotted had on him.

"Leave this place," Spotted told him again. "I am opening the bridge hatch."

"Power down the null singularity generator." Murphy took a deep breath, hating himself for giving in, knowing he'd never have done it if Spotted hadn't been holding the whole planet at the tip of his pink manipulator.

"Leave!" Spotted insisted.

"After you power the system down. When I see my planet and people safe, I promise, I'll go . . . Overone."

"Very well. Back away to the door."

Murphy swallowed and stood up. He stared at the monitors and watched the power ebbing out of the system, breathing easier now, feeling the hollow numbness of defeat. What else could he have done? Damn it!

The hatch slid open, and Murphy backed slowly toward it. He almost jumped as the white gliding shape of Wide rolled past his left foot and into the bridge.

Spotted piped shrilly. "Overone? It is you? *You are back?*"

"I am back. What are you doing?" Wide's spicules puffed and whistled.

Spotted released the consoles, flattening and thinning, fighting to control his body in a comical display. "I am now an Overone! Murphy called me Overone. This is now *my* ship." Spotted regained control, becoming ever thinner, voice deepening. "You will now address me as Overone."

"You, Nav-Pilot?"

Murphy saw his chance.

CHAPTER XXXIV

Murphy fingered the sharp edge of his fighting knife. His glare hardened as he looked at the two Ahimsa. He'd had to move like lightning in the low gravity to grab Spotted and roll him like an off-center bowling ball—shrilling and screaming—out the hatch. He'd stuck a boot against Wide's side and sent him sprawling after. Then he'd followed, hot on their tumbling tread feet with his bloody fighting knife.

Thereafter victory became a foregone conclusion. Murphy relished the thought as he looked about the small compartment which now penned two almost flat Ahimsa.

"So here are the terms. You're prisoners until we can get you out and drop you off somewhere where you won't bother us."

"Murphy, what have we done to you?" Spotted asked—hovering between flat and flat and knobby. "You promised if I would spare your world, you would allow me to civilize you!"

"I lied," Murphy grated. "Don't thin up at me, goddamn you! You damn betcha I lied. After Wide lied to us? And you? Yeah, I checked the transmitter, Spotted. I'm not Svetlana, but I know you've been keeping tabs on Earth, that we could have called home from the moment we took the ship."

"And you will persecute me?" Wide cried out. "Torture? Make me die?"

Murphy smiled. "Naw. Why should we? Just because you tried to have us murder innocent Pashti? Because you would have killed us—the very people who helped you? Just because you initiated the program that would have detonated every warhead on Earth? You think we'd pay you back for those trifling things? Think we carry a grudge or something?"

"We will not be harmed?" Spotted slowly puffed up.

"Naw," Murphy fingered the knife, aware that each of the Ahimsa watched the shining blade with rigid eyestalks. "So, Wide, when did you come around? Everyone was betting you'd be jelly by now."

He thinned slightly. "There was no reason for my dissolution. My brains slowly melded as I thought about my actions. Spotted sent me a message stating that he was an Overone. His training is incomplete. I realized I needed to take matters into my own hands again as he was incapable of—"

"I *am* an Overone!" Spotted sputtered, thinning with anger.

"He's an Overone," Murphy agreed sternly. "Treat him like one. He's smarter than you are, Wide . . . but not by much."

Wide looked at him with both eyestalks, thinning slightly. "Murphy, I will take that now because I must. But know, human, that no matter how long it takes, I will see you suffer for that!"

"I'm so glad Ahimsa are civilized," Murphy sniped snidely. "Maybe we ought to carry a grudge after all?" He shaved a thin slice of skin off the callus of his thumb meaningfully. Wide flattened immediately, providing him with a wry amusement.

* * *

Sheila ran trembling fingers through her hair, clouded vision trying to follow the incredible amount of data that was jamming the system from Earth. The fighting had stopped everywhere. A breathless world waited to hear the verdict of martial law, although Syria, Iran, Libya, and Vietnam had all been blacked out at least once when they rebelled. Lebanon didn't seem to care if it was powered out or not. Why did humans have to be such bullheaded louts?

Unbidden thoughts recreated Viktor's face. She felt his caress, remembered his cool efficient expression; her soul shrieked for the grief she had no time to feel. Under her heart, a hollow had formed, as empty as the distance between galactic clusters. A frigid blackness, it lay sodden, sucking up her vital energies.

Katya's face looked pale when it formed on the intraship monitor. "Major, I have received an Ahimsa transmission. I'm patching it through to your quarters. Murphy and I will watch from here. Anything you need, let us know."

"Right," she sighed, feeling Viktor's image slide from her mind. "What now?"

They formed, one by one, all the Ahimsa she'd seen on TaHaAk's monitors—or so she supposed. Mostly, they all looked alike to her.

"Sheila Dunbar?" the one called Tan asked.

"Bloody so. What do you wish this time, Tan? We are not harming you. Did you call to mend fences or pick at festering wounds?"

The Ahimsa ignored it. "Your monitors can observe your moon?"

"I suppose. It should be visible from here." She felt her gut tighten. What did they want with the moon? Were they trying something in spite of it all? Scare tactics?

A holo formed showing the moon. The familiar white face touched something inside her. "Tan, whatever you're about, don't do it. You will cause yourself nothing but trouble. We've been lenient. To date, no Ahimsa has been harmed. Leave it at that."

Tan rocked back and forth. "You have a rudimentary understanding of gravity by now, don't you? You understand the powers of the gravity beacons? They have, you see, functions beyond that of simply interdicting your planet. Observe!"

A flicker of fear ignited as she caught her breath and shot a frightened glance at the moon where it hung so serenely against a backdrop of stars and blackness. A shimmer appeared, a wavering of the image as something stirred just below the threshold of imagination.

The shimmer built into a hurricanelike vortex. A pinpoint of dust rose from the lunar surface as the mirage around it increased.

Tan's hollow voice informed tonelessly, "What you see

is light bent by gravity waves. We are generating local tides with the gravity beacons. The focus is quite superb, don't you agree?"

"Stop, Tan! *Stop now!*" Sheila snapped, seeing the dot of dust widen. Panic built under the threshold of her control. She wanted to scream, to throw herself at him in rage. Cracks, incredibly immense to have been seen from so far away, appeared as dark threads zigzagging out from the vortex. The eye of the storm had imperceptibly moved.

"Very well, we will stop it." Tan's voice sounded so reasonable. "You can see how it works now. That is sufficient. We need you rational for the moment. After that, we will start with your moon so that you get the impact of how we will eliminate your world and species from civilized—"

"What do you want?" The fear grew. Tan sounded too confident. Something struck her as terribly wrong.

Tan thinned ever so slightly. "Simply to say good-bye. It was unfortunate that Wide broke your interdiction. Had he not, your species would have been allowed to destroy itself in peace. That, or perhaps, someday, you would have developed to the point of civilization. Then, given the proper circumstances, we might have reconsidered and raised your interdicted status. As it is the damage Wide has done must be repaired for all of us. After all you *are* our responsibility."

"We have Pashti and two Ahimsa aboard." She spoke coldly. "Will you kill them along with us? We can still go null singularity and—"

"Blow up your precious planet, Sheila Dunbar? You are too deep in your planet's gravity well. Your ship will explode and take your planet with it." Tan puffed in exclamation. "As to the Pashti and Ahimsa, Ee!Tak knew the risks. Wide and Spotted caused the problem in the beginning. It is regrettable."

"You're a vile and despicable creature, Tan," Sheila snarled.

"I dislike the thought that you would apply characteristics we associate with humans when talking about me." Tan thinned slightly. "We have talked enough."

From the corner of her eye, Sheila caught the vortex building again on the moon. The dust cloud stirred and a faint pinpoint of red formed in the middle of it: plasma, atomic material ripped apart by the incredible gravity flux of the tides. The moon's surface began to crinkle and ripple. How much longer before. . . . Oh, Lord God!

"Murphy! Get us out of here! Get us up and away!"

His voice barely dented the horror. "Major, the systems are all down. It will take a while to power up."

"And before then," Tan added, "your moon will be gone."

"Tan, you don't want to do this. There's still—"

"You can say nothing. We're past listening. We're exterminating vermin. You have nothing to offer. Nothing to bargain with. You are simply an annoyance."

Her frayed temper finally snapped, as her impotence grew. "Bastard! You filthy despicable legless gutless bastard! If I could get out of here, I'd personally gut you and your worthless. . . ."

But what was the use? She'd lost everything. *Viktor, thank God, you don't have to see this.*

Tan rocked back and forth, admiring her anger. Sheila closed her eyes, breathing deeply to get her wits back. There had to be something? Some way—but how?

"How long until we're far enough out to save ourselves, Murphy?"

"Fifteen minutes, Major. That's assuming we don't blow anything up, powering up."

Fifteen minutes? She could see craters distorting.

"And before that we will shift the emphasis to Earth and suck you back down as a flaring gout of plasma," Tan promised. "Delightful! Oh, we remember your threats, Major. Animals! *You had the* nerve *to threaten Ahimsa?*"

What could they do? Sheila jumped to her feet, pacing, horrified eyes watching the moon's surface buckle like plastic wrap.

Too late! Her mind went numb with the realization. Too late! *I did it! I walked us right into a trap! How could I know the gravity buoys could do this?*

"You win, Tan." Her arms slapped her sides listlessly. "Whatever you want." She turned and screamed at the mocking holo. "Damn you! We'll let Wide and Spotted loose! We'll let them ship us to Earth and you can stopper the bottle! This is barbaric! Stop it! *You win!*"

The piping of Ahimsa laughter grated in the confines of the quarters.

"No," Tan added happily. "You are too dangerous. This is the only course. Your species is finished, Major—but we enjoy your capitulation."

She winced at more piping laughter. Mind empty, vanquished, Sheila Dunbar turned to watch the death of her world. "Please. Please . . . don't do this."

The moon shuddered, tremors visible as dust rose. *And the Earth will be next?* She shook her head, a strangled whimper sounding in her throat.

At first the tearing sound didn't affect her. But the loud crack from behind caused her to spin on her heels to stare openmouthed. Several of the Ahimsa literally bounced off the floor like basketballs as they flattened and their eyestalks twisted this way and that. Their individual holos shivered and shimmied, wavering like the horror on the moon.

Some flickered out of existence, their holos leaving blank places in the line. Oddly, occasional Ahimsa remained unaffected, eyestalks staring with surprise at their compatriots while their squeaked and piped questions drowned in the roar. Others completely deflated as, behind them, their imagers caught the buckling of bulkheads and the vibrations of explosions. Steel cracked and a gigantic metallic tube peeled plating from behind Tan's jiggling figure as it seemed to grow from the wall. A bulge formed, dimpling out immensely around the tube. Then the whole wall went, curled aside by the monster that thrust itself into the scene.

The translation sounded muffled through the confusion. "Tan, you will cease immediately! Shut it down! *Now!*"

Sheila simply gaped, exhausted. The storm on the moon kept raging, still a vortex; but the plasma in the center began to dull in color. The huge cracks and rents still crumbled, the dust still spread, but the threads grew no larger.

In other holo images, similar machines ripped through walls, huge barrels settling on flat knobby Ahimsa Overones.

She looked back in time to see the hatch on the front of the metal monster hovering over Tan flip up and back. The gnomelike features of Moshe Gabi rose smiling from the tank to utter a simple: *"Shalom!"*

He waved a greeting to a stunned Sheila Dunbar. "Assaf Company reporting, Major!"

She fought to keep her composure. *Assaf! They'd made it, saved their action until the last moment. Praise God!* She fought to keep from collapsing in relief, head shaking as she said, "Moshe, where have you been? We were worried sick when you wouldn't answer communications."

"Second law of Lebanon, Major. Maintain radio silence until contact with the enemy."

Tan, for the first time in several billion years, had gone completely flat.

* * *

Phantom spaced in null singularity again. The whole of the crew had managed, somehow, to make order out of chaos. Thousands of new recruits had been accommodated through days of shuffling while Ahimsa robot manufacturing built new quarters and factories to produce for the exponentially increased demands. An entire population of humans now headed for the stars. Pashti vessels scoured Earth for trade goods, delighting new markets with Pashti doodads and technology while they loaded exotic foods, fabrics, cultural items, and anything else that caught the attention of the Pashti traders. Ee!Tak, now Pashti Ambassador, had his own Micronesian island.

Viktor's body rested, home from the stars to be safely buried in Tula. Sheila had smiled, seeing the tears in Viktor's father's eyes. So the rent had been healed. A soldier's honors for a fallen son—second to last in a war that had finally ended—forever. *Viktor*, so far behind them now. *Viktor!* A solitary tear crept past the defenses of her eyelids and down her cheek.

A staggering Earth stared up in awe at the spectacle of their moon—peoples everywhere cowed at the changes in the face of that so familiar symbol. She looked out at the stars passing by—impossibly, as Sam Daniels had once told her.

"Major?" Murphy's voice disturbed her. "I could come back later."

She looked up and shrugged slightly, thoughts drifting far away, beyond space, beyond memory. "Anything wrong?"

"No, ma'am. Just thought I'd check and make sure you're all right."

She smiled weakly. "Are any of us all right?"

He worked his mouth. "I'm not sure, Major. None of us have had time to think. Hell, I don't know. I guess I'm all right."

She chuckled, awed at the sound her throat made. "I'm surprised. That was quite a binge you went on. I didn't think anyone could drink that much. Trinidad, Colorado, will never be the same. Is that why Cruz's little brother is aboard? The two of you made so much trouble you can't go back?"

"Promised Phil I'd check in on his family and eat some real food. Uh, his mom sent along a couple of coolers of tamales. We got 'em on ice if you're interested. His little brother just kind of wanted to tag along. You know, take a shot at becoming a hero like his brother."

"It was Katya who set off that little display, wasn't it? The Trinidad police weren't wild about letting you out—even at my request."

He hung his head, shuffling his feet nervously. "Yeah, well, I didn't expect her to stay. Never loved a woman before like that. I mean, she's right for the job—but I thought. . . . Hell, don't matter does it?"

Sheila shook her head wearily. "No, it doesn't. She's a good liaison for Ee!Tak. And she likes the sunshine and the swimming. Did you hear? Ee!Tak is going to take up scuba."

The silence lasted a long time.

"Well, I'd better get about checking on the ship. Barb might need someone else to help her keep an eye on things. I just thought, uh, nothing. Hey, if you want to talk about it sometime, let me know." He headed for the corridor, hands in his pockets, looking nervous.

"Just a minute, Murphy."

He stopped, startled by her voice, and turned to look back.

Sheila composed her thoughts. "When you killed Gubanya, how did it. . . ." She shook her head, frustrated at the inability to put it into words. "I mean it happened so fast. He hit Viktor and you had him. It had to make you feel . . . something."

He walked back and dropped to a seat, resting his back against the side of the observation bubble. "I just did my job. Don't worry about death, Major. It's just there—over the horizon—on the other side of the mind. As to Viktor, he didn't feel a thing. Mika was a professional. Gubanya didn't feel a thing because I was professional."

"But that's not the point. It's the incredible waste of it." Her eyes pleaded, begging for some understanding.

He smiled slightly, sighing. "It was the last gasp of the old regime, Major. There's no point or purpose to it. It just happened."

"Sam told me. He said to keep you close. Thank you, Leftenant. You and Viktor, you saved us all in the end. Heroes, both of you."

He dropped his gaze, scratching at his red hair. "I didn't do anything heroic, Major. I just couldn't let it all fall apart. We'd given too much. But what do you mean about Major Staka?"

She looked out at the stars. "I don't know why. Really, I don't. I suppose, indirectly, it was Viktor who saved us all in the end."

"How's that?"

"When Sam called and told me Chee'ee'la was up and about, I was thinking of Viktor and staring out at the stars. Chee'ee'la wanted to know what reason we had to survive, remember?"

Murphy nodded, eyes reserved.

"And there I was, talking to the most intelligent being in the universe . . . and I had no answers." A single tear had formed at the corner of her eye. "So I told Chee'ee'la that our reason for existence was to question. I told him that if we were exterminated, we couldn't question. If we couldn't question, we couldn't learn, couldn't find the answers. If existence wasn't learning, there was no point to the universe."

"So is the sun going nova someday soon?"

She shook her head slowly. "No. Chee'ee'la replied, as near as we can tell, that our goals were the same as his. Then he read everything we had on file about Hindu, Buddhist, and other mystical traditions, glowed a bunch of colors, and floated to his spaceship. Said he'd be back in a couple of millennia to discuss the nature of God—so long as our information processors were up to it by then. Funny thing, he said that Wide's understanding of spatial dimensions were grossly in error. He finished saying he would like his tape player when he comes back next time."

"And how many ways are there to win a game of chess? Did he say?"

"Don't know," Sheila looked out at the stars again. "The number he gave was so large it overloaded the Pashti system."